SWEET BLUE

Michael Kolanis

GW00599779

Tsaria Limited

First publication in the United Kingdom.

First Edition published 2006

Copyright © Michael Kolanis 2006

The right of Michael Kolanis to be identified
as the author of this work has been asserted
in accordance with sections 77 and 78 of the
Copyright Designs and Patents Act 1988.

All the characters in this book are fictitious,
and any resemblance to actual persons, living
or dead, is purely coincidental.

Conditions of Sale

This book is sold subject to the condition
that it shall not, by way of trade or otherwise,
be lent, re-sold, hired out or otherwise
circulated in any form of binding or cover
other than that in which it is published and
without a similar condition including this
condition being imposed on the subsequent
purchaser.

ISBN 10: 0-9552978-0-X
ISBN 13: 978-0-9552978-0-9

Set in 11/13.5 pt Times New Roman

Published by Tsaria Limited

Printed and bound in Great Britain by Bookmarque Ltd

Chapter 1

'It's not a machine's world, whatever you might *think*. Lust comes first. And jazz. And poker. And sex. And money... of course. Lots and lots of money....' Euroman caressed his tired eyes, and then his fingers slipped, cascaded round, playing ponderously with a nostril. 'You may think intelligence is a plaything of the geek; cunning the toy of a tyrannical lover; wit the basis of inventive schmucks eking out a living by the day, hand to mouth, desperation hanging over them. Well... it keeps them on their toes. Take it from me, cowboy, when you think you know it all, you don't know half the story.'

'Why?' said cowboy, with a savvy American edge, a USAman seated at the console, booting the computer into "Active" mode. 'Well?'

'Because it hasn't been written yet.'

'What are you trying to say?'

'It can wait.' Euroman prompted him, tapping his shoulder. 'Now, hook up the system, and log in to New York.'

The cursor raced across the screen, setting on the network alias:
NYC - Enable 101 ¦ Network 9: Node 4: Cluster 21: Server 6A: Connecting.... OK. Connected.
Profiling..... Please wait...
Profile OK. Status OK. Enter password: *******
03:20 a.m. Paris local time. Monday.

'We're in,' said the American; Brooklyn accent.

'Good. Catch the processor. Slow her down.' Euroman in Euromode with a Scandinavian drawl, directing the action. 'That's it; bring her right down. If you can, hover at the hibernation rate.'

'That's too slow. They're certain to notice.'

'Just do it.'

'It's not advisable.'

1

'Overruled. Just do it.'

The Brooklyn kid overrode his own misgivings, and brought the remote processor almost to a standstill. Suddenly, his fears were vindicated and he cried out:

'They've spotted it. I told you!'

'Damn! Get inside quickly. Snoop around.'

'The processor has surged back up.'

'It doesn't matter. Get in.'

'Now he's shutting her down!'

'Take a snapshot.'

'What? How?'

'A profile. Get a profile.'

'He's shutting her down.'

'Override the auto. Do it. Now!'

Hammering the keyboard with his fevered fingers, initializing the settings, sequencing the code:

Tracking... Processor rate at 83% and decreasing.

Please wait...... Remote host is OK.

Running Tunnelling Routines.

> *Angel_Red*
> *Angel_Blue*
> *Angel_Green*

Processor rate at 42% and decreasing.

Uploading to host... Please wait.... OK.

Optimizing host... OK.

Restoring settings. Please wait... Status OK. Path OK.

Processor rate at 15% and decreasing.

Caching data... Please wait... OK.

Time out 7 seconds....

End Run.

OK

'Got it!' gasped USAman.

'Now, sneak back out.'

'Reversing... Come on, baby; come on... Back out, come to daddy...' He's an American Theseus, his codes are the thread out of the labyrinth of global computer networks. 'Come on, sweetheart... Be lucky... Be lucky... Come to daddy...' he knows that the only thing of consequence in a machine's world networked with computers is to control the show – by a Greek thread, by a string of digits, by a promise, by a word, even with a conceit. Master and slave subsumed in the drama of machine and man, new-world and old world, silicon and flesh, a tale told by an android full of savvy code and circuitry signifying "Ain't I one hell of a smartass." Time is on the side of... *suckers?* Take five. What? Minutes? Transistors? Hey, who's counting? He's a guy; that's all that matters. The moral of his tale: it's life lived in a quintessentially male sense; he's an enigma with a hard-on getting off on battling with his wits what arms alone can never hope to emulate. Men are born to Fuck and Fight, in whatever way they can. Abuse of the f-word? Nah! F & F – kind of makes sense, male sense, that is, with a hormonal basis to underpin necessity. He does what he must, where the thread of his urges leads him, tying him in knots. Men.

'Easy, easy does it...' Euroman whispered after him. 'Lift it a touch... That's it.' Adroitly guiding him, his hand hovering like a maestro over the console, spellbound by his own daring and consummate cunning. 'Pull out the way you came in. Careful, damn it! Don't bounce off the server in Chicago, you'll trap us in their loop. Good. That's it. Don't let him see you.' Skillfully inverting the sequence, erasing their presence, deftly, from three thousand miles away. 'Are we clear yet? – What's happening?'

'We've no choice; I'll have to make a run for it.'

'Are we clear?'

'He's chasing us. The tenacious bastard; I can't throw him off!'

'Mask the DNS numbers.'

'Binary or Octal?'

'Octal. – And pop every third bit. Reset the parity.'

'Even or Odd?'

'Even. – And re-assemble on the bounce. No,' Euroman snapped at himself. 'Auto-correlate first, then re-assemble on the bounce. Come on, do it!'

'...Masking....'

'What's the delay?'

'Server's down. I've got to re-route.'

'What's that node there?' he pointed to the screen.

3

'Nexus. That's government.'

'Go round it. And that one there?'

'Let me check... Research Lab.'

'Go inside. Route the frames into the network, and look for a feeder into the Web. Make sure it's public domain; we'll lose him in the traffic.'

'Found one. Looks like a default proxy. Let me check.'

'Take the risk. Do it anyway. Jump out.'

'Engaging scramble... Bouncing.... Parity is even. Frames routed into seven channels, OK... Come on... Come on... Now back into the Web... Where are we? We'll lose control if we don't get out. There!' he gasped. 'Made it.'

'Have we lost him?'

USAman gazed at the screen, and saw the ominous trace of a hunter pursuing them. He hammered the desk with his fist. 'Bastard! He's still chasing us.'

'Update the routing tables and splice the IP numbers with a pseudo set.'

'Seventy-thirty?'

'Fifty-fifty. Keep it simple. Scramble the frames. Get us out, damn it! Try crashing the routers when you pass through. Bring them down! Bring them down!'

'Negative. The firewalls are throwing us out.'

'Damn!'

'We're going to lose this one.'

'Shut up and let me think!'

It's the biting reality of the chase, that sinks its teeth into your guts, and yet you know you can't give up. 'Fuck!' expletive recycled. 'Fuck! Fuck!...' like a hammer to the head, *whack!* It wants to knock you down flat, but you have to keep getting up. Spirit. Muscle. Stubbornness. It's the only way they know. Kind of a... male thing. Sure.

'OK... OK...' said Euroman. 'Stay in control. We'll handle it.'

'How? He's back in the thread. We've nowhere to go?'

Euroman was breathing hard. 'Go back to the primary host.'

'New York? Are you kidding me!'

'Just do it.'

4

'But he shut her down.'

'Go to the central processor. – Come on. Do it. Just do it.'

'Enabling remote host. It's up. Threading...'

'Hurry.'

'Routing packets through the proxy servers. This will take a bit of time to set up.'

'Just phase it in. Phase in.'

'It's too sudden. You'll alert them.'

'Just do it.'

'Latching the network alias. Factoring primes...'

'Hurry.'

'We're in.'

'Well...?'

A moment of tense silence and bated breath ensued. Then, 'Damn! He's still there.'

'Boot up the auxiliary servers. We'll fight him off with replication. Copy the signal and thread randomly. That'll lose him.'

'We might lose ourselves too.'

'Just do it.'

'And then what?'

'Compress the signals.'

'That will filter the packets. It'll slow us down.'

'It will slow him down too. It will give us some time. Where are we?'

'Engaging auxiliaries.... Come on, boot up you bastards. Done. Compression started. Done. Linking to router... Cut out on three, two, one. OK. Should I bounce off the remote server?'

'Try it.'

'Here we go. – Damn, it's not working.'

'Get out of the way. Let me see.'

'It's not working. He's still chasing us.'

'Damn!'

Euroman was breathing hard; he felt they were losing the struggle until his eye spotted the map of Arabia – the data traffic on the Arabian routes was light and the bandwidth immense: One roaring data packet amid a desert of silent information. It seemed absurd; self-defeating; ridiculous. But his intuition kicked in. He had an idea.

'I have an idea. Running is no good. The only way to shake him is to trap him in a loop. And we'll have to lead him into one, and build it on the fly. Take us into ArabNet Alpha. No... Wait. Put us in Beta. Those are the mobile bands, aren't they?'

'That's crazy. That's like a desert. He'll see us for miles.'

'Just do it.'

'Jesus!' USAman cried with a desperate shudder, as their prey became their hunter, and he stared at the screen with embittered doom. This was it. The final standoff; the OK Coral; the last shootout; you win or you die. 'You tenacious bastard. Come on, then!' taunting with the grudging pain of a man who fears for his life but loves the chase nonetheless. - It's a male thing, this, to defy and to dare, to hover on the brink, to win by a whisker. 'The bastard won't let go...' cried with angst but there's profound pleasure there, like a fix, a cocktail of sweat and spit and testosterone, a pitcher of adrenalin, that's all he really wants. Men lust for the challenge, they are passionate slaves of their own egos, and they crave for women, but men only s*emen! I see...* nothing but himself. A male eye on a male target. Women are divine, but they can get in the way sometimes. Still, they're around, they are always there, like space, like time, like an erection. And even now, as his fingers sweep over the keyboard, and his heart pounds furiously at the chase, life is a turn-on and he longs to be inside of her. It's deep in there, infinite, what the mind of man cannot measure but his body needs and aches for. A male harbor – the natural resting place for his restless desires. Full of threat. Full of danger. Full of himself.

Euroman was restless: 'Is it done? Let me have a look.'

'Dubai, Jeddah, Bahrain, Riyadh... Dubai, Jeddah, Bahrain, Riyadh... Come on, stay in there, you bastard. Get in the cage. - Who the hell is this guy? Who let you out of the desert?'

'Is is done?'

'Wait.'

'Come on, come on, bring him in. Damn it, don't get too far ahead. Put a delay on the signal; keep him in range. That's it; there. Hold the cycle. Good, let him maneuver; don't get in his way. Now, lock it.'

'Centers are locked. Nodes are locked. He's in the loop.'

'Come on. Hurry. Lock it up.'

'Everything but Riyadh.' USAman shuddered a mom
bracing himself for the climax. 'He's in. Gotcha! Closing
Round and round you go, sucker. Get yourself a camel and
desert for a change. See how you like that. – And don't call
call you.' He began to sigh and breathe more easily. 'Verifying...
Loop is locked. OK.'

'Now get us out.'

'Fading out the signal. I'll jump out at Dubai and lock it all up.
– Dum diddey dum... Do you know any Arabian songs?'

'Not off hand.' He heaved a sigh of relief. 'Good work... But don't
get cocky. There is nothing more certain in this world to screw you
up - except a woman, perhaps!' He couldn't resist being cocky. Kind
of a guy thing, that. 'Now, bring us home. That's it. Gently, fold it
up. Nice. Nice and easy. Erase our footprints. That's it, swing round,
and come back through Athens.'

'Where else, that's where this whole thing got going in the first
place.'

'Nice touch,' he patted him on the shoulder, and smiled. He realized
then just how much both of them had sweated it out. And it was...
exhilarating. Even better than sex... Almost.

Euroman paused, holding his breath as the computer locked
the network and erased all pathways. USAman hit the return key
to confirm; and the screen went blank. He heaved a sigh of relief,
leaned back in his chair, and smiled. 'It's done.'

And Paris went off line.

Chapter 2

23:45. New York City. Sunday. (PLAY...)

'Hey, buddy, can you spare me a smoke? Thanks.' His long spidery fingers clasped the butt-end, squeezing it into his mouth, like a nipple, and sucking deeply on its moist deliverance. 'Yeah! That's good. That's *reeeeeeal* good. Nice and easy...'

'I'm looking for Yvonne.'

'Vonnie? Sure; she's over there,' he breathed, thumbing with his saxophone. 'The lady in blue sitting at the table. You see her?' blinking his eyes as they bored through the weight of distance, 'Yeah, that's her at the table... dressed in a blue mood...' his gaze full of dreamy awe. 'Bluesy kind of blue... Sweet blue... Like the sun rising. Like lullabies dancing.' And fondling the keys of the sax, smiled. 'Knows her jazz too. And she's always drumming along some. Tap tap tap...'

'Blue?'

'Yeah.' - Gazing at her together seemed to multiply the sense, of a dreaming blue incandesce. - 'You know... I love that mood.'

'Thanks.'

'Any time.' He inhaled as if self-hypnotizing, sucking on that cigarette, downing all that nicotine as *her* juices quenched him with delicious ache. 'Ahhhh, she's sweet...' then enveloping the sax with his mouth, pumped out lyrical crescendos, booming like oxygen through the stage fanning the fire of the blues.

'Mister; do you have a light?'

'You're Yvonne?'

'You have a light?'

'Sure. - You're Yvonne? I'm looking for Roy Riemann.'

'Some nights I'm Yvonne. Some nights I'm Vonnie. Other times... I'm *Seduction*....'

'That's fine by me.'

'But tonight...' she looked at him intriguingly, 'I'm in transition.'

That last word reverberated, and entrapped him.

Smiling warmly as he struck a match, the phosphorescence of the flame blasting out an afterglow of engulfing light - everything is exposed, but still... everything is hidden, melting away a man's inhibition.

'Vonnie.'

'Yes?'

'I'm glad I found you.'

The match is a chorus of ancient spells, and she like an angel in the vapor trails of whispering sound, a flame slowly winding down.

'So, you're looking for Roy Riemann?'

'That's right.' He wants to say "Oh, by the way..." and his lips make the motion, but the woman draws him closer. And he waits. For...?

'He's around somewhere, I think.' She inhales the cigarette; holds her breath, a moment is all she needs; and sips lemon-gin, her tongue tasting the spirit, but it's his eyes she feeds. 'You're not in a hurry, are you?' she said.

'Yes. I am actually.'

'Still, have a seat.'

Men are the burn and sex the fire, and he is drawn into her flames with muscular desire, until the dimming glow of a match ignites his flesh – he feels the effect on his fingers, like brandy; neat; pure heat. She, like he, is human after all. But still, her smile, kind of takes his breath away.

He said. 'I'd like to take you up on that, but...' Watching her softly, inevitably, like the flame working down the match: 'I'm in a hurry...' Words are like color, full of light, full of performance, a luxury in breath: 'Yes, I'm in a hurry. This match is beginning to bite.'

They looked at the match, and she blew it out enticingly, pulling him nearer with her red-light eyes, like visual feelers snaking into a man and drawing him in. 'Please. For me. Have a seat,' she said, having trapped him with those red-lights.

He watched as she smoked, residing easy for a while – their time measured with a cigarette. She breaks the ash, lifts it to her mouth, just so, one two three... the sensual loading on her lips, the wafting haze enveloping the space with a sense of bassoons in enigmatic dreaming drone holding the night hostage to the moment. The musicians were improvising, the bartender dropped a tray, and the waitress protested.

'I ain't cleaning it up. No way. I'm sick of all this, Billy!'

'Yvonne?' he said.

She enjoyed being watched, it was a part tailor-made for her, like the hand of a lady to a voyeur's glove, shake, close fit, perfect, the preamble's a breeze, it looks sublime but really just a tease, his roaming gaze moving over her, fondling her, and his eyes loved to stare. The voyeur met his spectacle and, together, engulfed in silent conspiracy until he blinked, and she teased him with:

'Well, and what are you looking at?'

'You. I mean, I was looking for Roy. And...' stumbling into mutters, he hadn't realized sweet cocaine and quality hash spiced the air and baited his senses with magic trappings, his eyes blinking in the smoky light searching for a focus, her features filling out the drone of her voice with a soft frothy skin, and the deep angular lines pointing at a thousand things at once. She was someone of countless faces. The cool voice and masks of her face combined to mesmerize and, like heroin, fed its own addiction. Time and a cigarette. That's her world. And she slowed him right down. Real easy... Men, like tobacco with an aftertaste of women. You kind of take it whole.

'I am,' she said, consuming his time, puff at a time... he tasted sublime, tick tock... mmmm... you taste a piece of his ...*what?* Her tone playing with the soft gasps of voyeuristic breathing, 'I am whatever you want me to be.' They were whispers of immediate and puzzling intent; they were the essence of need, of sex, of spontaneous desire craving ecstasy, for the burnout of orgasm.

He pulled up a chair, sat, and ordered a drink. (He came to a full stop).

'Make that twice,' she added. 'And miss...' she smiled, power as a smile, 'go easy on the ice,' confidence as a smile, 'real easy... That's nice,' femininity as this, a smile, essential knowledge as softly curling lips painted ruby red and all... smiles. Breathy. Delicious. Powerful. *Smile...* She turned to him and said. 'And what should I call you? – Let me guess.'

'Go ahead.'

'*A man.*'

He chuckled with pleasure. 'I'm Nicolas Stokes. Just call me Nick.'

'Stokes? Hmmm...' she leaned back, pondering, consuming his time, winding him down, winding him around, unraveling him with her gaze. 'A, B, C... there's a letter,' she softly clipped her fingers together. 'I think I'll call you *Strokes*. - You see,' she said, 'there's something about that extra *r*...' inflecting the air with that sense of *je ne sais quoi*.

'Why would you want to call me that?' he asked her, as though any answer would do just to hear her speak.

'Because,' she began, reaching out to stroke his hair, 'you look so cute...' fondling his ear. 'And I can pet you like a cat.' Softly teasing. 'Do you like cats, Strokes?'

'They're all so cuddly and cruel.'

'Oh?'

'And they remind me of women.'

'Anyone in particular?'

'You.'

'*Meow...*'

Some women amaze, he felt, they cast a spell and make men forget what they are. And often, a man needs to forget himself, because he's always kind of alone. He would enjoy being her monopoly, but other pressing matters guided his sensual will. 'Vonnie, I really need to find Roy. I've tried everywhere. I've called him, but his phone is switched off. He mentioned you many times.'

'Was he flattering?'

'Naturally!' There, back under her spell, slowing right down, before picking up speed: 'Do you know where might be?'

'Perhaps.' She took her time, like her drink, consuming it in sips.

'Where?'

'Why the rush?' she sighed. 'Besides, do I look like someone who would ever let you down?'

'You seem like someone who would play with me,' he replied. 'That's nice, even flattering, but I need to find Roy.'

She licked the tip of her cigarette. And that lick had philosophy in thrall. 'Messiness, and men, when looked at honestly, make perfect sense. They go perfectly together. Cigarette?' - What did she mean? 'Nick; a cigarette?'

'No. Perhaps later.' Despite himself Nick felt irresistibly drawn to her, entangled with desire. It is this, that women are an endless seduction, conversation and all. For even amid doubts, Nick felt at ease, aroused and at ease. These were doubts devised to seduce a man, not to mislead him. And who was he to resist that?

'Trust me, Nick, the music will keep things alive for as long as it takes.'

'Things?'

'Events.'

'To do what?'

'To make everything come out right.'

'How?'

'If you know Roy, you know the answer to that already.'

'I'm sorry, you lost me.'

Vonnie laughed, playing with him, and kept the riddles flowing:

'A man's habits are like a map. His obsessions are a compass. You can always find him, if you really know him. If you open your eyes. If you had my eyes. If you see what I see.'

'Would I be amazed?'

'You'd be lost.'

'Even with your eyes?'

'But you'll still need me. It's only then that the eyes come alive.'

'Look, Vonnie, time is critical, things may be happening...'

'Men love the game, but often hate to play. Does that make any sense?'

'Excuse me?'

'The game. – Well, Roy's an exception, and women just love him. Love playing with him. – Are you growing jealous, Nick?'

'Not just yet. But I'll keep trying. You never know.'

'That's the fascinating part. But you can't keep it secret. You ought to take a lesson from Roy, Nick.'

'Sure.'

'He's pure man....'

13

Some women were a handful; but Vonnie was the world. And she left him feeling breathless, gazing at her and seeing.... sizzling infinities.

Everything went quiet. She played with silence, using it to bait and intrigue. He grew uneasy – not with her, but the silence:

'Please, Vonnie, if you're unsure where he is, just say so.' She said nothing, which he took as definitive, and began faintly mumbling to himself. 'I just don't know... Maybe I should wait it out, I guess? I suppose... Besides, there's nothing Roy could do. What could he do? I shouldn't have come here. I over-reacted. That's was rash of me. But what could I do? It was a bolt out of the blue. It will just have to wait until tomorrow. Damn this thing...' testing himself, his mind embroiled with sinister events, his computer network compromised by mysterious system-hackers and intruders. 'I can't do anything now. It's hopeless. I should just leave. It's getting late.'

'Where are you going? Come on, Nick, sit down. Come on, please... I might be able to locate him. I'll give it a try. Just give me some time.' She wanted him to stay; holding him with whimsical softness. That's all it took with a man, whimsical softness. Besides, she liked him. She couldn't say why. Well... he was someone to play with. It was a slow night, and she was careless of the time, just smoking a cigarette. 'What's the time, Nick?'

'How could you find Roy?'

She's like a hacker sexing her way into his brain, thread of a smart wile, reading the code of a man, his desire to know, boring through him with her soft tunnelling eyes.

'What's the time, Nick?'

'It's late. Why?'

'Oh... It's just the moment.'

'What of it?'

'We have to crack it open. – Nick. What are you doing?'

He nervously took out his mobile computer and logged on remotely to the data network, encrypting the codes, testing the firewalls and running a security check.

'She's quiet,' he said with quiet relief.

'Who?'

'I'm shutting her down.'

14

That's not a woman. So, for Vonnie, that's fine. Let him do what he likes. He's a boy with a toy. Let him play. And she smiled. 'OK... OK...'

He packed away the computer, and ritually looked at the time.

'You know, Nick, you look very obsessed with your boys' toys. Are you sure you should be shutting *her* down? After all, *she* may not like it. *She* can play you up in all sorts of uncanny ways. Just when you think you're on top, you find yourself under her.'

'What are you saying?'

'Desperation is the cage. And imagination runs on hunger. That's why you should never let your imagination go hungry.'

'Why?'

'It's how a woman always wins.'

He paused, and stared at her. 'Should you be telling me this?'

She laughed, filling everything with a breathless sigh. 'You're in my world now, you know. This is my web, my matrix, my network. And in here, you learn to use all of your senses.'

'All at the same time?'

'When you know how.' She lifted her glass and held it knowingly, studying him. 'You're rather conservative, aren't you, Nick?'

'Are you spying on me?'

'The way you talk. How you carry yourself. Hmm, it suits you. You're comfortable with what you are. That's OK. That's good.'

'And Roy?'

'A man should always glow where he shines most; and no one can dim his star.'

'Well, us guys, we're always learning how to shine.'

'Are you?'

'I think so... or perhaps I'm just dreaming. Why don't you tell me?'

'Men, they have invisible lights too: infra this; ultra that.'

'I'll remember that. - And Roy?'

'Roy can find his own way... blindly. Well, more or less.'

'I see. So you never have to hold his hand?'

'Just a finger perhaps... Occasionally.'

'Which one?'

'This little one.' She wiggled her small finger at him.

'Do I get to share? I'm only a man, after all.'

She placed her small finger to her mouth, and bit on it teasingly. 'I'll have to think about that.'

'With that one little finger, Vonnie, you could hold the whole world of men, and they'd never know because they would be too amazed to think otherwise.'

She blushed at the compliment. But only the barest touch, the red sufficiently soft to make her glow.

'Why are you blushing?' he asked.

'Facts are red. Fibs are blue.'

'And...?'

'Even I can be a little shy too... Sometimes.'

'And Roy...' he said, looking round at the club, 'him and his boozing and his music.'

'Always the music.'

He locked onto her eyes, aiming, probing. 'And his women.'

'For a man, what are women after all but booze and music mixed together into the ultimate cocktail.' She was effortlessly cool, censuring him, yet softly taking control; wooing him, but never condescending. 'As for me, well, Roy is like a deck of playing cards, half of them face up.'

'And the others?'

'Spirited away.'

'Where to?'

'Oh, in things and things besides...' With Vonnie, it seemed everything had to be riddled with whimsy, with fond but deceptively deep humor. Even a thought, unless it amazed, would simply bore her. 'Actually, his kicks are lyrical, like piano. I'm more basic, like a drum. And I play my part – like a good girl.

'I'm impressed,' he said. 'Are you open to a proposition?'

'As long as it's not an offer of marriage. Things would become... complicated.'

'Or interesting. It's a question of - '

'Taste?'

'Perhaps.'

'You're a clever boy, aren't you, Nick?'

'Well... I'm just a mamma's boy, really.'

'That takes training.'

'Well, I'm an expert. You know what to expect.'

'I expect nothing; I prepare for everything.'

'Like a good girl.'

'A daddy's girl.'

'What else!'

They laughed.

'And so...?' began Vonnie.

'So...?' continued Nick.

'If you're not going to marry me, what do you want?'

'What every man wants,' he smiled. 'As I'm sure you understand.'

'Do you know what I want, Strokes?'

'Are you a gambling girl? '

'I'm a daddy's girl, remember?'

'Well, then you want both sides of the coin. Can daddy give you that?'

'I like it when I can't lose.'

'Which doesn't guarantee you a win.'

'What business are you in?'

'Banking.'

'Ah, I see.' She considered a moment. 'Like Roy. Another drink?'

Winning and losing, it's not a question of margins, but psychology.

As the pianist performed a voluptuous variation on Schubert, a bassist joined the musical ensemble on stage, and two trumpets boomed in his wake with razzmatazz jazz, vying in the sexiness of its chaos, of a sensual lyrical blues.

Vonnie sipped her lemon gin and listened to the music, tapping her feet, drumming her fingers, la la la-ing with her tongue, she and the music and the club all part of a piece perfectly adjusted, while Nick sat in numb silence essentially alone of her sensuous world, and watched the clock for what seemed like a long time, but less than a minute elapsed. That was the rendering effect of music, and booze, and the sustaining aroma of cocaine. And women. Somewhere... always women, tying the parts together into a greater whole. The incomprehensible wholeness that men find so....

'Roy's here, isn't he?' he resolved, the thought spontaneously burst into his mind as the drummer whacked the cymbal with a frenzied thrash, and the giddy rhythm drove the tempo into improvised jazz. She gazed at him, and he repeated. 'Here's here. Where?'

'Perhaps he is. Have you a parking space for your skin?'

'What? Where is he?'

'Seek and you will find.'

'He's here. Why not just say so?'

'Outside and inside are two different places; like a man with two personas. Roy's sensible. He knows. He leaves his *other* persona outside, skin on the sidewalk, and steps into this.' She gestured with her hand, fleetingly done, contrasting with the spirit of a jazz score, tapping at the door of the moment – knock knock. 'You see, Nick, we are like sound, framed by whispers, jazz rhythm in a sense. Seek and you will find. Peek, even if you are blind. Because if you have the sense for it, for jazz, for life, for exotic things devoid of a skin, well...' she lifted her glass, and emptied it. 'A man's a chameleon shedding his skin as he steps inside here; the essence sucks you in; and you change. You become... sweet spirit, with a hint of blue.'

'That's a bit dramatic, isn't it?'

'Not if you love life enough to drown in it. You enter that door; you look around; take a table; order a drink; light a cigarette; sit back and listen to jazz... Another drink, Strokes?'

'Is that jazz or the blues?'

'Cigarette?'

He paused, irritated but completely enamored. 'OK, Vonnie, sensuous enigma aside, tell me: what is Roy? I see his skin out there, every day, he's a banker like me. What's it like inside of here?'

'Think of a number.'

'Zero.'

'Clever boy! - Try eight.'

Pondering the riddle, the glint in her eyes, like aces on a winning high, brought his mind to a scintillating ease. 'He's playing poker,' he concluded, then looked startled. 'Now! He's playing now? At this hour? Does he never get enough? I thought this was a jazz club.' He frowned. 'Where is he?'

'Private rooms.' she said, her eyes drifting upwards.

'Where? Upstairs? What's up there?'

'Restricted access. You can't just go up.'

'Why?'

'Because you're not music. You're not a song. Your skin isn't on the sidewalk...as we say. Cigarette?'

'Well, I forgot to take mine off. How do I get in?'

'Into what? The game? That isn't really you, is it, Nick?'

'And what makes you so sure? Are you judging me now?'

'I can tell.'

'And you think you can't be wrong? Are you that infallible?' Silence kicked in, loaded with her essence, and more weight than he could handle. 'I can play. I just don't get the time, that's all.'

Touché, rubbing it in, but teasingly so it felt like a soft massage.

'The thing with cats, Nick, is they have nine lives, and they're willing to risk them all. That's why I'm fond of cats.'

'And is a man really like a cat?'

'Poker gives him nine lives. The deal is to play; to spend them all. And Roy dies slowly.'

'How slowly?'

'As long as the money holds out. As long as you're liquid. It's like the Hindu cycle of the world, only the poker wheel has a pitch, and the game never repeats exactly. Tick tick tick...'

'You're a philosopher too now, are you?'

'It's depends on the cards, Nick, which particular skin I'm inhabiting at the time. You know,' she hinted provocatively, 'you can always wait. Cigarette?'

'Can I get in and watch?'

Her eyes fixed on him, holding him. 'You like to watch, do you, Nick?'

'I thought I was Strokes.'

'You like to watch, Strokes?'

'I like to play,' he said. '*And* I like to watch.'

'It helps to have money.' She lit another cigarette, chain smoking, synchronizing the left hand with the right. 'Lots of money.'

There is her glory, the multiplier of her hand to wave the wand and cast those spells a hundred all at once tantalizing, seducing, knowing the allure of words, of looks ever so beguiling. *Do you like what you see? Do you know what you see? Look closely now...* She is the crystal, the eternal eye to be gazed at and gazing through. Was that the voyeur's instinct, in a gaze, to consume the world whole yet feel themselves insatiable?

'I have money,' he said.

'And the others, they never cry when they lose.'

'Good for them.'

'Because they know, sooner or later, they'll win. And do you know why, Nick?'

'Because they're religious.'

'Exactly! Though their religion is based on roulette. You see, that pitch of the wheel is mesmerizing. – Are you a rational man, Nick? Because if you are, you'll wait.'

'No. I don't think I will.'

'Ah. I thought not.'

'Please, Vonnie, just get me in. If you like, I'll pretend to have another skin – anything to amuse your fancies.'

'And titillate them too?'

'Sure. And don't worry. I brought a handkerchief with me just in case.' (She laughed) 'Not that I'll ever need it.'

'OK.' She called the waiter to bring her a telephone. She made the call. Abrupt. Tight. Like a poker player securing her hand and tossing in a chip. Ante. Call. Raise you.

As an afterthought, he asked if she were a song? Did she ever play; tuned to the game?

'Only to win,' she replied, her beguiling eyes an ocean of delights, of gorgeous days and delirious nights that promise a man horizons he would otherwise never know. 'Shall we go?' Smile, lock-in his gaze, turn the key, and throw it away. For that moment expressed her as a woman beyond any mere beauty to desire and adore. She was sensual persona carved in flesh and worked in spirit, and the power of attraction became his fate. Sex is sophisticated fate. Addiction. Obsession. Mesmerizing and cool. 'Nick, are you ready?' For there, like a solitary ace turning on a suit of queens, she won the jackpot. Fate. And calmly taking her purse, led him upstairs.

Ante up the moment. He followed, and seemed destined to follow. For ever.

The first thing Nick heard as he entered the room was Roy Riemann's voice, the moneyed tone, breezy, cool, delightfully at ease with himself, like the sun came out and it was autumn and the leaves were turning red and you put your coat on and went for a walk in the park and met up with friends and had a beer maybe two and picked up a few chicks and got a call from mom and dad saying hi and sis' wants to know if you're coming home for Thanksgiving and bring your lady friend along too there's plenty of spare room no worries and the dog Sparky shucks he's not doing so well, ah, poor old fella, but he's had a hell of a life and that's more than most folks can ever hope to ask for kind of voice, the take-your-hat-off to kind of voice, full of confidence that's brimming over to bursting like a tuning fork resonating with money... lots and lots of money.

'I'll raise you a thousand. And...' as denominated gaming chips hit the table with the clamor of transient cash, 'raise you another ten big ones. That's nine for Lady Fortune, plus one for her mother Luck. Never forget mom, fellas. Always got to keep her happy.'

Mamma mia! This move was like opera. He was knocking them up, building pyramids in the center of the table. An opponent studied Roy's *gamely* features, calculation working his face as he weaved poker chips through his fingers, instinct daring him on: *Don't drop your nerve now. Go for it. Eight's bluffing my balls. No, dummy, hold back.* Grappling with the competing emotions of dare or run, chance and opportunity, calculation and risk - a divided mind is a weak mind, and he knew that: *You can't beat statistics; a queen is a queen. But that Hard Eight singing behind those scheming eyes.... Is he bluffing me, damn it? Is he bluffing?*

He tapped the table, passing, and threw in his cards. 'Fold.'

The next man swallowed his drink in a single round, and grinned. 'Call. I'll raise you. And another fifteen on top of that for the Pharaohs.' He stacked it on the pyramid. 'That's another five for Cleopatra, and ten for Nefertiti. Women... I'm not superstitious, fellas – you know me. You don't square them off against each other, or they'll circle you and divide your balls between them. But the pyramid is worth the risk. – Showdown! Let's see the cards.'

Wrong call. Beware of treating women unequally, especially a queen. Ouch!

Gasps all around as Roy, with a grin bigger than a royal flush, leaned over the table and hauled his winnings in. He was talking to an irresistible waif-like creature full of an explosive sex, a delectable kitten with a mighty roar, who drew up closer to him. For a man, her mere presence was a drug, and her warm smile an addiction. She was purring into his ear some enticing fancies that beguile the best of them: he was winning, and she wanted him inside her, deep inside of her. This kitten knows how to haul them in with her paws: men, money, and lifted a few poker chips for herself, knowing far better than any man how to cash them in. *Meow...*

Roy beamed, then saw Nick, and whispered to the kitten nibbling at his ear. She bit it teasingly before escorting Nick to a vacant table by the window; the cool blue curtains permanently drawn.

'Hard Eight asks you to wait.'

'I'm a friend of his.'

'Then you're a friend of mine.' She spoke seductively, her hand moving to his face and her fingers flirted with cuddles, stroking his cheek. She was tactile, perky, fresh. Her manner was habit, and her habit instinct, and the phenomenal power of her sex enabled her to penetrate the barrier of a man in the same way men seduced her. In her mind pussy is ante too, and she would raise you, and raise you, and raise you and out-bet the winners till they burst in orgasm and felt themselves a god inside of her heaven. And she would whisper in their ear, as she did Nick: 'You're cute. Can I call you Nicky?'

'He's Strokes,' said Vonnie. 'His name is Strokes.'

The gleam in the kitten's sensuous eyes glowed with the promise of money, and she ceded without a grumble: 'Strokes. Isn't that cute. Can I stroke you like a cat?' she teased his cheek with her delectable fingers.

'Bring him a drink, would you, honey?' said Vonnie, her tone now verging on sarcasm.

'What would you like, Strokes?'

'What does Hard Eight like?' he asked.

She paused, deferring to her essence, and said: 'He likes the taste of me.'

'That's not really practical now, is it, honey?' Vonnie interjected, cutting her short. 'So, bring him vodka martini. Make that two. And easy on the ice. Thanks, honey.'

But before she returned with the drinks Vonnie left the room, and the delectable kitten sat beside Nick, sipped vodka martini, stirring the ice with the fingers of one hand and, to warm him for the game, stroked his thigh with the other.

Meow.

*   *   *

The explosive sound of ecstasy at the end of the street stirring with anonymous pleasure – but no one hears the salivating symphony of animal submission. It is a long, lingering instinctive sound... deep within the recesses of the 'once-upon–a-time' stylized apartment block; minimalist Bauhaus cum practical whorehouse; bronze sheen soiled by wear and tear and sleazy, seedy, harum-scarum drunk molested fabric interior rounded to the nearest f***ing buck; third floor; apartment 307. The weathered smell of sweat, of discarded condoms, of grease and piss and booze; dingy interior, flaking paint, sodden stairs, there, the muffled sounds take form: behind closed doors; isolated; in an antechamber of oppressive sorts; cocooned; marooned. Dismembered from the gazing sky and sleepless lights of the metropolis, cut off from all spying eyes, the curious, the shallow, the sucker, the bore, the drunk, the sluts yanking at their punters' sleeves hauling them like sacks of spuds made to be mashed, roasted, fried, into rental rooms where the only things that work are the clocks (fast forwarded by ten) - it's flesh by the minute, sucker, minus ten! And the soiled bed where a cock grows hard and howls *cock-a-doo-la-dooo* then softens and she boots his ass out. Here, in sodomized Bauhaus, the only sound is a rank cacophony, but the sound of excitation in 307 is the sound of skin-tight leather sealing tender flesh, and the racking commotion of a whip, the stammer of stylized torture – that's his festish-fried thing, flayed by a lust bird for hire, feeding his desire, teasing his wounds with her fire. In 307, a sweetened hell became a fetish heaven, isolated from the world, from everything. Room in a room in a room... The lash of her whip gave pleasure; the force of her fist soothed him with hammering blows to the ribs. And he sighed... 'Yes... Yes...' even as he choked, even as she tormented him. He was in paradise.

Take two: Burn - man in suffering desire, the furnace of his lusts abated for a moment, and peace reigns. But it's only to tease the coming storm of her fire. Strike the match. Psssss... Her voice thunders with a roar, feminine venom multiplied by the decor, the leather, the whip in lightning bolts of explosive frenzy lashing his flesh to ecstasies. Burn. Burn. Burn. This inferno of a whore, submitting to her rages as she kicks him and he grovels at her feet, she spits on him, once, again, a third time. Then tyrannical in her humor acts sensual over soft surround, kneeling, there, the glove, silk, crimson at the fingertips pressing into his face; harder and harder, 'You are nothing. Nothing.'

'Yes... Yes...'

'Clean the floor – with your tongue!' she fires at him. 'Now. Lick it clean, you filthy animal. You worm! You dog! You pig!'

She kicked him again.

'You are nothing,' she growled contemptuously, looming over him. 'Nothing!'

Her body writhing, pressing onto his, her working hand erupts and punches him. Wearing a white thong over black leather skin, her wiles, like her accent, are *leather-deep*. Amusing? Yes. Until she clenches her fists and punches him, then it really becomes fun – leather deep; consummating the fetish of pain and desire as he stifles breathless in fulfillment.

She squeezed his flesh, breaking him, continuing until he was dazed. Taking him to the rim of unconsciousness, stop, tantalize, then turning earthquakes to tranquility eased the pressure all at once and gently stroked him, teasing the horizon between pain and tenderness, soaking up suffering and ecstasy as though she were the sponge dipped into his ocean of aching spirit: the suffered soul aching for love, aching for happiness, aching for pain... to quench his fragility.

'What are you?' she punched him with her words, then her fists

'Nothing. Nothing...'

Exhausted and languishing before her, his blood-drenched spit drooling from his mouth in a hideous flood. His soul burned, and he was in ecstasy.

Then she kisses him slow and tenderly over skin surreally bruised by her, impaled with metaphors of S & M, artiste and angel as she pummels him to pulp. 'Slave!' This marvel, this man, this catalyst of poems and of hymns; this spectacle of battered flesh is moved by blows to worship her, is touched by kicks and digging heels to render her obeisance, made doubly, triply, ...uncountably delighted by the sudden animation of her mouth, her fevered tongue assaulting him as he screams: 'Not now. Not now... Arrrhh...' is a raping punch-line of the fetish slave to feel himself utterly in submission, completely broken, reduced and turned to the lowest of the low.

'You are vile,' she rasped, disgusted. 'Vile.' And spat him out.

Punch line: *Ha!* And punching bag: *Ouch!* Hit him where it hurts, where he loves it.

'You disgust me. Don't speak. Shut up. I said shut up.'

'Yes, mistress.'

'Shut up!'

Seizing him by his hair and forcing his head back, she squeezed his cheeks until they almost bruised, and he begged her to love him.

'You disgust me,' she said, whispering into his ear, like a threat, like an omen, like a torture. And he was in paradise.

Then the lights suddenly extinguished and startled them.

When the lights went back on, the police forensics team never knew what to make of the scene.

'How long have they been dead?'

'About two hours.'

'That warm?'

'But the woman... less than an hour, I'd say.'

'Pretty hot.' With a puzzled expression he leaned over her, tracing the fractures in her skull, then down the profile of her long sleek and blood-lined body, reminiscent of the lifeline on a palm. He felt a sudden urge to touch her hand.

'What are you looking for, Detective, a pulse?'

'A clue,' he said, frowning, 'something to make the moment snap into place. You know, to get it to go *click*. A crime scene has to click.' Confused thinking hit him hard, and the scene just sputtered riddles.

Hovering amid the corpses, his mind struggled to decode the events before him: two S & M junkies overdosed on slaughter

25

that not only seemed bizarre, but looked revolting. For Detective John Forester of the NYPD, murders were the stuff of mishap, of jealousy, of greed, of error, of pique and anger. There was always a story there, seldom interesting, and typically a mess. But this murder proved exceptional: not one story, but a hundred; not one misshapen plot, but the entire script completely out of joint. – *It's hell out there. It always is; it always has been. So be careful what you look for. And don't be a sucker, kid, because life is a crazy game full of bums and queers and politicians. Are you listening to me, kiddo? Pay attention when your old man's talking to you.* – Those were Pop's words of wisdom popping up like an echo in Forester's brooding mind. His old man was very much alive, even though he was dead. *It's not always the heartache cases that spoil the show. But hey, that's the show called life. That's why we've got Broadway just a-ways, right?...* And Pop died with a bullet in the heart chasing niggers on the wrong side of town. But they don't call them niggers anymore. No way. Politics has turned all sweet now, sugar and icing: brown sugar and chocolate icing, that is. *Are you a wiseguy? Take it or leave it, schmuck head!* Pop had a way with urban words, those ones packed with muscle, brimming with semen, ready to screw the whole world, especially when he knocked back a few stout ones. *Whiskey. Give it me straight, shit head!* And he usually got what he wanted. *Ah! Those were the days, my friend, days of glory... We screwed around, and did our own thing then. Time meant nothing but a grand delirious party. Sex. Booze. Kicking ass on the streets; dealing with wiseguys – Wiseguys! Yeah...* A sentimental old pro was Pop. And besides, he'd be out of place now since, essentially, he was no more than a nigger himself. Black, white, blue, green, nigger is a nigger. That's a word you want to hold on to, keep it handy, in your pocket, in your mouth, on the streets. Use it. Because it has history. It has anger. And it's a word you use because others have lived it. It's grown with pain, nurtured on suffering. Nigger. Not something he hollered from the roof, mind, just something he earned – the hard way. *Bag up your nuts, nigger boy. Keep your women down; your enemies hungry; your friends close; your trap shut, and your eyes open. Hey, who's the hell's that nigger over there looking at? Ah, it's OK, it's me. It's just my reflection in the mirror... Jesus, I look great, don't I? Oh, what a handsome son-of-a-gun you are. Smile, my boy. Yeah.. that's it. Smile...* - And Pop just wouldn't leave it alone... the women, the booze, the cop's life, its legacy, vanity, myth... An urban cowboy cruising the mean streets, kicking his heels on the sidewalks, whistling, some kind of easy stroll taking his time, a deep leisurely step, one, two, he was the Zodiac man, Leo the Lion on Wednesdays, the Crab on Mondays, the Bull on Friday, the Twins on weekends. August the 3rd wasn't good enough for him: he wanted to be born twice, baptized at the Sacred Trinity Church Upper East Side when he was a month old (submerged in a crucible of holy water and a pinch of whiskey that time), and again more poignantly in the baptismal streets of New York City as a rookie cop when he was all of 22 (hey! still a baby – goochy goochy...but dropped him in the deep end that time when a street-bum split open the head of a co-bum who grabbed his stash of liquor, risking everything to gulp it all down his bottomless guts. What is life to a wino? - A deluge in booze). *The things people do. Does it shock me? Nah! Does it make me cynical? In a way, so what..? Hey, I was born cynical. You have a problem with that? Do I make any difference being here in this cesspool of crime day in day out? Hey, pass me a drink, butt-head. Whiskey. And as straight as the candy man, you cocksucking faggot.*

Like daddy like sonny. Like Pop like cop. And here was sonny bogged down in a bloody debacle in room 307 thinking to himself well, perhaps dad would have been a little puzzled too. But what would he make of it? Pop had a nose and ear for these things; and the touch too. Would he look for metaphors first before fleshing out the facts? Would he search for evidence, be systematic and sniff it out – be it up a whore's fanny or inside a wino's empty can, with not even a damn drop left? These boozing bums lick up the juice even by evaporation of the Great God *booze* - hallelujah, and pass the whiskey, mister. Or would a savvy combination of guesswork and experience do the trick? What do you make of this, Pop? Where do I start? *Sonny,* he'd grunt, *I've seen sluts banged and butchered. I've seen deviants die by mishap with a plastic cock up their ass. But I'll be damned if any of this makes sense to me. Damn, I need a drink.* – (It may not solve the problem one jot, but hey, it always helped him to think. He considered it an extension of cognitive development. And, as an instinctive student of the streets, he knew the urban landscape as the only school of substance in the world, as damn real as your boots, and you learn it on your feet. And he was always learning. Cheers! He'll drink another to that).

Forester paused, imagining he could smell something familiar, a sweetish aroma that had his thoughts sifting appellations, but a rookie cop, excited by his first *real* case, burst into the room and distracted him:

'Hey, Detective, there's someone out here who... *Jesus!*' The rookie took stock of the surroundings, the congealing pools of blood, the carefully aligned corpses abased and humiliated. 'What the hell is this?'

'Some find it arousing.'

'Detective…?'

'Never mind. What do you have?'

'A hooker; said she heard some noises down the hall. Hollering, and a bang.'

'Is that all – hollering and a bang? Can she be more specific?'

'She wasn't altogether there, if you know what I mean?'

'Excuse me?'

'She was preoccupied at the time.' He shrugged, grinning, 'Girl's got to make a living somehow.'

'And she heard some noises?'

'So she says.'

'Take a statement.' His grim look reflected his experience of never to expect too much too soon, especially from people. Often their misguided enthusiasm diverted cops into false leads. The greater part of what witnesses remembered was often imagined or fantasized - it's not their fault, but merely the shock of the moment, that sudden confrontation with the unexpected that sends human senses into a spin, and you recoil with a thud back to your bland everyday reality. It's what people are, what life is, essentially a balanced routine. Even the humdrum life is of a perfect order: without repetition, nothing would work, nothing would exist. The cycles of existence are a bore, sure, but they're fundamentally very deep. So the wise cop downs a pinch of salt with his neat tequila and aromatic lemon and examines the hard facts alone, because witnesses were unreliable. It's the bane of a crime scene – people surfacing out of nooks and crannies with embellished muck in their heads. But he's a cop, a tequila cop like his old man, bless him, so he had to do the rounds. The rookie seemed to sway his head uncertainly.

'Detective, shall I take her down to the station?'

Forester signaled him – No. And the rookie gestured back, touching his cap with a feathery clip of his fingers before leaving the room. He was still a cop with a smile. Jesus, did he have a lot to learn!

Forester sighed then turned to examine the room, psychologizing its fetishes, its peculiar motif, its deviant essence – some places, they can communicate with you. Inanimate things send feelers to your bones. But this? This room was a closed room, a sound-proofed room, a black box for deviants to expand their horizons to the limit and never be discovered – what you hide in shame out there, you can liberate with abandon in here. The only noises the hooker down the hall heard were the random farts of a blown-out punter who went limp all too soon on her. Well, even a whore has pride. *He can't even fuck me, the useless shit he is.* Well, what's he going to do, invite her home? Marry her? Tell her he loves her...? Come on, girl, get real. *Fuck you!* I have already. *Fuck you!* Again? *Fuck you*! Repetition... *Ffff* – Erogenous expletives?... Well, like 'have a nice day', or a streetwise gesture, they stand the test of time. Forester glanced at his watch and maneuvered around the room.

The victims posed the usual dilemma that confronts a cop – they were just ordinary people, nameless floaters in a floating world, with no apparent reason to single them out. But dead, the aura of paradoxical crime clung to them. Someone, the murderer, had entwined them in a fetal position, face to face, the man's right arm crossing her left in a strange coiling embrace. A surgical lesion on her left check, the same on his right – a scene gruesome but pregnant with symmetry. It seemed, geometry aside, even a strange ugliness can be poetic and inspire contemplation. Art for murder's sake. And there they lay, amid the grim silence of a dead peace, a room full of foreboding and cruel things, but echoing of emptiness. It would have been easier to understand were they chopped to bits and pasted to the walls. At least then you could call it abstract art: post-modern S & M, a fetish oeuvre, consummated in blood.

The murder, together with the general confusion, had a vile whimsy about it. The motive seemed less important than the idea of creating this *production*. The whole thing was too neat, too elaborate. It was sleazy, yet enacted with *style*. Irrationality with panache. Forester couldn't help but imagine he felt something, there, on the tip of his tongue, reminiscent of remembered things, but which eluded him and made him feel moody. He felt like having a cigarette, and a drink, and shaking his head with apathy, looked away.

Forester's colleague, Sandy, kneeled down for a closer look. 'We know who she is, this is her apartment. But him... no ID. Nothing. Not a thing,' she said ponderingly. He always felt Sandy was a bit too classy for this game, she had such lovely flowing hair, girlish, fresh, blissfully curly that made him often reminisce of carefree youth, and feel ever so tender and melancholy and wish himself smothered in their golden ripples. In less gory circumstances she would have displayed that dashing smile that graced her pretty face. Beauty amid the grim reality of the city: a landscape of blues with hopeful dashes of charming pink - that's the Apple of life, core of a dream, that's NYC^2 (New York City *squared – the emboldened heart of a dreamer that never sleeps).*

'So, Sandy, what else do we have?'

'Just what you see. Her… poor soul. And him.' She twitched her nose. 'One and one make…'

'That's not much.'

'You don't suppose they were married?'

He frowned at her: 'I guess not.'

'Well, they went on smiling till the lights went out.'

'Were they lovers?'

'By the hour,' she smirked irresistibly, for this was love kept hot by feeding the meter. No pay; no lay. 'What a crazy, crazy world. - Forester.'

'Yes, Sandy?'

'What a crazy world.'

He rubbed his eyes and knelt to examine them more closely. 'Why do you think they were tangled up together like that? Look how meticulously it's done.'

'I know. It's a strange performance.'

'But why do that? Is there a message? A code?'

'That's always bothered me. Does a murder scene tell you more about the killer than those he murdered?' She shuddered quietly. 'That's what makes them so scary. The contradictions. You're never sure which way to turn. They could pop up anywhere.'

'Overlook that for a moment.'

'How? That's impossible.'

'Look round at the scene. These victims: they were people playing out a role only a few hours ago. Fetishes thrive on role play.'

'And I wanted to be an actor. Am I in the wrong job?'

'Be serious, please. - These props, this whole scene is full of codes. It's perverse to us, sure, but theatrically exact for them. These guys are strange, but they're not random. Sandy, this means something? It must *mean* something.'

'And what's the language? What's the code? What are we looking for?'

'Look beneath the role play, behind the scene.'

'For what?'

'A sign. A signal of some kind. - Sandy,' he pressed his point, 'there *must* be a signal.'

'A signal with a jock strap attached. How deep is that?'

'Be serious; please. - Come on, Sandy, think, what can it mean?'

'What *can* it mean? It doesn't have to mean anything, does it? Just look at all this stuff, for goodness sake! Dildos, whips, full-leather body wear and masks. And what the hell's the thong for? Don't these people like the look of naked flesh? Do they despise it so much that they have to smother up the body like that? Asphyxiate it? Extinguish it? Pervert every inch of it? It's ludicrous. It's sick.'

'OK, Sandy, have it your own way.' He waited for her temper to abate, and then resumed. 'Does this strike you as a fetish encounter that just happened to lose the plot? Is that plausible?'

'It's so insidious, so bizarre, well... aside from a madman, it could be revenge. A vendetta, perhaps. And the woman, well... she was probably in the wrong place at the wrong time. Poor soul.'

'A vendetta, Sandy?'

'Yes, perhaps... It's too elaborate for anything else.' She noticed his disquiet, and continued. 'Who would conceive anything as bizarre as this, let alone execute it? This person isn't satisfied with simple retribution. He has to make a show of it. A grand opera of gore. For that you need not only a motive, but... imagination.'

'Imagination?'

'For want of a better word; yes, imagination. Even the devil is an enterprising actor. Give credit where it's due. Even applause.'

'Devil or no, someone was watching them,' Forester concluded. 'But who? And why?'

'A Peeping Tom?'

'I wondered that, but... No. This isn't a voyeur's scene.'

'Perhaps it was, and he just got carried away. I'm not ruling anything out, least of all where crazy people are concerned. And let's be honest, Forester, this is crazy, wouldn't you say? Even for New York City.'

'Bizarre as it seems, Sandy, they wanted intimacy; enclosure meant intimacy; just as pi to a mathematician reveals a circle. Doesn't matter how rough it gets, how menacing a spectacle it becomes, pain for them is intimate. It's beautiful; perfect; pure.'

'Like pi.'

'Yes. So they create their own world... and immerse theselves entirely in its space. This fetish hell that you see is their paradise. This is part of their drama; it's life fashioned with a fetish skin. You can't have role-play without that skin. And it's kept hidden. It's made safe. It's not something you can see from the sidewalk. It needs to be decoded. Yes...' He looked at the things around him. 'This room is encoded with them, their beliefs and passions are inscribed everywhere, encrypted in things, in stuff like this. This whip is an emotion; that chain is a soul. We are looking right at them, these people – but we don't always see. It's damn hard to see, I know. You have to be an S & M hacker to crack their code. But whatever the motive, whoever did this, no voyeur was here.'

'Are you sure about that?'

'Pretty sure,' he said. 'Even Pop, may he rest in peace, would back me up here.'

'After a drink...'

'Yes.'

'Miss him, huh?'

He paused and remembered, sharing his thoughts, his spirit chasing the fancies of younger days, when Pop was alive, and everything was so simple and not because it was simple but because Pop was around, so life seemed kind of... simple. Suddenly, reality pulled him back, and his senses kicked in with a start. 'What's that smell?' There it was again. 'Sandy?'

'What?'

A rush of emotion swept through him and, like a fleeting breeze, the smell vanished. 'It's nothing.'

'There's booze over there, I think. Some fruit too.'

'No. Never mind,' he said, and began lighting up a cigarette, but had second thoughts and put away the pack.

'How does it play out in your mind?' Sandy asked him.

'First impressions?'

'We have to start somewhere.'

'No voyeur was here.'

'Well... someone was. And it turned real ugly.'

'This was not a set up. It was improvised. They, or a lone killer, tried to make it seem that way.'

'Seem?'

'Staged on the fly.' He gazed at her and she cast him a doubting frown. 'Well, that's how it looks.'

'I don't see it,' she said. 'You can imagine almost anything here. This is a crime scene: you have to read from it, not rewrite it. Decode, don't write the code. - We need constraints. Speculation without constraints is no better than fantasy.' She paused a moment before justifying herself. 'I don't wish to frustrate your theories, but we've played that game before. And it got us no-where.'

'Stand back from the chaos and find a reference point. Without taking your bearings, an ocean will forever be an ocean, and never a road.

'Are you a philosopher now?'

'Hardly.'

She laughed. And he continued:

'So, from where you are, take an angle shot. Indulge me a little here, Sandy, please. - Your eye is the camera. Pan from the window to the door; the ceiling to the floor. Don't zoom in, just gaze at the landscape of the room, and keep to the wide angle.'

'OK. – What now?'

'Look at it, Sandy. It's just too tidy in some parts, a complete mess in others. The killer isn't familiar with the surroundings; he's alien to this fetish scene; with what went on here. He's not part of it. He doesn't belong here. Look how meticulous he is with the bodies – as if that's all that mattered. For a voyeur, every little detail counts: the fruit, the chair, the whip, the pin on the mantelpiece, the whole deal. These guys consume with their eyes like no other – no detail escapes them. They have complete knowledge of their surroundings; and everything has to fit. They are the easiest people in the world to figure out. No,' he concluded, 'the hand that did this had a technical mind guiding it, good at focusing on local details, not a strategist, more a tactician I'd say. Not the eye of Peeping Tom; but the eye of a stranger.'

Forester withdrew from the bodies, unfazed by the enterprise of murder. He regarded it not causally but methodically. A cop was like an alphabet: A B C... all the way to Z – an alphabeta man. Murder: these things have an order, even if they do confound and knock-up some strange words from time to time. Teasing little words. That sound surprising? Well, it's part of the psychosis of crime. As a man, what surprised him was that he wasn't surprised anymore. Fascinated? Yes. Perplexed? Yes. Surprised? No. Not any more... Consequently, the victims assumed roles in a reconstructed drama, following the speculation of a feasible time-line, token bits in a story around which weaved the specifics of a crime scene. The victims drew all the subplots together probably in much the same way this room attracted them in the first place. They have fevered cravings that are impetuous but irresistible to them. Forester knew, you don't need to understand these things to work them out. That's why a cop has his alphabet. He invents dialects, and phrases, and all kinds of nuanced rhymes, even poetry. A man and his desires are two sides of the same coin: in words, *I want, I need*, heads, tails... And in life, well, every alphabeta man knows – it's not every penny that fits the slot.

As soon as he entered, Forester felt intrigued with the room: its strange landscape of the seedy, the repulsive, and quite frankly the downright fascinating. Its features fleshed out an ugliness that coaxed and tore at the senses, oppressing them to a slow strangulation. Freedom, for some, is subjugation; liberation is wasting away in a cage; pleasure is being chained to a wall and tortured. *Some take sugar with their tea; others prefer pain.* And to achieve fulfillment, every detail had to be perfect. These were the signals Forester was homing in on. This was the essence of the room, beyond the savage fact of staring at death, assaulted by its plainness, there, the fact of slaughter in your face, pressed into its unimaginable uncannyness. Holding his breath, he turned away.

Death seemed so perverse a parody at times. But the reconstruction of the story had now begun, alphabeta man searched for a word and turned to Sandy, glancing briefly at her lovely golden curls, bursting with freshness, so full of life:

'Sandy, what's that over there? On the floor. There, to your left?'

'Where?' she looked and, spotting it, lifted it with care. 'This?'

'Yes.'

'A pen,' she inspected it carefully, remarking in aside: 'I wonder where that's been?'

'Hand it me, would you.'

'Careful,' she passed it over. 'We need to dust it for prints.'

Holding it by the tip he examined it closely. 'It has some mark or logo on it.' Traces of congealing blood obscured the details, but at an oblique angle to the light he could just make out the words as they flickered in the liquid red of blood and grime. 'NBS Banking Corporation. Got it. Here,' he handed it back. 'Get that analyzed first, would you.'

'Will do.'

He had something tangible at last, a money-connection, a pointer on the bizarre world of sadomasochism gone awry by the presence a third hand whose fingers weaved a strange murder, grafting riddles on the raw side of a thrill - man in the drama of his own semen. (It was ugly. Men desire ugly things. It excites them). Money and a sexual fetish – it *must* mean something, he thought. Then again, it could mean anything. Forester is that kind of a guy who knows he really knows nothing. Love is a smile, lust is a grin. And he sort of smiled, grinningly, and looked at his wristwatch.

'Forester.'

'Yes, Sandy?'

'What are you thinking?'

'Hmm...'

It was often the bane of a crime scene to have a glut of *something* offering very little of *anything*, like the signature of misleading clues written in invisible ink. If ever a crime needed a story, this seemed to be the one. But the narrative was muted; it told him nothing, and the central character faked the persona of a Peeping Tom. To Forester's mind, it couldn't be him – Tom's story would never have the kind of ending like this one had. The voyeur would never turn his world inside-out. His world, like his desires, were *outside-in.* There were no literal truths in Tom's mind, only an emotional amalgam of shadows and seediness. And like Tom's world, this was not a literal scene. It shared its ambiguities of strange lusts, the common melting of reality into fantasy, a primeval craze sparked by a stare, of things temptingly out of reach and available to the naked gaze alone. It was a stage for obsession; an uncontrolled, unbearable urge to liberate the frenzy of passion – perhaps a love – for things of perverted longing. And this explains the earnest desire of a man to become and remain a slave of his insatiable delights.

Looking round at the room, Forester said, 'Some crimes resemble a maze.'

'What was that?'

'Others are merely a parody of imperfect hopes.'

'Excuse me?'

'And failed dreams.'

'Forester...' she was growing irritable.

'Sorry, Sandy, I was just philosophizing.' He rubbed his eyes, then addressed a uniformed cop. 'Can we get some more lights in here, please? Thank you.' Then to Sandy: 'Who called it in?'

'Anonymous email.'

'Faceless medium.'

'A sexless medium.'

'Another enigma.'

'But a fact.'

'Where would you start?'

'Not with the message.'

'But how do we find the messenger?'

'Let's wait for the lab results and see what they come up with.'

'But look at it intuitively, Sandy, stand back, and tell me what you see?'

'The same as a voyeur would see. Knock knock, come in, Tom, and look at your handiwork.'

He shook his head, begging to differ, 'It's too... intimate. Too enclosed. Look at the quality of the paneling. These walls are polished wood; it looks like latex, doesn't it? Soiling any of it would be a sin. A voyeur needs a crack in the skin of the room to look through. Two-way mirrors; hidden cameras, something to spy with. A voyeur... this creature, he's like a fly. He wants to hide in a crack, in the fracture of a lampshade, the wound on a finger tip, if he could, even up your ass.' They laughed spontaneously, before turning serious again. 'Believe me, Sandy; there is more here than meets the eye. Much more.'

She examined the things around her and felt baffled at every turn, her curiosity throttled by the S & M scene, unable to comprehend what it was telling her. She shook her head in disarray. 'What is it with you guys? Why do you come to these places? My God! What's driving you? You're so weird.'

He tactfully averted her eyes and skirted the insinuation to his maleness – he liked it straight, not with a whip. But the idea of having someone on the inside, an S&M junkie, as it were, that might be able to crack the code, seemed rational. For now, he let it rest at the back of his mind as he continued probing the room, and said:

'This room is a cocoon. There are no cracks. It's sealed; tight. Hermetically shut in.'

'Like a coffin.'

Forester examined the ceiling. 'In the right, excited state of mind, one could choke in here. It has the sense of suffocation.'

'How?'

'You've been under water before?'

'Ah, OK, I think I see what you mean.' She shook her head, almost shuddering. 'You guys are really *weird*.'

'It's set up that way, as a construct, so the room feels like it's imploding in on you.'

'On them?' she pointed to the victims.

Forester considered the motionless forms where flesh seemed so alive; so sensual; so watched, so human. 'I see...'

'What?'

'Two people laid out like a card game; a King and a Queen with a Joker as the third card.'

'What did they play for?'

'Something… who knows. Perhaps we'll never know. But it took more than two to make a full house.' Was he being clever, or just pulling it all together? Hard to say. To her mind he's made of male stuff, muscular stuff, full of whimsy and brawn. And for a woman that's rather difficult to understand. Stuff. Male. Crime. Poker. Sometimes, they are no more than a numbers' game. Nice round numbers. Guy numbers. Simple. Silly. Totally male. Take five?

Sure, why not...

'So,' she said, 'what is all this telling us?'

'Telling us?'

'You're a guy. Is the killer throwing a scent?'

'No. The killer's throwing shadows.'

'You know, Forester, Peeping Tom or no, someone else was *here*; someone *was* watching them? And whoever it was, wasn't only playing games.'

He shrugged gloomily. 'And that's what really grates, because I'd sooner believe it was an angry ghost than a man.'

'I didn't know you believed in ghosts?'

'I don't. But it would make more sense.'

Sandy quietly smiled. That was his dad talking – Pop was in those words, articulated aloud with all guns blazing. Guys like him are the stuff of cowboys with Manhattan smiles, with New York tones, with a bustling energy that is America red raw with sizzling fire. Words are an engine ready to go, a story of a man strapped into a starship the size of Manhattan, revving her up, teasing her lights, and Pop hit the pedal hard in a burst of passion: *You bunch of fannies! What the hell are you doing in my police force? Do you think, even for a moment, this crazy case and these dead psycho deviants laid out like the Sunday roast have me stumped with their tricks? Do I look like the lollipop man? You see that plastic prick up that dead faggot's ass?* It's a cucumber, Pop. *A cucumber?* Yes, do you see, it's green, for pickling. *Jesus H Christ, what next! Is this faggot a vegetarian or something?* I've no idea, Pop. We haven't got around to that yet. *Holy Christ! I've seen it all, now. Pickled faggots in the middle of my crime scene. What the hell are you bothering the coroner for? Bring in a cook. Holy Mary Mother of God, if I can't crack this screwball case you can shove that thing up my ass, and I'll suck my thumb to boot. Get to work, you fannies. - God damn! What a world. Phew! No more salad for me. No sir. My salad days are over...*

Forester the younger knew this was a case that would consume him. Sandy offered him a cigarette. He smiled at her, and took one. 'I don't believe in ghosts, but I would like to believe in angels. I need to now.'

'What, an angel?'

'With a cigarette!' And laughing, he winked fondly at her.

At length, he walked over to the windows, parted the curtains, opened the thick wooden boarding with the soundproof panels, and leaned out. As he surveyed the scene below, the midnight flow of pedestrians and traffic, the faint sound of jazz wafted into his mind like the perfume of a rose carried on a breeze twenty meters away.

He recognized the song. It was a favorite. And he smiled.

*   *   *

'Susie, try it again in C flat.' The pianist, directing the vocalist, instinctively tapped on a piano key as he dubbed the tune: 'Da da da, rapid, like you're dancing on water.'

'Can we take five? Come on, Billy, please...' she pleaded, feeling exhausted, stretching out her arms, the microphone falling to the floor and sending piercing feedback through the sound system. 'My voice needs a rest, or it'll end up sounding like that.'

'OK, OK. Everyone back in five. Charlie, you stay away from the booze now. We've got work to do,' he told the drummer.

'I'm just going to see Vonnie,' he explained, resting his sticks on the boomer drum.

The saxophonist kept on playing as though he hadn't heard a thing. They let him alone, absorbed in his own sound, music maker of the endless night, jazz in a seamless mood – one two three four five......

da ba dub dub.

Upstairs, the card dealer called out:

'New deck,' and tearing up the used set of cards opened a fresh pack. 'Any one want to take a break?'

'Just deal,' a player to his left grunted, counting his losses by the meager stack of gaming chips remaining in his cache. 'Is there any more whiskey around here? Jesus, I need a drink.'

'Straight?'

'Yeah.'

'Ice?'

'Yeah.'

The players conspired in silence. It was an elementary rule of poker: gamble with what you know, not your fancies. The shuffle of cards was the only melody of consequence, the sweetest rustle that of money weaving through your hands, and the click clicking sound of poker chips an aria celebrating the great game: How many cards? Gimme two. Two? Yeah. Tap tap, throws two to the dealer and the dealer dishes a pair. Not a bad set, a six and eight of clubs. Hmmm, nice round numbers... wonderful what a shuffle of the cards can do. The ambivalent gaze, the long stare, the deliberate pause, studying the cards, observing each other, each pair, each triple - the cards have a strange power over the deck of men, of testosterone bunching into groups then spawning individuals. Chance, luck, intuition, poker – heck of a thing. It's all watched and watching, yourself and others, and Hard Eight coughs as his turn swings round.

'And the world goes round and round... Spin baby spin. Call. And I'll raise you five grand. Wait,' he coughed, 'make it six.'

Playing round after round, *Fresh deck. Anyone want a break? Nah!* And the chips shuffled across the table on the turn of a card, stacking up the heaps there, diminishing them elsewhere. Poker - you win or you lose. That's how you play. Coming out evens isn't even an anti-climax. The only thing a player wants to hear is 'Deal...' Always the game. Yeah, the game. While there's money around you play. You play your heart out. What's the time? Gimme a break, I ain't even got time to take a piss. I ain't leaving this table till the last buck's gone, into my own pocket or down someone else's. Anyone tells me to stop and I'll swat them like a fly. *Whack!* You got that? Time is measured

40

by your assets, not the hours in a day. *Deal!*

Amazed gasps bounce all around at the wiles of Lady Luck, as she waltzes a capricious little dance with the cards, seducing you with the tango, wooing you with the rumba, she's classical this chick, she pirouettes and sucks your heart out with an ace, tickles you with a jack, tempts you with a queen, ravishes your desires with a suit of tens. These guys are players and they love her and hate her and bless her bleeding bitch heart as they knock back the whiskey, and chips hit the table, and a player tapping a rib for luck makes his last wager, looks up, sighs, and folds with a smile. 'Not my day. I'm done. Outa cash. See you, fellas.' And he withdrew from center stage like a real pro – bowing out gracefully, sure, poorer by sixty thousand, but with royal flush dignity as only a real player can, the genuine article, the beauty of a complete set: spades arching into aces curving into clubs dancing into diamonds – the magic of the cards, and he broods in aside: *'Damn luck! It's just not my day...'* It's kind of a guy thing, this, as he slips on his jacket, swigs his drink, tips the waitress, and winks enviously at the winner, earnest to the last buck as he sighs: 'Hard Eight's on a roll.'

'What can I say?' Roy's exuberant grin frames the occasion perfectly, beaming with pride as he hauled in his winnings. 'What can I say? I love you all to death. You are my comrades, my friends, my buddies, and you bring me pots of money. You're all heart. I wished I loved myself as much; I'd be a happy man. This smile, it's all for you, fellas; all for you. - Come on, guys, look at me. Don't I deserve it? If anyone does, it's got to be an Eight with a Hard on, and surely that's me. Right, fellas? I've earned my brownie points, my right to life, liberty and all the rest of that stuff. I should be dishing it up in spades. Sandcastles aren't my game, but if they were, I'd be King of the biggest and the best. I'd have two point two kids and live in a three point three place on some four point four beach somewhere on the West Coast and God knows what else... n point n I guess, I'd have it all, the American point American dream. I'd be the consummate man. I'd be an ego thingy. A top dog top man in a top hat in a top act that's hard to beat. Do you think I'm boasting? Does this seem like over-confidence to you? Come on, fellas, it's natural hubris with a Yankee smile,' he said, feeling slightly bashful but looking *very otherwise*. If smugness was measured in tons, you're looking at a million plus, all metric and pure class. 'I'm not boasting just for the hell of it, fellas, but winning is my game. You know what my Ma said to me? She looked proudly at her handsome little boy and said: Son, a *smart* loser is just someone who hasn't won yet, that's all. It's the American way. Me, well, I'm just a regular all-round guy that happens to square the circle now and again. And it couldn't happen to a nicer guy. I grew up on homemade apple pie, me. You bet. – Ah, you see, the thing with me,' he said with mock humility as he stacked up his winning chips into denominated columns of one, two and five grand piles, 'is that I am religious at heart, while my head remains soundly pagan. Life: it's a gas! What can I say? Ah! I just love it when I'm winning. It feels soooooo right. Yes!'

The poker table had a gaping hole that needed to be filled; not necessarily with a skilled player, but anything that strives for the embodiment of symmetry, and keeps superstition at bay. Often *a player* fills that role, but his basis is money, not his character or assumed charm. It's money that carries a man, and gives him weight. At some point, if the man is a *real* player, he carries the money, and it all fits perfectly together. In fact, it's the most natural thing in the world. Like male stuff.

'Hey, Nick; over here. Pull up a chair. Come on, don't be shy.'

All eyes fell on Nick, and he blushed. Ouch! That move's just not poker. He went over to the table, paused, and conferred with Roy in a hushed tone:

'I'm a bit short of cash. And I'm not very good at this game.'

'Not to worry; I'll loan you. Just sit in with us. Fill out the circle. Go with the flow.'

Poker is an addiction to some, a superstition to others. It depends on character. And timing, too. And luck. And nerve. And money. Lots of money.

'Roy, what does it all mean?' he asked naively.

'What?'

'Poker.'

He leaned closer to him and whispered, so it sounded like an echo: 'Religion. An act of faith; that even though I can't cheat the cards, bribe chance, or bend statistics, still, I want to believe fate is on my side. – By the way, what did Vonnie call you?'

'How did you know?' he sounded surprised, and wondered whether he should have been. 'Strokes.'

'Strokes? Nah! Who pulled that out of the hat - Vonnie? Come on, she's just teasing you; playing around with your mind. You're Straight Ace. Take a seat. - Fellas, I'd like you to meet Straight Ace.'

'Straight?' scoffed the dealer with dry humor as he shuffled the cards. 'Straight at the corners maybe. But inside… Nah!' He had that look which leaves one with the impression of never being sure if he really meant what he said. Roy never doubted him for a moment, and brashly countered back:

'I always thought you'd make the perfect candy man. You have all the qualifications. You're as sweet as pie, and dumb to boot. And if you shuffle those cards any more, they're likely to wear away with friction.'

'I can't help it,' he said smugly, 'I just love fondling them.'

'They're not a pair of tits, you know.'

'You still have a *whole lot* to learn there, Hard Eight. A *whole lot* to learn…'

'Nick, stop standing there, and pull up a chair.'

The chair on the left was the chair for suckers. They called it *Speakeasy* after the wiseguys who overrated themselves: out-of-town cowboys mostly short of a horse. They came to the table with hope: 'Speak' - all smiles and yak yak. You just couldn't get them to shut up. And left as losers: 'Easy' - a sullen grunt, grrr grrr that knocked the stuffing out of them and sent them packing back to their turkey farms. Well, a mule was always more their style. Nick went for the left chair. Schmuck!

'No. Nick, sit on my right,' insisted Roy.

'He looks like an *Easy* to me,' said a guy seated opposite, weighing him up as he tossed thousand dollar chips between his hands. 'And I never misplace a face.' He grinned slyly at Nick. 'Speak *real* easy, fella. Real, real easy, because you won't last long.'

Roy cut in and confronted him: 'Are you warming up those chips for me?'

'Nope!'

'We'll see about that.'

He laughed and glanced obliquely at Nick: 'Grab yourself a chair. Left, right, take your pick, it's all relative anyway.'

'And skill, and the cards, and the nerve to go on winning,' Roy added with a defiant grin. 'Nick, sit on my right.'

'OK, OK...'

Roy smiled his *winning* smile and, turning to the kitten, gave her some money. 'Bring him some chips would you, babe. And get him a real drink.'

'Whiskey?'

'Yeah.'

'Neat?'

'Yeah.'

She brought the chips, the drink, deftly tipped herself a thousand, sat beside Roy and stroked his thigh as play resumed.

Nick wore a puzzled expression, like the quirky curiosity of a cat, which Roy noticed by glancing sideways at him. Lowering his voice, he asked: 'What's the matter, Nick?'

He shook his head, 'What does the gold chip mean?'

'Power. – Jack, deal the cards.'

'He in?'

'Yeah.'

Jack, a.k.a Jack of Spades, clockwise dealer of the session, dealt the cards.

'Roy,' said Nick.

'Don't call me Roy, not at the table. Call me Hard Eight.'

'Why?'

'Oblige me. Please. You can do that, can't you?'

'Roy – I mean Hard Eight,' he whispered tactfully, 'give me some hints.' And Hard Eight whispered back:

'Work the pairs; spades over hearts; diamonds over clubs. It's a gamble, sure. But it's an art, too. – Hey,' his voice rose abruptly. 'Is that Susie singing?'

'Yeah,' said Jack, quintessentially masculine in the phrasing of a sigh, 'Yeah...' mesmerized by her sensuous voice. 'Give me Susie and the blues over the rhythms of the sparrows any day. Yeah... any day.... I'll raise you a thousand.'

The waves of fortune ebb and flow, one round running gloriously in a man's favor, sweeping to a peak, then turn to a trough in the next – emotionally, it's a tidal wave, and you sweat it out or you drown; you grind it out to the end or you're ground down. It's relentless. It's amazing. It like having sex with money. You screw it, it screws you, either way, you get to come buckets of cash. - The capricious riddles of the poker table, ante up, sense the cards kiss the tips of fingers, teasing at the corners like a tongue, is that a french? like your lover, touch them in places only you can ever feel - up! - tantalizing victory in a sleuth's discovery of patterns, clues, signals, it's all instinctive heat in the slow burn of poker, a million degrees centigrade and it's only just warming up, you mix the numbers, you work the suits, you look for order to your hand – is it worth the risk to raise another ten grand? You call; you fold; the risk is all on hunches calculated over spasms of an eye, blinking, sweat glistening on the forehead, the breathing heaving hedonistic holding state of expectation wondering if Mammon winked at you. Ahhh. Yeah, Fate is a bitch in heat and a thousand more baby-lucks churning out of poker chips onto the table: 'Raise you,' and Spades Seven flashing his blue eyes gives his game away. 'Five thousand. And five more.' The smart money throws in the hand, yields to common sense and waits to see the risky money pile in more dough: 'Five big ones plus five and another five – three's my lucky number. Showdown! Let's see the cards.' And blue eyes flashes like a lighting bolt, *four queens,* and wraps his winnings with his hands, smiles, and orders another drink, generous with his tips. After all, it's just money.

'Hey, Spades,' says Jack, holding blue eyes in affected awe. 'Loan me twenty grand?'

'Sure.' And Jack stays in the game. Go another round. Fondle the chips, feel them up and tease a sense of luck that as he tosses them into the center they're like dice on a roll, feeling of victory, sweet, precious, hoping for sixes, sixes, come on sixes. Poker: is it a game or a way of life? The smart money plays both ways. It's an even bet. You're born. You live. You play poker. You die. But at the poker table not necessarily in that order. It depends on luck, skill, and a savvy way of mind. The bottom line is: when you're with the pros - luck depends on knowing what to do, knowing how to play. Hustle here and maneuver there and what is dream and what is real? It all boils down to...

'Money!' exclaimed Jack, throwing up his arms and getting to his feet. It was defeat played with panache. Not acted sentimentally, but with a knowing smile that he'll be back: he's a player and he'll endure. 'She's deserted me.' Luck, that is, because money is just a throwaway ticket to luck. Luck – feminine; noun; a kick in the head. Ouch! This is one dame you don't want to mess with. Treat her nicely, even when she's squeezing your balls. (Ahhh....)

The table yielded and wound up the game. The majority of players were reluctant to continue with a gap in the table – it was a lousy sign. 'It's like Lady Luck kicked your front teeth out,' Hard Eight explained to Nick, feeling irritable. 'An empty chair is like that. The table's got to be full. If its starts out full, then it's got to end that way, or you're playing with loaded dice stacked against you. Luck isn't a cheat. No. Just a feckless dame, is all. She won't make up her mind whether your balls are marbles or loaded dice. A lover one minute; a sadist the next. Love her or hate her, whatever, one way or another she's after your balls.'

'Marbles or dice?'

'Ask the lady,' he said, grinning. Then conferred with the others: 'We'll resume next week, fellas. Bring your dough. And easy come, easy go...'

Spades Seven was first to leave the room. A ritual ensued, an unspoken habit among the players. Each takes his leave in a fastidious, ordered way, even if appearances deceive, as they file out folding down shirtsleeves and pulling on jackets heading variously for the bar, the men's room, the phones to make that late call. 'Hold on, Nick. Let Spades shove off first.'

'Why?'

'Etiquette. It's part of good poker,' he explained, then, turning excitedly to the kitten: 'Come here, baby, and gimme a kiss.'

'Oh Roy!' she roused, lifting several bills from his horde of cash and sliding them into the wonderful crevice between her breasts. If ever there was a natural repository for money – holy Mammon, that must be it! He had yet to count this magnificent pot of honey, all lick lick and yum yum, this *fete du opulence* that drew the kittens in their grifty little hoards meowing their eagerness to lend a hand or two and, blinking coyly like an angel, she naturally offered to help him. But heaven had its price; and she meowed like a pussycat and looked winsome like an angel to the brooding ape that was a man with easy money, and said: 'It will cost you, Roy.'

'How much?' he asked, and he knew right away it was a price worth paying.

She took a thousand with the delicate tips of her fingers, and they watched the notes float into her purse like leaves from a tree. Is it autumn already? Someone must be singing in the rain...

Roy roared with laugher: 'You know, I feel like I'm growing money from all my orifices; like a tree sprouting leaves.'

'Do you mind if I help myself?' Nick chuckled.

'As a matter of fact, I do. Come on, let's go for a drink and have us some fun. We've earned it, haven't we, puss?' He kissed the pussycat ravenously, and she meowed and purred like a lioness on a roll. 'Stick with me, kid; I'm on a roll.'

'Naturally,' said Nick, and Roy roared with laugher.

'You're ever the laid-back Brit, Nick. The genuine article.'

The interplay of serenading jazz and tobacco, sprinkled with essence of cocaine, and swans (seductive dancers with gorgeous long legs) danced on stage in flesh enfolding lycra fashioned into dazzling red bikinis.

'I am a music voyeur with a gaze fixed on fingers fondling the piano keys, and an ear soaking up the dreamy beat of a drum worked in resonance with a bass. I watch. I listen. I feel. And I love it all madly.'

'Oh Roy... You're such a poet. Oh Roy!' cried the kitten with a dashing pride in him.

'Gimme a kiss.'

He slapped her ass and asked her to get in the drinks. Giving her a couple of hundred dollars, he felt a winner in more ways than one. 'And pretzels, baby. Nuts and pretzels. Don't forget them or I'll die.'

She winked at him and he blew her a kiss. Nick, the calm observer, coyly grinned. Roy resumed:

'Pussycat, pussycat... where would I be without my pussycat? I love her to death.'

'I can see.'

Roy coughed and turned to Nick: 'Thank God for sluts. I'd be a down-and-out schmuck without them. I'd be lost. I love them to death, even if they're the death of me. But hey, everyone's got to go one day. Right, Nick?'

'I imagine so,' he murmured.

'Christ! You're such a laid-back Brit. Where the hell were you made, Nick? Here, grab yourself a slice of this place, for God's sake. You're a real understatement Johnny in a jazz bar filled with gorgeous women, booze and slick amusements. Man was born to be a whoremonger; that's his nature. See? A slut is the fundamental prop of his life; and this is his playground. Don't start sucking your thumb around here, kiddo. Open your eyes. There! Take a look at her over there. Even if she is a fake blond, ain't that sultry enough for you? Ain't she magnificent? Just imagine how amazing it would be to drown in her ocean of ecstasy. Never mind the lifeguards; just dive straight in, and she'll do the rest. Take me baby!' The fake blond looked at him, and smiled. She was really rather lovely, but the kitten had his heart. 'Nick, forget all the moral bullshit you've learnt; if you can't be shameless now and again, what's the point? Go with the flow. Let go. Unwind. Relax. Shameless is good. Shameless is the heart of New York City. And hell, who needs a brain? Get with it, or get out of my town! Throw off the skin – leave it on the sidewalk. Who needs the skin anyway? It's the heart that counts! You're in paradise now. Grab yourself an apple. You can be a born-again whoremonger in this paradise of man, and worship sluts to your heart's content. The glory days are just getting started. This is the *real* Eden that men want to create on Earth. Who needs apple trees anyway – unless it's got New York City growing on them! Even the serpents are queuing up to grab a slice of the action. And who can blame them? Who's tempting who? Give them a break - they're only New Yorkers like the rest of us! Loosen up, Nick. Soak up the culture. Drown in it, goddamn it. Listen to music. Dish out some bucks here and a few more there and watch the adorable pussies swoon and curve and find their way to your suffering ego. And let's face it, Nick, I ain't boasting when I say I'm all heart, but your ego could use a few notches up the ladder of debauchery. You want to be saved, don't you? Well, what are friends for? Jeee – sus! Has that trumpeter lost it?' Incensed, Roy leapt to his feet and heckled the musicians with a piercing whistle. 'Ease up on the phonics, *jazz-ass*! Play jazz, or wait tables. Jeee – sus! Am I even hearing this? I don't believe it! Leave your goddamn skin on the sidewalk, pal. Outside. Throw it away...'

To a man, they declined to indulge him; but gradually into the piece the musicians adapted their play, evolving more methodical rhythms, building harmony over spiraling solos that had splintered the individual sound of authentic riffs into a wild cacophony of fits and bangs and roars, a hollering chorus that tries to sound cool and fun, but slips into a meaningless runaway sound. And Roy, hugging the kitten and tipping the glass to his mouth, exchanged his vodka with her gin as their tongues touched and tickled in a wiggly dance, and they laughed.

She bit his tongue teasingly.

'I love it to hurt. Do it harder, baby. Harder. They don't call me Hard Eight for nothing.'

And she obliged him.

'Ouch! Torture me, baby, torture me...' he yelled with ecstasy and roared with laughter.

It was strange, even touching as he enviously watched them spawn lust for one another, that the reason that drove Nick to find Roy in the first place seemed to wither in importance. *Make way*, the moment seemed to say. A flirting kiss had primacy over things – it mattered more, a kiss sucked up a man's loneliness, engulfing it, there, it appeared as a blessing, even though it wasn't his to share but merely as something to behold. Still, that fraction counted for much. Or perhaps it was the booze, the sound of ice cubes tickling the glass so that whiskey seemed to laugh and intoxicate itself, and the self-sustaining essence of cocaine spicing the air, and jazz creating other worlds, higher existences – *Look! Is that the Buddha over there? Ha!* ... And all that mattered was this dreaminess of things. Other things could wait, he supposed, until Roy, at the close of a titillating chuckle as the kitten deftly stroked his crotch before anyone could see, turned to him and asked:

'What's the matter?'

'How do you mean?' Nick asked, gazing at him strangely.

'Why did you come here? You could have phoned. – Perhaps you were lonely?'

'Your phone is turned off.'

'Ah. OK,' he said, looking at his wristwatch. It was late. 'So, Nick, why did you come here? You're not a *real* poker player; you don't understand jazz; the women here are a class apart; and let's face it, Nick, you're not exactly in your natural nest. So what do you want?'

'What is my natural nest?'

'You tell me. – What do you want? It's late. What are you doing here?' He began to feel wary. 'Well?'

Nick pondered a moment: 'We can't do anything about it now. We'll have to deal with it tomorrow.' He sighed unconvincingly. 'It can wait.'

'Perhaps it can't. What happened? Come on, Nick, you're making me feel all niggly now.'

Nick cast a sideways glance at the kitten, and Roy whispered in her ear, licked her voluptuous lobe, she giggled, took a couple of thousand to amuse herself, and a hundred more for miscellany (tips, candy, soda, baby oil for massage later, cigarettes, booze, etcetera, the typical New York City shopping list of insanely necessary things).

'That enough, babe?'

'Maybe another hundred or two. Yep! That'll do.' *Meow...*

And she let them alone to converse in private. Nick began ambiguously, as was his way:

'We have a *kind of* problem.'

'What problem?'

'At the bank.'

'What about it?'

'I don't know how to explain it.'

'Just describe it.'

'But it makes no sense.'

'Just spit it out.'

'Our computers.'

'Yes?'

'There was an incident.'

'What?'

'Some kind of intrusion.'

Roy looked alarmed. 'Get to the point.'

'Somewhere out there in the global network... There's a parallel system running amok. - What am I saying, parallel?... Anyway, it's something, and it's been watching us.'

'What do you mean?'

'For want of a better word, someone out there is *spying* on us.'

'Spying!' he gasped. 'Are you kidding me?'

'No.' Nick looked at him gravely. 'I'm not kidding you. That's what it seems like.'

Roy shuddered uncontrollably, and then froze, his face growing hideously pale. 'Are you out of your mind? What are you saying?'

'That's how it looks. I could be wrong, but... but I don't think so.' He shook his head indecisively. 'Well; I don't know. I'm confused.'

'Are you being serious with me? Nick...? Where's Frank?'

'I don't know.'

'Have you tried calling him?'

'His phone is switched off.'

'It should never be switched off! Never!'

'Why not? Yours was.'

'Have you sent him a message?'

'A hundred times,' he sighed. 'No response. Nothing.'

'Spying on us! Are you crazy? Are you sure? – What did Frank say?'

'I just told you. – Roy, are you listening to me? I said his phone was switched off.'

'The idiot!' he seethed. 'Where the hell is he when you need him? Off whoring and boozing, the bum. Damn it!'

'Well, you know what he's like. Boys will be boys.' Humor seemed misguided, if not in bad taste, so he resumed more soberly. 'Besides, Roy, it's the weekend. And perhaps I'm just overreacting.'

'Damn it all! I don't care if you're fucking an elephant. No one screws with my computers. This is my life. My living. What have I got if I don't have that? - When is he due back?'

'Tomorrow. Monday. As far as I know.'

'Shit!'

'Roy, what should we do?'

'Shit! Shit!'

The third man – Francis 'a.k.a Frank the Hack' Freiberg, systems developer with a talent for turning digital data into cash: greenbacks, euros, yen, rupees, yuan, Asian markets a specialty, Scandinavian blonds in shiny black leather a weakness, and with a gift for the markets renders him generally indispensable to the cause of Mammon: a money machine, that's their business. Now, Frank the Hack, he's like the paired part of quantum spin: you never know for certain whether he's above or under (a woman) left or right (politically) here or there (NYC or TB2 - Timbuktu).

'Don't worry, Roy. He'll turn up. He always does.'

'Where the hell is he?' He was breathing hard with the embittered intensity of fighting shadows in the dark, his powerless rage capsizing into an ocean of unknowns. 'Where are you, Frank? Damn it, where are you?'

'He'll be back.'

'When? When?' his words felt adrift, tumbling out helplessly as he struggled to comprehend what Nick had told him, what it meant, this threat, what it implied. Human reaction leans into strange motions when confronted with a shock, and even a winner with a charmed hand at poker failed to defy its onslaught. How to respond? That was the key to mastery of the moment; this was the joker in the pack of cards called life. So who was dealing this one? It was a cruel riddle that racked his mind.

'Roy?'

'I'm thinking. I'm thinking...' He was shaking. 'What do you want?'

'Do you think we'll be OK?'

Roy struggled with a choking rage. 'No one's poking their finger into my pie. No one!'

Nick paused, and then said: 'Would you bet on it?'

'When I see the cards, I will.' He answered thoughtlessly, thrashing like a blind man who holds aces but imagines the worse. It's easy, even natural, to imagine the worse. 'I don't understand. Nick - '

'Yes?'

'This is bullshit. This is crazy. What are you saying?' - Some riddles rattle a man, and he rushes impulsively at them. Others succumb to the softest blow, teasing open on the fall of a sunbeam. And some leap out and pinch you as you blink. Amid them all, how one bears and perseveres sets the pattern for a conqueror, or the fate of the defeated. 'A spy, Nick? A spy? What are you saying? We have the best firewalls. Our computer defenses are solid. Nothing can break in. Nothing. Not into our system. This is bullshit! Are you certain? It's bullshit!'

When your world shakes, you hold yourself firm. Man is the measure of all things, and the beginning is Man himself against the endless universe. It's big, this universe. But if you want something deeply enough, then not that big. Endless desire beats endless big any day. And Roy? He curses what he cannot see. Things of a tangible ilk are his sole measure, even as his imagination stirs, plunging him into bitterness, until the rages that consume him expend themselves in furies and the f word, then he becalmed himself as best he could, and said: 'Nick, we've got to be rational. What's the best way to be rational? Never mind.... Give me a cigarette. - Thanks... OK. I'm OK. Let's take it from the beginning. What exactly is going on? How did you find out? What do you know? From the top. No embellishments, just give me the facts.'

Nick took a deep breath, opened out his mobile computer, lifted the stylus and began drawing diagrams. 'We're here, at X, options and derivatives trading, NBS Bank New York City. Over here, at Y, is NBS bank in Europe, the Paris office to be specific, function and unit unknown. Our computers, our code, our operations, as far as I can tell, are being profiled and watched by Paris. That's my best guess. – Let me elaborate. Our code is our own code, written by us, running on our computers, all proprietary, right? We set them up; we isolate them from the network; and trade according to rules we set. That's the name of the game: program trading. – Now, today, as planned, I upgraded the processor and hooked up to the Bank's global network to download some software, just some diagnostic stuff, utilities and so on. While I was hooked up, some remote system out there somehow breached the security, grabbed the processor, interrogated it, built a profile of it, and slipped out again. They took control, so I shut down our system and gave chase. And they really gave me the runaround. I don't know how I kept up with them. I was sure I was going to lose the thread. But I got lucky, I guess. I didn't know what the hell was going on. Eventually, they led me into a loop. It was a duel. Their signal began to fade. So I just jumped out anywhere. Then, with nowhere to go, I routed back into the company network and threaded between nodes. I just wanted to get back. But by chance, I stumbled on their tail. So I kept them in sight until I bounced off at Paris. That was the end of the line.' He paused and gasped at the recollection. 'I guess I just got lucky in the end. But as always, luck only carries you so far. I slammed into a firewall, and that was that. I tried a few crack routines, but it was rock solid. I couldn't penetrate it. They shut me out. The bank in Paris was the last stop. That's as far as I got. NBS in Paris. After that – a blank.'

'This doesn't look like French kissing to me,' Roy gritted his teeth, rage consuming him. 'I find them, and I'll give those bastards a mouthful, you can be sure of that.' Roy knocked back the whiskey with passion, bringing down the glass with a hammering thud as though he wanted to nail it to the table. 'What the hell's going on? What did you do? You pulled the plug?'

'I backed up the data, cut the link, and then ran tests on our system, now isolated of course. No one was around. No one else knows.' He drank some whiskey to steel himself. 'Roy, someone out there is watching us. Maybe even more than that.'

'Fucking voyeurs. Freaks.'

'I suppose that's one way of looking at it,' he laughed half-heartedly.

'Are we compromised? Is it affecting our operations?'

'No.'

'Our code, our accounts, our clients, anything at all?'

'No. No, nothing. And that's what's so puzzling. Whoever it is... they just watch. And who knows for how long they've been watching us?'

'Bastards! What do they want? I'll kill them.'

'It appears to be harmless, but...'

'But what?'

'Why do it? Why would anyone go to all that trouble; to penetrate so deeply, to tunnel so far into the system, to camouflage themselves with such consummate skill, and then just loiter around and do no more than watch? It doesn't make any sense. Imagine the talent needed to go in like that and sit with the processor. It's ingenious. Brilliant! Sure, it crossed my mind that it may have been internal security monitoring our trades. But it's not those guys. No, Roy, it's not them. They sit on the top layer and watch. They couldn't breach our security and go in that far. We'd know. They'd trip the alarm as happened before. Then I thought maybe the Feds from outside nosing around for skullduggery and getting clever with their methods. But it wasn't them either. They're not that smart. We can beat them. It's someone in the Bank using and hiding in the Bank's own global network.' He looked with amazement at the drawings he made, before closing the computer and storing it away. 'This is not some computer hacker in the normal sense. I'm certain of that. It's something else. More personal. Something more intrusive; but very cleverly done. I would never have spotted it but for that one slip they made. It must have been hiding in our system... God knows for how long, watching... Just watching. But...'

'What?'

'Why us?'

'Did they plant any worms, viruses, anything?'

'No. As long as we're offline, we're clean. In any case, it just watches us. It pounces when we're active. Somehow, it just seeps in. It's like breathing; you hardly know it's there.'

'It?' exclaimed Roy, grasping at straws.

'It. They. Them...' Nick continued, baffled. 'Someone wants to know who we are, how we operate, how we behave.'

'Damn pervert. I've heard enough of this.'

'We shouldn't raise the alarm. My gut instinct is telling me that.'

'Then what do you propose we do? We have to respond. There's too much at stake here. Good God, it's our livelihood on the line. If it's the bag of tricks they're after, then they're not bloody having them. Their ours, damn it.'

Nick looked grim. 'It's watching us. Whether it's an individual working alone, or a team, who knows. It's just watching. They've kept it simple. That's the beautiful thing. It just watches. So...'

'So... What?' Roy anxiously read his mind, and countered with disdain. 'You want to watch it back? This is not a game, Nick. This is our livelihood.'

'I know. And *they* know it too. – They watch, but never seem to steal any of our critical data, or corrupt anything. Everything is left intact. Why? What are they gazing at? What do they see? Why do they only want to watch? How can they get in without tripping an alarm? Call this whatever you like, Roy. It's an eye that watches. And it wants to know everything. And I feel it's been watching us for a long, long time.'

'But why? There must be a reason. And damn it, Nick, give me a more compelling reason than money?'

'Reasons?' he shook his head. 'I can't think of any. It's just a blank to me, I admit that. What I think I see is something peering into our system, looking about, nosing around, getting a feel of our system like an actor would get a feel for a part. It's out there. It comes and goes like a ghost. And what does it do? Watch. It's watching. Just watching. And I don't know why. But it's just watching us.'

'They're playing with us.'

'Look who's speculating now.'

'Well, what else can we do?'

'If it's a game,' said Nick, 'then the only thing we can be certain of is that we're being watched.'

Roy leaned back restlessly, seizing his drink with his hand, steeling himself for battle. 'Sometimes, Nick, watching and doing, it's one and the same thing.' He swallowed his drink hard, and at that moment took a decision, made as swiftly as he would a trade and raking in millions: This thing, this network-eye, wanted to stare. Some trades are based on chance, some on a hunch, some on mathematics, and some on downright cheating. He resolved that moment to confront the challenge with all the resourcefulness of a poker player: the nerve, the skill, the staying power, to hold even a meager hand and play your way to the jackpot, grinding it out to the end. It was a matter of talent, ability and cool-headed determination. Winning, winning is a drug. And he was an addict. 'So, they want to play, do they? – Let me get this absolutely clear in my mind. What we have then is the following: There is someone out there, in the network, quietly feeling us up; sneaking around like a stalker, peeking and going boo! Getting in our pants and molesting the system. Poking us up the ass, and then just vanishing again. And they've been at this... God knows how long. - However you look at it, it's not seduction. It's seedy. It's rape. It stinks of a pervert. And I'll find who it is. I'll nail them. They may see Roy Riemann; but they don't know Hard Eight. And it's Hard Eight that throws the punches. It's Hard Eight who calls the shots!'

'That's not the point, Roy.'

'No!'

'It's too obvious; a gut reaction. They'd be expecting that.'

'Then what?'

'The question is *why?* When we can answer that, then we can act.'

Roy thought hard, qualifying his speculation with a double-headed fear: wishing he was right, yet hoping he was wrong. 'We must have something of value, stumbled on it perhaps, but don't realize it.'

'Come on, Roy, be realistic. What do we have that's so fantastic? We trade; we make money, good money. We can't complain. We're good, but in this game we're not the exception. My feeling is we were chosen at random. It's the only rational explanation.'

'So someone tossed a coin, and poked us in the eye?'

'More or less; that's my feeling. What else could it be?'

'Heads or tails?'

'Take your pick.'

'Damn!'

'And once chosen, it's fixed. They hold their position.'

'Damn!'

'In the circumstances, Roy, swearing is understandable, but it doesn't solve the problem.' He looked at him ambivalently, perhaps challenging him, perhaps testing him. In either case, his own confusion was palpable, and his calm exterior no proof of a fixed mind. 'The question is, how do we play?'

'A game. It's always got to be a game.'

'It's kind of a guy thing, Roy.'

'Screw them all!'

'Well, boys will be boys...'

'They're nothing but a herd of hard-ons in soiled-up jock straps.'

'That may be. But flattery aside, we still have no idea who they are, or what they're after. If they are playing a game, and let's assume they are - we can assume anything - then what kind of game? We don't know anything substantial. Roy, let's start with what we do know. We are being watched. And this spy can come and go whenever he likes. We have no idea as to why, or for how long he's been there.'

'Like a stalker.'

'You have a way with metaphors, Roy, I'll give you that.'

'We know Paris is the source, right? It's a start. I know people over there. We'll make discreet enquiries; nose around. Better still, let's go over and deal with them directly?'

'That's stupid. All we have is a location. Not a face. Not a clue. Not anything. And they could easily move around. It wouldn't take a genius to anticipate our reactions. In any case, the system in Paris may only be an intermediary. Setting up a proxy, even remotely, is hardly magic. Who's to stop them from moving around the global network at will? If I wanted to, I could. We can't play them at that game, Roy; they can hide in countless places. And they easily erase their tracks. Besides, we don't know what card is coming up next.'

'Damn!'

'The only things you'll end up chasing are shadows; or data streams through a network. And I've been through that game already. Believe me, these guys know how to tunnel from network to network as easily as tossing a poker chip into the pot. - You still think you can win?' Nick gazed at him, 'They're not stupid, Roy. At best, they're baiting us.'

'Damn!'

'Don't sound so beaten. We're just getting started. - Think, Roy; we need to think.'

'I can't.'

'Try.'

Roy worked his eyes, drilling him, as if for the last time, to finally settle where the battle lines were drawn. 'Let me get this straight. One last time – tell me, what are we dealing with?'

Nick took a deep breath and fleshed it out. 'The best there is of human talent, with whatever motivation is driving it along. Perhaps, Roy, it's like you say; it's a kind of game. But what game?'

'Then there must be rules; there must be structure; a plan; a winner;

a loser?'

That's what we have to find out.'

Roy bore the burden of a powerless self, and it felt crushing. 'So what are we in all this? Pawns? Fools? Pixels they can push around a computer screen. I feel manipulated, and I can't do a damn thing.'

Nick gazed blankly at his empty glass. 'God knows. Perhaps it's only an experiment; or maybe even a tease.' What was he saying? He glanced at Roy vaguely: 'I know it sounds crazy, but things often start out as one thing, and over time end up as something else.'

'What thing?'

'Who knows. Perhaps a game... of sorts. That concept is beginning to grow on me. - This began suddenly; who is to say it won't end in just the same way? Mystery to a mystery.'

'Or scam to a scam.'

'A double-headed coin. Who cares, as long as it stops and leaves us be.'

'Well, do you know what I think?'

'What?'

'Maybe we're the prize. If this is poker, then maybe we're the pot.' He struck the table with his fists. 'And I play to win. That's my game. Winning! Waiter... where the hell is he? Miss... Miss, yes, another round.'

Booze flowed continuously, and a short time later food arrived to soak up the alcohol, but it tasted mundane and felt like killing time – a game you can never win. The longer you play, the more certain you are to lose. Nick hovered amid the sweet aches of doubt while Roy consumed bitterness like booze, gulping it down by the tumbler-full, feeling he could conquer it by drinking more and more. And it was this, coupled with booze, that drained him of power.

Their spirits only began to revive when the kitten returned with several bags full to bursting with dainty *things*, her breathlessly perky way of flirting with the *things* in a style that boasted of superfluous *things* utterly essential to a kitten. And these *things* possessed a richness of meaning which, for a kitten, were utterly addictive *things*. 'Roy, do you like these things, Roy? Look!' And the mood changed to one brimming with thrills in the company of these delightful *things* that pampered perfectly to her whims. 'Look, Roy, look at this thingy....' She lavishes on herself, yes, she's game for a few millions dips with her paws into treats and treats, and the hers come coated with creamy bits, like sweets, which she shares. And that's just want a man needs to sustain his deeper health is a kitten purring winsomely over merry delights and things that luxuriate her pretty femininity. Sensuality, you know, is a thing. A big big big thingy. Serious is bad. Male-seriousness is a touch over sad. 'Roy, what's wrong? Are you OK?' She touches his face softly and he tries to smile. She hugs him warmly and shows him all the things she bought, making a great fuss over them. Her presence sparkles over the native complacency of his gloom, beating back glumness with a sigh, 'Oh my, isn't this night so magical-simple and a sight for sore eyes? Look at all these things, Roy. Look...' She is a breath of fresh air. Sometimes, she is more than simply there, when a man's spirit palls and yearns for resurgence, she is everywhere. Hope is the realization that there is something worth living for, and it comes on the wings of a warm smile, a kiss, a hand to hold your hand, a hug... Charmed things. She, devoid of complication, wholly serene, like... *a kitten dishing at the cream*! Men often grapple with the understated fact that an audience with God is not the solution to their woes, but the caress of a woman's hand to stir his muscle-bound bones, is. And the kitten knows that play for play's sake often works profoundly better than a prayer for a prayer's sake. 'Roy, I bought you something. Oh, wait a mo, let me show you.' Unwittingly or otherwise she brought something even more sublime, that magic of the woman's touch that she intrinsically possesses and men, alone, forlornly lack and can never hope to replicate. Kind of a girlie thing, that. Nice. Nice *things*, actually. 'Look, Roy, look; I bought you a necktie. Oh my God, isn't it so cute! I just love it to bits. I almost cried when I saw it. It's so... you! All youey and you!' She renders a pretty pretend cry. 'You.' And coos. 'You...' And finally sniffs. 'I bought it especially for you.'

'Gee, thanks babe, I love it too. Here,' he gave her a thousand bucks because it seemed the right thing to do, and besides, he had nothing else to say, and money always spoke handsomely. She could buy herself all kinds of *things* with that. And she gave him a deep kiss and a hug, which seemed to cheer him up.

Roy felt his passion stir, but then dwindle of a sudden, as if the tide of his spirit crept out. Hope was only a step away, but he wasn't willing to take it. Something was wrong, his life took a turn, and a dark mood set in. The kitten quickly noticed and gave him a hug. Love is a battle, and there are others fighting on your side, and far more often than he'll ever know. 'We may as well call it a day. - Nick?'

'Yes...'

'What are you looking for?'

Nick searched for Vonnie, but she was nowhere to be found. 'Vonnie,' he said. 'I was just wondering...'

'Vonnie?' Roy swept his gaze quickly along the bar, then over to her regular corner table: 'No, she's not around. She must have left. Well, every girl needs her rest. And even the best guys take second place to her sleep.'

'Second place to a dream sounds better.'

'Perk up, son. Perhaps she's dreaming of you!'

On their way out the doorman handed him a note.

'Who's it from, Nick?'

'Vonnie.'

'What does she want?'

He showed him the note. 'It's her telephone number.'

'There you are,' he said, patting him on the shoulder. 'If there's ever a woman to induct you into the pleasures of the flesh, then Vonnie's your girl. – Hey babe, gimme a kiss.'

'Oh Roy!' the kitten roused and pinched his cheeks before kissing him. He was smitten and hugged her passionately, the warmth of her body engulfing him. And, as the doorman helped her with her shopping bags into a taxi, Roy tipped him a hundred and offered Nick a lift.

'No thanks,' he said, reluctant to share a cab with the captivating kitten who was eager to get a move on, and tugging at Roy to pull him inside the cab. 'I'll just walk around for a while... down there. I think I'll find a place to park my skin on the sidewalk next time I'm around.' He briefly grinned. 'Besides, I need to think. It will do me some good, and help me to relax.' He saw dismay creep over Roy's face, and tried reassuring him. 'We've done all we can for now. I've shut down the system. It's secure. I've backed-up the files. They're safe. Now, get some rest. You're going to need everything you have for tomorrow when the markets open. – The world rolls on, Roy; on and on... Even without the best guys to share in it.'

'And Frank?'

'I'll keep trying to contact him. Sooner or later we'll get through.'

'Nick – '

'I'll see you tomorrow.'

And he watched the cab pull away with the kitten beaming with delight and miming and waving to him 'bye, bye,' through the rear window as Roy buried his weary head in her luscious breasts.

Strolling along the sidewalk and re-reading Vonnie's message, some twenty meters along, he noticed several parked police cars and paused to look.

'It's a hellova mess up there,' he overheard one cop remark to another.

'Yeah,' said the other sardonically. 'But he went out smiling, whoever he was. – Hey, buddy, can I help you?'

'No,' said Nick. 'Thank you, officer. Good night.'

'You take care, now.'

Chapter 3

L.V. (Mmm, gimme some more) how much? (Everything, bring it all on) a formula for indulgence (Formula?) L squared V squared (Huh?) Vegas, baby-face, Vegas Vegas... (Gotcha!) Cue me some lights, (Sure thing. Lights!) cue me dazzling lights (Razzle dazzle), cue me obese lights (Yeeha!) as the soul suffers burnout just add more fat to the flesh (How much you want?) dollops of it (One, two three... That enough?) more (Here it comes!) Gimme, gimme everything (Yeeha!) cue U (Me?) cue S (Eh?) cue A (Ahhh!) USA (I want her raw) Say cheese... (Yeeha!)

Got the picture? And into the picture strides a man dressed in a casual blue suit, Italian cut, and for him life is a breeze, like a suit cut to perfection (was that erection? – ouch!) He ambles along the hotel corridor, hell of a stride, wide, neat, as though walking were a gesture conducted like a cloud, man riding on a cushion of air. Ah! One step, two step, next next next... it's a breeze, life is a breeze, and he smiles, breezily, and presses the button once: *ping!* and waits for the elevator. Hmm, hmm, hmm... he's a witty kind of guy in a flirty mood for playtime, and heytime just musing to himself, no particular hurry to proceed, yet he's excited all the same: calm in the flow of sensual expectation, perfect like his suit. Cut. Erection. Ouch!

Life - it's a breeze.

'Going down, sir?' said the bellboy - a rather pretty girl actually with neat oriental eyes, European demeanor, American élan, and Vegas dreams. But despite the flourish of female exotica, our fella felt it should have been a boy in keeping with tradition. He's not an old timer, shucks no, but wood is preferable to plastic: the smell, the touch, the essence. Mmmm.

'Actually, I prefer up,' he wittily replies and steps inside, 'but down will do. Ahem! After you...' takes his place at the rear, slides his eyes down a touch and *a-hem!* peeks obsessively at a pair of dashing legs going up up up all the way to the thighs and beyond of a *creme de la femme* cutie as they smoothly descend to ground. (Mamma mia! time for a trip, lapping at sensual ambrosia on the Strip-side of a chick with golden legs delicious in her stride, all he wants to do is to plunge deep inside, "Open wide, baby, open wide..." His glazed eyes prove he's a drooling dreamer for the Strip-side of heaven, dames quenching a man's desire, tailored for effect, "Come for a ride, baby?..." feels like the right thing to do in this yausa-made town, built all of a piece, Strip at a time, and you can't beat a dame's legs for the perfect cut – they fit Nature perfectly as if custom-made for the whole world to walk over. As a woman, she could wear him any day of the week - fit him this way and that, he's her pussycat in slaves' togs, provided she's the one that meows. As a man, he's never considered himself shallow. Shallow? Hey, come on, look at his dress sense, look at his smile. Gee, he's sweet, ain't he? He can feel up the bills, divinely yawn an aside, "OK, gimme that..." he can buy what he wants, this guy, have what he likes. Strange? Nah! "Keep the change, honey, keep the change..." Besides, man is the measure of all things manly, women included. You gotta a tape measure? Try your dick, slick. Lay it down, and smooth it around. There, there, there...Ah! And by God he'd sell his soul to slip into her pantyhose, with her inside of them, of course. *This* defines the perfect fit. Ah! His eyes love a feast, the mind keeps pouring it on, and it's honey in his mouth, melting and sweet, lapping it all up, Strip at a time. Is this obsession with sex proof that man is but a toe of *her* gorgeous legs, set in place, fit into *her* infinite perfection? Nah! It's the normal cut, just the mind of man, that's all. He's a guy with a hard-on nosing for some action wherever he can find it. What is divinity on the 'Strip-side of life? There, *she's* standing right beside him). He ogles her completely, licking her legs with his ravenous eyes as she talks, in smutty Spanish, to her feisty *crème de la femme* friend who remarks casually that the masculine type behind her with the voyeur's eyes is staring at her perfect legs. In fact, the lecher, he's consuming them!

'Naturally,' he said with pride as they exited at ground, 'and that gorgeous ass of yours. Mmmm, and damn lovely it is too.' He smiled, fondling them with his eyes, the hanky-panky gaping look that slips into the note: 'My name is Frank; and please, regard me as your slave.' Frank, the epitome of avant-garde smut, connoisseur of superior suits and designer sluts, patron of the finest tailors and any half-decent whore that will have him inside of her. It makes perfect sense. It's a male thing. *Sex.*

Ah!

They ladies giggled marvelously and he raised his eyebrows a touch, preparing to move in on them but something unexpected made him stop. He received an incoming signal on his pocket computer, alerting the silent-vibrate feature and detaining him by the elevator as the Latin butterflies flew out of range and merged into the bustling Vegas crowd. Retrieving it from his pocket, Frank activated it and found a garbled message from New York City, which irritated him, and in response he tried to reply with a query message, but encountered problems with the uplink and the signal kept bouncing back with the error message: *Network down. Auto response from local host. Please try again later...* A crisply muttered *F**k You* was a typical header for an exclamation, and he let out a few f's to get the load off his chest, f..f..f..f..f...

Now that he's running on Vegas time – which is kind of an endless-day craze, this; you milk her lights until you're drunk with illumination, American ambrosia in shades of pink, and red, and orange, and magenta and blue, the only common feature is the Vegas dazzle, and time stands still or even runs in reverse - nothing is allowed to hinder a man's path to self-indulgence. Every man with a horny edge needs a rant, but some deeper intuition left him with a sense of gathering unease: 'What the hell do they want? Hmm... I know, I'll call Nick. Roy will just give me a headache, and I can do without his moaning right now,' he muttered to himself as he pressed the SEND key again and again, until the lights of Vegas licked at his spell-bound lusts and seduced him back to their enveloping embrace, to the primacy of the universal glow that in the beginning was infatuation, until the *Goddess* of the world's delights commanded: Let there be lights, more and everlasting lights... and Las Vegas was born of the sand dunes and the dreams of men who grasp the essence of the material world as love, desire, and money, with ambition as the glue. It is a riddle written in sand – *Vegas is a woman and a man plunged in a communion of flesh and spirit.* The result – legend is born. But that's only the beginning. For these guys know that eternal hope is the lighted key to the riches of things, and that the great dame Pandora *knew* what she was doing when she opened that box. Oh yes. But hey, she's a woman, she a babe, so what do you expect? A man can't help but search for Cassandra and beg her indulgence for a good smack of her worldly wisdom. She knows everything, this babe, inside and out, sees through men like what?... this... teases him like a pretty kitten as she licks his ear and whispers all, revealing the essence of things, even though she's literally *unbelievable!* – It follows, you see, women are the gateway to hope; but they kind of get a kick out of tripping a guy up. *Ha ha ha...* Kind of a girlie thing, that. *Ha ha ha...*

Switching off the computer, he returned it to his pocket, sighed as the shifting New York woes yielded to Las Vegas delights and, basking in the potential of a score, left his room key with the concierge and headed for the exits.

Resuming his stride along the gleaming boulevards of *his yausa town*, his footsteps fall into the saunter of an effortless beat, like sound to the rhythm of a song, neat, the patter patter tap tap of a soft dance but the motion is refined, poem of a man drifting down the Sunset Strip - his Sunset in a cool burn of everlasting delights, he paces to the rhythms and it feels... a perfect cut, tailor-made for a man like him. This is habit become ritual, slick piece like a clock going tick tock as he slides into a sequence of actions as though the Strip were his stage and he performs on cue: The speed of his walk, slow her down... tap...tap... he lights a cigarette, pauses on the sidewalk, gaze with awe at the scene, everything, inhale, another gaze, every little thing, exhale, feels great, inhale, sucking in that nicotine down and around and in, and looked at his watch: it was down-time down town in New York City: traffic jams, yelling, shoving, chaos, the meandering commotion of the masses, all of them in a hurry, while here, in the heart of Vegas, time slipped out, like shadows swallowed up by the overwhelming lights. Exhale. Ahhh... Knock back another nick of nicotine. Ahhh... Ready for the next act. Steady. Go.

It was existence defined in the parenthesis of life: that between drags on a cigarette all philosophy of time could be resolved, and seen in the Vegas light not as a glittering paradox, but essentially sublime. Here, you just forget about time. Simple. Ah...

'Excuse me, sir, do you have the time, please?' unless of course a *large* lady with Dixie heft and a lumbering gait strolling alongside him and wearing a pair of bursting red shorts stretched around her mammoth thighs feels compelled to ask him a perverse question completely antithetical to Vegas. That kind of thing just don't run here, babe. Time means *time to play, time for a lay*... things like that. This episode epitomizes her presence amid the giant chandelier that is Vegas: obese flesh strolling among obese lights dripping with photonic ecstasy. Not even the gravitational pull of a star can slow it down. Life just goes drip, drip, drip; and people just lick, lick, lick it all up. Ah!... Strip out the time, and it makes perfect *senselessness*.

He looks at her as if to say: *Are you insane, my dear? That's not a Vegas question? How do you expect me to answer that?* But his puzzled frown is all of a piece as he continues aloud: 'You know, it must be down-time in down-town New York City right now. Don't you think so, ma'am?' feeling sure it must be that – in any case, it never really mattered. For Vegas' time was ephemeral time, a fundamental otherness creeping amid the lights, not even a bum can burn time here, it was frozen in an ocean of lights, a trapped event horizon time, out there, in the desert, in the sky, on TV and the radio, in your dreams, memoryless, time meant another place. And in Vegas you don't get cocky with the clock. Roll the dice and f...f... f... the clock.

She said, looking puzzled: 'Oh, OK...' and continued on while he, gazing at her awesome rear, thoughtlessly suffered to amuse himself with hump 'n bump jokes before he turned away.

In his day-dreaming mind he indulged in a dialogue with himself, as though the *Dixie Chick* with all her legendary heft was still hovering around, looking for the clock, wondering what time was. And it went something like this:

'Hey, Dixie, do you know the vagaries of Vegas?'

'Excuse me, Mr. Tick-tock?'

'She's a lady's town.'

'Huh?'

'And men want her.'

'Who?'

'And that's just the way it is.'

'What?'

'Forever. Art. Science. Civilization. Life. Culture. A man wanting a woman – that's the fixed point of this world. All the rest is just posture, and charm, and paraphernalia.' The world revolves not on its axis alone, but through desire. To be human is to desire. *'Do you know what, Dixie?'*

'What's that, Mr. Tick-tock?'

'This is Vegas. And one way or another, we're all of us naked here. Bare ass in bare necessity, like in Eden. And we're all equal under the blazing lights. – Do you know what, Dixie?'

'What, Mr. Tick-tock?'

'There is nothing new under the blazing lights of Vegas. We're all starkers here. We're all the same.'

'So, would you sleep with me?'

'It never crossed my mind.'

'Well, how about it...?'

He mulled it over, and said. *'I think we'd better put on some clothes.'*

'I thought we were all equal.'

'It's not all dazzle, darling. Got to go home some day, babe, and get some shut-eye. See you later, Dixie pie...'

There is a purpose to his actions, he's like a homing bird, he's no fool, no sir, but the male dick is ever nosing around at the tip of its erection for a means to prove this assertion wrong. An irritating urge to contact New York stirs up in him again, the garbled message is turning in his mind, but Vegas is a lady's town, seductive, alluring, swallowing you whole, and he finds it easier to pretend that it can wait. It still felt like eternal Sunday here, Sun + Day in an arithmetical kind of way, it was a long weekend, L O N G and whatever it was, New York City; love you to death, baby, but she could wait. *And if she can't?* Well, she can always join me...

A perfect excuse in the perfect place - Vegas. Every nook and cranny of *Her* glittering space is a pretext for diversions, for *She* was the *real* reason for the desert's existence. V E G A S... silhouetted against the scorching sun.

What is Vegas - a religion? Perhaps not, but *She* is *religiously* real. And Frank is but an acolyte of her infinite seductions. For he is a He, and *She* consumes him.

Ten minutes later he finds the club he's looking for and goes inside, moving with style into the stylized interior, his eyes smitten as they roved about the scene in a sweeping gaze: people, lights, more people, more lights, indulgent people, obese lights, and feels he's in the right place.

He maneuvers to the bar, smiles, *hi there*, and sets the sequence running: pull up a stool, snaps his fingers, orders a drink, lights a cigarette, scratches his cheek, smiiiile, big smiiiiiiiiiile, then he asks the bartender for the time.

The bartender looks at his watch and said. 'Ten to...'

'Ten to what?'

'Ten. Nine. Eight...'

He quickly gets the picture and resumes his ritual: drink, cigarette, smile... He doesn't know the time, but he knows it's not time yet. And when only the twinkling melting ice remains in his glass he casts a glance over to the lounge, tossing it like something thrown by chance, aiming for the leftmost side where the communal seating is arranged for intimacy between single and single, pairs of lovers, triples of lovers, ménage à trois, and multiples thereof... it's all here, in the open, in the dazzling light, and it feels intoxicating, it feels wonderful, he only wishes he was born with ten dicks, life would be a heavenly debauch.

He waits, and stays his time timelessly.

Beside him at the bar a scene unfolds between a couple that mesmerizes him. The aura of smoky jazz tenderizes her voice, 'Hey, babe, you wanna play, babe?'... Although her lover's eyes seem surreally dreamy, he takes her tongue into his mouth, and tastes her. 'Babe, what are you thinking, babe...?' The smooth deciphering of her hand across his cheek, teasing him, poking him with her finger, with her tongue feline in felt-up fondling of her man. 'You like that, babe...?' Then down his chest seeking riddles in an aftertaste of danger and desire in the worldly miasma of cocaine suffusing through the air, like incense, like the taste of angels, coming....

Mmmm....

Suddenly, a stranger joined them and threw a Ten of Hearts on the bar.

'Stroke Ten!' said the woman, looking aloof but annoyed, 'why don't you knock?'

'Knock knock,' he said, pressing a joint into his mouth, holding it there for a time as though it were a trifling thing, before finally inhaling. 'Bang, bang, bang...'

The bartender notices his empty glass and starts refilling.

'No thanks,' said Frank. 'I don't have the time.' He tips him twenty and turns towards the lounge where she sits, simmering in sweet blue moods, watching the world, waiting for him.

Showtime.

There he is, in his casual blue suit, Italian cut, what a man, striding through the lounge, his gait, his posture an action of magnificence. Mamma-mia, he's a beautiful piece, she thinks; yet he wants to be racked. In line of sight of her eyes, blue magnums with a caliber gaze, the cross-wires of her desire takes aim, and fires at his beauty, ka-pow, pow, pow... firing flashes in a frenzy storming the face, the neck, the crotch. She is not a magnet, she is a cannon. And he, as the soldier of sacrifice, immolates himself as he strides towards her.

'What are you now, my lovely?'

'Live fire,' she said.

'Am I hit?'

'Bulls eye!'

The dream of being attacked, the tenfold imagination and desire of being racked piece-by-piece in public spaces arouses him. He watches to be watched, undressed, dominated, caged by her eyes. He sits opposite her. She gives him her hand. He takes it, leans forward, kisses it, and as she draws it back her gaze takes aim and unleashes war.

'What are you doing to me?'

'Having my way,' she said, her voice probing the margins of a whisper.

'Would you like a drink?'

'Straight.'

'Waiter. Whiskey. Twice.' He turns to her. 'Cigarette?'

She takes one, he lights it for her. Then sits and watches her smoke.

Burning time, wasting himself, the rippling smoke enshrouding them.

'I want you,' he said at last.

'Shut up,' was her curt reply. And re-loading, she sipped her drink in silence.

The color of sound is a mood, and humans are the hue, soft tones, warm tones, eclectic contrasts, there, inside the club, into themselves, painting life a rich and deep blue on a white canvas, the music playing slowly to a warm percussion, now notches up the heat and the lights dim changing in hue from white to tangerine – it's all seductive effect, atmosphere, sensation and phenomena, it seems even the Buddha would be a Vegas kind of guy if he were around today. He'd walk up to the bar, just lay himself down, and take in the sights piece by piece, overloading not himself but the moment with desire.

At length, she prompted him: 'What is it you want?'

'You.'

'You can't have me.'

'Then a piece of you.'

'It's all or nothing.' She contradicts him, deliberately, defiantly, softly, teasingly, womanly. 'Well?' - *Bitch!*

'Then all of it. Everything. I want everything.' – *She's a bitch.*

Her eyes seem to spy on him, to pry him open into fragments that she'd seen a thousand times before, each part, each piece of him dissected with a gaze, before reassembling him into patterns of a common moniker: Punter. John. Client. Boy. Him. It. Thing. Slave. A woman's mind is a weaving engine, and conceiving tapestries are her forte.

'What exactly are you after?' she said, knowing the answer, kind of.

'What can you give me?' he knew she knew. What a gas!

'Kinky. – OK. I do it to you; not to me. And straight. No violence.'

He smiled, enriched by mutual understanding. 'You're the player. I'm the piece. Tell me the rules.'

'Number one: I'm on top. Number two: *then* you're on top. Number three: no kissing. Number four: -'

'Why no kissing?'

'Mistress makes the rules.'

'Well the slave wants a piece of the action, or I don't play.'

She considered a moment. 'OK. But no tongues.'

'That's a shame. I like to fence. But... your move.'

'Number four: no skin-to-skin. Everything is with protection.' She paused, and he silently assented. 'Number five: I listen to your life story, don't ask me about mine.'

'It's not my head that's hard. - Shall we go?'

'One more drink.'

'You've not even finished that one.'

'Well...' she said, slowly lifting her glass, gazing at it, blowing smoke at it, 'I'd better put it away.'

Sexuality is performed in the simplest actions: as lips nibble at the glass and nip a sip of whiskey with the tongue, tasting it with swirly bliss before swallowing the bulk in cascade of icicles. Mmmmm, and the cigarette adrift in mid-air, barely touches her lips, then gradually overcoming the gulf to fit perfectly in her mouth and take it in, there, drawing the substance like a vampire sucking the life from the boiling steaming tobacco appearing to resist but in essence aiding its own destruction, like the doomed lover sacrificing its life for the ultimate fulfillment. The patterns of desire fleshed out in the immensity of a woman repeat themselves in a delicious daze, and everything in the jazzy overdriven sense of her, she is unquenchable doing in silence what a thousand yearning beasts would wantonly yearn for.

'I must have another, you know,' she said, pouting her lips and stubbing out the cigarette. 'Waiter. Another one. *And...* go easy with the ice, *please.*'

'Whatever you say, ma'am.'

'Good boy,' she smiled, coaxing her lips into the sensual surround of an oval blow, as though she were nibbling at him, nibble nibble... of the masculine aperitif. Hmmm... not bad, for a man.

And then she looked at her watch, casually, ritually, not really noticing the time.

Chapter 4

Speed!

The wheels of her car spin furiously as she pushes the gas pedal hard, harder, ramming it down to go fast, faster, per second per second she, the driven machine, storming into the Vegas night, into the desert starlight, this stillness so profound even the footfalls of a ghost can be heard clipping the rocks. But the Nevada tranquility smashes into her hard, making her swerve suddenly, braking then accelerating, and the car banks chaotically before she brings it back into the line of the road barely keeping control. And there, all around her, is mesmerizing stillness, is a fabled starry night, a holiness in sand so amazing it feels like a dream, while within the car she burns, pushing the pedal hard, harder, to go fast, faster. Fear is a furnace, melting even her stifled screams, the flame roars, an incendiary monster that she tries to outrun, but incinerates her, even as the stillness of the desert keeps an inexhaustible presence. There. Everywhere. Timeless. A burning.

Speed.

Just a drop more gas and she could almost fly. Her yearning intensifies but horror checks her, cages her, consumes her. The car throws up a shivering plume of dust flaring out like an umbilical cord that seemed to stretch all the way to the womb of Vegas. Vegas, it just wouldn't let her go. Vegas: immersed in light, a story by candlelight read in the sunshine, written with light, its words alone suffice to sweep out the dark, dark night. And it is Vegas' light, not Nevada night, that is deepest deep. What is a poem? Flesh plunged in light. Into the luminous bliss. A Rhyme. A riddle. Divinity. Kiss, kiss, kiss... As a man and a woman dispense with time and liberate themselves in wilderness – it looks empty, all this, but the landscape is a dream built with light: Vegas. This wilderness. This... Sure, it's crazy flirting with Vegas, it gets inside of you, it lights up your insides, and that's what makes it a spirit. The Vegas' ghost, sitting in a bar on the Strip, whiskey on ice, mmmm, nice, listening to jazz, sounding a toast – *"To Light and Life, let there be both. May their marriage endure, for a Vegas' day and more..."*. - Hookers yanked them in, one by one, winners, losers, grooming them in luxuries of body heat melting the nights to everlasting day. High rollers rubbing shoulders with slot machine junkies. Mississippi salesmen gaping at the wantonness of Mammon, roaring odes to joy – Beethoven, Elvis, bucks, yeah! and loving it. *I'm in paradise - yausa yausa yausa!* Excess became the Vegas' norm as night transforms to everlasting day. Fantastic Phantasmagoria - *je sais; je ne sais quoi; je puis*. A touch of panache amid the boldness of a town lit up on that one day meant to last forever. *In the beginning there was Vegas...* It makes sense, Vegas' sense, Sunset holistic Strip sense, and common cause among the many that life is meant to be lived, again and again with riveting abandon. *Count me in!* The hordes swarmed into the casino paradise and the promised land of lights. But she drove the other way, harder, faster, escaping the razzmatazz of Vegas receding behind her, its lights chasing her as she drove into wilderness out*strip*ping photons bursting from the 'Strip. This intangible light, like words, like metaphor, like Vegas, follow her everywhere. Her frenzied gaze bores into the horizon and the reddening, burning, ever yearning-to-burst sunset yielding that endless sheet of sky to a crescent moon, like an oriental eye watching her, a razor of a gaze; cutting, piercing, relentless.

Speed. Faster. In the beginning... *Vegas.*

Fear antes with the gas peddle, pumping it up and up, faster and faster, daring to see who burns first: her or the wheels of her car. *Raise.* It's to hear the screeching of rubber driven to a hideous shriek. *Raise.* The thundering pelt of rushing wind disturbing the streamline of the car. *Raise.* Turbulence and noise, a stifling heat, body heat and desert heat. *Raise.* If the wheels were rollers of a slot machine, they would have spun out quarters and decked the desert with silver millions; or like the revolving axis of a roulette wheel squaring the circle with absurd odds. *Raise.* It is to take the risk and burn, and set all chance on fire.

Speed.

Suddenly it all changed. She implodes reflexively and slams on the breaks, the car screeching to a stop. Time folded, but her fear just wouldn't abate.

All quiet inside. Then *thud! thud! thud!* She shuddered silently, semi-consciously. *Thud! thud! thud!*

If feelings were time then her emotions must have slipped past at a dizzying rate, pushing eons through a hyper-threaded clock, like time in a wormhole. But beyond the car the world was real, physically booming *thud! thud! thud!* as a burst of frantic motions stormed into her mind, hammering on the body of the car: *thud! thud! thud*

'Ma'am. Are you all right, ma'am? Ma'am...' The highway cop rapped on the driver's window to rouse her from her daze, crying out, 'Ma'am...' aiming his flashlight into her face now covered with her hands. 'Ma'am, can you hear me? Pull down the window?' He struggled with the door but it was locked from inside. Acting instinctively he pounded on the windows. 'Ma'am. Open the door, ma'am. Open the door.'

Suddenly he realized, not only was she terrified but possibly traumatized, and his presence perceived not as benign but menacing. He stopped and backed away, turning the flashlight on himself, allowing time for her trauma to subside.

In time, she overcame her fear, pushing faint feelers into the world around her to locate her bearings - the dash board, the leather seats, her purse, her own hands... Gradually, she worked her gaze beyond the threshold of the window and reassembled her world back together again, piece by piece, reluctant all at once to trust her own eyes – the desert, the sunset, the moon... things of the moment, of eternity. She could feel herself breathing and her throbbing heart, full of an aching sound. It was frightening and yet, strangely reassuring. And there, the hard surround of her car, its encasing shroud protecting her gave her the confidence to push further and she dimly saw amid the chaos of her emotions the faint profile of the policeman in shades of desert black, a lone cop trying to communicate, mouthing something to her, his gestures like wind-swept shadows in the desert dark. And then the echoes kicked in: 'Ma'am... Ma'am...' It must be his voice, the puzzling kindness that was him seemed to swell up and engulf her and she shut her eyes and opened them repeatedly. Staring at him again and again: would he vanish like a ghost, or stay beside her as an angel? Amid a cloud of apprehension she opened the car door and nervously climbed out, clutching her purse.

He waited, not moving, giving her time to find her own safe space. Then spoke softly to her. 'Ma'am, are you OK?'

Stifled by words that gushed out in sputtering gasps and made no sense, she panicked, her fevered eyes sweeping round as though fearing something, or someone, there, buried in the serene yellow-black of the desert.

He could see her clearly now, the shade of a woman in distress became a frenzied white light, her features a replica of imagined blondes in a cool blue dress blending beautifully with her long shiny hair and the languorous stillness of the desert moon. Even afraid, even traumatized, the cop noticed the classical lines, the perfume in candlelit wines, *a la femme* and a breath of that same soft silk air, she without a name and only the look to go on, is bare. It's enough, and everyone kind of knows her.

Shuddering, she tried to speak, but in her panic confusing past and present tense, the thundering roar of traffic making her flinch, headlights dazzling as vehicles rushed by, blazing, showering her in a hurricane of light. 'He... he's after me.' Trying to look everywhere at once and seeing nothing but the phantoms in her imagination. 'He was following me... Look! Look!' the blazing headlights swamps her rear-view mirror, blinding her. She was hallucinating and burst out, tightly shutting her eyes. 'Please, please, make him stop. Stop! Stop! Please.'

'Ma'am. Ma'am, it's all right, ma'am, I'm here to help you. I'm a policeman. You're safe.' She struggled and he tried to calm her, but his actions made her frantic and she thrashed out at him. He was losing control when all of a sudden she stopped and fell silent, and an eerie numbness took its turn, her eyes gazing blankly into space, into frozen time. It was a moment when the world seemed to stop. And it was only the soft shuffle of someone moving that drew her back to reality, and she saw the cop take several steps back tactfully, to wait it out. The grainy sound of sand beneath his footsteps felt somehow reassuring. Perhaps it was the nature of the desert – *Don't be afraid,*

and you won't be harmed it seemed to whisper to her. 'You're safe.
I'm here to protect you. Ma'am...' he spoke gently, reassuringly, 'no
one can harm you. Not any more.' He waited for a response, timing
her silence until he said: 'Ma'am, try and calm down. Just try and
relax. Take as much time as you need. I'm here. OK? - Ma'am, in
your own time, tell me, who was following you?'

'H... Him.'

'Who?'

'I... I don't know. I don't know. He was watching me. I saw him...
Why? Why me? Why...?'

The cop drew her safely off-road as the traffic thundered past,
setting the world around them trembling, and escorted her to his
patrol car. He called-in and requested assistance. At that point she
began to sob and he hurried his report. 'Roger that, ten four. Out,' and
helped her into the front seat of his car. She kept mumbling fitfully
through her sobs that someone was stalking her, who knows for how
long; it could have been days, weeks, months even.

'Why? Sweet Jesus, why me? Why me?...' A harrowing despair
ravaged her lovely face, fracturing its fragility, shattering its softness.
'Why? Why me? What does he want? Why me? Why?'

'We'll find him, ma'am.'

'Why me? Why me?'

'Guys like these... ma'am, they emerge from time to time. No one
knows why. Nearly always, they just fade away. Maybe it's Vegas;
makes them go crazy. You know..?'

She gazed at him, stunned: 'I'm not crazy, am I?'

'No, ma'am,' he looked at her resolutely and searched hurriedly
in his pockets, thinking fast, improvising on the fly to relieve her
pain. He found the pack and offered her a cigarette. She took one,
and simply held it for a while. 'We'll catch him, ma'am.' She said
nothing and seemed to just stare through him, as though he wasn't
there, an appearance fused into the desert. He continued: 'Fear; that's
what they thrive on. And you mustn't give into him, ma'am. We'll
catch him. Whoever he is, we'll catch him. He can't hurt you now.'
He paused and smiled at her warmly. 'We'll have someone drive
your car back. Is that OK? Good. You come with me. You'll be fine.
I promise. Where do you live?'

She gave him the address and he wrote it down in his notebook. He asked for her name too, Amber Gillespie, she said, and though it might pass as insensitive, asked her politely:

'Ma'am, it really helps if you have any ID. Anything.' Hoping for a driver's license he was rewarded with the same as she opened her purse and retrieved it for him. He noticed the gun there too, and she noticed he did.

She lit her cigarette with it, in a cinema moment, and he smiled warmly.

'Smoke?' she offered him her lighter.

He raised his arms in mock surrender. 'Thanks. I'll pass.'

She smoked deeply, nervously, her hand shaking. Was she hungry for amphetamines, or caged by those unremitting fears that a stalker was watching her even now, concealed among the shadows of the sand dunes, he was watching her, and those torments would never quit her mind. The cop was polite but remained wary of her. People, when excited, when panicked, could do the strangest things. He wanted to help, of course, everything he possibly could, but needed to stay abreast of events. As a cop he learned early this sobering fact – people are the surprise, not events or things. It's when the former cry *boo!* that you really have to watch out.

Suddenly, she broke her pattern and walked back to her car. 'I have to make a call.'

'Ma'am,' he followed her, careful never to touch or overpower her, only persuade; and interposed before she got inside to the telephone. 'Leave it for now, please. As soon as we get back to town, we'll sort all this out. We'll make sure your home and everything is safe and secure, and then you can do as you like.'

'Officer.'

'Yes, ma'am?'

'I'm not crazy, am I?'

'No, ma'am,' he assured her. 'You're under duress. I've seen it before, many times. And we all act a little strange under duress. You just take it easy, now.'

During the earlier commotion he never noticed she had music playing on the car audio system. The sound was sunny jazz, and he paused to listen, absorbing the rhythms; then instinctively leaned

78

inside and pressed the re-play button. An uncanny feeling caused him to move, a sense of soft spirit in this, sensation like a muse whispering in his ear. He needed to hear the song from the beginning. Perhaps it meant something to him.

'Why did you do that?'

'I'm sorry, ma'am. I wasn't thinking. I just heard the music and I...' and he proceeded to turn it off.

'No,' she stopped him. 'Let it play.' She paused there, listening, interpreting the sound, the easy percussion of a steady drum sending echoes to the stars, the piano gesturing to the mind, the tenor sax spreading its rhythms through her and deeper into the surrounding desert landscape. It was sensuous. It was beautiful. It was like spirit. Alive. A song is alive, and it soothed her. 'Let it play...'

When his colleagues arrived, two cops in a squad car working the late shift and looking slightly jaded, they took stock of the situation and asked if she were OK. 'We'll look after you, ma'am, don't you worry.'

'Thanks, officer.' She braved a timid smile. 'I can't thank you all enough.'

'How's the car? No problems? Good. Do you have the keys? Ah, they're in the car.' He started the engine and revved it. 'Seems OK. You heading back now, Luke?'

'Ma'am, this way please.' The cop escorted her back to his patrol car. He opened the rear door.

'Do you mind,' she said, 'if I sit in the front? I feel safer.'

'Sure. No problem.'

And he opened the passenger door, and asked her to secure her safety belt.

'May I smoke?'

'Sure. As much as you like.'

The drive back to Vegas felt unnerving for her. She rarely spoke, passing brief asides such as 'A-ha; OK; yes...' as her mainstay to any conversation the cop struck up. She lit another cigarette, then another, and then the sequence repeats: knock a pack of filters, taps it open, takes one between her fingers, wets her lips, presses the trigger of the mock gun, phzzzzz... lights, replaces it, inhales, stares at the road ahead, Vegas is looming in the distance, island of restless lights amid the golden sands, nods her head in approval, exhales, settles to a breathy mood... just killing time. Then quiet, until... 'It's a quiet night.'

'Yes, ma'am,' he said. 'You can almost hear the desert breathe.' Sometimes he's a Vegas cop; sometimes he's an American Bedouin. And sometimes, such as now, he is both. 'I love the desert. I find it beautiful. Serene. Like music...'

Home. Heimat. Bayt. – In every era, time and language, it always felt the same. Home.

When they reached the police station her car was already parked. The cop escorted her inside and reported in, introducing her to the detective on duty, an affable guy with a chubby face and curly brown hair called Mitch, alias Mickey Richmond, who was standing by his desk eating a ring doughnut and drinking coffee.

'A doughnut, ma'am?'

She smiled warmly but declined, and he said, easing himself into his chair: 'Please have a seat. Hey, Dave, bring the lady a coffee, would you? Thanks. Cream with that, ma'am?'

'Just black; no sugar. Thank you.'

'And hey, Dave, put it in a cup, not the plastic kind, the real kind.' Mitch turned to her, 'Sure you won't have a doughnut? Baker makes them fresh, just round the corner.'

She smiled, feeling shy, and he packed them away.

'They'll do for later. – So, what do we have here? A stalker?'

'Detective?'

'Call me, Mitch.'

'OK, Mitch.'

'It's not my real name. The fellas chipped-in with suggestions and invented an alias for me. I don't know why. You think it's my face, ma'am?' She laughed. 'I'm a happy kind of guy. Well, I can't say I'm dull. I like to laugh. Maybe it's just Vegas. I don't know...'

'Mitch.'

'Yes, ma'am?'

She wondered why he gazed so attentively, his expression quizzing her, scratching his chin then fondling his ear. He sighed *hmmm...* but his interest ran deeper than her name. Her features inspired him to ponder. He knew her from somewhere, or seen her before, and he muttered her name several times, but couldn't match either. Details seemed to turn at curious angles. Perhaps the hair had a soft shade of brown, the check bones a touch more feline, the smile more naturally set, her demeanor verging on ebony. He felt something there.

'I've seen you before, ma'am.' He snapped his fingers: 'Aren't you a singer? A jazz and blues singer?'

'No. That's my sister.'

'Wow! You sure as hell fooled me. The resemblance is striking.'

'Yes. I know.'

'Are you twins?'

'No. But people often think we are?'

'Ahhh...' he sighed, as though everything resolved itself and fell into place. 'Maybe our stalker hit on the wrong person. Maybe he thought you were someone else... Like your sister, perhaps.'

'But why?'

'You never know. Stalking is a form of voyeurism – Peeping Toms on the move, if you like.' He paused and discreetly noted her dismay. 'Ma'am, try not to let it upset you. Their behavior is predictable once you know their logic, which is a strange logic. But still...' he glanced at the time, 'that's how it is. We'll need to speak with her. Your sister, I mean.'

'She's out of town.'

'May I ask where?'

'Europe. She's in Paris.'

'When is she due back?'

'In about a month's time.'

'Do you have a contact number? An address?'

'Yes; we're constantly in touch; all the time. We have to be. Now, it's a busy time for her. For both of us, actually. Do you think he was after her? We have to tell her; warn her.'

'I don't want to worry you, ma'am, but it's possible.'

She searched in her purse and gave him the details.

'For how long has your sister been away in Europe?'

'More than twenty days now... Yes, twenty three.'

'May I ask what she's doing over there? Is she on vacation? Work?'

'Yes. She's working - singing that is. Jazz. Blues. Some new songs we've been working on. She's doing a promotional tour. It was arranged months in advance by her manager, Anthony Leoni.'

'I see. And you?'

'I write the songs. I'm soft. She's hard.'

'Excuse me?'

She chuckled. 'Just something we share, sis and I. Sis calls me *Soft* because I write the songs. I call her *Hard* because she sings them.' Software. Hardware. At the level of the voyeur it's all firmware, where software and hardware merge. Two faces of the same coin. Sunrise, sunset. Left hand, right hand. Physically, metaphysically, one.

'Care for another coffee, ma'am? It's no trouble, really.'

'No. This is fine. It's very kind of you.'

'Don't suppose you'd like a doughnut?' he hinted optimistically.

'No. But please help yourself.'

'Nah,' he blushed coyly. 'They'll keep.'

'May I ask you a question, Detective?'

'Please, call me Mitch.'

'May I ask you a question, Mitch?'

'Sure. Fire away.'

'Does this happen often?'

'What, exactly?'

'Being stalked? Being followed and watched?'

He pondered a moment. 'It happens. But it's not a common thing, mind. Not in Vegas, anyway.' He paused to see how she would react. She seemed disheartened, and he spoke candidly. 'Ma'am, in my experience, the people who usually do these things are harmless antisocial idiots; pranksters some of them; but mostly guys who are bored, robbed of something in their lives. Who knows what; I'm not a psychologist. For some strange reason they get their thrills from a distance, not by close contact. They're easily bored, and simply leave the scene, especially when the police get involved. They're seldom the kind to stick around when the juice gets hot. But rest assured, ma'am, we won't leave anything to chance. May I have the keys to your apartment, please?'

'Why?'

'We'll send a few of our guys round to have a look. Just to be on the safe side.'

She searched in her purse and handed them over. 'Should I wait here?'

'Yes, please. I'd like you to sit with our forensic artist and describe this guy who followed you. As much detail as you can. Then we'll have a go at some mug shots.'

'I saw him only faintly. He was always in shadows; a hand covering his face; obscuring himself.'

'Give it your best shot.'

'OK. And Mitch.'

'Yes, ma'am?'

'Thanks. Thanks for everything.'

'Here to serve,' he grinned. 'Any time.' And smartly slipped a doughnut into his mouth. Delicious. He couldn't resist it.

Chapter 5

The office appeared to be carved from a block of tinted glass laminated with silver and sanded down like a convex lens so the metallic hues played with light in ways that intrigued the eyes and offset the holographic Renoir on the wall: a slick gimmick in red laser and fusing shades of blue, topped off with a hint of magenta as symbolic of a guy who thinks he's so clever with light – playing with physics is a breeze, just do the math, as the laid-back kid does with American ease. Take wine with your burger? Please, (and smile) with cheese. Crackers and deli on the side, and apple pie with cream kind of along for the ride. Perfect. The perfect picture of New Yorkers savoring a mixed mood, climbing a skyscraper in an elevator that's as delicious as take-away food, quick, snappy, yummy yummy yummy as further down the roaming eyes discover picture-perfect oak wood flooring polished and shining of tonic reds and shimmering browns jumbled up like Jackson Pollock on a surrealist binge with a paint brush, working-class style - a curious amalgam of authentic elegance and modern perhaps vulgar sheen. Detective Forester gazed with fascination before he found the mind to speak:

'Excuse me, is Mr. Roy Riemann here?'

'Yes. That's me...'

And he briefly gazed around again before showing his ID. 'Mr. Riemann, I'm Detective Forester, NYPD.'

'What can I do for you, Detective?'

He hesitated and looked over the room, the act of a man who can't quite *see* what he sees and needs it verified again and again, then he turned to his left and noticed Nick, who paused what he was doing and asked. 'How can we help you, Detective?'

'It looks... I don't know, like a psychedelic spaceship in here or something...'

'It's to minimize static,' explained Roy, wondering what he wanted: 'The cabling interferes with the electronics. At the same time, we thought we'd jazz the place up a bit while we got the chance, since the designers made it look so bland. They offered us plants. I told them, who needs a goddamn plant? We have to work here, not them.'

'I see...'

'Can we help you in any way?' said Nick.

'Oh yes, of course. I'm sorry.' And he rummaged in his pockets needlessly. 'Do you know a man named Frank Freiberg?'

'Yes. He's our colleague. He's a bit late coming in today, but...' he looked at the clock and noticed how late it was, 'we're expecting him back any time now. Is there something we can help you with?'

'There's been an incident.'

'Incident?'

'Of sorts. Yes....' he corrected himself. 'We're not quite sure. We think he may have been... caught up in it.'

'What do you mean?' Roy burst out at him. 'What's going on? What are you saying? Why the hell don't you damn cops just get straight to the point? We're busy. We've got things to do, can't you see that?'

Forester shrugged absently, an act neither neat nor professional, but he yielded to normal reactions. 'We have very little to go on at present, so the details are rather sketchy. I hope you understand my dilemma.' They seemed unconvinced, so he resumed. 'We're still at the preliminary stage of the investigation. The incident in question happened late yesterday evening. We're not sure how Mr. Freiberg is involved, but other than...' he coughed to insinuate the fact, 'the obvious details. Anyway, I can't discuss that here.' He coughed again affectedly to test their reaction, which remained a mixture of stunned amazement and curiosity. Then, briefly glancing at the room again as if to take his bearings, he resumed: 'He's a bit elusive, your colleague. We can't trace a next of kin anywhere. That's really what I'm after. Does he have a next of kin we can contact?'

'No... No...' Roy began shaking his head in disarray, the agonized 'no' an expression of disbelief than a reply to Forester. 'It can't be...'

Forester waited for the news to sink in. He realized no one had asked him if the *incident* was fatal - the presumption settled by default. Human beings, in these trying instances, invariably assumed the worst. Forester was on the verge of resuming when Nick said: 'We're his family, in a way.'

Clearly, these psychedelic spacemen were typical humans after all, so Forester got straight to the point. 'Could someone come with me to the morgue and identify him?'

Shock, horror, disbelief. What is death but incomprehensible?

'I'll go,' Nick volunteered, touching Roy's arm in lament, who, at that moment collapsed into a chair, his grieving weight bereft of all cares; his thoughts, now prayers, going out to his friend and colleague - *Frank, 'Frank the Hack' Frieberg... Dead. Unbelievable!*

'Nick.'

'Roy...'

He looked up at him. 'You go.'

'OK,' he said, whispering, 'I'll go...' wondering what he should say, or do. 'Will you be all right on your own? Roy...?'

He cradled his head with his hands, 'Yes...' echoing faintly, solemnly, like a lament. 'Yes...'

Forester remained still while his eyes crept discreetly into motion, roaming with an irresistible urge to press themselves against the psychedelic walls and plunge into the glorious contrasts. Tones and tints seldom looked or felt this good, he thought. Despite the circumstances, human senses, all five of them, would never overlook a peculiar or glittering thing. The colors felt hypnotic and he would have loved to remain there tantalized forever and a day, but events intervened and jolted him back to reality when Nick said he was ready. Forester moved to the door, and Nick slipped on his jacket and followed him out.

While they waited for the elevator, Nick asked: 'How did it happen? Where did you find him? Did he suffer much?'

'The circumstances are somewhat confused,' he said, deliberately sparing with the facts. In his mind's eye the crime scene set off intriguing juxtapositions with the eccentrically designed office. The crime scene was a dark riddle, full of bluff, innuendo, and seedy facts, while the latter was a glittering feast: a doom-laden room counterpoised by a computer-generated landscape. He couldn't resist thinking about it. Space. Shape. Form. Spacemen. Dead men... What did it mean? *Sod's law, son, sod's law,* said Pop, all too eager to cut in at this juncture. *And to my mind, a sod's as good as a bum. No use at all...*

'Detective.'

'Yes?

'How did it happen?'

'We're not sure.'

'I mean, was he shot, stabbed? How did it happen?'

'That...' he began, recalling the room, the props, the bodies, 'is for the coroner to determine.'

Several colleagues passed Nick in the corridor and he greeted them glumly. Forester felt he was holding up rather well. In his experience the races betrayed their ethnic temperament when it came to bad news: blacks wailed with raw anathema and brought the house down; white Wasps shuddered with a kind of aloof disbelief; the Mediterranean ensemble automatically blamed someone and wanted revenge; the Slavs kind of accepted it quietly, not in their stride, but with resigned dignity; Asians sought harmony with events, and Orientals just prayed and got on with life. This guy Nick, well, he was definitely a Wasp in the luminous white category and portrayed the solid veneer of fortitude while going to pieces inside. Or was he? Forester's Pop once popped some bad news to a *posh* Bostonian with bohemian airs who groaned with a kind of crippled whimper, but actually he was having a heart attack – oh dear - and Pop never realized until it was too late, and *posh* popped off. Sadly, the shock was too great. The end, when it came, though unsightly to witness, was thankfully abrupt. *I couldn't do a thing, son, but stand by. He convulsed; he groped about and gasped for air; he said something arcane about herrings; then he popped. And that was that.* Herrings, Pop? *That's what I heard, son; that's what I heard...* This guy, Nick, well, he was a psychedelic spaceman. Forester could no longer resist the urge and asked him:

'You know, that's a very distinctive office you have back there? Who designed it?'

'No one,' he answered gloomily. 'It just turned out that way. Yes, I think so... By layers.' Grief diminished his voice, its power withering.

He seemed to be mumbling words than engaging in any conscious conversation. 'It was improvised. It was designed on the fly... We just went with the flow. You know...?'

'I see,' he felt intrigued. 'It's very interesting... Very *diverting,* one might say.'

'Yes,' echoed the gloomy syllable. 'Yes...'

'I hope you don't mind me asking but, are you still continuing to add more layers?'

'Why?'

'Oh... Just a thought.'

'Yes. I think so. Perhaps. Why do you ask?'

As they left the building Wall Street engulfed their senses with doses of a normal day's delirium: surround-sound hustle and commotion and pizzazz and *Get the hell out of my way...* razzmatazz. The seething masses of the world with their hedonistic syllables singing an opera of dollars and bucks and cents and dimes in thrall to the motion of Mammon, to the Statue of Mammon, New York City, as the masses of the world are swept into his arms. It's the velocity of life made manifest in *The Declaration of Decadence*; it's a city full of dreamers with sledgehammers running on turbocharged hormones. Knock on the door. Say what? Use the sledgehammer, buddy. And then get me the hell out of here. Where to? New York City, where else! Round and round she goes... When Liberty and Mammon embrace, it's fireworks. And when they make love, it's Manhattan. *Yausa yausa yausa!*

It's endless because it's life – a dream at the cellular level.

The traffic hammered the road, people everywhere walking, talking, eating, a carnival of hosts bleating out the dollars signs, fetish spelt with a $. That's the whole alphabet of life there in a single symbol. $. It's the driver of the human machine, it's an operating system for relationships, it's the protocol of affairs, it's the data-stream of a web that is universal and connected. It's irresistible. Get a move on. Only motion counts in this sleepless town and who the hell wants to sleep anyway? You? You? What about you? - Ask any New Yorker with a penchant for a pun, his gut commoditized by a barrel of carbohydrates and his arm dangling lazily from the window of his car - OK, he's stuck solid in a traffic jam and his car is going nowhere, *but what the hell are you doing?* that's the question, fella, as he roars out at them for crossing his field of view: 'Are you just gonna stand there all day, you dummies? Get the hell out of my way or I'll run you down. Move it!' and he honks his car horn like the car's getting mad and he revs his engine and the fat greasy geezer's going nowhere but it kind of feels right to him. Motion. Movement. 'Asshole!' That's it. That's the spirit. 'Asshole!' and on and on and on... F U 2.

And on it rolls; Forester took no action – just another day in the life of the Apple's hard core - and looks the other way for his parked car and his colleague at the steering wheel. Where's he gone?

'Damn!' he looked around. 'Where did he go? The idiot, I told him to wait. Where the hell is he? Damn him!' He fretted for an instant, then turned abruptly to Nick: 'Listen, Nick - can I call you Nick? OK. Look, my *colleague*... (the prick!)... he's obviously got called to another job, so we can take a cab and risk sitting in traffic all day, walk, or take the subway.'

'I want to get this over with as quickly as possible.'

'I understand,' he concluded in a businesslike way. 'I apologize for this; but it can't be helped. These things unfortunately happen. - The subway is the quickest route. Is that OK with you? Good. This way, please.'

And they waded headlong into the restless throng, steering a path as they weaved and wrestled among the tortuous maze of people from all corners of the Earth. *It was a cosmopolitan soup* – Cue another angle: *a melting pot* - A deeper perspective: *a social milieu* – An informed opinion: *an integrated process of nation building* – Just get to the point: *a fucking mess!* OK.

'What a mess, hey?'

'Excuse me?'

'New York City,' breezed Forester, sweeping out with his arm, which he rendered, perhaps unconsciously, with a rather majestic turn. There was pride in his gesture. 'What a mess...'

'You sound almost cynical.'

'Who me? Naaaaah!...' he brushed away all doubts, yielding to irresistible America that was New York City. Now Pop was gone, it was just him, one-to-one yielding to the one-to-many. Me against them. You're alone in the Big Apple, right at its core. You're smothered with them. With it. With that. People. Ethnics. People. Noise. Bedlam. Car horns. Noise. Ethnics. Trucks. Taxis. Noise... weaving in and out in endless restless winding synthesis, threading like a helix, multiplying in numbers like a gene, hooked up to a blood supply pumped by a limitless heart of wealth and power and technology; smoldering with roaring opulence on hamburgers, pizza, Chinese, Malay, Indian, Thai, Mexican tacos spicy as sin. The American heart takes a pounding, but she still roars: *Yeaaaahhhhh...* NYC, it never stops mixing, never settles down, car horns blaring, salesmen prowling, afterburners, rap, street traders, hustlers, free-wheelers, movers, shakers, peddlers, thieves, beggars, millionaires, millionaires, millionaires... It's not like Paris – a fine wine; London – a blend of Asian teas with English names; Rome – ancient roars: Caesar? Gimme a break, sunshine. Uncle Sam, now you're talking, sweetheart! That's the way. It's the idiom of the World. The BIG Apple – crunch! dynamism defined by bucks and billboards and limos and movies and hustlers and jeans and ponytails and sounds and scents and... and... phew! The absolute sense of dreams, of mammoth endeavors, of individual will surging through Midtown to the heart of Manhattan, *May I have this dance?* Music, let's roll: Fifth, Madison, Park, Third, Broadway, Avenue of the Americas... the sheer spectacle and scale and wealth and glass and steel and flies and money and excess and corruption and blacks and whites and indecipherables. What the hell are they? Well - what the hell are you? I'm a New Yorker, butt-head! Yeah, screw you! Me? You! And some...

Then softly goes the city's voice: 'Hey, man, have you got ten bucks for me, man?' holding out his hands.

'One for each finger?'

'Sure.'

'Here.' He gives him five. It'll do. Like being on the street, or in a penthouse. What does it mean? Ask any New Yorker:

'Love.'

'Love?'

'Sure. Love.'

'I see.'

'Hey... You loan me twenty bucks, man?'

'Sure. Here you go.'

'I love you, man. Peace.'

'Thanks.'

'Don't mention it. Peace. Peace.'

'You all have a good day, now.'

What do you say to all that?

Yausa yausa yausa!

The subway seems so far, the sidewalks busy, and the motion speeded up. Forester racks his brain for an easy way out, shoves a guy in the back. He gets the middle finger in response.

'Asshole. Watch where you're going.'

'Screw you already.'

He's getting into the swing of it now. He seldom walks these days. He cruises the streets in cars, he's earned that. He's usually in a car, honking at them, packing a punch with his words: 'Get out of the way. Move it, asshole!' Now he's on the receiving end and it stirs him furiously. The car honks madly as he tries to cross the street, traversing its path. The driver won't have it. He brakes hard, seethes, gives him the middle finger and a bit of colorful lip: 'You freak. You butt-head. You pervert. You asshole! Get a goddamn car.'

'Get out and walk, why don't you? When is the last time you even walked, you sack of spuds, you lazy good for nothing slob, get out and walk. Yeah, and screw you too!' Forester booms like a hailer. He's finding his way now; he's pitching his place among the masses again. You think he's not having a good day? Get away with you. He's on a regular NYC roll of a day full of sound and fury signifying...

'I'm telling you for the last time,' flashes his police ID at the irate driver. 'Get back in the car, and move your ass, or I'll have you, and that car, impounded.'

The sidewalks are like soup kitchens crammed with the masses, the throng heaves and breaks like a tide, never stops surging, pushing, shoving, even the uniforms get in on the act. To Forester they're like a signpost and he makes his way across. A tourist gets there first and tries to be nice.

'Excuse me, officer, do you have the time?'

'For what?'

'Errr... the time?

'Oh, the time. Yeah, sure. It's almost two.'

Forester walked right past, onward to the subway. Uniforms. What the heck...

'Detective.' Nick breaks in beside Forester, making him adjust his brisk pace for a saunter.

'Yes?'

'What time is it?'

'Ten past two.'

'Is your wristwatch fast?'

'By ten minutes.'

'Why?'

'Pop...' his said. 'It's what Pop used to do.' He diverted a glance at Nick, wondering what he was after. There was something else on his mind. 'What is it?'

'You're not telling me everything, are you?'

'If that's true, and I'm not saying it is, it would only be procedure, because we're not sure ourselves. Well... at least not yet.'

'In that case, isn't a guess better than nothing at all?'

'No,' he said empathically. 'Definitely not.'

Nick felt disturbed, and Forester noticed his unease. He hated to see people in a grind, in agony of any kind, so he grew more considerate – after all, it was his nature, and at bottom he was smart enough a cop to know that thoughtfulness is often handsomely rewarded, if not in heaven, well, then certainly in New York, in this city of intermingling contradictions. Besides, it seemed like a good idea to talk, Nick seemed a nice enough guy, and there was nothing to lose, and it becomes a man to ease the pain of a fellow human being: it's what Pop would do.

'You find me crude, don't you?'

'No,' replied Nick, 'I'm used to the city. I don't judge anyone like that.'

'Like what?'

'On appearances. That's too superficial.'

'But aren't we all superficial? Caught up in it.'

Nick pondered and said, 'You can't live in this town and not be a part of it. Whether you like it or not, it just soaks you up.'

There it was again. This sixth sense become a landscape. A room.

A cell. A spaceship. A city. A silhouette. These things press on you and make you behave in ways... you think only drugs and alcohol are mind altering. Think again. New York City is the biggest drug of them all, prescribed in doses you can hardly bear.

Forester resumed the conversation, trying to pull the threads of the mystery together.

'When was he expected back? Your friend Frank, I mean.'

'We were expecting him today. This morning in fact,' he glanced briefly at his wristwatch. 'I've been trying to contact him since yesterday, but his phone was turned off.'

'Has that ever happened before?'

'The phone? Yes, he wants his moments of privacy. But being absent like this? No. Never. We're a team. There's a lot at stake.'

'And you heard nothing from him?'

'No. - What are you getting at?'

'How can I put this? Excuse the cliché, but things may not be as they seem. We discovered pieces of information, here and there, and put what we could of the puzzle together. And we *think* it may be your friend.'

'You said think, not is?'

'I never meant to alarm you. I handled that part of it rather badly, perhaps,' he admitted, looking apologetically at him. 'But that's right; we think it may be him. So far, it seems the best shot.'

'So maybe it's not him,' his voice leapt and his heart beat faster.

'That's why we'd like someone - to be perfectly frank, at this point *anyone* - to take a look.' He looked warily at Nick. 'It's not altogether a pretty sight.'

'Detective, what happened? What did you find? Please, be frank with me. I know his habits, his tastes, his likes and dislikes. If you describe the circumstances to me, maybe I can help. Let me help. Please.'

Forester considered, eased into deep thought, and stopped on the sidewalk as the throng passed by:

'This guy, whoever he was, he found this woman with a taste for whips. He played a game with her, the "You do it to me kind. Sweat me hard, baby, sweat me hard..." And then...' raising his eyebrows.

'It went too far.'

'No. Someone butt-in and broke the house rules.'

He could see in Nick's forlorn expression recognition of his friend's vices. It was a pointless question, but he asked anyway in a tone of despair. 'Who?'

'That's what we're trying to find out. - Shall we?'

Nick bowed his head, and they resumed their journey.

But New York City continued to intrude and wouldn't let him grieve in peace. Walking ahead of them were two disheveled youths strolling side-by-side and arguing loudly. Suddenly, they broke into a scrap. It was a job for the uniforms, but Forester got out his badge and warned them.

'You boys run along now and let it alone, you hear?'

'He owes me,' raged one against the other, shoving him.

'No way. Bullshit!' contested the other, scowling.

'I'll arrest you both. Now be good boys, and scram.'

Some jostling and sparks of incendiary rhetoric exploded all at once, but it eventually settled down to rebellious grunts, sexual slurs and mischievous teasing – it's not exactly religion here, or morality, or even right against wrong. It's more fundamental than that. It's the *street* – having credibility, like a great set of wheels, or a dazzling pair of sneakers: it's the fashion, and you've got to be seen. That's the essence of identity – a state of mind, an attitude. Before, you couldn't. NYC (Now You Can).

Nearing the subway, Forester's face suddenly lit up with an amazed frown. He spotted his car in the distance and headed straight for it, jogging, crossing the street. Empty! Where was his colleague? He tries the door; it opens, and warily looks inside. He's left the keys in the ignition. Dickhead!

'Get in.'

'What about your colleague?'

'Screw him,' said Forester, revving up his cruiser and sailing along Fifth Avenue like a stallion on wheels swaying with the prairie breeze, Manhattan as she breathes... Yeah, that's good. That's really, really good... He was back into his stride, a cowboy's glide. This is how he wanted this town, behind the wheel of a car, nudging the gas pedal, testing the overdrive, elbow on the window, a smile on his face. It was like his spirit returned to him. It felt like *his* town again.

'How long did you know him?' he stole a glance at Nick, who seemed to accept that Frank was really dead, and a fixed gloom descended over him.

'Twelve... thirteen years. A long time. We were good friends.'

'Do you mind?'

Nick shook his head.

'Would you like one?'

'Not for me. No thanks.'

Forester lit a cigarette. He needed that – not as addiction, but the sheer pleasure of a free choice, exercising his lungs with the stinking mess that is nicotine, his clothes even reeked of the stuff but hey... 'It helps me to think.'

'We all need to think,' added Nick somberly.

'You should be aware, Mr. -'

'Just call me Nick.'

'Sure. Nick. You should be aware that it could be someone else.'

'You don't sound very convinced.'

'You must be wondering why I never brought along a picture of him, or something similar like that?'

'It never crossed my mind.'

'Maybe you *felt* it was him?' He paused. No answer. 'That it *might* be him.'

'I was too shocked to think,' his beaten expression seemed of years beyond his own. 'I didn't know what to think. What is there left to think?'

'When did you see him last?'

'Thursday. I told you.'

'Where? At work?'

'That's right.'

'Given what we know already about him, what other... *lifestyle* choices would he entertain?'

'Lifestyle choices?'

'Things.'

'Oh....' he closed his eyes briefly. 'Those...'

They stopped at some red lights and the car alongside boomed a relentless rap sound: humping and thumping its muscular roaring odes, it smothered the senses of those inside, four young men dancing

96

and swaying in their seats, moving to the beat, miming the lyrics: *If you tell your bitch, You talk too much, bitch. Be careful, man. She'll chew up your dick while she's sucking on it. Ouch. Yeah, ouch! Ouch!...* ad infinitum on a macho theme that for all it's muscular verbs, was full of male whimsy. Kind of a guy thing, that. Tasteless? Sure. Exotic? Who cares. Does it change a single thing? Nah.

But hey, this is New York City.

The lights turn green and the ricocheting sound accelerates around a corner.

'Welcome to New York,' said Forester ironically.

'I've been here ten years...' he replied, but sometimes it felt like ten minutes. The BIG Apple, it just rolls on... changes all the time. *Crunch.*

'Look, Nick, if it's not too much to ask, and you're up to it, perhaps you can tell me something of your friend's lifestyle choices, his habits, that may be of some help to us. Did he have any enemies?'

'No. None that I know of.'

'What about the other guy? The guy you work with?'

'Roy? What about him?'

'Where was he last Thursday?'

'Who knows,' he said absently. 'Perhaps he was playing poker.'

Forester grinned and latched lustily onto the subject. 'Poker! My kind of game. Yes sir! Is he any good?'

'What has that got to do with it?'

'Nothing' he sounded rather deflated. 'I was just asking. – Damn, not again! What now?' Turning into a street he hit stationary traffic. Lowering the window he asked some passers-by what the problem up ahead was. Several shrugged and one just complained it was always the goddamn same. But another, a jogger, explained a cyclist had been hit by a delivery van. 'Not a pretty sight,' he said, holding the momentum of his run at a single point during the exchange, praising the diligence of the uniforms tidying up the 'bloody mess up there' with laudable efficiency, before turning and jaunting away.

'Stupid bastard,' Forester cursed, sliding the window back up.

'Who, the cyclist?'

'The van driver. And the cyclist too! Yeah, why not, the leg peddling moron should have more sense than cycle on these streets.

These streets belong to four wheels, not two.'

'Oh, I see,' Nick remarked as an afterthought that verged on pointless commentary.

Forester frowned briefly, as Pop often would, in disdain for things, gestures and attitudes, quintessentially pedestrian. 'I suppose...' he said at length, 'we'll just have to wait it out.'

God gave us legs, sure, but wheels to a New Yorker are like the seeds of an apple: they naturally grow out of you. Immaculate Conception is a living myth running on four wheels and pumping gas as hard as you can on that pedal that roars vroom vroom, and not the teasing little poke of a toe, but the hammer of vroom vroom... all the way down Park Avenue. *Vroom!*

She was walking by, in a dainty red dress, and saw two ordinary guys in an ordinary unmarked car waiting for the traffic congestion to clear. But men are always up for it, so she slides up to the car, taps on the window, Forester slides it down. He smiles:

'Greetings, my lovely,' he said.

'Hi, handsome, are you looking for some fun?'

'Leave me your number.'

'Fuck you!'

'Yes please.'

And she saunters away with the air of a queen, the strut of a harlot, and the body of a plump Venus. It's better than having a wife. It's more convenient than a cozy mistress. Better even than a girlfriend who invariably makes demands. It's not that hard for a man to be beguiled by sex if that's all he wants - just a fuck, a simple fuck. And this enterprise of loose women is a lay with no questions asked, physical theater with a crisp storyline: a beginning, a middle and an end. (Er? Huh? Ah!:-) No fancy prelude, no postscript, no footnotes, only a clean, crisp smile. And you just keep on smiling. Yes sir! Just ask any man with *that* smile. Nick, however, in moralizing mode, moodily confronted Forester with the following:

'Aren't you going to arrest her? Or at least caution her. I mean, she strolls up in broad daylight and solicits the first men she sees.'

'Why make things difficult? It's just life. All I care about is getting a move on.'

'I see.'

98

'Besides, we're sitting in an unmarked car; I'm in plain clothes; I've got more important things to do; and she doesn't know I'm a cop.'

'What about the law on soliciting?'

'What about it?'

'Aren't you meant to enforce it?'

He was getting fed up with this damn Englishman and his funny ways. 'Look, *Nick*, if the law can't prove itself against the real menace of society, and all it does it strut around petty misdemeanors, then who is the real whore? I say then the law is a whore if that's all it does,' he argued rather passionately despite himself, gazing at the amazing sprawl of NYC. 'If that's all it boils down to, then it ain't worth a damn in my book. - So long as she doesn't molest children, rob or cheat people, I say, let her be. Adults can take care of themselves. She's not Caesar with an army and imperial ambitions. She's just a local hooker with a purse of condoms. Always take protection - that would be my advice to her.'

'But it's your job, your moral responsibility, to *at least* caution her for soliciting in public the way she did?'

'Give me a break! The only morality is to mind your own business. Look. Do you see that woman over there? There, in the dark blue pants.'

'Yes.'

'Imagine for a moment she's a hooker - it's not uncommon around here. So, she has four kids to feed and look after. Do you have any idea how tough New York City can be for someone like her? It's a burden, even with the hand of an angel. Just imagine the expense and responsibility for someone in her circumstances. Who do you think she is laying on her back for, day in day out? I know it would crush me; yet these people seem to go on. Stop and think for a moment, it's really amazing these attachments people have. Compared to her, I'm tiny. I'm puny. That's the rub. Do you think I could carry all that and keep my sanity? And never mind the ulcers eating me up. Could you? Ah! The philosophic shrug. You're a real cosmopolitan gent you are, *mister morality*. Are you willing to give her a handout? A part of your income? Well? - No. I thought not.'

'But it's not my responsibility.'

'No,' he said dismissively, 'it never is.'

'But it's your job. Why become a cop? This is not a marketplace where you can pick and choose the laws that suit your conscience. You must have accepted that. I mean, you're not stupid.'

Tell that English fuck to shut his trap! Give the bastard a wallop, son. Give it to the fuck; the limey smartass, wiseguy knowitall ffffffffffff....!

'I guess you're right,' he said with resignation, knowing it was the thing Pop hated most, these moralizing moaners, their puritanical theses (read feces) of the streets they knew nothing about, the dialectic clichés pampered in the media, while people were hungry and in want and trying to earn a buck. 'Let's get this over with.'

'Yes. Let's,' Nick concurred, grieving quietly for his friend.

'It's not him!' Nick gasped uncontrollably, shuddering.

'Are you sure?'

'It's not him,' his heart pounded frantically, the pain of relief shattering him as he gazed with horrified amazement at *that thing*.

Forester watched the harrowing expression work over his face as Nick studied the corpse, the sense of death swamping his senses with a burst of faintness, and Forester hurried to steady him.

'Nick, are you OK?'

'Yes... Yes...' Instinct kicked-in with a thud, as the powering surge of blood flooded back into his face. In that moment he felt he was burning inside, and was overcome by a hideous wave of cold sweat. The overwhelming physicality of his own body felt immense, and his hands shook nervously as he reached for a pack of cigarettes, muttering to himself again and again with an uncomprehending stare, relieved and horrified at the same time: 'It's not him. It's not him...'

'You can't smoke in here.'

The morgue attendant routinely pushed the body back into the fridge rack, sealed the door, and left them alone. Nick shuddered as the door broke with a thud. The morgue, though illuminated brightly throughout, was a cold, eerie place, devoid of the dignity of graves possessing the spirits of worn ages. Here, memories were white-washed and blotted out, the sense of the softness of a heartbeat betrayed, the improbable mystery of life erased. It announced death as a noun, not as a verb. And spoke nothing but the cold sense of lifelessness. Sheen without a soul. Dead.

'Nick, can you talk?' He nodded yes after a while, looking dazed, clutching his head with his hands, and Forester resumed. 'Before you thought it *could* be him. All the pieces seemed to fit.'

'It's not him.'

'We know that now. But before, you imagined otherwise.'

Nick shook his head. It was hard to think clearly as the surge of relief engulfed him. He mumbled something that made no sense, until the wounds of his spirit ached and he said: 'You never know what to expect. Do you? You never really know yourself... What I would feel inside... How can I?'

'Where is he?'

'Who?'

'Your colleague Frank.'

'I don't know. But that's not him.' He indicated the faceless door entombing the corpse. He froze, and then an acute sense of revulsion made him convulse suddenly. 'Good God, are there people inside each of these cubicles?'

'Well... yes.'

'Dead people?'

'I hope so. That's what they're meant for.'

'Shouldn't this be a shrine or something? Something holy?'

'Excuse me?'

'It's so dead. This is horrible. Horrible! It's not dignified. Jesus!'

Forester followed the progression of his trauma and swiftly escorted him out. 'Nick, it's over. I'll have someone take you back.'

Walking along the corridor, Nick saw a bench near the main exit and sat down. He felt his face and the sweat pouring from him. Could this really be happening to him? It was incomprehensible.

'Are you all right?' Forester asked him. 'Would you like some water; a sedative or something?'

Nick shook his head and Forester offered his handkerchief. Nick recovered sufficiently to retrieve his own. He held and gazed at it, as if proving to himself it was really there.

'Nick, I need to arrange for a car to take you back. Just bear with me a moment.' And Forester withdrew.

Breathing hard and fitfully, Nick waited alone, but his mind was in turmoil. Only the conviction that Frank was alive gave him the strength to confront his fears. He thought of Frank, and Roy, and Vonnie – Vonnie! Her presence in mind surprised him and tempered his gloom. There was the stir of hope, alive in him. These precious thoughts empowered a sense of forgiveness of things – all things, a deep toleration of the world and its strangeness. *Live and let live* sprung ever so true. And he wrestled with the fact that those dear to him were alive. This alone mattered. He discovered then that even in despair, reserves of energy are there if one has the will, and the intelligence, to seek them out. Glancing at his wristwatch, he made a decision and rose from the bench. He informed the duty sergeant not to trouble himself with the car; he'd make his own way back.

'Are you OK there, fella?' he asked gruffly, but meant it kindly.

'Yes... Yes. Thanks.'

'You take care, now.'

And Nick left the police station and walked out into the late afternoon sunshine.

He made for the subway because the traffic was bulging at the seams and getting back by cab would be fraught with unbearable delay. Heading south waves of pedestrians surged past him and he felt he was asphyxiating in a swarm of people, magnified in mind than in actual fact, but he felt vulnerable, his feelings were in chaos. Acting impulsively he hailed down a taxi that swept suddenly into view. He wanted to escape things, to break away, perhaps, even from himself, and plunge into an ocean of silence. The taxi swerved to the side and screeched to a piercing stop. The driver never seemed to mind and looked lively. 'Taxi, mister? Get in.' What Nick saw was Irish pluckiness on a Latino face with a Midwestern smile crowning a grin, an everyman running on whiskey-wisdom and tequila-humor and bourbon-bounce topped off with All-American-ice. And this cocktail of delights was bustling with energy.

'Where to?'

'Wall Street.'

'I know a short cut.'

'Good.'

'Leave it to me, sir. Leave it all to me.'

102

'Thank you.'

Being laconic, it's part of the make up of this town, just another facet of business and business-sense permeating everything.

Nick reclined back in the seat and lit a cigarette. He noticed his hand had stopped shaking, and this calmed him even more.

'Do you mind if I smoke?'

'Nah. Go ahead.'

Gradually, he began to feel more at ease. The drive, swaying him to and fro, was a lullaby motion. New York City from the back seat of a cab, time was a symphony of place, this town a tempo and he within it, a sublime song. Painful self-absorption left him, and the tempo of his will was restored to an even keel – we sail in an ocean, sometimes boiling, of own imaginable feelings - and the cigarette helped. He gazed at the panorama of New York City before him – it was a metaphor for life; that life must always go on, despite everything, life is a dance, it's a waltz, it's a New York tango, shuffling along, doing it your way. Feeling... at ease among this self-energizing shiver of humanity was life, that was New York City on a summer's afternoon, inviting you take a share like a ripe grape bursting from the tree of life... and you suck, and suck, and suck, this ambrosia quintessential. And you pull down the window; and the noise and the air and the sense of it smacks you. 'Traffic is hell today,' Nick remarked, dreaming of serenity, basking in tranquility. This.

'It's hell every day out there. Monday, Tuesday, Friday... Man oh man, it's the worst! It's hell out there. But it's like love; so what can you do!' He seduces the City with that Irish pluckiness, that Latino visage, that Midwestern smile crowning a grin. Being a New Yorker is equivalent to Immaculate Conception. You are born anew every single goddamn day. And today is the first day of the rest of your life. 'Yes sir, next week's the Grand Parade. Man, I love New Yorkers, they sweep me off my feet,' chuckled the cabbie shuffling in his seat, pausing occasionally to scowl at the static traffic, to have a blast on his horn, to swear at a cop, to prattle nonsense with the passing crowds, to sweet-talk the majority, to pick a fight with the heat. 'Streets'll be empty of traffic like a wino's bottle then.'

'Tomorrow's another day,' said Nick, heaving a sigh of relief... *It's not him.*

'Yeah. You got it right there, buddy. You sure as hell got it right there. – Come on!' excitedly honking on his car horn. 'What the hell is holding up the traffic?' *Vroom vroom...*

'It's not him.'

'Are you certain?' Roy shuddered.

'It's not him.'

He gasped as though he would faint. An enormous pressure lifted and he breathed with such rapture that it surprised even him. 'Thank God!' A moment later he stopped and looked up, emulating Nick's smile with a grin of his own, then grew stern of a sudden and demanded: 'Then where the hell is he?'

Nick slumped into a chair and looked at the trading screens. The markets were steady. Paris was up five points – a rally. The Dow up a touch. Profits were slim today.

'Maybe,' said Nick, moving his hand over the console to execute a transaction, 'he's shacked up somewhere dreaming of riches.'

'Then he'd better wake up fast and call us first, the bum.'

Roy threw a fist in frustration, punching the air before returning to his desk. Nick turned and looked at him, prolonging the stare. And together, at length, they slowly began to laugh.

'He'll be back,' said Nick. 'Wherever he is; he'll be back.'

Chapter 6

Prelude:

Frank unfolds the pocket computer, face upwards, and fires it up, hits the control key, nothing, hits it again, ah! polishes the screen as though fine-tuning a violin, then draws it closer, almost tender with enquiry, a conspicuous conceit of a man who handles the tools of technology in the palm of his hand as something intimate and dear to him. It's his pathway to delights, to blessed lays and seismic nights, to things of palpable need, of music and finance, and technical aspects of tie and tease - *stoke the bloke while she's having a smoke and drinking a coke.* Easy! 'Ready for action' declares his little computer, and he's titillated by it all... *he he he*...mesmerized by the self-indulgent call of his hormones: fondling the cosmos of cyber-space with a probing hand, feeling up events in time and space with the swift cascade of a thumb tapping the touch screen, highlighting options, selecting from a menu with a randy forefinger teasing the world at his fingertips. Ah...What should he have? Clearly, everything!

He scans the text, scrolling down to the rollover sections, searching M for Mistress and goes into overdrive for XXX, rated fireworks time, *yausa!* selects her number from a list, and dials.

It's ringing. Once. Twice. A third time. A forth time... She picks up:

'Hi there.' Her voice. Contact!

'MX?'

'A-ha.'

'Are you open for business?'

'A-ha.'

She's monosyllabic in a bimbo kind of way, but a sweet throaty voice all the same, (full of endearments that turn nasty when she strikes him with her whip. *Ouch! That's nice...*). He adores the way she sounds, a cute fornication performed sublimely with the tongue, licking you in a ritualistic kind of way. Mmm, he likes that... He likes that a lot.

His imagination arouses him; he coughs, timing his response: 'I want to see you. Can I come over?' He looks at his wristwatch. Damn thing, it's stopped.

'Now?'

'What time is it?'

'You have a pen?'

'I know the address.'

Cut to the chase girl. 'Come over.'

'I'll be there in forty minutes. OK?'

'A-ha.'

She hangs up smartly and he follows suit. The phone. His life. The universe. God. All meaning of things demystified into the phallic necessity of man - he's horny, so all intelligence is suspended for the duration while semen gets the signal from the brain (The brain? The cock, perhaps). *What day is it?* he wonders to himself, agonizing and shuddering with thoughts of her. *A-ha,* she sighs in that fuck-me voice that is worth traveling to the end of the world for. Who cares: today, tomorrow, the day after... Time, it's just one big hangover. Nighttime, daytime, he's here to party-time, he's on a roll; he can't stop now. Yes-sir-eee, can't stand still and can't look back. Got to get a move on. Take a quick shit, quick shave, quick shower and get the hell over there. Yes-sir-eee...Vegas, Vegas, the cocktail of lights, full of heavenly delights. And boy can she sing, and the mermaids swing, and gaming tables rumble to the roll of the dice. And boy ain't she nice: dames, money, liquor. Slop, slop.

'Your car, sir,' chimes the pageboy, all delightful-like, a six foot bundle of efficiency.

'Thanks.' He's all smiles, he's a master of smiles, his dick's a directional homing device autonomously pointing the way, his hand reaching into his pocket the same time as he leans into the car. Then he pauses of a sudden. 'By the way; what day is it?' He tips him twenty from the wad of cash.

'Tuesday,' the bundle of efficiency smiles back at him, a face flirting with envy, he knows it's rude to stare at the scrumptious cache of greenbacks, but it's irresistible, really. 'You must be a high roller.' He says, and covets a mysterious slice of his luck. 'Any tips?'

'Tuesday? Did you say Tuesday?' the echo kicks-in as he wonders what the hell happened to Monday; and the loud honking of a car queuing behind his on the driveway adds to the mystery. Quickly he enquires: 'What time do you have?'

'What time do you need?'

'Eh?'

'Cadillac time; boulevard time; The Strip time; casino time...'

'Are you humoring me?'

'Las Vegas time.' He winks; this fella's all smiles, showing him his wristwatch. 'You have a real nice day now, sir.'

It's eleven-thirty in the morning and he can't help wondering whatever happened to Monday? But as he pulls out smartly into the street, the niggling thought subsides and he glides into the drive and the ceaseless flow of traffic. - Power. Motion. Restless America. He knows this town like the back of his hand. Clap clap (slap slap). Life: you wrestle with it, it wrestles you back, and he cruises down the Sunset Strip like a sunbeam from a star.

'You know what I love about the desert?' he asked himself, gazing at Vegas.

'What?' his alter ego asked back.

'*Its desertness*,' he replied, never for an instant removing his transfixed gaze from the constellation of dazzling lights. All this, in the beginning, was desert, was a man's dream that something can be done with anything. It's a testament to the human will, a triumph of benighted hoodlums with a suntan, sharks and cowboys who carved a niche in wilderness, and made it gleam brighter than the sun, hotter than a blazing star. And they named her *Vegas*. Yes-sir-eee. *Las Vegas*. A place. A spell. An idea. *A She*

It was searing out there. Desert heat. Vegas heat. Dollar heat. Intermingle them into body heat, and rub it in, yes sir... rub it in.

Round One

He was greeted at the door:

'MX?'

'A-ha.'

And once inside she offered him a drink.

He looked her over while they went through the preliminaries of chat, chat, chat. She's dyed her hair flame red since he saw her last. She flashes him some rubber knickers and he wanted to taste her there and then but she invited him to sit down. The tease was merely a ruse to drain the masculine brain of reason and fill it with testosterone. And when it comes to turning on the tap, no question she's the babe with the wrench. He looked at her lips, ogled her breasts, stared at her legs, watched as she walked over to the table and retrieved her phone.

It was quick, conducted in whispers, a shy giggle, a glib return of plaintive sighs. She hangs up and gives him a smile. 'OK?' She beckons him with her finger and he follows her into the bedroom. He looks around. *Stop! Stop everything!* What's this? A bland box not worth a soft stroke in. Is he merely a jerk-off to her? The day's just getting started. Come on, girl. He had better things to do with his hands. White sheets, white curtains, white carpet and a black pair of panties over a drawer. It's like a hotel room minus the porno channels. Not his thing. He wants what he had before, multiplied a thousand times.

Cut to the chase. 'Where's the dungeon?'

She showed him a picture. Girl packs her assets, from picture to a pussy, she knows the enticements that swamp a man's senses with oceans of lusts. His eyes gape, his intestines grovel, he's become a six foot one cock - no surprises there. He's been there before. She's installed some new gear.

'You like?'

'I want,' he said hungrily, consuming with his eyes.

'A-ha.' She points temptingly to a door draped with a full-length mirror. He pauses, looks at himself, those voyeuristic eyes immaculately crafted for the gaze, his brown hair cut neat and groomed perfectly back. Sure, he's a handsome kind of guy. Using the mirror they exchange a gaze. Her eyes say: *Hmm, not bad... for a mid-day John.* His suave answer is just a touch above cliché: *Yes-sir-eee!*

He is first inside and removes his jacket, throws it anywhere, and takes a seat on a small metallic stool; effectively, he has to squat. She looms over him; looking down; examining, prying him apart with her feline eyes – feminine cat, teasing a rat, closing in for the kill, well, it's all part of the thrill... of being a man. Details of his persona begin to ripple and turn, the way he stares at her, seedy and prolonged, evokes a restless desire. At length, she recalls something...

'I've seen you before, haven't I?' Her voice was spicy, more curious than questioning. But he remains silent, seductively silent. He wants her to guess; to remember; to arouse him with the stir of recollection. Is he just another John to her, or something more? She winces, tightening the muscles on her face. Her mood follows the seductive idioms of a ritual. It's all coming back now... He arrives, undresses, lays out to be inspected, poked, probed, whipped, teased into submission and then comes, then leaves, exhausted, exhilarated, rejuvenated. Hungry for more. Please, may I have more. *More?* More and more... (Ring's a bell? But it's not grub he's after.) Always more.

'A-ha.'

'Yes...?'

'I remember you now.'

'Tell me.'

'I know what you need.'

'Twice over, my love.'

'Are you sure?'

'I'm twice the man and half the trouble.'

'Greedy!'

'I know.' He confessed. 'I know...'

'And I know *exactly* what turns you on.'

'Hmm...'

'You are my slave.'

'Do you have time for me?'

'Do you have the money?'

Money creates time. Time created money. The Big Bang. Free Lunch. Cosmic Inflation. It's all weird and wonderful stuff. But only money talks. Yak. Yak.

'Do you take credit cards?'

'Cash only.'

There's no arguing with the fundamental laws of nature. He wants to know: 'Will you make my day?'

'If you have the money, I'll make it last a lifetime.' She confides to him, dropping an aside, 'This is Vegas after all.'

'For old time's sake.'

Old time. New time. Elastic time. Relativistic quantum time. Multi-dimensional time. Been-here-before time and seen-it-all-before time. Who's counting? Tick tock...

'Cash!' she insists. And he pays up like a good boy. 'One. Two. Three. Four.' Bills. Hundred is the floor here. Nobody speaks of dimes. The only sound that counts is the crease of paper. Greenback. Back to back. Pile it up high. Lovely. Yes-sir-eee.

Her kit - a suit of squishy rubber, the shiny black material, pristine, antiseptically clean, pure, elastic, colorless, odorless, intimidating, powerful... like the desert. It was more than merely garb; it was tease become necessity, like spacesuits out in deep space, or a diver's suit beneath the deep blue sea. Nothing else quite cuts it. It's got to be rubber. It's got to be black. It's got to be shiny. It's got to be pure. It's got to be squishy. Like human flesh - one of a kind.

'I want you to wear the tight rubber suit.'

'A-ha.'

'The black one.'

'A-ha.'

'I don't want to see your flesh. Not a speck of it.'

'You won't,' she said. 'You're not worthy to see my flesh.'

'I know.' He's scum. He's shit. He loved it. 'I know.'

Round Two.

Two hours latter he's cruising down the Strip. It's a long time till *sunset* and time rolls on. Well, talk the talk, walk the walk.... Could the Pharaohs ever have imagined all this? Have the stomach for it? The nerve? Vegas! He slows, pulls over to the curb, stops, kills the engine and frisks in his pocket for the mobile computer. It bursts alive and he scans the list of names, scrolling down to S & M and selects a number from the list. He went for someone spanking new, a babe combining All-American cool with a French heart, her motto was: *Je t'aime, baby. Cum to me...* and she sounded like a darling in the ads. So, naturally, he gave her a try.

110

He lifts the handset and dials. It's ringing. Once. Twice. A third time. A forth time... *Come on, you bitch, pick it up. Pick it up...*

She picks it up on the seventh. It makes him moody. Cut to the chase:

'Are you open for business?'

'Yes.'

'Can I come over?'

'Yes.'

'How much?'

'How long do you want?'

'An hour?'

'Three hundred.'

'Make that two hours.'

'Five hundred.'

'Done.'

He drove his car into the gas station for a top-up and, like his balls: 'Fill her up,' it'll take some knocking up the miles until the tank is fully emptied and he has to drag himself back to New York City and the routine of his life. Las Vegas, after all, was a kind of afterlife. Reincarnation as a flight plan. The only difference is you live and live, and resurrection is a seamless thing – the ten o'clock shuttle from New York to Vegas explains everything in a cascade of light and boarding passes. Drink, sir? *May as well.* Champagne? *With a cheery, please.* One or two? *Make it three.* Here you go. *Ta...* Next stop, Vegas. You're welcome. Have a nice day. *Ta...*

This princess was a different slice of cake, baked with feminine sweetness and topped with sultry cream, and real courteous too. Those cherries of hers were a real bonus. He took a fancy to her almost immediately, living proof than men's eyes were engineered for eating out cream cakes tasting real sweet. Unlike some other well-rogered royalty eager to cut corners, like chopping twenty minutes off an hour, or working slaves mechanically to a climax, this little number was a perfect pro. If whoring were a science, then she's the highest state of the art. Ten out of ten, and well worth a bundle of bucks just to have her poke you with a whip. Ouch! Progressing from straight sex into tie and tease and domination went deeper than a staged routine. Give her a man and she plays him like a card, always keeping several stashed up her delightful sleeve – surprises were her forte, and they don't half tease you with a pinch! Wager at your peril or your pleasure. You should see her ante with a whip; she packs the chips like only a real pro can. Graces are not measured with moods, but with firepower, and this little number is a hyper-power in thongs and thigh-length boots with stiletto heels. More tiny and cute than large and domineering, her sexiness transcends any man's advantage in height as she towers above him, those muscular stiletto thigh length boots elevating Tiny into Mighty Mouse – there, now looming over him, the menacing tinyness of her glare, *Bad boy, you bad, bad boy...* The dominating vantage she commands is the main prop for a slave to worship, where his fetish craving to submit meets her power head on, and he obeys her every whim. Even as she taunts him: 'You are a filthy, worthless slave. Lick, you dog! Lick hard. Harder!' The soles of her boots, she wants them spotless, a sheen like a mirror so he can see his own vile face being crushed beneath them when she condescends to grind them in his face. (Not bad for a five foot two kitten! Meow.)

She is more than provocation, this feisty young thing with the feline stare, an orgiastic power ravaging the scum beneath her. There is sacrifice and menace in those sweet savage eyes, staring, probing, leering at the seediness and infamy of his helplessness, the sacrificial juices that he spurts when she touches him just there, ouch! those tiny hands make ecstasy, escalating when her voice rouses his emotions, taking control of him.

'No more!' he squealed.

Which meant moremoremore... It's like that; yea bucks nay; yes attracts no, when dry he means wet, when he's finished it suggests he's just begun. It's not a contradiction. It's chaos. It's ecstasy without a reference. There is no mind, and only flesh counts.

'I am not an animal!' he screamed out wildly like a caged beast.

And plug his mouth, because she's sick and tired of listening to him. And she left him there, gagged, languishing, while she went into the kitchen to do her bits and pieces.

Round Three.

Refreshed, back in his car, relaxing with a cigarette and a beer, he scans the list. There. Dial that number. The Savage Nurse. He needs to be taken care of.

'I'm ill. I'm sick. I need taking care of.'

'Then come to Nookie Nightingale,' she teases. 'We'll make your day; and soothe all your sorrows away.'

The plural *we* fires off a fantasy in his brain, and he excitedly requests the extras: 'It's a job for two nurses. A trainee and a pro.'

'I see...'

'Do you have the right kind of girl friend? Let's try it with three.'

'Her?'

'Plus you and me.'

'Three?'

'Yeah.'

She giggles and sounds delicious. 'Sure, whatever you like.'

Ménage à trois... or the meek and the mild; the submissive and the slut, the humbled and the whore; the tamed and the shrew. Two is too few: he needs three to burn. And he tells her meltingly. 'If it gets too hot, you know... she can always watch.'

'Yes, she can...' Watch, that is, provided you pay, schmuck, provided you pay she'll watch; she'll wash your cock and slap your ass and pee all over you she'll do whatever you want... 'OK. Do you prefer blonde, brunette..?'

'Red head,' he chooses, instantly aroused. 'Like fire.'

'Then fire it is,' she assures him, and gives her address.

Perhaps he's using his dick as a pen because he's breathing hard like he's working himself crazy. She interposes and asks his name.

Without thinking he spurts out: 'John.'

She cocked a merry smile and sighed with an air of cool routine: 'John. OK, *John*. It's cash only, *John*.'

'Frank. I meant to say Frank,' he corrected, thinking to himself – the hell with it, why bother to lie? If she can be honest and admit she's a whore, can't I be honest too and a whoremonger? After all, it's more fun being honest; you strip away your shame and no one can ever seize that handle to poke you with. As a womanizer and a man's man, he knew this: never allow others to manipulate him with his own hands – especially his best hand. 'Frank Freiberg, to be exact. Frank to my friends.' And precision is something even a whore admires, so she responds in swanky mode.

'See you soon then, Frankie boy. *We'll* be waiting.' Is she a tease, or a girl with a pretty attitude? Speculation was the last thing on his mind just then as he starts humming a tune he was particularly fond of, which had a tinge of seediness in its rhythm, but it managed to get him into the mood just nicely.

She hung up and he folded down the handset and fired up the engine. Suddenly, it hits him again, *What the hell happened to Monday?* But it doesn't linger in his mind, as Vegas' lights flood his senses, he devours the spectacle and eats *her* up. Vegas fills up an appetite not to bursting, but just deliciously filling enough so drowning in *her* feels like a dream. 'I'll call the boys when I'm done with the dames.' Yes-sir-eee.

Typically, with a nurse, (decked out in pure white rubber, of course) after probing about and examining him, the diagnosis arrived at (he's horny and needs the whipping cure) the therapy would be formulaic. With a dog chain bound around his neck, he would be dragged into an enclosed room kitted out as the surgery, the smell of wood and the aftertaste of sweat would seep into his senses as he was tied up, spanked, and molested to completion. This time, the third person added her fire. Despite her petite frame, she had long swanky legs tailing, it seemed, all the way down from her pointy little nipples to her ravishing toes (on which he had a good long groveling suck), and her piping little screams did the trick handsomely as she took an incredible whipping from Top Nurse. And that red hair – well, it's a wig, but imagination transforms those small discrepancies to the creamiest delights. Top Nurse had them both as slaves, tying them up tightly, tormenting them beautifully, making it feel like honey-coated agony as she played with the girl while doing delicious things to him. She made them come several times and he collapsed feeling knackered and wanting moremoremore.

'Please, nurse.'

'Just wait your turn.'

It's all an act, but he loves it.

'I want to watch you two doing it.'

'Next time.'

'I have money.'

Johns have money. Johns can always find the money. Their dick is like the handle of an old time slot machine. Yank away and it coughs out the quarters. It's a money machine. Ding dong. The lady knows. It's her business to know. Hitting on a John is like hitting on a lopsided slot machine. You're sure to win. Just hold the Dixie cup, and the dollars come pouring out. Men: blessed with semen and not the sense to use it wisely. It all makes for a:

'Cocktail, sir?'

'No thanks.' His buckets are empty, and Frank hangs out at a bar at a casino on the Strip and indulges a grin of fulfillment Ahhh... and takes a moment to breathe, Ahhh... basking in the warm afterglow of exuberant pleasures. 'Waiter.'

'Yes, sir.'

'Are the slot machines here rigged?'

'No, sir.'

'Are you sure?'

'Absolutely, sir,' he insisted. 'The casino likes to win honestly.'

'Don't we all!'

'Sir?'

'Here,' he gave him a hundred. 'I'd like a beer. And bring me some change for the slots, would you?'

The waiter's efficient. He looks like a student working the holidays. He returned, gave him the beer and the coins, thanks him for the tip, and wished him honest luck – well, casino luck, anyway.

The slot turns - but Frank? Even as his manhood makes more semen, he can't quite hit the jackpot. And you know, he puts it all down to sheer bad luck.

Round Four

As an afterthought, Frank took out his phone and switched it on. Almost instantly he receives a call from New York City. Until that moment he renounced it as a meaningless device while screwing for the world record on how many times he could come in a day. At heart, he's an Olympian athlete of sorts – he has tremendous respect for *cumming* first every single time. And his rationale ran something like this: *To hell with it. Who needs this thing on all the bloody time? Leave me alone. Leave me in peace. I need to practice for the*

Olympics.... until a flood of hectic screams spew out frantically from the phone at him:

'Frank! Frank, is that you? Damn it!'

'Nick. Is that you?'

'Where the hell are you?'

'Me? I'm here.'

'Where?'

'In Las Vegas. Listen to me a moment, Nick, something strange must have happened, because I seem to have lost... Hello. Hello.'

The voice down the line drifted and faded into a chaos of jumbled sounds, which took the form of frantic voices wrestling questions and retorts like a stream of bullets: *He's alive, he's alive. Yeah. Gimme the goddamn phone, Nick, I'll kill that butt-head. Keep calm, Roy, don't panic. He's back. Screw him, Nick, screw the selfish bastard. Just get him back here. Give me the phone. No. Let go. Damn it, let go. Shit...* and so on as a fitful struggle ensued over possession of the phone in New York. Frank muttered into the receiver with a puzzled drone.

'Hello. Hello. Is anyone there? Hello. Nick. Roy. Hello...Is anyone there?'

'Asshole!' Roy won the contest and screamed down the line. 'I don't give a damn where you are. Get back here. Now, you idiot! It's an emergency. You get it? Get back here.'

'OK, OK. But listen to me for a minute. Roy -'

But Roy hung up.

Frank looked at his wristwatch, and despite his will it seemed to hold his stare. It was working again! At that moment, as he gazed at it strangely, all he could register in his confused mind was: *You stop, and then start up again just like that. What the hell is going on?* (Time he got a new watch, perhaps).

'Sir. Excuse me, sir,' said a gent with a drawling Southern accent and a barrel gut, nickname Bud and in need of a top up, wearing a sunshine shirt and carrying a Dixie cup full of coins.

'Yes?' said Frank.

'Could you tell me the time, please?'

Frank looked at the gut, then the cupful of coins, and swayed his head from side to side, wondering what to think. 'I have no idea...'

116

Chapter 7

Paris. Slant the inflection to an E, and out climbs *Pareee...*sung with an easy *eeee...* See? All feminine riffs and flow and poise, and reverberations of honeysuckle noise made by busy bees when flirting with the rosaries, picked up by gents swaying to the tune, and giving them to mademoiselles in love with a twirly moon reflected in the ripples of the River Seine, easy as she flows, from the tip of the Eiffel Tower to the bottom of Champs Elysees toes. It's lovely beyond compare, this E, this Pareee... dazzling in the sunset bonanza of orange, red, purple, cyan and magenta hues, nothing cuts you a French like Par*eee*, sung with an easy E...M...C... squared. You long to embrace her, feel her, be seduced by her, flirt with her essence and suckle on her *eeee* like she were the breasts of the world's desire, to slip inside her and take her and ravish her. She's magnificent, this legendary dame, *Parisienne* in everything of mood, and time, and space. But *eeee* turns into a crass cliché of *ooooo* when a scruffy Frenchman with a knack for a spoil spits pointlessly on the pavement when he spots a foreign punter, cagily approaches him, and croaks into his ear:

'Psssst, monsieur, can I interest you in some stuff?'

'Stuff?'

'To make you happy?'

'Me?'

'Oui, monsieur. Very happy.'

'Nah.' The punter shakes his head, an American with a boozy grin gazing back at Frenchie and tossing a coin into the River Seine. Is he wishing favors from mermaids and fairies, or paying his dues for being contrary? He looks at Frenchie leering back at him with cagey eyes: 'Hey, fella, you know of any half-decent chicks around here decked out for a feast and ready for a roll in the hay?'

'Pardon, monsieur?'

'Dames, buddy, dames.'

'Ah!' He grins, acknowledging the baser fancies of a horny Yank and nods knowingly at the *hormonal-sapien* (with star-spangled eyes) before pointing him towards the riverbank. 'Down there.'

'There?'

'Yes, monsieur. Look. Do you see them?' He points at something. Are they dames or ducks? He needs a lay, so let's go and find out.

'Oh yeah. Thanks a bunch, buddy.' He winks and tucks in his collar. *Show time!*

But he's a schmuck, because chicks with dicks is all he'll find ambling along the promenade like over-embellished swans: a masculine idea of how cosmetics should be applied over the face – smack it on with beefy strokes, and overload your mug till it's a cliché of a slut: luscious gobbling lips; sleazy eyes, ruby cheeks, face like a pussy. *Yeah! Eat me.*

But hey, you never know, he might even enjoy it.

'Hi there, honey, today's your lucky day. What's your pleasure?'

She grabs his dick like only a man can, and the schmuck realizes he's on the wrong side of paradise. – *Eden's that-a-way!* - He soon discovers a capacity for sprinting and knocks up a good hundred meters in a shave under ten. Adrenalin is an amazing tonic – it fires up like no-body else's business. 'Jesus Christ. Shit! Holy shit!' The world seems crazy as he blunders along and hails down a passing cab: 'Stop! Stop, you fuck! Stop!' And it screeches to a stop.

'Taxi, monsieur?'

A dumb question. The Yank dives in and just stammers frantically. 'Drive.'

'Monsieur?'

'Just get me the hell out of here.'

'Monsieur?'

'Drive.'

'Where to?'

'Bléu Doux. To the jazz club Bléu Doux, on the Avenue Alizee.'

'You want to go to Avenue Alizee, monsieur?'

'Move it, asshole. Move it!' Cough, spit, cough up some what? Halleluiah! The muck that people carry in their innards... I know... it's not a pretty sight. Some might pause and ponder what this intestinal juxtaposition means? - Man, the Universe, God, phlegm! Religion or mathematics? I dunno... tap tap, busy busy loaf. But most guys with a hard-on just curse their rotten luck. - Cue to the schmuck: 'Fucking fake-queens! Bastard fucks!'

'Monsieur.'

'What?'

'I can see you've been running, monsieur?'

'Just drive, will you!'

'Would you prefer I take the scenic route?' he said. He was pure composure, this man, not a single wrinkle of his middle years out of place. 'It's longer, but it will give you time to get your breath back.'

'No. Just get me there pronto, damn it!'

'As you prefer.' And he's the kind of guy never in a hurry for a single thing, and resumes the drive with that cool, unruffled Gallic grin on his effing French face. What's he smiling at? thinks the American to himself, and grows irate when the driver starts whistling a bland melody.

'Enough already!' he reproached him. 'Jesus Christ. Can't you people just drive?'

Driver hits the brakes. Wheels spin. Car jolts to a hard stop. And all this is achieved with seamless panache. He pauses, then calmly turns to face him. 'Just so you know, this is my cab, monsieur. Mine alone. If I say we stop for a glass wine and some cheese, we stop. And we take our time about it too. I'm never one to rush a meal; not for the world. And if I bolt on rockets and choose to blast off for the moon, then that's where we go. Voila! And if you don't like it, well, you can open the door, get out, and I'll leave you a parting smile - *Au revoir*.' And he did smile, this man, handsomely, and waits patiently for a reply. But none came, so he resumes by way of casual humor: 'The day is still young, monsieur. We could always head back and pick up *le cherie, mon amie.*'

Now that's slippery, even for a Frenchie, one who likes to act cool and suave all the time, with a smile as wide as frog's spanning ear to grinning ear: the epitome of smugness. The American growls, but only softly, the bleak frown of a challenged man sullying his face. He's a guy that considers himself handsome, dresses well, always looks great. And when called on he can really deliver a dirty look - real gutter-class, sewer level stare. That's a talent, sure, but in reality what else can he do? Get another cab? He turns uneasily in his seat and knows he has to make a quick decision. But events uncannily turn in his favor.

'Monsieur.'

'Yes?'

'Would you care to listen to some music?'

He's offering a truce all of a sudden. He's being nice; real nice. Is this a trick? Is he for real? *Can this guy really be French?* The American has to grapple with a conundrum that throws him into disarray. The last thing he needs sloshing around in his head right now is the riddle of the Frenchman acting out of kindness of the heart. This kind of thing jars. It makes no sense. But he's in a tight bind, an excruciating one, so he takes a deep breath, imagines the improbable and hopes for the best. 'Yes. Please, sil vous plait. Jazz... or Blues if you've got it. Thanks. Merci.'

He resumes the drive. The Frenchie is an angel after all, thinks the American - *Viva la France!*

'You are welcome, monsieur,' And he hits the switch, music plays, and the American, Anthony Leoni, music promoter extraordinaire, reclines back in his seat, begins to relax, and slips effortlessly into the embracing robes of melody, settling into the musical mood like a scrumptious warm cashmere as he easies by a log fire with a glass of wine and a lover to sing to him – tenderly, sublimely, profoundly, the whole world hanging perfectly on the cusp of a note. Yeah.... 'You're not in any particular hurry, are you, monsieur?' No, replies the American, giving deep meaning to the notion that to be a man is to immerse yourself in music, and feel divine. *Yeah*, he thinks, *Yeah*, he feels, *Yeah*, looking at the sunset, listening to the Blues. *This is wonderful. This is paradise. Yeah...*

The jazz club Bléu Doux was blessed with the subliminal voice of an angel.

'What a voice.'

'Remind me, what's her name again?'

'Cindy Gillespie.' Anthony frowned at his brother. That was the

120

third time. 'Remember that name, dickhead. I'm not going to repeat it again.'

'Why?'

'Don't be a wiseguy. And get yourself a new set of ears. – Waiter, excuse me, garcon, sil-vous-plait, the bill please.'

'Monsieur,' he acknowledged, bowed and strode away effortlessly and with such panache is made Anthony wonder aloud: 'How come we don't do it like that more often?'

'Do what?'

'Have a bit more... how can I say... *élan*. Yes, that *continental* style. It's a cultural marker, and it comes with taste, a taste for the best. And you can't learn that on a diet of burgers and beer.'

'What's wrong with beer? I like beer.'

'It's not beer, or burgers for that matter. It's what you bring to them that I'm referring to. Not just service; but style. That's being *cosmopolitan*. Like matching a beautiful voice with a lovely song. Like Cindy...' he turned to her, mesmerized by her repertoire of soulful blues, easing back into his chair, lighting a cigarette; and dreamed... her singing was exquisite. 'Doesn't it inspire dreams?'

'What?

'Music. Songs...' said Anthony, pushing the bill towards him. 'Here, pay the man. That's it. Good. Put your hand in your own pocket for a change.' He paid, grudgingly, and was rather sparing with the tip, so Anthony topped it up. Pride alone had him reaching for his wallet. Dignity had a price, and he was more than willing to pay. 'How you ever came to be a banker, stingy miser that you are, I'll never understand. You don't have the class to step foot in this place. Your mere presence is a scandal, and I should have known better for inviting you. Sometimes, I'm ashamed you're my brother. The world is too big and amazing for a mind like yours. You should have stayed at home.'

'No thank you.'

'You should have been a pig farmer, that's your forte. You're small town. You'll always be small town. You'll carry it with you wherever you go. Sophistication will always elude you. Your fate lies with a shovel and a field full of dung. It's makes great fertilizer, and you learn to appreciate it.' He chuckled. 'You get used to the smell.

121

Especially guys like you.'

'Don't lecture me. I'm careful with money; that's all.'

'You're downright mean. *That's all.* Now belt up and listen to the angel sing the blues.'

'What's her name again?'

'Screw you!'

As you wish... taking it in his stride, thinking to himself how smart he was, that he wasn't named Michelangelo for nothing – although he was christened Michael, and his brother preferred the broadcast acronym FM (fucking miser). He sat and drank champagne (after all, he was paying for it), and the angel on stage really did have a captivating voice, smoothly unfolding for an aria, perfectly pitched for duets, and the phrasing quite a feast of sound, filling the senses with its dreaminess - but he couldn't purge the torment from his mind: *I paid a hundred-fifty for a bottle of champagne. Am I stupid? Am I out of my mind? Am I insane?* In an effort to tackle this imponderable, he slipped off his spectacles and cleaned them with a napkin, his myopic gaze roaming around the space as things fused and details dissolved in a common sea of blurred light. The floating chandeliers seemed to hover like spaceships; the stage looked like a cosmic spectacle of galaxies exploding with sound; the cigarette smoke left halos of cloud, reminiscent of the after-burn of an explosive universe. It was wonderful to be blessed with imagination and intelligence. The things you could do. The wonders you could imagine and understand. Then he put his spectacles back on, and the sharp lines of the early universe gave way in his imagination to a chic club with patrons gaping at the star on stage. After all, humans can be stellar objects too, the majority invisible planets or like the hulking dark mass of asteroids enthralled to the wondrous stars, in worship of their power, like hers, Cindy Gillespie... He remembers her name, of course he does, and as the applause intensifies and she takes a bow, the sound swells like a raging starburst. And she's damn well lovely too.

'Anthony.'

'What an angel.'

'Anthony.'

'What a voice.'

'Anthony.'

'Made in heaven.'

'Yes, I know. Anthony.'

'What is it?'

'What do we do now?'

'We go back stage and beg an audience with higher beings. Leave your drink. OK; quick... just bring it with you, I'm not arguing.' And he strode ahead through the throng, past the security guards who recognized him and let him through with a nod.

'And him, monsieur?'

'Oh, he's with me,' he said off-handedly. 'Can you let him pass?'

'OK.'

Anthony was industrious to a tee, the smooth operator, his taste for music and sense for business going hand-in-hand like a tenor sax to piano in a Holiday suite - Billie, that is, the hard life and the unforgettable voice. - You have to stop and gaze. That's a star.

'Although you're a miser,' said Anthony, 'and I loath that part of you, you're my brother, my mother's son, may she rest in peace; my father's offspring, bless him too. And that's just how it is. Despite your failings, I'm glad you're here, I wanted you along tonight. - You're a miserable bunch, you bankers.'

'She, I mean Cindy, has a great voice, I admit that. But I know nothing about jazz.'

'She's singing the blues. You haven't heard the jazz pieces yet. You'd be amazed. Amazed! The songs seem to glow, if that makes any sense, like a halo shimmering with sound. – Very poetic, I must say. It must be the music making me feel this way.'

'I don't want to leave you with any false impressions.'

'Don't worry.'

'I don't know what you expect of me. I don't understand music the way you do.'

'That's true,' he said. 'You've never had that feeling, that passion, that... savoir-faire.' Anthony transcended a devotee: his horizons ran deeper and closer into what made sound a living thing. Music, if you listen closely, *breathes*. He excelled in the instinct of music, in the business, in knowing the power of a great song. Greatness and the common will are not opposing tides, but part of a complete sea. Our ears, our minds, our souls, they're hungry too and yearn to satiate the hunger in our bones. Life is the whole universe, and it says: feed me, with songs, and sights, and fancies too. Anthony, feeling suddenly philosophical, reflected aloud: 'I regret you never shared the wonder, that you lacked the instinct or the sense or whatever it is, because it's the most beautiful thing in the world is a great song – after a woman herself. A woman and a song, when they gel together, is the most exquisite thing in the world. You want to be touched by life. Love a woman. Love a song. Together. Yeah.'

'You know what I am. Why invite me along? I'm an engineer. I'm a banker. I work with information. You want to feed me, then feed me data, feed me code. This glass, fill it with algebra and let me drink numbers. Cheers to that, Anthony.' He drunk a little, and continued: 'To be honest with you, the things I know, and the tricks I can do, well, I would probably make the ideal automaton. I can think outside of any simulated framework. How about that!'

'No need to invent a robot then!' Anthony grinned. 'You're a mug you are, dear brother.'

'People, gifted people, *the elite,* can only dream of doing what I do; to know what I know,' he said defiantly. 'You want to bet on it?'

'I bet a thousand bucks you're full of bullshit.'

'I'm a smart banker; especially the *smart* part. Take a good look.'

'At what?'

'You underestimate me, Anthony. You underestimate me.'

'Oh yeah...'

'I am dynamic potential. I am power. Power!'

'You're a pig farmer.'

'Power!'

'Oink oink.'

'You know what I do? I'll tell you. I do *more* than make money. I turn *ideas* into code. You get it? Ideas. I take *the craft* of banking and turn it into software that trades and makes money – sometimes we even lose money, OK. So what? But we learn from our mistakes. Even me. In fact, mistakes only make me stronger.'

'Can I be honest with you, Michael?' he said. 'I've heard more sense from a pig than I have from you today. Perhaps they should be breeding you, you banker guys, than the other way round.'

'If you knew only a *fraction* of what I know, you would cry.'

'Ha ha!'

Michael, unable to impress him, changed the subject. 'Cindy's a great singer. OK, she makes me want to stop and listen. But I'm not a music connoisseur. What else can I tell you?'

'Well, I don't need a dummy's opinion, that's true. A-hem... No offence intended.'

'I can't always believe that, Anthony.'

'You've got me all wrong.'

'Have I?'

'You ought to change your job.'

'And do what?'

He grinned. 'Be a pig farmer!'

'I'm leaving.'

'No, stay. Where are you going? Come back here. Come on; don't start sulking. Can't you take a joke... as well as a few provable facts? I invited you, didn't I? Don't be silly. Come on. That's it. - What did you think of Cindy? Isn't she a star?'

'Listen, why are you asking me this? I'm poetic in other ways. Computing and banking, with astronomy thrown in, that's my forte. In that field I'm a star. I'm a superstar, in fact.'

'Music is dreamstuff. Sometimes she's a slut; sometimes a princess. You can't resist either. So you rely on instinct. Trust me, I know.'

'With our techniques and systems, we're developed beyond that. I can beat instinct. I'm a super-superstar. Take a look.'

'Bullshit! Your computer systems are bullshit. You're naïve in your taste for music, I accept that. But you have intuition, and that's what I'm after – the gift in your bones to sense out a good thing, songs included. And instinct does the sniffing. - You ought to have more savvy, Michael. You can learn a great deal from a dog – especially a bitch! Listen to your big brother. Intuition will always win.'

'I told you, but you don't seem to be listening to what I'm saying. We've moved beyond your primitive notions of dogs sniffing things out. Intuition takes second place to what we're doing at the bank.'

'Nothing can top that. Nothing. Least of all a machine. Not even a fuck can top that. Intuition wins. Hands down.'

'With a computer, I'm King.'

'And with a woman, a clown.'

'You don't know me.'

'No!'

'You're in for a big surprise, *big brother*.'

Anthony laughed. 'Gimme a break! You even sound fake.'

Michael grew increasingly bitter, and took the offensive: 'With a computer I'm a different man. Are you listening? You wouldn't recognize me. I'm Action Man, goddamn it! Action Man.'

'Schmuck! You can't call yourself a man until you've hooked your cock around a woman, who's a thousand times what you are, and shown her who's the boss, and learned how to haggle with the *true* masters of the world. *Them!* – Only then, you can call yourself a man, mister *Action Man*.'

'You're crazy.'

'Am I?'

'I'm an engineer.'

'I thought you were Action Man.'

'I can match anyone in my field. Anyone.'

'I told you before, *Action Man,* your computers are all bullshit. That's not life. Your only enduring strengths as a man are your instincts and intuition. And women are better at that game than we are, so we're always at a disadvantage, anyway. Listen to your big brother. Intuition will always win.'

'Why?'

'Because it can; and it will; and it does. The real players are the instinctive types. Even you, you miser. Instinct brings in the riches. It's not mathematics. Never let your instincts wane, because there's nothing more certain to wear a man down. Don't grow too infatuated with machines. They're maybe real, sure, like a rock is real and you can whack it with a hammer and it won't hit back. But it doesn't know it's real. Instinct does. Trust me,' he said, 'I know. It hits back. If you screw around with it, it hits back. And harder than a hammer.'

They waited outside Cindy's door; increasing applause a reminder why she was delayed. How many encores would she have made by now? At least five. And listen, yep! She's started number six. No question, she's a star. Michael's opinion was rather redundant, but Anthony couldn't tell him that. Besides, Michael felt aggrieved at having his ego trimmed by Big Brother. Big Brother can be insensitive and tasteless at times, and small brother suffered wounds to his computable pride, (x plus y equals Action Man squared kind of thing) and couldn't leave it alone.

'Listen to me, Anthony, with the new smart gizmos we've got at the bank, we're on a roll. No network in the world can keep me out. No password. No firewall. Nothing. I can go anywhere I want to, grab anything from any network, download it, change, it, possess it. It's mine. I'm a Peeping Tom with eyes as big as the world; yet invisible. Isn't that terrific? Isn't that clever? Isn't that amazing? If only you knew.'

'That bullshit isn't worth knowing. Intuition is. Be master of that, and the rest comes naturally.'

'Just listen to me, will you? Anthony, this stuff is dynamite. It's amazing. These systems are smart. And I mean *smart*. Do I have to spell it out for you? S - '

'H. I. T.'

'You don't understand a thing.'

'Yeah. Yeah... Suck on a lolly-pop, pal. Listen.' The applause was fading out. 'She's finally let them go. They'd applaud all night if she'd let them, like fish in her sea. She'll be here shortly. Spruce yourself up. Look decent. Jesus! Am I going to say you're my brother? Here, have some respect, straighten your tie for the lady. You're about to meet an angel.'

'No, really Anthony, the new stuff we're developing is amazing. Really powerful. Damn it! Get off, you're choking me.'

'Don't be a mug. Look at me! Trust your instincts. Always. They hit back. Harder than a hammer.'

'But that's what I'm trying to tell you, if you'd just listen. Let me explain what we - '

'Cindy. Cindy. My angel...' Anthony rushed to greet her as she turned into the corridor and strode towards them. Embracing her hand he kissed it infectiously, and then her cheeks, first the left, then the right. 'This is Paris, after all.' And then he hugged her in the all-American way, with gusto.

'Very romantic.' She blushed blissfully. 'And yet I feel right at home.'

127

'Well, you know me. I can't resist a great song.'

'I know.'

'You're the best.' Lifting her other hand he lavished it with kisses. He noticed her looking past his shoulder and remembered who was waiting there behind him. 'Ah, meet the baby of the family. Mike, this is Cindy. You may bow at her feet and worship at her pleasure.'

'Flatterer,' she teased him, blushing.

'Perhaps some other time when *Big Brother* isn't around,' said Michael, stepping forward and taking her hand. He was too shy to kiss it, though she could see he dearly wanted to try. It was hesitation born of inexperience than unfamiliarity with things. 'You sing like an angel,' he said.

'Thanks. That's really sweet of you to say. Why don't you boys come in? We'll talk inside where it's more comfy. I have some wine and goodies. Do you like hors d'oeuvres, Mike?'

'Mike's got to shove off now, don't you, Mike? He just wanted to pay his respects,' said Anthony. 'Besides, he's a bit of a tea drinker, aren't you, Mike?'

Foolishly, he stammered and conceded to *Big Brother:* 'Well, I... Yes, I really do have to get going. I hope we can meet up again some time. And Anthony...'

'What is it now, my son?' he grew uncommonly tolerant in a blasé way, glancing at his brother with a question mark wrapped in a frown: *What are you doing here? Run along now, why don't you.*

'Oh, it can wait.'

'We're very pleased to hear you say that. Very pleased indeed.'

'I'll tell you later about all the new things I'm working on.'

'New; old; immutable...' he chuckled glibly, 'we take everything in our stride. After all, tomorrow is another day.' He looked at Cindy and she laughed, 'Well, it may as well be, right babe?' She entered her dressing room, followed promptly by Anthony who winked at Michael, smiled, and then shut the door on his face.

'Yes...' he uttered blankly to the door, and the name-plaque with *Cindy Gillespie* engraved in golden lettering. Just as he was getting his tongue around the name, the commotion increased inside the room and the door opened. Anthony, surprised to see he hadn't shifted asked him what he was doing. 'Thinking,' he replied naively. About what? 'Things,' he said. Well, replied Anthony, didn't he know that little boys lurking outside girls' dressing rooms thinking really only had one thing on their carnal little minds?

'Oh. Such as?'

'Schmuck!'

Broodingly, Michael turned to leave, but Anthony detained him:

'By the way, I almost forgot to mention it – you see what happens when an angel sings? Careful they're not sirens leading you astray.'

'What is it now, *Big Brother?*'

'There's a woman at the bar, red top, white pants, hair in a bun.'

'I didn't notice.'

'It doesn't surprise me. You're losing it, Mike. Your instincts are burning out before you've even lit a match.'

'What about her?'

'I'd give those machines of yours the boot if I were you. They're only useful if they're under your foot, like women used to be!'

'Save your wit for someone else. - What about her?'

'She was watching us, you mainly, which really puzzled me, because she's not that bad looking. And so I asked myself - why would she be looking at you?'

'Just get to the damn point, will you. - Well?'

'Mischievous eyes staring like a hawk. A calculating look. But be careful, it's hot. It's soaked in sex. Don't jump in unless you know what you're looking for and can climb out again. That gaze is a door leading you right into a chasm. She's got something in mind, if you ask me. She's full of intrigue, that one, I bet. If it were a guy, I'd say watch out. Since it's a woman, better write your will before it's too late.'

'Are you sure she was looking at me?'

'Don't flatter yourself, pal; she's not that kind of hunter.'

'What?'

'When I see a woman, and she doesn't flash an eye at least once at your crotch, it need only be a wink, to weigh you up, then she has other motives in mind.'

'What the hell are you talking about?'

'Don't get excited. Calm down. Never let a woman see you rattled. Just go and see if she's still there on your way out.'

'Why not mention this earlier?'

'Women watch if they want to, what can I do about it? But it just struck me this moment, if she's not after a shag, well, think about it, what is she after? Is she a voyeur or something? If a woman gives me the old eye routine and misses my crotch, I want to know why. It's not normal. Women *use* sex. Men *consume* it.'

'What should I do if she's still there?'

'Give her a good beady look-over; remember to peek at her crotch; then go home.'

'What for? What use is that?'

He heard Cindy call him and hurried his reply. 'Just do it, please. I'll talk with you later. Cindy, my love, I'll be right here.' And he winked mischievously at his brother, and closed the door.

That was the second time in succession he was staring at a blank door, shut firmly on his increasingly touchy face, and he damn well had enough of it. 'Who the hell does he think he is?' he grumbled as he strode back to the bar, pacing hard steps, and only when well into his stride did apprehension dawn on him, and he paused to tilt his head around a corner and examined the area around the bar. There was no red pants, no beady eye, no trace of a woman with hair in a bun anywhere, and Michael wondered if his brother had invented it, before setting aside his doubts and continuing on towards the table where he had dined. To his dismay, it had been cleared, and his one-fifty bottle of champagne gone to oblivion.

'Can I bring you something, monsieur?' offered a waiter.

'I was looking for someone?'

'Who?'

'She's not here now. Thanks.'

The waiter bowed and strode away with instinctive élan. This wasn't servitude; it was service. It was sheer class in the grace and sweep of a step, in sway of a hand, the motion of a head, the cultivated warmness of a welcoming sigh. It was actually quite beautiful to behold. Almost worth the one-fifty price tag in itself. Ouch! One-fifty! That bit him; and Michael had second thoughts. Having a scientific mind made him a natural skeptic; and being a miser only consolidated that fact.

Feeling frustrated with his brother, he decided to have a drink at the bar before leaving for home. The bartender was English, and sported a snappy cockney accent. Michael felt a headache coming on, and requested the first palliative that came to mind.

'Do you have tea?'

'Tea!' exclaimed the cockney. 'Rosie Lee? Tea?'

'What? Yes, tea.'

'No, mate. Not here. Across the English Channel. You'll find lakes of it over there. Lakes, both man made and natural.'

'I have a headache. Can you recommend something?'

'Straight whiskey.'

'Are you crazy?'

'No. I'm English,' he quipped, and he made up a concoction that included lime, 'Got to add this stuff; it won't work otherwise,' and some green liquid from an odd shaped bottle, 'And this too, made by the Dutch, but they don't drink it too much on account it makes the Dutchman fart like mad,' and some angostura bitters and salt, 'To top it all off. Here you go, sir. Down the hatch, and you'll feel like a million dollars. Trust me; on the word of an Englishman, as we say.'

Michael lifted the glass and inspected the concoction against the light. 'What's it called?'

'I learnt it from a guy in Brazil. Works every time. Shifty looking bloke he was; but an ace with the babes. He gets my vote any day.'

He examined it warily, sniffing the potion. 'Smells like foul limes.'

'What! Do you take me for a Limey? – Knock it back, son.'

He did as advised, and his face flushed instantly. '*Je – sus!*'

'Care for another?'

Shaking his head wildly he choked on his words and shuddered. 'No. No. Did... did you see her? Where's she g... gone? Gone?'

'Who?'

'The woman...' he hammered the glass down on the bar, staggering, 'in the red top.'

'Oh her... She's right over there.'

He choked again as he spun around and saw her, there, seated intriguingly at his table staring right at him, her gaze demure and fixed, her right hand holding her chin at an elegant pose for comfort. She

131

softly cut a smile and began to laugh and light a cigarette as though it were the coolest thing in the world to do. She saw immediately he lacked the initiative to make the first move so, rising from her seat, superfluously tapped her cigarette once to break ash, strode forward, maneuvered onto a bar tall stool beside him, and said:

'You could use a drink. Bartender, bring him a drink, would you.'

'He has a headache, miss.'

'Then bring him something for a headache.'

'No!' Mike shrieked agonizingly. 'I'm driving. Just bring me a glass of wine.' He composed himself. 'Make that two, please. Is white OK?'

'White is fine. Sara,' she offered him her hand, 'Sara Capstan.'

Without pausing, Michael instinctively kissed it. He seemed a little dazed, and she chuckled.

'You've taken to Paris, I see... or perhaps it's taken to you.' Her accent was sophisticated French, not native, perhaps originally Slav. Her voice carried that educated caliber of manifest learning that sets apart intelligence from mere savvy.

'Michael Leoni. Call me Mike.'

She smiled. 'Do you recognize me at all, Mike?'

'Excuse me?' he uttered, startled, trying to think.

'We've had, how can I say... brief encounters.'

'No. I'm sorry. Forgive me, but I don't recall.' He felt embarrassed and began to blush. She felt it was charming that he was shy, and she smiled.

'We work for the same bank.'

'But I've never seen you before. I'd remember. I know I would.'

'Fifth floor, mortgages and small business loans.'

'I'm first floor. Program trading and financial instruments.'

'Yes, I know,' she said, lifting her glass. 'Cheers.' Their glasses softly touch, more in gesture than an earnest tête-à-tête, but an ideal ice-breaker when the general conversation threatens to stagnate. 'We've actually brushed into each other several times, along corridors, elevators, in cafes...'

'I must be really dumb. I'm sorry.'

'You always seem so preoccupied.' She smiled in a way that was irresistible, but somehow seemed affected. And being a man much infatuated and flattered by her, he was naturally a slave to her every whim. Clearly, he would drown in her ocean of intrigues, so long as it tasted of sex. And being a man, he would want to drink her all up. Every last drop. Even now, as she dipped into that cool chic reservoir of femme fatale wiles: 'Just think of this encounter as two glasses of wine touching; just so,' and she broke a toast with him once more, softly. 'Cheers... Again.'

'Well, we've broken the ice now. You have my full attention.'

'Thanks.'

The conversation petered out too soon and seemed stuck in an awkward silence. More frustrated than upset, he wondered what to do. Although she possessed the confidence to take the initiative any time she pleased, she deliberately left him dithering, playing with his naiveté, and toying with the pause: a coy smile here, a winsome wink there. Feeling exposed and somewhat of a fool, he wished Big Brother was around now to kick-start the conversation into play.

– Action Man is nice; but it's a ladies' man that melts the ice.

'Nice wine,' he said.

'Yes...'

'Better than red, I think.'

'Sometimes...'

'You like to smoke?'

'Occasionally.'

'It's a nice place they have here.'

'Yes. It's rather wonderful.'

That's it, time to press the pedal and pump the gas. 'And so... What are you doing here?'

'Oh... Having a drink... Listening to the music... This and that.'

'Cheers,' he lost the flow and hit the brakes. 'Salute!' he drank the wine, which tasted rather dry. He had a sweet tooth.

'Are you learning French?' she asked him.

'I'm trying.'

'How is it coming along?'

'Rather slow. But I'm keen to learn. It's the vowels, you see?' The wine had the uncanny effect of steeling his nerves, and he confronted her politely with his misgivings. 'You know, Sara – may I call you Sara?'

'Please do.'

'This is not a coincidence, is it? I mean, it's unlikely, wouldn't you say?'

'It's a fortunate encounter,' she replied cleverly.

'But you want something, right? What can I do for you?'

She tackled him head on: 'OK. I'm looking to make a career move. I have a proposal that might interest you. Have I come to the right man?'

'I can't discuss what I do at the bank. You must know that. If you have something to contribute, then my advice is to go through the normal channels. They're always on the look out for good people with bright ideas.'

The muscles on her face tightened, and her confident smile tapered to a frown. 'I know what it is you do. And you're not on the first floor; you're in the basement. In the place they call *The Vault*. Well, that's its alias.' She had the location right: the basement, aka The Vault. His best guess, and his hope, was that she knew very little what was really going on down there, but it was sufficient for Michael to feel alarmed. She continued, 'I've been watching you with both eyes wide open. And I like what I see. That's why I'm here.'

He was taken aback by her boldness. Averting her eyes, his own vulnerability confused him; and he paused not from a failure of will but a complete lack of ideas. At length, he finished the remainder of his wine, (dry, but shores up the nervous spirit nicely) and said: 'You'll have to speak with my boss. He deals with this, not I. You need to speak with him.'

She waited a while, sealing the moment, resting her chin on her free hand: 'Will you speak on my behalf?' She slipped a finger in and out of her mouth, probing it with her tongue, maneuvering around him with visual feelers from enigmatic eyes spiraling in to entrap him. 'Mike, will you do this for me?'

'I can't. I'm sorry.'

'I know things... little secrets... bits of the puzzle...' Was she teasing him, or softly threatening?

He met her eyes, challenging her. She dared his gaze, adding:

'You've been tunneling your way through computer networks, into domains and places you're not supposed to go. Unless one has a reason, or a motive, such as... spying, perhaps? Hmm, let's call it eavesdropping, that's more your style.' He coughed, choking on stifled laugher, or possibly the wine. She continued to work on him. 'I have my own secret ways of finding things out. I don't have the resources you do, but it's enough. And almost always, for a woman, enough is enough.' He drank his wine, forgetting the taste – it was perfunctorily done, a maneuver, something to do. She resumed at length: 'You must have built yourselves quite a system down there. It sees everything; watches... everything. And swallows it all up like a... woman with a glass of wine. Cheers.' She drank her wine, spying him over the rim of the wine glass scintillating in the light. 'It's cleverly done; masterful method. Bravo! It's very hard to trace. What clever boys you are. And it is all boys, isn't it, Mike? Not a woman in sight I bet. Ah!' she sighs, with the knowing smile of a man's surprise. 'Are we that powerful? Do we rattle you that much? Is this soft hand of mine, this gentle touch – may I? It's soft, isn't it, Mike? Soft enough to make a man's world tremble? - Let me give you a taste what it would be like.' And she leaned over and licked the lobe of his ear. He closed his eyes and trembled. 'You've been watching us, haven't you, Mike? Well, I grew curiouser and curiouser, like Alice in her Wonderland... And I've been watching you too. Surprised?'

'It's nothing. We were just running some tests, that's all.'

'You're using A.I, aren't you?' she said, and he blushed.' Your system may be *Artificial*, but it's *Intelligent*, isn't it, Mike? Your *voyeur* has voracious eyes. Perhaps one has to be a *voyeur* to join your team. Well, I can be a voyeur too. We see things no machine can ever see; no man can ever match. Mike,' she said, softly breaking open her words, hatching a metaphor, 'would you like to share my eyes?'

He shook his head, confused. 'It's not our style.'

'Ah, men and style. - How can men, all on their own, know what style is? Would you like me to show you, Mike?'

'We're just running tests.'

'Have you never considered a flaw?' She sighed effortlessly. 'Such men you are.'

'A flaw?'

'My my... I spy with my little eye something beginning with A.I.'

He remained silent, watching her until her empty glass was gently placed on the bar counter, and then took the opportunity to order them more wine. He was too perplexed to retort, too undecided to take his leave. It seemed the obvious thing to do. 'Shall we try red?'

'Have you ever watched, Mike?' she said. 'Have you ever spied on someone who knows you are watching them watching you?'

'Bartender, your best red. Thanks.'

'And they enjoy it. So it becomes a performance. And you see in your voyeuristic gazing not truths, not the things that are, but... voyeuristic embellishments, shall we say. That is, computers can't distinguish lipstick from tomato sauce. Machines can't be seduced. Well, not yet anyway. But being a woman, rest assured, I'll find a way... sooner or later. And nor, alas, can they even be teased – which is a shame. But... give it time; give it time...' She paused, and readied him for the next blow. 'But, just like a man, A.I. *can* be fooled. Here...' She lifted his hand, caressed it, fondling a forefinger and drawing it sensually across her lips, a touch open, teasingly, but enough to slip inside, so he wonders endlessly what's within. 'No machine can ever do that. Feel that. Want that. Sense that. – So, if you want to watch, it won't be me you'll see, but something else. A mask of me. Flesh without the essence. – Do you know?'

'What?'

'I like a man who sweats.'

He gazed at her for a length of time, mesmerized, and then sighed: 'Oh...'

Schmuck!

'Here we go,' the bartender brought the wine and grinned with mischief: the woman was overwhelming the man, *and* he had to pay. It was picture perfect. And Michael, surrendering to the seductive confusions cast upon a man by the sexual intrigues of a woman, took leave of his parsimonious mind, smiled with a kind of dreamy daze, and said:

'Keep the change, bartender. Keep it all.'

'You're a gent. Thank you very much,' he said smartly, and withdrew.

'Sara, we can't be fooled that easily. You can't subvert our systems just like that. We can distinguish false data from the real thing.' Michael turned to her abruptly and said. 'We're not fools.'

'Of course not,' she smiled. 'You're men.'

'We're smarter than that.'

'Smarter than men?'

'Than what you think.'

'Ah. I see.'

'We know what we're doing.'

'That's good to know.'

'And we're in control.'

She breathed supremely: 'You haven't the faintest idea, have you?'

'What do you mean?'

'You rely on machines. You depend on a system.'

'So what?'

'A hundred percent.'

'And..?'

'The *whole* hundred, Mike.'

'So what? That's perfect, isn't it?'

'So long as it's understood it is *I* who am in control. *Me*. It's a matter of... *style*. I can manipulate and mislead. It's a woman's way.' Her tone played with soft wiles but maneuvered with deeper intrigue. 'Your one-hundred percent is actually *my* one-hundred percent. Don't you see that?'

'No.'

'I let you see only what I want you to see. Have you the slightest idea how many angles a woman has at her disposal?'

He shrugged, guessing: 'Quite a lot.'

'Countless.'

'What do you want?'

'A piece of the action. Please, Mike, I have a lot to offer. If you understand a woman, you know she'll give back a hundred times whatever you give her, if it's done with love. Give me a chance, that's all I ask. Speak with your boss. Set up a meeting.'

He never had the wherewithal to ask what ratio her bitterness would provide. It came out thousands to one, but he just couldn't see it. Few men do. Instead, he looked at her bravely a moment, then turned aside, gazing at the glasses on the bar, holding them in a fixed stare, making time for himself. Then, as if to sweep away all shyness with a dare, lifted both glasses, looked at her straight in the eye and handed her one. He tasted it without saying cheers. 'This wine isn't chilled.'

'Red wine is normally that way. The warmness keeps it rich.'

'How warm?'

'*Body* temperature.'

'Oh...'

'Just give it enough warmth, and the wine does the rest. If you hold the glass just so, that's it, let it rest under gravity in your hand, it's like holding the wine itself without the separating glass between. And wine feels... feminine.'

'I feel something,' he said.

'You see, good wine is matched perfectly to good sense. Not only smell and discerning taste, but the eye too, and touch. And of course, not forgetting the spirit. Good wine *looks* right; it *feels* right. Just like a perfect thing.'

'A hundred percent.'

'*My* one-hundred percent.'

He gazed at her skeptically a moment, and then shook his head. Desire for a woman, and wine, played with his mind and aroused him until events grew overwhelming. *A hundred percent.*

'Cheers,' she said, and maneuvered them back into ritual.

Wine glasses touch; eyes entangle, minds mutually hypnotize, and the masculine self is all but forgotten in the impetuous rush for sex.

'Sara.'

'Yes?'

'To us.'

He's learning... But feminine tutor sets the pace. He has to be taught, she concludes to herself, trained in the multitude of small things that tip the balance in affairs of the heart, affairs of the pocket, affairs of life, affairs of affairs of affairs of whatever you like. It's the details that count. And she, mademoiselle of a multifaceted mind, takes the lead again, signals to the bartender who cheerfully plays along, his grin as wide as a Cheshire cat as he glances at Michael and thinks to himself - *Aye, aye, there's a sucker born every day.*

And Paris just sucks them all up. Suck, suck, suck... And he hits him with a barrage of feisty tasting cocktails: bloody-marys, manhattans, sidewinders and the rest. And before Michael knows what hit him, her arm is locked in his, gelled by ambition and desire, heading for the exit. 'Keep the change, my friend. Keep the change...'

And the bartender replies: 'Thanks. You're a gent.'

Smug bastard!

Chapter 8

The perfect secret has a basic rule: *Always keep things simple.* The perfect secret has a name: *Hush.* The perfect secret sports an easy smile - *Ahhhh* **:-)** The perfect secret is perfectly self-adjusting, and all that's needed to meddle with perfection is a man with the horn to screw it all up.

Simple really – there's no secret there at all.

The Vault is nominally a store of money, a honey pot of dough. But here, it's testosterone that's boiling in the pot, not cash. A bevy of whiz-kids yelling yippee yi yea! smart guys and polymaths full of technical potential and the power of dreams to make a cake from nothing and eat it all up, crumbs and all.

The ingredients: an ample measure of male hormones, well-groomed men of various blends, a pinch of women – any kind will do: in photographs, on calendars, in blue movies downloaded from the Internet – a dash of greed, a sprinkling of technology, lots of schmucks well roasted in the heat of the financial markets, top easy cheating, and a good smack of pure will.

And don't forget the spice… Knock knock, let's go inside.

Ah, what's all this? Activity, intelligence, mesmeric things in ceaseless flux. The sealed surround of an enclosed room polished from floor to ceiling and purring with *the best* machines performing countless computations, watching the world outside, feeding on its thousand inputs, sending feelers into the global data networks of the world, the mission was: *Get out there, with hands the size of oceans, and scoop everything up, suck her all in.* What? *Information.*

The seething human presence was rendered through muscular egos trailblazing with gizmos, guys with the technical edge flexing into action and seizing control of events, commands executed mostly by fingertips tripping smartly over keyboards, others on touch-screens zeroing in to the financial centers of London, Paris, New York, Mumbai, Tokyo, Rio, Dubai, Shanghai, the whole world on the end of a fingertip, on the swagger of a lip saying *Gotcha!* coordinating the inputs onto a giant projection screen marked with grid lines and time zones, displaying the guts of the world before their eyes: *Money*. Global casino and the gladiatorial ordeal of merchants and market makers and movers and shakers and gamblers and hangers-on and bulls and bears and governments and crooks and saints and angels and the whole shebang masses of the world sipping on a soda as they make a deal, take a cut, agree a commission, buy, sell, barter, hope, beg, sell your soul and do whatever it takes to make the lolly come to you – lick, lick, hmmm... money. The only kickback is a profit. Losses are a kick up the ass and get your ass and *move it move it move it*, sucker. That's the deal. Whatever you are, wherever you are, boot-up your machine, jack in the codes, plug yourself in, give it a good shake, and throw the damn dice. Roll, baby, roll...

Are they on a roll?

Let's watch.

And all the while they're watching, and watching, and watching...

'What are we seeing, Jay?'

'Shanghai was rolling a moment ago, boss.'

'Bring her up. Let's take a look up her skirts.'

'Come to daddy, puss puss...' He entered some code and pressed the RETURN key. 'There.'

They pondered over the price of bonds that initially got aroused in Geneva, became horny in Milan, started sweating in Bangkok, reached full erection in New York, began petting heavily in Tokyo, went to full penetration in Shanghai, finally hitting the climax with a bang in Mexico City. Some trader with deep pockets or a talent for risk stretched the margins and came out laughing, while the herd bucked into the stampede of chasing the market when it had already peaked and felt the torment of losses. What goes up comes...

'Down with a salsa,' said Jay. 'This punter has really cooked the meat and made it hotter than a Mexican chili.'

'Water! Water!'

They chuckled before shifting focus and debated the ordeals of a trader in Montreal who took a position on metals to corner the market by spinning out long-term contracts from nickel to cadmium to lead to copper to steel but ultimately getting cold feet and selling short and pulling out. 'He took the whole market down with him,' observed Jay. 'It's like burning the whole house down just to kill a flea. – Do you know what, boss, people never cease to amaze me.'

'Well, human nature under pressure is a fickle thing.'

'Shall I follow it up?'

'Pass it on to Yasser. Get him to take a look.'

'Will do.'

'Anything else?'

'Nothing special, boss. Just busy bees at work, making the honey.'

'Margins?'

'About average.'

'Profits faring OK?'

'Steady so far. They're heading in the right direction.'

'Commodities?'

'Just the quiet numbers: easy, easy... No unusual contracts or movements at present. Wheat spiked about an hour ago, but swung back into average territory after I fondled her parameters a touch with my algorithm, and gave her a couple of boosts. She likes to be teased.'

'Speculators? Where?'

'Arabia.'

'Hmm,' he pondered searchingly. 'Keep your eyes peeled. There's often something exceptional about the unusual ones... I once knew an Arabian princess. Quite beautiful to behold. Unforgettable. But the most difficult person in the world to deal with. Not merely a handful as such. Just overwhelming.'

'Lucky you.'

'OK, Jay.' He touched him on the shoulder and spoke louder so everyone within earshot could hear him. 'Yank up the system a touch, fellas; let's start pushing the envelope. Get stuck in there. Probe. Mine the networks; flesh them out. That's it, don't be shy, the best voyeur doesn't only watch, he extends his gaze right up to the skin, and fondles it with his eyes. Flirt with the markets, fellas. Flirt. But don't let them see you.'

This was Ice talking: I. C. E. Ice Cool Euroman inspiring his team of specialists: computer programmers, traders and scientific wizards, philosophers, linguists, chemists, a nutter or two, and those with dreams of Mammon in their bones. It was his show, his creation, his universe. 'The world is our oyster, and it's all there for the taking.' He smiled infectiously like a big fish, nosing around for the best pearls. 'Never wait on luck. Get out there and make it happen.' Molding their responses, honing their aims, notching them up and up and up.... I.C.E, roaming his domain like a conqueror. Ice. Nice.

The financial markets heaved and turned and pitched like a leviathan, the global push-pull velocity of trades presently smoothing out in the average to a 'steady as she goes' scenario, no stampede of greed to contend with, no insatiable surge of traders stirring the pot of gold to acts of immolation for a buck. It was riding easy, easy, easy... like dancing with your lover in the moonlight, swaying to the mood, gently, softly, taking her to places where you've never been before... perhaps... you never knew existed and... events evolve on the flow of chance, intuition kicks in, and you feel that special something is about to happen as you begin to kiss. Delicious calm, delicious tenderness... the world is at peace. Then suddenly out of the blue, someone, somewhere, starts a raging stampede. *Bang!* Traders let loose a few ticks ramping up a speculative burst that died down almost as soon as it began, five seconds hit the peak and vanished into thin air, a trail of numbers that left a track – history fifteen seconds old, redundant, forgotten, erased from the terminals in every market of the world – data that went delirious in its famed fifteen seconds. Even moments, it seemed, went breathless with wonder at their brief spell in the limelight. It's the way they play: flick a switch; hit a key; instant dip; instant rise. The market is a beast, in steady-state don't think she's resting, no, never imagine she's abated, because she'll suddenly burst into life, and before you know your egg from your chicken you've yoke on your face and left wondering: what the hell happened? No beginning and no end; that's money; that's the markets. Ice. Nice.

'What are you guys doing? Billy? Leonardo?' Ice strolled over to the derivatives traders, their algorithms pushing the envelope of the riskiest trades.

'We set them a trap,' explained Billy.

'Ah, I see. You pitting London against New York.'

'And L A as the joker in the pack.'

'Keep an eye on the joker. Who knows what he has up his sleeve. You never know, the foil might be on you.'

'The best foils always are.'

'And the worse.'

'We'll see if they fall for it.'

'Good. Record it. Finesse the data for later analysis. Filter out the mess, and get me some nice smooth curves. I need it looking pretty, so the *guys upstairs* will understand and keep the tap open. This operation needs funding, so let's feed them the dream. Spice it up a little. Throw whatever you have to at it. Improvise if you must. And then let me know when you've done.'

'Will do.'

One of the team cultivated a habit of working to music - the ambient spell of easy jazz, light classical and mellow pop. It was an eclectic mix that circulated and found a home in everyone's heart. For music, like water, spread everywhere eventually, seeping into everyone's life, and nothing was going to stop it. Presently, Ice strode to an opera mood and stood by its source. And there he listened delightedly. 'Puccini, isn't it? Beautiful. Just beautiful!'

The diva singing an aria in *Madama Butterfly* delivered it with such ache and moment, that it made his eyes glisten with pleasure, the glint of delight cascading down his cheeks, and he sighs at the sense that such power resides in softness, such strength holds to tenderness – that he felt, deeply, is not a great song like a loved one, a lover, a destiny? Music, for sure, was more than merely profound sound. It so consumed him at times it made him forget where he was, here, among the elite technical traders, examining data on a console, watching the financial markets unravel the riddle of profits, probing currencies and swaps, fine-tuning the program trades and algorithms of their system to spy on traders the world over, to the point where it would replicate their human skill-sets, and anticipate market movements.

Leonardo stole a gaze at his colleague seated opposite him, who watched mesmerized the trading screens displaying transactions amounting to tens of billions. The ancient Pythagoreans believed the basis of existence was number, and kept root two secret from the world. They believed it was too irrational for men to comprehend and might lead to turmoil. Today, modern Pythagoreans saw root two everywhere reaping currencies in every denomination, and were amazed. The old Pythagoreans failed to understand the essential essence of number: it was too playful to be a sober god, or a bearer of immutable truths. Its promises are a set of maybes, a set of perhaps; a collections of what-ifs. Numbers fit neatly into the scheme of financial markets and men with a network of computers to endow them with an element of *risk*. For numbers to work, they have to give you a kick, and a thrill, and a whole lot more besides. One, two, three... A dollar for each prime. Prove that. The rewards are astounding.

'How is it running, Willy?' asked Leonardo, his Italian accent rounding the w's.

'*Billy!* My name's *Billy!* How many bloody times must I...?' he exclaimed, exasperated with him. 'Please, *try* and remember that.' Billy was a touch over-sensitive, but felt himself justified. After all, he never called him four-eyes, but at times he wished he did. 'What do you want?'

'Are you still seeing that woman?'

'Who?'

'The one you spent all your money on.'

'No!' he said bluntly. 'She cleaned me out, anyway - the bitch! Why are you asking?'

'I thought I'd have a go.'

'Fine by me,' he grinned mischievously. 'But all she's after is your money.'

They both laughed. Men, paradoxically, are perfectly content to enter into relationships with *beguiling* women fully aware they are going to be shafted. But all that Leonardo wanted to know was:

'Is she really that good in bed?'

Billy gazed at him with muscular pride. 'Awesome!'

'Can I have her number?'

'Sure,' he said, suddenly noticing a flurry of market activity that his intuition told him would swell into a huge surge. 'We've got a hurricane from Asia coming in. This is going to be a big one, Leo. I feel it. A tidal wave; a damn tsunami. Get ready... Here she comes. Now. Grab her! – Yes!' he roared with exhilaration, punching the air with unquenchable delight. 'Yes... Yes... Yes... *Fucking yes!* That's it, baby. That's it! Yes! Yes! Yes! Give it to me. Yes!'

The ultimate climax is to *win!*

'Yes!'

Ice strode through his domain and paused by a poster that read: "I'm scxy. So what!" which hung enticingly over a group of wonder-kids and watched as they plied their clever tricks at the energy markets. These were skills not of the gifted or the brave, but of stealing your way into the guts of decision makers, be they governments, bankers, charlatans or speculators. The big boys with the big hands avoided risk at all cost; they loathed it. But for Ice, the best hand to have is one with invisible fingerprints.

The glass of orange juice resting on the table by the wonder-kids was chilled, and the glass half empty, or half full, depending on the timing of a glance.

'We've spotted something interesting. - Ice, over here,' cried out one of the wonder-kid's excitedly.

'OK,' said Ice. 'Lock it in. Fade your presence out. Whoa! Slowly. Don't let them see you.'

'Switching into stealth mode. On three... two... one. Done. That's it, Ice. It's working beautifully,' he assured him. 'We could be up their ass and they'd never know.' He began laughing and talking to the screen. 'We're watching you... suckers.'

'Never get too cocky, David. There is always something to upset the perfect ruse.'

'It's not a ruse. It's skill. It's talent. And it's all under control.'

'Good. Keep it that way; *and* keep out of their way. Never rely on stealth alone. Stay on the safe side and observe from a distance, but make sure you follow their every move.' He reached for the orange, and drank.

Karl Lomberg, aka Iceman, or straight ICE, (mixed with vodka when relaxing) strolled among his team of technical wizards in the basement complex of HBS Banking Corporation, Paris. The pet-name Ice featured as an amusing fancy on several counts: one, he was the

147

boss; two, he took all his drinks chilled, even tea; three, he was from Iceland; four, his mother used to make him take cold baths; five, he loved cold baths; six, call him a big kid, but he builds snowman, even to this day; seven, eight, nine and ten, well... he liked ice. Tall and blond, all of thirty-five with a handsome face and sturdy jaw, he had an eye for women, heart for money, brain for computers and time for everything else, especially women, money and computers.

'It's steady as she goes, Ice, steady as she goes...'

'So long as it's not the Titanic.' He looked at him superstitiously. 'What else do you have?'

'Tokyo is on a roll,' said David with breathy confidence, having predicted the outcome, and it was all just a matter of waiting it out. 'They're following the curve with barely a deviation. I sometimes believe men are no more than numbers in a box.'

'Let me have a look,' said Ice. 'That's perfect. A box of numbers is fine, David, so long as they don't leak. Why? Well, that would be like cheating. - How's our baby doing?'

'The program is fine. Ticking over nicely. I'm really proud of her.'

'Have they spotted her?'

'No way. She's like the perfect puss, and can sneak her way into anything with a man at the controls.' He chuckled. 'So long as he stays horny and doesn't wise up.'

'Good. Keep it that way. And be cautious, because even a horny guy can stumble into some luck. – Mike. Where's Michael? Has anyone seen him?'

'He went outside to make a private call.'

'Someone find him. Tell him to meet me in the simulation room. Thanks.'

*   *   *

Meltdown.

It was only a simulation, but as financial catastrophe swept across the display monitors, the dazzling spread of multicolored disaster was like a diseased field of changing patterns that obsessed their gazing with the thrill, the fear of market meltdown, and made them shudder. The global repercussions would be catastrophic, unless one could control them, finesse their terrible effects, tame the beast before it consumes everything of value and renders it worthless. It seems, financial markets were like a man with a suicidal psychosis intent on proving the value of life by threatening to throw himself from a cliff. It was bad enough with one, but the global financial system is a whole crowd of madmen vying to see who could dare the most and bear the greatest risk. And the world, as it were, leans on water. Sure, it's ice. But how thin? Do you dare to jump up and down and find out?

'God, what a mess...' gasped Michael Leoni in awe of the spectacle, breathless at what he created, like a prairie cowboy with a yearning for the final scene - puts on his hat, clips it, kicks his heels and says: *Saddle up, son, and let's ride into the sunset.* He was the educated Brooklyn Kid saddled-up in his superman-seat surrounded by gizmos, his skeptical USAman eyes conferring with Euroman: 'Well, what do you think, Ice? Should we shut it down?'

Ice remained silent, the greater part of his mind distracted with a purpose that went beyond immediate catastrophes – albeit simulated on computers. He stood there, composed and unshakable, his cool pose raking in the ice-sheets of intention in calculated fondling of floes, easy as he goes. But he's a banker too, Euroman rubbing his money fingers together. They had to be oiled, or they might blaze with friction and melt his cool veneer. Michael continued:

'Ice, I hate to admit it, but this just isn't working as we intended. Computation isn't enough. There's something missing. We need to be clever as well. – Should I shut it down? Ice, what should I do...?'

Ice pondered quietly to himself, only his mind worked, and then he spoke: 'Let's not be hasty, Mike. We need to get a handle on it first. What do you think it resembles?'

'It's hard to say.'

'Indulge me. Take a calculated guess.'

Michael started thinking, USAman riding the landscape of speculation, pointing the stallion into the sunset, lifting off his cowboy hat with a languorous hand, wipes the glistening sweat from his brow, and gazes at the horizon: *God, it's endless this land. Endless...But it fascinates too.* At length, the blank expression on his face prevailed, the lonely cowboy gazing at the monitors, and Euroman suggested:

'Mike, we need to find a pattern. We need something, damn it, something we can work with. And it has to be plausible. What about a tiling structure? The colors *suggest* dynamic cells.' Ice rubbed his eyes, struggling with ideas, and Michael looked skeptically at him. 'Is this just wishful thinking on my part?'

'That would be putting it mildly,' he said, facing facts, like the cowboy pointing his horse into an endless journey. It was a long ride, and he had to be rational; dreaming only made the journey perilous. 'We can't just push the boat out like that. We need to be sure where we're heading; and whether the tide is with us.'

'We can't always be sure – not a hundred percent of the time.'

'It's a risk.'

'Of course it's a risk.'

'In that case we need a calculated risk.'

'Some calculations yield zero. What then? The boat stays? No, Mike. We push it out. We have to. It's only human.'

'Maybe I'm just thinking too hard. I like to rely on certainties. I am what I am, Ice. I'm methodical. And method is first with me.' Michael felt then that sometimes thought itself is the hurdle, and it was better at times to suspend belief and rely on faith, or blind luck, or even irrationality. 'You know, Ice, life proves to us again and again that the truth can be formidable; it can even crush you. But you just have to deal with it.' He glanced at Ice and pointed at the monitors. 'This is formidable, and kidding ourselves won't alter that fact. You can't just change the settings like that, Ice, like you're suggesting. It's too arbitrary. It's a leap in the dark. And we're not ready for that. In fact,' he gazed at him candidly, 'we're not even built for it. Push the boat out. OK. But it won't go anywhere, not without something more. Even if it's no more than a feather to show you the direction of the wind.'

'A feather...? Then consider this: if we filter out some of the sovereign debt, we can reset the ratios on interest rates, suppress the differentials on some of the credit ratings, and dampen the effects of the secondary markets. You see, Mike, we've got to knock these perturbations on the head. If we concentrate on just the majors, a pattern might begin to emerge.'

'That won't work. Shifting the numbers around like that, you'll collapse all the data-sets we've accumulated. The model is sensitive to small changes. That was the idea to begin with, wasn't it? That's where profits lie, in the margins between trades.'

'Once we get a pattern, we can step back and massage it to fit.'

'Fit what? That's a fiddle. Come on, no one's going to buy that. We'd be no better than amateurs playing that game. And besides, we'll still have all these random numbers to worry about.'

'There's too much data anyway, right? So let's average them out. That might smooth out the overload. Let's burn off the fat. After all, all we're looking for is a pattern, Mike, not the whole solution.'

Michael countered with insightful arguments, adhering strictly to the science. He was just being methodical, he explained, doing his job. But Ice persisted: 'What about imposing more constraints? That's worked before.' But Michael disagreed. It would be effort wasted, he argued. Ice challenged him. 'Come on, Mike, I need a way around this thing. Give me a pattern. *Any* pattern. Push the boat out.'

'There is no right way; or a wrong way for that matter,' he reasoned. 'Perhaps, only a *clever* way.'

'Then be clever and find me an answer. A clever answer.'

Michael picked up a pen and toyed with it thoughtfully. 'We need a workable model, not just any model. - Look at it this way, Ice, we have heaps of data; every second we're scooping it up, masses and masses of it. But we don't know how to define a pattern with it; or *where* the signal is; or *how* one could be built up, even using the model we presently have.' He paused, intrigued with the challenge, because it had the testing weight of fact. 'How can you build a solid house on an ocean of data? That's the trick. And maybe we need magic to do that. Like it or not, we've built a maze around ourselves. And not just any maze, but a labyrinth with a million doors.' Michael's throat was dry, and swallowing saliva he felt like a drink, but he chose to wait. 'Just because there's a door, it doesn't mean you must go through.'

'What do you mean?'

'Not all exits lead you out of the maze. Some take you right back to where you started.'

Ice considered quietly to himself. Michael continued:

'Imagine a drama. And we are players in that drama. We are not outside of events, so our observations are biased from the start.

We're looking from the *inside-out*. We're embedded. Our actions, our thoughts, our will even, are the landscape.'

'It's a neat idea, a perfect philosophy even; but we need answers?'

He thought aloud with a smile: 'Some mazes are just too circular.'

'What?'

'What you can't pass through - leap over.'

'How?'

'We won't get there all in one go,' he concluded. 'The easiest things to overlook are the details, and it's often the details that make the model work.' He reflected a moment, and then resumed the analogy. 'Some actors, sure, they don't understand what they're saying and merely mouth the part; and they can get away with it, at least for a time. But that's not an option. Understanding is the key. That's what unlocks the right door. Because sooner or later the audience will spot a fake. It just a matter of time.'

Ice studied the simulated events sweeping across the monitor. 'Do you believe in what we are seeing, Mike?'

'How do you mean?'

'Are these simulations misleading us? Are our scenarios worthless, after all the effort we put in? Is this depiction of meltdown no more than a fake? Are we just mouthing words, or getting to grips with what *could* happen?'

Michael seemed to reminisce in turn. 'We're worked hard and have come a long way with this project. We've learned a great deal. We can crash data networks. We can break into systems, no matter how well-protected they are. We can tunnel through anything; we can crack them. That's an astonishing achievement in itself. But the trading model..? Look, Ice, it was a great idea. And even now I really want to believe that if we just knuckle down and press on this still has a chance of success. Getting this to work has been an obsession of mine. But who knows if it's really possible? You never know. Push the envelope, and what guarantee is there it won't recede further than you feared? - Imagine yourself as a cowboy; and there, it's just you and the immensity of the world. You gaze, spellbound, and it holds you. Then ask yourself: how far is the horizon? What am I reaching for? - Sometimes, science is about chasing ghosts.'

'Do you think there is any real signal there?'

'I think lots of things. But are any of them true? Do they make any sense?'

'And?'

'Well...we can all speculate. It's not a crime. – I'm thirsty.'

'We have to try a lot harder than that, Mike.'

'Science isn't a magic wand, Ice. It's a tool. And it has more in common with a craft than many people on the inside care to believe, limits and all. Sometimes, it's an act of faith. But we're not dealing with belief systems here. Ask the right questions in the right way. That's our best shot. In fact, it's our only shot.'

Ice closed his eyes, which gave the impression he was meditating because he conveyed a serene quiet in the stillness of his pose. Then, opening them again, he gazed at the monitor, which filled out his expression with dynamism. Michael too stared at the monitor, before they glanced at one another, vying for ideas in a shared gaze. Ice began: 'Mike... what if we had a system which is essentially simple, but *behaves* in a complex way. I'll give you an analogy. About a month ago I met up with a friend, and he had this deck of playing cards specially made, the reverse sides of which were of various colors according to the suit. To be specific, the spades were green, the diamonds blue, the hearts red, and the clubs magenta. – I thought it was an amusement for his poker-playing friends, but he was actually studying their psychology, and he hit upon this new tool.'

'It sounds like a case of loaded cards to me.' He chuckled, but continued to listen with interest.

'Now, this is the clever part: he *manipulates* uncertainty. He *reduces* it, because now you know what suit the card facing down belongs to. But of course you don't know the actual value of the card.'

'A one-in-thirteen chance,' he said, following the argument through. 'Better odds than before.'

'Yes, that true, in an absolute numerical sense. The numbers seem to add up in your favor.'

'OK,' he looked puzzled. 'So what's your point?'

'The point is this: the uncertainty in the deck of cards was *reduced*, that's clear. But the complexity *increased* because the *way* you play with the cards changes, the kinds of risk you must take, changes.

In short, your *behavior* moves out of familiar territory and into the more untested range. That's where the complication kicks-in, despite the better odds. And bear this in mind, Mike, you are playing against others who are themselves taking unfamiliar risks. So what was once normal to you, or familiar odds, now seem more puzzling. – You see, it's not complexity that baffles us. It's just a question of familiarity with things.'

Michael was intrigued, and smiled at the subtle but clever device of controlling risk by reducing uncertainty in a system (a deck of playing cards) only to increase complexity elsewhere (human behavior). Cause and effect were strongly coupled, and could be correlated with certainty. This seemed to work his mind in novel ways as he watched the monitor and studied the dynamics of meltdown: following the course of events as they deteriorated, but this was an unraveling full of strange signals and clues suggesting impromptu things and others more permanently rendered.

'Yes, there's something there, a pattern... But what can it be?' He studied more closely, taking his time. 'It *does* suggest behavior, or a process, perhaps, hovering at the threshold of breakdown. There are these self-functioning parts; here, here and over here, independent but connected: Tokyo, London, New York, Moscow, Shanghai, Sao Paulo... There's overlap; there's similarity - even in confusion there's overlap. After all, Ice, market behavior is one grand overlapping dance of left feet trying to find the right.' They laughed, for traders were a tango, the currency guys the cream of the salsa, going *cha cha cha*. Michael resumed. 'For want of a better analogy, the whole thing resembles a construct whose autonomous parts can no-longer coordinate, and it's every part for itself – like the left foot trying to go its own way of the right. You see, it's not intentional, but incidental events that convey the impression of order or chaos, depending on when you look. After all, take a snapshot of a storm and it looks beautiful. Go inside, and it's horrendous.'

'Are you saying this construct is random?'

'I'm saying it depends on how you *interact* with it. You can be thrown about chaotically by the storm, or glide through cleverly with an aim. It depends. We have a will, and that makes a difference.'

'That's good, Mike, that's good. But let's take a look at it from another angle as meltdown progresses. What happens to the markets? They start by being connected together in the global matrix of overlapping networks. Data exchange is essential, and integrity of that data vital. So, during meltdown, the financial centers will try and protect themselves by breaking as many of those connections as they can, so they can control events. But there's the catch, because to recover you need connections, yet the only way to survive is to sever them. There must be a tradeoff – an equilibrium point. The financial center that can get the right combination of breaking and re-making those connections in a particular sequence, in the shortest possible time, survives the crisis, and comes out on top. And that's where we want to be. On top.'

'That's a scary thought.'

'Not really. It's like a game of poker.'

'Poker?'

'Yes, like a game of poker played by a man who's down on his luck and begins to believe he's jinxed. But he can't leave the game, he can't quit, because still, deep down inside himself, he believes it is his game.' Ice brooded, quietly reflecting on a previous ordeal with a tinge of gloom. 'He knows. But he shuts his eyes.'

Michael chuckled. 'Poor guy. He's really taking a hammering; down a cool million. His wife's left him and the kids loathe him. His mother won't stop reminding him and bitching about it, and his father drinks himself senseless and stays quiet.'

'Yes... Poor guy.'

'He has a lot on his mind.'

Ice juggled several thoughts at once, and then spoke in a studied tone: 'This necessity to break the very connections that you need to save yourself with is... statistical; or would you say determinable? What do you think, Mike? How do we model it?'

'That's a question with perhaps many different answers,' he said. 'Like an object reflected from many different mirrors. They all look alike. So, which is the real one?'

'Like a paradox from Greek drama.'

'Sure; why not. After all, a man can't be in ten different places at the same time. Causality would break down.'

'So what's the solution?'

'You tell me.'

'*Managing* those connections,' said Ice conclusively. 'Turning them on and off at the right time. We can't rely on experience or history alone. This can only work in real time.'

'But that implies working with incomplete knowledge.'

'It's a gamble, I know.'

'We're scientific, Ice, we're engineers. Your scenario doesn't call for mathematics, but a kind of behavior. If you're going to gamble, gamble on psychology.' He paused and breathed hard, struggling with the dilemma. 'If you're going to gamble like that, then your risks stand a better chance by mastering psychology. It also helps if you're a wizard.'

'Or a poker player.'

'Poker?'

'Yes. This is the guy who makes and breaks connections all the time; risking everything; juggling the odds in his head in ways that are beyond computation.' He hinted intriguingly. 'Trust me, Mike, I know.'

'Then science is only one of our props; and the task is really beyond our current tools. I wouldn't gamble until I have something to work with, some intuition.'

'We need a novel way to handle the unknown.' Ice folded his arms and looked at the clock. He had something on his mind, and at length he began to speak, almost narrating: 'Imagine the following. You have a deck of cards. You unpack them; you shuffle the deck and offer them to the guy next to you. "Cut," you say, and he cuts. He gets a king. You reshuffle the deck and offer him again: "Cut," and he cuts. He gets a three.'

Michael watched him enigmatically: 'Is this a riddle, Ice?'

'It's a warning from the Gods, that they refuse to let you know too much. And they punish those who dare to know what only they know.'

'The Gods are jealous Gods.'

'Perhaps...' he speculated ironically, 'they are only protecting us from a worse fate.'

Risk was like motion, it took you forwards, but it could also run you back. Guessing and having complete knowledge amounted to a compromise – leap across the chasm of the unknown, and maybe you make it, maybe you don't. *If you're smart you work the odds; but never play with the Gods. Because they're not your friends. You may know your origins; but only they know your ends.* The answer to the riddle was not *to do and to know*, but *to dare and not know*. This, perhaps, is the guiding angel of the man of ambition. You may get it wrong or you may come out right. It was all a matter of...

'You know, Mike, ultimately, we can surrender to events, or put up a fight.'

And together, in silence, they watched the running simulations of market meltdown, inferring what they could, guided mostly by speculation until this standoff challenged their pride as powerless observers, and they began directly interacting with the system by deploying more elaborate algorithms that, correctly triggered, attempted to intervene in the meltdown and restore market advantage. They concluded this dynamic was not about speed, at least not in isolation; it was about being smart, anticipating, knowing where to look, and how to get there. It was about behavior, not mere computability.

'What can set it off?' asked Ice, thinking aloud.

'No one single cause; various triggers come into play. Some of them are vague, or at least ill-defined. Some are human and, I suppose, certain market mechanisms play their part in pushing the market over the edge.'

'The invisible hand of the market?'

Michael laughed: 'Fingers full of mischief, more like.'

'That's the magic of the marketplace. What else?'

'The speed of meltdown varies from scenario to scenario, but the outcome is the same. The initial conditions don't affect the final crunch. - *How* we get there, well, that's another matter entirely.'

'The *how*?'

'We can't tame the beast, but knowing its behavior is what counts.'

'That's the real prize.'

'Call it what you like.'

Ice considered the options. 'Given our resources, our knowledge, limited as it is, if anything happened now, could it be turned off?'

'I wouldn't bet on it. We might be able to slow it down, but we're talking... what... if we're really lucky, a matter of minutes. Anything beyond that requires a coordinated effort on a global scale. It's not only one financial center pulling the plug, connecting and disconnecting, they'd all be at it – governments; banks; corporations; individuals... you name it. There are too many players. Everyone speaking at once. We would need to clear the stage.'

'Could we do anything?'

'You mean could we take a position and hold it?'

'Yes.'

'For a time; briefly. Well, in theory it's possible. But human nature being what it is... competition, fear, greed, a stampede is inevitable, and someone's certain to knock us down again.' He took a moment, thinking. 'If a thousand people are drowning, and they can't swim, and they're clinging to each other for dear life, how do you hope to reason with them?'

'You're outside of the financial markets now, Mike.'

'No. That's what it would be like. Logic isn't the solution. Brute force, maybe. But a drowning man is going to go under anyway, whatever he does.'

'How do we deal with market confidence?'

'That's the trick.'

'And perfect knowledge...'

'Leads to a perfect cock up.'

'If it happened for real, now, would we survive or be wiped out? What are our chances?'

Michael leaned forward, considering: 'There's always going to be an element of luck here, Ice. And timing – that's crucial. And it depends on the players as much as anything else.'

'What is the most important factor?'

'Are you referring to computation, or human behaviour?'

'Anything. Either. At this point they amount to the same thing. So, what would we need to make any reasonable impact?'

He thought for a moment as he watched the simulation of meltdown reach its climax, as markets tumbled, as economies the world over went bust, as savings were wiped out in the frenzy that gripped everyone. 'Not to be afraid,' he said. 'A certain deft boldness. A cool head. When all else fails, be intelligent; be brave.'

'Do you mean a bluff?'

'No. I'm talking about a bold move, though it could take the form of a bluff.'

'I see...' said Ice, his thoughts entwined with deeper thinking. 'Anything else?'

'Anything more would only complicate the problem. It would blur your resolve. And some problems can't be simplified. You must take them as they are.'

'I see...'

'That would be my gut instinct, Ice, looking at the simulations, knowing what we know thus far. But if it really happened, how would I react? Who knows. I guess I'd just be pulled along with the tide. - Well, it's irresistible, isn't it? Most of the time. Besides, what could we do without computers? Nothing. That's our boat – sail or sink. It's our best shot of staying in the game.'

'Machines are our third arm, our third eye on the world, Mike.'

'When used wisely.'

'And smartly.'

'They're part of the human mix.'.

'That's right. But we don't want just any machine. That's not good enough for us. We want systems in place that won't crash, that gives us the reach and the confidence not to panic in a crisis, fearing what's going to happen to the mortgage, or those savings for your old age. It's the little details that screw things up.'

'It's not so little if that's all you have. Humans will be human, Ice, you realize that? After all, that's why we're here. To replicate their behavior as best we can,' he said, contemplating. 'To beat them at their own game. That's the aim, isn't it? To win.'

Ice seemed to stare through him as though his thoughts dwelled elsewhere. 'Replication... yes. That's fine as far as it goes. But then there is *innovation*, which implies greater risk. Like the analogy with the deck of cards - you know more, but you have less. It cuts both ways. Ultimately, all that matters is getting this thing to work.'

Michael was unsure what to say, or what he should think, so he simply remarked: 'We've come a long way, Ice.'

'Yes.'

'We can be proud, I think.'

'Yes...' he echoed, almost whispering, deep in thought.

Would it be unnatural to imagine, Michael Leoni wondered then, that someone, perhaps even he, or Ice, or any one of them, on impulse or design, might trigger an event that could spiral out of control? These systems, in attempting to model the markets, drove those models all the way to financial meltdown. Once started they wouldn't – couldn't – stop. And all it needed was a feather-light human finger pressing on a key to set the system in motion, from the smallest tremor to an avalanche. Should anyone ever be so bold, believing he could persevere and understand it, or even control it, attempt to engineer that process, and so hasten catastrophe upon the world? Was this possible? Is greed really so blind, that it always gambles on the heart, rather than the mind?

'You know, Ice, it dawned on me lately, and I tell you honestly, the more we develop this project, the more I begin to fear the likely mishaps if we expose these tools to the wrong hands.'

'What?'

'The big boys upstairs who are funding this enterprise of ours. They must be wondering what they're getting for their money. What are they thinking, Ice?'

'Thinking?'

'Do they really appreciate what we're doing down here, or trying to do? Do they understand the limitations? Ice,' he gazed at him gravely, 'what do they expect?'

'How do you mean?'

'You meet with them regularly. You must have formed an opinion by now. Surely. You must know what they're thinking about. Ice..?' He seemed to insinuate, but Ice looked distracted, so he spoke louder. 'What are they really thinking?'

Ice remained silent, brooding.

'Ice, do you really trust them? I mean, look at it from their side. Without thinking, perhaps one of the lesser sparks eager to impress the top man might take a risk and precipitate something... You know,' he pointed to the monitor, 'humans will be human.' Their eyes met, conferred in silence, then folded back onto the monitor as the simulation reached meltdown.

The thoughts that stir in silence, that ripple gently and have a long-term effect, these were the shudders that they felt then – ripples of trepidation, intelligent concern and the hard stare into the forbidding void. Michael recalled what his brother had said the previous evening outside Cindy Gillespie's dressing-room door. Those words resonated more powerfully than he could imagine at the time, and they felt difficult for him, an exertion on the part of faith, and seemed to sweat from him:

'Ice, if you see a chance... do you take it? Is it a risk worth taking?'

Ice never answered. The instinct to silence seemed compelling then, because he had considered the possibility but kept it to himself. As the project developed in size and sophistication, he found himself deliberately omitting facts to his superiors, minor ones at first, then more substantial editing of reports on the simulations. Some accounts he doctored were within bounds, just playing with words, but others packed real weight and had a hard edge. It was explosive. And men on high adore explosives. Knowledge is the prize, and the Gods exact a price, sometimes even fateful, as on Prometheus for stealing the secret of fire from Heaven and bringing it down to Earth. Why did he do that? Trust is a virtue incompletely comprehended until one is tested by it, until it kicks you in the guts and you confront it, head to head, and it demands to know: Can you trust? Should you trust? Yourself? Others? Can you believe in yourself more than in your opponent? Is the guy holding his cards closely to his chest covering a full house? Does he hold an unbeatable hand? Or is he just bluffing? - Sure, life often poses moral questions, and they can check your haste to judgment. But that alone is rarely a guarantee of the right choice, in the short or long run. Savvy, and the will to win, takes you to the top.

'Mike.'

'Yes?'

'Keep the system running on, all the time. Don't turn it off. We'll watch and see how it develops. And Mike,' he looked at him curiously, a stare full of ambiguity, of quiet schemes, 'Let's keep this quiet. OK? Just between ourselves.'

He whispered back softly, 'Sure...' uncertain why he did so.

Ice turned to leave, and then suddenly stopped. 'By the way, I want you to snoop in on Roy Riemman and his boys at UBS in New York when the markets open there. They gave us quite a fright the other night, remember?' His humor seemed affected; out of place; strange. 'Go inside their operations. Penetrate the inner layer. I want to know what those guys are up to.'

'Why? They're alerted now. Surely, it's too hot to take a peek. Wouldn't it be wise to let things cool down?'

'It's always wise to be cautious,' he said, evading an answer. 'But still, go inside. Use the new tunnelling software.'

'It's're not ready.'

'It's good enough. Just keep the ciphers ticking light. Don't push them.'

'Why the risk? Why New York? Why them? Why now?'

Ice tried to smile, but his expression hovered uncertainly, giving tangible proof of a divided, perhaps a scheming, mind.

Just a hunch,' he said.

'That's a very specific hunch. And full of risk, too.'

He shrugged uneasily. 'Call me when you've locked horns. And hold them,' he said, preparing to leave, 'I want to watch this. And be sure they don't see you. Go under and around if you have to, connect through the peripheral networks; but don't let them see you... Well, not until I say. The timing has to be just right.'

A strange hesitation followed. Why was Ice standing there, his fixed stare moving between Michael and the monitors, and then, some way in to this brooding pose, shifting and looking at the clock? One moment he seemed to have something on the verge of being uttered, stirring on his lips, but then the same hesitation intervened and the intent folded. Michael waited with growing disquiet until Ice gave him a lukewarm smile. It felt affected, rendered as a prop. Michael sensed premeditation in the absence of things Ice did, in the chilly stillness he rendered, and the expression on his face, worn as a mask over the muscular exterior of his ice cool eyes focused with single-minded will. Ice behind Ice, it seemed, cooler than cool, a permafrost of hovering doubts.

'Are you all right, Ice? You look a bit dazed.'

'I'm fine. Just thinking, that's all.'

Michael grinned. 'A late night again?'

Ice gave an unconvincing sigh, leaving ambiguity answer for him. 'I guess so...' he said, resuming his composure. 'I'll see you later.'

As Ice left the room, Michael knew that Sara, promising her the world while he was deep inside her, would never have a place in the team. The project had progressed too far, had grown a personal dimension that it never should have, and the team was too well adjusted to accommodate new members. Ice had firmly shut the door. But Michael felt that eyes beyond *The Vault* were more powerful than those that watch from within, here, rendering power, but sometimes lacking the foresight to deal with it.

He lifted the telephone and called her. She wasn't there. He decided to leave her a message and began:

'Sara, hi, it's me, Michael. I... I'll see you later. Meet me at the club. Love you. Bye.'

In love already! Twenty hours old and a night of passion and yet they put se**men** at the heart of global networks. Life is a mystery.

Nah, it just sucks!

Chapter 9

Frank Freiberg grumbles and sighs: *Damn it, I don't want to leave...* but it's time to wind down the dream on the Strip and open his eyes. Vegas is a swell chick, she's all honey and licks his –

'Excuse me, I need a ticket?'

'Where are you traveling to, sir?'

'New York.'

'City?'

'Where else.'

'Round trip?'

'Don't tempt me pal, Just don't tempt me.'

'OK... let's see what we have available,' and the salesman busies with the timetables and schedules and filters out a list of available flights. 'A-ha. There's a flight leaving in an hour.' He gazed ironically at Frank. 'Are you fond of traveling the long way round?'

'As long as it's to New York City; or Las Vegas.'

'You have a cowboy hat?'

'What?'

While the least favorable route from Las Vegas to New York City went via Dallas, it was the earliest available flight with a free seat. 'Take it or leave it,' croaked the salesman, who seemed to be having fun at Frank's hapless expense. It was definitely a schadenfreude moment.

'What else can I do?'

'Grow wings.'

Frank shrugged, 'I'll take it.'

So he took it. A forty minute stopover to offload passengers with big Stetson hats and bigger guts full to delirious bursting with guzzled experiences of their sleepless nights in dazzling Vegas: aka slot-machine junkies bound for the southern belt of sweet 'ol Dixie and the Rio Grande. They're buffalo tourists packaged by the planeload tumbling out and finding their way home on ranches, towns, regional cities. Memories here have a short life span – a hiccup or a belch away from reminiscing. And it's back to normal in the morning...

Meantime, Frank gets to wonder: Life, I love her so, but she's such a bloody grind, she works you to the bone and you say, 'fine... like, what do I know?' She's a tempestuous pixie with a dollar sign pinned to her wings, she sighs at your fate and sings 'la de da de da....' and doesn't care a blessed thing whether you perish or flourish or make a pass at her with the drone, 'Hey darling, be an angel and throw me a bone... Pleaseeeee...' And this pixie takes a walk in the sky, laughing at your plight, she's a peach, but the bitch seems always beyond reach, Oh my! what the heck does it all mean, this life? She giggles and replies: 'A pixie dream of endless days sashaying down the Sunset Strip.' It's teasing him, she knows, with a quip. But that's just fine. If he's a real man, he'll survive.

Life, the pixie cow! But still, she's divine... ain't she? Wow!

Meanwhile, Frank Freiberg slept right through the tedious routine of the airplane descending and coming in to land, touchdown, taxi-in, off-load, pick up, taxi-out, and take off again, which proceeded like clockwork, (they're pretty cool, these airlines) so perfect that even, hours later and over a thousand miles of flying in a comfy tin can, a discreet shove from the Air Hostess as they started their descent to land at New York's JFK airport:

'Sir, your seat belt please.'

'Eh?'

'We're about to land. Belt up, please.' (Cheeky!)

'Miss,' Frank called her back as she slipped away.

'Yes, sir?'

'There's a nasty rumor going around.'

'Sir?'

'They're saying it's Wednesday.'

She nodded her head affirmatively like a robin, looking rushed, but sweet all the same. Appearing dazed, he asked her.

'What time is it?'

'Ten past three Eastern Standard Time on Wednesday.'

'There you go again,' he gasped. 'How can it be? It's a rumor, surely...'

She smiled stiffly at him, but sweetly all the same (it's her smiley nature), suspecting he was priming up his chat-up lines – you know, the guy's meant to dazzle the girl with all kinds of whimsy clichés and she's meant to laugh and sigh *Oh my, isn't that such a thing. I've never heard the like in all my life. That's sooo original. Well, here I am babe,* says he, *I'm all yours...* But she wasn't having any of it; not a syllable; not today. Bye bye, honey-pie. - So, gazing at him with soft persuasion that he *Now be a good boy,* and *belt up, please. Thank you...* And, with a *have a nice day* pose, slipped effortlessly away down the isle in swanky mode like a fine swan. She really was cute. She had the perky look of a bruiser that clips your pecker if you push her flaps too far. *Lock and load, baby – Sure, in your dreams, maybe...* Nevertheless, she could be a touch cool, but impeccably so. This was ice with fire inside of her, he felt, the playing-hard-to-get kind that's so teasing to a man. Her iciness only baits him and draws him to her fire. He's a man in heat, who would like to have her neat – raw actually, because her less is so much moremoremore. He followed her with intoxicated eyes as she sashayed down the aisle and vanished from view. And it is close to perfection, this moment, as he twitches his nose, yawns, and discreetly scratches his crotch as he looked out of the window. Hmm, not a bad view... The sun was still high and it was a beautiful day. The airplane was cruising in circles around JFK, a holding pattern waiting for controllers on the ground to push this tin can he was flying in into the next available landing slot. Clearly, those slobs on the ground didn't seem to mind keeping them up there, and the passenger next to Frank smiled effusively and began rambling about the Big Apple.

'You'll been here before, sir?'

Is he Dixie-man who forgot to get off at Dallas, or just a jolly fella with a hefty drawl? Frank rubbed his eyes and massaged his neck as he gazed at him absently and kind of smiled back. 'Have you heard the rumor?'

'Rumor?'

'It's Wednesday,' he said breathlessly. 'Wednesday. Can you believe it? Isn't that just incredible?'

'I believe so, sir. Yes sir, I believe so.' He was cheerful and plucky, chuckling and bouncing and sharing jokes not sequential with any seasoned logic but sputtered all at once. This may have been peculiar to him - nice guy, a bit daft, color of green urbanwise and full of civil gesture to strike up a chat. Or he could have been in tourist mode keen to acquaint himself with the local customs. Or, of course, he could just be a plain old schmuck. They let them fly on airplanes too, you know. Schmuck Airways Inc could make a killing selling seats on airplanes staffed by hostesses dressed in tiny hot-pants and frilly kickers sashaying down the aisle saying "Belt up, please". Is that meant to be kinky? Perhaps...So, who the hell is this guy? Spare time for a guess? Nah! Frank failed to make any sense of what he rambled on about and cared even less.

'You'll been here before, sir?' he asked again.

Frank groaned with a boozy air. 'I think so... *Wednesday?*'

As the aircraft started its final descent and his eardrums began to strain and pop, Frank grumbled to himself *What does the schmuck want now?* He couldn't work out what this barrel of a man was yakking on about until this barrel chuckled heartily, rolled his grin, and offered him a sweet mint. He showed him how it was done, and chewing hard on it seemed to do the trick nicely of easing the pressure on his eardrums. When they finally landed the barrel offered Frank his card, tapping it with a sporting finger. 'J. W. Branson, sir. Metals processing. At your service, sir. You have yourself a real nice day, now.'

And clipping his obligatory Stetson hat he pressed on ahead for the exits while Frank lingered back so he could think what to do.

He needed a drink. He needed to sleep. He needed a woman. And preferably all three at the same time, and all in sufficient dosages so he could forget himself. What he dreaded most was the inevitable confrontation with Nick and Roy. But he had to get it over with and braced himself for the furor that would greet him, especially from Roy.

It was Nick, waiting alone, who met him at the airport.

'Jesus, Frank. You look terrible.'

'I feel worse,' he moaned. 'A lot worse.'

'Where have you been?'

'Don't ask.'

'Jesus Christ.'

'Forgive me, for I have sinned...'

'You idiot!'

They shook hands belatedly and Frank sank back into his gloom. 'My head's all mixed up, Nick. Please, don't ask me any more questions. Not now.' It was clear Nick had several ready to throw at him. But knowing Nick as uncommonly polite, he shamelessly took advantage and asked: 'How's Roy?'

'Screaming mad.'

Frank shook his head as they made their way to the car. Nick brought him up to date with events: the intruder from afar with the spying eyes that stole its way into their computer system and watched them like a Peeping Tom was still lurking in the data network. It was too much for Frank to absorb at once. A lucid state of mind eluded him and he replied at length, more from his own sense of exhausted gloom than any prompting:

'Nick, I lost a day.'

'What?'

'I seemed to have lost a day.' Frank rubbed his tired eyes, leaving him feeling more dazed than before. 'I think something was put into my drink. But I had so many; I can't even imagine which one. I'm an incurable degenerate, I know. That scene... it kind of gets to you. It's addictive. I... I can't explain it any other way. I'm sorry, Nick.'

'Are you being serious?'

'Well, I remember the slots, the roulette wheel, the bar, the brunette with the cream-white blouse and short skirt, beautiful pair of tits, worth going to the moon and back for, I remember her. And then in the bath with all the soapy bubbles smothering us as we sipped champagne, she kept rambling about tropical fish and the Florida Keys, and then...'

'What?'

'Nothing. A complete blank.'

Nick erupted. 'You're out of your bloody mind! You are your own worst enemy, you know that? You'll wind up boozing and whoring your way to an early grave.'

'We're all going up to the casino in the sky one day, Nick.'

'Frank!'

'Sorry...'

'You're undermining everything with this reckless attitude. Look at yourself! Have you no shame! You're like something that crawled out of a slut's ass.' (That brought a teasing smile to Frank's indolent face. You see, even amid the cesspool of his own deepest yearnings, he considered himself something of a swell guy. So, naturally, let the good times roll). 'You're totally shameless. Our computers are being hacked into, compromised, perhaps even damaged in some subtle way. Our livelihoods are at stake. Are you listening to me? Frank, this is serious, damn it! For God's sake, get yourself together.'

'Who? Who's watching? Who's doing it?'

'Someone. Somewhere. Out there in the network. And we've got to find out. Do you understand?'

'But what are they watching? What do they want?'

'I told you, you idiot. Us. They're watching us.'

'Us? What for?'

'Our system. Everything. Who knows. – Frank! Are you listening to me? Damn you! Acting up at a time like this.'

Frank sunk into gloom: 'I'm not up to this, Nick. Not today.'

'Pull yourself together. We've had enough of your pranks. For God's sake! Look at yourself. Look! You're a degenerate. What were you thinking? Frank, are you listening to me?'

Nag; nag, nag... 'I know. I know,' he echoed lamely. 'I'll work it out. I won't let us down. Just give me some time.'

'We've run out of time.'

He meant computer time. This time. Not past time. Not future time. Only real-time. The here-and-now-time. That was it. You took it, or you lost it forever. T. I. M. E. Time.

'Have we lost money? Are we down?' asked Frank.

'No. Not yet at least.'

'Then what are you raving about? They want to watch. So, let them watch. Why provoke a harmless thing?'

'What's the matter with you, are you crazy?'

'What the hell, Nick. All that counts is liquidity. At the end of the day, all that matters is who owns the buck. And we're liquid, right?'

Who owns the buck? Was this boozing wisdom, or a rhetorical chant codified in slang to mean money, ownership, spending power, liquidity? The sense of oneself amid the dizzying spectacle of oceans of money storming through the financial system feeding the greed and liquid might of capitalism, that the velocity of aggregate longing gets swept up in countless billions, and you take it in your stride to bet a nation's wealth on a margin of zero point zero, zero, zero, zero, zero, zero one percent, and you rake in millions; run it and run it... billions. Money. Time. The cosmos. Pussy. Booze. Who owns the buck? Does it matter, so long as you have it to burn? Cash. It's liquid.

That's a wrap.

'Frank.'

'Yes, Nick?'

'Do you want something to eat? A coffee?'

'No,' he droned with resignation. 'Let's just get back to the office.' He struggled to get a firm grip on his senses. 'Let's deal with this thing.' They get into the car. Nick revs her up, and drives. Frank continues: 'Let's find this Peeping Tom, this network voyeur, and shut him down for good.' His mind wants to wander, but he forces it back. 'We'll give him something to stare at.' Leaning his head back on the head-rest he closed his eyes, letting the motion of the car sway him like the breeze to a soft ease. Just so. Yeah. She can do that nicely, this gal, swaying him in her breathy glide, her neat consummating ride, where consciousness lingers half and half with sleep, and in time, as the commotion of the city dawns, it's like an endless day, like Las Vegas awakening to the rainbow of tomorrow.

'You know, Nick, I adore this city. I love New York.'

'Sure... sure...'

Metaphors move with the stream of life. You never grow old in New York City. Like the river: you change. Or you simply melt and die.

The twenty-second floor of NBS Banking Corporation, financial instruments and derivatives section, was a sprawling floor partitioned into autonomous units. They referred to them fondly as *Chinese Walls*, but it could have been a donkey's balls for all they cared. These units consisted of teams: men, women, and every hybrid cock and cunt that this corrupt and lovely world affords us. There, they are a breed driven by the animal instinct, steered by greed, disciplined by intelligence, and their sole *raison d'etre* is to win. In the restlessness of late afternoon, bets and trades were hedged not with a question mark over time, but with margins and profits foremost in the minds of those driven individuals that hook up their labors into networked computers, and raked in the trades like the trawler men or yore fastening to the whale ships as the leviathan thrust through the surging waves, and tested men with its might and animal will. Then, they used to have nightmares of the giant swallowing them whole. Here, on the twenty-second floor, the nightmares were a liquid rush of capital dwarfing the mind of Man to comprehend the magnitudes involved, the speed with which it surges through the financial system and, most potent of all, the instinct of a man to hoard as much of it as he can grab in the least possible time. Not merely to gulp, but voraciously to plunge in the mad sensation of having it all, with endless more to follow. In the past, the leviathan was physical and weighed tens of tons. Today, the goliath is a number with eleven digits and more and weighs absolutely nothing. Yet it awes all the same as it sweeps through the mind of Man with the shuddering awe of obsession. Can't let it go. Can't get enough. A curse. A lust. A God. An inevitability.

Money.

In an ordinary corner of the twenty-second floor the iris security system registered Nick as 'Valid OK – Permission to Enter', but Frank must have been dazed into anonymity because it failed to recognize him and triggered the intruder alarm, and Roy had to override the controller and drag him inside.

'Is he drunk?' Roy seized on him furiously, forcing him into a swivel chair at a trading desk, 'Sit!' turning it around and confronting Frank with a bank of computer monitors blazoned with market data generated by their system. 'Just shut up and look.'

'At what?'

'The blue numbers.'

He gazed for a time, afraid to tempt fate and provoke Roy by rubbing his eyes to soothe the ache, even though they were watering from an itch of over-indulgence. A very large itch. In fact, *the* itch! And there was nothing worse than an itch you can't scratch, though the memory of it was warm and lovely. Frank deferred to discretion and said: 'It looks normal to me.'

'Shut up and keep watching.'

Several moments elapsed of unremarkable transitions in the numbers, just the normal pattern of a typical day's trading: the random burst, the abrupt collapse of interest in a stock: they come and go like fleeting things of almost no account. Then, suddenly, a timed sequence of cascades pulled the blue numbers in a most unusual way. It was not the numerical values themselves, but the actual *behavior* that was striking. Many traders all over the world would have to synchronize their trades to facilitate such a block move in such a seamless fashion. Statistically, outside of a crisis or comparable external shock, it was unlikely to occur of its own accord. Frank's gaze latched onto the monitors with amazement. He was back. This had his attention. And Roy cut in:

'Peeping Tom is starting to have a poke.'

Frank, stunned into silence, heard Nick say something which no-one seemed to grasp. He just gazed intently at the monitors. The grim expression on his face gave relief to the stark fact of events spiraling out of their control. The voyeur became a seducer, and was not content to simply hide behind his gazing any more. Peeping Tom became Poker Tom and pushed his evil finger in their eye.

'Frank, do you see now? These events aren't real, are they? There's a thread somewhere in the network. It's simulated. But from where is it being generated? And how does it get into the system?' Roy turned to Nick and sighed with dismay, tapping Frank indicatively on the shoulder. 'Nick, did you update this moron with what's been going on?'

'More or less.'

He turned the moron around, glaring at him an inch from his face. 'When Nick first uncovered Peeping Tom, he was grabbing an eye-full of us from Paris. Well, that's as far as we got. Now they're coming at us from random locations. It's pseudo-random, I'm sure of it. There must be a pattern. Get some strong coffee inside you, and find it. Find them, Frank. No more women. No more boozing. Nothing. Not until you get this Peeping Tom hammered down and we nail him to the ground. Do you understand?'

Frank nodded his head passively. He was still stunned, but

his response only incensed Roy. Gestures were too feeble, too meaningless now.

'Do you understand, Frank? This is bread and butter stuff now.'

'Yes. Yes...'

'Good! - Nick, I've thrown everything I could at it, ran all the trading routines, booted-up the algorithms, I've tried the bloody lot. I just can't see what they're up to. They come and go, appear and disappear like ghosts. It's driving me crazy. I can't trust myself anymore. I'm not sure if what I see is real or a simulation. I don't know why they're switching stocks the way they do; why they work the margins so narrowly; and then change the whole pattern in an instant. Sometimes they take a position, hold it, then let it go without achieving a single thing. It's crazy. They're trading on a whim, it seems. I... I just don't know. I don't get it. What the hell is going on?'

'Perhaps it's a game,' said Frank suddenly.

'What?'

'A game.'

'What are you talking about?'

'Maybe they're gambling.' This idea seemed to leap from him spontaneously, like the ball into the pocket of a red ten at a Vegas roulette table. Prayer doesn't mean a thing, but you kind of feel invincible when you win. And Vegas – she makes no promises, she ain't a guarantee; but a wink is enough to get you going, and you're smitten completely. 'Like a game of cards. Like poker, perhaps.'

'Poker?'

'It's just an idea.'

'Talk sense.'

'Maybe they're playing a game.'

'Game? What game?'

'I don't know. The idea just popped into my head. It *could* be a game, that's all I'm suggesting.'

'Then why all these odd tactics? They're bizarre. They're even ridiculous. They show us their hand. It's good; they fold. It's bad; they fold. There's no pattern. Nothing. What are they playing for?'

Frank frowned, looking puzzled: 'Us.'

'What the hell are you talking about?'

'They're playing against us; for us; towards us. Well... there's probably a better way of putting this.'

'What?'

'You know, Roy, you do this all the time. You manipulate – no, more than that, you *play and manipulate* those clueless guys riding into town on a cushion of bucks looking for a serious game of poker. You throw a few games; sometimes more. You toss them to the guy seated opposite. You deliberately lose. Why? Because it's basic strategy. To understand your opponent. To see how his mind works. To test his strengths; his weaknesses; to unravel his method; to see how he plays; how he reacts – to decode him. Put a guy on a high, and see if he's a sucker and watch him fall. How hard does he hit the ground? Does he bounce? Does he get up again, brush himself off, and have another go? Is he a sore loser? Can he take the hit? What are his limits? You see...? Strategy. Strip away the layers from your rival until he's an open check. And you're the one who's cashing. When money is no limit, it's not the cards that matter; it's the guy on the other side of the table daring you to raise him.' He looked at the monitors, studying them. 'Are we players? Do we want to play? Do we call?' He turned to face them, 'Roy, do we raise?' front loading a stare: 'Nick?'

Roy replied, looking hard at him: 'Find them, Frank. If anyone can, you can. I'd love to throw you out of that window head first, and twenty-two stories are nowhere near high enough as far as I'm concerned. But we need you, damn it. So do it, Frank. Get it done. Find Peeping Tom. Find him. Before he antes up, and wipes us out.'

Chapter 10

The air was sensuously warm, an evening warm, New York City heat and body heat combining in the elemental mix of razzmatazz heat, the sunbeams crisscrossing the street bouncing by reflection from the New York sheen, that's City sheen, Cadillac sheen, the kind of glow that only deep Manhattan possesses, and it seizes you, intoxicates your spirit, like breath from an evening star, heavenly and Broadway theme. Yeah.

Detective Forester was standing by the window, his gaze drifting among the sunbeams as ripples of his cigarette smoke floated down the valleys of Manhattan to Lady Liberty herself declaring to the world: *'Who loves you, baby! Come here and hug me...'* An irrepressible cry to those teeming millions who yearn and dream of her giant embrace. Yeah!

The phone started ringing and Sandy, working at her desk, lifted her coffee cup, drank calmly, and then, on the forth ring, she picked it up.

'Yes. A-ha. OK. Sure. Yes, we're working on it. No, we're still developing the case. Sorry, Captain, but what do you expect me to say? Sure. OK. – Forester,' Sandy called him and he turned to her causally, stubbing out his cigarette against the windowsill and throwing the stub down into the street below. Dreaming of the stage, he smiled with Broadway flair as she handed him the receiver. The whole moment was one eclipsing the mundane with something quite exotic, and he seems the man of occasion and of few words – the meaning resides in the gesture, friend, like a controlled hand, a sigh, a sudden flicker of an eyelid. He has the taste for it, it's easy, it's American, and it's kind of... *normal.*

Just as they always did, they talked frankly, Forester explaining, his Captain interrogating in his husky no nonsense way.

'Do you have any leads?'

'We're working on it, Captain.'

'Working on it?'

'That's the idea.'

'I need more than that.'

'Don't we all,' he whispered in aside.

'What's that?'

'Nothing, Captain.'

'OK. Come and see me in five minutes.'

As Forester sat down a colleague at a neighboring desk made a muscular remark. Sandy frowned, and Forester discreetly grinned.

'He's just a jerk' said Sandy. 'All men are jerks. Aren't they, Forester?'

He coughed. No answer. None. And just looked at the window again, almost day-dreaming, and felt like having another cigarette.

Forester grew uncommonly quiet of late. For several days now his conversation drifted absentmindedly, his mood growing more sober and detached. His normal snappy asides yielded to ambiguities, replying with polite but pointless shrugs at every other thing. Cops can become introverted and moody at times, particularly during periods of prolonged reflection; when curiosity seems to vie equally with obsession. His life's knowledge of crime was his mainstay, and nothing was meant to really surprise him anymore, the narrative that was America grew superabundant in New York City, and he'd lived the tale, out there, on the streets, where his steps echo with the rhythms of the free, of the brave, of endless possibility... That's him, a cop on the beat, smart on his feet, eyes on the ground, nose to the air and ears to the sounds of the street. New York City heat... simmering.

Yet people never ceased to amaze him. Solving crime often amounted to this, that a simple wink was enough to get you thinking, and lead you into who knows what horizons. Shucks, he was turning all philosophical now. His eyes turned down to the objects on his desk, miscellaneous evidence of a crime scene, and that blue packet of cigarettes stirred his curiosity. Like a muse, he wondered what they tasted like: a lemony-apple; a mint-candy; a sweet beer. For Forester, it had to be paradoxical, because the crime was laden with enigma and sleaze in equal measure, with fantasy and fact, wisdom and depravity. Philosopher. Slut. Teacher. Politician. What are they? – Just marbles in a bag.

'What are you doing?' Sandy asked him.

He glanced at her and then, in that brief moment, fixed a stare: she looked so pretty; those smoochy-flowing locks of hers, all blonde and shinning and bright. He would have loved to run his fingers through them, but in the meantime made do with a flirty wink, an expression that could have meant anything in the circumstances, and he held up the cigarettes intriguingly.

'So what?' she said. 'We found a packet of cigarettes.'

'French cigarettes, Sandy. French cigarettes.' Did he philosophize, she wondered, or was he just posing – a cop with cigarette-wisdom? It annoyed her. And she stubbed him out dismissively with:

'Is that so strange?'

'Perhaps... You never know with French cigarettes.'

That's quite an act to follow, she thought, but she couldn't tell *him* that. 'Well, I don't see anything of note. Nothing at all.'

'Look closer.'

'Read my lips, Forester.'

'Which ones?'

'Pervert!'

'Look, Sandy, I have a hunch. This may mean something.'

'Something?' She frowned, not resenting for a moment he had a hunch; no, hunches were welcome in the general scheme of things: it's part and parcel of being a cop: part sleuth bound in the maverick parcel of risk-taker. But his general attitude dismayed her: the unsubstantiated peddling of facts, without context, merely stated, lacking any rationale, based merely on notions that could be no more than a headache. It would need a great deal more to persuade her round than that.

Sandy drank her coffee and waited, leaning one arm on her desk in a skeptical pose. To her mind, this crime, lay it open for inspection and take a good look inside. What do you see? Forget forensics; leave aside the gimmicks of the trade, just butter your loaf a touch with a dollop of savvy, and let the stinking mess that is a crime scene float up. What do you find? Psychos, perverts, twisted voyeurs that lost their cool and exchanged their fetish craving for a knife, and turned the dreaming masturbation of a fertile mind to dreadful slaughter. Humans were capable of anything. Was this lust gone bust in a crazed mind, or something so absurd one would be forced to describe as... ludicrous? *Is there a comic in the house? If so, encore, you prat, and show your bloody face.* And if a twisted mind gained nothing from this evil handiwork, then who did, and why?

Forester leaned back in his chair, feeling restive. 'Have you stopped being curious already, Sandy? Have you just given up?' Was he being facetious, or pompous, or just plain dull? 'Is this just another murder case to you, and you're going through the motions?'

'Just another case!' She struck the desk with her fist. 'Forester - '

'Look at the evidence. Look. These cigarettes for example. Look, they're French. That *must* mean something.'

'Are you out of your semen-soaked mind? Is testosterone made in your head? Are you thick? You might have the horn over this case, *mister,* but you'd better control that erection of yours, because it's pissing me off. Forester,' she snapped, 'if you can't keep it down, get a jock strap. But don't take it out on me.'

He remained unmoved, or perhaps stupid would describe him properly in her eyes. He was baffled by the drama of a murder seeped in bloody chaos and turning on a thread of speculation. Why, even Pop was mystified and waded in with a roar: *It's all a load of queers whacking themselves, son. These bums'll do anything for a lay. Sometimes, with cases like these, well, you've got to ride it out as best you can, and leave it at that. – What twisted things bubble up in a pervert's boiling head? Who knows! It's nothing but a stinking stew of fornicators and bums. What can I advise you, son, other than to find yourself a good wife, and make sure she doesn't screw you up like the last one did. Hey, come to think, you don't suppose she might have had a hand in this malarkey...? Find yourself a good woman, son. That's my advice.* Thanks, Pop, but I've got other things on my mind right now. *Well, always remember this, son - it's only a woman that can butter your toast. But make sure she doesn't eat them all.* Thank's, Pop.

Just then, Forester began to feel hungry and imagined he sensed the aroma of fresh toast. But Sandy's pretty face hooked him with a frown, and he soon lost his appetite.

And so on it rolls, the measly evidence, the meager fragments of fact rendering even conjecture hopeless, he was determined to investigate any feature, any clue, no matter how vague or bizarre, and with any luck persuade her to the same conclusions.

'Sandy, we have nothing substantial, only crumbs. But we're cops, so stir your savvy mind and tell me: what did we find; what do we really know? What happens next? Even metaphors have the weight of fact now. So don't be shy; hold nothing back. Consider everything: the smells, the colors, the whole saga. Put it all together and tell me what you really think.'

Sighing condescendingly at first, she then took up the challenge. Opening the file on her desk and examining the photographs, she transposed them in her mind, distilling the recollection of things, the smells, the intrigue encoded as carnage, the distinctive pastiche of black and white and red, the suffocating sense of the room, the horror and yet the farce of death made to seem like a gruesome fetish. Or was it more ancient than that, a visceral hankering for pain as sacred rapture? It's not the strangeness; it's the sheer... *improbability* that strikes her most. It was a puzzle in an enigma within a riddle all wrapped up like a Russian doll minus its neatness.

'It's not the handiwork of a freak at work here,' she spoke at length, taking her time. 'This was not done on impulse. And yet it was improvised.'

He raised his eyebrows with interest. 'Go on.'

She grinned, 'I have my hunches too.'

'Touché, Sandy. Touché.' Actually, she was a fencer and practiced regularly at her club.

'There is one thing, though,' began the fencer, thrusting her thoughts to the mark.

'Go on, I'm listening.'

'Whoever committed these murders probably watched lots of cheap thrill movies, read fetish magazines, taking ideas from everywhere and amalgamating the bizarre into a single script. This whole event seems garbled to me.' He twitched his nose in confusion at her, so she undid a few steps, explaining: 'Whoever did this never simply tried to murder, but to do it twenty different ways at once to be sure and let us know that this kinky scene went too far, and even the dumbest cop would get the message.'

'Are you saying the killer was some kind of theatrical amateur?'

'I mean someone who has never done anything like this before; someone who has never even imagined it. And he's set about the task... well, as a kind of *game*. He must play. But how? Crime is like that, it's a game of confusions. This too is a crime of confusions.'

'You mean he's acting?'

'He's performing, yes.'

'Acting?'

'No. Not acting. It's not planned that way. This is not a role he knows how to play; not really; but he knows he must be methodical. What he does must appear... *labored* – because that's what gives the impression that there's a story, a narrative to his crime. He's kind of bluffing. That's it! Bluffing! Yes, and managing to make a complete mess of it.' She grinned knowingly. 'Men are expert at that.'

Forester skirted that last remark, and wondered aloud: 'And where does that lead us?'

She grinned mischievously: 'To a packet of French cigarettes.'

Forester softly tapped the sweet blue packet of cigarettes on the table, and then glanced at his watch. 'I had better go and see the Captain.'

'Give him my regards,' she lifted her coffee cup, smiled, and drank with a quiet passion a triumphant aftertaste making her go mmmmm.

The Captain, a savvy cop with more than thirty years in the job, a taste for the best whiskey, a hard stomach for bearing the absurdities of the legal system, and a peculiar drawl that sounded Irish with German timbre and an overtone of Scotch with the sweetness of Italian – aka your run-of-the-mill all-American Brooklyn kid who could have been a baseball star, perhaps.

He was a cop's cop, the kind Pop grew up with on the streets and thumped from time to time when occasion called for it: they were sparring pals in the boxing ring from rookie days.

'You know, Forester, your old man whacked me in the jaw several times.'

'Sorry about that, Captain.'

'Nah!' he gestured with a contender's pride. 'I had it coming. I let my left drop; and he let me have it.'

'Oops! There you go. Live and learn.'

'Yeah,' he reminisced with a chuckle, and then grew more sober. 'Fair and square. Which proves the point - and never forgot it, kiddo – when you're in for a hard slog, never let your guard down, or someone with a point to make is going to let you know it. Your old man and I learned that the hard way.'

'Perhaps Pop should have been a lawyer.'

'A lawyer!' he shrieked in horror, 'Nah. Are you crazy!'

'Why not?'

The Captain glared at him. 'Never let your old man hear you say that. He'll jump out of his grave and sop you one, sonny.'

'Sorry.'

The Captain sat at his desk and immediately began rummaging through some papers. It was difficult to imagine this man ever retiring. He was that perfect testament to natural law that men exist to work, not slop around all day. 'So... What have you got for me?'

'We found some cigarettes.'

'And?'

'French cigarettes.'

'So?'

'Well... we think, though it might seem early days, that maybe he's French.'

'Who? The victim or the perpetrator?'

He hesitated, shrugging: 'Either. Both.'

The Captain frowned. 'Because of French cigarettes? - Come on, Forester, that's a well-known brand. You can buy it at thousands of places.'

'Even in France.'

He eyeballed him. 'You'll need a lot more than that to get a free trip to Paris.'

'Captain - '

'Save your breath, Forester. I know what you're after, and I not buying it.'

'It's just a hunch.'

'I'm all for hunches, so long as they lead somewhere, and don't put the Department to unnecessary expense.'

'For now, it's all we have to go on.'

'Well, you run with your hunch, pace it awhile and see what you come up with. But do it from your office, or out there in the streets.'

'You're the boss.'

'See you, Forester. And keep me updated.'

He had a half empty (or was that half-filled?) pack of French cigarettes; a pen with the NBS Banking Corporation logo embossed on it, and a peculiar hunch. This may seem a puzzle composed of many puzzles, but life was often like that. As in most things, it seemed so much simpler in hindsight, and more than likely this case would bear out the virtue of that experience. But only time would tell, and the clock was ticking down. Even Pop burst in on cue, blaring away: *Am I the only one around here who can tell the time? Has the NYPD become a dumping ground for donkeys? What the hell does a cop need to get a job done around here these days, a block of evidence the size of Texas? Figure it out, you fannies. Get to work; or get the hell out of my police force.*

'Sandy.'

'What did he say?'

'This and that.'

'So, where do we go from here?'

'Press the lab guys and see what else they can come up with.'

'Maybe their own urine,' she murmured quietly to herself.

'What was that?'

'I said OK, I'll give it a go.'

'And here, take these,' he tossed her the pack of cigarettes. 'See if their bag of tricks is any use on them.'

'They've dusted them already. There are no clear prints.'

'I know. But see if there is anything else.'

'Like what?'

'I don't know. These guys have got gizmos, haven't they? Just ask them to do their best.'

'Maybe they can piss on them,' she murmured in whispers to herself again.

'What was that?'

'I said OK, leave it with me. I'll see to it.'

184

'Thanks.'

'And you?'

'I'm going back to see those banker guys.'

'What for?'

He shook his head, churned a frown with a grin, and said: 'A hunch.'

She's seen it before. Sometimes, it was a long shot. Sometimes you hit the bull's eye. Was it gamblers' luck or simple statistics? You never know until you throw the dice, turn the cards, figure it out. The thing with being a cop is that he only ever really knows so much. And the best cops understand that they only ever know very little.

But it's enough to get the job done.

Bingo!

Chapter 11

The phone call to their office was received in late afternoon: enigma or inconvenience? Who knows, but it carried every sense of being a spoiler. The guard at the Information Desk got directly to the point: a plain-clothes police officer, Detective John Forester of the NYPD, was on his way up.

'Did he say what he wanted?' asked Roy.

'No. He just smiled. And asked me for the time.'

Roy met him at the door; his foot pinning the base, he held it slightly ajar, just so, pitched at a slim angle, not inviting him in, though Forester worked his eyes and could see though the gap the other two milling around inside: Nick first, with whom he exchanged an affable smile, while the other grungy looking one glanced over indifferently, before returning to his desk and resuming his work.

Roy was polite but firm. 'What can we do for you, Detective?'

'Can you spare me a few moments of your time?'

'We're rather busy now. Can it wait for another time?'

'Not really. It's important. Do you mind if I come in?'

Roy conferred quietly with his colleagues, the grim probing of eyes signaling a vague assent, before yielding the door to. 'Sure, I don't see why not. Come in, Detective. Can I offer you a drink?'

'No thanks.'

Forester's eyes roamed discreetly around the room and observed Frank engrossed in some work. He seemed wholly incongruous within this 'psychedelic' setting, like a stain on an otherwise pristine surface. But Forester was a cop, experience his mainstay, intuition his primary tool, and first impressions one thread among the multitude of competing considerations. The cop's eyes presently took the heat and did the real work this time round. And to Forester's mind this disheveled looking character had profound aptitude; the tell-tale

187

signs revealing him, from the way he worked and sifted data around from one console to the next, coordinating his actions in a seamless way, made manifest the enduring fact that human beings were the true catalysts of data, not machines. This man was in full control of his actions, he could see in and through and beyond things, the industrious persona, grungy looking or otherwise, that obsesses over details, that understands the challenges and can shut out the world and get a job done, oblivious to everything but the task at hand. Such people ranked above the common moniker of the dedicated man. They were driven individuals, fanatics of the moment, powered by their own unique steam, and Forester concluded to himself, and asked for confirmation:

'Excuse me, are you Mr. Frank Freiberg?'

Frank reluctantly stopped what he was doing and turned to face him: 'Are you the cop who's been snooping around?'

'That's right. I'm conducting an investigation into a - '

'If it's all the same to you, reports of my demise are wholly exaggerated. In fact, you've missed the mark by miles.' He grinned briefly. 'Better aiming next time, Detective.'

Forester remained muted and seemed a touch embarrassed. Frank continued:

'And I'm busy. We're all very busy. You can see this is not the best time for paying us a visit. And if it's all the same to you, Detective…' frowning and resuming his work. 'We have things to do. Goodbye.'

Clearly, they wanted Forester to leave, and gave him the cold shoulder, except for Nick who paused to smile and grin alternately in polite contrariness to his colleagues. Forester felt the sense of alienation, of being excluded, but continued regardless.

'We're in a sort of a bind, Mr. Freiberg, and we thought you might be able to help.'

'How?'

'Oh, you know, just answer some questions... Assist with our enquiries. Things like that.'

'This is crazy.'

'I was hoping you would let me be the judge of that.'

'How long will this take?'

'Not long.'

Frank grudgingly paused what he was doing and leaned back in his chair. 'Fire away.'

'The last time I was here your colleagues informed me you were in Las Vegas?'

'That's right?'

'You go there often?'

'Now and again.'

'How long was the trip?'

'Four days?'

'Have a nice time?'

'I try my best to enjoy it.'

'And?'

'Practice makes perfect.'

'Good for you.'

'Thanks.'

'You returned today?'

'Yes.'

'Do you know a woman by the name of Sandra Ellis?'

'Sandra Ellis?'

'Sound familiar?'

'Sandra... Yes, we're old acquaintances.'

'Sandra Ellis was killed three days ago. She was found, brutally murdered, together with a *friend* of hers at her apartment.' Frank went pale, Roy froze with disbelief, and Nick sat down and looked dazed. Forester continued. 'I'd like to ask you some questions.'

'Am I a suspect?'

'No,' he replied convincingly, although it wasn't strictly true. He had so little evidence to go on he was reluctant to rule anything out at this stage. What he really wanted from Frank was corroboration for his hunch, not to implicate him in this episode of blood and gore. 'Mr. Freiberg, can you tell me when you last saw Sandra Ellis?'

Frank ran his hands over his face, which felt cold and trembling, pulling them across and around his head, smothering himself, the shock of her death reverberating no, no, no... his throat tightening as if to stifle him. Eventually, his breathing eased, and a vulnerable presence of mind drifted back, and he found himself reminiscing, lamenting in whispers:

'I remember seeing her about... about a month or so ago. More... Five, maybe six weeks. Yes...yes. I can look it up in my diary. Where's my diary...?' Frank fumbled and Forester remained quiet, just gazing at him. 'What are you thinking, Detective, that I should have been dead?'

'I'll be candid with you, Mr. Freiberg. I'm not investigating any act of passion. There's a story here, if I can put it that way. And I need your help.'

'My help? How? What do you want from me? I'm not the author. I'm not part of the story. Damn it, I wasn't even here. I was in Las Vegas. I can prove it.'

'A hunch.'

'That's all you have to go on, a hunch?'

'It's a start.'

'I...' he shuddered, 'I don't know what I'm supposed to think.'

Forester paused and turned down the heat. It was time to act the 'nice-guy' role, to show understanding, to be the sympathetic cop with a heart of gold whose warm considerate smile lifts the pressure and puts you at ease. A cop with a smile, gee, that's the thing, he's just doing his thankless job and wants the whole world to be happy – especially you. It may sound feeble, but to anxious men, like Frank, it often worked, so Forester gave it a try. As Pop was keen to advise him, when dealing with reluctant guys: *Son, get the fuckers to think straight. Be nice, but don't put them to sleep. In my day, we'd whack them in the chops, and follow it up with a volley to the guts, which got the proceedings going just smartly. Then you tie them up by their ears to make sure they're listening and beat it out of them, the proper way, like it should be done. But today, the pansies rule the city, and have screwed it all up.*

'Mr. Freiberg, it's shocking what happened; it's horrible; it's unimaginable. I know how you must feel. Just try and calm down. Take all the time you need. It helps no one by jumping to conclusions. Please, try and relax, and let me worry about the questions.'

'I'm sorry, but what use am I to your investigation? Yes, I knew her. I grieve at her passing. It's shocking. I can't believe it. But I don't see how it affects me. It's a coincidence. They happen all the time.'

'I think there's more to this than meets the eye,' Forester pondered over the Peeping Tom theory: *Eye for an eye become eye for a life.*

'Excuse me?'

'I'm being cryptic. I apologize.'

'Do you think someone was out to get me?'

'I don't wish to alarm or scare you with this, but - '

'This is insane. It's ridiculous. I have no enemies.' Frank shook his head. 'I have hurt no one,' he spoke in sorrow, 'expect myself, perhaps.'

'It's a hunch.'

'So you said.'

'And would you like to know what my gut instinct is telling me?'

'No.'

'Well I'll tell you anyway.'

'What?'

'That whatever this is, it's not just going to go away. We have to resolve it.'

'That's as maybe, but it has nothing to do with me. Nothing.'

Forester, the man, believed him. Forester, the cop, wouldn't rule anything out.

'We found this Valentine's card in the garbage bin with the name Cassandra and the message "If *Daddy* don't sing; then the fat lady ain't his thing. Love and hugs, Frank." Is that your handwriting?'

He looked briefly. 'That's mine,' he said, and seemed wholly unperturbed. He's either a cool character, or a cunning one, thought Forester, who pressed him with:

'Well, is there something you're not telling me; something I should know about?'

'Not particularly.' His face changed to an involuntary grin. Why was he smirking, thought Forester? That look was an echo of his misspent youth in ladies' toilets wearing crotchless body leather and getting spanked, he wondered with derision. They made him confess his sins many times past, no doubt. Pervert!

'Who's Cassandra?'

'A plant.'

'A plant?'

'Yes. A plant.' Frank became blasé. 'I sent her an ivy... some time ago now. For Valentine's Day. She put it in the kitchen betweent the fridge and the stove.'

'Is that meant to be kinky?' Roy cut in irresistibly, his face flaring with a broad grin which, though natural for him, seemed entirely out of place. 'Sorry. Please continue.'

'So, it's just a plant?' Forester resumed.

'She must have kept the Valentine's card for a time and thrown it out only recently. Women: who understands them!'

'A plant?'

'That's what I said. A plant. Don't you like plants, Detective?'

'Like them..?' his voice ached with the echo: *Damn! There goes another lead.* But he refused to give up.

'Is that all, Detective?' said Frank.

'Will you accompany me to the scene of the crime?'

'Excuse me? Scene? Where do you mean?'

'The apartment. The scene of the crime.'

'What for?'

'I'd like your opinion.'

'On what?'

'The room.'

'The room? What room?'

'Where the events took place.'

'Are you out of your mind! Why?'

'Just a hunch.'

'I don't have the time. I'm sorry. We're very busy here, as you can see. We have things to do.'

'Please.'

'I'm sorry.'

'It would really be a great help if you would.'

'I'm sorry, I can't.'

'Please, Mr. Freiberg.'

'Why don't you just go?' Roy cut in impatiently. 'Just go!'

'Why should I?'

'To sort this mess out once and for all.'

'It's not my mess. Why the hell don't you go?'

'Because it has nothing to do with me.'

'Nor me, either, damn it!'

'Please, gentlemen, please...' Forester intervened. He turned to Frank, 'I can't compel you. You are not a suspect. I am asking a favor to help with our enquiries. No, I don't know off hand what good it would do. But it might. You're just a free citizen assisting the police, that's all. And if it will encourage you, I'll mention you for a citizen's commendation. You get to meet the Mayor and all.' *(Duh!)*

'Nah...' Frank grew bashful, taking a moment to reconsider and then relenting all at once, shrugging at things, just any old things, and reaching for his jacket. 'No need to put yourself to any trouble over me. Let's just get this over with. Do you have a car waiting downstairs?'

'Yes. And don't worry, I'll drive you back. I really appreciate this. Thank you, Mr. Freiberg.'

Nick was silent all this time, standing apart, watching, and now cut in: 'Would you mind if I came along?'

'What for?' said Roy. 'It's not a circus.'

Nick shrugged and looked optimistically at Forester. 'Curiosity.'

'Curiosity's fine with me,' he said. 'Sure. Why not.'

'Yeah,' said Frank, sniggering. 'Curiosity never killed anyone – expect the cat!'

Smart ass!

Forester, like Frank, never seemed to mind Nick's presence and struck up an easy rapport with him. Frank, ever the observer, ever the quintessential voyeur, sat in the rear seat of the car sprawled out for comfort and listened to the conversation which ranged through stories of the city: it's big, it's crowded, it's dirty, it's mean, it's wild, it's frenzied, it's electric, it's magnificent. Car horns sounded out a symphony of passion packed into the fevered chorus of city narratives and the looming epic of rush hour traffic as the masses swarmed and walked and strutted and ran and huffed and puffed and felt the microcosm of the world in their bones at the unceasing pace of life. Fall down and they'll trample over you; so move your ass because the world rolls on, it's *got* to roll on and no one's going to stop it – take a deep breath. OK! - and lights light up the Manhattan skyline and you dream the great U S of A dream, the immigrant dream of deliverance, of hope. This is something that you do because you believe it; you want it; it's yours; it can be all yours. Because the spirit never dies. Got the stomach for a fight? Fists up! Gloves on! You toil and push through the muck of events, past every onslaught of bad luck and irrational omens trying to pull you back, but you tell yourself "fists up", you push yourself to that almighty next step and scream at the Devil, "I ain't going back, sucker. No way. Just get out of my way..." and your heels catch ablaze, clipping with incendiary faith through everything life throws at you, through splendor and the Bronx: snap your step and let the fire that burns within you blaze. Because unless you light it yourself – what the heck, you'll burn anyway, so you may as well give it a shot. Give it your best best best shot. It's always the best.

'Yeah...' Frank said eloquently, breezing in like a summer song. 'I love this town.' He smiled. Kind of warm. Kind of big. Kind of wow! 'Yeah. She's my kind of town...'

So did Forester's Pop; and his Pop before him. They loved this city. And they just hated it, too. *Son,* Pop would brag, *listen to what I'm telling you, and listen good. Quiet down now, and listen. You hear it? Do you hear it?* He never got the chance to tell him: Yes, Pop, I hear it loud and clear. - By the time he realized what he meant, he was dead.

The city has its own voice too, made up of millions and millions and millions of them all talking at once, and sometimes they synchronize and tell you things only a city can. And that voice was going to tell Forester who the killer was.

'Detective,' said Nick, as they entered the apartment, 'do you have any idea who might have done this?'

'If we listen hard enough...' he said, thinking of Pop. 'If we listen, eventually we'll hear. It's only a matter of time.'

Forget city lights. It's city voices that capture the imagination.

Nick smiled; perhaps one day he'll understand what he meant. 'Only a matter of time...' Tick-tock, it's a wise man who bets on the clock. And a fool who thinks it's ever going to stop.

'There have been a few changes,' Frank began quietly, gazing gloomily around the room. People had died here, brutally murdered, and this fact cut a punch. He moved warily into the kitchen as if looking for something. There she was, Cassandra the ivy looking beautiful as ever in her pot beside the tulips (who bought her those?)

and the germaniums (that could have been the corporate lawyer from Taylor and Marsh downtown) and the irises (that was definitely the Mayor! *Kinky*.)

'How does it feel to you?' Forester asked him.

'Some things...' answered Frank emotionally, looking at Nick, 'never change.'

Forester hoped Frank would navigate independently through the apartment, and that's exactly what he did. Apart from the inner room that functioned as the dungeon, he behaved normally, although tempered with deference for the deceased. But once inside the dungeon he became withdrawn and was anxious to leave, which he quickly did, shutting the door behind him before any sense of it could attach and burden him with painful reminiscing. It was strange and hard for him to imagine that those intimate things one takes for granted can be swept away in an instant. Things so alive, so real, die. Why?

Thus far, the atmosphere of reflection, of gentle grieving, continued from room to room. Despite himself, Frank was becoming a mourner, rekindling her memory with affection. But it wasn't leading anywhere and, in particular, Frank was evading the dungeon. Forester concluded he would have to intervene and steer their progress.

'I'd like your opinion on the room.'

'Which room?'

'Where the events took place,' he said, indicating. 'In there.'

'Oh,' Frank seemed lost, wondering what to say or do. Nick came to his assistance.

'Well, this is why we came, Frank,' he said thoughtfully. 'Let's just get this over with. Give it your best shot. OK?'

He closed his eyes, yielding without effort, 'May as well...' and followed at a distance as Forester guided them inside, eased the door open and switched on the lights. It was quiet, eerily quiet; the only patter was their footsteps scraping across the floor, vanishing like clipped echoes amid longer pauses.

Frank briefly shuddered, crossing the threshold for a second time.

'What's that smell?' Nick asked.

'Sweat,' said Forester, conferring with Frank, 'and other things...'

The bench. The leather. The straps. The whips. The tools of his desire – humiliation a thousand bucks a throw. Ouch! The cage for punishment, the bucket, empty now, but he remembers filled with urine. A room masked with the habitation of shadows, the stale invisible breath of ghosts languishing in an immaterial cage, a suffocating, hollowed-out shell of a place where, failing to arouse, is a doom-laden womb pregnant with darkest desire.

'So, this is where the hanky panky went on...?' Nick wasn't thinking, and it sounded insensitive and tasteless. 'Sorry. - Frank, are you OK?'

'I'm fine.'

Forester took up the slack. 'Does it say anything to you? Anything at all? - What do you feel?'

'How do you mean?' Frank asked him softly, fearing to raise his voice above a whisper as though the echoes would perturb the dead. 'Are you a psychologist now or a cop?'

'Both. It depends on the circumstances. And the case.'

'I see... memories,' he said without the faintest suggestion of shame. He is what he is. He likes it rough. That doesn't make him bad, just kinky (nor good for that matter, just kinky).

'I asked the forensics team to put everything back as they found it. Take your time; we're in no hurry. Your observations, please, would be very helpful, Frank. May I call you Frank?'

He shrugged OK, answering both questions and began moving through the room. Instinctively, he ventured out alone, his steps tentative at first then, with the confidence of memory, took possession. The wall on the right was re-painted with a fresh coat of velvet black: suffocating, oppressively delicious. The floor, yes, the deconstructed floor, its solid timbres conveying the mystery of primeval seduction. The mood S; the place M; sadomasochism - S & M. Over on the left lay the trappings of her trade arranged like a cache of wanton delights, whips, chains, a leash, sex toys... giving tangible weight to imagined ritual as she breathed her incantations with a purring lust and convulsed her charges to their pleasure. Was this the bait that led them to her lair, the deeper symbolism inherited from a fetish brain? Is S & M the echoes of ancient man animalizing kinkiness to his taste? Sex is in the mind. *Phew! What a mind is man!* And Mistress Sandra, her corporeal essence gone, no ghost nor the mocking timber of her voice, her velvety hair, black, shamanic, sultry, slutty; her exquisite menace, her howling rasps: "Shut your mouth, you filthy scum..." and delivered with such passion, such power, what a *tour de force* she was, that he loved her acting most of all. Yes, she can act, and played the part wonderfully. And someone, for some reason, in the audience of a voyeur, perhaps, decided to cut the drama, to edit her out, and put her to rest forever.

At length, Frank began: 'Do you know, Detective, I get the sense she had no idea someone was watching her. Yet he was here all the same, able to melt into the background; and wait, wait, wait...'

'That's what I suspected.'

'She had a gift for sensing things around her. One time, a cat crept into the room quietly and slunk into a corner. She felt it, found it sleeping, and took it outside. – Occasionally she was moody, and then she showed surprising vigor for her role, surpassing herself. But that was rare. She was never detached from reality. She knew whose fantasy was being played out. Her job was to be in control, first and foremost.' He reminisced than remembered precisely, recalling tenderness in moods and themes of pleasure than tracing out exactness in events. There was gentleness in his voice, in his expression, in the way he handled her things when he moved over to her *pleasure tray*, and fondled them, his hands exploring the language of pain and power - the thumb-screws, the whips, the canes, the leather straps (their smell engulfed him completely) the metal pins and candles. These were the prizes that men like him craved; even now amid the awful tragedy, it was difficult to quell their visceral power arouse in him a deep yearning when all he ever wanted was a good flogging. He was a simple man nipped by the tip of her flailing whip as he licked her toes. Playful. Silly. And he misses her dearly. She was an artiste of S & M, and he adored her.

With a quiet, intimate smile, he thought of her. He'd never handled the whip before, and it felt powerful in his hand. Gripping, it infused him with a sense of animal strength, of primeval master. Mistress and slave: this was the other side of the coin; he flipped it over, and it felt good. Then moving over to the all-body harness, the smell of leather still deliciously pungent - this was aroma not to taste but to devour. What must he have seemed bound to that? Merely helpless man, or burning temptation? Like memories drained, these were relics now. All these things, existing in endless limbo without her spirit to rouse them; to set them on fire; to consummate them with his flesh. Without her here he felt their meaning, their quintessence, had vanished forever. Her sun had set, and he felt sad.

Straining to clutch them tighter, his strength suddenly drained away as he powerlessly let slip the whip and other things from his grasp, his hands trembling as he reached for his face, recoiling with muted horror. Something within him posed the awful riddle: perhaps, this fatal *event,* this wretched drama was meant for him – deeds not intended to tease out desire, but to crush him.

Horror and an agonizing 'if' aroused revulsion of him cheating fate. Was this doomed episode intended for him? The stifling gasp *Oh God!* dazed his imagination. Suddenly, the room felt cold, alien, bleak; a cruel space of frozen time – like a coffin.

There, bound with straps, his head pressed to the wall, his body chained and shivering, there, three days ago, was finality. Someone had taken the final blow, but this end was meant for him. Perhaps?

'Detective, there's something else I should have told you.'

'Yes. I'm listening.'

'I don't know how to put this, but… things are not as they seem. This whole episode... it *feels* wrong.'

Feeling. Instinct. A gut reaction. Those are human powers divining with potential, smoldering with magic. They sensed clues, latent echoes of the city, conveying a sixth sense. Forester latched on and listened closely.

'She was *kind of* expecting me.'

'How do you mean?'

'It was always provisional with us; that's the way we did things. We work; we lead busy lives. Unplanned events can arise and...' Frank pondered deeply as he spoke, 'how can I put this into context? Circumstance intrudes.'

'Did she have a diary?'

'I don't know. I think so. Maybe...'

'We never found one. But go on, please continue.'

Frank took a deep breath. 'I would call to make an appointment; we negotiate a time, and agree. Then, nearer the time, I would call again to confirm, as a matter of courtesy to make sure everything was OK. It's very normal, like visiting a doctor or a dentist.'

'How many calls did you make?'

'Just the one.'

'And?'

'Well, I arranged an appointment and planned to return to New York City three days ago. But I got caught up in Las Vegas. So I never made that second call. She must have taken that as a cue, and booked-in someone else.'

'Caught up with what?'

'I'm not quite sure,' he said, looking dazed. 'It's still puzzling me.'

'Go on.'

'As I explained to Nick earlier, while distracted, I think someone may have slipped something into my drink, because a whole day is missing, and I don't know what the hell happened to me or it.'

Forester looked quizzically at him. 'Do you take drugs?'

'No.'

'He's a boozer,' said Nick, trying to be helpful. 'Moderately; most of the time.'

'Did you report this to anyone?' asked Forester. 'The Las Vegas police?'

'What am I going to say?'

'Did you lose anything? Was anything stolen, or...'

'No. Nothing. Not a cent.'

'Nothing at all?'

'Just a day,' said Frank. 'Just a day.'

The upshot of this visit, and the new facts in particular, added to the confusion that beset Forester. The quirks of the crime were infuriating, he felt they were grinding him down than adding to his stock of useful facts. But he persevered with quiet determination. Some crimes are like that, you burrow away, but mostly, you just have to wait it out. He was convinced the pieces to the crime were there, scattered and in fragments, and someone had really stirred the puzzle. But he was determined to put it back together.

Suddenly, Forester received a call on his phone. It was Sandy.

'Yes, I can hear you clearly. It's fine. What is it?'

'Forensics said they found a micro photo-sensor.'

'A what?'

'A device that detects and amplifies light.'

'Where?'

'They say it's effective in the visible band and down to the near infra red.'

'One thing at a time, Sandy, one thing at a time.'

'OK. They found this tiny thing that sees in low light: it picks it up and amplifies it. They shoveled up some scattered artifacts by the wall on the left, near the chains. Among them they found this tiny device. Seem unusual to you? I'd say it was bizarre.'

Forester abruptly turned to Frank and asked him: 'Did she ever shoot film here, make movies or record anything?'

'No. Not that I know of.'

'Does it seem likely she would do such a thing?'

'No. She was a pro. She would never do anything like that without the client's consent. You see, Detective, you've got to understand these women. It's business to them; sure. But the good ones, like her, don't want to rob you. They provide a service, and they do it honestly and well.'

Well spoken, thought Nick, who otherwise remained silent as Forester pondered this a moment before resuming the conversation with his colleague.

'Sandy, did they get a trace on this device? How old is it? Where does it come from? Where was it made?'

'Oh sure, that's the other bit of good news. Guess where?' she teased him, and Forester grew annoyed.

'Spare me the agony, Sandy. Where?'

'France.'

Bingo! Paris. Yes sir! Come here and cuddle me, darling. Ha ha. Paris! Who loves you, baby? I do! *Yausa yausa yausa!* And that mighty smile on his face sang something sweet and dear to his heart; it sung *Paris!*

'Sandy, did you mention this to the Captain; to anyone?'

'No. Not yet. I'm still writing it up.'

'Good. Wait till I get back. Don't mention a thing. We'll do it together.'

'Hokey-dokey,' she agreed good-humouredly, and hung up. He folded away the phone and looked at his wristwatch.

'I think this is a good time to leave, if you're both ready. I can give you guys a lift back.' He never waited but led them briskly out.

Frank, his feelings confused as Forester shut the door behind them in the corridor, braved the moment and took a last look inside, and said, 'I just realized, the door has been repainted too. Same color; new coat.' He drew closer and touched it. 'It must have been repainted about the same time as the wall inside the room.'

Forester made no comment but let that detail ferment in his mind. By the time they reached the car, Forester and Frank were thinking the same thing. Nick was a little late getting there, but eventually as they sped away and turned the corner and a truck hectically rushed past them:

'I ought to book that bum for speeding,' said Forester, and Nick replied.

'Perhaps these micro devices are embedded into the wall.'

'That's what I was thinking,' he said, turning and heading south. 'Would you guys like to be dropped back at your office?'

'What about the paint?' Frank asked him directly.

'I have some friends in forensics. They owe me a favor, and it's time to cash it in. I want this done quietly?' he looked over at Nick seated beside him, pressing the point. 'And I'd like it to stay that way,' before glancing in the rear-view mirror at Frank reposing sullenly in the back. 'Frank.'

'Yes, Detective?'

'Will you be all right?'

'Sure. Sure I will.'

'You can stay over at my place,' Nick tried to insist, but Frank declined, resolved to have his own way.

Forester offered him his card, taking one from his pocket and holding it over his shoulder. His eyes never left the street:

'That number is available twenty-four hours a day. It's a private number. It's not recorded, so no one will know.'

'Thanks. But I won't need it.'

'Take it. If you think of anything, give me a call.'

Frank took it.

The ride back was swift and generally quiet. Cruising along Avenue of the Americas they caught some traffic and Frank looked about him with a surge of interest. The animation of the city stirring him perhaps, and he briskly got out when the car stopped at some red traffic lights.

'I'm getting out here. I need to do something.'

'Wait, I can take you there.'

'No thanks,' he said, 'I prefer to walk,' giving a thumbs-up sign to Nick and shaking hands with Forester, who wished him well and thanked him again for his help. They watched him walk a while before he turned and vanished from view.

'He'll be OK,' said Nick. 'After all, he could use some time to himself. He needs to think. He's still shaken after what happened.'

'We can't escape the possibility that it could have been him.'

'But it wasn't.'

'No,' said Forester, shifting the car into gear as the traffic started moving. 'You guys have any connection with France?'

'Not really,'

'What about Frank?'

'We've all been there, of course.'

'Business or pleasure?'

'Both.'

'Could you be more specific?'

'Sure. We often travel abroad; that's part of our job. We attend business meetings, conferences, training seminars... Well, the show never ends. There are always new tricks to learn, new techniques and methods being devised. Basically, the world is a giant trading shop. Imagine the volume of transactions, and the range and variety they embrace. In this game, you can never be complacent. Traders are like singers always looking for the next great song, remembering the good times, learning from the bad, and wishing it would roll on forever. The risk is to do nothing. There's too much at stake, and someone somewhere is always innovating. At times, I imagine to myself that numbers were first invented just to keep a tab on finances. The world needs accounting or we'd all fall flat on our face. Maybe that's why zero was devised, and the digits too. Zero to nine are like the fingers of the world; hands embracing everything, handling everything.'

He paused, expressing a whimsical smile that flirted with pride in humanity, its passion for a buck, its embrace of innovation and risk – men, women, and the markets, what a remarkable cocktail they are; in combination, what a gas! That takes some beating, don't it? The trading instinct. Civilization galvanizes around the desire to trade. We are traders first; homo sapiens last. And that's a wrap! Nick continued: 'We usually gather at the bank's own premises. But occasionally they hire out a venue. It could be anywhere in the world. It's the events' team who arrange the time and place. We just turn up. It's that simple. And let's face it, why make life difficult?'

'When was the last time any of you were in France?'

'Let me think,' he mulled it over for a while, naturally at ease as he watched New York City breathe with the spirit of immigrants, the will of the whole world; the brimming desire to embrace a dream, and live it. At that moment the world seemed entirely in step, it felt normal, beautiful, amazing. 'Roy went alone that time, around six or seven weeks ago. He was there several days, four or five... I don't remember exactly. But it was a small affair; only a few people turned up. I think they met at the bank's offices in Paris. Yes, that's where it was. Roy was none too pleased with the topic. What was it again? Oh yes, Trading the Long Bond with Inflationary Models.'

'Roy, eh?'

'That's right.'

'And is Roy... you know, kinky like your other buddy?'

Nick laughed. 'He has his soft spots that he likes teased and tickled from time to time. We all do. After all, he's only human. But not in *that* particular way.' He wondered aloud. 'Roy, well, to be honest, he prefers the horny, sultry type. You know, women with sweet looks dripping with sex - a whole lot of sex, flooded with it - but who inside are all soft and cuddly like a kitten. It's his nature. Maybe it's his weakness, too.'

'Not only his...' Forester smiled. 'For a guy, heaven is just one long hard-on.' Then back to the normal tempo: 'And you?'

'Me? What about me?'

'You go to France?' he asked, trying to appear discreet, but it wasn't France that interested him. He wanted to know if Nick too groveled at the rapping of her hand – not the hammer, mind, because it's not auctions that interested him, but the naughty boys that deserved a good spanking from Miss archetypal Peterson the generic school*mistress*.

Nick laughed. 'It's not really my cup of tea, Detective. I'm more the shy type... I like to take my time... I go with the cool blends.'

Forester laughed, embarrassed first, then with an amused air. 'We men are insane, aren't we?'

'How do you mean?'

'If a dick had a face, do you know what it would look like?'

'What?

'A man.'

'That makes sense, I guess.'

'Why do we distort women into all these weird, strange sex objects?'

'Maybe they liked to be morphed. You make a fuss over them any way you like, as long as they have your attention. Besides, women do it to us too?'

'Do you really think so?'

'Perhaps; but not as much as men. We're kind of obsessed.'

'Why?'

'I suppose it can't be helped. It's the nature of the sex drive.'

'To produce offspring?'

'No. To imagine.'

'Imagine what?'

'Weird and wonderful things.'

'But still, can't we be more practical than that?'

'No,' said Nick, 'I suppose we can't. Basically, I think we're happy as we are.'

'Why?'

'Because if we weren't, well... then we'd change, wouldn't we? There must be some deep contentment with things, even if it's a paradox.' He started to chuckle with an idea: 'If you had a spare moment to kill, like now for instance, would you prefer to peek up a woman's dress, or think about art?'

He needed only the barest moment to answer that, and said: 'Looking up a woman's dress *is* art!'

They laughed with a roar that was muscular in tempo, and as sweet as pie in titillation. And naturally, for men, it seemed rather fitting at the time. They understood each other perfectly, and appreciated the value of the discourse, even if it wasn't leading anywhere and was just killing time. After all, men, well... that's just the way they are: suckers for sex, grovellers for sex, slaves for sex, obsessed with sex. S. E. X. Sex. And the finest artists in the universe. (Well, wouldn't *you* like to *draw down* what's under a woman's skirt? A-ha... Yes *you* would, wouldn't you... *Naughty***:-)**

A police siren sounded and the traffic slowed and pulled over to the side to let the squad car race by. 'There go the hormones,' said Forester.

Nick smiled, at ease with the conversation, 'It's a man's way...'

'Well, as long as it gets the job done.'

The traffic started moving again and a car behind, seeing the opportunity to slip ahead, took the chance and swiftly pulled in front of them. No law was breached, it wasn't a dangerous maneuver, and Forester took it in his stride. The car carried the emblem of a religious sect who sported bald heads and were attired in strange regalia. Forester started to laugh and narrated to Nick.

'One case I was on a while back involved this religious sect, some offshoot or other, I couldn't make it out. Anyhow, a member of their group was apparently kidnapped, and the villains demanded a ransom. Normal so far, OK? Well, the details aren't important, just the gist that counts. The victim, it turned out, was the actual kidnapper.' He let out a breezy laugh. 'This guy, one of the brothers of their order – it was an extended family, they said, based on spiritual genes, that the soul had a genetic makeup. Crazy idea, huh? Anyhow, this guy abducted himself and set up a scam to extort money from the sect that, for some reason which they wouldn't disclose, barred him from meddling with the accounts. Anyhow, it was all uncovered in the end, and I just got the hell out of there as fast as I could.'

'I follow,' said Nick. 'But what point are you making?'

'Well, a lot of them, these people - and not just religious sects, but take them as an example - they clothe themselves in values; engineer a dialect of exclusivity... But they know, in their more honest moments, that they're not special. Not people of destiny. Not like those that take it in their stride, and couldn't give a damn, but that

205

fate deals them a certain hand and forces them to action. And that defines their identity. It's the bane of their existence, and their gift.'

'You're quite a philosopher,' said Nick.

'Not really. It comes when it comes. I just watch and I learn; that's all. – Fancy a beer?'

Without being in any way self-conscious, Forester genuinely enjoyed conversing with Nick. It was a considerable time since he enjoyed a good conversation. You know how it goes? Your mouth opens and words dribble out, but they don't mean a thing because you're not *really* thinking because your counterpart's not *really* listening so you yak and babble and sigh and shriek and yawn and swear and swig your beer and chew on pretzels and repeat the whole damn circus night after night after night... Then one day, you find yourself *actually* having a conversation, really talking, truly listening. And it's such a priceless, precious thing that you wonder why you don't do it more often.

Just then, seated at a table in a bar drinking their beer, ambient events unfold and they overhear a commonplace couple, the booze still in their mouths, walking past them at the bar. She pokes her dog-on-string Joe Romeo in the ribs meaning it to hurt, and he cries out:

'Shit, babe, what the hell you do that for?'

'Ricky,' she turns on him and barks: 'Shut the fuck up!'

Talk, talk... It's so damn easy.

Barely anyone stirs and few bother to look. Forester leans the glass of cool beer to his lips, tilts it gently, and drinks. Give a moment for the taste to take, ahhh... and it makes him feel all good inside, like a hard day easing to a soft ending. At length, he asks Nick.

'Are you married?'

'No.'

'Ever been?'

'No.'

'Why?'

'You?'

'Yes.'

'And?'

'It came. It matured. It went.'

'Are we talking about cheese?'

'Perhaps.'

'Where did it go wrong?'

'Where? Good question.'

'Another beer?'

'Perhaps later.'

'Cheers,' said Nick, drinking his beer and swayed with the mood for guy-talk and manly narratives. Forester took the lead, with the intruding visions of his wife, his marriage, his hopes and dreams tenderizing him.

'Well, it was good while it lasted. But we hit the rocks. These things happen, I guess.'

'You guess?'

'Her fault. My fault...' He looked around, seeing nothing, just sensing the past. 'You know...?'

'Oh...' was all Nick said. Without a reference point - namely being married himself - it was all he could say, adding a passive aside to fill the silent spaces: 'We live and we learn.'

'No. Not really,' said Forester. 'It stares us in the face, but we don't learn a thing. Or maybe we do...?' he shrugged. 'Well, not that it really matters, because it's all after the fact.' His face carried the inscribed experience of knowing, of being there. The understated expression of a man fed up with a woman who dogs his mind wherever he goes. You see, even failure has its compensations. Kind of... You hitch up with the bitch and get knocked around by a great pair of tits. Heck, so you miss the bruises like hell, and hate her totally but you feel, hey baby, knock me out! So what? Are you looking for a parable? Take a lesson, son. It's the way of the world, this. Live and...

'So why did you marry her?' asked Nick.

'She married me.'

'Oh...'

'I'm a man,' he confessed. 'I'm stupid.'

'And you had no chance at all with her; to make it work?'

'Look!' he struck the table, not hard, but with the sense of doomed bitterness. 'You climb a female mountain, and you're going to fall on your ass. What do you think? She's never going to let you get to the top. Never! She keeps the summit for herself, and only tempts you with it. Like a mug, sure, you try and climb her. But she'll push you off. She'll cause you to slip; stumble; hesitate and falter. And she's laughing all the time, ha ha ha... Yes, ha ha ha. She'll seduce you with every kind of siren cry and feline sigh. Men are drips! - Scaling *her* isn't a journey or a challenge, but a doomed assault course.'

'What can I say to that?'

'Ride on, baby. Ride on!'

Nick bulked. 'I need another drink.'

'Cheer up. I'll get us in some more beer.'

'Excuse me a minute,' said Nick, hesitating with a purpose, and going outside to make a call on his phone. He dialed her number, and she picked up. 'Hi, Vonnie. How are you? It's me, Nick,' he sounded a little nervous. 'Roy's friend. I mean Hard Eight.'

'Hi there. I wondered when you were going to call.' (Not if, but when: a woman always knows). There were soft noises in the background, perhaps a TV, but it never dulled the smooth sheen of her voice, a take-what-she-pleases tone made to measure for a queen of cool.

'Would you like to meet up?' he asked.

'Where? At the club?'

'No. Well... maybe later. Let's have a meal somewhere first.'

'Chinese?'

'Thai.'

'Close enough. You'll pick me up?'

He waited a moment and took a deep breath: 'Absolutely.'

'Good. Nine is fine for me. OK with you? Good. I'll give you my address.'

A while later, flush with achievement, Nick returned to the bar. A fresh glass of beer awaited him. It took Forester barely a moment to figure it out.

'Did you call the bitch?'

'Excuse me?'

'Your woman?'

'Oh,' he lifted his glass. 'Yes. Cheers.'

Their glasses touched, beer rattled and bubbled, and Forester mused aloud: 'Hard habit to break, wouldn't you say?'

'Absolutely,' he agreed.

'We're idiots.'

'Still... however that may be... we're still men. Cheers.'

'Born suckers! - Cheers, and down the hatch.'

As their glasses emptied and refilled, Nick felt the aura of gloom, and it resolved quietly over his face. Forester gave this consideration. Often, being a philosopher and a boozer work wonders in a cop. Forester said:

'Don't tell me, I can guess.'

'What?'

'The last one gave you the boot. Straight down her mountain; the steep side; landed right on your ass.' He confided with empathy, 'I can see it in your face. It shows through the happiness.'

'Ouch! Is it that obvious?'

Forester shrugged in camaraderie: 'Do you want to talk about it?'

'Is there any point? It's over.'

Good conversation is cathartic. Forester knew that intimately, and he'd never seen a shrink in his life – not in private, anyway. He'd arrested several though: for murder, blackmail, public indecency, and the general dispositions that come natural to a quack. 'It's up to you,' he said, and left it there. But at length Nick felt at ease and began to relate:

'I loved her. Followed her around. Did everything for her.'

'Until... What? She dropped dead!'

'She told me to get lost.'

'Why?'

'Who knows.'

'Bitch.'

'Yeah...' Nick yielded. 'I guess she was.'

'You guess?'

'Near enough.'

'Bitch.' He repeated in earnest. The easiest, best categorization of them all. *Keep it simple,* that's what Pop would say. *Don't let the bitch rule your life. Keep her busy with the kids and the cleaning and tell her to keep her trap shut.* It don't work like that these days, Pop. *How the hell would a bitch know unless some stupid sonofabitch opened his mouth in the first place?* It's men's fault, then? *Dumb bastards' fault. Remember that, son.* Sure, Pop. Sure...

Chapter 12

Showtime! And the stage bursts into life, breathing stories, dramas, dreams, fables about to be enacted in lyrical themes from a meter of action to rhythms of desire. And at the center of it all – a song. The lights hint at her beauty, reflecting off her soft skin like percussion cascading from a drum, like sparkles of tone rippling from a bass that storms into your amazed mind and you take a deep breath and gasp *Wow! That's something. Sing, baby, sing...* Applause resounds like endless voices. And some, they just want her to go on forever. And a day... Yeah.

Passion shivers in the tuning souls of jazzmen, shaping rhythms from a bustling frenzy, lifting worlds of harmony out of the primeval chaos of a drum, a horn, a sax, piano and a bass, sifting though divine improvisation until the scores of ecstasy catch hold, and you're hooked, like the brunette by the bar baiting her john, drawing him in, fish on a line, reel at a time: *Gotcha, sucker!* Nabbed by the balls. Irresistible really. He's a guy. He takes the highs and the lows. And she's a-humming *'Come to me, baby...'* And fun cocaine consumed by revelers in a smooth vice of soft intoxication. *It's a wrap. It's a laugh. It's a gas; ha ha ha...* Isn't it divine? Well... Some differ and regard self-indulgence as a drag, kind of an unlit cigarette drag - suck all you like, it just ain't gonna burn. Is silence their thing? With prayer, hey, you can't really have a fling. Can you? That ain't jazz. Or is it? Quiet moments, sure, they're kind of cool, interlude cool... And besides, among the roaring crowd no one is really alone - it's intimacy fashioned in delirium. And that's the prize of a sexy song, circumcised all along its pumping riffs... It makes the flesh shiver: spine, toes, cock – that a real master-shake. Let's rock. Music, maestro, don't stop. This is communal therapy jazzed up as entertainment. It's Life – and you don't sit this one out. Get up and dance. It's what they want. It's what we need. There's ecstasy in suffering excess, sometimes, having it always on tap, going way-way-way-over-the-top, much as the life-juice of the drunken bum guzzling the liquid majesty down deep into his guts, because that's the only way this stuff will reach the brain, where it's really needed, where it sings sweetly to him, and he can dream. Up there. The seat of craving. He's a guzzler of the world, him, this bum, laying idly on his back gazing up at the stars – although it's still broad daylight. But he can see them because he has a friend that opens his eyes – *booze*. And these guys are best buddies, real close. They're star-men. They travel through the cosmos together faster than the speed of light. And all done with a smile as wide as the world. 'Come for a star-trip?' says booze, smiling. Yeah. Cosmic haloes; red giants, Andromeda and Orion, he wants to do the grand tour; it's what he needs, what he wants. And even if it don't listen (because, hey, it's just stuff in a bottle: when full, he's a pal; when empty, she's a bitch) in the star-burst of desire, something comes of nothing. It's primordial. It's a first cause. It's human. You want it. This. The notion to have, the will *not* to resist, to abase yourself before it – *gratification.* Yeah! That's all it takes. That's the essence *burning* for your meat. Desire. Longing. Life. This. *Sizzle....*

And Roy bathes in the swell of the music, soaking it all up. Drip, drip, drip...

'Well, babe, what do you think?'

'I'm tempted, Roy,' says the kitten winsomely, licking his ear, touching his... *Meow!*

'Ah. So am I...' he sighed indulgently. 'So am I...' *Meow!*

They gaze and listen, embracing the spectacle, enraptured by the sound, because the diva's left the stage and the band, too intoxicated to stop, plays on, the muscular notes of the drummer beating *boom boom boom*, pounding out stories from the essence of the score, jamming on and on, clearing the way for the easy speed of a sax taking its time, sliding into blues, the curvature of melody is saxophone blues, knock knock, opening doors for the pumping leaps of a bass scaling the breadth of decibels, bridging the rapid dash of piano joining in the chase, rhythms in the mind of the flesh in a whiplash of sounds and frenzy made to measure from a dream leaping over each other. Can't stop! The band plays on because that's what it does.

That's what it wants. A desire. A need. A passion. Infatuation. Instant love. Climax in the tempo – Ahhh! And you can't fake that. And the audience holds its breath, enraptured, and listens. Moremoremore... Ahhh!

At the next table there's a party of three wiseguys, not the religious kind, unless it's jazz and women that form the canons of their faith. Philosophy came in starlight packed in bottles of booze; in whores dressed up like queens pouting 'I want you inside of me... baby,' as cigarettes hover on their lipsticked lips and the billowy smoke curls up in a smooth whirl. When they inhale and the tip burns red - Ouch! That hurts. Do it again. Do it again... As the band plays on it swallows a hectic rhythm and out comes a giddy beat. The experimental side of jazz explodes on stage, and it's fireworks time. The audience erupts. It's one, long climax.

Even the wiseguys are connoisseurs, and know when jazz leaps into the throes of invention, and they chirp in seedy sequence:

'What's happening?' begins the wiseguy with the loutish air, Mr. Lout, mouthing his ignorance in a shameless tease. 'What are they doing,' wonders Mr. Lout, a decibel above the music, 'hypnotizing us?'

'No. They're tearing at sounds, savaging them, and creating new ones,' said the sleazy looking geezer, Mr. Sleaze, sweating to his knees, eyeing up the girls, gazing on those chandeliers and pearls – body jewellery that the hookers wear to dazzle a crowd, to pull a cock, sensual idioms of her spirit that says: *Pay, and you get to come with me. And even slap me around a little. Ha ha ha....* Her flesh, well, her flesh is a tease. Yes please... And Mr. Sleaze wants to know: 'What's the brunette by the bar like in the sack?'

'It's all sweet music,' adds Mr. wiseguy number three, ra-ta-ta-tat. 'You can always sing along to it, I guess.' And off he goes, yanking at the beat, tapping his feet, discovering meaning in the music again and again and again...

'Yeah,' added Mr. Lout, knocking back a whiskey. 'It would blow my mind.'

'While she,' dared Mr. Sleaze, pointing to the lioness at the bar, 'blows you.'

'*He he he...*' adds number three, superfluously.

The best, and the worst it seems, come in threes: wise men; wiseguys; *he he he*...

And the musicians pack the weight of rhythms in a visceral punch and blow the roof away to the resounding roar and applause of those aficionados of the perfect score. Encore! Encore! Don't stop. Give it to us raw. Moremoremore...

'Roy,' purred the kitten, hugging his arm. 'What are they doing?'

'Playing jazz.'

'Jazz?... Can't they stop?'

'There's no beginning; so there's no end.'

'I don't understand,' she said, twitching her inquisitive nose at him. 'Roy?'

'Jazz.'

'Huh?..'

'Jazz.'

Listen. Jazz. Spell it out J. A. Z. Z. Jazz. Say it – Jazz. Again. Jazz.

'Got it, babe?'

'I... I think so.'

'Jazz.'

It's hot in here. Damn hot. The air fans are down. The smoke, static. Only the music moves. He came in quietly, unnoticed, and nosed around a bit. Casually, he wanders to the front, eking out space between hookers and the drunks, and slaps a fifty on the bar. Beer. Make that two. The guy's alone. Maybe he's thirsty. Change? Keep it. He's in a good mood. A generous mood. The bartender smiles and gestures to the band. Yeah, says the stranger, sipping his beer, he's here for the jazz. So why is he staring at Roy? The hookers tease him with a smile, but he takes no notice. One asks him for a light. Says he doesn't smoke. She moves away – he's queer, she mumbles in aside. He takes it in his stride. Anyway, he prefers brunettes, not sham blondes. Women are art. A work of art. You can't screw around with the colors. It messes things up. He takes out a deck of playing cards and beckons a waitress. He throws an eight of diamonds on her tray and places the other beer on top. It falls hard on the eight and he gives her ten. She's cute. Her smile's cuter. He makes it twenty.

'That guy there?' she says, pointing to Roy.

'Yeah. Take it to him, sweetie.'

'OK.'

He followed her with his eyes as she weaves between the tables, the tray aloft floating like a comet on its weaving trajectory to its final destination. Roy looks at it, gazes at the beer, sees the card, and picks it up. He's curious, grins, then his eyes follow the guiding finger of the waitress.

'Has he been here long?'

'I don't think so, sir. Would your lady friend like another drink?'

The lady friend's not the humble sort. A pitcher of beer is not her thing, bubbly cream is more her style, and she meows and orders champagne.

'French or American?'

'French, of course,' rebuked the kitten. 'What do you think? They make it in Kentucky!'

While the girl-girl banter heats up Roy slips away and replaces the card in the middle of the pack, the stranger holding out the deck in halves, part in each hand, now folding them over and placing the deck on the bar.

'My lucky card,' says Roy.

'I'm partial to the queen myself.'

'Brunettes your thing, eh?'

'So long as she's a princess,' he replies, smiles, lifts and shuffles the deck, finally holding it out. 'Split,' he said. 'Highest card speaks first.'

'After you.'

Confidently, he selects and turns over a card. It's a ten of clubs. Not bad. Good odds. Hmm.

Randomness rolls, and Roy picks a king – diamonds.

'Luck,' said the stranger.

'I'm on a roll,' said Roy, and finally they shook hands smiling fondly at each other. 'Long time no see, Steady.' His name is William Banks, alias Steady Hand because at poker he's as cool as the moon. Nothing fazes him, not even his own hand.

'Who's the lady? I've not seen her before. Is she new?'

They looked at the kitten as she argued with the waitress. She was really kind of beautiful; her naiveté was the source of her confidence, it gave her a breathy way with words, with managing relationships, and her soft prettiness always easy on the eyes. You can't help but smile. A warm smile. And Roy was proud of her.

'It started out as a casual fling. I picked her up at a game in Vegas. But damn, I'm hooked on her now. I can't let her go. – So, Steady, to what do I owe the pleasure? Are you just passing through?'

'Bartender. Two beers.'

'I heard about the game you had in Rome with Zander. That's the second time you two have sparred at the poker table, right?'

'The last time he squeezed me like a lemon. I had to win my money back, Roy. I'd lose my nerve for ever otherwise. You know how it is,' he said. 'Plus interest. I needed my confidence back. It's a fragile thing. And I can't be losing that, not for anything.'

'How much are you ahead?'

'A cool million-five,' he beamed with pride. 'Plus a half. He got a bit cocky with his kings, and I had to use my nines' trick.'

Roy gazed with awe. 'You have real balls to stake that much and hold your nerve. I take my hat off to you, Steady. You're a real pro.'

'To tell you the truth, Roy, I got a bit lucky in there. I almost folded with the nines. That kind of bluff tests any man. After the game ended Zander rose, shook my hand, and strolled out with a big warm smile, a lemon-crusher smile. He'll be back. That smile says he'll be back.'

'We can all use some luck around here.'

'Did you know he went head-to-head with Diamond Bedouin?'

'The Diamond?'

'Yeah. That guy packs Arabia in his pocket. He's got it all rolled up.' He chuckled. 'Arabia! Talk about a starry sky. Bursting with diamonds.'

'When? Where?'

'A couple of weeks back at a private game in Paris. Zander strides in with that big cozy smile, a lemon-crusher smile; that myth-making look, and starts flirting softly with the threat: "Dionysus is dancing for me tonight. Wine. Cigarettes. Light..." and he takes his seat; orders coffee, deep black; soda breeze on the side; lights a cigarette; and the shows begins.'

'That's theatre for you.'

'What a game!'

'He won, didn't he?'

'Rumor says twenty-five.'

'Ouch!' he cringed enviously. Zander, his lemon-crusher smile and all, apparently had some deal going with the Gods on Olympus. It would seem to serve a man handsomely to befriend the legends. Roy sighed with awe and they nestled elbow to elbow at the bar.

'Roy, while I was there in Paris, around ten days ago, your name came up.'

'Me!' He was astonished, gaping at him. 'Are you sure?'

'I was just killing time at a casino, and a group of guys strolled in and started knocking around, just dime stuff, you know, testing their nerve, fondling the chips more than playing with them. Anyway, while dipping their toes in at the tables, they started talking about the bank you work for. It was just rambling stuff at first, but then your name came up. And that English guy you work with.'

'Nick?'

'That's the guy. They kept on referring to him as *Tom Thumb*. Is that a pet name, or a riddle?'

'Are you certain about this?' This was startling news, a quixotic mix of precision and fecklessness: men will brag, men will shoot their mouths off and feel themselves invincible, pouring out bravado and daring - shaken, and not stirred, and knocked back all at once as though they owned the world. Roy breathed hard, the muscles on his face tightened, and he grew more assertive. 'How did - '

'Excuse me, sir,' the waitress abruptly cut in. 'The *lady* says you'll pay.'

'Who?'

'Your *lady friend*, sir,' she fumed. Only another woman can make her mad like that. And the prettier the madder.

'Pay for what?'

'Champagne. French. She *insists* on French.'

He glanced over proudly at the kitten, 'Well, she's my girl.' He paid, waved to Barbie (yeah, that's her real name) who excitedly watched a waiter pop the cork, and Roy continued the conversation.

'These guys, Steady, who were they?'

'I have no idea; but they were speaking way over my head. Technical jargon mostly mixed in with some guy quips and casual banter. Altogether, they must have uttered the word *network* a hundred times or more: go into this *network*, go into that *network*... They're experts of some kind. My feeling is they're way out of their depth where gambling's concerned – they weren't a casino crowd. They weren't naturals for it. They're uncomfortable with the character of chance. Poker would whack them any day. They're more the exact kind: science, math, engineering, that kind of thing. Some of them drank too much, started shooting their mouths off. Kind of bragging. It's cliché. But you could read between the lines. At bottom... it was serious. You can tell; it's a guy thing. They meant business - whatever it was.'

'I know you're telling it straight, Steady; but are you sure? I mean, what you're saying is quite incredible.' He gazed at him, mesmerized and wary at the same time. 'You weren't perhaps a bit worse for a drink or two?'

'I know where you're coming from, Roy, and I'd feel exactly the same way. But there's no doubt.'

'None?'

Steady breathed-in hard, looked him squarely in the eye, and said. 'It's a question of instinct, Roy. Instinct.'

Roy prized the player's instinct above almost anything else. And *Steady Hand* was not merely a pet name to amuse a crowd. It defined an instinct in him. Poker was his game, the outward expression of his leanings, but his instincts were the real champ. They had foresight; they called the shots.

'Steady, these guys, what were they doing there?'

'It beats me.'

'Did they have any real intention to gamble?'

Steady shook his head. 'Whatever it was, they weren't there to play. Not to gamble; no sir. To observe; perhaps to learn... I can't say. But not to play.'

'Steady, can you remember what they said? The order it was said too, it's very important.'

'I can do a lot better than that.'

'What?'

He took out a small voice recorder. 'I always carry it with me; wherever I go.' He smiled with pride. 'You can learn a great deal from the things people say, and how they say it. The whole nature of a tone is very revealing. Voices have always fascinated me.' He fondled the recorder, tantalizing it with a tickle. Sure, it's a machine; and fondness aside, it meant something to him. 'A tap leaks water. People leak themselves through words. You can't catch water; you can't hold a word. All you have to do is *listen*. In fact, that's all you can do. But this makes us wise. Here, Roy, now it belongs to you.'

'If I was the Pope, Steady - no, if I was God - I'd make you my right hand man.' He heaved a sigh of utter gratitude. 'I owe you for this, buddy. More than you'll ever realize.' He took possession and smothered it with his hands, fearing it would vanish if he blinked ever so fleetingly. Here, he felt, he was holding keys to those voyeuristic eyes of AI spying on his business, gaping into the data networks, fondling his operations from afar. In any machine, any system, any process where the hand of man lays claim, the human is the perfect foil. Somewhere, there is always a sucker. And sooner or later he spills the beans.

'Roy,' began Steady, sounding a note of caution, 'there was one guy that stood out. He *was* the exception. The others I could sniff out; but he was a puzzle. He kept away from the gaming tables, aloof, but involved in an odd way. He was being deliberate in that. He wanted to be invisible, but there; if that makes any sense. A kind of *presence*.'

'Like a fly on the wall?'

'Kind of. But he also tended to steer them.'

'How?'

'When they drifted to the bar, or the lounge, he would guide them back to the gaming room, gently, so they almost wouldn't notice.' Steady took a sip of his drink, consuming time as well as licker as he recalled: 'You could tell, even in glimpses, he was a player. He had that expression, that look of a man used to the cards, holding them close to his chest. I've seen it. I know it. There's no mistaking it. Even when he spoke, the sparkle of intrigue, of a dare, of gamesmanship, resonated in every syllable. – I must sound poetic to you, Roy.'

'Yes, you do.'

'And you know that isn't me. I'm straight thinking. I see it as it is.'

'So he was a poem?'

'Well, he's a player, and there's nothing prosaic about that. We could charm the wings off angels if we had to. And he had *that look*.'

Roy knew exactly what he meant, but repetition was a source of strength, so he asked. 'What look?'

'Winning eyes. The man that spots the ace in the pack. He can ante with an angel, raise the stakes to heaven and beyond, and win. Those eyes don't just see; they play. What's a needle in the haystack to these guys? Nothing. Hand in a glove. It fits. He finds it. He had it, Roy.'

'Damn...'

'He studied how a man played cards; how often he called; how people placed bets at the roulette table; who yielded first at baccarat. He wasn't just watching. He was predicting. He was simulating them. He could put himself in their place and tweak his mind until he got them just right. Just like me, at whatever game I play, I am a player, an actor, and a spirit all in one. I don't just sit with my rivals; I conjoin with them; with the game. - That's what I saw, and he had it in abundance. Roy, he had it all. And he used it. All of it.'

That look – to write a scene in real time, to improvise, to draw with instinct, to see things not as objects, but as pure potential. *That look.*

For some guys, you perhaps, a deck of cards can never be just something that you play with. To handle them is to dare the riddle of life. The turn of a card prompts you not with ah, but with a wow! You breathe them, you smell them, you taste them, you live with them and dream of them and speak to them. They equate to a separate identity, a spirit, an obsession.

'Who was he?' asked Roy, absorbed.

'Some guy. I've never seen him before. Tall. Nordic looking. Mediterranean smile.'

'Did he have an accent?'

'Faint. Why?'

'You overhear a name?'

'Name? None that I remember. But they found it amusing when a waiter asked if they wanted their whiskey with ice. "Yes", says the Nordic guy, "make sure it bites first." Then he hugs the blonde babe next to him and plants her a kiss. They start smooching and she bleats something in French. Then her tongue's all over his, fencing away. I think to myself: is she biting, or is it the ice?'

'Cute.'

'He seemed to take it sentimentally, though.'

'How do you mean?'

'You know us guys, Roy, our idiosyncrasies; they're part of our ego; part of being a man. Sloppy? Sure. A failing? OK. But they're clues to our nature.'

'Maybe you're pushing this a little too far.'

'OK, I admit, it's just a hunch. But it seemed to mean something to him. Ice bites. He latched on to it; even if done softly.'

It's just testosterone; a guy thing. Men tend to incorporate the most incidental details as personal adjuncts of their character. Not that they have any real significance. No. It's just the way they are. Guys.

Steady caught the bartender and gestured for a refill:

'Two whiskeys please.'

'Ice, sir?'

'Make sure it bites!'

'Coming right up.'

'You look as if you know something already,' said Steady, hinting. 'As if you know what's in there?' he indicated the recorder.

'Let's just say I have a pretty good idea.'

'Sure,' he chuckled. 'After all, what use is a secret if it doesn't tease, if it doesn't brag and offer a dare to have itself exposed? That's why women are the best kept secret. No matter how many times they disrobe, they're still a mystery. And we always want them to be.'

Roy clutched the recorder superstitiously. Fear, excitement, power, hope, together these coalesced into a heady mix and left him feeling vulnerable. 'Part one is closed. And this is part two.'

'Let's hope you find what you're looking for. A lucky two, Roy.'

'This,' he tapped the recorder, 'is a start. Perhaps more than a start, maybe even an end game. Perhaps part three. But...' he hesitated, struggling with deeper anxiety that rose to check him.

'But what?'

'The past few days have tested me in ways that... well, quite frankly, I'm not equal to. I don't know what to trust anymore. I've realized, anything that can be manipulated is suspect. And machines, well, they can be manipulated in all sorts of ways; and yet we depend on them.'

'What are you getting at, Roy?'

'Some clues, Steady, they send you the wrong way.' He reflected on the past several days, and felt humbled by events. 'Sometimes, there are missed opportunities; and other times there are things... how can I put this?... *arranged* in the wrong way, and made to seem like something else entirely.' He chuckled nervously. 'I know this must sound strange, but some pictures just don't fit the frame.'

'Like some poker games I've known.'

'You're spot on, Steady. Like those card games that drag on and wear you down, this whole episode epitomizes that. I've bet more than I have, and playing on borrowed time. - I just hope desperation doesn't get the better of me, and I start reading clues into things that were never there.'

'Play it slow,' he advised him thoughtfully. 'That's what I would do. It's perseverance that counts now; and you've just got to grind it out. It's tough, sure. But what else can you do? When you can't dictate events, do what you must to preserve your hand. And never show until you have to. The secret to keeping a secret is – Ah, thanks. Keep the change.'

The bartender brought the drinks, and the ice cubes looked like silver crystal balls suspended in a golden liquid of whiskey. They shared a quiet moment of reflection. Sometimes, even a brief spell of silence is worth a thousand words.

'Things are not as they seem, Steady. Odd things have been happening at the bank that I just don't know even how to begin explaining. And I'm not only speaking about prying eyes, not just fingers frisking through the networks. I'm referring to intrusion. To deep infiltration. A threat. And all done with the greatest stealth. I've got to hand it to them - it's magnificent what they do. Whoever they are, they possess amazing skill. I'm inspired and terrified at the same time. I confess, Steady, there are some real smart people out there, who really know how to spin the dice. And they're playing for high stakes. They scare me.'

'Loaded dice?'

'Yes.'

'And whatever this is, they won't let you play. That's it, isn't it?'

Steady had lifted the curtain and cast the spotlights, and there he was, Roy, on life's stage, alone, overtaken with events and staring out into an arena of hidden eyes that see him, while he knows not a single one. Hitherto, he had persuaded himself that aggression and confronting a ghost made sense, but all that a spent force thrives on are the echoes of defeat, of frustration. Sometimes, you have to gaze in the mirror and admit: I'm wrong. *Maybe I'm not up to this. I'm an ass*. Pride gets in the way, sure, but the will to win runs deep in him and, committing himself to battle, clutched the recorder like he were unsheathing a sword, and said. 'I've been fighting blind. I've been an ass. But now, with this...' he held up the recorder, 'with this, I'm not playing blind any more. No one's cutting me out of the game. I'll be able to see the cards. And it's my turn to call.'

'But not the face. To win at this, Roy, you have to see the other man's face. Close up. Proximity is the only threshold that matters. You have to see the player sitting at the same table. If he can see you, you had better see him. Close up.'

Roy breathed deeply, troubled with the challenge but determined to confront it. The human will, when stretched, takes one hell of a pounding. 'I promise you this, Steady,' he said, steeling himself in that emotionally charged moment, 'I'm just getting started. And I'm going all the way.'

'Well, I hope you know what you're doing.'

'Tell me more about these guys. Everything you remember.'

'Like I said, they're not players, apart from that Nordic looking guy. They're not gamblers. Whatever they are, they're not that. I can spot a player a mile away. These guys are probably engineers. Deal them a Royal Flush, and they think it's the Queen of Spades in Alice in Wonderland raving to her men: *Off with her head!* Poor Alice,' he chuckled. 'They'd give the game away. – Do you want my advice?'

'Every time.'

'If a man insists on playing his own game, by his own rules, the only way to win is to play by your own ones.'

'That's like the blind playing the blind.'

'Well, at least you're on equal terms. Cheers.'

'Cheers.'

And they touched glasses. For luck, that is. Luck. Ancient luck. Superstitious luck to chase the spirits away. But now the spirits are machines. Engineered with precision, computable, devoid of emotion and lacking awareness of the meaning of a game; the desire to compete, to dare, to win. You can't just approach them and say *Tell me?* It's the essence of consciousness as you ponder to yourself the riddle... *And will machines ever whisper in the dark?*

'Roy.'

'Hi, babe. Meet Steady.'

'Hi, Steady.'

'Hi, sweetie.'

'Oh Roy...'

'Yes, babe?'

'I'm lonely over there. Come... join me. Bring your friend. Join us, Steady.'

'Sure.'

That's nice. That's sweet. She's so open and cute and precious. She has a mind of her own. And she prods the waitress as she goes stalking by, 'We'll have another bottle of champagne.' She smiles. '*French,* of course.'

And sure she's seething back at her *You effing bitch* behind that immobilized stare. But who cares? Barbie gets to pop another bottle of the best bubbly around, and pop the waitress one at the same time. It's a game, sure, but fun too. And ladies being ladies, well, whether dressed or disrobed, on the moon or in a sinking ship, they are going to play, and try and have their own way. Every time.

And it makes life just that little bit more interesting. Because what is life if not to win, even if the spoils are no more than conceits, or the mere fluff of flattery? Occasionally, even the smallest things can make you feel a giant; a real swaggering colossus. And getting one over a rival, even a nipper of a victory, is sooooooo sweet. Time rests neatly on your shoulders then, and all you want to do is touch glasses and laugh and drink champagne and...

'Just listen to her sing,' said Roy amazed, as the diva turned on her soprano voice and gave her heart and soul to a song. Such passion you can only be born with. Mighty. Sublime. Deepest human. And it takes a great voice to open your mind to wonder.

Yeah!

Chapter 13

Midnight. Zero. And the night had just begun. Roy started warming up, loosening the brace of his wristwatch his hands felt tense but he stretched his fingers all the same, nighttime was the right time, though the kitten had misgivings and began to purr, meowing softly:

'Roy.'

'Yes, babe?'

'I'm tired...'

Steady checked out before Midnight Serenades beat the clock by some twenty minutes, and jaded punters were kept feeling lively with a bevy of routine numbers croaked out in tune - a blond chick and balding geezer in matching blue outfits swooning lullabies to one another: I love you. You love me. We love our love. Great love. This love. That love. Love... riffs fine-tuned in a whiskey glass, honed in lyrical decanters, perfumed in sweet wine, matured in sentimental spirits murmuring in dripping cask of soothing tempo, a grape song, a harvest mood made lazy-whimsical sweating not from heat, but the blandness of a time-filler, an interlude, a song to know, to sing along with, a ballad to smile at, and then forget... It kind of goes around like that, and the early birds among the crowd slipped out during the interlude and headed home to get their seven winks. One, two, three, four... snooze. Some sleep to kindle a dream; others because it's a fact of life, and for them, life ain't do darn dream, but a story narrated by authority demanding to know "Why the hell are you late this morning...?" These guys take the heat, because basically though it seems hard, their life is really neat – in a practical everyday sense. It kind of fits: hand in a glove. Sure, listening to the soprano sing and feisty jazz shaking their bones, it makes them giddy with desire, the atmosphere kicks and embraces them and says *Come here, you gorgeous bitch, and kiss me*. These guys are like the rest of us, they feel eternity's soft breath in those moments – *God, what a thing!* - And darn thing is life it makes them yearn to be top-heavy – guys with style and dames with panache, laden with liquid cash, all brimming with indulgence. They can dream, can't they? Sure. Look close – hey, not that close. And you'll see contentment is seldom a fixed thing, even for your bottom-heavy types, the kind that let fly off-the-cuff expletives and sigh *Oh my, ain't life a bitch...* but accept their predicament all the same. It's called resignation with things, with what you are. And even though they see the things they're never likely to possess, or ever taste a pinch of in this ironic contradictory world, all the same, they're just like us – only different. Life, it's ironic. Drunk from a whiskey glass, with ice, it's a tonic. It sings you a song, and you listen and dream, and reply when it's done, *Goodnight.* What else can you say? And you pay your bill, adjust your neck-tie, slip on your blazer, climb into your car, slide in the key and turn on her ignition, ahhh, she revving, she sounds OK, notch her up a touch, a bit more gas, that's it, and get her moving, easy there, babe.... stop at the lights when the whimsy of the night turns them red, push her back into gear when they switch green, pull over to the side when the boom of a squad car roars and races by, casually sigh, light up a cigarette, turn on the radio, look over your shoulder, start her up again, drive, twenty minutes later, *Hi honey, I'm home,* and hit the sack. Because life, like the song, knows you'll be back. Again, and again, and again...

Roy received a call on his phone. Usually, that's ecstasy ringing, the sound of someone who wants to know you, but now it made him feel moody. One moment he seemed busy, morose, anxious, and then sounded pleased. The kitten moaned and he hung up.

'It's Nick. He's coming over with Vonnie?'

'Who?'

'Yvonne. You know, Vonnie.'

'Oh,' she griped. '*Her!*'

The kitten's a cat. Meow. She knows how to bite, flexes her jaws just right, she looks at things and slithers her gaze, like a sidewinder weaving through a maze. But hey, don't be a fool, Vonnie's cool, she's part of the scene, this having your cake and eating it too, with cream, mmm, true... things of the moment destined to endure: champagne, cigarettes, jazz, love, living it up. Sure, she's one of them; part of the troop, guys and kittens entwined in a loop. It makes perfect tasty sense, and Roy naturally came to her defense: 'Look at it this way, babe, in my addicted eyes you're worth a thousand times more to me than her; but we can't do without Vonnie. She's like champagne; like jazz; like cigarettes; like love. It would be a mistake to do without her. And I'm a businessman. I can't make mistakes.'

'Why?'

'Do you want to be poor?'

'Oh...'

Compromise or common sense? Back to back, they're the same thing. That's a wrap!

Ten minutes later the stage clears. Showtime yields to audition-time and the bandleader takes five and lights up a cigar. He smiles at Roy and conveys him a greeting, which was more than merely gesture, it was buddy-talk: a breezy wave with a hand is worth a thousand handshakes. Roy replies in kind and the kitten kind of stares like she's lost in the wilderness of midnight jazz until the bandleader strolls over and shakes Roy's hand, taking a seat at his table.

'No game on tonight?' he said.

'Fellas took a beating on Sunday,' said Roy, matter-of-factly.

'So I heard.'

'And then there's always the woman of the house to contend with. She wants to know what the suckers have done with *her* hard earned money.'

'They lost it.'

'No. I won it.'

'You're the man, Roy!'

'I guess I am,' he boasted smugly, grinning. 'And the woman of the house -'

'The boss?'

'Yes. She knows hubby better than he knows himself. And she makes sure he knows his place in the greater scheme of things.'

'Under her thumb.'

'Where else!'

'Takes all kinds, Roy. Takes all kinds...'

'What have you got set up for tonight?'

'Some kid's coming in to audition.'

'On what?'

'Piano.'

'What's he play?'

'Old stuff. New stuff,' he smiled. 'It's jazz in the mix.'

'Great. Can't wait.'

'Speak of the devil. There he is now.' He rose from his seat and headed for the stage. 'You're early.'

'Sorry, boss.'

'No problem.' He parked his cigar in the astray, and climbed up on stage, strapping into the jazz quintet like he was a rocket man about to blast off for the stars. 'Let's see what you can do.'

Technically, it's mere improvisation, but ranks as something deeper to adore. The sound's not sentimental - he's pure energy, this kid. He's not content to work the formulas and tease out yet another revival number, but makes it sound fresh, energized, undeniably exciting. It's the toxic exotica of soloists blending into an orchestra of virtuosos reinventing pastiche pieces of the past performed with pizzazz and timing out to the future.

'The kid knows how to rock.'

'It's jazz.'

'I know. But jazz can rock too, can't it?'

'I guess it can.'

He's a young man, draped in an amalgam of feisty wear and slick soles to boot, his eyes a-dazzle with the afterglow of dope, his hands big like they could hold the world and caress it, just so, easy, like rolling up a joint, and infusing that consenting spell like magical intoxication.

'What's your name again, son?'

'John.'

'John?' he seemed to question it. It didn't sound right.

'John.' His soft reply sets off the boom of the big boss chewing on that cigar, fondling a guitar, plucking the strings not to make any melodic sense but as a counterweight to tapping his feet. 'Where you been at?' he threw him a glance, more friendly than the last.

'Playing bars; places and some... You know?'

'Let's hear you play some more. On that big mamma over there.'

He makes his way self-consciously over to the grand piano, takes a seat, looks up at the boss chewing that big, big ciiiiiiiiiigar, and waits.

'OK now, you relax and follow me.'

Cat and mouse or hare and the fox – is he going to lose him in the sweep of the piece, or be gentle and lead him to the grand finale? Those big wide eyes floating above that big cigar - cunning or benevolence, what's his intent? The boy looks up and waits. 'OK.'

'On my cue; one; two... Ease yourself into the tempo.'

'I don't understand.' He breaks the sound and the big boss leads in with:

'The beat.'

'Huh?'

'Don't you understand?'

Sure he understands. He likes this boy, he was a kid just like him once; eyes wide, big hands, a jazzman piece by piece stitching the soul of harmonies together till the music drums and beats within you like a second heart, reverberating: *Boom, Boom. Boom...*

Those big white teeth pin that big brown cigar and the big fat boss lets out a big wide smile and cocks his yes-sir-eee head at the kid. 'I done gone and found me a jazzman. *Yeah!*' And the tuned strings of his big guitar thunder into motion all at once, and it's rapture in sounds galore, a medley improvised on rock and roll and blues and soul and classical recital with a bang and pizzazz and rat-a-tat-tat... audio firepower pounds the stage with crescendo-tipped styles, harmony-charged notions innovating to the beat and muscle of the drums, bass men trained in hustling and pimping their instruments to the soft swell of a breezy stride across the stage. No one can remain still here as imagination and sound make love. He's damn well hot sophisticated, this boy, he's well traveled - to the Bronx and back. What does he know?

'Jazz. I know jazz.'

Kinda like jazz, according to custom, mood, taste, even after-taste, bitter at first, then turning sweet, cum-coated sweet. A hangover boom from a trumpet charges the air, sexing expectation, the accumulating ensemble of bassoon and sax take him on, until the whole shebang dissolved into homogenized sound, top heavy cymbals on the rocks, percussion as raw as it gets, as frantic as discipline allows, each finger on the piano key burning with velocity tapping micro movements in microseconds in the swooning serenades across the ivory and nigger keys, like an atomic particle racing through the cosmos. This is rapture. This is love. Mad love. Sex. Jazz.

'Roy?'

'Yeah, babe?'

'Can we leave now?'

'Sure. In a minute. Just wait a moment more.'

'Roy...'

'You see, babe, we can't just leave like this.'

'Roy...'

'It's like a child being born. It's a miracle. We have to see it through.' Tragedy, happiness, completeness, incompleteness. It was jazz all over again, morphing the volume until silence wept, and the only thing that was left in the whole universe was... *the sound.*

Like jazz. Jazz... A now. A never. A forever. A...

Twenty minutes later the kitten perks up. She's a moody character at the best of times, and at the worse – moody, what else? *Oh Roy, isn't it lovely. Love you to bits! Kiss kiss...* She gets ninety-nine percent for consistency, and one for fascination. But he loves her deeply, infatuation manifestly sensual and serene at the same time. It's a guy thing, sure, enraptured with a blonde, a babe, sweet as pie, with a body made to be adored, so it's love like a jazz-set, improvised but fundamentally profound, so that ratio ninety-nine to one gets inverted as swiftly as the musical stars on stage jettison symphony and take flight with their instruments, seizing the raw moment and pounding it with sound - Star-men. Jazzmen. Synonymous on the stage of music, the stage of life, of love; of life and love. Yeah. Man star. Man jazz. A*men* to that.

'Hi, Roy, sorry we're late.'

'Nick, about time. What took you so long? Have a seat.'

'Hi, Roy,' said Vonnie, looking only at him, and then referring obliquely to the kitten. 'And you are..?'

'An angel in disguise,' she said perkily.

'Ah,' jeered Vonnie softly, 'I thought so.'

Seated side by side in mutual disdain bound up with perfect manners, the ladies yielded to a formal (though very personal) truce, ordered their drinks, Vonnie lit a cigarette, the kitten prettied up her pretty face with a mirror, lipstick, and mascara, and they listened to the music while Roy conversed with Nick.

'Has Frank headed off home, or is he sniffing around the streets again?'

'Home.'

'And that cop; he keeps snooping about. What's he after?'

'I'm not sure. But he thinks what happened... you know, was perhaps intended for Frank.'

'Is he in any danger?'

Nick shrugged and looked baffled. 'I really don't know.'

'And Frank? What does he think?'

'He seems, how can I say, to take it in his stride.... in his own peculiar way.'

'I think it's bullshit,' Roy hammered the table, turbulently stirring the drinks and spilling them a piece, and the women gazed indignantly at him. 'Sorry, ladies.'

'Listen, Roy,' Nick continued, turning to something that was troubling him. 'This cop thinks that there may be some connection with France.'

'France?'

'You were there recently, right? I told him you were.'

'And what of it? Nothing, Nick. It was just a routine affair. Why even mention it? I went to a seminar at the bank. I arrived; looked around; went through the motions; and came home again. Voila!'

'What happened?'

'Nothing happened. Well... just some open discussion, some wine, a little poker when I got the chance. It was tedious, Nick – apart from the poker, that is. That's never tedious. Anyway, three days and back home again. What's this damn cop after, a blow job?'

Now that was crude, idiotically crude and uncalled for, and the women were furious, glaring at him with contempt. Roy raised his arms in mock surrender and ordered more drinks by way of apology. 'Go on,' he said, 'knock me one on the chops; I deserve it.' Moody like the twinkling stars in their feistier moments, the kitten rose first and went to the ladies' room. Vonnie, a moment later, joined her.

'Well,' said Roy, 'at least it got rid of them for a while.'

'Crassness has its compensations, I suppose,' Nick remarked with understated humor. Roy showed him the voice recorder, explaining what it contained.

'Did you listen to it?'

'Yes. They even mention you?'

'Me.'

'All of us. They refer to you as *Tom Thumb*.'

'Tom Thumb?'

'Yes. Does that mean anything to you?'

'That's sheer whimsy, wouldn't you say?'

'Whimsy?'

'*Tom* I can accept; but *Thumb* is the butt-end of a joke, surely.'

Roy shook his head. 'Never mind...'

'Who are they? What are they up to? What do they want?'

'Steady reckons it's a kind of *game*.'

'*Game?*'

'Well, he's bound to see it that way I suppose, isn't he?'

'See what? How? Who are they?'

'I don't recognize any of the voices. There's an American among them sounding feckless. His accent I'd say is New England. He talks with a slurred drawl. Perhaps because he's drunk. Is this guy really a boozer? I can't say. But for sure, it's booze that's doing the talking, not him. I know booze. I know how it sounds. Here,' he passed him the recorder, 'I've listened to it again and again. I'm too anxious and it's screwing up my mind. You're more rational than me, Nick. You're better at keeping your head straight in a crisis. Being conventional has its advantages, I guess. We can all profit at times at being a little bland. No offense intended.'

'None taken.'

'You're a pal. Take it home. Listen to it. See what you can figure out. We'll compare notes tomorrow, and listen to it again.'

'Why don't we call Frank? Let's do it now.'

'It won't make any difference. Not now, Nick; not tonight. This thing is digging into me. Like it's testing me. My head's in a spin. It's exhausting being so close and yet so far. This kind of tease, this riddle, is a torture. I don't want to be tantalized to death by slow, cool words that could mean a million other things. - This is so damn disabling. Someone out there is mocking our rages. It's the same method that the Gods on Mount Olympus used all the time to screw up the Greeks with, drunk out of their minds on Ambrosia, wallowing up there in the clouds and having a great big laugh at us suckers down here. It's the same old game, only now it's with technology. It's wearing me down; it's screwing me up. I'm sick and tired of being handed a bent key, and there you are, stranded by the door of your desires. It's getting to me, Nick. I'm even beginning to sound strange.'

'Booze, more like.'

'No. Not the booze. The booze is keeping me sane. It's honest. It speaks to me like a buddy. It's showing me where my true limits lay, and saving me from tearing my hair out. I hate to admit it, Nick, but I guess I'm a vulnerable kind of guy, more than I care to disclose.' He paused, feeling relieved by confession and yet defenseless to the vagaries of a stranger's hand invisibly playing with his mind. 'If these guys were clever shrinks, or something worse, I would say they were toying with our heads, and not our balls. If you must have an enemy, better a woman than a man. At least then you know what you're up against.'

'You're talking crazy.'

'I know. I told you so. This thing… it's driving me nuts.'

The women returned in a huff, and Roy felt their combined passion. Why did life play a hand like that, when sorrows arrive in pairs of irate chicks rooting for a spoil? Men needed space, and Roy, now, needed a galaxy-size of it. They remained standing glaring down at him with disdain, looming over the men. (Kind of sexy in a way, if that's your thing. Frank would definitely have approved).

'Well!' began the kitten, fretting at Roy.

'Well what?' he said imprudently. (Well, he's a man, kind of normal, no?)

'Have you grown up yet?'

'I'm trying. You know, it's harder than you think, love. But boys will be boys.' He tried smiling and humoring her and she remained defiant, so he yielded: 'OK, OK...' asking the waiter for the bill. 'The boy has grown up into a man. Reluctantly. OK.'

'Shrunk down to smaller than his cock, more like!' retorted Vonnie, and the kitten concurred. - Wherefore this bizarre alliance? Weren't these two alley cats going head-to-head only a moment ago? Well, don't that beat the chicken and the egg! What came first, women's egos, or their alliance against men? This riddle scrabbled up his nuts, and Roy came to believe he'll never eat scrambled eggs again as long as he lives. No sir, it's fruit juice and toast from here on in. OK, he'll miss his morning eggs, but principle is nothing if it's not buttered thick and creamy on your homemade bread. Christ! All this philosophizing was making him feel hungry. 'You make me sick, Roy, do you hear!' ranted the kittens. Now, they've gone too far, he feels. Of course, being a man, he never *really* blames himself but puts it all down to feminine quirkiness running amok. After all, a woman, she's not *really one of the guys*, is she? No, sir. Birds of a feather, just don't go the *brotherly way* together. However, this time around, he said nothing, not diddley-do. Knowing when to keep your mouth shut is a talent up there with philosophy, physics and Greek. And he had the booze to thank for that. A guy thing. A savior with balls. Knocks it all back. Cheers, son. Thanks, booze...

Nick settled the bill, and they left.

'Share a cab?'

'No thanks,' said Roy, arm in arm with the kitten. 'I've got my car parked around the corner. And besides, it's a lovely night, and I want to walk a bit. Don't we, babe?' He winked at the kitten and squeezed her hand.

'I'll see you tomorrow,' said Nick. 'Be early.'

'Is there really a tomorrow, Nick?' he said, then whispered to himself, 'I think there might just be....' and he strolled on, bearing an easy east towards the waterfront and heading for the river.

'Where are we going, Roy?' purred the kitten after a while.

'I parked the car down here, further along. Here,' he gave her the keys, 'you drive. - Ah, it's a gorgeous night, isn't it, babe? So beautifully clear.' He gazed up at the night sky. 'I think I know what the ancients used to dream about.'

'Roy?'

'Let's drive down by the river.'

'Let's just go home. We can go another time. I'm tired.'

'I want us to go there now,' he said. 'To unhinge my mind. Please, babe, do this for me.'

She sighed, assenting in silence. And that was why he loved her so: because she knew how to read his mind. The small details that fill out a life were important to a person; the details of relationships, the nitty-gritty parts that stitch the whole and hold it all together. She gave them space, the quirks and aspirations, and set them not on a leash, like some women are apt to do, but afforded them room to flourish. And, because she is innately smart, would turn them to her advantage *without* taking advantage. It was so damn simple. Learn by listening; do while learning. And if you have nothing to say, keep mum in mind. However...

'It's a lovely evening. Look, Roy, look at all those stars.'

'Huh?'

'The stars. There are so many. Could we ever count them?'

'Huh?'

'The stars. Count them. One, two...'

'Less is more,' he whispered.

The words scintillate in his mind as his gaze sweeps the horizon. There, the constellation of Manhattan, a star field filling the skyline. More is more is more...

'...ten, eleven, twelve...'

'What are you doing, babe?'

'Counting the stars.'

'Oh...'

'Roy.'

'Yes?'

'Shall we count them together?'

He paused, gazed at Manhattan, gazed at her, the river, the bridge, the stars, her, his watch, the lights, her again.

'Sure. Why not.'

Yeah...

Chapter 14

'Nick,' said Vonnie.

'Yes?'

'Close the door quietly.'

He entered her apartment and, casually with his foot, shut the door behind him as she switched on the lights and strode on ahead of him, throwing her purse into a cushioned chair, this neat series of actions conducted as a single smooth motion, like ballet, staged in a perfect setting of time and space, an enigma of simplicity, a cinema.

'I'm drowsy,' he said, trailing after her.

'Nick...'

'I'm drowsy.'

'Would you like a drink?'

'Whiskey.'

'Neat?'

He smiled. 'Like the drowsing sea.'

She kicked off her shoes – dancer's feet emerged, prim, trim, exciting. Walk on by. Walk on you. Walk on a man.

'Your drink,' she passed him the glass and their fingers touched.

His turn. Kicks off his shoes, stretches his toes, smiles, laughs and glances at his feet: 'I prefer yours; but I'm fond of my own.'

'It shows.'

'I know.'

They reclined on the sofa, close together, palpably close, closer than touching.

'How was work?' she asked him.

'OK.'

'What did you do today?'

'The last couple of days have been hell.'

'Oh?'

'But it's settling down now,' he was a touch vague, but with the essence of hope residing, like cream topping an Irish coffee, it kind of makes you want to sip, and sip and sip all night long. Mmmm...

She smiled briefly: 'And Roy?'

'The same as always.'

'And the other one?'

'Frank,' he inflected with a touching sigh and gazed at his glass, lifting it to his lips as if to catch the swell of words that came gushing out and poured inside, melting into the whiskey. 'Frank the hack. He'll soon be back in action. No worries there.' Pause for a reminiscing chuckle, a sense of relief that he was safe and sound. 'He'll be back into the swing of things in no time. He'll bring it around. Good old Frank...'

'You seem very fond of him.'

'I'd miss him terribly if he wasn't around.' He finished off the whiskey and she refilled his glass with an ample measure. 'Whoa! That's enough; I'll be drowning in the stuff. Are you trying to get me drunk?'

A moment's hesitation caught her eyes probing, her chin pushed forward in tantalizing enquiry like an elegant sleuth – all gesture and shadow and suggestion.

'Did you want to know something in particular, Vonnie?'

'No, just making conversation.'

He paused and smiled at her with affection. He never wanted to appear cool, it was the last thing on his mind as he stumbled into a throaty chuckle which left an impression of being forced, but it broke the ice and lent an air of credibility: 'You know what Roy is like, Vonnie,' he said, half gasping.

'I try to.'

'Well, Frank is more... idiosyncratic shall we say.'

'Interesting.'

He stared at his drink and rocked the glass gently till the ice, like a tuning fork, struck a note as it collided together. 'Imagine these ice cubes. If Roy was the water, then Frank would be the temperature.'

She laughed, 'I have to think about that one.'

He laughed with her. 'I think I will, too. Cheers.'

'Cheers.'

'Frank was out of town for a few days.'

'Business or pleasure?'

'Oh, pleasure,' his lips curled into a scrumptious grin. 'Very much pleasure.'

'Lucky him.'

'But he's back now.'

'All good things must some to an end.'

'Alas.'

'Or to those who wait.'

'That's probably me.'

He probably meant far more than he could appreciate that moment, but he was too tired and worn out to pursue it any further, other than to pose the question with a sense of humor:

'Are you spying on me?'

'I'm watching you,' she said.

'I meant it lovingly.'

'I know you did.'

'What are you watching?'

'You.'

'I thought I was the one who liked to watch.'

'Shall I bring you a mirror?

He smiled, 'I'm only partly vain. It depends on my mood.'

'Then I'll bring it for me.'

'Perhaps it will complete the picture.'

'Ménage à trois.'

'What's the phrase for four?'

'Double couplet.'

'Almost like a poem.'

'Almost.'

They gazed at each other with the weight of longing, the complexity of suggestion, the intensity of lovers. And it was all in the momentum of his hand to draw her towards him, press her onto his lips, slip his tongue into her mouth, and taste her.

After, when they parted, she looked surprised.

'That was a deep kiss.'

'Yes.'

She meant a *desperate* kiss. Passionate and desperate.

'Nick.'

'Vonnie..?'

'I want to turn the lights down.'

He concurred silently with a smile and she dimmed the lights till the room became opaque to everything but the essence of suggestion – colors in fusion just above a silhouetting grey, a warm shadowy hue where shades of imagination lend the power of thought to things observed in a glance, painting layers and layers on a man, on a woman, with the deft brush strokes of desire.

To be a lover is to be an artist – weaving patterns, weaving a web to entice, to catch, to have, to consume.

Nick spoke softly. 'A cop came to the office today.'

'A cop?'

He chuckled, 'It's been an emotional rollercoaster of a day.'

'What did he want?'

'Missing persons.'

'Who?'

'Ah... It was a mistake.'

'That's...'

'Fortunate.'

'A coincidence.'

'Why?'

'Oh, nothing.' She brushed the issue casually aside. 'Kiss me.' She seemed either anxious to distract or, fervently clutching in embrace, desperate for love.

To be a lover is to be a fighter.

'And what did you do today, Vonnie?'

'I slept late.'

'How late?'

'Till mid-day.'

'And then?'

'Oh,' she gestured with her hand passing smoothly to her side, 'I day-dreamed and did other things besides...'

'Besides..?'

'Then I went shopping, then day-dreamed some more...'

'Sounds like a pretty full day.'

They laughed together in the smooth synthetic twilight, sharing earnest ecstasies.

To be a lover is to be... naked.

Your soul, your ghost, your ego revealed and laid bare to be seen, touched, tasted, imagined, smelled, and heard in the deft secrets of a palpable humming heartbeat, lyrical, enchanting, magical. Naked.

'Nick,' she whispered.

'Why are you whispering?'

'I got a call today.'

'From whom?'

'A friend from back home.'

'And?'

'She had a baby. A girl. They're naming her Amy-May, because it's May.'

'It's June now.'

'Yes. But she was born in May.'

'And?'

'Just thought you'd like to know,' she said softly. 'And I wanted to share it with you.'

'Why are you whispering?'

'Oh... I don't know.' Her meditations ran on a murmuring tide. She touched his face, tenderly, folding her fingers through his hair.

'That's OK,' he whispered in reply, gently yielding in her wake.

'It feels natural... kind of...'

He paused, and smiled deeply. 'It's OK.'

To be a lover is to be decipherable.

'You're very introspective,' she said.

'What are you looking at?'

'I spy with my little eye...'

'Something beginning with...'

'After you.'

'V.'

'Voluptuousness.'

'Mmm... perhaps. - Your turn.'

'E.'

'Exotic.'

'Essence.'

'Exotic essence.'

'Near enough.'

'Can I watch you undress?' he said.

'How does the angel play..?' she murmured softly and began to undress, slowly, sensuously, clothes like a code enshrouding the body like a cipher, encrypting a being with surface, with color, with texture, with exotic essences.

'You look... L.'

'Lovely.'

'And luscious.'

'And?'

'Luxurious.'

'Well, I'm all M.'

'Mine.'

And he consumed her with his eyes, engulfed her with his being, made love to her – fucked her.

To be a lover is to be one.

'Nick.'

'Yes?'

'What time is it?'

'About one I think.'

'Are you tired?'

'No. Not anymore.'

'You're a wonderful lover.'

Silence. A feeling of fulfillment. He kissed her.

'Nick.

'Yes?'

'Shall I make us something to eat?'

'Yes.'

'I have some soup in the fridge. I can warm it up.'

To be a lover is to be normal.

Chapter 15

H-foo. H-foo. H-foo....

It's not a humming bird he's listening to; it's the slut snoring at his side, the tempo of her grunts reminiscent of a hog. She drank too much, cocaine worked it's overkill and sent her high into the purple realms of smoky heaven, from where she coughed herself awake and drawled in queasy French gratuitous expletives that had a kind of remnant elegance attached (*fuck you* in French is kind of cool...) as she reaches consciousness with a hangover frown and dried vomit festooned like soiled pearls down the bed sheets.

He looked at her and felt disgusted. Recoiling with an exclamation *And so it's all my fault? Screw you already!...* kind of stare that sees him toppling from the bed, bullock naked and dragging himself to the bathroom for a long overdue piss where, as he hits the pretty light, the glow blinds his eyes and dazes him and he felt even more disgusted as the dazzle of the mirror booms *Hey, psssst, over here, you. Yes, you...* and he observes himself in the mirror... *Come closer, that's it, over here...* and his reflection seemed to wobble and distort like he's about to spawn shimmering copies of himself, multiple universes, parallel idiots and mocking piss-takers *...would you get a load of that pathetic crowd!*

'Sweet Jesus, is that really me?'
You bet it is!
'All of it?'
Every single copy.
'Oh my God!'
Sing it again, sunshine. Sing it again....
'That's not me!'
Playtime. Knock knock..
'Holy shit!'
Wakey-wakey. Time to hit the brakes, wouldn't you say..?

'That can't be me. It can't. It just can't...'

The shrill cry fires off alarm bells in his head and the moralizing motor in his mind starts up: whatever happened, how did he sink so low, he was a good boy once, scouts, church, good family, Sunday roast, 4th of July... 'I'm telling you, that's not me!'

But the inner voice loses patience and thrusts at him: *Take a good look at yourself. Look at it. Look! That's you. Alright? Get yourself a wife, you schmuck. Get a normal life, you schmuck. Buy yourself a dog, schmuck. Hammer yourself down in the sprawling suburbs like the rest of the crowd, schmuck. Normalcy. Get it, schmuck? That's a wrap.* – But the fact remains, even with a wife, even with a *normal life,* a dog, a mortgage and two-point-two kids tucked neatly away and cruising down the freeway in a camper (like normal families do, you know) he'd still be whoring his way all over the shop and rolling in the *Fuck You And I Do What I Like* All-American Way. Life, liberty, and the pursuit of whoring to my cock's content. Happiness is only a starting point, like fable – it sets the dream in motion. They sort of teach this stuff at school. Cue to the routine; it runs something like this: *One day, son, you'll grow to be an upright man.* – Will I really? - *Sure you will.* - Will I have a hard-on? – We'll have to ask the science teacher to answer that one... 'Excuse me, Miss Peterson, can you tell me the right steps to get to heaven?' – 'Be a good boy,' she says warmly with a reassuring smile. - 'A good boy?' he wonders aloud – 'Yes. Every single day,' she emphasizes with another Peterson smile. And the boy, well, he has his imagination working at full throttle and gets all kinds of ideas, and puzzles over her words from every possible angle. He thinks to himself: Good boy. Boy Good. Boy O boy. Goody good. Sooooooo Good.

Pontificate or fornicate. A choice?

Nah!

The slut starts moaning and tossing and turning in the bed, falls off, and hauls herself into the bathroom, gapes at him a moment, feels awful, wonders who the hell he is, and then turns towards the shower groping for the door, and grappling with the appliance as though it were a snake coiling around her misfit, misspent youth (she's not exactly a spring chicken, mind, but worth a bang or two... make that three, four, five...), struggling with the cords, hitting the taps.

She likes it hot, really hot, and complains when it's boiling down in buckets - but so what, it's hot. And he joins her for the duration.

'Shit, it's hot!' he rants in Anglais.

'Shut up!' she returns in Francais.

'Fuck vous!' they conjoin in *Franglais*, and eventually settle down to the steaming experience of a shared shower. He rubs her tits, she strokes his balls, it's a fair exchange, and besides, better to be clean than *dirty*.

Last night, it all seemed so good. But people just don't get it. Not these guys, no, I'm talking about the moaning majority who lack the balls to plumb the depths and then some. People like the way they are, they just rave a bit against it, that's all. No harm done. And everything remains the same. Semper Eadem (that's the Latin equivalent for *Don't waste your time, sunshine, what will be, will be. – What's the French for that?*)

Oui. Yeah. And h'asta la vista, baby... (Derivative Latin always does the trick).

Within the hour they were themselves again, and he began to get a bit horny and suggested, you know, a quickie. She, being practical, tempered his arousal and lifted the telephone and ordered some breakfast. She was expert in that. Eating and screwing (in either order), you can't beat the French. So be a wise-guy, and learn from them :-)

'By the way,' he asked her, as they tucked into the toast. 'What's your name?'

'Marie Claire,' she said, though is sounded like the first thing that came into her mind to stop the schmuck from yakking so she could eat her meal. 'And you?' she asked, shrugging with indifference.

'Anthony. Anthony Leoni. Music promoter, impresario, showman, and all-round great guy. Ah!' he said, lifting his coffee cup, 'I just love myself. Don't you?'

'Love you?'

'I meant yourself.'

She shrugged in an off-hand way. 'Oui. Je m'aime.'

'Well,' he rejoined, 'at least we have that in common.'

And it only takes a little to get the ball rolling, and off they go.

She wanted eight hundred for her services. He rounded it to a grand. She kissed him on the cheek. He winked at her and suggested, you know, a quickie.

'Maybe later,' she said, and gave him her card. She liked him. He was generous. He was fun, a bit moody perhaps, sure, oui, but no one's perfect.

'See ya, babe,' he says breezily, waving her bye bye; and as he closed the door the phone started to ring. He puts on his jacket as he heads for the phone. He picks up and leans it on his shoulder, securing it with his left cheek, manipulating his cufflinks with his free hand. For a freewheeling whoremonger who couldn't give a damn about most things, he's especially slick and fastidious with his dress sense.

It was Cindy Gillespie. She was calling from the airport, which surprised him. His fingers paused, leaving the right cufflink loose, and grasped the receiver.

'Hi, honey, how are you doing?'

'OK. You?'

'Fine. Are you planning a trip or something?'

'No. I'm meeting my sister. Amber's flying in today. I'm meeting her.'

He heaved a sigh of relief and resumed fixing his cufflinks. 'That's great. When is she due in?'

'About forty minutes time.'

'Great. We'll show her the town.'

'Anthony?'

'Yes, babe?'

'There's something else. She called suddenly last night and said she had to leave Las Vegas.'

'Why?' His fingers stopped working the cufflinks again. 'What's going on?'

'I'm not sure. But she sounded frightened.'

'Wait there,' he said, arranging where to meet. 'I'm coming over.' And he hung up, leaving his hotel room and finishing the cufflink while making his way to the elevator. The bellboy looked at him and grinned. 'What's the matter with you?'

'Your neck tie, monsieur,' he said amicably. 'It doesn't quite go with the shirt.'

248

Anthony looked down and considered the apparel – pale blue shirt and a red tie, the kid had a point. Instinctively he thought to return and change it.

'A nice beige would look magnificent,' the boy added with the flair of a connoisseur.

'Never mind,' said Anthony, handing him a tip for his good sense as he stepped from the elevator. 'It can wait.'

Daytime in Paris contrasted with nighttime in one significantly French sense – there are more of them around: the French, that is. The buggers are everywhere and they insist on having things their way. Even the grumpy looking cabbie that pulled up adroitly and nods his head at the trade.

'Taxi, monsieur?'

'Do you speak English?'

'Non!'

Of course he can, but what he really wants to know is can you speak French? A numbness follows this conundrum, stare for glare it's not worth the bother and Anthony finally settles for a cab with a black driver who speaks French, English, Portuguese, and Spanish.

'A bit of each,' he boasts to Anthony who is anxiously worrying in the back of the cab as it plowed through dense traffic towards the airport. 'Do you know what the Spanish is for good morning, monsieur?'

'Fuck off!'

'Not quite. Not quite,' the cabbie responded affably, rolling up the windows to subdue the restless sound of the city. 'How long are you staying in Paris for, monsieur?'

'What's that?'

'How long have you been in Paris?'

'Almost a month,' he replied, resigned to the conversation as something inevitably to pass the time. The cabbie was a nosey fellow, but it was wiser to amuse him than risk a protracted journey, and Anthony tried to smile, learning that this chap was a part-time student, he had three kids, two wives (the French didn't know about the one in Africa) four brothers and three sisters. All of them educated. And he was the youngest by just over a year.

'Can't you drive any faster? I'm meeting someone. Their flight is due in soon.'

'From America, monsieur?'

'That's right.'

'I know a short cut. But the traffic may catch us. Would you like to take the risk?' he chuckled. 'Are you a gambling man, monsieur?'

'Not really,' said Anthony, but urged the cabbie take the risk anyway. In response, a shriek of rapture shot from him, he glanced at the dashboard clock, pushed the vehicle into overdrive, turned right, and there followed the most tangled excursion through the streets of Paris that Anthony had ever experienced. 'Jesus Christ, man, do you know where you're going?'

'Just sit back and relax, monsieur.'

He sat back, but he couldn't relax – not until they pulled out all of a sudden onto the highway, heading directly for the airport.

When they arrived, Anthony briskly glanced at his watch and paid him, including a large tip as a *thank-you* gesture.

'You are very generous, monsieur. Thank you.'

'Well, what the hell. You can't take it with you; so you may as well spread it around.'

'You are a gentleman and a philosopher, monsieur.'

'And a pure womanizer to boot,' he added. 'Good day, au revoir, and give my best regards to both your wives.'

The airplane arrived on time, and in the Arrivals Hall the sisters huddled together in intimate proximity anxiously conversing.

'What's wrong, sis?' Cindy pressed her. 'What happened? You had me worried sick.'

'I had to get away.'

'Why?'

'I had to see you.'

'You see me. What's wrong?'

'I was followed,' she burst out uncontrollably.

'Followed by whom?'

'I don't know... A stalker. Someone.'

'Oh my God!'

No, I'm OK. I'm not harmed.'

'Was there any physical contact?'

'No. The closest he came was while I was driving.'

'How close?'

'He pulled up beside me at the lights. He half hid his face. I... I wanted to...'

'He never tried to force you over or anything?'

'No, he stayed behind. But always close enough to see me.'

Cindy gasped deeply with a mixture of fear and relief as her sister continued with her story.

'The police think that the stalker may have been after you, and that he thought I was you. We have to be careful.'

Cindy paused briefly to consider, then looked at her skeptically. 'You could always be mistaken, sis. Never believe everything you see, least of all in Las Vegas.'

'Try telling that to the stalker.'

'Maybe it was just some stupid guy, decides to play a game. I mean, why would anybody be stalking you, or me? Maybe it was a fan or an admirer who just wanted to talk in person and ask for an autograph. It happens all the time. You sometimes get the shy types; they don't know how to handle it, and a simple little thing like that... well, it easily gets interpreted the wrong way. - There's probably a rational explanation. I think you're jumping to conclusions.'

'Well, it scared the hell out of me. And I'm not imagining it. He was there. He was following me. How close does he have to get?'

'OK. But must that mean it was malicious?'

'Until I know for certain, yes, it's malicious. And we should both be careful. I won't take chances, sis', not for anything.'

Her fears felt stifling and Cindy, glancing briefly at the clock, said: 'Listen, I've got to get back. I have a show.' Instinctively she began searching for Anthony, looking among the crowds that flowed incessantly through the Arrivals Hall.

A moment later she heard the distinctive bedlam of an American cadence heat up the air, followed by a strange shriek in visceral French. Anthony had collided with a hefty woman, the *Don't screw with me* kind who heaved herself around and glared indignantly at him, firing salvos from her reservoir of expletives. Her arms pounded the air with passionate sweeps, her fists like cannon balls, shot after shot. This was a warrior class woman nourished on carbohydrates with a capacity for flattening any man in a single bounce. He kept a safe distance and gave back a piece of his own mind when his apologies fell victim to the imperative French refusal to accept them. But this was a lose-lose situation, so he simply withdrew when he heard Cindy's voice and spotted her over the crowd.

'Anthony. We're here,' Cindy called out and waved nervously. He advanced swiftly, feeling disgruntled but looking dapper. – Being, and looking smart, was just part of his nature.

'Jesus! What a fat cow. If she weren't so damn fat I could have seen around her; but she damn well blocked out the view. What is any man in my position meant to do? Ah!' he saw Cindy's sister smiling coyly at him. 'Amber, my sweet, we are together again at last. You look lovely. Lovely. Hmmm...'

'Watch him,' teased Cindy, 'he's in his element.'

'Thanks, Anthony. How are you?'

'Overjoyed,' he said, charming her in his classic flirty way, looking at each of them in turn. 'Simply overjoyed and delighted.' As he had often done he paused and reflected at some length on their striking similarity – a casual habit performed unselfconsciously. Sure, he could distinguish Amber from her sister by features pertaining to hairstyle, gestures and the like. But still, he remained overwhelmed by the resemblance and gazed with wonder. 'It's hard to believe you two are not really twins.'

'You're always saying that,' said Amber. 'One day, I'll write you a song about it.'

'Ah! But if only you could sing it as well as Cindy.'

'If only she could compose as well as I can.'

'And I, my sweet, worship at the shrine of a great song.' He embraced her hand and fondly kissed it. 'Welcome to France.'

'Do you speak French?'

'In a way,' he grinned mischievously. 'In a way.'

'Anthony, I know I shouldn't have shown up like this out of nowhere, but - .'

'I'm over the moon you're here. We're a team. In fact, I'm glad you're here. Cindy, didn't you say you wanted to rework some of the songs?'

'What songs?' Amber looked at her, frowning.

'That can wait,' said Cindy, quietly, keen to avoid the issue.

'Well, since Amber's here,' he added, 'you may as well *finesse* them to perfection.'

'Oh, and that's what you think?' Amber stared hard at her sister.

'We'll discuss it later,' she said hesitantly. 'It was just an idea.'

'An idea. What idea?'

Cindy knew that altering any composition Amber originated was anathema to her. 'Look, Amber, please, we'll talk later. I have to get back and prepare for a show.'

Amber was uncompromising, stubbornly refusing to budge, and Anthony felt obliged to intervene. 'I love this creative friction, it's what makes us great,' he began whimsically, but neither woman responded. So he tried coaxing them with compromise. 'Agree to disagree. There's more than enough to be getting on with.' But no reaction. He tried humor, and even that fell flat. 'This impasse, ladies, well - it's just not jazz.' He looked fondly at Amber, 'Cindy tells me you felt a bit anxious in Las Vegas. What's the matter, babe?'

'A stalker was preying on me,' she cried. 'At work, at home, on the freeway, everywhere I went... Someone was stalking me,' glancing icily at her sister, then back anxiously at him. 'But she thinks I'm over-reacting. But I'm not. It happened. Damn it, it was real! Someone was there. How close does he have to get before anyone believes me?'

Anthony gasped in amazement: 'Are you being serious? Did you report this to the police?' She nodded nervously yes, she did, and he asked if they had detained any suspects.

'No. But it scared me to death. And I just couldn't take any more. I had to get out.'

'Las Vegas can be a crazy town.'

'Tell that to *her,*' she replied bitterly. 'She won't believe me.'

'Why not? Why don't you believe her?'

'I never said that,' Cindy protested. 'I said she could have been mistaken. It could have been something else, shadows, paranoia, who knows. Besides, she's here now, so why keep making a fuss?'

Amber, both puzzled and infuriated, sensed a strange disjunction in Cindy. It was abnormal of her to be dismissive, to subvert Amber's fears as frivolous things and not register their omens. It was hard to gauge which fact hurt Amber more: Cindy's cool passion, or the menace of a stalker.

'You seem so cool, Cindy,' said Amber apprehensively.

'Why shouldn't I be?'

'Because...'

'Because what?'

'Because it's not like you. It's as if I don't know you any more.'

'I think you're over dramatizing.'

'No you don't. That's a lie. You know me better than that.' She confronted her, 'And I know you.'

'Come, come girls. Let's have peace and reconciliation,' said Anthony.

'Anthony, tell her,' said Amber.

'Tell her what, my dear?'

'Tell her she's being stupid.'

'Cindy, lovely as you are, your sister says you're being stupid.'

'Tell her I'm not listening.'

'Did you hear that?'

'No!'

'She said she's not listening. – Now, both make up and we'll take our leave in peace.'

Reluctantly conceding that each knew the other too well, they shrugged in turn and exchanged a grudging smile. It wasn't perfect, he thought, to have them at loggerheads, but given the circumstances it would have to do. Moreover, he perceived his role as perfectly adjusted to be man in the middle. A yum yummy ménage a trios popped into his sordid mind, but lingered less than he would have liked it to as the fat woman came marching his way, and he eagerly positioned the sisters for their exit.

'Ladies,' he offered an arm to each, his cufflinks dazzling. And thus, they swiftly made their way out.

The multi-lingual cabbie was milling around outside, leaning patiently on his cab passing the time and enjoying a cigarette. As soon as he caught sight of them he dispensed his cigarette, cried out excitedly to beckon them, and started his engine. They strolled over and he opened the rear door for his passengers. A smile, wide as a sunny day, beamed from his friendly face.

'I've always wanted to go to America,' he said.

'And you will. You have the face of someone with luck on their side.'

'You are a gentleman, monsieur. Thanks for that.'

'Don't mention it. Don't mention it....'

'Shall we take the same route back, monsieur?'

'Spin the dice,' he said, alluding to the risk of traffic congestion.

'Where would you like to go? Your hotel?'

Cindy gave directions. He said that she was very beautiful and looked remarkably like the other woman.

'But you are not twins,' he observed intuitively, and drove to the jazz club *Bléu Doux*.

Chapter 16

The New York City cacophony orchestrates sonatas of gorgeous anarchy from a cocktail list: whiskey arias, bourbon odes, brandy phrasing, champagne chorus (the best of course) and a cheery that exploded sending the whole shebang up skyward to the towers of Manhattan. A living, breathing sound. It's inspired mayhem set loose upon the resonating, reverberating bounding pulses of a populace, their passions chewed and spat and seeded to the bone of life. It's raw here. Raw – *like life.*

On the twenty-second floor of NBS Banking Corporation Frank, Roy, and Nick, expunged all sounds of the city from their midst and convened in conspiratorial silence listening intently to the audio recorder reproducing the whirring sounds of a roulette wheel spinning the ball, dice chasing themselves across crap tables, the smooth drones of the croupiers trawling in the chips from bets placed by patrons clinking their glasses and laughing their hurrahs and cheers and faint booms of despair as the fates teased and tantalized them - well, the casino has advantage on its side, and the house prevails, sooner or later. *That's the only certain wager.* Bets, packing them in, on impulse or by design; it's the ropes, sucker, because there is no way to bet around a certainty. You stop when you're ahead and pack up your hormones and head for the exit, or leave empty handed and try again next time. Good luck; bad luck. Good day; bad day... Comes and goes... comes and goes...

Savvy isn't a virtue. It's a formula. Like E equals M C squared. E is for Easy. M is for Money. And C is for chance – *Squared!*

'It's a riot of gaming and fun. Those bastards are having the time of their lives, while we're stuck here with swollen ears. Nick...' Frank cried out bitterly having labored at the task in vain, 'I can't make any sense out of it? If there's any kind of signal, it's washed out in the background noise. We're just wasting our time.'

The sounds from the voice recorder were not merely a tease - as oftentimes riddles play on the mind before yielding a clue - no, this lacked the seduction of a mystery that whispers *Come hither, my sweet, and listen to what I have to tell you...* This was dissonance framed like a brute, a paradox of sensory torture that enslaves men in cages of enigma, that tormented their minds with faint abstractions: could be, maybe, perhaps is, is not... the pervasive neuroses of gamblers and swingers and high class rollers and whores and charlatans and money-makers and dime-shakers and credit-breakers and the tap tap tapping of gaming chips, round and around, plowing dough and baking bread and shoving great wads of it down guzzling mouths and sighs and grunts and the phzzzz of champagne running all bubbly over avaricious lips, mmmmmm. These were not vague idioms to suggest things, but magical temptations to choke on, nuggets of pure bliss swallowed whole with the sweetest kiss as the perfect aftertaste. Sensual world - it doesn't come deeper than this. You can sweat just thinking where these people have been, what they've done, how they live their prodigal lives, consuming the best, screwing like the rest, only... it just felt a whole lot better, more fulfilling, with lashings of ecstasy on top. *Hurrah!* It's the crazy decadence that the world adores, a licentious Rome, a sleepless festival of ancient orgy, a bordello that sweats you to the bone, raw, the painful ecstasy, a home away from... home. 'It's like I'm staring right at something, but I just can't *see* it. And the damn thing is poking me right in the eye.' Ouch! That *thing*, there, (where?) staring you in the face, is the most elusive thing of all. And it sweats him mercilessly, sounding something that he dearly wants and cannot have, as he sets the recorder to repeat, again and again in a futile cycle. Turning again to Nick, he fretted: 'Who's the American?'

'I don't know. Why ask me?'

'He's acting like a jerk.'

'So what? He's drunk. And everyone acts like a jerk one time or another. For goodness sake, Frank, you don't have to be a magician to make a fool of yourself. Just concentrate.'

'It's useless, Nick. This is getting us nowhere. We've listened to this damn thing over and over, and if I hear his voice one more time, I'll explode.'

'Stop taking everything so personally.'

'The imbecile!' he griped. 'For some reason, I think I should know him. But who is he?'

'I've no idea,' said Nick, sounding deflated. 'Roy?' he glanced at him, but Roy just twitched his head. And Nick, at length, signaled his misgivings. 'Perhaps we need to take a step back. Frank?'

'He sounds like a complete idiot. The imbecile, he should act with more class. If he can't hold his booze, he should consider his dignity and drink orange juice. There's no sin in that, is there?' Frank was full of gloom, sounding reflective. 'I'm not like him, am I, Nick.'

'No, Frank; that's not your style,' he said, exasperated with him. 'Besides, why are you taking this personally? It's just some guy.'

'Wait!' Roy cried out abruptly, his face clouded with riddles, tracing out the cadence of the American's voice, its expressive banter, like the exuberance of a child running wild at a funfair whose fireworks and lights amazed him. 'This guy is totally out of his depth. You can tell by the voice. You can hear it from the booze. He treats the casino like a candy store; and this guy loves his chocolate. He has no control over himself. It's just as Steady said, this guy is all logic drowning in an ocean of chocolate chaos. You can tell by the voice, the way he sounds, the things he says. It's not the booze. It's him – whoever the hell he is.' Roy paused and rubbed his forehead, thinking out loud. 'He gets his kicks with a computer. He's a lab man; not a gambler. He uses dice to derive formulas, not take his chances at the crap tables. There, he's like a kid at a funfair that wants to ride all the carousels at once.'

'And eat chocolate at the same time.'

'Yeah.'

'Lucky him.'

'Ha. Ha...'

'Yeah...'

Each man grew silent and brooded in solitude for a time, with only the roaring odes from the recorder spacing out intervals of time. It was Nick, resolving his doubts, who suggested, 'Look, guys, perhaps we're focusing on the wrong things. Forget the American. What about the others?'

They considered that before, but gave up because it seemed to offer even less. They were defiant men loath to begin again. An early clue felt so compelling, an American sound seemed to hold the key, but the lock was foreign. And the paradox was unforgiving. Damn! They were confronted with riddles whose syntax was everyday speech, the idioms of profligate life, hustlers' laughter and guys on a roll, the giggling voices of angels sipping champagne and nibbling the ears of rich patrons at the bar, the amalgam of sleaze made irresistible. An answer. But what was the question, what were they looking for? Frank struck the desk with his hand.

'Come on, Roy, you were the last one there. You must remember something. Anything at all.'

He stared at him with hard beveled eyes:

'What do you want from me?'

'Put the pieces together.'

'What pieces? How do you expect me to remember anything in all that delicious chaos of gorgeous sound? Listen to it. My God, just listen to it! The fevered laughter, women eating men, the rustle of gaming chips and spinning roulette wheels and tumbling dice and the brouhaha of a paradise... it's amazing. Sounds like that make you want to make love and love it. They speak to my guts, not to my head. These sounds don't tease the ears; they rake the mind of anything resembling order. Screw the mystery, I'm full of envy. I want to share in it.'

'Are you crazy!'

'Gimme a break. I am what I am. I'm no more than a man.'

'Money! You moron, the sound is ringing with money, cash-register syllables singing ha ha ha. Ain't that a laugh! Aint that a bang! Ha ha ha, get it? Every note, every jingle, every whisper. Even the yawns are a cash machine. That's the clue. Listen.'

'I know. I can hear it. Everything is sounding money, money, money... money songs, money words, money farts. It's an ode ringing in my bones, seizing my guts. I'm drowning in songs. Drowning. – That's not the point. I don't recognize any of the voices. Who are these people? Who are they? – I don't know.'

'You must remember something?'

'I'm trying.'

'Try harder.'

'OK... OK...'

Moneyed voices full of restless delights swayed and jostled and made Roy cringe with bitter envy as he grappled with the whimsy tenors, the register of blending voices speaking all at once, dialects in the global mix of fantastic rhythms in the melting pot of sound: French frisson, German odes, Japanese chants, Arabic prayers, Scandinavian mid-tones of revelry averaged to the global standard, Italian tones sounding like punctured singing, American English in prosaic reflection on the merits of a six of spades... "Oh damn, I wanted a three. Excuse me, are you in charge here?" "Yes, monsieur, I believe so." "Well, is that card any good?" "Monsieur?" "A six." "Six?" "Can I swap that for another one?" "No, monsieur." "What do they call this game again, Blackmack?" "Jack, monsieur. Blackjack." 'Oh... Jack... I see... Well, is this card any good, Jack?" "No, monsieur. Play again?" "Why not – same again, Jack." "Monsieur..."

'That damn stupid idiot again!' Frank seethed as the cackling voice cascaded into gibberish from too much booze, frothing up its rhythms and tripping on a hiccup. 'Roy!'

'What now? I'm listening aren't I?'

'Anything?'

'Nothing. Just words. Voices... Don't they all sound the same? It's driving me crazy.' He listened in turmoil, struggling yet enchanted with the sense, syllables of money and voices, tumbling out with a visceral cadence. 'This is mad. Mad!' And he bristles with anger and desire, wanting to despise what he heard, but consumed in the fire. 'Mad!'

At length, the elastic strain of his concentration snapped, and he descended into a fitful cliché of gloom, mocking the accents as a foreign bedlam, the casino roar as an opera of gaming chips and roulette wheels, calls for placing of bets, *Bets, please. Last bets...* and the wheel spinning around, and the dice giving off their distinctive clipping sound – it was money singing in a thousand voices a thousand songs at once about money, money, money, and all it seemed to tell them was: *Let the good times roll, because here, you have no need of a name. All you need is money. And a voice that laughs. Ha ha ha...*

With all their efforts proving in vain, Frank finally conceded:

'Fellas, this is getting us nowhere. What did we expect, that this would be easy? I mean, what the hell are we doing? I'm the last to fold, but look...' he lifted his arms in surrender. He fell silent and rubbed his eyes, consuming time, wishing someone else would continue or extemporize. But no one did, so he concluded. 'Let's just start at the beginning. OK?' It cuts hard, this, when a man feels he's on a road to nowhere, heaving a stone around in circles, the journey never ends. It defines mental paralysis, stark and cruel, to shine the light of hope into a void and wish for miracles to emerge from the endless darkness. At what point does a man capitulate to fate? They came pretty close then. Sure, they were just ordinary guys, finding relief in cigarettes, but in adversity need to be heroes. Perhaps it was better not to know the odds. There's shut eye and there's blind eye. One offers you a dream. The other, what – hope? The immensity of an ocean of doubt would challenge your will with such a raging passion, that death seems no less enviable than risking the tide.

Frank stopped the recorder and the silence was palpable, like a heartbeat closed. Someone, somewhere, had obsessed their common mind, had seized control and they wanted it back. This, like the power of belief, of superstition, is a ghost powering its way to tyranny. The question is - who controls it? 'Listen, fellas, this is exhausting. And it's not my bones taking the strain, but my head. This recorder is next to useless unless we have some idea what we're looking for; an outline, however vague. We have to work this from the ground up; outside-in. You can't disrobe a ghost. You have to put flesh on it first. Perhaps *it* has the answers... Perhaps not.' He gazed defiantly at this *thing*, this little machine less than a human palm in scale, in weight, insignificant; in complexity, a trifle. Yet they prayed to it, beseeching this, wishing it would whisper them a message and end their sorrows at a stroke. Ancient man imploring a stone; modern man pleading with a machine... and time out of time, always hostage to events. 'What have we learned so far? Nothing. What have we heard? Just a flood of voices. This is a cocktail of accents all jumbled up. We've listened to these people time and again, washed out of their minds with booze and dames and money... We know the game, fellas, we've all been there before. It's the same old story; it doesn't need anyone to keep it alive. We're just chasing shadows. I've been in bars and talked to twenty different people. Ten minutes later, I can't remember a single one, or even what I said to them. Not a word. - Booze, fellas. Booze and dames. And life on a roll... It's not people thinking. It's their emotions going boom, boom, boom. We could have made this story up ourselves; that's how close we are. But filling in the pieces, that's what counts. We need faces to fit the voices, not the other way round. Give me a clue, any clue.' He looked at each of them in turn. 'Come on, fellas, we're not idiots. Let's ask ourselves: what would a shrink do in these circumstances? What's he after? Quack that he is, he knows how to take your money, and the answer just pops out the other side. There has to be a method, right?'

Roy exclaimed, 'Are you a shrink now? Give me a break!'

'You're too stressed out to think. Don't think; just sit down and relax. Let it come to you; don't chase it.' Frank tried imposing himself but Roy countered back, protesting it was a waste of time, that they should call Steady Eddy and ask his advice. Rashly, he drew Nick into the fray, accusing him of idleness. Nick reproached him:

'You have a nasty side about you, Roy. You can be petty and mean.'

Roy answered. 'Nick, you're far too sensitive. Just calm down.'

'And you're a womanizing, gambling drunk.'

'Guys! Guys! Guys!' Frank struck the desk, hammering it several times, and the others grudgingly yielded. 'Let's not start turning on ourselves. I look up to you guys. And is this how we cope in a crisis? We're running out of time. We have to get back to work. We're skating on thin ice here. - Think, fellas, think. This is the bottom line. Someone out there is playing with our minds; they've tangled us up like spaghetti. Roy, you know I'm right. Think with your head, not your balls. This is not the time for indulging a mood. And I know that better than both of you. I thought I was the... *exceptional* one, shall we say. – Hey, give me a break here, fellas, I have feelings too!' They briefly grinned at the confession: it was unusually honest of him. 'Come on, guys... Nick, you're so tense you look as if you're about to snap in half. Get up and move around. Bring us some fresh coffee, would you, please? In fact, bring us all some tea as well, and anything that takes your fancy. Ta.' He used the English idiom for thanks because it was a neat adjunct to a Yank's blithe way of rounding off a quip. And besides, it had a charm all its own. One ta meant thanks. Two ta's, as in *ta ta*, meant goodbye. Call it contrived lazy-speak or stylistically astute, whatever, when Nick returned with a tray crammed with coffee, tea, cocoa, biscuits, buns, sandwiches and a lot more besides, Frank succinctly said:

'Ta.'

And their feelings settled down just nicely, the mood turned cozy, and Frank resumed:

'Roy, it's your call. You were the last one most recently in Paris.'

'So what? I can't see how that helps.'

'You're the starting point. Whoever those people are recorded in this machine, they must have seen you; you must have met them, even if only briefly. How come they know so much about us? However it came about, you came into contact with them, somehow. So... what do you remember about Paris? Think. Even the smallest details count. Never omit them from the plot. They're often the most important pointers. And I should know; I'm a sucker for detail.'

Roy closed his eyes and started thinking aloud. 'I've been running this through my mind non-stop. Even the kitten tried to yank it out of me. But nothing; nothing at all. It's like I told you, nothing happened to write home about. It was a routine affair. I met these guys at the bank. No, Frank, I never saw any of them before, not one. Outside of the fact that we worked for the same firm, we were strangers. No, I was the only American present. It was a small affair, seven in total... Let me think, yes, seven,' he paused, and lit a cigarette. 'So, there we are, seven strangers in Paris. The seminar went smoothly, but nothing useful was learnt. So we traded tips and strategies; you know, tricks of the trade. One guy, Chinese, he had this strange ancient method that helped him track the markets. I couldn't really grasp what he meant. I suppose you had to be Chinese to understand. It was untranslatable. Anyway, he seemed keen and knew what he was talking about. No, Frank, they weren't mugs. They were a savvy bunch of guys, deeper than your average hack at a trading terminal. So what if they were a little peculiar, it gave them an advantage. It made them interesting. So, we hung out. You know, after business, we went out on the town. We were men all alone after a long day. The seminar was a bore; and we were horny. So why not?'

'When? Which days did you go out?'

'Every night.' He looked defensively at the others: 'Give me a break here, fellas; it's Paris! What do you expect from me, lullabies!'

Frank grinned enviously, Nick soon after, and Roy continued:

'We went downtown; hit a few bars; tried out the clubs; played some poker; you know...'

'Who won at poker?'

'Why?'

'I don't know why. I'm chasing shadows. I'm looking for clues. I'm prepared to try anything.' He snapped at him, 'Do you want my help or not?'

'OK. Why are you so touchy all of a sudden?' He had a glib thought and grinned, 'Frank, are you seeing a shrink or something?'

'Who won?' he repeated firmly. 'Well?'

Roy shrugged and said, 'It was evens overall, I guess.'

'You guess?'

'More or less.'

'So *you* never won?'

'Won? What the hell are you talking about?' He was starting to grate Frank's temper, so he asserted himself and tried again. 'OK, let me think back. Yes... a couple of grand either way. I think I was ahead. Or maybe I was down. I can't remember which. I must have been a bit too indulgent with the whiskey. It's how I am; once I get going. Besides, what's a couple of grand to a guy like me? It's not something I would take any notice of. So, I'd say evens overall. I've had better days. What's the big deal anyway?'

'Who lost?'

'Eh?'

'Lost, asshole! Who crashed out first? You?'

'What's all this about? What are you getting at?'

'Just answer the damn question. Did you bail out first?'

'No.'

'Then who did?'

Roy pondered, reviving the thread, the sequence of events tending to flow from his loins, the kind of reminiscing he was prone to. There, the dolls in red dresses with frisky French accents sliding their lips over yours, mmmmm, their tongues smothering them with wine-laden spit, delicious; and the scented babes undressing in twos taking it in turns to... Frank was staring right at him, and Roy began to focus and mull over the relevant facts: The tall blond handsome one from Iceland played his cards in an intriguing way. Nothing could be gleaned from those prized icicle eyes, impermeable as a stonewall of silent confessions. Roy considered him a risk taker, judging from the hands he played. Was he losing; was he winning? His image climbed sharply in Roy's mind. 'The first to fold was a guy named Karl Lomberg.'

'Who?'

'You don't know him. He was a cool guy, smart, charming, really quite refined in fact. You could learn a lot from him in matters of taste. I think we all could.' Roy recalled, pondering aloud as the memories shuffled in his mind to a semblance of order, like a full house. Raise. I'll see you... 'I'd never seen or heard of him before. Like I told you, we were all strangers. But at poker, yes, he was a different persona altogether from the sober guy at the bank. He'd always start out firm, but gave into pressure when the game went against him. You felt he could crack, with enough time... Softly crack. I called him Ice.'

'Ice?'

'Yes. On the final day we got chatting about our respective teams. He asked about you guys, who you were, how long we've been working together, and so on. Anyway, I told him over here we give ourselves pet names... you know, playful aliases. He found it amusing and suggested I make one up for him. Thinking of poker, naturally my first instinct, I thought of Diamond Jack, after the card he was fond of holding - the Jack of Diamonds. That, by the way, biased his playing method. You can't stroke Lady Luck like that; she just cuts you to pieces.' Roy smiled reminiscently. 'He'd take exceptional, even careless risks to try and obtain that card; you'd think it was a talisman or something. Otherwise, he was a cool guy. We got along well together. So, I spun him a tale and came up with Ice instead. I gave him to believe the reason was because he was from Iceland. Besides, diamond has a semblance to ice, don't you think?'

'How much did he lose?'

Roy thought back, using his fingers to tally:

'Eighty; maybe ninety grand. I don't recall exactly. But he took it all in his stride. He was a cool guy.'

'Was he a good player?'

Roy nodded. 'Yes; you can tell he was a talented player. On a good day he could be lethal.'

'Then how come he lost?'

'It was an unlucky day for him, I guess. Spin the coin; throw the dice...Win. Lose... It's all a question of measured risk. It's part of the same game. It's a human thing, this game. I've tried sharing that with you guys before, but you just don't feel it the way I do.' He thought deeply, a hankering for desired things stirring his imagination. 'It comes with the territory, within the framework of probability. Skill and chance weave together in the most amazing human way. You don't really want to unravel it, even if you can, and the math becomes common knowledge. - You regard it as a living thing, a mystery. That way it retains its magic. And you keep coming back for more. In fact, it's like a relationship; and you grow with it; you learn to love it; and respect it. Sure... when you're betting your last buck and you raise, you really feel the heat. The burn is irresistible.' He sighed, feeling the warm currents of obsession stir his being, for in the realm of poker Hard Eight felt himself a King. 'Turning that last card; raising the ante; holding your nerve. God, it's exhilarating! – If I was a Hindu, I'd want to be re-born as a new deck of cards. Ace of diamonds at the top; Queen of Hearts at the bottom; and the joker on the side... just to keep me on my toes.'

'And what did this Iceman want to know about us?'

'Just ordinary things, you know? Stuff like... Damn!' Roy suddenly leapt to his feet. 'I'm an idiot! An idiot! An idiot! Ice!'

'What the hell is up with you now?'

'Ice!'

'What about it?'

'Nick, replay that part near the end, when the American orders the drinks.'

'What for? Aren't we all sick and tired of hearing his voice?'

Roy fretted with passion, punishing himself. It was so clear now; everything fell into place. How neat things are. How faultless. How could he never have seen it? It amazed and infuriated him together. Life is a shower of confusions that subside of a sudden, and out comes the rainbow, bursting into beautiful, simple color. *Here I am!* it sings, and all you have to do is clear your mind, relax your eyes, and listen. The word *Ice* connoted meaning beyond the respiration of a syllable: ICE signified fire, and like a cannon primed with clues it went *bang! bang! bang!*

Nick replayed the recording at the relevant sequence where the American's voice rippled with giggles, his voice tripping over one too many vodka martinis, *he he he*... giggled the American, while Ice's controlled tones played with quiet zeal. They listened intently and Roy smiled with recognition. 'Steady was right. He said *ice* in the whiskey was a loaded word. It's because it's a *name*. Ice. Alias Karl Lomberg. Alias Peeping Tom.' It was a tempting speculation. Perhaps too tempting, but it was too seductive then to resist the conclusion. 'It *must* be him. It's *got* to be him.' Nick pressed the play button and they listened to it again. There, the jingling of ice cubes imitate the rough staccato of a tinny drum amid the whiskey glasses and patter of laughter, *ha ha ha...*

Nick, thinking quietly, finally said: 'What happens now?'

'We have to be sure,' said Frank, looking anxiously at Roy. 'And I mean beyond a shadow of a doubt. - Roy, do you understand? Get a grip on yourself. The tiniest shred of doubt is unacceptable for me; for any of us. It's got to go beyond a doubt. We're not dealing with amateurs here. They've devised something that can break us at any time. And they have the nerve to use it. Roy, I'm not starting something I can't finish.' He looked anxiously at his wristwatch; they were pressed for time, and the trading screens were competing for their attention. 'I'm not betting my future on an ice cube.'

'I'm certain it's him. It's him!' Roy seemed confrontational, on the threshold between assertion and conviction. This was psychological warfare played raw, like an open wound that wouldn't heal, that thrived on its own pain.

Nick cut in anxiously, 'But if this is the case, shouldn't we expose them? Confront them? Bring things to a head?'

'No!' Roy cried. 'That's not good enough. I've been screwed around with like a toy and I want to know why? What do they want? What have they found out? Why did it start? Why are they driving us crazy? Why us? I want answers, damn it! First, I want answers.'

'And do what with your precious answers?' argued Frank. 'Will they heal your pride; will they soothe your wounded ego?'

'No.'

'I'll tell you what they are – *they're nothing.*'

'I want answers.'

'Nothing!'

'This is a challenge. This isn't over by a long way.'

'And so now you're a tough guy? A big shot. Tough guy.'

'You're in this game too. Remember that.'

'Game?'

'Yes. A game. It's always been a goddamn game.'

'And what do you think you're going to do, tough guy - play?' He was scathing. 'They're not stupid. They'd be expecting that. They'd be ready with a thousand contingencies. You're small fry. And that's what really grates you, isn't it, Roy; that we're *all* small fry? – Go ahead, throw a punch, scream, rant all you like. But it's true. What I bloody care about is saving my own skin; keeping my head down; holding onto my job. Does that make me a coward? Fuck you! I'm using my head. I've got everything to lose, and I'm not risking that for anyone.'

'It's them, or us.'

'Fuck you! You want to play the dumb hero? Go ahead. But leave me out of it.'

The truth is sometimes a booming voice from an angry man who reads between the lines and sees clearly that with some games, you throw in your cards early, because the chips are stacked against you, and you're betting above your weight. No one said anything for a while, until Nick broke the fractious quiet with:

'Roy.'

'What?'

'We have to be realistic. – Frank.'

'What?'

'It's not all in our hands. We can't just turn and run; and we can't stand still either. These guys won't let us. We're being preyed on by a machine: set it running and it never stops. We can't just lash out and fight. In any case, we don't know what we're fighting against. Yet we can't turn our backs and run either. Doing nothing is not an option.'

'So what can we do?'

Nick, feeling the burden suddenly upon him, said: 'We have to be absolutely certain it's him. That's the first thing.'

And Roy impulsively reached for the telephone: 'I'll ask Steady and see what he says. - I want answers, damn it!'

Nick looked at Frank and then briskly at the trading screens. He pointed out to them both, 'Just so you know, we still have a living to make.'

'Hi, Steady, it's me, Roy. Yes, Hard Eight, buddy. I need to ask you something. No, no time for a game right now. Maybe later. At the club? Sure. The kitten? She's fine. You know women... Steady, about the recording. Yes, it was a great help, I can't thank you enough.' Roy laughed nervously at an impromptu joke Steady made, then straight back to business. 'Tell me, the guy who took his cues from the word ice. Yes, the ice cubes. What's that? He swirled them gently against the glass. I see, and you noticed him do that? You found that action what? Labored? OK, I think I know what you mean. It was personal. Right? - Well, my guess it's an alias; a nick-name he's grown attached to. Remind me, what did he look like again?' Steady described him, and the details matched perfectly. The height: 'Yes...' The blue eyes, blond hair, the style of clothes he wore, the controlled cool voice pitched perfectly between charm and intrigue. 'Yes...' His whole demeanor, look and character were a perfect match. 'Yes... Thanks, buddy, I'll see you tonight.'

Roy turned and confronted Frank decisively, replacing the phone hard: 'Read my lips.'

Frank frowned. 'OK, so it's him, but - '

'No buts!' Roy cut-in passionately; his temper volatile; a man oppressed by defeats who suddenly transcends them and gave him the chance to hit back. When you grab a piece of fate, it's electric in your hands, and you can't let go. It was a raging power expressed from the confines of a cage; and he, as a man, is consumed in the vice of his own tormented life.

Nick, ever the pragmatic man, observed each of them in turn. The men he saw seemed distant, cool, mechanical even, languishing in an inevitable solitude. This must be what ancient war was like, those soldiers of eons past languishing for days in trenches, where the enemy on the horizon separated whole worlds, before computers brought everything up close and erased time and distance. Yet here, within this modern skyscraper, built equally for men and data to work together, designed to be information rich, with intelligent walls, sensor packed, capable of knowing and monitoring even when a flea breaks wind – there was still the primeval sense of men at war – although now it was a game. Almost a virtual game, but it was real, because emotions (and money) rendered it real.

'Would anyone like some coffee?' said Nick, diverting a glance at the tray of beverages. 'Actually, I fancy hot chocolate myself.'

So they all drank hot chocolate, and calmed down.

Ten minutes later someone knocked on the door. It was a woman. The clock stops dead; and men begin to grovel with their eyes. She came in, said hi, sighing prettily *Isn't it a nice day today, guys?* and smiled. In that compelling moment an immense passion of unknown force (the semen engine fired up) seized the men and they gazed obsessively at her exquisite legs as though they were the whole meaning of the world wrapped in pantyhose – the fixed point of time, of space, of all existence. If a man was tasked to create the universe, self-evidently he would begin with those exquisite legs. Matter, energy – huh! It's legs like those that started it all. Believe it, as a universal fact more fundamental than pi, men far and wide would marry her just for those legs. Legs like those make numbers seem *sooooo* derivative. They, (and she, by God) look so erogenously delicious in a skirt, in slacks, in jeans, in shorts, in tiny panties with a v-line. For a man, it makes perfect sense. When he says I do, it's not to her as such, (that's taking it too far, come on!) it's really to those gorgeous pair of legs. It's not a riddle one has to try and crack. It's an *inevitability*. In fact, the most natural inevitability in the whole world.

She turned to them and said something (no, not about her legs, so it wasn't of the slightest interest to the men), something about audits, and accounts, and reviews. It was all a bit nebulous and vague and outside of reality for the men, but her voice was mesmerizing and they seized on that with a passion. But it was those legs. Mamma mia! Above everything, those legs! They just kept staring at those spellbinding legs. It was like a compulsion. LEGS.

'Are you guys deaf?' she yelled, throwing the file down on a desk and storming from the office.

'She ought to wear pants,' remarked Roy.

'Seriously consider getting married and settling down,' added Nick.

'Yeah, I'd marry her just for those legs,' Frank contributed his share of worldly wisdom, and left this afterthought to inspire, tempt, puzzle and dazzle men. 'What does this reveal about deepest Nature when *She* makes legs like those? Isn't *She* really a man? Isn't *it* really a he?' (Gosh! gasp the men, I wish it were *me – he he he...*)

This was men-talk. Pure male-made syllables and masculine verve. Temptation and torture go hand in hand. A makes B seem like C to D and E makes an effing grand proof of the origins of man in the belly of a woman who's in the bones of a man. Appetite is just sex. And sex is hunger. And the origin of logic is therefore sex. QED! Sure, there's the common way home to a woman's heart. Some you buy a wedding ring. This dainty little piece you adorn with a stock of pantyhose, and just lick those legs, up and down, up and down... Mmmm.

At length they perused the file. (They could smell her scent around it, and that made them feel breathless). The auditors had been over the accounts and the report praised their trading pattern as holding over the previous quarter, profits were on track to exceed the benchmarks set last year, and trading volume curving up in the right direction.

'What do they know?' said Nick.

'Whatever we tell them,' answered Frank, becoming distracted by the blinking numbers on the trading screens. He leaned forward and pressed the ESCAPE key to terminate the loop. The program had taken a speculative position in copper futures, and had overdriven a trade, recording a loss.

'Was that for real?' asked Roy, looking grimly at the prospect.

'No. It's a simulation. It just worked its way through.'

Roy sighed with relief as Nick took a closer look. 'It looks real enough to me.'

'Well it's not. I've had it running in test mode since this morning. Go ahead; check it out for yourself if you like.'

Nick took the graphic pen and opened another window on screen, selecting data that displayed actual real-time transactions, and pasting it into the virtual simulation. He then overlapped data-sets, thus threading them together.

'Are you trading, Nick?'

'No. I'm just steering the simulation. I want to see what it does if I take it over into real time.'

'Why now? Just leave it; we'll do it later.'

'Let's ask ourselves this,' Nick continued, 'how closely can a simulation replicate the real world? And, inverting that, how accurately can the real world reproduce a simulation? *Could the world make a copy of itself?* Surely, it would need to *simulate* it first, right? It has to go *through* itself to make itself.'

'Do you mean a clone, Nick?'

'An *informational* clone. A body of pure data – quirks and all. Pure data.'

'Are they watching us now?' Roy drew closer and whispered. 'Well, is Peeping Tom creeping in the network?'

'If he is, let him watch,' said Frank. 'I like a cat to watch. What are you whispering for?'

'It's a Peeping Tom, not a tomcat?'

'What are you saying, Nick?'

Nick looked at him and grinned: 'Curiosity killed the cat.'

They held their breath a moment, then began to laugh. 'For a man of quiet talents, you're a crafty devil, Nick. And a subtle one at that.'

'A perfect cat, you might say.'

'Meow.'

In the past some philosophers saw the world as the stuff of dreams. Presently, *dreamstuff* gets a rehash as computer simulation. A dream. A simulation. A game? Stuff! Is there something here combining the improbable fancies of a dreamer with the rigor of the believer? What magic unfurls for us? Is the whole greater than the parts? Is this, *that?* Is a sphinx, a cat?

Don't hold your breath; it's not worth a sigh. It's all just a ream of words. Mere words... Open your mouth and out pour... dribble, dribble, dribble, noteworthy syllables that taste of this and that. Go on, pour them into a bowl and offer it to a cat, and watch it nose around and lick lick lick up, mmmm, dreamy semantic cream, tastes wonderful, like a lullaby, better even than a dream, mmmm... more scrumptious than a simulation. One could lap away at this forever.

Meow! Simulated meow. Dreamy meow. Kind of sounds the same meow to me... To you?

They watched Nick finess the data-sets. They were seeking those vital threads that tie ingenious ideas to reality, and weave a simulation distinct from mere chicanery. It had to be realistic, look real, feel real, and even smell real to a discerning mind. Something even a magician can believe in. Something nifty. Something smart.

But without the action of a human hand to guide the simulation, to bias its progress, it would drift into its own pre-defined randomness. Human ambition, calculated risk, the gut instinct that proves your moves against your rivals, creeps in, always. The conviction that the market could take the slides, the falls, the rises, the turbulence and the gamble that makes it not only dynamic, but *human*. The tenuous link holding the data-sets together was the human hand; the toolbox of endeavor is the one that prevails. It relied on mind to measure the odds of a winning bet. After all, even a random gust of wind can turn over a prized card. But what does it know, other than to howl and to blow?

Suddenly, Frank began to agitate, picking up the random card of life. 'Fellas, I just had a thought.'

'If it's about business, I'm listening,' said Roy. 'If not, keep it to yourself. The less I hear from you, the better.'

'Nick. Roy.' They both ignored him. 'Are you listening to me?' No, they weren't. 'Fellas.' They looked at him with irritation and asked him what he wanted. 'I understand. I see it now.'

'What?'

'Peeping Tom. I understand... I see what he's after. It just now struck me. It's not our systems he's been poking around with. It's not machines he wants to control. We're the prize. It's us. *Us.*'

'What are you talking about?'

'*Us!* You; me; us,' he pointed significantly at each of them in turn, working his hands as if trying to sculpture something from thin air. 'What it means to be *me*. If you could simulate *me*, like data, and all you had to do was *finesse* the plot, just as Nick was doing a moment ago. All this... this *game*. It's about men; traders; us. Not machines. I was right first time. It's like throwing some games in a match to test how the other guy responds. Winning; losing; no matter what the hand is, you toss them to the other guy to see how his mind operates; how he behaves. We are guinea pigs in our own space. All this stuff,' he indicated everything, the trading screens, the technology, 'this is our world, a controlled space where we sequence our actions to make a profit. We never considered it necessary to spy on ourselves. And there they are, out there, feeding us signals to see how we react. We're reading from a cue, even though we can't see it. They control the environment by taking over the system, *our system, our network,* so everything looks and feels familiar. And all they need do is just tweak the details to obtain a response. It's like training a dog. It's cunning. It's simple. It's so damn clever.'

'Woof, woof.'

'That's not funny, Nick. I was being serious.'

'Sorry.'

'You least suspect the one place where you feel most secure, most strong. Here,' he said emphatically. 'Fellas... you know I'm right.'

Roy frowned. 'You're crazy,' he said. 'You're talking crazy.' After all, for him, smart guys work with smart tools, reluctant to admit that the smartest tool of all is simplicity itself, which could be no more impressive than a blank card, and you find yourself occupying the same intellectual space as a schmuck. Playing simplicity in an endgame is the perfect ruse, because it is often overlooked – you judge yourself too smart for that. As the wise man knows, it's patience and perseverance that unravels the plot of life. And Frank realized this with cool passion. Like pain, like pleasure, they are simple unadulterated facts. He knew this intimately, instinctively, as when Mistress X grasps the whip and brings it lashing down on his back, breaking his skin, it is pure rapture simulated as pain. *Ouch! That's nice...* And he can stomach a few more of those any time, thank you very much.

'Don't you suckers get it yet?' Frank resumed, raising his voice. 'We aren't leaking numbers, not data-sets. That doesn't mean a thing to them. *We've been leaking ourselves.* Like Achilles' heel? They sucked us out, and put us back in, the way *they* wanted to. And we never even noticed a thing.'

'You're crazy.'

'Our systems, our code, our clients, never meant a thing to them, except as bait to trap us with. Somewhere we would be certain to go, and lock ourselves in. Here. This. We're right in the cage.'

Achilles' heels can be elusive. If you love a thing passionately, are you weakened by its embrace; are you vulnerable where you feel most strong; where you are least conscious of the stakes?

'Even if you were right, what do you expect us to do?' Roy tested him. 'Stop trading? Stop work? You're crazy! Trap or no trap, this is all we have.'

'Don't be so stupid. Of course we continue to trade. We couldn't stop even if we wanted to. We'd be fired. But we *must* change our habits; alter our lifestyle; anything that suggests what we are.'

'How? Do you expect me to trade less, to make less money?'

'Don't be so naive. That's the least of our problems. - Are you listening to me, you dummies? I'm talking about lifestyle. *Lifestyle!* They know *what* we are. They know our drives, what keys to press. They know my love of *strong* women. You, Roy, poker, music and your boozing. You're a degenerate. - Nick,' he turned to him abruptly, 'you're still a bit of a closed book. What have you got that's a big part of your life, that's a passion?'

'Things.'

'What things? Where are the leaks? What are the vulnerabilities?'

'Nothing that comes to mind.'

'Whatever they are, blank them out. Blank everything out. Fold the cards. Fold them face down.'

Nick was a voyeur. He loved to gaze. He loved to watch. He was an eye the size of the world, and it was watching, watching, watching...

Obsessed with an endless stare, like the smell of leather, a Dominatrix, S & M, the fetish scene, like fable irresistible. Is it an opera in belief and action; it is an orchestra in being drawn to its overwhelming power, a repertoire of desires trapped in its sense of perfect enslavement. Watch. Be watched. Abase yourself before her, for she, *the fetish*, is the ultimate Achilles' heel.

Voyeur.

Nick lifted his hand and, like a magician, made the simulation disappear with a tap.

The markets, what were they? Entities opposed to prediction, reality composed of a fiction, simulated animals working machines, fleshing out pixels weaving dreams, like water that eludes the grasping hand, as it flows past fingers animating a man... in the restless information flow – like life, what it is, and what is seems to know... A game, whose ceaseless sum is mostly zero. And the residual part of being me, confounds the riddle of uncertainty. Markets, like a god it seemed, were made in Man's image. Success is ever the hope, motivating even angels to participate in the *Great Game*. Profits created through the interplay of numbers spinning out odds as you speculate on tight margins from a dollar to a yen redeemed or devoured by the process of a speculative trade, going where the wind blows, leaping in, scrambling out, chasing the buck. People. The markets are people. The invisible hands with the weight of spirits grasping at the informational tides of life and risk are people, people, people. And some of those people, clever, resilient, persevering, disposed to an amalgam of beliefs, scientific, holistic, agnostic, crave the desire to surpass human instinct with machines, and try their luck with code, tying their fate to the binary bits weaved by people, unleashed by them, and set into the pool of market hysteria to make a buck. And amid it all, in the flow of things, of time, you may pause, light a cigarette, drink some wine, sigh to a colleague, and wonder: is any of this real? Is money, real? Is it just information? Does it really exist? *Is money just a simulation? Is life a....*

'Let's get back to work,' said Nick, trying to unravel the deeper meaning of a deal, of things. 'We'll deal with this other stuff later.'

An ocean of money, weighing absolutely nothing, yet they drown. Metaphor or a trick? Who knows...? It's a deck of cards, that the wind blows.

*   *   *

Across town, rays of sunlight burst through the partially opened blinds of the Homicide office like a patchwork of laser beams, turning the interior grayness to a slick shade of white. Scraps of paper littered the floor among some vacant desks; computer terminals basked in the sunlight as the screen-savers swept into wild gyrations of improbable

277

geometries. Several detectives huddled over their desks and sneezed and whined, and yanked coffee down their gullets after shoveling in spades of chips, pretzels, buns and dried fruit. The uniforms strolled in and out, witnesses and arrestees sat solemnly and gave confession, the junkies couldn't give a hoot, the hookers sighed and manicured their fingernails, the secretaries cackled, and a janitor tripped over a bucket. It was a normal kind of day.

'Are you going to answer the phone?'

Forester let it ring, oblivious to its shrill tones an octave lower than Sandy's own repetition of the same.

'Forester, are you listening to me?' But he was too absorbed in reckoning the sparse evidence before him to maneuver his hand and lift the receiver. At times, she felt, he was particularly obtuse and selfish. Somewhat less than infallible herself, and too proud to recover her composure, she exaggerated her upheaval, lifted a file up above her head, held it threateningly aloft a moment before bringing it crashing down on her desk; waiting for a response and, with none forthcoming, followed these tantrums with a frown, resentfully rose from her chair and picked up the phone. Her shrill ripostes were venom aimed at him.

'Yes!'

Women will never forgive, *ever,* being ignored, even in the slightest degree.

'No!'

Her voice rose, becoming vicious.

'Why?'

Twisting her mouth into contortions.

'Who?'

She was boiling, damn it. Boiling.

'When?'

Forester began to stir, twitching his face in reaction to something, perhaps a fly, but otherwise remained unmoved.

'Now!'

She was reaching breaking point, and he scratched his neck.

'Over my dead body!'

He sighed, leaned back in his chair and yawned, lifted his coffee cup and took a sip. He shuddered feebly, 'Cold.'

'Tell him to go to hell!' Sandy slammed the receiver in its cradle and folded her arms, glaring down at him. Forester glanced at her, appraising, (you know, for a cop, she was a terrific looking piece of ass) cocked a wink at her and said:

'Is there any more hot coffee around here?'

'Asshole!' said rasped, and less than gracefully strode back to her desk.

Don't take any lip from the bitch, son. Cuff her one across the chops. Knock her down to size. Forester gazed at her and felt his old man's words resonate in his mind – a real muscular tempo, that. Naturally, he was inclined to agree, and like a good protégé listened to more of Pop's thundering good advice which, though not of the style, had the effect of a parable on a susceptible (one hundred percent pure male testosterone) mind. *Get up on your feet, son, and stare her down. That's it, stare down the bitch and show her who's boss. They're getting bolder, these wenches. They have a nerve. By God, they've got to be whipped and tamed, son. Tamed into submission. Show her who the real boss is. Show her who's the man. You're the man. You! Boss equals man. Go for it, son. Go!*

'Have I done something to upset you, Sandy?' The old man's method didn't quite pan out, and he sat back down, quietly.

'Are you a moron, Forester? Does it take a genius to figure it out?' Seething; she took up her pen, more in gesture to spurn him than a means of effecting a meaningful display of work. 'What the hell's going on? What are you keeping from me? I can't work like this.' She beat her fists on the desk, hard, and the old man had something pertinent to say about all that female malarkey.

In my day, by God, any bitch open's her mouth like that would soon get it plugged, properly plugged, and she'd know when to belt up in future - or else! Cuff her one, son. Gag the bitch. Tell her to keep her trap shut. Or else!

Being eternally male and heterosexual (just like his old man), Forester was apt to listen but, unlike him, seldom acted on this worldly wisdom. Although *feasible* in theory – for who was he to argue with his old man? – it seemed a touch impractical, but that touch was enough to quash Pop's counsel. It was challenging to gaze at Sandy when she's fuming mad and not be intimidated, and sexually aroused by her, in equal measure. It was a tantalizing fact, that she was a terrific piece of ass, a real turn-on babe with a badge. She could spar with his balls any time she liked; *any* time; even if he did get knocked about a bit, it's the best sport a man could wish for, and he was passionate for overtime. Thus, he confided in her, sounding cautious: 'I have a suspicion that our man is a foreigner.'

'Whom do you mean?' she answered him curtly. 'The pervert?'

'Come on, Sandy, be fair. Live and let live. Have some respect; the man's dead. Whatever his tastes and fancies, he didn't deserve that.'

'OK,' she yielded, regarding his sympathies odd and misplaced, but never dwelled on the matter. 'Where do you suppose he's from?'

'White; age about forty years...' He glanced over the evidence on his desk. 'It's anyone's guess at this point. I'm riding hunches here, Sandy.' - *Pity you're not riding her, son. Teach that bitch a thing or two. Take that, you bitch. Gidde-up!*

'What are you grinning at?'

'Nothing,' he said, mulling over his old man's tempting words of encouragement. *Gidde-up!*

'So what do you have in mind?'

'Well, for a start, I was thinking we could start with the hotels,' he began, thinking more coherently. 'My hunch is some hotel is missing a guest. Now, chances are he would have left his things there. The hotel would keep records; his passport details and so on.'

'OK. I'll see if anything like that has been reported.' And she interrogated the crime database using her computer, but nothing matched any of the keywords. 'No luck there, I'm afraid.'

'Perhaps this hasn't been reported yet. It's only been a few days, after all.'

'So, do we just wait a few more days and follow up other leads?'

'No. There are no other leads. We'll have to do it ourselves. A bit of legwork never hurt anyone, least of all a cop.'

'Do you have any idea the number of hotels in this city?'

'Use your loaf, Sandy. Narrow it down. Check only the top tier ones and leave the rest. This guy had means. Do you have any idea how much his kind of *amusements* cost? We'll, they don't come cheap. He'd stay in Manhattan, downtown, where the action is.'

'Where do we start?'

'You take the west side.'

'From where to where?'

'Central Park. And we'll work our way down south.'

'What if he took an apartment on a short let? What if he had his own apartment here for years?'

'I thought about that...'

'And?'

He shrugged: 'Let's hope he's a normal tourist. It's less complicated that way.'

That was typically him. 'It looks to me like one hell of a long shot, Forester; not to mention the amount of work. You never change.'

'Do you have any other bright ideas?'

She thought and quizzed him: 'Are you a gambling man, Forester?'

Rubbing his forehead, he consoled himself with the afterthought: 'Maybe... Well, when I'm in the mood. It depends on the kind of game.'

The telephone started ringing. This time he picked up and gave his name. It was a lunatic witness who claimed to have uncovered fresh evidence of an unsolved crime committed several years ago. Forester rolled his eyes and Sandy slumped back in her chair, yawned, retrieved a grubby copy of the Yellow Pages, thumbed through to the Hotels' section, singling out the five stars first, and began making calls.

'Sure, sure,' Forrester tried to be polite, but cut into the lunatic's rambling. 'Thank you for the information, Mr. Frankfurter. No, don't bother coming in, we'll let you know if we need you.' And he slipped the receiver back in its cradle. He stared glumly into his coffee and thought wistfully of his Pop. – Give me some advice, Pops - was a plea to abate his troubled mind. And Pop, as always, was on top form. *Listen, son, being a cop ain't just about getting all the facts. Facts are sometimes lazy things. They kind of stroll in at their own leisure. What really wets the pickle is you've got to use your savvy, son. Work a bit of mustard into your loaf, drink a beer, have a smoke, flirt with the babes, shoot a few low-lifes. The innocent? Fuck the innocent. Who's innocent around here? – Habit. Perseverance. That's what this is all about: habit and perseverance. And some luck stirring in*

281

the pot of life always helps too. Rub that bit of relish into your bread, son, any day.

Again, acting on a hunch, Forester made a phone call. He held the receiver to his ear, a pen and paper at the ready, listening anxiously to the ring tone: once... twice...

The third time, Roy picked up.

'Hello. Yes. You want who? Yes, he's here. Who's speaking, please? Well, he's very busy right now. Could you call back later?' Roy turned anxiously to Frank, covering the receiver with his hand. 'It's that cop again.'

'What does he want now?'

'You.'

'What the hell for?'

'I don't know. Here.' Roy passed Frank the telephone and, lowering his voice almost to a mime, said: 'Get rid of him.'

'How?' he returned in mouthy whispers.

'Who cares; just do it. He's beginning to give me the creeps.'

Nick, following closely, stopped work and watched from his desk. Though air conditioning kept the room cool he began to sweat, as did Roy, their respective roles limited to facial cues and shrugs full of disquiet.

Frank, however, became animated with the conversation. The sunlight pouring through the glazed windows intermingled with the blue tones from the trading screens. It seemed atmospheric, and gave him the surreal sense of an actor gesticulating as the dialogue unfolded, a punctured soliloquy of denials and the echoing retort: 'I don't know. I told you a hundred times already. What? When? I've never heard of it? No. I don't know. I wasn't even here, I was in Las Vegas. So how could I possibly know?'

Forester, hindered by Frank's anxiety, decided to work him more gently by sharing some information - a gambit to elicit a response.

'Frank, let me confide some recent facts that have come to light,' he paused, stirring anticipation. 'We think we're getting somewhere. We have a lead.'

'Good.'

'Chances are, and this is still preliminary, that he's a foreigner.'

'Oh?'

'Yes.' He paused again, waiting to draw him further, but Frank remained stubbornly quiet. 'Have you been anywhere recently?'

'How do you mean?'

'Anywhere different from the norm; exotic, unusual even?'

'Idaho.'

He's being facetious, thought Forester, not expecting sarcasm at this juncture. 'Anywhere overseas. That's really what I meant.'

'Then why not simply say so?'

Forester dearly longed to lunge at him with the roar - *Because I'm a cop caught between a rock and a hard place, you shit-head. And if you'd shut your mouth for just one minute and stop trying to be so damn clever and help me solve a crime, I'd leave you alone to rot in your own perverted cesspool you degenerate S & M junkie freak. Do you get the picture, Frankie boy?* But alas for etiquette, he had to beg the slob for cooperation, so he cut to polite blandness: 'I apologize for the oversight.'

'Accepted unconditionally, Detective,' said Frank smugly.

'Well? Where have you been?'

'I went abroad last year. Well before any of this happened.'

'May I ask where?'

'You may.'

The smug, cocky bastard, he thought to himself. 'Where?'

'London; visiting a friend. Stayed for ten days. Not a drop of rain anywhere. That's strange, don't you think? I even took an umbrella with me. I felt very confused and lost,' he concluded. 'It must be the weather.'

'Anywhere else?'

'Why; have you somewhere specific in mind?'

'Please, just answer the question.'

'Tokyo. That was on business. I've never felt so suffocated by so many people in my entire life. I stayed a week, followed by three stifling days in Hong Kong, and four in Shanghai. God, where do all these people come from? Is it *really* women having all those babies? I mean... is there *really* that much fucking going on in the world, or is it just China?'

'Frank, this is important.'

'Sorry. That trip to Asia was several months before London.'

Forester hit his desk fretfully. He fired two arrows at the globe, and both missed the intended target. It was no use being close: in crime, you had to hit the bull's-eye, or nothing. Forester thought quickly and asked: 'Your colleagues; have they been abroad recently?' clutching at anything he could. But he knew the answer, so why did he ask? He wanted to determine Frank's reaction who, in a sense, by being brash, had backed himself into a corner.

Frank felt a stifling sensation in his throat, and his boldness dissolved as he gazed at Roy, miming him something that Roy found incomprehensible, and in exasperation he advanced towards Frank and took the phone from him. He answered abruptly as he listened to the same questions put to Frank. Roy explained:

'Look, Detective, we're in banking. That's our business. We travel all the time. It's part of the job. In our position, if we didn't travel, well, *that* would be something worth investigating.'

'I understand. - What's your most recent trip abroad? Could you tell me that at least?' He heard Roy grumble with irritation. 'It would really help with the investigation. To be candid, Mr. Riemann, we need all the help we can get.' Still no answer, just mumbled expletives. 'Every little bit helps.' Nothing. 'Even the most trivial facts.' God, did he have to beg? 'Please.'

'OK. OK,' Roy finally acquiesced. 'I went to Paris about six weeks ago on a brief business trip. I was there several days. No, Detective, I don't speak French. Is that all?'

'Thanks. I'll try not to trouble you again.'

'Goodbye.' And he hung up abruptly. 'Damn cop, what's he after?'

'There's something spooky going on, and I don't like the look of it,' Frank concurred, looking troubled.

'His snooping around is the last thing we need.'

'Maybe he's trying to intimidate us.'

'He'll have to try a lot harder than that.'

'Perhaps not so hard,' said Nick. 'This is no time for second guessing a cop. I think he's as confused as we are, in his own way.'

'It's one more stupid thing to worry about,' said Frank, bitterly. 'And I just can't cope any more.' He rushed to the windows and tried forcing them open. He knew they were sealed shut and it was hopeless, so why did he even bother? 'Maybe I'm hoping we're not really here, but somewhere else.' He gave up the struggle, and sighed. 'Well, I can hope, can't I?'

Roy shook his head; while Nick grinned and remarked:

'Something tells me we're running in *parallel* here; even if we aren't aware of it.'

'Eh?' Frank grunted as he returned to his desk.

'Events. They're pushing the cop to conclusions that *may* overlap with our own.'

'Eh?'

'Never mind... Never mind...'

Roy continued to agonize, traversing the office and muttering aloud to himself: 'What, with Peeping Tom creeping around our network; and that damn cop with nothing better to do than keep snooping around. With everyone else watching us, what the hell are they seeing that we can't?'

'Themselves, perhaps.'

'Spare me your cryptic riddles, Nick. I want a straight answer.'

'Maybe there isn't one.'

'There is *always* an answer.'

'Then perhaps what I mean is a blank answer. What question could you pose to elicit that? A blank. One and one make one...'

'There you go again,' he said, frowning. 'Stick to the crossword puzzles, Nick. Don't bring that stuff in here. We can do without it right now.'

'What do you mean, Nick?' Frank, feeling curious, asked him. And Nick replied:

'I think that if we knew, or even if we found an answer, we wouldn't know what to do with it.'

'And what would such a thing be? What would it look like?'

Nick thought before answering: 'Something that leads to nothing. Like a fun game. Like a bluff...'

They fell silent for a while, and their space echoed with the soft purring of machines. In that moment empty space felt like a womb, a cocoon, a soft cage.

'Does anyone smell something?' asked Frank suddenly.

'Burning?' said Nick, speculating.

'No. It's like cheese.'

'That's my feet,' said Roy. He had removed his shoes, discreetly, to air his feet. 'Sorry, guys, I sweat a lot down there.'

Frank found the aroma rather kinky, and promised to treat himself with a diversion into the eccentric world of foot fetishes once their current ordeals were over. He kept this to himself, of course, delights of the flesh being a profoundly personal matter. And, shrugging in the manner of an afterthought, said: 'We may as well get back to work, I suppose.'

And they melted back into their routine. Nick turned to the trading screens. Roy picked up the phone and made a call. Frank smiled and took a private little sniff: cheese. Mmm, reminiscences of the French variety, that, with a warm log of crusty bread, goes down handsomely with dry red wine – and a good whipping! Ouch. How can you better that? Never in a month of Sundays... (*Je ne sais quoi!*)

*   *   *

'Sandy,' Forester caught her attention while she was preoccupied with a call, and she froze him a moment with a halting gesture, continuing her conversation with rapt intensity. She gave him a sign with her hand, forming a circle with her forefinger and thumb symbolizing a lead. He quieted down and waited, carefully following as she spoke on the phone:

'I'm sorry, would you mind repeating that, please? How long did you say? A-ha, yes, three nights. Right. Yes. Did you notice anything unusual in his behavior? When? Who did? OK,' she hurriedly wrote something down. 'And what happened then?'

The concierge at a hotel downtown explained that a male guest had booked a room in advance, checked in six days ago, and vanished several days after that. He related the events formally:

'We received a phone call from someone describing himself as a colleague of one of our guests. He related that this guest had met with an unfortunate accident, not fatal, but nevertheless having incapacitated him, and he was recovering at a private clinic. No, he never said where, just a private clinic. He confirmed the guest's details, a mister Maurice Goustan from Paris, France, and someone was dispatched to settle the bill and collect his things.'

'And?' she gasped at this.

'Well, we closed the account.'

'You closed the account?'

'The outstanding bill was settled and the account closed, ma'am. That's the procedure here. It's perfectly normal. There was no need to inform anyone.'

'And you just let them stroll in, on a phone call and a wad of cash?'

The concierge paused, coughing, feeling utter incomprehension at what was troubling her: 'Excuse me, ma'am, but is there something wrong? The account was closed. Did we omit anything?'

Incensed at the impersonal way he conducted business, she had to struggle to remain calm. 'Did it never once occur to you to do something, to double check, to be on the safe side? It only takes a phone call. Is that too much to ask?' She paused to cool herself. 'You should have informed someone, anyone, as a matter of routine. Routine saves lives. You should know that. Damn it, everyone should know that.'

'We're very sorry, ma'am. We had no idea what to look out for. But I'm sure you can appreciate that such things seldom occur. It was a rare event,' he said, 'and wholly unremarkable. In effect, just like a passing transaction.'

Sandy acutely felt it was *behavior* like this that hurt society and filled it will gloom. As long as you pay, others mind their own damn business. *Closed accounts are invisible accounts, and no one gives a damn.* - But she had a job to do and needed his cooperation. 'I trust you kept a record of his *transactions*, his personal details, bills, receipts...? You still have those at least?'

'Can you wait a moment please, ma'am, I'm sure we do, but I'll have to check.' And he put her on hold.

During the conversation she warded Forester off with her frantic gestures, telling him to wait, just shut up and wait, though he grew ever more restless. Now she had the opportunity to share the information, and packed it with a hefty barrage of cursing.

Forester fumed: 'The dumb bastards! And we have to be polite to get anything out of them. I tell you, Sandy, my old man would never have stood for all this bullshit nonsense we have to put up with nowadays. Never! I know what he'd say.' And sure enough, the old man kicked in like a raging bull: *Hand that swine over to me, son. Pass him over. Now, stand out the way. Come here, you cocksucker. I'm gonna ram your head up your ass and through the presser, you shit. Take that! And that! And that! – Throw me the next one, son. Give me 'em here. Let me at the bastards.* One at a time, Pop, one at a time. *Grrrrhhhh!*

The concierge came back on line, his voice in the same bland register. 'Hello, Detective? Yes, ma'am, we still have the records.'

'Good. Thank you. Would you send everything over to us, please?'

'Sandy,' Forester impatiently pressed her for the telephone. 'Hello, this is Detective Forester. Yes, thank you, send it over as soon as you can. We'd appreciate it. Also, do me a favor and check whether he made any phone calls, or ordered anything from outside using any of the staff. You may have discarded the receipts. I know it's not your job to look through the trash. That's our job, but it would be a great help.' The concierge grudgingly agreed to get someone 'under him' to carry out the task. 'Would you? Thanks, I appreciate it. Thanks for all your help.' He tossed the phone back to Sandy, who adroitly slipped it in its cradle. 'The dumb bastard! We can't become a set of transactions. Life isn't a business. Its consequences aren't a receipt. Economics fucks up the integrity of things if left unchecked.' Forester, the "no-holes barred, take no bullshit" philosopher needed a smoke and a leak and a hot coffee and an egg-salad sandwich on rye bread all at the same time. He chose to go to the men's room first.

Sandy smiled and stretched out in the chair, advancing her hands up and massaging the back of her smooth, delicious neck, easing out the tension and gently drew back her hair. Very feminine. A great piece of ass for a cop.

(Phew!) What a day.

Chapter 17

French, the way it was *meant* to be spoken, can really only be appreciated by a foreigner, and a canny American at that. Add in a New York City cop with a smile, and it really becomes articulation with that... *je ne sais quoi* effect. Forester was that unique person, and he had a great deal to say.

All in French, of course. *Oh la la!*

It wasn't only how Forester laughed into the telephone with Claude, his counterpart in Paris, (and pompously at that), but rather the way he conversed that most impressed Sandy, listening enviously to his cackles and his tempo, the measured pitch of his verbs at glancing angles to the nouns, fondling them with his tongue. Watching him with perfect envy, she was all ears.

It was the first time she heard him speak French in such a sustained way – she knew the rumors, of course. But *actually* doing it? Well, it never seemed quite him, characteristically speaking, and quite honestly she imagined she knew him better than that. It follows the first rule of witchcraft, namely the feminine credo, that they know men better than they know themselves. *Ha ha ha...* (What a business women are. *Ha ha ha...*) In hindsight, she still had everything to learn, and her sense of hearing took up the challenge.

Even his gestures retuned to a Gallic fluency, resonant with pomposity, elliptical flights of a hand, the wiggle of cheekbones ponderously lifted to a sigh then held a touch, just so, before cascading to a crescendo: *Oui!* His proficiency was crisp and flawless, the cadence refined like a tuned string plucked to perfection. Was he dieting on frogs legs? she wondered, how could he be *that* good? A cop can never be too obvious: it's a basic rule, he has to be cool, rough cut, polished at the edges, a 21 carat cop - but elegant too? Forester made it look *too* easy, as if she was lacking in something, inside, outside, short of a carat or two. It made her feel inferior, damn him! She felt the urge to pounce on him with: *Well, what's so funny, Forester? What are you laughing at, you frog?* particularly when his humor assumed a flair she wasn't too keen on, the deep nasal rendering of infinitive j's splitting *J'adore notre peu cause, mon ami!* and the crisp pirouettes with his tongue leaping out into *ho ho ho's...* in gamely little echoes that amused the fancy of a grinning man. Forester embellished his nimble train of syllables with various quaint asides spanning the weather, the food, the best wines of the season and, of course, women. You can't have a man-to-man dialogue in French and not discuss women. *Ces't impossible!* They concluded the intros with a brief diversion into the everyday realities of policing either side of the Atlantic.

'By the way, Claude, how's the weather like in Paris?'

'Fuck the weather!'

'Not so good, then...'

'This job is nothing but a constant fucking headache!' ranted the French cop in grungy English, hammering his nouns with vowels, real working class slang this, a battering ram for pounding down bulwarks of pompous eloquence. No superior French for him. Oh no, he was perfecting his urban English with *uber*-grit slang and getting the weight of policing the concrete sprawl off his chest. 'Nothing but a fuck-load of hooligans and thugs out there. I'm telling you, Forester, society's going down the pan. Talk about a fry up. And I haven't even finished my lunch yet. Can you believe it? Christ!' His tongue thrashed about as he munched on a sandwich. 'I arrested some useless good-for-nothing cocksucker who hijacked a bus dressed up as a Viking. Fuck me, what's the world coming to? Does that make any sense?' Munch munch! 'Is this the Paris of my youth? Fuck the lot of them! I've had it up to here! – What's in this bloody sandwich? Mayonnaise? Jesus Holy Christ! Where's the mustard?'

Forester empathized more thoughtfully. 'I see. Yes. Oui...' droning out clichés that the world was going to pieces right before their eyes. 'It's all going to pots, Cluade. Going to pots...' And it was they, cops, who stood between civilization and chaos. Cops against the whole shebang going to pots. The burden was theirs by necessity, not choice; that a *loose* society had thrust the riff-raff onto them. It's a messy business, full of loose ends; but it needed to be done. In fact, he ventured to say it was a vocation, feeling very sanguine at the time because in French it sounded very snappy, and he would love to have danced to his speech as Claude swigged his wine and dug in to another sandwich.

'Mayonnaise again! Fffs-sake! What am I, a cow?'

Forester coughed and resumed. He said policing the *loose* society demanded they reflect coolly – Why was it loose? How did it ever get that way? – and try to understand. That nifty bit of discourse sounded so superior to Forester he beamed with pride, and self-consciously digested his French verbs like the best brandy from the swelling fields of Champagne. Adjectives, he nibbled as hors d'oeuvres. All perfect, of course. *A la carte.*

'Well, Claude, all I can say is that we, as cops on the frontline of the urban jungle, must take the initiative. We're frontline men. That makes us narrators, story-tellers, we read it as it really is. We don't just solve crime; we use our imagination to understand and master the complexities of criminals and set them in context. There's a story here, Claude, and it has to be told by us. Amid the crazy wayward intellect of a hoodlum, there are... how can I put this, sociological considerations to consider.' Forester paused and took stock. He was pleased with the vowels, they were sounding just great, but the consonants he felt could benefit from a smidgen more emphasis to balance out the phrasing. He took great pride in this, more concerned with achieving perfect rendition of the language than any meaning attached to the words, although *sociological* was a bit iffy for him; it sounded a bit bland, and needed more body in the mid section. - His old man was a pug, the boxing ring his playing field, and he was a champ in that setting. For Forester, language was his forte, and he felt he had round one in the bag by a hefty margin in the Eloquence Stakes. 'It's a tough call for a cop; cops like us, Claude, I know. But it's got to be done. Solving crime is like perfect grammar. And you should never compare perfect grammar with anything less than perfection. Only a man committed to eloquence has a shot at getting this job done right, so we may as well do it with *style*. Voila!'

'Style! Fffs-sake, Forester, get with it!'

'Pardon me, Claude?'

'Are you out of your goddamn mind? This Viking moron has interfered with my digestion - *my digestion!* - and over here that counts as capital C crime. C I'll *crucify* the sonofabitch! C I'll chop his head off and ram his C you know where.' The mayonnaise was troubling his guts, but he persevered for round two. 'Have you any idea how serious this is? This is my digestion, damn it. My God! And you want me to understand him? I'll boil the bastard alive in vinegar and feed him to the pigs, I will. So help me God, I will.' (Well, digestion *is* a soft spot, especially for the French. - Round three).

Forester shook his head. Something wasn't quite right. Something jarred in the interplay between urban English and *eclectic* French that had his mind working overtime. He resumed speaking, picking up rhythm as his phrasing aspired to pompous heights of precision, the gilded vocabulary of an American in Paris sounding exquisite to him, but colliding with the guts of *le cop Francais.*

'Are you nuts, Forester? Who taught you to speak like that – a fairy? Are you turning queer or something?'

Forester (particularly his pride) was taken rather aback by this vulgar French retort, as if Claude had landed him a grammatical punch right across the chops, blow for blow it felt like language molested by a man who should know better, and Forester frowned, saying something like he wished for better prose from a Frenchman than what he was presently hearing. It was a riposte aimed with style, and in its turn of language and the swivel of his tongue, came out sounding rather splendid. 'Are you trying to tell me something, Claude? Because if you are, well, I'd really like to know.'

'Oh you would, would you? That's rich coming from you, Forester, after the earful you've just given me. You're bruising my brains, you are. You're using words even I don't understand. And I'm French, goddamn it! What the hell is going on over there? Who am I speaking to?'

Forester asked him, in the best French of course, why he had to swear so much.

'Because I'm a f...f...fucking cop!' he shrieked at him *a la rant.* 'And these streets are exploding with expletives. There's an f-you on every street corner; a goddamn on every sidewalk. You want to know more? A crap on every grinning face that wants to take a copper for a ride.' He gasped for air. 'You've got me all hot and bothered now. What the hell's the matter with you, Forester? What is this crazy talk you're speaking? When, and if, you get here, spruce up - or rather down – your lingo, or you'll undermine the credibility of the Paris Police Force as European toughs. We're hard-nuts over here - you got that? We don't bend for anyone. We make the goddamn rules, like it or not. And we don't want citizens thinking they can fuck around with us. Start speaking like that over here, and you're asking for a riot. Jesus Christ, what's the world coming to! - Forester? Hey, Forester, are you still there?'

Forester sighed, pained that life can be an unforgiving arena for the finer features of language, and a man of his caliber, alike. He concluded with *Au revoirs* uttered with panache, and Claude crudely belched out his own adieus gurgling on too much wine and grub. This is Parisian bye-bye with an American twang and, just so he would not be misunderstood, Claude signed off with a shriek at a low-life who was escorted to his desk by a uniformed officer: 'Guilty! Just shoot the bastard! And bring me another sandwich. Make sure it's got mustard, damn it. Friggin' mayonnaise!' And the line went dead.

Forester had no doubt in his mind that the investigation would lead him to Paris and, confidently replacing the phone in its cradle, said: 'Did you hear all that, Sandy?'

'Oui, oui,' she murmured with a tinge of envy.

'Not bad, eh?'

She looked at him suspiciously: 'Was that *really* you, Forester?'

'I'm afraid so.'

'OK. I'm impressed.'

'Practice makes perfect. And I'm a persevering man.'

'I see...' He seemed in frisky spirits and she knew immediately what he was thinking. 'So you think you're off to Paris, do you?'

'The answers are all there,' he reminded her. 'Need I say more?'

'Ah, I see, so it's good news from the French?'

'We're getting close.' He posed a forced smile, 'Very close.'

'Look, Forester, you need more than a hunch and fluency with French to convince the Captain. You'll make us both look fools if you get this wrong.' He began to fret in his quirky way of mumbling to himself, but otherwise said nothing; just glancing at some papers on his desk that he handled aimlessly. 'Besides, we have to be certain the victim is the same man.'

'Our French colleagues have left no stone unturned, and are working away at it night and day. We can learn a hell of a lot from them, Sandy.'

'The only things they work hard on are on grooming their dicks and taking three hour lunch breaks. We should be so lucky!'

He looked at her haughtily: 'It's a question of style, Sandy.'

'Style?'

'Yes; style.'

'And *we* lack *le style*, do we?'

'I can assure you, Sandy, that *I* am up there among the best. The very best, in fact. *Voila!*'

'Frog!'

'Yank!'

'Look who's talking.'

'You're too cynical, Sandy, that's always been your trouble. You need to have more faith.'

'In what?'

'And trust.'

'Trust?'

'Faith in ourselves, trust in what we are, in what we do.'

'Are you running for public office now, Forester?' she mocked him. 'I don't vote for frogs.'

'Faith and trust have proved themselves indispensable in the past. And you should never doubt a cop on a roll. We're partners, and partners stand together.'

There he goes; he imagines they're unpacking a cozy chair for him in Paris, all luxury, airing the fleece; and warming up a bowl of scrumptious soup; they're pouring him wine and filling his glass to the brim. The fool, she thought to herself, racing ahead of himself that way. He's a cop with years of experience of the city, the raw reality of urban policing, the bitter-sweetness of the job, sickly sweet with crushed hopes, and he should know better.

'I prefer to wait and see.'

'Look, Sandy, New York started the ball rolling, but the endgame is in Paris. The French passport is forged. They're following its trail along with the other things we sent them. And it's not leading us back here. It's over there.'

She gazed at him silently, skeptically.

'Well, I'm convinced,' he continued.

'I say wait and see.'

'For what? I'm ninety-nine per cent certain of the evidence that's come to light. The passport is forged, you can't deny that. All bills and transactions were settled in cash, so there was no financial trail left here in New York. Everything leads to Paris. It begins there, and ends there. This is our man. And the staff at the hotel remembered him clearly. God! They even conversed in French. And that does it for me, more or less.'

'More or less?'

'You have to know French to understand.'

'Well I don't know French, and I understand perfectly.'

'It's all coming together. Why is that so difficult to understand?'

What is it with a man when he feels the urge for something, be it Paris or Apple Pie? Does soft obsession cloud his intelligence, that he overrates a hunch and inflates the facts? Fancifully, she wondered whether to learn French; but in the meantime proceeded skeptically. 'It's still too provisional if you ask me.'

'And don't forget the phone calls. Look where they lead.'

'I bet I can guess where.'

'The French cops are checking them out.'

'Naturally. What else would they do?'

'For starters, they've traced calls to that jazz club in Paris; what's it called again... Ah, here it is, *Blèu Doux*, or *Sweet Blue* in English.' He held the slip of paper aloft. 'The victim called there several times, and Claude is checking it out this very minute as we speak.'

'Of course, it's *Claude* now, isn't it?'

'You've got this all wrong, Sandy,' he leaned back in his chair awkwardly.

'Have I?'

'Events are moving fast. We can't afford to just stand still, or we'll miss the boat.'

'Or airplane.'

They sat confronting one another across a wall of mistrust. Such feelings jeopardized the ethos of a team and harmed the basis of a partnership. The obligation lay with him to prove that the direction he was leading them in was a risk worth taking. He was smart enough a cop to know this, and said:

'Ultimately, it's not our job to be sure, but to solve crime?'

'What good is one without the other?'

'We'll never be sure unless we take a risk and run with a hunch that has enough evidence to give it momentum. And the only way to be sure is to act *ambitiously*.'

'Ambitiously! That's a *fresh* one, Forester, even for you.'

'Well, I am what I am.' He tackled her misgivings not as a challenge, but an earnest appeal for her trust. 'Sandy, are you with me on this?'

It was her call, but the decision was already settled in her mind. What persuaded her was the continued cohesion of their partnership. Sometimes, against the odds and beating against the tide, you just have to do your best. 'OK. I'm with you.'

He heaved a sigh of relief and winked at her, rising from his chair. 'Can I kiss you?'

'No.'

'Just on the cheek.'

'My *ass* is hot and bothered right now,' she grinned cheekily. 'And you might get more than you bargained for.'

He laughed. Although kissing her bum cheek was not something he would likely turn down. In fact, this was a treat he thought often about. Hmm, tasty...

'I'm going to see the Captain.' he said.

'You don't waste any time, do you?'

'Why wait!'

'Well, don't forget me. We're partners, remember? If you're going to Paris, then so am I.' And out of earshot sighed wearily to herself, 'I could use a holiday.'

It was open slightly ajar, and he pushed it a touch, hesitated, then knocked on the door, and took a peek inside. The Captain wasn't there, so he went into his office and waited by his desk. Instinctively, he glanced at the pictures adorning the walls, fixing on one in particular taken many years ago portraying rookie cops on parade. There was his old man. Look! He was in uniform then, a proud smile vitalizing his face, muscular shoulders and broad torso: he could have been a boxer, but he ended up a cop. *That's life, son,* he would say. *And don't argue with the bitch. Take what she dishes out, and make the best of it.*

'OK, Pop,' he whispered back softly, reminiscing, and saluted his old man.

'You!' The door suddenly slammed shut behind him, and Forester turned to see the Captain in a foul mood heading straight for his desk. He sat down heavily. 'Well!'

'Captain.'

'What is it?'

'I need to see you.'

'You've been doing that a lot lately. You're not turning queer are you, Forester?'

'I have a lot on my mind. And I thought, perhaps, if you could spare me a moment of your time...'

'Can't a man take a leak around here? Jesus Christ!'

'He's a Frenchman.'

'Who? Jesus Christ?'

'No. The victim.'

'Which one?'

'The S and M guy.'

'The Smile and Misdemeanor man...'

Eh? Forester quietly overlooked that remark as the Captain threw him a searching look and began rummaging with some papers on his desk. 'And?'

'We're getting hot now, Captain.'

'What are, your chestnuts?'

'After many false starts, we're finally on the right path.'

'Oh yeah..?'

'All roads lead to - '

'Brooklyn.'

'Paris.'

He set down the papers and rubbed his chin as though Forester had just sopped him one right there with a left jab and then a right hook and then a left again smack on the chops. Not quite a knock out punch combination, but it hurt. Ouch!

'I have good news, Captain.'

'Hmm,' he growled guardedly.

'You'll be pleased to know the pieces are beginning to fit into place. The evidence we found is being verified by colleagues in Paris even as we speak. They're good men, Captain.'

'Who?'

'The French.'

'Oh yeah..? You seem pretty keen on them.'

'They helped put the pieces together. It's been a tough case.'

'I need plausible reasons as well as evidence.'

'I speak French.'

'You!'

'Fluently. Oui.'

'Give me a break, Forester, I need more than that. I'm a cop, not a travel agent. Where do you think you are?'

He held his breath a moment and looked gravely at the Captain. 'The answers are in Paris. That's where the knot is tied. That's where this whole thing hangs together.'

The Captain hesitated, stroking his jaw, caressing the fleshy part of his cheek where the molars would have ached under the impact of a blow. Was he soothing them, or grounding down a morsel that particularly bothered him? Perhaps, but mainly that morsel was a dilemma, and the Captain wasn't ready to digest it just yet. 'What about Interpol? That's what they're there for, to liaise and mediate and save us the trouble.'

'And a great job they do too. I love those guys, Captain. They're amazing.' But his enthusiasm seemed too beguiling for the Captain.

'That's comforting to know.'

'I've been on the phone with them several times. They're digging up what they can; within their limits. But the boys in Paris have their nose to the ground. Come on, Captain, a cop that can sniff out a fact from a flea's ass is one mutt you want on your side in this game.'

'And what have they found out, these mutts?'

'They're checking the integrity of the evidence we sent them. You need mutts for that, Captain; guys on the ground who know the streets. Guys like us, not bureaucrats. Give me a dog with a badge over a king with a crown any day. Hey, I'll even take a bitch.'

'What does Sandy think?'

'She's agrees with me; her nose is to the ground. Just throw her a bone. And all we need now is a leash. But don't tell her that.'

The Captain shook his head from side to side with the weight of fond memories: 'Just like your old man, wiseguy and philosopher rolled into one.'

'But he never spoke French.'

'No. But he can throw a right hook!' He rubbed his jaw, and the memory felt the pain, even as the flesh remained becalmed and pristine. 'I don't know. I really don't know...'

'They're checking the leads from the passport as we speak.'

'Forged?'

'Yes. We think so.'

'Boy oh boy...'

'And the phone calls. We're certain they're significant. Before he left his hotel for the last time he made several calls to Paris, late at night. He called the same numbers the night he arrived. I guess he was checking-in with someone.'

'There's a time difference, don't forget.'

'I know. But someone took the calls, and they lasted several minutes each occasion. The longest one went on for over ten minutes. That's a long time, Captain.'

'Who did he call?'

'Various places. We know he called a night club; popular as a jazz hangout.'

'Well, at least he had a taste for music,' he remarked sardonically. 'Better than his women.'

'The others are private addresses. The Paris boys are checking them out.'

The Captain paused, threading the pieces together in his mind, and concluding bluntly: 'Correct me if I'm wrong: so far you've made some progress; but basically you're still riding a hunch, and want a free ride to Paris?' Short and sweet: that's how Pop always referred to the Captain. And he's still the same man. Character is immutable, withstanding the assault of time. Forester looked at him thoughtfully, the stare that is long, sincere, and by necessity optimistic. The Captain shook his head and mimed a laugh, then said. 'We'll see. I'll need to make some calls. Make a few nods. Twist a few arms...'

'Is that a yes?'

'It's a maybe,' he replied. 'You're a smart cop, Forester, you know the system. You can only bend an arm so far.' - It's not getting away with it that's the key, it's knowing how far you can push.

'Thanks, Captain, you're a fella and a half, you are, as the English say.' He withdrew with a smile and the French word for *victory* tickling his tongue. And it felt giggly and sweet.

Sublime moments are like luck, which have a knack of making you feel great. And, as Pop succinctly put it: *It was during the regional championships; we breezed through the semis with style. Within a minute of up-time, when the bell sounded in round four, I knocked the Captain flat out on his back. And I tell you something, son. It felt... Great!*

Sandy received a call from a friend over at the District Attorney's office. A girl, one of twins, went missing, and there was a French connection.

'I understand you speak French, Sandy.'

'A handful of expletives, perhaps,' she replied.

'I was informed you were fluent.'

 That's Forester.'

'Is he around?'

'No. But what has this to do with us?'

'Maybe nothing. But I'm sending her over to see you.'

'Is she French?'

'No. American.'

'What's her name.'

'Alice Long.'

'OK. We'll be expecting her.'

Alice showed them a picture, and it looked exactly like her.

'That's my sister, Zoë. Zoë Long.'

Forester looked at it first, the sweet face, the self-conscious pose, the blond curls tumbling over her shoulders, the sparkling eyes of a girl dressed as a woman. They grow so fast, he mused quietly to himself, before passing it to Sandy who gazed at it for a while. 'One and one make one,' she spoke softly, and looked at Alice.

'Excuse me, ma'am?'

'I'm being cryptic, that's all. How can we help you?'

'My sister went to Paris two months ago. We always kept in touch. But for the past ten days no contact from her at all. No email; no message; nothing.'

Sandy and Forester briefly glanced at one another, and both were of the same mind: what has any of this to do with them? Sandy said:

'It's something you need to take up with the French authorities. We can pass on the information, and if you leave her picture with us, and any details of her past whereabouts, we'll do what we can to help with enquiries, and try and push things along. But you must understand, we're here, not in Paris. It's not our turf.'

'Zoë worked at a club,' Alice began abruptly, pushing her burden back onto them. 'She waited tables for a while, helping out, finding her way around. She befriended an American jazz singer, Cindy Gillespie, who has a sister that resembles her. People often mistook them for twins. But she isn't a twin. Not like Zoë and I.'

'Alice. Here, have a seat. Please...' said Forester.

'What happened to her?'

'Tell us what you know.'

'Where is she?'

'Give us the details. Write it all down, everything you know. We'll look into it.'

'She wouldn't do this, sir.'

'I know she wouldn't. I believe you.'

'She's not like that. I know her. There's something wrong.'

'I believe you. I do. I'll look into it personally. I'll let you know as soon as I have any information.'

'When?'

'As soon as possible.'

Unsteadily, and with a nervous hand, she began writing, tears trickling down her cheeks. Sandy passed him the picture and he gazed at it warmly, full of an overflowing pity. A deep sense of pathos framed the moment, and he held his breathing to a slow resuscitation, fearing to disturb her. And the hardest part of all – he felt powerless.

Even Pop cut in with a heartfelt aside: *The kid needs a break, son. Give her a hand. You've got to help her. That's what it means to be a cop. You get involved, whether you like it or not. Shutting it out will just kill your soul. It's not just a day's work any more; it's a vocation. This is NYPD: **N**ow **Y**ou're **P**ulled-in **D**eep. And there is no way out.*

I hear you, Pop. I hear you...

Chapter 18

Paris by night. (Whispers, *sssshhh*...) Call of the dreamer catches two winks before insomnia kicks in, and he's revving up the system reaching for the nicotine pack and lights a cigarette, coughs then ahhh... knocking back a coffee, hot as sin and black as the devil, while watching TV day-dreaming of the dames he could have had, and football, and horses. He's fond of horses, considers them serene, beautiful, graceful. The TV hacks at his mind with video monotony, but is the perfect backdrop for imagination to meander among the sleek form of women's legs, pantyhose making them dreamy length, necessarily starting at her toes, and then climbing up the ankle to the fabulous smooth calf, up... up to her thighs, then deepest high to the topmost glistening wet surround of sensual heaven.

Paris. *La Femme.* Evocative by candlelight but it's the streetlights draw the moths, the creatures, the lovebirds, the swingers, the feisty young things after the hullabaloo of hungered pleasures. The insomniac takes a walk and ambles down the quiet boulevard. He's an American in town just killing time. *Bang bang. Seconds are dead.* He rummages in his pockets for another smoke. Finds one. Slips it in his mouth, but can't find a light so uses his eyes and spots a hooker swinging her purse (heavy with condoms) softly to and fro as she loiters by the pavement on the corner.

'Do you have a light?

'Pardon, monsieur?'

'Cigarette.'

'You want to fuck?'

He thumbs it at her and she shakes her head. She kind of smiles and he wants to smoke and instinctively draws-in air, but tobacco ain't tobacco unless it burns and burns like a bitch deep in your mouth, so he ambles on spying out the scene, not hungrily but with time to spare, and looks at his watch, killing time, sighs, looks at his watch again, and this ritual almost grows purposeful. These avenues of writers, dreamers, idealists, women, nightingales... the narrative of timeless time and other fanciful contradictions... and starlight looks enticing, but all he really wants is a light. He hears a van pull up behind him and stops. He yanks the cigarette from his mouth and strolls over. The driver gets out and leers at him a moment before tossing him a casual gesture. Strangers in the night stuff. (Hi, Hi. Bye; Bye. Who the hell are you looking at? Just passing. Get lost. Au revoir. Catch you later...) All they need is a breeze to set the boulevard in motion and the moment becomes mythical. (Camera. Action. Perfect. That's a wrap.) He's an iceman delivering ice to the sweltering hotspots of a Paris club scene. The overloaded ice machines can't keep up. People want to party, party, party. They want to f**k and f**k and f**k and they never get enough. Insatiability – synonymous at times with emptiness, with loneliness, with hopelessness. Burn up time. Waste yourself away in ecstasy. And ever fear to stop and wonder who you are, what you are, why anything exists at all. That's just the way it is. Isn't it? - Paris. City of...

'Pardon me, monsieur. Do you have a light?'

He obligingly nods his head and slips back into the van and retrieves the lighter from the cab. The American sets fire to the tobacco and inhales. Time, life, light, all expand as nicotine hits the spot, and the American smiles, offering his savior to share in his salvation and opens the pack, exposing sixteen cigarettes neatly trimmed and waiting to be devoured. The driver takes one and stores it behind his ear, grinning belatedly. Later he'll have a smoke and a glass of wine before hitting the sack.

The American strolls on, late into the languorous night.

You wanna fuck, you wanna party, you wanna smoke, you wanna dream, or just wanna stroll and gaze at architecture and the stars? Well, go ahead; it's your world. The American pauses by a lamplight and chain-smokes from one dying butt end to the next, meandering to a part of town he knows. It gets busy as he looks both ways and crosses a main street, and then it grows all quiet again as the flipside of animation is a soothing silence – just interludes of the city moment.

A taxi races along the quiet boulevard, midweek in mid June;

and it's lusciously warm. He looks at his watch – it's the other side of midnight. It's a breezy kind of time, a twilight time between streetlight and moonlight, between sleep and dreams, that ocean of tranquility ensuing heavy sex. Two lovers giggle coyly as they turn into the boulevard, saunter twenty paces, and get into their car. A cat, its huge searching eyes glowing diamond, its petal shaped ears erect and alert, watches them as they drive away before turning its attention to the American strolling down the same boulevard, lighting another cigarette with the butt end of the previous one before casting it into the gutter. The cat crawls up to it and sniffs. Ah, nicotine. It benignly purrs and lingers a while nosing around the ember, then casts an envious gaze at the American heading for the night-club. Ah... To be human and enjoy a cigarette. Perhaps, in another life the Hindu wheel of chance slips the cat a suit of aces, and its *yausa yausa yausa* kind of life till the cat comes in. And with that afterthought to muse on, the cat slips away into the night. *Meowwwwww.*

'Good evening, monsieur, Mr. Tomka.' The doorman politely greets the American and steps to one side.

'Sam. Please, call me Sam.' This eponymous *Wham bam, Thank You Ma'am* kind of guy is a laid back, womanizing, money- making engine of a man with mousy hair and romantic eyes that flatter the light and make him seem appealing to friend and foe alike. He has that look that makes you want to trust him. And tipping the doorman smiles breezily like he's everyone's favorite cup of tea: (sugar; cream, not so much, just a touch...) And the whole of China loves him, if only they knew he was Sam. Like the doorman:

'Thank you, Sam.'

'Don't mention it,' he says breathily. 'It's a pleasure. It's always a pleasure.'

You just can't help liking him. Oh, and he fancies himself a connoisseur of poetry too. He knows a medley of verses off by heart and recites them to himself when walking, thinking, eating, having sex, making money and, of course, during a game of poker. 'Who's upstairs?'

'Ice. And someone I haven't seen before. Some Greek guy, I think.'

'Greek?'

'Or maybe Italian.'

Some nights you get a Mediterranean crowd, sunshine smiles and laughs galore and a way of conversing that's easy as you please, wooing the candlelight of romantic nights, and sometimes the sensuous torches of Sicilian delights: red wine, a song, a kiss... sunsets and serenades... But tonight was a quiet night.

Sam, a.k.a Sam Tomka, alias Double Heads (he always carried a double headed coin for luck), entered a password into the electronic lock and slipped upstairs, pausing only briefly to light a cigarette. It was silent inside the room as he eased open the door, the motion as quiet as his steps. Ice noticed him with a brief flicker of his eye, while the other guy kind of guessed:

'Sam?'

'I can't sleep. It's these sensuous nights keeping me awake.'

'Close the door, Sam.'

And never took his eyes from the cards. He was Italian, refined, he had the face of easy life, the good life, and like Ice seemed to sense the things around him. It was poker, perhaps, or the human fancy that he is so engrossed only the game matters. As with all poker games it emanates a power, a silence like sacred moments. 'Raise you ten G's, Ice.' And he taps the table, talisman-like. Next step. Call. There isn't much to see or do – but it's everything in the world to a poker man.

'Cigarette?' offered Sam.

'Maybe later.'

The only stir was the lone sound of poker chips tossed onto the heap swelling up at the center of the table as they raised the stakes first to ten, then twenty, then forty thousand. When he hit fifty, the Italian turned his head and glanced at Sam. Time for a smile. 'You look good?'

'Thanks. I try my best?'

'I'll take that cigarette now.'

Ice pondered his next move as the Italian laid his cards face down and massaged his face. Ice waited until he lifted them again and said, 'Raise you twenty more. And I'll see you.'

The Italian sighed spinning out time. 'Did you know the numbers in roulette add to six-six-six? And three six's add to eighteen. And eighteen times thirty-seven is... Sam?'

'Six-six-six.'

'I was about to ask you to recite us a poem.'

'Maybe later.'

'Well, Ice, what must be, must be.' And he revealed his cards, one at a time. Six. Six. Six. And two nines. Ice folded his cards with dismay, (a triple five, jack and a king). The Italian hauled in his winnings and withdrew from the table, asking as he passed. 'Sam, you still have the coin?'

'Only for luck,' he said. And for kicks too, but he was quiet about that. Sentimental, I guess.

The Italian quietly left the room, closing the door behind him.

At length Ice sighed, a man down on his luck but not defeated and, collecting them up, began slowly shuffling the cards, glanced at his money and remaining chips, then fixed a stare on Sam. 'Are you in?'

Sam moved to a tactical seat opposite him, took out his money, lit a cigarette, and said: 'I thought you were coming to see me today.'

'Things became complicated.'

'How?'

'Just the usual things. You know...'

'Far less than I should like.'

'Well, you know how things are.'

'Do I?' he insinuated. 'It seems you guys down there in *The Vault* are very busy bees these days. What's happening to all that golden honey? I'm beginning to worry, Ice. I hope I'm not missing out on anything. That would be most unwise. And very unfortunate for everyone concerned.'

It was a poker moment, and Ice thought quietly in the ensuing silence, his gaze roaming aimlessly for a while, before his fingers fired up and he dealt the cards, opening play with a thousand.

'So, Ice, what's happening? I was expecting to hear some good news.'

'Good news? What good news?'

'This isn't a game.'

His eyes fixed deliberately on the cards, arranging them, swapping them around, his fingertips fondling them for luck. 'I told you this before, Sam, we don't make things; not in the way you imagine.'

307

'But you have the means?'

'The means?' he glanced up at him. 'We work with what we have. We manipulate, yes; and *embellish* with technology. After all, in this game, computers are like mascara.'

'I never noticed that.'

'Well, they are. They make even the plainest eyes look fetching.' He sounded irritable. 'That's our business.'

'To put on mascara?'

'To look! And to look the part. That's all we do: is look. We crack networks; we spy; we simulate the markets. If something is there, we'll find it. If it exists, we'll break into it. But… you know all this, so why am I telling you again?'

'You know why.'

'It's a big world out there, Sam, with deep pockets. We don't make the rules any more than you do. We go around them. That's the trick with rules, we go around them, not break them.' Ice argued, the greater part of his mind enamored with the cards. 'That could easily get out of hand. You know that. Ask for the impossible, and all I can offer is an illusion, even a beautiful illusion painted with mascara. Is that what you want?'

'I want what you promised.'

'You have to be realistic, Sam. You guys, you sometimes lose the thread of what we're doing. We're trying out new concepts and, well, the future is full of surprises. It's a fact of life. I made that very clear in the beginning. I never gave guarantees. That's impossible. Do you want to play cards or not?'

'I'm in,' he said, challenging him softly, throwing in his chips. 'So what about the project?'

'Like anything born of an idea, or even a dream, one is always competing against the great unknown.'

'What unknown?'

Ice grew impatient, he wanted to concentrate on poker, 'Greed, then, for want of a better word.'

'And there is nothing as capricious as greed, is there, Ice?'

'You're the expert, Sam.'

'I try to be.'

Spontaneously, they both began to laugh.

'Ice, on the level, what's happening? We need to know.'

He evaded answering and focused on the game. 'How many cards?'

Sam studied his cards and smartly threw down two. Ice dealt him the same number of fresh cards and himself three. It took Ice only seconds to respond: 'Call. And raise you a thousand.'

'We're growing restless. You understand that, I hope? We trust you're not going to let us down. We have an enormous amount invested in this enterprise.' He paused to give weight to what he said. Then coughed as he reached for his money. 'A thousand.'

'Everything is under control. Trust me.'

'I hope so. – I'll take one card.'

'Only one?'

'Yes. A nice easy number to remember.'

'Have I ever let you down?' Ice dealt the card and himself two, deliberately keeping control; looking over his cards and then at Sam, playing a game of run-and-chase done subtly to keep him guessing without working him too much or tiring him too soon. You need your opponent, you need his endurance to test yours, to make you stronger, to empower your mind in mastering the moment. It's the details that count, sure, but the broad sweep of perspective is an eye-on-the-world you never want to be without. What is a knock, even to the ground, if you can get up again? Just another event in the wholeness of time. It happens, you learn, you move on. In cards, as in life, rashness has checked countless heroes. It was wise to be wise, but wiser still to act wisely. Ice should know, and he does, but even he sometimes forgets. While the wager was rendered with money, the prize was information.

Sam was a senior executive at NBS Banking Corporation. His role was managing people, in building teams. He stove for perfection, which seldom emerged alone but of many things converging. Luck is really a thousand invisible hands performing a synergy operation. The right people were the keys to enduring success; to make a fortune from trading in currencies, from bonds, commodities, intangibles and tangibles alike, even from nothing. Luck lies with the hand of the right man in the right place at the right time playing the right card. And this informed him of the wisdom: *easy come, easier go.*

Getting it right, doing it right. That wasn't science but sheer savvy. And this is the root of abundance.

Like his smile, the prize of success, he tended to share it around. And Sam liked to smile, more than most men, though that smile cut a definite purpose. It expressed a satisfaction in the people around him, in skill, in hard work. In savvy.

He respected his own decisions, because he worked so hard at them. Risk was a bastard, but this *guy* he respected too. Risk was basic to existence – you needed it to thrive, it was spliced into the mind like a mental gene. Man is a kind of avalanche waiting to happen. Getting it right was essential. In fact, it was everything in the world to this man. And risk? Well, he knew, at any moment, even perfection could collapse. Respect. That's the thing...

Ice worked independently and Sam befriended him by chance at a poker game, in time learning of the project piece by piece until he built up a picture of its overall potential and aims. Inevitably, Sam became involved; initially at the fringes but then deeper as temptation grew - which came at a price. As a man that admired horses for their refined power and grace, he nevertheless felt that banking had features more in common with a cat: nimble, quick, sleek, alluring, *purr-fectly* there, seductively dangerous – a cat. One could be mauled by its sweetness, stifled by its softness, beguiled by its eyes, seduced by its meow... as its ears rise to absorb the shudders of the world around it.

At some point Sam took a risk, and Ice tantalized him with pieces of information which he had to pay increasing amounts for, one way or another. It was poker that started the process and had kept the momentum going. And driving it all was money. It oiled ambition, and greed, and desire. There are few things more tempting than an addiction, more relentless than an obsession, and you run the risk of being consumed in your own fire. - Money. America. Pillars of abundance. But it ain't the whole story. No, sir, not by many a mile.

'Tell me, Ice, how is the project coming along?'

'Ticking along nicely, Sam. Tick tock. Tick tock...'

'Cute! And the troops?'

'All in step,' he said.

'One two, one two...'

'Shoulder to shoulder.'

'Good. – What about Roy Riemann and his merry men? Did they take the bait? What are they doing?'

'Showing all their cards, as usual,' he said. 'Some guys are never sure quite how to play the game. They see the queen as a woman. But she's really a man. She acts like a man. She has the power of a man.'

'But the queen aside, they're not resting, are they? – Ice, there have been rumors that Roy and his perky little team of Tom Thumbs have been poking around. They're growing restless. Did you plan for that? Was that meant to happen?'

'Who can say.'

'What have they found out?'

'That a ghost has not one but many faces.'

'What?'

'Can you ever be certain what you're seeing is real?'

'How close are they to finding anything out?'

'The closer they get, the less they know.'

'I don't believe you.'

'Do you know the easiest thing in the world to simulate?'

'Whatever it is, I'm sure you're about to tell me.'

'Yourself.'

'That's a novel idea,' said Sam. 'Why?'

'Because you're liable to believe anything. Especially the sweetest part. Flattery being what it is.'

'Do you know what I think, Ice?'

'No. Not really.'

'Life thrives on risk.'

'In that case, you know you could lose.'

'But it's a *calculated* risk, not any old risk.'

'I'll keep that in mind.'

'Ice, about Roy Riemann...'

To Sam, it felt as though Ice was on the verge of revealing something significant, but only gazed at him ambiguously instead: 'You know, Sam, I sometimes like to imagine that people would be a lot better off living in a cage. Especially men. It's much better if women hold the key. After all, relationships, they are a kind of cage, aren't they? And commitments too. And your job. And even the draw of the cards. You're a captive of external events and things.'

'What?'

'Of chance.'

'And your point is?'

'Roy and his merry men are really a suit and a half - diamonds, of course. It's amazing what they can do when they put their minds to it. Men, you see, are arrogant beasts. Being what they are, well, using their savvy must make a real change. I like that word – savvy. Did you know that a word can be your best friend? These days, I measure almost everything by them. Even poker. Even you, Sam.' Ice grinned. 'Does savvy always grow so well on American soil? Or is it just New York City?'

'Have you... spied anything; heard anything? Anything at all?'

'Did you have something specific in mind?'

'Just some rumors floating around. Things might have got a bit out of hand over there, and spiraled out of control.' He looked at him evasively. 'It's just a rumor, of course.'

'Rumor or no, that's your problem.'

'*Our* problem.'

'*Your* problem.'

Sam tried pushing the envelope before, but Ice always pushed back.

'You know, Ice, we're in this together.'

Sam fidgeted nervously with his cards, turning them over in his hands to regain control. He was working his mind, striving for a clever rhyme: 'I think we need to pause and face; the repercussions that unfold in a known and distant place.'

'Look! whatever happened over there has nothing to do with me. I break into networks. I don't break necks. You're a smart guy, Sam. You guys, you know what you're doing. You cut the cards; you bear the consequences. You calculate, remember? A calculated risk.'

Sam lit a cigarette, taking his time. 'Raise you... two thousand.'

'Besides,' he said, counting two thousand and another three, 'we reap what we sow.'

'Give me three cards.'

'One. Two. Three.'

'Now it's my turn to play the piper. And you're going to dance.'

They laughed spontaneously, releasing the tension that festered and threatened to engulf them. Smart guys know the limits; understand how far they can stretch events before they snap and overwhelm them. Self-interest and survival mutually reinforce, like a king and a queen of the same suit, they are cards closest to their chest, and you don't want to give them away. And smart guys know, above all else, they should never start something they can never successfully complete. Smart guys, like them. And did that include poker?

Poker? - It's just a game. *Isn't it?*

'When I was a kid at school, around fourteen, I won a prize in a lottery,' began Sam.

'Lucky you.'

'It was a date with a girl.'

'Was she worth it?'

'At first, no. After all, someone gave me the ticket, and I'd rather have the bike. But ten years later I ended up marrying her. - Do you believe in fate, Ice?'

'I never buy lottery tickets.'

'I don't mean blind luck, I mean fate.'

He pondered quietly. 'Coincidence. I can appreciate that, perhaps.'

'And fate?'

He shook his head and gazed irritably at him: 'Am I really the person to ask?'

'It depends on the prize. Match the man with the method – does he apply it? Offer him a prize; does he aspire to win it?'

'The prize?' Ice leaned back as if laboring under a weight of thoughts, and Sam took the double-headed coin from his pocket and pressed it between his fingers in a ritual that seemed stranger than reason could unfold. The act of powerful persuasion is entrenched deeply in the psyche of a man, and he, as a spirit of ancient trusts, yields to its fearful promises.

The project to design innovative trading systems for gaining advantage in global financial markets was the real prize Sam played for, and that had obsessed him for months. Although the details mystified him, the implications - the prize - proved irresistible.

313

'Ten thousand; and I'll see you.' Having resumed play, Ice made the call to see him.

Sam smiled a royal smile, and showed his cards: 'Three kings.'

Ice folded his cards, his eyes reflecting the gleam of the believer. Sure, his resources were dwindling, but to an instinctive gambler that was no more significant than conceding a fact. Luck is a bitch, she scratches, she mauls. But this lady has the last word. So you whisper hopeful wishes into her dice and take a throw. They're numbers. Clumsy numbers. But the cards speak sweetly to the gambler, tickling his obsession. They are shades under a scorching sun even if you're down. You just take it in your stride, you smile at the deck and say to yourself *Use your savvy,* even if you can't always win, margins count. Margins matter. Margins make the difference. In business. In life. In poker. In the next game.

'You deal,' said Ice.

'It's in my nature to,' replied Sam, handling the cards fondly. They felt easy in his hands, pliable, soft, engaging, and he flirted with them in a gambler's sense by teasing them in a shuffle and bending them to, till they snapped back reflexively in his hands. Then, he started to deal. 'Your team of wizards is keeping us all awake these days. This project must be a handful and more.'

'You know how it gets, Sam. We do our best to make it work.'

'Dedication. I admire that in a man. That's what attracted me to you.'

'I'm flattered. I am what I am.'

'And Mammon made bankers.'

'Well, someone had to; it may as well be him.'

'And this enterprise is keeping us all on our toes, isn't it, Ice?'

'Our toes can bear a great weight. They lift us up by the smallest of margins. And sometimes, those margins make all the difference in the world. Never underestimate the small things in life. Like your lottery ticket, for instance.'

'But you never buy them, so what advantage does that give you?'

'It trains my mind never to rely on blind luck.'

Sam rearranged his cards, taking his time. 'A theatre company is putting on Oedipus Rex in Greek. I've seen it before, many times. I can recite the whole piece off by heart. Different interpretations of the same play have always fascinated me. It's fascinating how many faces a chorus can have.'

'That's life.'

'That's drama.'

'Same thing.'

'I speak Greek, by the way.'

'I know.'

'Great stuff.' Sam maneuvered his cards again, fidgeting. 'The wonder of the Greeks is that they taught themselves *how to think*. It's like pulling yourself up by your own boot straps.'

'Remarkable,' he thought aloud, studying his cards, leading his thoughts, taking his time. 'Remarkable...'

'What do you think of Homer?'

'Raise you five thousand.'

'I'm in.'

Driving the dream on, another ten, another twenty, another fifty thousand, this flawed belief that he can overwhelm the odds, that he can play against the Gods, desperately taking on *one more game, just one more, one more, one more...* blinds him with the joker's hope, then shudders when he's dealt a five of clubs promising him victory, but which subsequently turns to a loss around a pair of queens and three fives against the weight of three tens and a pair of jacks. The cards beguile him; there's no pattern he can fix on - like a drug, addict himself to. It's only the softest ones, the unnoticed ones, that speak to you, and so quietly done, it feels like dreaming. The rational mind that defines Ice... melts; his eyes narrow in prayer to the fates, his fingers crossing superstitiously evoking the ritual he despises as a man. The faint cough is the plea: *Please, God, give me a break!* But only chance dominates the dynamics of the game, with skill at the fringes, calculated reason in the middle – you bake your cake and eat it. OK, so long as you can. But for Ice the game is a capricious hand meddling with his wits, not a hand to hold his hand, but to push him over the edge, the fall prolonged by the vitalizing flow of bitch-black coffee and strong cigarettes shoring up his nerves for one more game, just one more game... until realization dawns that he has pressed too hard too long and built up a running debt. It's insane, but he antes up again and looks forlornly at his last ten thousand. It's all credit. But

315

for him, now, credit is like life; so he wagers it all, seduced by the gambler's obsession to win. But Lady Luck threw the dummy card and called his bluff, and he gasped, exhausted, gulping down heaps of air as though he were drowning, before resigning to the inevitable and slumping back in his seat. Defeated. Humbled. Broke.

'The cards are winking at me today.' Sam hauled in his winnings. 'I fondled the hearts, teased the clubs, and stroked the diamonds – they like that kind of tickling. And the rest, well... they couldn't resist me. That's how seduction is meant to be *played*.' For Sam, winning was like champagne. And it all went *pop!*

'It just wasn't my night.'

'But the pearly lights of Mammon are glowing bright,' he rhymed teasingly.

'What goes around, comes around.'

'And in for a penny, in for a pound.'

'Perhaps I should get married and settle down.'

'Well, it's the only way to get a real divorce. And I'm always willing to play the best man. Especially for a poker player.'

They touched glasses and drank, not as a gesture, or even rivalry, but in mutual recognition of what it means to win and lose, and above all, to play. You're in a ship, and sometimes you run aground; other times you sail all the way to the New World. But what needs to be understood is this - in a calm sea, never rock the boat.

Sam felt completely satisfied: 'Winning is an infectious. But...'

'But what?'

'You ought to try poetry, Ice. It relaxes the mind wonderfully. When you're lost, it navigates you back to your senses. It gives you a clearer horizon than anything else I know.' He felt at ease philosophizing, and it showed profoundly in him because he spoke wisely. 'Circumstance is very much like these cards: you feel you have them in your hands, but in reality you are in *their* hands.' Ice looked at the cards, then the money, the gaming chips, the drinks, then Sam. 'Let me see... Ah yes, start with Shelly and Wordsworth to get you going. Then, since I'm in a generous mood, get yourself some Shakespeare to get the motor really rolling. Poetry won't touch you unless you get up close. You have to embrace it because it wants to be your lover. It's an intimate thing. Let it move you.'

'You're all goodness and heart.'

'Don't forget smart.'

'OK, and smart too.'

'Here. Take a couple of thousand and treat yourself to some classy editions.'

Ice laughed. But he took the money anyway. When a man riding on a wave of luck gives you something, take it. He means well, and you can always use a break. Sam continued:

'True poetry is like holy incantations. The Gods listen to you. In fact, that's the only time they are listening to you, because you're speaking in their language. Take it from me, Ice, I know.'

'It's not a prayer I need, it's a break.'

'A break. Ah,' he lit up another cigarette, and the mood changed. 'So far, we've been lucky.' The *other* conversation kicked in. 'The information you provided us with is neither hot, nor cold. It's, how can I say... tantalizing. - Ice, I don't like exposing myself to these kinds of risk.'

'What I provide you with is information. That's all. How you choose to use or interpret that in the financial markets is entirely up to you.'

There are three persistent dangers that can try a man, and that Sam feared: being in someone's hands; being in the hands of fate; and having access to something that may be beyond your capability to control. He laid it out. 'I've taken risks based on that information. *Big risks*. There are *serious* people involved who take this very, very *seriously*. Ice, are you listening to me? We can't take unnecessary risks. They must be avoided *at all costs!* What people will do for this.' Grasping a handful of money and clenching it passionately, before letting it slip back from his hand, and looking down at the cards scattered over the table, uncertain what to make of them. 'After all, this is not a game.'

'Double or quits.' Ice trapped him with a fixed stare before reaching out and gathering up the cards. He fondled them, stroking a queen of hearts as if arousing her, before placing her under the king of diamonds. This soft and tender addiction betrayed the doomed gambler who monetarizes knowledge in the hope of success. Desperation dazes him as he shuffles the cards, handling them with reverence, caressing them for power, shuffling the magic, redeeming the spell. The compulsion to gamble grows religiously in him and he, the disciple of a sixth sense, prayed not at the shrine of reason, but senselessly persevered, deaf to all the inner voices urging him to stop. Nothing, nothing but the desire to play and hope to win possessed him. For that yearning is the ultimate believer; it defines the man and his life, and rakes his consciousness of the thousand things besides that could save him from the terrible abyss.

'Well?' said Ice.

'Well what?'

'Double or quits.'

The cards were a lover, and as he slowly shuffled the deck, picking up rhythm and speed, he waited – and would wait forever if he had to, for in that moment, this was all the world to him.

Sam deliberated, taking his time, smoking his cigarette as though he were counting time. 'How will you pay?'

'With information.' He spoke plainly, casually, conducting a transaction, assured of its value and lure.

Sam noticed his obsession, watched him cradling the cards as they bedazzle him with the narcotic suits of spades and diamonds, hearts and clubs, the register of queens, kings, jacks, the penultimate set of aces: to be dealt them, to possess them, to have them drawn is to have the world in your hands... the wheel of chance favoring your score, number and dream, man and his schemes, are an irresistible lure. He can't stop. He persuades himself, as he continues to lose, that victory is just a game away. Next card. Next game....And it is only when he is down a million plus that it kicks him hard in the head.

'You'd better stop, Ice. You've already gone too far.'

Ice stared incomprehensibly at him, then more deeply at the cards, the table, then the money, and then the cards again, *things*... the voices in his head thundering him to *Stop!* But desire says *Go!* Next card. Next game, it will all come around... He hears; but he doesn't listen. He is unable to listen. 'Deal.' He can't feel a thing. 'Double or quits. Sam... double or quits.' It is a relentless romance that must run its course; infatuation became submission to the game. Next card. Next game... Ante up, again and again, ante up.

'I need a drink,' said Ice gloomily.

'You should go home and get some rest.'

'After I've had a drink.'

'And pay off your debts, of course,' said Sam, lighting a cigarette, looking down at the IOUs resting atop his cash heap. 'And a pretty big one at that.'

'How?'

'You said it yourself: information.'

Feeling resigned but not exhausted, Ice took a cigarette from the pack, lit it nervously, and reclined back in his chair.

'What I have to say will clear the debt. OK?'

'We have faith that it will.'

'Trust me.'

Five minutes later, Sam handed over the paper IOUs. Lighting another cigarette, Ice put the match to the IOUs and watched in silence as they fizzled in the flame and burned his debts away.

'I wouldn't let it become a habit.' Sam fingered the cards while Ice, catching the nip of the flame, released the IOUs, letting them fall to the floor, feeling a surge of relief as the flames consumed them. Then his eyes lit up as the sound of music emanated from below.

On stage, jazz was melting into soft blues. It seeped into his mind like a twilight mood and left him with the sense of expectation, a soft motion stirring on his lips and eyes transfixed for a song. He seemed hypnotized and grew unusually still, as if the slightest shudder would dissolve the world, and he himself vanish into nothing.

Sam looked puzzled. 'What are you doing?'

It was a while before he answered. 'I'm listening to it.'

'Listening to what?' He regarded him strangely, glancing at the cards and shuffling them, a diversion to occupy his mind than with any intention to deal. 'It's only music playing. – Ice, are you all right? You seem pale. Would you like a cigarette?'

'Don't you feel it?'

'What?'

'The song.'

'Song? What song?' He stopped to listen. 'No one's singing. No. Nothing, it's just the music alone. The band never stops playing. That's why I love it here. And poker, of course.'

Harmonies rippled out of the soft rhythms of an oboe, enchanting, oriental, deep, and then: 'There. There it is. Do you hear it?'

Sam listened intently, for the song had not yet begun, but all of a sudden: 'Yes... Yes. I hear it now.' Was Ice telepathic, or did he simply yearn and it came to pass? Sam grew whimsical again. 'It's a pity you never had that same knack of foresight during poker. Perhaps life is telling you something, Ice. And you ought always to listen to life. I'll write you a poem about it, and you should learn it by heart.' He listened to the song as it grew louder. 'By the way, isn't that Cindy Gillespie singing?'

'Yes. Yes... It's her.' Her voice was booming with desire, sound that's alive like a part of her being. Her voice is a pen composing the poem of life, words fashioned to be sung, phrasing the story in pitch and tempo so perfectly hung on syllables, that the whole world felt delicate then, like a snowflake, it would melt on the tongue, and you could taste it, mmmm... Ice knew the words, miming them with the richness of a whisper.

Sam grew restless and offered him the cards. 'Ice.'

'Yes?'

'Cut.'

Ice, absorbed with the song, looked at Sam, bridged the gulf of lyric and a man, and cut.

'Double or quits?'

Ice prayed quietly. Sam dealt the cards. And the song grew louder.

*　　　　　*　　　　　*

Hush... Though it's not silence but amazing sound that holds the audience in awe, as she sings the pearly message in a ballad. It is soft but deep, the power residing in the tenderness of rhymes. Words, made of music. Time, made out of sound.

'That's amazing...' says a guy.

'Yeah..,' replies his lover. 'Truly amazing.'

And this defines the register of her singing, to ripple with divinity, to be like memory so that she was an endless part of them, there, listening to her, singing with her, coalescing with her. With words in a score. With music to adore. With gesture so profoundly set. With character, so you never forget... *that's a star.*

320

She sung three ballads in succession with the intensity of an aria and followed them with earnest bows to tumultuous applause and the roars of Bravo! *Cindy! Cindy! Bravo!* crying for more, for the opium of a song that burns them, and then soothes.

She waves and blows them kisses, encoring several times, yielding to their raging passion for *moremoremore*... Messiah or a Blues singer, sometimes the one is synonymous with the other, even if the symbols play a different tune. Prayer and a song. Sun and the Moon.

The emcee bounds onto the stage, feigning a stumble and an expression of wonder, enacted so often it becomes meaningless to improvise but he plays his part flawlessly and joins in the applause, his outstretched arms evoking the scripted theatre: 'Ain't she something? Ain't she..?' he jabbers almost unnoticed into the microphone and then hurries off for the next act waiting ready in the wings. One, two, three...

And on they glide in synch to the intro, catching the crescendo in step, ten dancers unfolding onto the stage from one wing to the next in a continuous flight of kicking legs and swaying hips and swinging arms. *Ra-ra-ra,* it's the hullabaloo for eternity, where eternity spans the length of a stage. As flesh bursts in a fevered dance, the patrons take it in their stride, light another cigarette, toast themselves with champagne, clap thunderously as the dancers take a bow, and they all deliriously believe themselves part of this living, dreaming, bursting world of entertainment. That's Jazz! The one constant presence is the band of musicians drenched with sweat and spiritually consumed in the thrill of their own sound. Music is an endless heartbeat pumping life into their bones. Passion is a string quartet taken to frenzy; it is a drum booming out the beat, ra-ta-ta-tat; it's a sax playing so serenely sweet you can taste it with your soul, lapping it all up – he's hungry, that man, he can eat out the world and play at the same time. Music wasn't simply sound, it was desire cast as sound that drove them from one improvised piece to the next with the certainty of life. Because like life: music just *is*.

'When these guys play and pack a smile they really mean it,' said the emcee, bounding back on stage as the lights dimmed and he blabbered into the microphone. 'And our dancing troupe, ain't they something special!' French accent of course with an American twang teetering on parody, he turned to his left and held out his arm for one of the dancers hesitating just off stage, and calling her back on cue. 'Jessica. Come here, baby, mon cherie. Come.'

She took a deep breath and leapt back into view, her face lit up by an array of spot lights revealing a multitude of dazzling smiles as she waved and kicked her legs high in rhythm to the synchronized beat of the thundering drum made more dramatic by being amplified and playing alone: Thud! Boom! Bash! Bang! Hsssss...

'Ain't she something!' Jessica ran trippingly off as the emcee feigned a little dance and exaggerated the unfeasibility of him ever being able to kick high like her, fanning his little fat face with his little fat hand, morphing from exertion to a grin in a single motion. OK, this sucker gets to have a few derisory grunts of laughter from a jaded audience who had seen it all before. And sure, they clapped and let the sucker make a fool of himself – why not, it was all part of the act. He's just hustling to make a living like anyone else. And before you yawn, remember, in a moment or so this sweaty little man in the shiny blue suit will just evaporate. If nothing else, jazz will just blow him away. *Whooooosh! That's jazz!*

'Maybe one day I might be able to dance too. Right, folks?' Let the sucker have his moment in the spotlights; give the schmuck a break; he's trying his best, ain't he? 'Later, we'll be bringing you someone really special. Yes; just for you, and for you; and for you,' he indicates randomly before making a giant embrace: 'For everyone! Tonight, we have with us the unique talent of that great comedian and entertainer... *Henri Lebeck!*'

WHO?

The audience clapped feebly and boomed their displeasure with gasps of oh no's and poo poohs and a few well timed expletives. Meanwhile, standing off stage on one of the wings was Anthony Leoni frisking in his pockets for a cigar and observing the ludicrous spectacle. He sneered at the emcee and said: 'Take your comedian and shove him up your ass!' Jessica, the dancer to whom he was giving his phone number, swelled up in blushes. But he smiled at her warmly and kissed her hand before returning to his table, where his brother Michael sat despondently waiting. As he did so, he paused at several tables to exchange greetings with friends and acquaintances, garnering all manner of smiles and hi's and gee's, long time no see, how are you doing..? shake hands, share some amusements, slip in a quip or two, make merry with the laughter, round and round it goes, and then, on reaching his table, promptly took a seat and threw a dubious glance at his brother, who stonily gazed back at him.

Anthony got straight to the point, pointing at his brother with his unlit cigar. 'Are you horny for some action, or something more prosaic? This ain't a library, son.'

'What?'

'You look knackered and right out of it. I hope we're not related.'

'Tough luck.'

'Take it from me, you could use a good lay. It'll straighten your hormones out. They're down in the dumps, I can see. What you need are a couple of wild babes to pump you up a bit. Quite a lot actually! Well, do you want me to arrange it? Why not try two? They'll knacker you for sure. But hey, at least you'll get pumped up ten times your normal size. How about it? Tempted?'

'I'm going steady with Sara.'

'Schmuck!' He turned round and looked at the stage, as the band picked up a gentle improvising rhythm that lacked the commitment of passion, but made ideal background sound for just killing time – ambient time, like a cool serenading mood. Easy as she goes...

Anthony struck a match and lit his cigar, sucking luxuriously to coax the tobacco to catch fire and retain the burn, pumping it up with the afterburner relish of inhaling it long and indulgently. Some people live for these moments, savoring their pleasure as infinite delight. At length he addressed his brother:

'Are you sure you don't want a good pumping? You're in Paris, you know. One means two here – especially when it comes to frolicking with the babes.'

'I'm certain. Why don't you just back off, *big brother*.'

'Waiter. Garcon,' he turned his attention to more indulgent matters.

'Yes, monsieur?'

'May we have more wine, please, and some hors d'oeuvres.'

The waiter changed the ashtray, dispatching any flakes of dust from the clean one, cleared the table, and withdrew.

Anthony said: 'You'll have another drink and some grub?'

'I might as well,' he shrugged.

Anthony seldom troubled himself with his brother's vagaries or moods and, glancing at his wristwatch, rose from his chair suddenly. 'I won't be a moment. I'll be right back.' He made his way backstage to Cindy Gillespie's dressing room to see how she was. He knocked several times on the door, but there was no answer. Calling for her, he tried the handle but it was locked. Feeling concerned, he walked further along the corridor to the stage manager's office. He immediately knocked twice.

'Unless it's an emergency, go away. I'm busy.'

'It's me.' Anthony burst in and the stage manager, with a cigarette dangling from his mouth, was arranging some files on a shelf and he turned wearily to face him.

'What do you want?'

'Cindy's not in her room.'

'I know.'

'Then where is she?'

'She said she received a phone call. She said it was important.'

'When?'

'About five minutes ago.'

'From whom?'

'I don't know.'

'Where has she gone?'

'To see someone.'

'Who?'

'I have no idea.

'Who did she go with?'

'Alone. She took a cab.'

'That's strange. She never mentioned it to me.'

'Perhaps she forgot. Perhaps she was in a hurry.'

'Why?'

'Don't worry; she'll be back. She'll be here well before curtain call.'

'I know she will,' he said, feeling that she would, because she was a professional. But it continued to worry him. 'Let me know as soon as she gets back, will you? Thanks.' He stood outside in the corridor brooding for a while, but through sheer will power alone drove the disabling sense of suspicion from his mind. Anthony harbored a repressed undercurrent of superstition. He felt, secretly, that holding negative thoughts induced disaster in the stream of life. He had only to look at his brother to confirm this idea. However absurd, belief was a hard thing to tackle, let alone control. And at times he found himself struggling to restore his reason. A fair portion of best whiskey often helped here enormously, and he was no exception to the rule: that a stout heart, weeping or otherwise, sad or confused, can benefit immensely from some fine Scotch spirit. And now, he was stoking up a good thirst for the golden stuff. He tried humming an improvised melody to pass the time – he wanted to savor his moments. Five minutes later he returned to his table; the cigar was slightly shorter, the grin visibly broader.

'Miss me?'

Michael, now perked up and indulging in hors d'oeuvres and wine, said: 'No. But he did. These are really delicious. Try some. The prawns are lovely.'

Anthony, quizzically turning, saw the day manager looking rather bored, his arms slouched on the bar and staring right at him. He was a large brawny man, like a bouncer with a distinctively shaved head. A moment of mutual grinning ensued before he made his way over to Anthony's table and they shook hands. He rarely worked this late, and Anthony remarked, by way of causal conversation:

'Are you out partying tonight, Andre?'

'No. Not tonight.'

'Is there a game on that's running late?'

'Yes,' he frowned. 'So it seems. So it seems...'

'What game?' Michael interposed, his curiosity stirred.

'Poker,' Andre explained. 'We have a private room upstairs for some of the more - how shall I put this? – better endowed patrons.'

'Money,' said Anthony. 'Guys with loads to spend; who can really grease the pot with the stuff. Ha! Talk about baking a cake.'

'And it doesn't stop with the icing,' added Andre. 'Oh no, not with these guys, they must have the cherries and the fruit on top too.'

'If you can ante up the zeroes... well, the clock keeps rolling, and it buys you a lot of time.'

'So it seems,' he said. 'I wish someone would just win and get the damn thing over with. I want to go home.'

'Or lose it all and call it a day. It takes two to tango.'

'Cha cha cha...' Andre worked a few steps amusingly with his feet. 'Perhaps I should take up dancing.'

'Or gambling.'

'Poker isn't gambling.'

'No?'

'It's more of a... a...'

'A calculation,' Michael cut in smartly as he ate hors d'oeuvres. 'A calculation with wings so it can fly. - You know, this salmon isn't half bad either! Try some.' They both stared at him oddly and he wondered why before concluding. 'Oh, gambling. Well, that's just my opinion. Not that I know everything; but I know enough,' he asserted. 'I've been around.'

'You!' gasped Anthony. 'Where the hell have you ever been?'

'A lot further than you imagine. That's where.'

'Oh yeah... Give me a break!'

'Do you know the most important difference between risk and measured risk? Think before you answer.'

'Why?'

'Go on, *big brother*, let's see you answer that. You always think you're so smart with all this showbiz baloney. Fine, let's hear it. Come on, mister wiseguy with the blue tie.'

'OK. With one you use your brains, the other your balls.'

'You're so predictably *showbiz*, big brother. A cliché answer from a cliché mind.'

'Balls and brains carry the whole world; especially the balls; and especially when there's pussy around, as there always is. But you wouldn't understand that, would you, Mike? Because basically you're nothing but a sooped-up pig farmer in a cashmere suit.'

'I'll be more specific, then. The question is, what does a *game of chance* look like to a machine, to a computer? How would you code it?'

'Who cares! Screw your machines. I wouldn't even waste my time pissing on them. Not a drop. They're not worth pissing on.'

Andre, however, was intrigued and asked him to explain. Michael ate a pastry to create himself some time, and said:

'The numerical odds are calculable. That part we can do easily. And we can even simulate a character to make it seem like a person. But that *extra* bit, that tantalizing piece of *dare*, the intuitive part of the equation... Well, I'm still working on that.'

'And how far have you got?'

'Well, we know that human intelligence plays a strategic role.'

'How?'

'He means cheating,' said Anthony bluntly. 'When you're dealing with people and money like that, mixing them up, corruption kicks in – it's part of the human makeup; it's part of the landscape. That's why I told you, Mike, again and again, your computers are bullshit.'

Anthony offered the plate of hors d'oeuvres to Andre. He smiled and rubbed his belly at the full load, and at length, with nothing more to add, glanced at his wristwatch and wandered away with a dwindling smile on his face - a simple man waiting for a poker game to end.

Anthony remarked casually to Michael: 'Those guys must be playing for some seriously major stakes. I wonder who they are? Hmmm... Shall we order more hors d'oeuvres? I'm still a bit peckish. Waiter...'

*　　　　　*　　　　　*

Upstairs, in the poker room, as fortune slips from hand to hand, wagering higher and higher, and fingers dips into the pack and lights up another cigarette, and casually ease out caviar gram by gram from the pot, wash it down with the best whiskey money can buy, the one thing that goes unnoticed is the time.

'I'll raise you fifty thousand,' the poet's voice grows melodic, and he smiles.

Ice said nothing. Just folds. And Sam hauls in the riches. 'I told you, Ice, you weren't going to keep it for long. Lady Luck has been sleeping in my bed. I know just how to treat her.' He chuckled. 'Tease her; slap her ass around a little. She likes that. Even more than I do! - Ice, shall we call it a day? It's getting late.'

'One more game.'

'Are you sure? Would you prefer some poetry instead? Who's your favorite poet?'

'I'll deal. - Here, cut the cards.'

'How would you like to hear something magnificent in Greek? What about one of the great speeches of Pericles? He was a great orator, that man.'

'There is a method to poker, Sam, just as there is a method to most things. Drama included.'

'But this is not most things. This is poker. Played with cards. All fifty-two of them. And face down. You are in *their* hands. Have you forgotten that already? - Never underestimate the cards, Ice.'

'Never overestimate luck.'

'Well, you know me - striking a balance is my forte.'

And so, to the soft and sensuous sounds of improvised jazz, they resumed play, with increasing amounts of information monetarized into IOUs when Ice ran short of cash.

As this entire episode proved, trusting in fortune was a fickle thing for Ice, a mere foil to defer the pain and magnify his losses to a later hour. For when Lady Luck roused and peppered him with some of her favors, he just wouldn't learn when to stop. And this Lady took it personally, punishing guys risking everything on a punt. So, as men suffer the crisis of a lack of liquidity, if money is in short supply, you either borrow or bluff your way by inventing a capital base.

'I have information potentially worth a hundred times what you've won today.'

'You know what I would do, Ice?'

'What?'

'I'd cash it in.'

Cash it in. Before it's too late. Because nothing lasts for ever; not life; the planets; stars; nothing. Even the universe is a gambler. It cashes itself in... Eventually.

While Ice was mulling things over, applause climbed lazily and quickly snuffed itself out as the comedian, *Henri Lebeck,* came on stage. He bounced on gurgling up mundane quips and clichéd asides in his grainy voice that jarred with the mood of a jaded crowd. *'Bonsoir mesdames et messieurs. Welcome to the show. Bonsoir. Je t'aime follement - I love you madly.'* He shut up a minute and waited for applause. (Wait a lifetime, sucker. This ain't your day; and this ain't your forte). Even the French patrons took an early twenty winks. But this *comedian* just wouldn't take the hint, no sir, this one is a *regular comedian*, and he goes *ha ha ha* and rambles on like he's having the time of his life. 'Tonight, I have got jokes galore and more and so let's rip the place up and get started. Did you hear the one about the ox and the farmer?' Someone in the audience cried out defiantly *At least a thousand bloody times already, mister comedian...* The number, perhaps, must have held some significance, because Henri found that very funny and belched with laughter, really giving the audience a great big blast of his thunderous wit 'And the ox said to the farmer....' *ha ha ha*. Old Henri could barely contain himself as he buckled around the stage dribbling out jokes and re-used asides that left him in tears, while the audience mostly yawned and moaned.

Like the majority, Anthony groaned at the stream of mundane jokes probably dredged up off the Internet or picked up from some seedy hive. This was humor tailored not for a sober audience but pulped together for a drunken crowd washed out of their minds with one-hundred percent pure proof booze and who laugh at anything, especially themselves, and their reflections, and the reflections of their reflections, ad nauseam. While it remains established fact that Nature abhors a vacuum, it is arguably beyond conjecture that she loathes a fool. And proof of this is that he, Henri, unable to entertain his audience, proved gifted in becoming despised. Even Michael, half way through a comedy sketch, groaned to his brother:

'I need to take a piss.'

It remains the primary rule of the theatre, which you run against at your peril: never screw with an audience. Even when they're serious, even when they're patient and forgiving, ultimately, they are out for a good time. An uplifting time. *Never bore them.*

Draining every drop from his pride, down to the last reluctant dribble, even by sustained evaporation, seemed preferable to returning to his table while the *comedian* continued on stage, so Michael leisurely loitered with his pride dangling there and just taking his time and mulling over in his mind that wasn't the salmon good, and the prawns, and the shrimp. And the wine, especially the red, yes, he was growing rather fond of it now. It beats soda any day.

I mean, you can't have hors d'oeuvres and soda, can you? Come on! Get serious...

'Are you stuck there or something, buddy?'

'Uh?' Michael, jolted out of his daydreaming, wheeling around and seeing a guy with a gaping grin ease open his trouser zipper and relieve himself luxuriously.

'Ahhh... I needed that. Taking a piss is almost as good as drinking the stuff in the first place. Pleasure in, pleasure out; wouldn't you say?' He gazed at Michael with an amused expression that bordered on the inquisitive. 'Are you offering me something, friend, or just making a statement?' and sloping his eyes down indicated a glaring indiscretion.

Standing there with his limp pride in his hands, Michael hastened to restore his dignity; frantically drawing up his zipper but it caught in a kink and stuck half way. Struggling with it, the damn thing just wouldn't budge, and Michael cringed with shame.

The other guy smiled, taking everything in his stride. 'Some things are meant to be taken slowly, with a feather-light touch. And handling your pride takes top priority there. You don't want to mess around with that. You know, this reminds me of college days and the pranks we used to pull. Women love all that bullshit. Deep down, they are a dirty load of whores. Don't listen to any of their bullshit. Hey, wait a moment,' he grew more sober and shook the droplets free before zipping himself up, *gently*. 'I've seen you before, haven't I? Come to think, yes, you're American, aren't you?'

Finally, the struggle over, Michael zipped himself up. 'Bloody thing! - American, Yes. Yes, I am.'

'*The little things in life; forever cause the greatest strife,*' said Sam, the poet, gazing at Michael with the glow of recognition. 'You're with Ice. You're one of the wizards, aren't you? Yeah, I've seen you around. Yeah...' They moved together to the washbasins and began scrubbing their hands. 'I'm Sam, but you can call me the poet.'

'The poet. Yes, I know,' he answered without thinking. 'I've seen the file.'

'File!' He stopped what he was doing. 'What file?'

'No. Not a file. I meant to say I've seen your name listed on the meeting schedules.'

'Ah...' He resumed scrubbing his hands. 'How come you get to see the schedules?'

'Because I help prepare the reports. I'm Michael Leoni.'

'Leoni...Yes, I remember you now. Leo the lion, right?'

'Excuse me?'

'It's nothing. - Do you come here often?'

'This is only my third time.'

'I thought so. And I should know. Me, well, let's just say this venue is a home away from home... whenever I get the urge. And that happens a lot more often that you think. But hey, that's the price you pay for the good life!'

'Oh. I see. OK.' Michael searched for something to say. 'So, what do you think of the comedian?'

'What comedian?'

'Exactly!' he grinned, as they dried their hands. But Sam honestly never knew who he was. Michael realized this and assumed the first thing that came to mind. 'You've just arrived, then? Good for you. Even if it is pretty late.'

'Who, me? No. I've been here a couple of hours.' He looked at his wristwatch and exclaimed. 'Damn! Actually three and a half. Time flies when you're having fun. Well, one more drink for the road with Ice, then it's home sweet home.'

'Ice is here?'

'Yes.'

'Here?'

'He's been here most of the night, I think. Longer than I have, anyway. I never asked him.'

'Where?'

'Playing poker.'

'Here?'

'Sure. Upstairs, where there are no comedians.'

'With you?'

'And Lady Luck sure screwed him tonight. I warned him not to flirt with my women. But he just wouldn't listen. Guys, huh!'

'He's here? Is he still here?'

Irresistibly bragging, Sam took out a wad of cash and a string of IOUs. 'Am I a champ, or am I *the* champ! Take your pick, Leo.'

331

Michael gazed with amazement. 'Jesus!'

'Yeah, go ahead, look at it. If it weren't all mine, I'd believe I was pimping Lady Luck. All I need now is a fancy hat, huh!'

'Oh my God!'

'Why look so surprised? When you're as good as I am...' He stuffed the booty back in his pockets, dropping a couple of bills and briefly kicking them. 'Ah! Leave it for the cleaners. Come on, Mike, Ice is waiting at the bar? Let's go and have a drink. - Well, what's wrong? What are you waiting for?'

Michael stood there stunned. He couldn't explain, even to himself, but an inexplicable sense that something was wrong seized him. It was only the half-drunken jostling of Sam tugging his arm and escorting him out that Michael re-established a presence of mind.

Entering the auditorium he could see Ice sideways seated at the bar with a drink hovering in his hand and staring absently at the stage, obviously not watching the show, but his mind drawn to inward preoccupations of his own.

Gag followed feeble gag, the comedian having the loudest laugh cramming *ho ho ho* and *ha ha ha...* while the audience conducted their private dialogues. - Some interludes are filled with sound, but it's the deeper silence that reigns. As Ice instinctively turned and saw Sam and Michael approaching, his gaze appeared to freeze. He remained seated as they advanced, and he briefly shook hands with Michael as Sam got in the drinks.

'I didn't know you were fond of jazz,' said Ice.

'I'm always open to new experiences,' said Michael, wondering what he was saying.

'I must remember that.' Ice repressed his surprise with skill.

'You fellas work together, huh?' Sam butted in and embraced their shoulders with rough but good-spirited camaraderie. 'Surprise, surprise... Small world for us guys, huh? The wizards meet!'

Michael could see Ice working his eyes, and those eyes glittered with intrigue, studying the setting for advantage. The conversation flowed but he was probing very subtly. Ice was trying to engineer an outcome, grooming the characters for roles he was devising in his mind. Like the best jazz, Ice had a natural talent for improvising. Sam finished his drink and asked someone to call him a cab, but Ice created a ruse and persuaded him to stay a while longer.

'What's the rush, champ?' he flattered him. 'It's Friday night.'

'Saturday morning, actually.'

'Then what's the rush?' Sam bought it easily and Ice ordered more drinks. 'Besides,' he said, glancing at the stage and the comedian winding up his act: 'she'll be back with us soon.'

'Who?

'Cindy Gillespie.'

'Ah... That's worth everything in the world.'

What were they saying? What did this mean? Michael felt alarmed at the double meanings. Even a gaze suggested conspiracy.

The emcee, sweating and clapping frantically in a futile exertion to rouse the audience, boomed:

'Wasn't that something? Henri Lebeck. Give him a hand. Come on, folks, give him a hand.' The impervious majority, either taking pity on the fool or being simply polite, obliged, accompanied by the customary booms of a drum that amplified the faint applause. But this only served to define the bulk of entertainment, of whatever form, as mere effect. 'Madames and Monsieurs, the show continues. Musicians, take it away!' Now the applause and cheers was genuinely sincere, and the band pushed into overdrive, pounding the audience and emcee alike with a sound long repressed and bursting into freedom all at once. A hunger drove them as the deep drone of the bass went wild too early and came tumbling to a melodic crash, and was pushed and kicked aside by the blaring trumpets racing each other tripping and scratching, like bitches they were fighting over their man, and over-stepping the high notes at a stammering pace, yielding the lead to the sax that cruised-in on a cushion of harmony, before the drummer muscled in and took everything high – beat like a fix, they trailed in his wake following his giddy percussion on an improvised riff. Take five...

Michael watched the raw artistic power, the passion and energy, convulse the stage with delirium. Men, it seemed, who played only to burn themselves out, to become cinders in their own dazzling inferno, before the phoenix of their sound raises them again - to odes, to joy, to odes of joy. And on they play, born from music, to music, outperforming the wonders of themselves, again and again and again...

Michael, over the riveting sound, said to Ice: 'It's amazing.'

'Yes. Watch.'

'Do they want to set the stage on fire?'

'Just watch.'

'I'm having a great time,' said Sam, drowned out by the music. 'Ha!' And he rapped Michael on the shoulder, who smiled briefly before asking:

'Ice, what are they doing? What are they trying to do?'

'Watch.'

'Why do the other musicians let the drummer lead? Is it a contest?'

'Not exactly.'

'Are they hesitating? Are they intimidated by him?'

'No. They take turns to lift each other on a high, like positive feedback. There is no overall plan. It all works in real time.' He drew closer. 'What does it remind you of?'

Michael shook his head, looking puzzled. The ulterior meaning Ice wanted to convey, or perhaps the deception intended, failed to register in him.

'Ice, what's happening to them? What are they waiting for?'

'What do you mean?'

'Is it all about timing? Are they waiting for something to happen?'

'That wouldn't be spontaneous. Watch.'

'For what? Ice, what am I looking for?'

'For what you least expect.'

The acoustic rhythms of the strings contrasted with the raw freakiness of a cymbal. The piano performed with hammering beats time-picked for synthesis, a glue to a tune, leaning lyrical on the tenor sax, pressing him into melodies of uncompromising speed and beauty - humming birds gone crazy with sound - it was the brisk attack as the hammer hits the strings, lips suck the trumpets, muscles wade in to the drums, lungs pump the horns, fingers strum the bass, mouth slams into the oboe as flesh chases the envelope of sound, totally orgiastic. This is music. This is sex. You feel love, but you want to fuck to this. Yeah!

Michael frowned. 'It's just a series of affects, isn't it? There's no thread; no harmony. Nothing I can see. Nothing.'

'Now, compare that with what happened yesterday in the markets. You remember when chemicals dipped below the benchmark. Then energy futures soared. Remember metals at eleven o'clock? Copper bounced and took the rest of them up. Then they leapt over the leader and it rolled in, tide after turbulent tide. It seems chaotic, but... What did *you* think?'

'I thought it was crazy. Just one of those days. It was hectic. Sure; the financial markets can be like that. They can be moody; they can be delirious; and they can be downright dull.'

'So why wouldn't jazz be like that?'

'Because there's nothing to clash over.'

'Are you certain about that?'

'There's nothing to compete against.'

'Look closer.'

'At what? It works or it doesn't work. That's all there is.'

Ice drew closer, ensuring Sam would overhear. 'There are no fixed rules in the markets, no more than in jazz. But there are patterns – emerging, vanishing again; turning on a moment. This music has the sense of the markets. They share a common dialect.' He pointed to the musicians. 'Listen, the clarinet is off key, and if it stays like that long enough the threshold begins to move his way, and the rhythmic tide will follow him wherever he goes. Musicians, traders, we're all just leaves in the wind, just flotsam on the sea. - That's how the markets operate too. That's how they move. That's how it all works. That's what we do.'

In time, as the clarinet found the breath of harmony, drawing first the trumpet to swirl around the tempo, then the sax in a swaying mood gracefully entwined with them, then the bass coasting on, deeper than deep, into the improvised mix, followed by percussion synthesizing all that's dear to the raw and primitive sound of beat, beat, beat... the shifting patterns of jazz discovered a new world heralded not on a note of whimsy, but on the hurricanes of passion. But hey, that's jazz. And new worlds are as common as serenades from a smiling piano.

Michael shook his head, hesitating, reflecting. Ice was manipulating him. It was a show for Sam, or so it appeared. And Michael was a mere pawn in an act of subtle, bold, curious story telling.

Several minutes later the emcee came back, said nothing, and merely gestured with an outstretched arm inviting the audience to gaze to his left. Their applause soared several octaves higher when Cindy Gillespie walked out on stage. She seemed to rise, to radiate something special, *kinda like jazz*. And taking the microphone, the lights dimmed, the spotlights struck, the band steadied the melody and, sailing straight for the heart, she began to sing.

'Now *that's* what I call poetry,' said Sam, mesmerized. It was a beautiful song, the lyrics perfectly matched to her tenor, the music blending with the timbre of her voice. 'This song is a favorite of mine.'

'It's been changed,' said Ice, listening intently.

'But I know this song. I'm certain of it.'

'It's different. It's not the same.'

'You're crazy! I know this song.'

'You know something, but not this one.'

Michael, watching Ice closely, said: 'What makes you say that?'

'Something has changed. It's different.'

'What?'

Ice rubbed his eyes. Alcohol and a long sleepless stretch were beginning to take their toll. The conceit of overconfidence proved irresistible, like the song, several bars of which he began to recite softly:

> 'You yearn for more; and I close the door,
>   And you knock and knock...
>   Until twilight strikes out the clock.'

Ice explained: 'In the second stanza; someone has changed the lyrics. It should be "Until twilight melts into the sunshine," not. "Until twilight strikes out the clock..." '

'But then it doesn't rhyme,' protested Sam. 'It's perfect just as she's singing it. This is my song. I love this song.'

'Perhaps she's hiding something,' added Michael, abruptly.

'Excuse me?'

'Relax, Ice,' he said. 'It's just a song after all, isn't it?'

Michael could see he had struck something in Ice, and Sam looked warily at each of them as though deep suspicion had been stirred. Michael, by acting in the dark, had switched on a light. But what it revealed eluded him.

Ice revived when some friends invited them to their table. Sam accepted, but Michael excused himself and returned to join his brother. Before separating their eyes dueled. Michael yielded first, since he had no idea what the stakes were.

'Who is he?' asked Ice, looking at Anthony.

'My brother.'

'I see.'

And they parted.

Back at his table, the first thing his brother said was:

'Who were you talking to?'

'A colleague.'

'I've seen him before.'

'Who? Karl?'

'Is that his name?'

'Ice. We call him Ice.'

'Ah. That name rings a bell. He comes in here a lot. I've seen him around. He's always with the same crowd.'

'Perhaps you're mistaken. Perhaps it's someone else.'

'No. It's him, Mike. I'm sure it's him. Yes. He even bought me a drink once.'

'Ice? Why would he do that?'

'He was in a winning mood.' He chuckled, speculating, 'I bet he was playing poker upstairs. Was he? Ah, I thought so... And that other guy with the smooth smile – I can't explain why, but he reminds me of a cat. Look at him now. Meow! He looks as if he's about to topple over. I've seen him too; many times.' He examined them from a distance, especially Ice, watching as he turned his head, lifted his glass, sighed with surprise at something that was said among his friends, laugh, then resume the conversation. It looked contrived. Ice lived up to his namesake and was cool, but it seemed all of an affected piece. 'It's him, Mike. Trust me, it's him. - What's the matter with you now? You look dazed. Do you want me to call the babes and have them pump you up? It's not too late, you know.'

'I'm just tired, that's all.'

'And by the way, your icicle chum likes his music too. He went up and introduced himself and kissed her hand. He's a calculating man, sure. But he has style.'

'What are you talking about?'

'My angel,' he signified Cindy Gillespie. 'He wanted to meet her.'

'When?'

'About three weeks ago on her opening night. No, tell a lie, it was her second night. That first night we had the press and media people over. Hmm…' he pondered quietly and drank all his wine, as though he needed the time that emptying the glass gave him. Then, refilling, he began: 'Your chum walks over late one evening, bloated up big in a winning mood. – What are you gawping at now? Are you listening to me, you knuckle-head?'

'You said a winning mood. What do you mean by that?' They both turned and looked at Ice. 'Did he look like that?'

'*That's* not a winning mood.'

A feeling of disquiet transpired that Michael could neither understand nor dispel. He lifted his glass and drank all the wine in a single gulp. This greatly surprised his brother.

'Are you out of your head? What's the matter with you?'

'I have something on my mind. I'll get over it. I'll be OK.'

'Women? Work?'

'Among other things.'

'You're too soft. Assert yourself with a woman; never be under her thumb. That thumb of hers is specially made for pinning down a man. If she thinks you're weak or kinky, she'll shove it up your ass. Be careful. OK?'

'Thanks a bunch for that *holistic* advice,' he said with sarcastic glumness, preparing to leave.

'Where are you going now?'

'To make a call.'

'Are you leaving already?'

'I have an appointment.'

'It's a bit late for all that now, isn't it? Look at the time.'

'I try not too. It's giving me a headache.'

'But I've ordered some food.'

'I'm sorry. I have to leave. It can't wait.'

'But the food. Wait, damn it. Maybe we should invite your chum over.' This was just teasing him, but it provided an impromptu cue, and together they turned and gazed at Ice, who at that moment was engrossed in an enigmatic stare of them. He studied them, fixedly, until someone at his side touched his shoulder and shattered his intensity, prompting him with a question. He turned only briefly and answered with a smile before lifting his glass, and miming 'cheers' with a clandestine weight to Anthony and Michael

'Weird,' said Anthony, 'I feel as if I'm being watched. Spied on... That's really weird.'

Michael's face clouded over with the same troubling confusions, until the song burst through and the trombone flexed swiftly into life sweeping the burden from his midst, while deeper within him lurked an agonizing chaos.

In time, the song dovetailed to a crescendo of applause which shook him back to normal. He had the presence of mind to gaze at his brother who was on his feet clapping like mad and crying out 'Cindy! Cindy! Bravo! Bravo, Cindy!' Hastening away, Anthony left these words trailing in his wake: 'I've got to rush, Mike. See you later. Bye. Cindy!'

'Anthony, wait a minute, I wanted to...' The waiters suddenly appeared with several filled trays and obscured his view. He leapt up and searched for his brother; but he was gone. Michael muttered, as if to a ghost: 'The food's here...' Then, as the waiters set the food, he waited, thanked them, and then left.

Outside, it was just starting to rain which, in the ubiquitous sheen of streetlights, seemed like a faint mist. He called Sara from his mobile phone. It rang five times before redirecting to an answer-machine. He hung up and hailed down a passing cab, driving directly to her apartment. The rain grew into a shower and the raindrops sounded serene. He was tired but instinctively noted the details: raindrops; the sound of a passing car; the wild groans of a drunk flailing his arms at the world; lovers laughing as they crossed the street wooing a rainy night.

Arriving ten minutes later he got out and asked the driver to wait. The driver agreed, lit a cigarette, reclined back in the seat and watched the rain trickle down the windscreen; at length switching on the radio, in no particular mood just tuning through the channels. Most were talk shows, so he settled on jazz. And, at ease, listened to a midnight saxophone playing a timeless, labyrinthine jazz piece which, in the rainy night, sounded kind of blue.

A few minutes later it all changed. Michael was back, wet from the rain and looking disheveled. He immediately pulled down the window to let in air.

'Where to?' asked the driver, stubbing out his cigarette.

'We wait.'

Lumbering in his seat, he turned around. 'I don't get paid to wait. I drive.'

'I'll pay. What's the problem? Imagine you're driving. You can do that, can't you?'

'Sure,' he replied, 'I can do what I like…' before folding back around in his seat, smiling approvingly at the sublime wetness of the night, closed his eyes, and relaxed to a rain swept jazz drizzling with tender soft sounds.

Sweet as Blue…

Chapter 19

Meanwhile, amid the pandemonium backstage, Anthony ambled towards Cindy's dressing room, his spirit swift as his steps weaving through the throng of performers rushing to the wings, barely a superfluous breath expended in their frantic flight as they scurry to the stage, the multitude of showgirls, dancers, singers, the up-rush of applause signaling frenetic motion as they hauled their props for the one minute call: *'To your places everyone. Get ready...'* rushing, shoving, gesticulating, some hurrying a smoke, knocking back a gin, a ramshackle shaking of nerves sending them ricocheting the wrong way *'The other side, get to the other side...'* of the stage, that is, because they're on next and the show can't stop, won't stop, refuses to stop for anyone. That's showbiz! Actually, no, that's life. And showbiz takes a cue from a heartbeat and just keeps rolling on: *boom... boom... boom...* 'Watch yourself there, babe,' Anthony lends a dancer his hand as she stumbles and falls. She smiles warmly, mouths *Merci, monsieur*, but doesn't have the time to stop. 'I know,' he said, 'The show must go on...' And with barely a second to spare she up and cuts a perfect pose for curtain call and swoons on to the stage, catching the envelope of the intro just in time as the drummer pounds the drum *wham! wham! wham!* A dynamo *whoosh!..* Then others of the troupe in identical costumes cascade on after her, leaping to the beat as the stage-hands holler and steer a path through the restless throng of performers skipping and turning, navigating and scurrying along the corridors with props and costumes and things, and even a menagerie of birds and cockatoos wailing yahoos and chirping for life. *That's showbiz! That's life!*

Amid the hullabaloo of being on time and getting it just right, the show goes on and there is barely a step out of place, the stage-hands gasp that it somehow always manages to work, and Anthony, with a luxury smile, fell into an easy stride, riding a cushion of air borne on the breezes of an easy mood. Ahhh... easy, life's a breeze; an easy breeze. His steps had the snappiness of a child about to take possession of the sweetest sweet around. Mmm... Apple pie, my-o-my, catching sight of Cindy's door raised his spirits higher and he ambled up, stopped smartly, ahem! cleared his throat, adjusted his necktie and finessed his smile, then rapped excitedly on the door. Yippee-aye-yea!

'Yes? Who is it?'

'It's me, babe. Anthony.'

Hushed voices within rattled awkwardly then swiftly subsided, like the faint rustle of a fall. A drawer closed, loudly, deliberately, furniture shuffled, shudders of nervous activity resounded in fits and starts, then she opened the door, looking serene and the epitome of controlled nerves – it wasn't an act, but an instinct harnessed from years living in awe of the stage.

'Hi.' She smiled; he smiled back.

'You were great,' he said, peering irresistibly past her into the room with a desire to be invited inside, but where instead he saw her sister register his presence with a hesitant smile. 'Hi Amber, I didn't know you were there.' Amber lifted her eyebrows. She looked nervous; something was troubling her. She was smoking a cigarette and drinking orange juice from a champagne glass. Together, the two seemed to jar. Turning his attention to Cindy: 'I just had to come and tell you, you were wonderful. You know exactly how to pluck the heartstrings of an audience. They're a tuning fork in your hands. That's innate talent, when it resonates like that. Cupid may have his arrows, but Cindy Gillespie has the voice. Way to go! Perfect.'

'Thanks. You're a godsend, Anthony; more than you'll ever know. And I adore you for it. I always will.'

'Nah!' he blushed, something he seldom did, throwing his hands in a bounding gesture, both of them knowing he would move mountains for her.

'Look, Anthony, I don't mean to rush or be impolite, but can we meet later? After the show.'

'Sure. Sure, that's fine. I'll be at my table. You both come join me. I want you to meet someone.'

'We will. Thanks.' And she abruptly shut the door.

He heard the latch snap into place, sealing the moment. He paused there a while, thinking, caught between curiosity and concern. But not one by nature to brood, he shook his misgivings and sauntered away, dismissing apprehensions from his wake.

'What did he want?' asked Amber.

'He was just making sure I was OK,' said Cindy, the ripple of stage jitters keeping her nerves on edge, taking a hairbrush and sliding it through her hair to calm herself, to prolong the moment. 'It's normal. He does it all the time. And I'm glad he does. I feel safe when he does.'

'He's checking up on you.'

'Stop sounding so damn paranoid over everything!' she screamed, full of tortured bitterness, throwing her hairbrush at the wall. 'Don't provoke me, Amber. Don't you dare! I have to go back out on stage, and I won't have you tearing me up. I've worked too hard and long for this chance. Do you understand? Do you? Amber? I'm talking to you, damn it!'

'Yes. I'm sorry.' She stammered, facing the floor with sorrow. 'Forgive me. I didn't mean it like that. I... I can't help myself from...' and lifting her eyes, the yearning for pity seemed immense.

Deep pain clouded her eyes, her tenderness under constant siege, the agony of fearing to look behind her when she walked through the park, of turning a corner, amid the crowds of a bustling street wondering what menace lurked among them, of answering the telephone when alone, afraid of a voice, intimidated by a whisper, of a gentle knock... imagining what horrors hold behind a door. Light, shadows, even stillness seemed to agitate and make her shudder. The ordinary things of life tore at her mind, and broke her spirit not with sticks, but the barest palpitations.

Fear; staggering fear; that the body, the mind, the spirit can possess such fear makes her wonder that she is a host of infinite sorrows. The torment of being pursued by strangers, stalked, the relentless menace of generic man, unknown man, faceless man. Why her?

Cindy felt Amber's desperation and pain. Remorse came quickly to her and she yielded to its passions. Amber needed her as refuge, even as an angel. But there were things tormenting her too, things she wished were forgotten, that Amber resurrected. Fears, frozen deep in

Cindy's mind, roused again to spur the softness of her being, and make her shudder. Cindy, in her own way, was beginning to break.

'Things just don't happen, Cindy. They happen for a reason.'

'I know,' she said softly and sat beside her. 'But we can't be certain.'

'You just want me to forget; pretend that it never even happened, don't you?'

'No.'

'Just close my eyes and forget, don't you?

'No.

'Cast it from my mind. As if I can. – Well I can't!'

'No! No! No!'

'Then what? What are you saying?'

'Just shut up and let me think. Please!' Clenching her fists, Cindy shook them powerfully at the ghosts that haunted her, beating the air then covering her face, moaning in pain that this suffering release her; and she could walk out onto that amazing stage, bathed in light, and breathe free air – let them see, let everyone see that she wasn't afraid, not her, she wasn't afraid of anything - and sing her heart out, sing for the world. For everything. Just to sing. To sing.

'These things don't just happen by themselves. There must be a reason. There must be. Cindy... are you listening to me?'

Amid her sister's pain, Cindy's own spirit shook, and she felt the sense of dreadful things about her. 'Why is this happening? Why?' She gazed at Amber, encompassing countless things in the frenzy of her eyes. 'Why? Why? Why?'

'You want me to believe I just imagined it, don't you?'

'No.'

'Liar.'

'Amber, you know I wouldn't lie.'

'Why should I believe you? Why should I believe anything you say?' Amber's voice broke. 'No one believes me. Not even you.'

'It's not true.'

'Yes it is.'

'I just don't understand. Why? Why?'

'It is! It is!'

'You're...' Cindy started to panic, holding her head as though it would explode, bracing herself for detonation. 'You're confusing me. Listen... Please, just listen to me.'

'Bullshit! I should never have come. I should never have trusted you. That's all you have to say. It's bullshit. It's all bullshit!'

'I'd do anything, but - '

'Bullshit.'

'Because I...'

'Because what?'

'Because...' Cindy's shuddered, divulging the ghosts that haunted her. 'Because I was followed too. - Someone was stalking me. Someone...'

There. She said it. It was out. Finally it was out; and a surge of fears lifted all at once. But it was tranquility broken, for no respite settled in its place. Confronting her fears neutralized the paralyzing pain, but a deluge of worries stayed their turn and burst upon her consciousness. She fractured sorrow into a million pieces, like shards of glass fragmenting into confusions, and the multitude spawned other woes, unforeseen, and no less troubling. She now realized, before her confession, when the threat of a stalker still seemed a cruel fancy, that hope had kept her sane, but now resounded of fact. And there, gazing into Amber's aching eyes, and herself reflected in their trembling light, an unknown stranger, somewhere, somehow, gazing at them both.

At length, in the aftershock of a prolonged silence, Cindy began:

'I thought he was a fan.'

'A fan?'

'He came to the stage door; and waited there a long time. He was alone.'

'And?'

'He asked for my autograph.'

'What else?'

'He talked about the songs.'

'Which songs? Why?'

'The ones I want to change.'

Amber caught her breath, and just listened.

'He scared me. Not overtly, but I felt afraid. He made me afraid to sing them. That's why I wanted to change them.'

'What did he want? What was he looking for?' Their fevered stare held them, as though each were in a trance, and bound them not for intimacy but the wondering stare of trepidation. Bound not only by blood ties, but by fear.

Together, in hushed tones, they conducted a whispered series of speculations, each sister second guessing the other as they pored through scores, studying the songs, probing them for clues, sifting through each verse and line for anything to explain the mystery.

'What are we looking for?' said Cindy, switching randomly among the scores.

'Just keep looking.'

'I know them all so well. It's difficult to see among the familiar. Amber, are we looking for one song, or several?

'I don't know.'

'I can hear them in my mind even now, singing to me. How should I read them? As songs; as poems; as voices...?'

'Perhaps there's a riddle somewhere; a scattered message.'

'What?'

'Read between the lines. Use your head, not your heart. What's wrong with you? Just keep looking.'

'This is crazy. Amber!' she cried, forcing her to stop and look at her. 'This is crazy.'

'I don't care. Something isn't right. I don't care how crazy it looks. Or how mad it is. – What about this one?' She singled out a score covered with scribbled notes in her handwriting, and Cindy yielded without a struggle.

'That ballad is an old song,' she said. 'We agreed to re-write it. You wanted a clarinet in the piece. Remember?'

'And this one? What about this?'

'That's a favorite of mine. I often save that for the closing number.'

'And this? This is an old one too.'

Cindy began to laugh softly with a resigned sense of aimlessness.

'Why are you laughing?'

'Sorry, sis, don't take it hard, I was just being absentminded.'

'You were never any good at reading the right moment.'

'That's not fair.'

'It's true. You're too soft.'

'Soft? Do you mean weak? I'm not weak. Let me see you go out there on stage, night after night, and sing.'

'Maybe I should.'

'Oh, I'd like to see it, miss almighty. Go ahead!'

'I will.'

'As if you had the guts.'

'I have the brains.'

'And so do I.'

'Then pay attention, for God's sake. I'm wetting my pants here.'

Cindy drew back from the confrontation: 'Look; I'm tired, that's all. Can't you see, you're putting all this pressure on me?'

'We're both tired. But that won't help us, will it? Now come on. Please, help me. All we have is each other.'

Cindy quietly yielded and pressed on with the search; not with any hope but the effort counts as much, as Amber fell to the task desperate to discover anything. Sometimes, willpower alone can spawn the things we seek - even out of thin air. Wanting something, yearning with all her anxious might was an emotion so overpowering, so driving, so much a part of her being, that if it had a voice, and a capacity to sing, then words alone would be sufficient to create the world, and the whole damn cosmos follow in the chorus of desire.

'I'm not giving up. It's here. I know it's somewhere here.'

'Amber, get a grip on yourself.'

'It's here. I know it's here.'

'What are you looking for?'

'The connection between them.'

'Between what?'

'The songs. There's a link. They are more than the sum of their parts. It must be here. It must.'

'You wrote them. You would know.'

'But you changed them. You shouldn't have changed them.'

'That's a damn cheek! Why are you blaming me? You agreed.'

'I know,' her temper snapped. 'I know. I know. I know. But I liked them as they were. Why didn't you leave them alone? Why did you have to insist? If only you left them alone, maybe none of this would be happening.'

'That's absurd.'

'It's all your fault.'

'That's stupid. – Amber?'

'What?'

'That's stupid. Stupid!'

Arguing was futile. And at length, as the balance of what unites them far outweighs the divisions, forgiveness settles in.

'Amber, we need help? We can ask Anthony; he'll help?' No answer. 'Amber..?'

She never answered, and resumed searching through the scores, looking for patterns, for something to seize her intuition.

A while later, as Cindy began her breathing exercises in front of the mirror, Amber picked out a score that attracted her, and she held it up. 'This one?'

Cindy walked over and studied it without touching it, her arms on her hips as she continued with her exercises, breathing in and out rhythmically. In. 'Ah!' Out. 'That one.' Hold it. In again. 'Yes.' Hold, longer than before, longer than she should have. Out. '*Take me over the edge.*' She looked at her suspiciously. 'What of it?'

'This is the one.'

'Excuse me?'

'This is the one,' she repeated, her mesmerized stare fixed immovably on the score.

'That's impossible. How do you know?'

'I know,' she said, apparently addressing the score, whispering intimately to it. 'I just know...'

*　　　　*　　　　*

Certain things, at your peril, should never be neglected; while others are invariably designed to be drooled over as a matter of course. Anthony struck a match and relit his cigar. Tightening his lips and sucking hard, he brought the resistant brute back to life and exhaled a luxurious cloud of smoke high into the air where the extractor fans, silently whirring, weaved it around into gentle spirals and devoured it with style. Lighting up was all part of the pleasure of devouring these Havana cigars; they demanded a persistence to sustain them, as if smoking them seemed against the grain of their existence and were merely to be prized in the show, than in the pleasure of consumption. If the world was a stage, and we actors all, then the Havana was the quintessential prop of the singular man of taste: wine, if he really must, he could do without. But his cigars – *never!* Absurdity, it seemed, was all part of the persona, although some would defer to philosophy and call it life.

There are sins in this world that are in essence meant to be forgiven, and smoking a Havana comes top. The waiter brought him, as if by heavenly decree, a fresh pristine ashtray molded of sparkling glass, even polishing its base as a natural, not perfunctory, part of waiting on a man with a cigar. And Anthony, exceedingly that man, parked his ample Havana there to rest it a while, because it needed to breathe, and it lay there with a gravitas as the world spun around it. Anthony passed his gaze over the food and his brother's empty chair, then rose and strolled over to the bar to talk with some friends, unaware that someone was watching him. Indulging himself with adlibbing asides and joking and fun, he ordered whiskey on ice. A sexy slick creature with long red hair and fiery eyes winked at him irresistibly and he winked back, but before he could put one foot forward to steer himself there, a strange hand tapped him on the shoulder.

It was Ice smiling confidently. He offered Anthony a drink.

'Thanks. But I'm full. Perhaps another time.'

'Rain check?'

'Rain, snow, sunshine... whatever the skies. A party's a party. It's all seasonal to me. I'm dressed for every kind of weather.'

'That sounds like fun.'

'Well, I'm like the weatherman, I just follow the signs.'

'By necessity?'

'By nature.'

'Ah. Where's Michael? I've not seen him around for a while.'

'He called it a night and went to see his lady friend.'

'Restless or lonely?'

'Who knows. You work with him. Your guess is as good as mine.'

'You're his brother.'

'But only his brother; not his mother. That's not as significant as you think.'

'No?'

'I guess you don't have a brother. No matter, you can share mine.'

'We live and learn.'

'We might as well.'

'What's he like as a brother?'

'At times, he'd make a better sister, I think. But that's just my opinion.'

'I see.'

'Just kidding.'

'I know.'

Since the start of this odd encounter Anthony wondered to himself: what the hell does he want? This wasn't chance, there was motive behind it. But what? Ice's cool gaze shone with calculation; his words calibrated for the measured response; his expression tailored for effect. He was clearly up to something.

'I wanted to tell your brother something,' he said. 'Do you have a contact number?'

'Thankfully, no!'

'Oh...'

'Well, considering who he is,' he said, turning to ogle the redhead, 'it's probably best to leave it for another time.' Anthony made ready to leave, but Ice detained him.

'He's a smart guy, your brother.'

'Good for him.'

'You're Anthony?'

'Someone has to be. It may as well be me.'

'Yes.'

'And you're the top guy, the one they call Ice.'

'Ice, yes. But we're a team. No one's on top.'

'Someone's always on top. If there wasn't, the world just wouldn't work.'

'No?'

'No. I mean yes. Even religion acknowledges that fact. God holds the chair. And rightly so in my opinion.'

Anthony dealt with him capriciously, and Ice changed tactics.

'You look similar to your brother,' said Ice. 'Faintly. You do.'

'Is that so? Hmmm. Well, I'm a believer in appearances. Sure, it's shallow, I know. But you'll agree, it makes life simple. If you don't like something, for whatever reason, or if it bothers you, then just brush it aside. – Sorry; I must rush.'

'Be seeing you.'

'Sure.'

And Anthony smiled mischievously at the redhead. She was cute, this one, she had a delicious voice, and she pinched his cheek. He liked that; it tickled, and made him feel happy. He beckoned the bartender and ordered a bottle of champagne, requesting it be sent over to his table. And, arm in arm, he escorted her there.

'What are you doing?' she asked, giggling, as he struck a match.

'Stoking up this lazy brute,' he said, puffing away hard at his cigar. 'He won't stay awake.'

'You're funny,' she said, laughing.

'Thanks.'

'Yeah. You're really funny.'

'Babe.'

'Yes?'

'Is that guy I was talking with still at the bar?'

'Who?'

Impatient for an answer he never waited but turned and searched. Ice wasn't there; nor was Sam. Apparently they left together, and Anthony looked ponderously at his brother's empty chair and imagined those intrigues Michael often spoke about with such excitement, and Anthony regarded as ephemeral conversation.

'Are you OK?'

'Sure,' he said, the cigar again in full flourish. 'It's this cigar, that's all.'

'What about it?'

'You can't put it down or ignore it for a second. As soon as you do, you begin to lose ground.'

'Huh?'

'Just a thought, love,' he said, making an effort to smile, and taking a long deep chug to ensure the cigar would burn down to the butt end and conclude its existence as an ember. 'I need to have the whole cigar. And I ain't gonna let this sucker go out again.'

'That's funny,' she laughed, as the bottle of bubbly went pop! And the waiter filled up their glasses with frothy champagne.

Chapter 20

He caught the traffic lights just as they were showing amber. In that instant he wondered... Red or Green? Rain, like time, measured in ice sheets that barely move, frozen time. Red. His heart relaxes as he slows down and stops, engine still running. It's a long wait, measured in milliseconds, so he counts them by the thousand... two... three... four... He lit a cigarette and offered one to his passenger. The passenger takes one, lights up, looks at the lights. 'They're green. What are you waiting for?' He inhales the nicotine, looks at the clock on the dashboard, and turns right into the Champs-Elyseés, a Parisian constellation of lights effortlessly cool, he longs to describe it, to work out his feelings to a lasting definition, *je ne sais quois*... Yet for him time is a drive measured in milliseconds, everything runs slow, every motion of the traffic stream flowing, like music improvised, melting into the night, stylized, radical, yet soft. A slow burn. Like life.

Unless, like him, it's felt in milliseconds... one... two... three... four...

The passenger lowered the window and took in the scene 'Isn't it great to be alive? Isn't life good..?'

The sixth sense is the mystical sense of place, and time; life is like poetry, and you are the rhyme: reading between the lines... life, even suffered life, can be extraordinary; so give me moremoremore. But the six is on the slide, and it's back to five – his senses, opening wide as they drove the golden mile towards the financial district. The rain was thinning to a drizzle and the moon sailing to the horizon. Unexpectedly, the driver was asked to take a detour:

'Up ahead, along here on the right,' said Sam, not searching for lone details but the wholeness of things, the essence of a floodlit night, he knows it's not day but the radiance dazzles, leaving him with a sense of mystery. 'Here. Turn here.'

'Where?'

'This boulevard just here. Here. Whoa! Slow down, Iceman. Pull up anywhere along here. OK, Drop me here.' He started to open the door but hesitated suddenly as his hand caught the handle. 'Are you going in to work?'

'Why do you ask?'

'I thought so.' Sam frowned softly and got out but no further than a step, holding the door open and leaning slightly forward. He was always instinctively sure to be comfortable before he spoke. 'Be especially careful with your emotions, Ice. Feelings can lead us astray. Moods can get us into trouble, if *you* are not careful. Moods - this is a feminine game. And being men we're easily distracted.' He grinned: 'We're not women, after all.'

'And men don't have moods?' he said, annoyed at him.

'Sure,' replied Sam, 'we do. But unlike a car, or a woman for that matter, we have a mind that runs on testosterone. So we have to be more careful. Slow down. And think. Or perhaps... don't think. Moods: they give the game away.'

'What game?'

'That's something you never really want to find out.'

'Is this a parable?'

'No. It's a fact.' And he levered the door shut.

Ice pushed her into gear and drove her hard back down the Champs-Elysees, all along her length, towards the financial district. *She.*

Apartment six. Second floor. So what, it's late: fuck it. He's already here so up the stairs he goes. *Shush, you prick*, he scolds himself, *don't wake the grannies and the snoring old dears.* Quiet steps, one, two, three... getting there... Knock, knock.

'Who's there?'

'Double - '

'Heads?'

Sam coughed: 'Let me in.'

The lock sundered from its socket and the latch turned: click! The door yielded to and there she was in the splendor of the moonlit dark, naked, available, at his disposal, his – for a price. *Ask, and you shall have. Seek, and you shall find. Pay up, sucker, and it's all yours!*

He pressed a thousand into her open hand. She feels the cash with sensual relish, tactile in the measure of its grams exceeding the equivalent of gold and begins counting it, carefully, a woman accustomed to these moments of commerce – *I open my legs; you open your wallet.* Nice.

He drones at her impatiently, 'It's all there...' but the restive tone is too formulaic to impress or move her. The power of the moment lies in the ritual, not with emotion. He begins to move closer, she looks at him abruptly and he stops.

'Why are you late?' she said.

'Because I am.'

'What made you think I'd wait up for you?'

'Because I'm on a roll. Here,' he hands her a piece of paper. She was expecting money.

'What's this?'

'An IOU.'

'You owe me what?'

'I'm collecting, not paying.'

'Let me switch on the light to see.'

'No.'

'How will I know what it says?'

'I'll tell you.'

'And why should I believe you?'

'Because no one fucks you like I do.'

She laughed mockingly. 'You'd be surprised.'

'Bitch!'

'Bastard!'

And they kissed: deep french, the whole licking way. She bit his tongue. He teased her lower lip. It seemed just about perfect. *Nice.*

'You've been drinking,' she observed, subverting his delights and he frowned at her.

'Are you my mother now?'

'Would you like me to be?' she teased him, scarcely intimidated.

'Shut your mouth,' he demanded, and opening their mouths resumed passionately kissing, devouring the sense deep and whole, tongue rimming her teeth, his teeth, entwined in a spit gurgling plunging orgy of ravaging mouths lost in the wild giddiness of ecstasy. – *Nice.*

Next.

'Turn around, you whore.'

She swore back at him and obeyed, wheeling around in a slutty flaunt, revealing her slender back. She had soft, gorgeous skin, tender to the touch. She was desire, his thirst to be quenched with her juices, and she tastes of fire. He felt her lower spine, fondling up along its smooth length in titillating ripples.

'Do three-sixty,' he said, and she turned around. Her eyes had the velvety texture of cats' eyes, blue-green, the cardinal mixture of sensual nights, moonlit, sex-obsessed nights, drizzly nights abating in the wet warm of a Parisian summer. Mmmm, delicious. *Nice.*

Next.

'Put on some music.'

She moved over to the Hi-fi. Sleek as a cat prowling through the dark, and turned it on. 'What kind?'

'Jazz,' he said.

'Fast?' she guessed.

'Then slow,' he said, resolving the mood. 'I like it just perfect.'

'Yeah.'

He increased the volume a whisker before sliding his hand over her breast, fondling it, then the other, then both, and then she started to undress him. She tickled him a little, playing.

'You like that?'

'Yeah.'

'Good.'

A shudder fills his being until the music kicked-in, a smooth piece gracing the silent dark. Then, as she sunk her lips into his moist chest:

'Hey.'

'What?'

'Fuck - '

'You.'

And they kissed, tenderly. *Nice.*

It's inevitably far from perfect: sex, work, life in general, it stinks unless you can play from time to time, entertain the spirit with asides, with bites of fancy, cavorting with silhouettes that dance a merry dance like a boy, like a girl. Like them.

Nice.

The sound is the sound of pleasure, of foreplay, and smooth jazz serenading the obscene, consummating the scene. He takes her, she has him, his muscles glisten and bake in the furnace of passion, her skin blue, moonlight blue cools him only to ignite him more, for fire is the essence of the sexual union – to burn, to immolate, to immortalize in moments such as this the sense that the world is pure orgasm. The space between desire and love, between dark and light, a touch and the dream of kissing her breast, this hunger, all along her body sucking the threshold and raid her paradise: 'Ahhh...' the sigh is deep ecstasy, a sanctity of dripping cum as she echoes worldly karma, sound become physical turned transcendent-sex in moonlight-flesh and awakening jazz sounding time tomorrow, and the day after when...

'Did I make you come?' It's important that he knows, and he watches as she lights a cigarette and sits at the end of the bed, smoking erotically, just staring at him, her eyes full of mystery, full of mischief, full of... a woman.

'Yes. I came.'

'Why are you over there? Come closer.'

'No.'

'Why?'

'I want to see you whole against the moonlight.'

'Just turn on the light.'

'No.'

'What are you afraid of?'

'Moonlight is enough.'

'What's that playing?'

'A song.'

The sound of a lone sax fills the space like erotic incense casting aromas of sensual delights – spirits, days, nights...

'Is it our song?'

'Our song?' she wondered aloud, taking her time. 'Yes. Yes...' turning to the window and the emerging dawn, the tweet tweeting of birds suggesting the unchanging parts that weather every age, each epoch sweeping up the multitudes and still it all remains the same, each note, each moment, each scent of rose and lavender, each drop of cum and sweat.

Distracted thus for an uncertain time, she heard a thrashing sound and turned back to him anxiously. 'Sam. Sam, you sound as if you're choking. Sam!' she rose in panic, rushing to him. 'Sam!' she cried in horror. 'Sam. Can you hear me? Sam!' Consumed in a throttling fetish, he tied a cord about his neck and squeezed... until aching ecstasy rippled through his body and choked him, almost, at the threshold of this last breath. 'Sam!'

It was abysmal in her eyes, but he opened his eyes, and smiled. Crying, she embraced him powerfully and damned him for being mad, before assaulting him with fevered kisses and making love to him again.

'Don't you ever do that again,' she pleaded with him, angry with him, passionately naked with her love. 'Sam.'

He smiled, promising her by moving his head gently, barely, under a weight of thought. Then he asked her, 'Honey, did I make you come?'

Dangerous but... *Nice.*

*   *   *

Across town, in another bed, with the curtains drawn and the lights on, a man with something on his mind and a satiated limpness never had the wherewithal to ask the most fundamental question to a woman following a bout of passion, but was rather more casual about the whole thing – he even preferred she wouldn't smoke. He said it was bad for her health. Of course, he meant well and obviously had a considerable weight on his mind, but still, concern can be carried so far.

'Was it OK for you, Sara? Did you enjoy that?' Michael asked her, and she smiled at him rather condescendingly, understanding his limitations far, far better than he ever could.

'Sure,' she said softly. 'It was great.'

He grinned and swayed his head delightedly. 'I'm glad,' was an epilog appropriate to the occasion, and he thought it improper to ask for a second round so early on. It might appear unduly forward. Besides, he felt troubled by Ice, and Sam.

'What's on your mind, love?' she asked him.

'Ice, and Sam Tomka.'

'Ah, Sam Tomka, the smoothie man. Someone, they say, difficult to dislike. He's sleek like a cat; like a tomcat! Are they acquainted?'

'Intimately,' he said, sounding nervous.

'Is there anything odd in that?'

'I don't know. I just can't think straight. It's a feeling I have. Sara, I'm suspicious; something feels out of place. Something isn't right. There are loose ends everywhere.'

'Perhaps it's work related - their relationship, I mean.'

'I have a feeling it goes much deeper than that.'

'How deep do you mean?'

'Into all kinds of things.'

'What things?'

'Too many to mention.'

'Name one.'

'Poker.'

'Poker!'

'Among others.'

'I see...' She leaned over and kissed him, reaching down and taking him in her hand, working him.

'Wait!' He suddenly pushed her away and leapt up, staring enigmatically at the foot of the bed, focusing all his thoughts. 'I'm going to the office. The project.'

'Now?' she glanced at the clock. 'It's past five in the morning. Are you crazy!'

'There's always someone there, monitoring it. It's running. It stays on.'

'What?'

'The project. It's running all the time. It's never turned off. There's always someone there finessing, improving, learning, watching.'

'That sounds kinky; like a voyeur,' she giggled. 'Can I come too?'

'No. Not this time.'

'Please. Why can't I come?'

'Next time.'

'You promise?'

'Sure. I promise.'

As he left the apartment she blew him a kiss. He smiled briefly, looking distracted, and closed the door. Then, she immediately lifted the telephone and made a call.

*   *   *

Ice, looked haggard and tense, glanced periodically at his wristwatch. A colleague, realizing his discomfort, brought him a cup of coffee.

'Thanks,' he said.

'You look tired, Ice, like you've been through the mill. It's a quiet night, nothing stirring; nothing at all. Besides, it's the weekend. Why not go home and get some rest.'

'Later.'

He returned to his desk and thumbed through a magazine, but found he couldn't concentrate. Wondering about Ice, and why he seemed self-absorbed, felt more interesting, so he started up a neutral conversation as Ice studied the markets, examining the numbers and graphs: data a day old, but he seemed mesmerized. The conversation never tempted him at all, only the occasional diverting asides such as *Yes, OK...* and *Oh, is that so?...* and *What did you say?...* comprising the bulk of Ice's casual contribution, so his colleague resumed thumbing through the magazine without really looking at it, watching Ice, there, more curious than anxious at his appearance, fascinated with his behavior beyond the man he knew, one hundred percent Ice, permafrost frayed at the edges, withering from within, melting in his own heat. Ice was absorbed in whatever he was doing, and nothing, it seemed, could disturb him.

At length, as his eyes floated over the pages of the magazine, he saw an advert for a bank, the faces of ideal people, the everyman and everywoman everyone supposedly wants to be, and they had holiday hats on, their sunshine smiles adorning their twenty-something faces, and it prompted him to try again, and he said to Ice. 'You know, Asian market indices moved up three percent yesterday. The markets closed early for the holidays. It's Chinese New Year. It's the Year of the Tiger. I like big cats. Which reminds me, I must book my holiday before the deluge starts. I hate having to rush.'

'Do you know what three percent is?' Ice spoke coolly, never taking his eyes from the monitor.

He shrugged: 'A fair day's trading, I'd say....considering it's holidays and all. Some guys, they like closing on a happy note. They see it as a sign of better things to come.'

Ice never heard what he said, but seemed to continue a dialogue with himself. 'It's a number. That's all you need to know. It's just a number. – Who's there?' He turned around fretfully and stared hard at the door.

'It's just me,' said Michael, not in the least bit surprised to find Ice there, although he never understood why. Each step was based solely on a hunch, no step necessarily following the one before, and he feared how long it would last. 'Are you working late, Ice? Or is it just early?'

Ice frowned as Michael exchanged pleasantries with his other colleague, who felt himself fortunate to have company at this hour. 'Please, don't expect me to return the favor when it's my night off. But now, since you're both here, you're welcome all the same. Coffee, Mike?'

'No thanks,' he said, positioning himself at a desk opposite Ice.

'OK. I'm just going to the men's room.' And he withdrew.

'I made a bet,' began Ice.

'With who?'

'Sam.'

'On what?'

'That the dollar would plunge.'

'Why should it? The market seems calm; the numbers are steady. There's nothing to induce it, Ice. - Is there?'

'We'll see,' he said, typing on the keyboard with seamless synchronicity, like a performer, like a jazz pianist on a lyrical high. 'We'll see...'

'Ice; what are you doing?'

'Doing? What can anyone do?'

'Why don't you tell me?'

'OK, I will,' he said, steadying himself as he *seemed* to be trading in real time. 'Don't push the markets hard. Ease them gently, softly... *over the edge.*' He sighed, at peace with himself. 'There.'

Chapter 21

New York City roused this side of the sun kicking in, as moonlight licks her fiery skin, deep red, color of an apple. She never really slept, parts of her always in the throes of pleasure, always on tap like a cocktail stream, like a junkie's dream. And twilight wasn't a moment, but all part of a piece.

Vonnie lit a cigarette and watched the rolling swirls of early sunrise hint at an oriental pink, discovering daytime in an unfolding of delicious light. She had the radio playing softly the echoes of an old song, yearning, turning, a poem tenderer than a healing wound is love played in the soft weeping of violins, the clip of a yielding drum, the heartbeat of piano, the boom boom boom of acoustic bass interspersing the oboe's call to love. Tranquility was power, vast and sublimely set; but the song was a celebration of the cry: lovers dream, and time creates the fractures.

Lying naked in the bed beside her Nick stirred, ever so lightly, but never awoke. The moment suggested to her deepest sense an untying of rules and, gently raising her hand, moving along the contour of the headrest and down to the sheets, pausing for a second... two, three, four... eased them down and lifted away, unpeeling him like a skin, slowly, softly, imperceptibly, revealing the surreal surface of his nakedness, the sense of his body seeping into her mind like a slow cool drink. And there, intoxicating, she tasted his perfection.

Voyeur.

And she watched him, gazing, fondling with her eyes.

Suddenly the telephone started ringing. She answered it quickly, whispering hurriedly, 'Hello!' But it was too late, the harmony of the moment shattered and Nick began to stir, the murmuring heave as he rouses from his stillness, as sleep and wakefulness compete, and he can slip either way as the caller briskly intones:

'Vonnie; it's me, Roy.' No answer. 'Vonnie? Are you there?'

Whispering back as Nick slides in his sleep: 'Shhh, yes,' anxiously watching as the motion increased, as though her gazing alone would wake him, the smallest stir of her eyes rouse him from his naked slumber. She held her breath, as if forever, defying time to stop.

'Vonnie... I need to speak with Nick.' No answer. 'Vonnie, are you still there?'

'He's sleeping.'

Roy laughed crudely, connoting sexual mischief. 'Been *working* himself *hard*, has he?' the slur of his giggle frothed and bubbled with innuendo. This was something he could never resist, the petty triumph of facetious wit, he found too tempting to ever tame. 'Well, you're the one to stir his hormones for him, Vonnie. And they could use some stirring. You bet! Oh, and don't forget to add a pinch of your illustrious spice, babe.'

'What the hell do want this time of the morning? - I'm hanging up.'

'No. Vonnie, please, don't do that.'

'You've woken him now. You're such a total dickhead, Roy. What do you want?'

'Put him on the phone. Let me speak with him.'

'No. What do you want?'

'It's an emergency.'

'What emergency?'

'Tell him to get over to the office, right away. Tell him Victor just called me from London, and he's raving mad.'

'Who's Victor?'

'I don't have time to explain. Nick knows everything. It's serious. Tell him, Vonnie. He'll be mad at you if you don't.' Roy sounded grave, even grim, so she listened. 'I'm meeting Victor at the airport; he's arriving around nine. He's cutting it tight, so tell Nick I'll call him at the office. Tell him he should decouple the system from the network, set the flags on the trading system to yellow, and back up everything into the pot. You got that, that's most important, back up everything into the pot.'

'You're playing with me, aren't you?'

'Just tell him. He knows what to do.'

'Are you being cryptic?'

'See you, babe.' And he abruptly hung up.

Nick roused and she switched on the bedside lamp, its amber glow shedding a diffuse light, like a mist, soft on the eyes, romancing the imagination. A naked man - sleeping. A woman beside him – watching. The moment was serene; it was gentle; it was power. He. She. They.... Parts that orchestrate a play on things of a dream, everything feels surreal and love most of all, but it's very real.

'Nick... Nick...' whispering as the ambiguity of his consciousness climbs, his breathing rhythm of awakening sighs... 'Nick...' she watches although she spies, like a voyeur with a million eyes, that tantalize... He's getting there, climbing out of the labyrinth of sleep, 'Nick...' her echoes are a thread leading him to the light, and finding a lover, there, naked skin and naked clues in naked time. Beautiful. Naked.

His eyes moved in drowsy reflex. 'Hi.'

She smiled, 'Hi.' An Ariadne smile.

'What's the time?'

'Time?' it felt lovely to watch him as her eyes brave the moment with an endless stare, the consummation of her gaze with the naked flesh of her lover excites her, thrills her, but it is the steadfast, innate softness of a calm gaze that connects her to the shared and conscious moment, and she whispers: 'It's time...'

'For what?'

'Oh...'

'How long have you been awake?'

She breathed gently, easing out time, yielding into its flow. 'A while...'

He felt his nakedness and looked down at his body; then hers still half covered with the sheets – the exploration of voyeurs had begun. Mind is but the spirit of flesh but believes itself physical and bare, the expression of touch, of longing, of desired poses in the faint light defining his stare to see and be seen long, long into the moment. Poetry is a smile, an intuition, a fact, a lover, a kiss; and she leans over and kisses him deeply. And they... all part of a piece, attain perfection in the moment.

At length, they mutually spied into each other's eyes.

'Vonnie.'

'Yes?'

'Vonnie, what are you thinking?'

'Thinking?'

'What do you see?'

'Things. You,' she said. 'Nick...'

'Yes?'

'I was thinking about us.'

'And?'

'I was just looking.'

'At what?'

'You.'

'At me?'

'Yes.'

'Why? What did you see?' he asked as though he knew the answer. 'What did you find?'

'This.'

'And that...'

She laughed. He laughed, and they continued in this playful vein.

'Did the sheets fall away all by themselves?' he asked.

'No. It was me.'

'How?'

'With this hand.'

'That hand?'

'This.'

He reached out and touched it, his fingers melting into hers. 'Why?

She smiled. He smiled. And lovingly caressed his face.

'I wanted to watch you,' she said, and kissed him. 'That was for you?'

'What?'

'The phone.'

'Oh. Who?'

'Roy. You're a very light sleeper, Nick; easily stirred.'

'Roy? What did he want?'

'He asked that you go into work early.'

'Early? Why? What's the time?'

'Half past five.' She glanced at the clock. 'He said Victor called him from London. Roy sounded a bit tense. He's flying in today, and Roy's going to meet him.' She watched him transform swiftly from dreaminess to anxiety, and he started searching for his clothes. 'Nick, is everything OK? Aren't you going to take a shower?'

'Later.'

'Shall I make some coffee? Who's Victor?'

'A colleague.'

'From London?' No answer. 'I can make some coffee, it won't take me a moment.' Still no answer. 'Roy said he was going to meet him, and will be a bit late into work. He also asked that you back up everything into the pot. What's the pot? Nick?'

His actions accelerated considerably. 'Anything else?'

'No. That's all I remember. Shall I call him back for you?'

'No. I'll speak with him later.'

She watched him frantically slip on his things and clasp the watch to his wrist, looking utterly disheveled. She concealed a grin behind a tone of concern. 'Can I help in any way?' He was utterly distracted, and she raised her voice a touch. 'Nick...'

He turned abruptly, stopped everything he was doing, and rushed over to her. 'I'll call you later,' he said, and kissed her. 'Thanks.' Then he left.

*   *   *

The kitten was adroitly painting her toenails a velvety pink, finessing the edges with surgical dexterity, her concentration fixed nimbly on the task. Suddenly, she slipped and clipped her skin with the pink varnish as Roy hammered down the telephone with fury.

'Oh fiddlesticks!' she shrieked, mortified.

'What the hell is going on?' Roy scowled at the telephone, lifting it again and pressing the buttons with such fury he seemed on the verge of exploding. He wanted to throttle someone, to squeeze the life out of him, the person he was trying to contact.

'You made me mess up my toenails. Look, Roy!' she cried. 'Look at them. Oh fiddlesticks!'

'Sorry, babe, but this damn thing is driving me crazy.'

'Who are you calling now, Roy? Who?'

'That pervert shirker – Frank!' he seethed, seizing the phone as if to crush it. 'He's taken the phone off the hook. He's up to something... The filthy swine.'

'Maybe he's sleeping.'

'Sleeping? Huh!'

'Or maybe he's busy.'

'Yeah... Busy!' he fumed, fearing to think, drumming his fingers on the sideboard. 'That's what I'm afraid of.' But the only answer for his agonies was an unremitting engaged tone and a scowling pussycat wiping pink varnish from her big toe.

'Fiddlesticks!'

*   *   *

'Scum!'

'Yes, Mistress?'

'What are you?'

'Scum. I'm worthless scum.'

'You're lower than a worm. You're less than scum.'

'Mistress, please...' pleaded Frank. 'Have mercy on me.'

'You wretch! You groveling maggot! Get down on your knees. Now!' crushing him with her boot, as he strokes the rubber, smells the leather, licks the whip: 'Slave!'

'Yes. Yes. Oh Yeeeeesssss... *Ouch!*' he gasped, yearning for atonement (fetishes are pure ritual without the cumbersome ceremony of religion or the formality of flagellation. Guys like him know, you can't get off by knocking yourself up. Come on, that don't cut the loaf! Eggs are fried sunny side up. If you're going to roast, shucks, you may as well have the full menu and bake with the cake before you eat it. Make sense? Nah. Not a bit. It's crazy talk just making men feel hungry all the time, is all. But that comes with being a guy. Right?). He is craven, gutless, the rump end of a dog pressed into submission howling to the heavens for a leash, for a kick up the backside with sleek pointed heels – *ouch!* – and reeking like a slave: fresh-smelling sweat touched up with *eau du cologne*, actually, very manly and sweet (to the unjaundiced eye), all macho with bouquet – but he's still nothing but a stinking slave as far as she (and he) is concerned. And yet it's claimed man is spiritual. Sure, provided it comes wrapped in spit, a big dollop of the gunky stuff from a wench's mouth spewing and slutty and purring those sparkling endearments: "You filthy stinking slave. Take that!" Whack. Ouch! "And that!" Whack. Ouch. Whack, whack. Ouch, ouch. "And that..." It's the dialect, you see, finessed by a whore. And she loves him dearly, you see, because he pays her bucket loads of money for bucket loads of her pee. "And take that!"

'Yes. Oh yes... Ouch!'

Paradise is distinguished for its frame of reference, (relatively speaking, seventh heaven is seven senses to bewitch a man on Monday, Tuesday.... every day of the week): each man has his own, and perhaps women have one too, but they keep mum about it, just like a good mummy's girl trained in the immutable mantra of relationships: *Don't tell the man anything. Screw him, all the time. Keep him spinning in circles. Round and round you go, sucker. Round and round you go*...Whip! Ah, that's nice...

He can't help it, but even if he could, he'd delight in breaching all the moral norms and lurk amid the sewers waiting for rats, female rats, that is, to devour him. A lick ain't enough. A bite won't do. No, sir. Guys being guys, they've got to have it all. And when aroused, doubled. Her boot in his balls – *Ouch!* And that lash of her whip over his back - *Ouch, what a cow! The filthy bitch. Ouch!* will do just nicely, thank you very much. Oh yeah. Thanks a bunch, honey-pie. Way to go, love. Merci, mon cheri. J'taime, my-one-and-only...

Sucker!

'Get down and lick, you filthy scum; you shit, you nothing, you vermin...What hole did you crawl out of? Who told you to come out? Down, and lick my boots. Lick them clean. Harder. Lick harder. I said harder, you slave. – You make me sick!'

He yanks out his tongue and pours on the spit like its honey and strawberries and cream, frantically working and smothering her boots with a lapping gratitude. Mmm, yummy, delicious. Sluicing around the juices with carousing gurgles like he's licking up the world. Heaven tastes of leather, of black rubber, of this. It's paradise in his mouth. His only longing is that his tongue were the width of an ocean, and he could suck her all up. Lick lick. Mmm...

She's a BBW (Big Beautiful Woman), tits the size of mountains about to collide. She storms up close and engulfs his head in them, and squeezes. He almost suffocates, grows giddy, before she curses and releases him again.

You or I would call her a BFC (a Big Fat Cow); but she's an angel to him: GMM (Give Me More) riding on a cloud of satin steel, AWT (Amazing Woman This) if she's your bundle of delights, she'll make your day, and crucify your nights, if that's your ding-a-ling, GGG (Gimme Gimme Gimme...) MMM (More More More).

The lust for pleasure perfected with pain, for **S**oft & **M**ean arousal, convulses the fetish obsessive with powerful urges, as it tickles the mind with a trembling lick: the role play, the action of her fist in bruising his flesh, crushing him with a whip with an ice cold stare while his spirit floats in flaming ecstasy. She glares at him with venom, he spies on her like a voyeur, the one creates a hell, but he feels only heaven. The entire encounter is a play on paradox: taking pleasure in inflicted pain. It's not psychological, it's... redemptive. Imagine bright questions with dark answers shadowing a question mark. Fetishes are a solution defined in one language seeking a problem posed in another. Understanding is mostly by suggestion. She is cruel by design, not nature; she is cool by decree that this is what the customer is paying for, and the customer is always right. Right? It's a transaction; it's commerce of the flesh. You bid, you agree to exchange the goods. Simple. Right? And yet... something in the mind provokes the question, and the body tests the answer: I know it's wrong - but it's right. Culture, language, civilization, are not nouns, but verbs.

His only yearning is to be a billion layers thick so she could strip them off his back, one by one, tormenting and discarded like the scum he is become, the seedy, vile and loathsome minutiae of insect insolence to be stamped on, battered, squashed, enslaved and humiliated. Whack! Kick! Punch!...

But why?

After the session ended, he rewarded her generously in cash and she saw him to the door, feeling the texture of the cash between her fingers. No problem there; it was real, and it felt *right*.

'Come again,' she said sweetly, and pecked him on the cheek.

'I will.' He grinned with self-satisfaction. 'And next time, I want to be watched.'

'What do you have in mind: beady eyes; soft eyes; old lady, old man, couple, fat lady, thin chick, a - '

'Just you and me,' he interrupted, subverting her expertise in the tested range of willing participants always happy to oblige a lecher or a saint - for the right price: MM...M (Money Makes... the world go round, Mammon).

'Huh?' she frowned at him as though he were a deviant unwilling to settle for a good deal. 'What do you mean?' She's a business-woman, right?

'Mirrors.'

'I supply a dungeon, love, not mirrors. Besides, how many do you need? I just can't see it. This ain't a beauty parlor, you know. It wouldn't work.' She's the epitome of expertise at its best and ablest. 'It's not the business if you ask me...' expounding wisdom at its plainest. 'I provide authentic scenarios. Authentic! No one's fussier with the details than me, love. What do you need mirrors for? To watch the world go by?'

'Just fit mirrors in the room. Large ones. Wall to wall. My eyes crawl everywhere. I want to *watch* as well as *feel*.'

'Eh?'

'Feedback. Client satisfaction magnified a thousand fold.'

CAR (the Customer's Always Right). Vroom Vroom; no brakes; drives you crazy just thinking about it!

'Ah!' she sighed, winking at him knowingly. 'Kinky suggestion. I need to figure out the lighting; it's got to be just right. OK; leave it with me.' - She's a perfectionist.

'Good.'

And waving him bye-bye, she closed the door.

ASC (Another Satisfied Customer).

As he waited by the elevator he overheard two men, double Ds (Drooling Deviants) lurking by the stairway engaged in whispered conversation while waiting their turn with the BBW at the allotted time. One was a veteran of the S&M scene, the other a confused fella with a yearning for atonement - after he had a good whipping.

'Make sure she hammers you with her tits early on,' said the vet.

'Why?' asked the novice.

'She gives you a real good walloping, and if she were lactating, you'd drown in a sea of cream.'

'Marvelous!'

'Yeah. Now, don't try and boss her around, because she's sure to get moody and boot you out.'

The novice was suddenly overcome by shudders of doubt and wondered at length, 'Do you ever regard it as degradation?'

'Fuck, no! It's what you want, isn't it? I mean, why are you here?'

'The experience, I guess,' confessed the novice, wondering. 'I can't stop thinking about it.'

'Ask yourself, is rubber the same as leather?'

'Well... I guess not.'

'Well then, there you are. You know what you really want. What you need. Right? So why deny it?'

'But what *am* I looking for?'

'What?'

'What drives us? Is it something inside, deep down?'

'Down. Up. In. Out. It's just sensation; like an erection. And you want one of those, don't you?'

'Sure.'

'Well then; sit back and enjoy the ride.'

'I guess so...'

'You understand now?'

He hesitated, 'I think so. Kind of...'

'That's OK,' he reassured him. 'That's fine. Just let her do all the driving. You're only here for the ride.'

'Yes. But it would make it easier, wouldn't it?'

'Easier? How?'

'If you knew exactly why?'

'Look, I told you already; it's not a problem. We are what we are. Needs are precious, they need to be looked after. You get it?'

He shrugged lamely, 'Sort of... I guess.'

'That's good enough. Oops! My turn.' And he leapt into the corridor just as Frank entered the elevator and pressed ground.

When Frank returned to his apartment he switched on the lights, locked the door, instinctively looked at the clock on the wall and replaced the phone in its cradle. He barely had time to sigh with relief before it started ringing and jolted him. Staring at it hard, he felt a wave of troubles about to engulf him.

He paused, took a deep breath, composed himself, and then lifted the receiver. 'Good morning.'

'Where have you been?'

'Hi, Roy,' he greeted him calmly. 'You're up nice and early?'

'Where the hell have you been?'

'Me? I've been here. I took the phone off the hook. I wanted some quiet time to myself. A lot has happened lately, and I couldn't sleep.'

'You've been out whoring again.'

'No. I swear.'

'Bullshit!' Roy fired off expletives like a cannon. 'It's bullshit!'

'OK. OK.' he yielded, improvising. 'By chance, not by design, I had a little diversion. My spirit was low; it needed perking up.'

'Where have you been?'

'Calm down. She came over here to my place. Besides, she has three kids to feed and needs the money. You can't begrudge her that. Come on, Roy; you know how hard it is to bring up three kids these days? It takes an awful lot.'

'I don't know and I don't want to know. If it bothers you that much, just marry the bitch. Don't screw around on my time. Inside; outside. Doesn't matter where.' He stopped to catch his breath. 'Don't you realize? This is serious. The stakes are damn serious.'

'Sorry, Roy. You're right. But I needed to unwind. I'm on edge. All this is getting to me. And coping isn't easy, you know. Look at it from my side. I'm in a state of shock. Be fair. I just took a little dip in the pond, to relax, like.'

'Then dip it somewhere else. Try a rubber doll. Or get a dog.'

Frank recalled all the women he had known: big ones, little ones, fat ones, thin ones, all kinds, and the analogy rang a bell. A big bell. A very big bell. Thousands of bells shaking into song all at once in the tempestuous reminder that the world is a smallish kind of place after all. There's not that much new under the sun. Rubber doll. Dog. A hard on. A women. Think about it a mo. Rings a bell?

'Sorry, Roy; it won't happen again.'

'Make sure, damn it. Think with your head, not your balls.'

'OK...' he conceded, raising his eyebrows while admiring his reflection in a mirror, and imagined the BBW adorning the dungeon with the glittering things – Irresistible! 'OK...'

Roy recovered his composure and became more businesslike. 'I called Nick about an hour ago. Victor called me from London – don't talk, just shut up and listen. He's hot on to something and he's flying in today. No, no he didn't say what; just shut up and listen. Nick's gone in to the office and started cleaning up. He's backing up everything in the pot.'

'What about Victor?'

'I'll meet him at the airport and keep him busy for as long as I can. I'll take him somewhere. I'll bounce around town and stall for time. Get to work pronto and encrypt everything. Hide everything. Use your own codes, and leave the rubbish in the network to keep prying fingers busy on their keyboards. We don't want them fondling our ass at a time like this. And one more thing.'

'What?'

'Track those guys in Paris. Give Peeping Tom a wink. Lead them on; woo them; make yourself visible. Let them know we know. We're taking this to a head.'

'Are you sure about this, Roy?' His voice echoed with misgivings. 'Roy... We'll have our pants down. Are you sure about this?' He saw this step as irreversible. Each day, most moments have a neutral basis. Only seldom does the balance weigh so heavily that it makes one stop and think: How smart, or how lucky, do you really think you are? Roy shared his anxieties, but was unable to articulate the ache, other than to say:

'No,' his voice trembling with apprehension. 'No, I'm not certain of anything.'

And he abruptly hung up.

Ten seconds later he received a call.

'Roy, it's me, Nick.'

'You shouldn't be making outside calls. Not from the office. They're all logged.'

'Someone's been snooping around.'

'How do you know?'

'The furniture's been moved,' he sounded alarmed, whispering anxiously, fearing to be overheard. 'And other things. I don't like it.'

'Did you check the pot?'

'The pot's fine.'

Roy sighed with relief. 'Calm down. Don't get paranoid; it's just the cleaners or someone. Frank is on his way. He'll fill you in.'

'What does he think?'

'Ask him yourself when he gets there. I have enough on my mind to worry about.'

'Victor?'

'Don't remind me,' he sighed despondently, but the persevering instinct pulled him through. 'Nick, don't let your nerve slip. Not now. Resist the temptation to panic. There's nothing as seductive as fear - expect hunger perhaps. It can make you do anything. Anything...' His voice grew soft; reflective; he was philosophizing. Events were beginning to take their toll on him, and this disclosure of advice was as much for himself as for Nick. 'And Nick, don't call me again unless it's really urgent.'

And he hung up.

By this time, the kitten was becoming agitated and felt neglected. Several times she tried to attract his attention, purring, 'Roy, don't you love me anymore?' Naturally, he said he did, every atom of her being, but continued working on his computer non-stop, never pausing until around seven o'clock when the kitten grew bored of the TV and started at him again.

'Roy... What are you doing?'

'I'm working, babe.'

'Come to bed.'

'Later.'

'When?'

'Tonight.'

'Tonight!' she gasped. 'That's *ages* away. *Ages*. What'll I do till then?'

'You'll just have to think of something, babe,' he said decisively. 'That's how it is.'

'Men!' sulked the cliché bimbo with the cliché moan in the clichéd way of dribbling her vowels over her consonants that seemed puny by comparison like she couldn't care less. An intrinsic part of her nature is having him inside her. It made her feel wanted, desired, important, powerful. 'Men!' There she goes again, rising then slumping back immediately on the bed, whacks the pillow, picks it up angrily, and then tenderly hugs it, then lies down moodily like she wants to cry and cry. 'Men!' She painted her toenails a dashing pink just for him. But he just... 'Men!' Doesn't he realize it needed meticulous genius to get the strokes just right? Is he dim or something? she sobs to herself with pretend tears dramatizing the epic in her mind. And she shut her eyes not meaning to sleep, but this ceaseless angst and grumbling eventually took its toll, and she fell into a clichéd kind of sleep – sound enough that she never stirred a jot when the telephone began ringing.

'Hello. Roy?'

'Victor, where are you?'

'Ten thousand meters above the North Atlantic. We've over Iceland now. The pilot informs us there are active volcanoes down there. Live ones. Not exactly reassuring, is it, Roy?'

Roy coughed superstitiously. 'Iceland?'

'Yes. And it looks very pretty from up here. Despite the menace, I'd probably be tempted to take a stroll. Care to join me, Roy?'

'Rather you than me...'

'I'll be touching down in a couple of hours.'

'I'll be waiting.'

'Good. – Are you on-line?'

'I just logged on this minute.'

'Check out the markets. Dollar's tumbling a wee bit.'

'It's just a glitch.'

'You think so?'

'Sure. A technical bounce, that's all.'

'Keep watching. We'll talk when I get there.'

'I'll be waiting. Bye.'

As soon as he hung up Roy hastened to check the exchange rates for the primary currencies. He noticed some unusual movements in the dollar apparently initiated from Riyadh. *Riyadh!* Roy shrieked.

That's a spooky one, he thought. Of all places, Arabia seemed the last to cross his mind. But he knew, never to underestimate men with conviction, especially quiet conviction.

'Kitten,' he called out. 'Hey, baby, are you awake?' No answer. 'I'll have to make my own tea then,' he grumbled, thinking in context: 'What use is a woman if she can't bring you a cuppa when you fancy one? May as well settle for a robot instead.'

Then, while returning from the kitchen, he caught sight of her sleeping and stopped to gaze. In that ineffable moment he was captivated and in awe of her. She, a sense of pearly candles in the dark, of gentleness unbeholden to time for the world to see and breathe her, that to be alive is magnificent consummation. How did she get here? Where was he before? It was as if she was always there, an innate part of him, and imagination flowed from this realization. 'You are so lovely,' he whispered to her as she slept. 'You are so gorgeous... God, aren't you a picture? Aren't you incredible? Aren't you something else..?'

Softly, in cushioned steps, he tip-toed towards her, leaned over and kissed her. Tender was the moment, and timeless... and then the phone rang. He rushed to answer it. 'Hello?'

'They spotted us.' It was Frank, sounding very somber.

'Are you sure?'

'We've shown our cards. They got the message. They know we know.' A long pause ensued, intense and protracted. 'Roy. What now?'

'We play,' he said.

And he hung up.

Twenty to nine, the kitten was awake and feeling feisty. 'Roy, where are we going?'

'To pick someone up at the airport.'

'Who?'

'An English gent.'

'A Limey?'

'Don't call them that, babe, not when they're around. Be discreet, he's an important friend.'

'Ah…' she sighed in afterthought. 'OK.'

The kitten's a peach; she's all heart; she's got it where it counts. She knows her man, and doesn't hide it. She knows a hug makes all the difference in the world, and a well-timed hug something to treasure. The kitten's a dream; she knows warmth costs nothing. Lick lick, her, like whole cream. Mmmm...

'Roy?'

'Yes, babe.'

She kissed him and gave him a hug. Her emotion and warmth engulfed his body. She was so physical that the delights of the mind, with her, were even more physical than a touch. And then she looked at her nails to make sure they were perfect. They were, and she smiled.

Meow!

*   *   *

The hubbub at JFK felt like a sign of things to come. Movement, people, controlled pandemonium with the fascinating sense that each part had an aim, a destination, a route through the labyrinth of international travel. Tickets, boarding passes, passports, together with the virtual tags digitized in an information stream, identified and transmitted people with their luggage and wares flawlessly. Humans invent machines to control and manage their lives, and in time, what do these inventors inevitably become? Resentful; grumpy; and downright bloody moody.

'I hate these damn places,' Roy groaned as he searched for a place to park.

'There, Roy. Look! There's a free space over there.'

'Well spotted.'

'Quick!' she gestured frantically with her hand. 'That car's going to grab it. Shoo you!'

'Gotcha, sucker.' Roy swept his car into the vacant space with speed and agility. 'What would I do without you, kitten?'

She blushed and smiled with great pride, and that seemed to say everything. Just a few words, spoken at the right time, can make all the difference in the world to a human being. It costs nothing, and is priceless.

Weaving among the multitude in the Arrivals Terminal, they confirmed the flight and landing time. 'Ten minutes, babe. Good timing, wouldn't you say?'

He preferred to be outside in the sunshine, smoking a cigarette, and conferred with her. She nodded yes and took the opportunity to visit the ladies' room. Besides, he needed to compose himself and a cigarette always helped.

A swanky looking guy lingering near the exits by a stretched limousine approached him. He was smartly attired and seemed like the driver of the car. 'Do you have a light, buddy?'

'Sure,' Roy passed him the lighter, not realizing until moments later that the guy was lighting up a joint.

'Thanks, man,' he said contentedly, and strolled away.

Takes all kinds...

The kitten joined him and they held hands for a while, watching the airplanes glide into town. After another cigarette and a brief walk they returned inside and waited at Arrivals for Victor. He was traveling light, first class, just an overnight bag. He was a thin, mousy haired man with a crystalline angular face, pushing six feet in his handsome heels taking up less than an inch of pure leather that tapped the ground like a tap-dancer's gait.

'Roy.'

'Victor.'

They briefly shook hands; their eyes warily competing.

Turning to the kitten, he asked Roy:

'Who's this?'

'Barbie.'

'Like the doll?'

'Yeah.'

'Hi, doll.'

'Hi!' said the doll, winking at him.

As soon as they began walking light conversation kicked in, Victor feeling reluctant to raise more pressing concerns while the kitten was around, the main reason Roy brought her along – to stall for time. When they reached the car Victor asked: 'Where are we going?'

'I'll take you to the hotel.'

'Never mind the bloody hotel!' he erupted; then amended his tone with a cheesy smile. 'Jet lag, you know. Makes me a bit moody.'

'Happens to us all,' said Roy sympathetically. 'Happens to us all...'

The kitten looked for a relevant role and waded in smoothly with: 'Would like a chocolate, Victor?'

He looked at her and smiled, shaking his head, 'No thanks. It's a bit early in the day for me.'

'Go on,' she insisted with enthusiasm, holding the box open for him. 'Take one for later. Go on, Vic.'

He politely acquiesced and picked one wrapped in gold foil. 'Thanks, sweetie.'

'OK.' She smiled at him quaintly, and blew Roy a kiss.

They were quiet for a time as they left the airport and picked up speed. Roy informed him. 'We'll just drop Barbie off at the beauty salon, and then be on our way.'

He pushed his luck too far. Slanting his eyes to the right he observed Victor's expression, the hard-edged eyes, shrewdly intolerant and pressing for answers. You play cat and mouse like this at your peril. You can persevere at first, sure, some scheming, a measure of bluff, but sooner or later Humpty goes all Dumpty and you are left with your pants down – not a pretty sight. Victor broke the strained pause with a cough and remarked, as though in passing, that the kitten seemed lovely as she was, and meddling with perfection was unwise. 'You're asking for trouble, if you ask me.'

Roy sighed, rubbing his eyes, playing for time. He needed to improvise fast to forestall the impression he was dragging his feet. 'We'll head straight for the bar after that.' He threw him a colluding stare. 'We have to meet someone there.'

'Bar. What bar?'

'A place, nicely tucked away for occasions such as this.'

'Such as what?'

Oops! Foot in it again.

'Relax,' said Roy. 'We'll get there in good time.'

'Good!' he fired like a bullet. 'Good!' and marveled at the view of Manhattan just a-ways soaring through the skyline, lifting the world up and up and up like a rousing giant, to breathe, to live - monoliths of the endless moment pregnant with potential.

Some moments last for ever. New York City...

Thirty minutes later Roy pulled the car over to the side, and stopped. He left the engine running, still in gear, the kitten got out and he rolled down the window.

'I'll pick you up later. Call me when you're done. Do yourself up real nice.'

'OK.'

They pecked each other on the lips and she briefly waved to Victor, who forced a smile and waved back. Roy waited till she entered the salon, and then he turned to his passenger.

'Deal,' said Victor.

'They don't call me Hard Eight for nothing.'

'How's the gang?'

'Nick is fine.'

'And Frank?'

'Alive and kicking, as always?'

'Roy, what's going on?'

'That's what we're going to find out,' he said, turned and looked over his shoulder, found a space in the oncoming traffic, pressed the gas pedal, and cruised downtown to the bar.

Inside the salon the receptionist misspelled her name, and the kitten became annoyed. 'Like you can't even spell a simple name like that. What's the matter with you, lady?'

'Sorry, ma'am,' she replied, a woman in her mid twenties not as pretty as the kitten but considerably more patient. 'Please, go on inside.'

'Has Jenny Risbin arrived yet?'

'Yes, ma'am, she has.'

'OK.' And she sauntered into the lounge area where her brunette friend, Jenny, while speaking on the phone, was being served with a cappuccino coffee and croissant. She waved to the kitten and they kissed, quickly on the cheek - one two, kiss kiss - and the kitten looked with yummy eyes at the attendant who got the message instantly and went to fetch for her a cappuccino coffee and croissant. Jenny continued the conversation on the phone, drawing it to a reluctant close now the kitten had arrived:

'Make your move, baby...' She was an oral dynamo, this chick, speaking with her lover. 'Oh yeah... Just there. Ah! Slowly.' She was a wet dream, this one. 'Ouch!' and a hard-on. 'Ouch and yummy ouch!' Someone was getting it laid on thick and creamy. 'And?' she was not one to hold back. 'Charm me some more, baby.' She sighed, 'Go on...' then giggled. 'OK.' Louder. 'OK.' Even louder. 'Good.' It was time to hit the brakes. 'I'll call you later.' Prolonging the ending. 'Later.' Damn hard to let go of a good thing; even remotely on a phone. 'Yeah, you too, baby... ' But it had to end, for now. 'Ciao.' And there would always be next time. 'Bye bye...' She hung up, slips the phone into her purse, and then leans back in the couch and smiles: 'How's it going?'

'Great,' says the kitten. 'Just great. And you?' hinting at the phone call.

They laugh together as if the question were the greatest tease imaginable. And at length take it nice and easy as they drink their cappuccino coffee and tuck in to their fresh croissants.

The salon is entirely devoted to the service of kittens, in pandering to their whims, and not just a few, but whole litters of them. As a business it's guaranteed to thrive as few others can, the commerce of vanity being liquid in every corner of the universe where a kitten lays her fussy paws. From opening the door to greeting them with: "Felines, you are most welcome..." the staff at the salon ply them with a luxury smile, with care, with attention and endless details. Sure, you can buy a smile, and the hundred-dollar smile is honed to perfection and feels just great, even on a rainy day, here, in the salon, one takes the smiles for granted because they are part of the furniture: they come naturally with cappuccino coffee and croissants.

Twenty minutes later the pussycats are seated side by side under computer controlled hairdryers softly whirring as they thumb through glossy magazines, admiring the pictures and forgetting the words are even there, or possibly, perhaps wondering *why* they're there. Something catches Jenny's fancy and she brings it to the kitten's attention:

'Look at this,' she said, holding out her glossy magazine.

'Nice.'

'Yeah.'

'And this.'

'It's even better than that one.'

'You think so?'

'Sure.'

'Hmm, maybe... Maybe...'

The hairstylist returns and releases them from the hair-dryers, propping up their hair meticulously with a perfect comb.

'You comfy?' she enquires.

'Thanks.'

'Coffee?'

'Thanks.'

'Sugar?'

'Thanks.'

'Milk?'

'Sure.'

'I'll take cream,' says the kitten as she yawns a little yawn. 'Not too much, though.'

'Certainly,' and she saunters away like the coolest breeze on the sunniest of days.

'Jen.'

'Yeah, Barb?'

'You ever thought of having a kid?'

'Kid?'

'Yeah.'

'Well...' she mulls over the life-shaping conundrum and then out pops the answer. 'Not just yet.'

'When then?'

'Later.'

'Oh...'

An unexpected silence ensues: what to speak about now? The dilemma stretches their mutual mind this way and that, as lounge music hushes smoothly in the background, and one glossy magazine is exchanged for another. Boredom begins to seep in, and they need to do something fast. The kitten takes a cue from the previous topic, and spurts out:

'I'd like a boy.'

'What?'

'I'd like to have a boy.'

'Oh,' Jenny pondered this a while. 'I like girls.'

They agreed on the outline of child-bearing, more or less; vaguely agreed on the timing; disagreed on the gender; agreed on the hair color (light brown) eye color (blue) and diverged on the preferred method of education.

'I think it has to be a private school, Jen.'

'I'd teach them at home.'

'Do you think so?'

'Yeah.'

'Oh. OK.'

Has she been persuaded of the virtues of self-reliance? Not really, but at that particular moment it seemed like a pretty neat idea. And neat ideas can be like chocolates – they melt in your mouth, taste yummy, and then are gone.

'Would you like a candy, Jen?'

'Thanks.'

'What about a biscuit?'

'No thanks. - Oh look,' Jenny darted her eyes to the left and gazed out of the one-way window into the street. 'It's started to rain.'

'I like the rain.'

'Yeah,' she mused at length, as though it were a masterpiece. 'It's nice.'

'Yeah,' the kitten echoed, as thunder wracked the clouds and lightning blitzed the sky.

'Yeah. Kinda nice, really. In a way...' Pause. A dainty sigh. A yawn. A pretty little yawn. 'Ain't it?'

'Yeah...'

*   *   *

'So the heavens open, old sport,' remarked Victor, feeling peeved over everything. They were presently stuck in a traffic jam and he felt it impossible to resist the conclusion that Roy was steering them into obstacles and stalling for time.

'These things happen, Vic,' he said, trying to humor him. 'The pouring rain, traffic congestion, moaning and groaning... Look at it this way, it may be boring, but at least it reminds you of home.'

'Very witty.'

'Well, the Brits fly in and they bring their weather patterns with them. What else can you expect?'

'Ha ha,' he retorted. 'Who are we going to meet?'

'Someone from New Jersey who has government connections.'

'What's the government got to do with this?'

'Who knows.'

'Do you know what I think, Roy?' No answer. Just a blank stare. 'I think this is a load of bullshit.'

'Oh look! The traffic's started moving again.'

'I want some answers; or I'll pull the plug. And I don't care who goes down the hole.'

Roy was cornered. He had to respond. 'Understood,' he said, his foot pressing the accelerator teasing the cars in front, all bumper-to-bumper. Although the city was bustling and noisy, it felt uncomfortably quiet in the car.

'Have you ever heard a ghost fart, Roy?'

Ahem! - 'No, Vic, I can't say I have.'

'Do you think they empty their bowels, like we do?'

He raised his eyebrows, smirking. 'It wouldn't surprise me,' he said. 'After all, this is New York City!'

'That's a real touch of American panache, Roy. Bravo! And let me tell you, my old mate, I'm a religious man. So when someone starts spreading rumors about Jesus being an ordinary Joe and farting, and angels relieving themselves in public up there in the clouds, all that thunder and rain, it makes me think they're up to something real dodgy. Like pulling a bloody fast one. Do you get my drift?'

'I can't see what you're getting at, Vic. There's a problem. OK. We'll sort it out.'

'Not a problem, old mate. No. But intrigue; machinations. There are things out of joint; little things that add up to a lot. And they shouldn't be happening at all, because it looks about as normal as an angel farting. Or Moses taking a crap while the Pharos's up his arse.'

It was a bit crude, both the pun and the parable, but Roy could see the point. 'He was human after all, Vic. It's normal. What's the big deal, if you look at it logically?'

'But his reputation stinks when you imagine him constipated and begging God Almighty to send him down a mighty fart to force the gunk from his bowels. I mean, would you follow someone for forty bloody years through the middle of nowhere preaching the Ten Commandants, and yet craps in the desert and wipes his arse with a stone? It ain't right, Roy. It ain't the business. It ain't religion anymore. It don't cut the mustard, old son. We expect certain things to happen a certain way. Do you understand me, Roy? Are you getting the message loud and clear, old son?'

'Clear as day,' he said, relieved that the traffic had started moving again. 'But bear this in mind; we're still in the dark, just like you.'

Victor remained quiet, looking impassive as the famed stones of the desert (the ones with the Ten Commandments carved on, not the practical pebbles most guys would use when they need to spend a penny in the deserts of Arabia), just staring hypnotically ahead at the dense traffic crawling slowly forward, honking horns, competing for a finite space as if the whole world hinged on this maneuver. It seemed, among the mass of cars and restless people scurrying from shelter to shelter, and the few lucky ones with umbrellas braving the storm with advantage, that the animated picture exposed a ritual of the city, like religion practiced day in day out, obeyed, abided by, conformed with, a sentence not of death but of endless toil to the capitalist machine that drove the whole relentlessly on to... to...?

Life - it's all a guessing game, really.

Victor, tired from his flight, muttered: 'What the hell am I doing? I must be crazy.'

'What did you say, Vic?'

'Nothing,' he rubbed his eyes. 'Just get us there in one piece.'

The rain abated to a peppering mist by the time they arrived and looked for a place to park. The morning was warm and the feathery rain felt like droplets of sweat showering the skin, covering it with thin layers.

Victor avoided speaking at all; but he had the pent up expression of a man about to explode on any incendiary thought or remark. Roy proceeded cautiously, trying to keep his mouth shut for as long as possible until they reached the bar, some fifty meters from where he parked the car. He kept looking at his wristwatch every few seconds and this irritated Victor.

'What the hell do you keep looking for?' he finally snapped, wiping the sweat-rain from his face with a handkerchief.

'Just making sure,' he replied. 'We're almost there. – Ah, here it is.'

Soft blue lights shaped into the name *Tango Man Bar* and turning sepia with dirt lit up the entrance to the jazz bar. Its less than subliminal message was *'Don't come in here, unless you want to party...* a kind of urban cocktail of missives written in seediness tempting any stranger to stop and think, notwithstanding the grime, as *Tango Man* uttered sweetly, *You know, really, all I want to do is play you a song. And then, you know, share a joint. OK? And then, you know, make out at the long bar. Why don't you nice folks come on inside, huh?* - What voice a stranger listens to depends critically on how much he drinks. A soft voice. A hard voice. A soft fuck. A hard fuck. A love song. A melancholy song... Whiskey on ice...

Tango Man was a hang-out and venue for sensual blues and deep jazz, fashioned with subdued lights and flaking walls looking surreal in the shadows; a low profile downtown down-market backstreet behind-the-scenes bar whose dubious renown was measured by the musical notes pumped out per second to a predominantly dazed clientele of singles, couples, triples, people on crutches, rolling in on boozed-up wheelchairs, day-time hookers with confetti looks. Buy her a drink. Have one yourself. She touches your thigh. Smoke – a joint? A guard on the door, an ex-con with swanky garb and a dazed face, who makes extra money on the side spinning hash and weed to the patrons.

'You looking for some stuff, man?' he croaks.

'No,' said Roy curtly, but the guard is a businessman and offers them a girl. 'No,' he says again flatly, and the guard lets them through and says:

'You have yourselves a real good time around here, now.'

'What the hell is this?' Victor exclaimed. 'Roy?'

'We'll be incognito here.'

'We'll be fucked here, that's what!'

'Don't worry, Vic. Trust me, I know what I'm doing. It's all been arranged.'

'It's your head on the block, mate!' he warned starkly. 'It's your bloody head.'

'Relax, Vic. - Come on, let's have a drink at the bar.'

'This time of the day?'

'Don't worry. We'll order you some tea.'

'Fuck you! And fuck the tea!'

They climbed on stools, Victor reluctantly, and Roy, with renewed vigor, immediately leaned on the bar and fondly ogled everything around him, taking in the sheer sweep of the bar as if he wanted to embrace it. Flashing a grin, he felt indulgent beside the multitude of liquor on display. To Victor he seemed much too elated; his spirits unjustifiably excessive and out of sympathy with the occasion. But Victor stayed his time and waited to see what would happen.

'Bartender,' Roy beckoned him over excitedly.

'Yes'r?' he said in a single syllable.

'Two whiskeys, please. And bring plenty of water.'

'Yes'r,' he threw himself into action. 'Coming right up.'

Roy dipped his fingers into a bowl, picking up savories and filling his mouth. Then, sliding it over with the back of his hand to Victor: 'Pretzels, Vic?'

He gave Roy a dirty look; the filthy, low-life scum-in-the-hole gaze. But he was a wee bit peckish and helped himself anyway. After a few pretzels and some nuts, he laid it on hard and uncompromising.

'I'm not impressed with all this bullshit.'

'What?'

'When is he coming, this government bloke?'

'Soon, Vic, soon,' he said, nodding and smiling at the bartender as he brought their drinks and he gave him twenty bucks. 'Keep the change.'

The bartender thanked him and smiled. It was always nice to see a smile.

'I've just realized,' Victor began suddenly, 'there are no clocks in this bar.'

'That because they don't have time here, only moods. That's what they adveretise. See?'

'So what's the time?'

'Whatever your fancy tells you.'

'Cute,' he said, adding water to his whiskey from the jug. 'But I'm not impressed. - Cheers, and down the hatch.' And he knocked it all back.

'Well, as long as it works.'

'But we don't have all day.'

Roy shrugged. 'There's always tomorrow.'

'Not if you wanted something yesterday, there's not.' He stared at him hard and implacably. 'The codes, Roy. Who's using them? Where are the codes?'

'I don't have them.'

'Then where are they?'

Cornered; boxed in; forced to respond - but how? Precariously parting his lips to tease out a ruse or a downright lie, and phew! Lady Luck flew to the rescue and anted up the action with a blast of jazz just as his grin melted away and his face flushed with doubt, the musicians kicked-in with a flurry of warm-up riffs. On stage a quintet set the volume booming and the auditorium ricocheting with sound, wall to wall, floor to ceiling, it soaked them up and sucked them in and spat them out as only jazz can. He couldn't resist a smile, a big smile, and Victor heckled him with questions but Roy said he couldn't hear, and worse, the band starting playing like it was losing its breath, sputtering out discord and chronic sounds that left all sense of harmony in tatters. The musicians plunged into deep solo performances creating a conflict of sax and percussion, trumpet and trombone, flying into whimsy tunes that failed to gel or harmonize, fracturing coherence and tempo. Roy grew agitated despite himself. The sin of disharmony was in full swing and he was horrified. The sedate A minor of the long horn was intended to tame and balance the defiant B major of the trumpet that overdrove the drummer who stormed à la kamikaze into his own long, suicidal solo. This was sound become dictatorship, the tyranny of a sharp E stamping on a flat A with all the wantonness of a B major.

Roy thumped the counter with indignation. 'It's all crazy! Listen to him, the imbecile. The trumpet is overdriving the whole balance of the piece. He's started fighting. It's war.'

Victor shook his head, unwittingly getting involved, 'What are you raving on about now?'

'It's improvised mayhem. They've got their gloves off – the hooligans! This isn't a Roman pit. Music deserves better than this. They're assailing each other, vying for sound slots in the audible spectrum of our minds.'

'What? Where are the codes?'

'They're competing, Vic. Molesting sound.'

'Competing. Why? Who gives a damn! Where are the codes?'

'But they can't do it any other way. The trumpet could never make that sound unless it had something to dominate.'

Victor's head rattled with doubts, but he suffered to indulge him. 'So you're saying the bass is the fall guy? He thinks he's the leader, but he's not watching his back?'

'Yes. It's a kind of lyrical sacrifice. The piece they're playing can only slaughter him in the long run.'

'Maybe it's suicide.'

'Then it's a death adored.'

'So who gets to survive?'

'They all do. One dies, they all die. One lives, they all live. It's all part of a piece.'

Victor shook his head. 'I don't get it.'

'Yeah...' Roy smiled, 'you have to be a connoisseur to really understand. And that takes time; and style; and love.'

It still seemed baffling to Victor:

'OK. So why don't they just fake a duel? The horn against the drummer, say, and blast away?'

'You would get a different sound. You might get the blues, or rock, but you wouldn't get this flavor of jazz.'

He shook his head defiantly: 'Where are the codes?'

'We're trying to find out.'

'When?'

'They're all been changed.'

'When?'

'They run different sequences on different days.'

'When?' he demanded. 'How?'

Roy had not the faintest idea what he was saying. He simply blurted out the first thing to enter his mind. 'It depends on the state of the markets.'

'So tell me about the markets?'

'Erratic.' Roy looked anxious. 'Sometimes, they just go crazy.'

'Who's poking them? Who's stirring it up?'

'It's something to do with the government. That's why we're meeting here, to find out.'

'I've lost a lot of money. – Roy,' he seethed, 'someone knows. Someone bloody well knows why.'

'Probably someone very like the trombonist over there,' Roy diverted him swiftly to the musician just as he ramped up the volume. 'The quiet guys, it's their market. If the uncertainty persists, time is on their side. The tyrants just don't know when to stop. They exhaust themselves. You see,' pointing to the trumpeter. 'He'll tire soon, while the trombone and percussionist, like peasants, have the staying power to thrive, if given the chance.'

But it was the loner, the sax, which intrigued him the most. But Roy wasn't saying. No. Instead, he started to grumble at the unruly sound and pressed the bartender with questions.

'Yes'r?' he smiled in expectation of another hefty tip.

'The musicians; who are they?'

'Dunno. Some new guys. They came in a couple of nights back looking for work.'

But jazz isn't work. It's a way of life. Roy pressed him: 'Where are the regulars? Did they quit?'

'No. They're inside, in back of the house, jamming with the strings. I hear they may be cutting a record deal.' He intimated, eyeing him for tips. 'It's just a rumor, mind.'

'Thanks,' and Roy slipped him ten bucks. It wasn't much, but not bad for a rumor. And besides, the bartender liked to smile.

The hectic sound booming from the stage continued to intensify, the musicians not teasing but beating out of their instruments a raw medley of solos colliding against each other. It was aimless instrumentalism, a slushy repertoire of vintage and modern that seldom converged and when it did seemed to shatter all at once. Testosterone music. Roy finally lost his temper and, though reluctant to make a scene, struck the counter with his fists, got to his feet and confronted the musicians on stage. 'No! No! No!'

An anguished shriek of trumpet hailed the retort.

'What's up?' leaning his trumpet on his arm and polishing the horn.

'I'm suffering,' cried Roy, more in sorrow than anger.

'So what's that got to do with me?'

'Your sound.'

'Yeah?'

'It's shapeless. There's no discipline. You're too loose, hanging rhythms on to the ends of solos, kicking your heels at what? Nothing. – Well, that's just not good enough. Not for jazz. I've heard alley cats sound spiritual compared with you guys. There's the back door, get in tune or take a walk.'

'I'm trying my best,' he was sweating and breathless, and his anger seemed more a folly than a threat. 'Who the hell do you think you are anyway?'

'A connoisseur.'

'Who?'

'Don't take it personally. It's about the music, not you. I'm sure you've got it in you, somewhere. But it's not there today.'

Music is not enough. You need the drama of music; you need the essence of something profound, something sensuous to believe in, a harmony, a feisty twang, a sublime voice, a spirit in a piece that is as soft as air, yet tears your soul apart with its wonder.

That's jazz!

Roy returned to his seat, tossed a pretzel into his mouth and gushed it down with whiskey. He made his point and that, perversely for him at the time, was the most important thing in the world.

'What about the codes, Roy?' Victor pressed him again.

'I was just coming to that. I had to straighten out my mind with their sound.'

The musicians resumed, playing on defiantly, but it was obvious in their register that they took the criticism to heart, despite that they resented it. But Roy was a patron, and more, he was a connoisseur. And if you're a smart guy and you want to make it to the top, you never question a connoisseur – except to ask him his name.

'Roy, I'm losing my patience.'

'Bartender.'

'Yes'r?' he hastened briskly to their service.

'Another round. And make them doubles. Large doubles.'

'Yes'r, coming right up.'

'And have someone bring them through.'

'Yes'r.'

And taking their unfinished drinks, Roy led the way:

'Let's go inside and listen to the regulars. It's more comfy in there.'

'Where are the codes? When is this guy coming? What's going on?'

'Soon.'

'Bullshit!'

'Have a seat, Vic.'

'Fuck you. Where are the codes?'

'Let's see how good these guys are.'

'Roy!' he was fuming with controlled rage. 'I'm warning you, I'll pull the plug.'

'Wait till he comes. He'll be here soon.' He glanced at his wristwatch. 'Ten minutes; max.'

Victor groaned and sat sown uneasily as the waitress, sporting greasy unwashed hair and glazed eyes, strode up with their drinks and lazily placed them on the table. 'Whiskeys. Here. - Sorry, but it's not my job to clean the ashtrays.' Roy informed her they were expecting someone in around ten minutes time, and when he arrived to bring them a fresh round of drinks. Extra large doubles.

'For three?' she said.

'Unless you want to join us.'

Smirking her greasy smile she strode away, Victor grumbled restlessly, and Roy reclined in his seat and listened to the musicians on stage, mainly strings but with some brass instruments. With few customers this time of the day, even the cleaners were milling around, and the caterers too on the fringes loitering by the doors, mingling with the stage crew and chatting and laughing and having a smoke.

The auditorium was compact but comfortable, providing a low-key elegance of sorts, the lighting tailored for intimacy, the acoustic characteristics honed by luck more than engineering, but Roy felt a deep appreciation for these fortunate features born of a chance, like immaculate conception on the throw of the dice, and he grew more discerning as a consequence, listening for the multiple threads of harmony and processional beats, particularly the piano which dominated the stage, and the pianist a burly man in his mid-fifties with greased combed back hair, a gut nurtured on beer and hamburgers, and a ladies' man by the look of him, a wow with the hookers when they tired of the punters and the flirting housewives bored with hubby. The theatre lay in the players as much as the music, the mood always on tap with the beer and the whiskey and the songs. These places are for unloading your self, not only your burdens. Because often, the self is the greatest burden of all.

It didn't take long before Victor started hammering at him again.

'Roy.'

'Have your drink. It's hot in here. Never let your ice melt. It leaves a bad impression with the ladies.'

'Which ladies?'

'They'll be around soon.' He glanced about expectantly. 'In any case, here or otherwise, you should never cultivate bad habits,'

'That's it. Fuck you! I'm going to the office,' Victor threatened and got to his feet.

'Why? There's no need.'

'I want answers.'

'You'll get them. That's why we're here, to sort this out. It's touch and go. Trust me, Vic. Sit down. Please. We're almost home.' Bluffing is an art; having the nerve to bluff a science. And Roy? Well, he was artfully crossing all fingers and toes and hoping for the best.

The pianist, for a reason Roy couldn't understand, began pushing a minor key to its limit, and the sound induced was overdriven.

'Roy, I'm growing very pissed-off with all this bullshit.'

'I can't think straight right now.'

'You have to play fair, damn it! Or I'll bring everything crashing down on your head. And I'm not kidding.'

'Hey, mister. Yes you, on the piano. Could you lighten it up a little? You're way off key. Lift the scale; space the timing out. That's it.'

'Roy, for God's sake, are you listening to me?'

'I'm listening.'

'I need the codes.'

'Can't get them.'

'I need the damn codes.'

'Sorry.'

'Then get me access.'

'The bank has them locked up. What do you expect me to do, bluff my way through?'

'If that's what it takes. Yes.'

'Hey, mister. Now that's too smoochy. You need to lighten up a little. Easy on the keys...'

The pianist stopped playing, angrily pounded the keyboard with his fists, rose in a huff, and strode over to Roy.

'You have a problem, mister?'

'Yes, I do.'

'What's your problem, huh?'

'Minimalism. Even if you push the limit of a bass, go for the limit, not beyond it. You're not a bad player. Here,' Roy gave him a hundred bucks. 'Play me some blues. I need to think blues, because this gentleman has set me a challenge.'

'So what's that got to do with me?'

'With the right combination of notes, the correct rhythm, the balance of harmony and pitch, I can always solve the problem. Thinking, well, it's just like playing a song.'

'You want us to take five for you, man?'

'No,' he said decisively. 'Play.'

The pianist smiled as he remounted the stage, striding into the realm of the blues, swerving by the horns and basking in their throaty roars, shaking his head with mounting pride as he swept by the strings and bassoonist, and sat at his piano like on a throne. Cuing the band, one, two, three, he led them into harmony, synchronizing the sense of melody and time. It's was music that lends suffering minds a friendliness, and helps troubled ones see a way through the confusion that besets them. And Roy, tapping his feet in step with the rhythm, drumming his fingers softly on the table, from sound alone emerges an end game; and France rose into his thoughts then, inspired by the melody, driven into being by music so at home and at peace in a man's psyche, that he knew then Paris was the next stop. The key to misgivings is often a sublime song, a gentle sound, a moment of subdued reflection, pure idea: piano, flute, violin.... This.

'Roy, what are we going to do?'

'Let's just sit here a while and listen. When it comes to me, I'll let you know.' And he lit a cigarette, lifted his glass, and drank, smoothly, before the ice melted.

Ten minutes later, as the music drifted to a lounge mood and Victor showed signs of fatigue, he looked up and saw him standing there, and curtly asked Roy:

'Who's this?'

'This is Roger.'

'Roger, eh?'

'Pleased to meet you.' Roger grinned extravagantly, but in a way that seemed normal for him. He promptly took a seat. 'So, you're from London?'

'Never mind that. You work for the government?'

'That's right.' He laughed to himself, hogging his amusements. 'I'm a G-man. I even wear a G-string. You see!' And he quirkily thumbed his necktie at them.

'And?' Victor demanded bluntly.

'And...' he grinned, cobbling together a mischievous reply, 'and they don't pay me enough. I need a pay rise.'

'Perhaps you don't deserve it.'

That surprised him, and he hesitated before answering: 'I never thought of it that way before. You know, you might just have a point there.'

'Live and learn, sunshine. Live and learn.'

The G-man metamorphosed swiftly into a different persona as he dramatically cleared his throat and, lifting his briefcase, placed it significantly on the table and opened it out, keeping the contents concealed from the other two as he fumbled frantically with unmarked envelopes and papers, rummaging feverishly among nondescript articles and sifting through folders with SECRET written in red on them, turning and tossing, opening and closing, lifting and putting down, studying and dismissing, speeding up erratically before slowing to a dramatic stop.

To Victor's aching eyes and weary mind this whole scene seemed a charade, appearing in equal measure both suspicious and ridiculous. Then Roger suddenly concluded his machinations, slammed the

396

briefcase shut, and placed it on the floor beside his chair.

He cleared his throat again, this time with composure, and held aloft in his hand a piece of paper that Victor reasonably expected to relieve him of and reached out to take without further ado. But the G-man held onto it, drawing his hand aside, like a poker player teasing away his hand from prying eyes. That slip of paper seemed to carry the weight of a gaming chip, and you don't play this baby unless you're willing to raise really high, for the creamiest stakes, the kind of game you grind out to the end, and bet the whole pot on. And as every instinctive poker player knows, *you play the man, not the cards.*

Roger cleared his throat affectedly, and said. 'As you know, there have been odd movements in some of the market indices. We've been watching them closely. Very closely...'

'What the hell are you talking about?' cried Victor, pounding the table with his fist.

'We noticed the markets behaving erratically, and wondered if it was triggered by normal market forces or...' he emphasized that *or* for effect, 'something else. But it always slipped back to normal trading patterns when we began to take a closer look. There's something going on.'

'That's not news, mate!' Victor convulsed with fury, bracing himself for murder, full of a seething rage at being scammed, stung by a hustler with a grinning face. The waitress abruptly appeared, yawning as she plopped the drinks on the table – straight whiskeys, extra large, blocking Victor's view of the proceedings. He badgered at her angrily and she shuffled back, waiting there beside him with the bill, attached idly in her greasy hand and poking it in his face. Victor resumed, ignoring the waitress and blasting away. 'You're full of crap, mate! Everyone knows that. What's that slip of paper for?' He had his eyes fixed on it constantly, and the G-man was playing with his vulnerability, his compulsion to know.

'Look, Victor, I'm just telling you this as a favor to Roy.'

'Tell me what? You've told me nothing, mate. Get to the point, or fuck off! I'll rip your fucking head off!'

An inauspicious pause, then: 'I don't think I like the look of this,' said Roger. 'Excuse me, folks, I need to visit the men's room.' And he slipped away faster than the blazing curses erupting from Victor's mouth.

Without thinking and incensed with rage, Victor seized a glass and swallowed the whiskey whole. Within seconds his eyeballs began to roll and his guts turn and he collapsed with unwieldy chaos over the table, slumping with a crashing thud before he could mount a fist and throw a punch at Roy.

'What's the matter with him?' the waitress barked, accustomed to the shenanigans of punters, all sorts and flavors that visit the bar, having seen them maul and grope each other in turn, and typically taking the world of loutish behavior in her feminine stride. But today, she was covering the day shift for an idle waitress, and it was too early for all this mischief.

'He's had a rough day,' explained Roy.

'Rough day! Who hasn't?' she grumbled, presenting him with the bill. 'That'll be twenty dollars. - You know, like it's *dozy* me all the time that has to clean all this mess up. What do you think I am?'

Roy shook his head wearily, rummaging in his pockets for some cash. He gave her fifty bucks: 'Here,' he offered, letting her keep the change. She perked up instantly and flashed him a smile, her eyes glinting with surprise.

You see what money can do? It presses all the right buttons. *Say cheese.*

Roger gingerly tip-toed back into the picture and discovered the repercussions. Surprised with what he saw, but pleased with the outcome, he expressed relief. 'You knock him out flat?'

'No,' said Roy, as they maneuvered together for the best way to carry him out. 'We got lucky. He lost his cool and knocked back the whiskey.'

'Whiskey?' He lifted a glass and tasted it. 'I thought it was brandy. You know how I like brandy, Roy.'

'Take hold of his left arm, would you? Lean him on your shoulder. That's it.'

'How long do you think he'll stay out like this for?'

'Not long enough,' he groaned, struggling under the burden of self-doubt and the anxiety of having to improvise. Although Victor was neutralized, at least for a time, which one could always prolong, by fair means or foul, it simply wasn't a feasible plan even in the short term. Realistically, Roy presumed an interval of perhaps twenty-four hours. He felt the pressure of events work powerfully on his mind: *You can't hold back the tide indefinitely. Sooner or later, if you try to hold it back too long, your schemes will break, and the tide is going to sweep in and drown you.*

'Is that enough time?' asked Roger, alias King Stud to his chums and poker playing buddies.

'For now,' said Roy, driving to his apartment. 'That's all I have. I can only work with what I have.'

'You're making this up as you go along,' he said with surprise. 'Is that a wise thing to do, considering... you know?' and he glanced over his shoulder at Victor slumped unconscious in the rear seat of the car. 'I hope you have some contingencies. After all, it wouldn't be poker. Would it?'

'I don't have a choice.'

'Good luck.'

Roy brooded anxiously. 'I'll keep him at my place for the time being. Damn!' he snapped, as if anything would ignite him. 'It's started raining again.'

'This guy's brought it with him. He's almost the perfect storm.'

Roy grimly glanced at Victor in the rear-view mirror, irrationally fearing he could rouse at any moment. Emotionally drained, Roy gazed at him without feeling a thing, and the clock was ticking. With Victor's presence life seemed suddenly surreal, all parody and farce. But there lay the threat, latent, ominous, and all he could feel was that disabling refrain: *What the hell am I doing?*

'What are you thinking, Roy?

'Of where all this mess is leading me; and how it might end.'

'Do you want to talk about it?'

'No. Thanks, anyway. The less you know the better. Besides, I'm too worn out with all this to think straight.'

'I see.' He looked over his shoulder at Victor, then the rain, then Victor again, before turning to Roy. 'Whatever this thing is, this guy has storm clouds written all over him.'

Roy frowned and schemed for ways for Victor's inclusion in his plans.

'I'll have to tell him eventually,' he thought aloud. 'But not just yet.'

'Pull over; let me out here.'

Roy pulled over to the side, and stopped. He cut the engine, but quickly started it again.

'Roy, are OK? Are you sure you won't need a hand with him?'

'No. The doorman will help.'

'I'll see you later for a game, then?'

'And a drink, perhaps. I need to keep the kitten happy; and unwind myself a little too.' He sighed, deeply, 'Quite a lot, in fact.'

Roger looked encouragingly him, and said; 'Remember, I'm only a phone call away.' Then he chuckled briefly and glanced at Victor whose posture seemed quirky, if not a little amusing to him. 'Give him my regards when he wakes up. And tell him to stay away from poker. He plays the cards, not the man. Like that, he'll never stand a chance.'

'Thanks again for everything. You're a pal.'

'And Roy.'

'Yes?'

'Next time, tell him to bring an umbrella!'

Chapter 22

'Nick, would you like some coffee?' asked Frank, carrying a tray into the office.

Nick never looked up, his gaze glued to a monitor: 'Make sure you lock the door.'

'It's cold in here.'

'You're imagining things.'

'No I'm not. It's cold.'

'Frank.'

'What?'

He briefly glimpsed at him: 'You're imagining things. – Is the door locked? Good. Come over here and help me with this. The network is playing up.'

Their psychedelic office, to a stranger, might seem like art, like sculpture, like toys for the boys, even down to the screensavers and customized PC desktops taking tapestries of data and weaving it peculiarly for human senses to drench entirely in signals, feeding the faculty of sight, touch, intuition, smell, yes, even smell, the clear aroma like desert air, the beautiful emptiness devoid of fragrance, nothing but pure... thing. However, to Frank, it felt unusually cold. 'Cold...' he muttered as he poured coffee, his senses fine-tuned to slick surroundings, and the imperceptible purr of machines keeping perfect time, atomic time... and the sense of something... what?... the bare echoes of relentless computation. He understands that. He felt safe by the knowable, but alone. 'Nick.'

'Yes?'

'Would you like milk or cream with your coffee?'

'Get over here,' he told him bluntly, 'I need your help.'

'Meow.'

'What?'

'Nothing,' he murmured quietly, pouring cream into the cups. Suddenly, the telephone rang and Nick quickly answered it.

'Roy? Where are you? Where's Victor? What's going on?'

'Resting. How's the pot?'

'The pot's full? What do you mean he's resting?'

'It's a long story,' he sighed. 'Is everything there OK?'

'Yes. Apart from some glitches in the network, we're fine.'

'Good! At least that part's OK.'

'What do mean? Roy, you sound anxious. What did Victor say?'

'I am anxious. Victor isn't happy. He's not happy at all.'

'Why is he resting? – Let go!' Nick tugged the phone back from Frank as he tried to pry it away from him. 'Roy, what happens now?'

'Let me worry about Victor. - What has Peeping Tom been up to?'

'Paris is quiet. They're probably reflecting. I know I would be.'

'Probably surprised...' Roy reflected uneasily. 'I can't imagine what they're thinking right now, what it would be like to be in their shoes. - Nick, it's unwise to second guess them, isn't it?'

'I guess so.'

'But sometimes we have no choice.' Was Roy theorizing, or conceding? Nick waited a while and then said:

'I guess so.'

It went quiet, then Roy asked: 'Nick, tell me again, is everything under control?' - When one's world feels on the brink of collapse, anything that hints of order resounds as a blessing; it signifies hope. 'Nick...'

'I heard you the first time. Yes, everything here is under control.' He spoke not only to reassure, but to galvanize each embattled man, for Roy's sense of purpose faltered. He was vulnerable. Alone. A man alone amid other men equally alone, friends and colleagues notwithstanding. Alone. He. Nick. Frank. Sometimes, the broad sweep of events muscles in and forces you to look honestly at things. In truth, they were cameo players in this episode that swept them up whole, and spat them out in pieces. They were just ordinary guys embroiled in a drama that eluded their grasp. If they never took fright, it was because they never knew what to fear. Bravery and daring was not their winning hand, but a reckless persistence sometimes sounds the winning bet. A hero is often a guy who just tries his best, does what he can, keeps his head down, and hopes that everything will turn out right – a naive gambling on life. 'Roy, are you still there?'

'Yes.' He was breathing and smoking heavily, the cigarette wrestling with his lips as they clutched it and smothered the tobacco: burn it all, suck it up whole, he needed an ocean of nicotine to calm his nerves. 'Yes, I am.'

'Roy, Frank and I have been thinking, we have an idea.'

'Me too. But my instinct tells me it's too soon for ideas. The timing is all wrong. I can't explain it. I'm asking you to trust me on this. We're not ready. We may never be ready. - Let me speak with Frank.'

'Hi Roy, it's me.'

'Did you secure the codes? Did you hide the profiles?'

'Yes.'

'And the client data?'

'Especially those. Locked and sealed.'

'And you encrypted everything else?'

'Yes,' he said. 'And I even tossed in a few riddles. Peeping Tom is not the only one with a card up his sleeve. Always save one for a lullaby day, as my daddy used to say.'

'Everyone gets an appetite for a song sooner or later. And this Peeping Tom, his eyes lap up the world even while he's singing. He's always on the prowl; his imagination is never at rest.' Roy took a deep breath, 'Frank, how much time do we have before they start unraveling things?'

'They have the resources, so... a couple days; three maybe if we're really lucky. Where's Victor?'

'Resting at my place. – Listen, finish up there and leave. Sneak out. Let the system run in safe mode. Set it to "Auto" and let it coast in the marginal stocks and float with the tracker funds. Set up an external connection and nudge it remotely every few hours to give the impression we're there actively trading. Then you and Nick go to a bar or some place. Just get out. Get an early lunch. Try and relax, loosen up, stress does no one any good. I'll be in touch.' He looked at his wristwatch. 'It's still early. I have some things to do. I'll get back to you soon.'

'What are your plans?'

'What are yours?'

'This has to end,' he said candidly. 'We have to confront them. We're punching in the dark otherwise. And what's the point of that? After all, who do we think we are - Hercules? Roy, can you hear me?'

'And Nick?'

'He agrees.'

'I'll call you later. Give it some more thought.'

'And Victor?'

'Please! Don't remind me.' And he hung up.

Frank threw himself into action: 'Nick, let's lock her up. Throw her into safe mode. Set her to coast the marginal stocks and hook her up to the tracker funds. Leave open an external link to poke her remotely; set a new password; then let's get out of here.'

'What's happening?'

'Your guess is as good as mine.'

'And Roy?'

He shrugged apprehensively: 'Let's worry about ourselves first? That's his problem.'

'And Victor?'

He shrugged again: 'Fingers crossed.'

Nick intoned ominously: 'This does not look good, Frank.' Staring with misgivings at the monitors, 'This does not look good at all...'

*   *   *

Life is an easy fella. Look, he's winking at you now as he spies out your rut. He knows you're screwed, but kind of shakes his head with a grin and cosies up to your ear and says:

"Boo! – Ha! Just kidding!"

"Hey there, fella?" says you.

"Yeah?" says Life.

"Cut me some slack here, would you?"

"Slack?"

"Yeah, you know, fella? Cut me some slack on my predicament here. How do I get out of this stinking mess? Give me a break here, would you?"

Life ponders a wee bit, sighs, chuckles just a touch and says: "Nah! Sorry, old chum. I just can't do it. I don't have the time. It's not my style. And besides, you know..."

"What?'

"I can't be bothered. See ya!"

So, just take it a step at a time. Easy, easy there, fella; touch and go, OK? You improvise where you can. You hope for the best, sure; but come on, plan for the worst. It's just strategy; right? You work it this way and that and a thousand other things at once; the wet-in-your-pants thrill you would rather do without but events conspire and throw you into a spin. So what? Hell of a time to get giddy. Sure. What do you do, grumble? Go ahead, but you'll always find Life has the last laugh, ha ha ha... there's a singing fella for you, ha ha ha... *You want to call the shots, fella?* says Life. Be a smart guy, and back off. Life ain't joking with the rules. Bend them, and it's you who'll break. Thing to do is, you grin and bear it. Not for you? OK then, ball your eyes out and cry all you want. Water's for free, fella. But you carry on, you yank at the problem and who knows what might arise. Don't stand still, that's the ticket, which as every fella knows is not the same thing as rushing headlong into panic. You ferret out alternatives, you re-jig a context, and even as you pick your way among them, there is always some nagging doubts hammering away at your brain: some threads left untied, some doors still left ajar for the spooks to sneak in a peek and scare you.

"Boo! – Ha! Just kidding..."

That's Life. But what can you do?...

*   *   *

It was almost midday and, mounting stools at a local bar to avoid the rain, Frank ordered some coffee.

'We don't serve coffee here,' croaked the bartender. Frank gazed at him with disbelief and lamented its absence from the menu. But the bartender took a swipe at him with the words. 'Not a drop, unless it's got whiskey in it, sunshine.' And he pointed to the rain outside the window. 'You can always try singing in the rain. Need an umbrella there, fella?'

'I'll have tea, then.'

'Nope.' Now he started to grin, a torturer's grin, and folded his arms. 'Unless you want it packed with gin.'

'Lemonade.'

'You're kidding me, right?' he said, reaching for a bottle of vodka like a gunslinger, drawing the weapon and firing pow! pow! pow! with seventy-percent pure proof spirit, and knocking a man out flat.

'Just bring us two beers.'

'Welcome to the real world,' he said, grinning, taking two glasses and hitting the beer tap, filling them to the brim till they frothed over and he placed them on the bar. 'Enjoy!'

'Grub, Nick?'

'I'm not hungry.'

'Me neither.'

Frank looked languidly at the clock above the bar, then at his own wristwatch: they were misaligned by two minutes, and he wondered a moment which one was right, which one should he believe? But then it all seemed so pointless he dismissed it from his mind. The beer was light and cool, and they drank slowly. Then Frank pondered aloud.

'I wonder what Roy is doing?'

'Call him.'

'No. Let him call us.'

Looking at his wristwatch again, and then the clock above the bar, he addressed the bartender. 'By the way, do you know your clock is running fast?'

'So sue me.'

'I was just saying, that's all.' As the glass reached his lips his phone began to ring. He expected Roy but was startled to learn it was someone else. Nick threw him a puzzled look and Frank paused the conversation, put the phone on mute and informed him: 'It's that damn cop again Forester.'

'What does he want now?'

'Search me.'

Frank shuddered and took a moment to compose himself before resuming the conversation. Forester was calling from the Borough of Queens; he had just parked his car, and was walking through the tepid rain. He was calling on a hunch, he explained, rather circumspectly, acting typically *copish* of teasing out a point and seldom going directly to the heart to the matter. What hunch, asked Frank sounding vexed. A cop's hunch, he said (there he goes again...) 'Can you get to the point, Detective,' Frank snapped. So Forester elaborated. He explained he was looking for a link, for coincidences that trigger connotations, that lead to a clue, that result in an outcome he can stand back and wonder why he never thought of that in the first place. (Well, he's a cop. What is he supposed to do? Apart from never getting directly to the point, that is! A-ha, semper eadem – ever the same, like a cop with canny brain...)

'There is a young woman,' Forester continued, 'an identical twin who some time ago hung around boxing clubs and similar places like that. Perhaps she had a boyfriend who was a sportsman.' Frank cut in and explained that young twins were not his kind of sport, and boxing less so. 'I never implied either,' said Forester. 'I noticed a very vague link with your late lady friend. Oh, I'm sorry, I hope you don't mind if I refer to her in that way?'

'Not in the least,' he said, feeling a gust of unease chill his bones with recollection, but keeping the tempo of his voice steady. 'I may have been fond of her, Detective, but I assure you the acquaintance was far more prosaic than you imagine. At bottom, it was a business-to-business relationship. – And that's the American way, right?'

'Would you mind visiting the police station and going over a few details? It won't take long, I promise.' Frank grumbled and said he was busy, and couldn't see the use, but Forester persisted: 'I'd really appreciate your help.' Frank suggested they conduct this over the telephone, but Forester explained he wanted him to look at some new evidence, and examine other *possibly* related facts in greater detail. He emphasized that *possibly* with a certain vague tension, offering nothing to seize on but leaving everything to the imagination.

Frank was exasperated. 'I've told you everything I know. How many times must we go over this? What's the point?'

'Every little bit helps. Even negative results often help; far more than you imagine. It eliminates false leads. Besides, this girl is missing, believed somewhere in France, mostly probably Paris, and her family are deeply troubled, as you can imagine. Please, Mr. Freiberg.'

Frank stared glumly at Nick, mouthing an expletive. 'OK. OK... When?'

'Well, as soon as possible really. Would now... be OK? Can you? That's really very good of you. I appreciate this. If you would call in to the station and ask for my colleague, Sandy... Oh good, you know her,' Forester felt pleased and chummy all of a sudden, finding success where he least expected it, and leaping in with: 'Well, I don't know if she'll go on a date with you considering your exotic taste in women but, well, ahem,' he coughed abruptly, 'but she'll get things started until I arrive. I'm just on my way to a boxing club in Queens to follow up on some leads. I'll get back as quickly as I can. Have a coffee. Hang around. Your help in this matter is greatly appreciated. Thanks. Yes. And thank you again.' And he hung up.

'That cop is the limit!' Frank vented his anger, livid at his own supineness, at Forester's presumption. 'This is all baloney, Nick.' He finished off the beer quickly and hammered the empty glass on the bar. The bartender glanced at him menacingly, but Frank didn't care. 'Let's get this damn charade over with.' He looked at his wristwatch and conferred with Nick. 'I'll meet you back here in about an hour.'

'I'm going to the library.'

'Why?'

'I like it there, I can think there. It calms me.'

'OK. I'll be in touch.'

As they left the bar the rain began to ease, but dark-grey clouds still hovered ominously in the sky. They parted briskly on the sidewalk, the sound of a police siren reverberating in the distance.

Chapter 23

That morning Detective Forester awoke late and never had time to shave. A cigarette, tuna bagel with relish and piping hot coffee got the system going, and presently, as he fondled the stubble on his chin and pondered the rain, his mobile phone started to play Beethoven's Ninth Symphony (the rousing choral part). He listened for a while, day dreaming of empires and the great marches and heroes metamorphosed into perfect sound, until his lips curved up at the sides and he smiled at the blazing sunburst of the chorus. *That's my baby. That's singing! Triumphalism at its zenith.*

'Forester, are you there?'

'Go ahead, Sandy.'

'You have a message.'

'What is it?'

'The Captain wants to take a bite out of you.'

'Why?'

'Because he feels like it.' She laughed, actually a rather scruffy laugh, like a cackle, before continuing in good humor: 'Just kidding. Actually, your pal from France has sent you some stuff.'

'What does it say?'

'It's in French.'

'Does it have *Pressant* or something similar written on it?'

'I don't know. I don't know French.'

'Does it have *Prèmiere Priorité* written anywhere on it?'

'No. That's not it. But it does have something like... let me get my tongue around this, *Pour vos boules seutement*.'

Forester started to laugh.

'What does it mean?' she sounded pretty peeved. 'Is it lewd? Forester, you damn frog, it wouldn't surprise me.'

'You'll have to learn French, Sandy. Besides, even then, you wouldn't completely understand.'

'Why?'

'It's a man-to-man thing.' He paused and heard her grumble an expletive, and he poked a grin at the rain, wondering if it was raining in Paris too, before resuming. 'It can wait till I get back. I spoke with Frank Freiberg, and he'll be coming over to see you. Show him the mug shots and get what you can out of him.'

'Will do.'

'And Sandy.'

'Yes?'

'He's not that communicative, so lean on him if you have to, but be gentle.'

'Shall I tease him with a whip? He'll probably like that.' - Ha ha. She's a plucky kind of gal, is Sandy, temperamental like the weather when it amuses her (and a great piece of ass for a cop). But still, she's his partner, so what can he say other than:

'Work him softly, Sandy. Use you charms, as only a *woman* can.'

One-up*man*ship - it's kind of a cool thing, really, especially with a wo*man*. Naturally. Oh yes...

He folded the telephone and stored it in his pocket. He paused, inhaled deeply, felt like a cigarette but glanced at his wristwatch instead, noted the time, asserted a masculine frame of mind, and started to walk.

He sauntered with a manly pitch and crossed the street, parabolic in his stride, hyperbolic with his arms, coasting like a march, gun slinger kind of gait, the *You looking at me, kid?* momentum, a pure Ninth Symphony in his motion because he was about to enter a man's world.

But besides the physicality of place, other things of substance presently preoccupied his mind. The strands of a strange case, ambiguous details, disconnected facts, sometimes conspire and resolve themselves to something approaching a persona. It doesn't always happen, but when it does, it's really rather marvelous. You experience the dynamic of life as you watch it work in strange ways right before your eyes. The answers to the riddle manifest in the strangest places: in the blink of someone's eye, through the quirky tone of suggestive conversation, a teasing frown on a child's face, a passing stranger suggesting commonplace moments. But deeper goes the mind, all it needs is a spark and the flames begin to glow, warm at first, stoking up the paradox of chance, snaking into several suppositions at a stroke, moving with the circumstantial drift into scenes, places, characters, events, completing the puzzle as he went along. Does it mean anything? Who knows, he just follows the heat, wherever it gets warmer, so long as you don't burn. You keep your wits about you, treating coincidence with respect, holding superstition in check unless, of course, that's the only thing around driving you on. You take its leads, sure, but never its goal. Everyone needs a break now and again. Hunches are like stepping stones, leaping from one to the next. The old man would often beat on the solid drum of experience, and he came through loud and clear: *Son... are you listening to me, sonny?* Yes, Pop, I hear you; loud and clear. *Remember this as though your life depended on it, because it does, and your sanity too. And don't get cocky with me, sonny, just shut up and listen to your old man.* OK, Pop, I'm listening. *In this business, never leave things to the wiseguys. You've got to help yourself by pushing things along. Are you listening to me, kiddo?* Yes, Pop. *Just shut up and listen to your old man. Now, son, don't ever waste time belching out your sorrows over bad luck. Fuck that game. It's a loser's game. I've met my share of suckers and they all have this is common: they have lazy minds. That's their fate. And they bake it themselves, the dumb bastards.* Not every man is a great cook, Pop. *Shut up and listen to your old man. Never leave things to chance alone. Anticipate where you can. Guess in the dark if you must - that's life, it's a risky business. But always be conscious of the game. And life is not one game, but many games played at the same time.* Thanks, Pop. *Nah. Don't mention it. That's what fathers are for.*

Walking along the sidewalk he spotted a human marker, there, and approached an aging whore vamped in the garb of a tacky decade, timeworn, banged and reused. Striding towards her, she throws him a clichéd look, kind of a smile dribbling from her lips, chewing gum and killing time leaning against a wall as a hundred cars sailed by, and no one noticed her. She was the replica of discarded hope living in the afterglow of a make-believe world of better days ahead, just around the corner. Her gaze seemed expendable, a throwaway worn-out look, the sleeper's woebegone frown, a narcotic dreamer's

411

wondering at life, at the great game.

'Excuse me, ma'am, I'm looking for the Rowntree Club?'

'You what, hon?'

'The boxing club.'

'Oh…' She kind of sighed in afterthought wondering if it had any value. Undecided, she frowned and thumbed him to her left. 'Come see me when you've finished, darling, I'll show you a good time in the ring.'

'Thanks,' he said, moving past her, instinctively wary of, and perhaps fearing, the social contagion that besets us – you mind your own business; you just don't want to get involved. It's her life, and if she screws it up, well, what's that to do with me syndrome… Was that a sad reflection on mankind; something profoundly to be ashamed of? Was it ultimately an admission of your cowardice, your powerlessness? *Nah,* said Pop, cutting in, *it's just part of life. And you are less in control of yourself or events than you imagine you are. Just keep moving, son. Never look back.* Thanks, Pop. *And, son.* Yes, Pop? *Next time, get a shave before you leave home. You look like a goddamn mess!*

Zoë Long was rumored to have to an appetite for men, and the will to indulge that appetite: a woman that knows intelligence is akin to sexual prowess, cleverness made feminine with pouting lips, smartness made demure with a sultry look, genius made her own by teasing a man with her eternal essence – *come taste me, baby…* A smart babe, and not slow to show her street cred. And how many takers must she have had? Forester was hoping to find that out.

His enquiries revealed that before Zoë left for France she was mixing in the singles' scene; frequenting bars, clubs and other maverick hangouts that defined a social milieu, wandering amid the spectacle of romance and chance. Why wait for love? It seldom comes of its own accord. You have to go out there and bake your cake yourself and eat it, and with effort and luck, you'll find someone to eat with you, and before you eat each other out. Man. Woman. Not a state of mind, but a *state*, pure and simple. Intelligence. Passion. Desire. Hunger. Cock and a cunt. Love. Mix it all up and what do you get? - A cake. Munch munch… mmmm.

The janitor asked who he was. Forester showed his ID.

'You're a cop?' he said, his face a blend of cool and curious.

'Do you mind if I take a look around?'

'Fine by me.'

'Does it get very busy here? And do women hang around here much?'

'Only to meet their guys. Not inside. This is a man's world.'

'Amen to that!'

The janitor laughed good-humouredly and continued on up the stairs to resume his work.

The noises, smells, the essence of the place reeked of the physical proximity of men. Muscle and physicality combined with sheer willpower, dreams and the craving for fame and wealth to create a framework that was uniquely noble in the male sense. These things focus the nature of man more fundamentally even than a fuck. A fuck filled the gaps, like in ancient days when athletes built physique into a temple, and women, if they had a place at all, spied *his* place with envy.

A real man's psyche resides not in his balls, but in his instinct to dominate, to outperform the best and become superabundant. Men must grow in this, or they wither and die.

Kind of a guy thing... Sure.

The Boxing Trainer with the graveled face, (who was taking a break in his office), was the first call.

'This woman you met, could you describe her?' asked Forester.

'Sure.' Sparing with his syllables, and considering each one with the weight of thought, he just waited and stared. Forester waited and stared too. Eventually the trainer wiped his lips in surprise and said: 'Now?'

'That's the general idea.'

'She was a typical West Coast girl.'

'What did she look like?'

'Just like her pix. Nah, even better, an incarnate slut with the *You want me well here I am you faggot what you gonna do about it fuck me or just stare at me all day...* look. But it's a real gas when she looks straight at you and smiles. Gee, she looks so pretty and takes a...'

'Yes?'

'I was about to get lewd.'

'Oh, I see.' He shook his head with affected surprise. 'Please continue.'

'She takes some beating, Detective, I can tell you that.'

'What, her acting talents?'

'Acting maybe, but she deserves an Oscar for the performance. One minute you're driving your car; next thing you are in the land of porno-dreams.'

'Why did you go there?'

'The miss's was away and I felt as horny as hell. What would you do?'

'Why her?'

'Looked at the pix. They turned me on. I fancied her. Magnets attract magnets. You know?'

'Do you remember anything in particular about her?'

She had a boob-job, and her nipples stood to attention like a couple of guards at Fort Knox.'

'I see. Anything a bit more prosaic?'

'Like what?'

'Think.'

'I never went there to think.'

'Try.' Forester was becoming testy, his voice strained. 'For me. Please.'

'For you?'

'For me. Yes. Please.'

He brooded at length, rolling his eyes pointlessly, then said. 'OK, let me think a bit.' And he got up and broke open a six pack and waded gluttonously into a can of beer, gulping it down whole in a single shot, belching, then turning to Forester with a bewildered expression and said: 'Detective, what was that question again?'

'Details. Something likely to be helpful to an ongoing police investigation.'

'Am I in trouble or something?'

'No. Not at all.'

'Oh. Good. Well, er, let me think...' he folded his arms and ogled the remaining cans of beer with a covetous gaze and suddenly out popped the following disclosure. 'Yeah, of course.'

'Yes?'

'She wanted me to kiss her; so I obliged. That was nice of me, no?' he said, appearing very pleased with himself. Forester sighed glumly, thanked him for his time, and left. 'Happy to be of help,' he said, and saw him to the door. 'Call me anytime. Anytime...'

Son, grumbled the old man kicking in on cue, *when faced with a mug, don't waste time becoming one yourself. These citizens don't know what's good for them. The hell with the rules and sucker's rights. What rights? Human rights? Bullshit! These people aren't human, they're New Yorkers! Smack them around a little; show them who's boss and make them cough up or belt up. These suckers want a decent police service. Well; this is how you provide it, not by pussyfooting around. Hard hand, son. Take a hard hand. And not for jacking off with, but for cuffing the bastards in the chops.* Sure, Pop, sure...

The Promoter (smoking a cigar by the boxing ring).

'I handed over the money, she smiled, and asked me to take a shower. After the shower she was waiting for me on the bed in nothing other than a red thong. My cock stood to attention immediately and she didn't waste any time. I was manhandled to perfection. Her ass is superb, plump, round, a peach butt just begging to be squeezed and massaged. I willingly obliged. I soon got her to mount me and she moaned as my length slid into her. Her first orgasm occurred right after she rode me, then I took her doggy style giving her a good pounding before mish and again giving her another intense orgasm as she lowered herself onto my pole. Had a little rest, coffee and a piece of homemade cake. Really rather tasty, if I say so myself. She's a darling little cookie. Anyway, got going again and picked up steam. Pounded her like mad but couldn't come a third time. This was epic. This was how the world was made.'

'How?' said Forester.

'In the beginning...'

'God created light?'

'Nah, someone had a real good shag. And thereafter reality is just a long wet dream.'

'I don't suppose you're a philosopher?' (He was being sardonic, of course).

'Do philosophers fuck?'

'Yes. I believe they do. Some, anyway...'

'Then count me in, pal; count me in.'

'Thank you for your time.'

'Don't mention it. Cigar?'

'Thanks.' He took one, for later. 'Don't mind if I do.'

The Boxer (in the dressing room).

'She was a slim pretty thing and very tight. She's very passionate and eager to please. She tasted wonderful and was very responsive. Tits not too big; but hey, who am I to complain. Right, Detective?'

'Right.'

'There you are then.'

'Can you tell me anything about her?' asked Forester.

'She's a breathtaking sight. Out of this world.'

'You like the pretty ones?'

'You bet. But I'm not stupid, man.'

'I never suggested you were. I apologize if I ever implied it.'

'I read. I educated myself because school was a lost world for me.'

'I'm sorry to hear that.'

'I've taught myself philosophy, astronomy, botany, and I dig insects. They're cool.'

'Entomology?'

'Yeah.'

'So tell me some more about her?'

'She's like a Greek Goddess, the way she strides, her posture, her movements. She has a lyrical, refined, graceful beauty like a swan, a liquid, serene presence, and you just melt into her. You don't ride her, man, no way, not like your ordinary babe, this is something more sublime. You're aroused, yet enchanted at the same time, like tender passion that burns. You're on fire, yet it's ecstasy. She's the pure form, not over-painted like the dames hustling along the park, but a soft, porcelain princess, made to be seen and admired as well as touched. God made a masterpiece with her, and I take my hat off to him! She has unbelievably soft skin, luscious in its gentleness; almost marble-like in its smoothness. She has the kind of face Renaissance artists loved to paint, and the kind of body and skin that a princess would be jealous of. I confess to shaking with awe, and there were times when I really couldn't look her in the eyes. She was that beautiful, too much to take at times. She's an artist. Ha!' He began to laugh. 'You think I am a romantic, don't you? That I can't stop myself waxing lyrical about her? I just love words, that's all, man. It's my language too. She was great fun to talk to. I could have spent ages just talking with her. And to hear her laugh is something magical to savor. And you haven't had sex till you've waltzed to The Bolero. That's music for love, even tragic love, made for passion. - I've been around, man, tried them all. Some, they shine because they're like porn stars and seem insatiable. Others shine because they're like playful sex kittens that you can't get enough of... But her luster is entirely unfathomable. She is stellar. You know what I mean, man?'

'Thank you for your time.'

'Don't mention it. Call me anytime. Always happy to help the police.'

The Referee (strolling outside and having a smoke).

'What a wonderful girl. I've yet to pick the rotten apple.'

'And?' said Forester.

'She seemed to be open to gentle seduction. My favorite.'

'What else?'

'Tall and attractive. Nice smile. Beautiful eyes. Demure.'

'Is that all?'

'I was awestruck when I saw her flawless body.'

'Can we get to the point, please?'

'She was very shy and needed coaxing. But once she gets going and you hit the right rhythm, the sex is explosive and noisy.'

'Did she say anything?'

'It didn't take long and I popped. She said she wanted me to last longer, which probably isn't true but a great touch - I tipped her an extra fifty for that. I'm only human. An average guy needs a reasonable lay now and again. We have egos too, you know? Anyway, we chatted a bit afterwards, and split. Just chatted about football and home sweet home. Why do people leave? Do you ever ask yourself that?'

Forester sighed indifferently, folding up his notebook. 'I suppose that sums it up?'

'I guess so.'

'Thank you for your time.'

Stitch, the Ring Hand (picking his nose by the boxing ring).

'What did you do earlier that evening?' Forester asked him.

'Saw a porn movie.'

'I see.'

'Yeah, Jennifer Flame. Boy! I love watching that sexy bitch pounded hard.' His eyes watered thirstily and his expression grew lusty. 'Watching Jenny enjoy it was wowie. Yes-sir-eee!'

'Good for you.'

'What do you think I am?'

'You tell me.'

'If I want to watch a movie, it's no one's fucking business,' he insinuated fearlessly, standing his ground. 'I ain't asking for permission. I ain't asking no motherfucker to approve. It's no one's business but my own.'

'I couldn't agree more.'

Stitch gazed at him hard, feeling himself judged and shoved into the crude category of porn junkie - the fella that gets his shakes by watching the birdies rock and the bees roll in a hullabaloo show that leaves nothing to the imagination. Night after night feasting on the porn lovely with a body to boot and mouth full of cum-soaked words that dribble clichés like a slut on a high. "Shut your mouth / Screw you! / You whore / Yeah. Fuck me. Fuck me hard..." See what I mean? - And I ask you, honestly, is this what men really want? - You bet! There she goes, and you get to see the director's cut of her coated in a chrysalis of spunk, network of spit, of sweat etched like a circuit in the grunting exertions on their faces, Ah! Ah! Ah! Yesssssss. Ah! – Remind you of philosophy? Well, not quite. Flesh ain't a topic for discussion, you know. There's the thinking man's bit, and then there's the man man's bit. All in all, this unravels as an incredible mess, easy to see, provided you think with your balls - and the *harder* the better. Men understand that perfectly. For them, it's obvious. Women? Well, what can one say...?

'What did you do after the movies, Stitch?' asked Forester.

'Had a drink,' he said assertively. 'Went for a walk.'

'Where?'

'Downtown.'

'Women?'

'What else!' he grinned. 'What do you think I am?'

'You tell me.'

'I went looking for pussy.'

'And?'

'I found it.'

'Please continue.'

'Her place was a dump. Outside it looked revolting, and I dreaded what inside might be like. Look, copper, I have my standards, you know. What do you think I am?'

No comment.

'But anyway, things sometimes look different with some booze inside of you; and my hormones started nosing around for some sleazy action. Filth is sometimes a turn on, and downright dirty is the way to go. - What the hell are you looking at, copper?'

'Nothing. Please continue.'

'Well, as I was saying, I often wondered at the seediness of the walk-up scene. But me, venture inside and have a poke around – never! Up until then, copper, I've never been beyond the smell of the doorway of one those places. It's a septic, mouthwash, sweaty kind of stink; strange and revoltingly seedy - but nice. I ain't breaking no law. What do you think I am?'

'You tell me.'

'I ain't a pervert. In the past, I was as careful as sin.'

'Then what happened this time, you discover religion or something?'

'Nah! I was horny, copper. What do you think I am?'

'You tell me.'

'I told you everything already.'

'Tell me again.'

'I ain't got all day.'

'Nor have I.'

'I told you already. Her place was a dump. And I don't care what anyone says, no way was she Hawaiian - Tennessee nigger more like. And that crazy maid called her three different names within five minutes, like she couldn't make up her mind who the fuck she was. Stoned out of her head.'

'The girl?'

'No. The fucking maid. Dumb cow!'

'Did she appeal to you in any way?'

'Fuck, she did!'

'Tell me more about the girl.'

'She's got this ugly damn tattoo all down her back and around her ass. I mean, what is she, a reptile? I felt sick, like I was fucking a snake or something.'

'Then why didn't you leave?'

'I told you, I was horny. I had a few, too. Drinks. I needed several inside of me just to get it up her. - I tell you, my pole just ain't made for docking into that kind of dirt. Damn! What's the world coming to!'

'You're precious.'

'I try to be.'

'So what are you telling me, Stitch?'

'OK, in looks she was a dog; the place needed a serious makeover; but for a tart she was friendly. She had heart and did her best. I've got to give her that. I gave her a ten dollar tip.'

'Any distinguishing marks, apart from the tattoo?'

'Yeah. She had a clit ring. That's a new one for me.'

'Anything more prosaic.'

'Let me think.'

'Yeah. Do that!'

'All said and done, and apart from the blemishes, she was a good little runner at a great price. No rush at all, and polite too. And that counts for a lot in this racket,' he laughed, but it sounded like a grunt. 'That's the lot, copper. What's your thing? For me, if you want some cheap fun minus the frills, you want to fuck hard and aren't too picky about the surroundings, go see this girl. She really is spunky.' He nodded his head as though he were pondering a philosophical point.

420

'Would I recommend her? Yeah. Would I return? Yeah, I'd get in the ring with her any day. I'd pay. So want. I'd fucking pay. And leave her a tip too. What do you think I am?'

'Thanks for your time, Stitch. But no thanks.'

'Don't mention it,' he said gamely, and strode away with a bucket and towels towards the washroom.

On the way out the janitor saw him and chuckled sympathetically. 'Did you find what you were looking for, Detective?'

'No.'

'Waste of time, eh?'

'Yes.'

He paused, scrutinizing him: 'Are you a boxer yourself, chief? You look like you can box.'

'No. Not me. But my dad was in his day,' he said with pride, reminiscing.

'Yeah? What'd they call him?'

'Charlie Forester.'

'Forester, eh?'

'Yes. Charlie the Wild Cat Forester.'

'Name rings a bell.'

'Here,' he took a picture from his wallet of his old man posing in boxer's garb for an attack.

'Yeah, that's a boxer!' said the janitor, laughing pleasantly. 'You have yourself a real good day now, Detective.'

By the time he got back to the station, Sandy was showing Frank some pictures on one monitor and correlating his comments with another. Forester noticed she looked disgruntled with the progress and, as he shook hands with Frank and slumped down in a chair:

'Nothing,' he said, looking exasperated. 'She's in France, Sandy, the answers are over there.'

'The Captain wants to see you about that.'

'OK.' He looked at his wristwatch and then Frank, who was staring back at him blankly. 'Did any this trigger anything? I was hoping...'

Frank shook his head, regretting he couldn't be of more help to them; thinking inside: *I told you so, you know-it-all smartass cop.*

'Oh well...' said Sandy. 'Can we offer to take you anywhere? Give

421

me a moment to arrange a car.'

'No, it's fine. I'll get a cab.' Frank rose, smiled hesitantly and began to take his leave. 'Please, don't trouble yourselves. I can see you're both busy. I can see myself out. Goodbye. And good luck with the investigation.'

As soon as he left the building he called Roy, who was still baby-sitting Victor in his apartment.

'Cops!' he shrieked. 'What the hell do they want now? This is the last thing we need.'

'Nothing. It was a waste of time. That cop is just crazy.'

'Is Nick with you?'

'No. He's at the library.'

'Good. You know Freddy McCourt?'

'Never heard of him.'

'He's a hustler and a good friend of mine. We went to school together.'

'That figures,' he put in a skewed aside.

'What was that?'

'I said I never heard of him.'

'Go to The Blue Moon Bar in Soho. You know it? Good, ask for Freddy.'

'OK. And you?'

'Just take things one step at a time,' said Roy, rushing him. 'I need to think. I'm picking up the kitten in twenty minutes, and we're heading for the club.'

'This time of the day?'

'I need to relax; somewhere to think.' And he hung up.

Frank frowned and proceeded to call Nick, who was reading *The Twelve Caesars* by Suetonius at the library.

'Have you ever read it, Frank?'

'Can't say I have.'

'I'll get you a copy.'

Frank brought him swiftly up to date, hinting at Roy's vagaries and strange itinerary, and then expressed his own misgivings and doubts. Nick empathized, though he sounded more circumspect about it. But at length they agreed to meet at Roy's favorite jazz club in downtown Manhattan in about an hour. Nick, in an almost offhand

422

way, asked Frank who the hustler was he was going to meet. Frank got clever and replied 'Roy's alter ego!' Half-hearted chuckles aside, Nick confirmed he would proceed on schedule and log-in remotely into the office data network, tweak the trading computers, and check the status of Ace, an alias for the pot - the major program and file store of all their leading-edge software, code, client data and account numbers, and big bag of tricks. In the past, firepower was packed in balls of iron hauled at castle walls and sandbanks more than a meter thick. Now, it rolls off as invisible bits of data, and is just as lethal in the wrong hands. Or was that the *right* hands?

Folding over the top corner of a page of his book, Nick left the chapter on Julius Caesar unfinished at the part where Caesar, on the day of his Gallic Triumph, ascended the Capitol in Rome between two lines of elephants, forty in total, and on the decorated wagons one bore the eternal inscription:

I CAME. I SAW. I CONQUERED.

Way to go!

And closing the book, he cleared his throat, looked at his wristwatch, set the timer, and proceeded to his task.

*　　　　*　　　　*

Rumble rumble... It started raining again by the time Frank strode into The Blue Moon Bar, a clap of thunder stirring overhead, wafts of a faint breeze gusting here and there, but no traces of lightning to awe spectators of the mighty sky.

Expecting something more exotic, Frank was surprised by what he found and was immediately struck with the plasticity of the decor. A grin of discrimination washed over his face as he examined the interior, the tasteful, oddly delicate features of a new design, updated, sophisticated, like walking into a slick dream.

Frank detained a passing waitress, 'Excuse me, miss, is the club under new ownership?'

'That's right.'

'And what happened?'

'They updated.'

'To what?'

423

'This!' she chuckled. 'They wanted a breath of fresh air.'

Frank shuddered slightly, took a longer look and felt to himself: *Not another fashionable joint. What's the point?* The furnishing was excruciatingly post-modern in the me-too sense of groveling to urban taste – a man's interpretation of *The Modern Mood*. Or was it a woman? Bets are on! Either way, pretty lame when you think about it. He preferred it when it looked seedy, tacky, like the backside of a slut, and had the hard smell of a whore, her cheap perfume, the reek of sweat after the sixth punter had been inside her and seven is heaven if it's your turn and you're banging her bonkers because your brain in awash in testosterone and nothing beats a good friggin' ride down the reeking pussy of a cheap thrill. What is money really for, after all? For men to earn and women to burn, that's what. Style is OK, but style alone lacked any kind of purpose, or a reason to get you excited. You need action, with a hint of sleaze, to fire-up the hormones. Take two. – That's a wrap.

'Would you like a drink, sir?' asked the waitress, her red hair combed back in a school girlish kind of way. She looked cute, and had a dancer's trim body.

Frank said he was looking for the hustler.

'Who?'

'Freddy McCourt.'

'Ah, him,' she grinned. 'The pool tables; through there.'

He dropped twenty dollars in her tray; she said thanks and smiled; he said don't mention it and seemed a touch despondent as he walked among the renovated interior and reminisced on the good old days when the place looked sleazy, where a brunette whore could convince you she was a blond because you were either stoned or drunk out of your mind and the bitch could be purple by the time you had your way with her, and she of you. This is the kind of place a man needs to frequent now and again to restore the proportionate animal instinct that essentially defines him. In the past they had rituals, orgiastic bursts of frenzy lasting for days, not to understand the meaning of life, but to amaze – to freak out the system and burn it to exhaustion. It wasn't just a fuck, but delirium. As simple as that. As mad as that. As *religious* as that.

'Freddy McCourt?'

'Who wants to know?'

'I'm Frank, a friend of Roy Riemann's. You're expecting me.'

Freddy leaned on his pool cue and ogled him for a moment, his dark eyes and cropped brown hair trimmed like a convict but he never looked like a convict, more like a surgeon who would rather be playing pool and whoring on the circuit of club to bar to venue to club to walk-up to bar ad infinitum... than saving people for a living. They drew together warily and shook hands.

'We've met before, briefly as I remember,' said Freddy. 'Long time no see.'

Frank remembered him now, at a party about three years ago. He had a woman on each arm; a grin about to burst from his face, and a laugh that convinced you he really enjoyed life. Every delicious minute of it.

'Do you play pool, Frank?'

'Not much. It's not really my game. And now is not a good time.'

'I understand,' he said, bending low over the table and taking a final shot before handing his cue-stick to a friend, and they passed through to the bar. They sat at a table by the small low-set stage and ordered some beers. 'You've got some guy that you want to keep on ice?'

'Is that what Roy told you?'

'He asked for my advice.' Freddy paused, deliberately. 'Roy's an old friend of mine. We go way back when. Thanks, sweetie,' the waitress brought the drinks. 'Put it on my tab.'

'You have something for me?' said Frank.

'I don't *have* things, I *do* things.'

'Excuse me?'

'I'm a computer hacker,' he told him bluntly, lifting his glass. 'Cheers.'

Frank gazed at him with mixed curiosity and surprise, murmuring 'Cheers,' the word seeping effortlessly from him. 'So... what have you been hacking into lately?'

'You,' he said. 'Roy asked me to hack into Ace. He wanted to see how tough it was.'

A shudder. Hesitation. A numbing disdain barely noticed and inferred only by a silent rage that Frank struggled to contain. 'Me?'

'Yes.'

'Why?'

'Roy asked me to.'

Another breathless pause. Another shudder. Anger; deeper; more penetratingly silent.

'And?'

'She's a tough one, I'll give you that.'

'But you never got in?'

'No. But I found something else.' He took out a pocket computer and turned it on. 'I'm not the only one trying to crack Ace. There were three others: one in Las Vegas, one in Paris, one in Riyadh, of all places. You have an Arabian connection?' No response. He shrugged and resumed. 'These three units coordinate in a peculiar way. They don't base the sequence on time, like you would expect when breaking into fundamental tier networks, for example, but on a pattern or... perhaps *behavior* is a better description. It's bizarre. Each system is playing the other in a kind of *game*,' he looked at him strangely, 'a bit like poker, I'd say. One starts a move, and then the others seem to try and *guess* what it will do next, like they're raising stakes and drilling into the system.'

'You mean they're *learning?*'

Freddy snapped his fingers, struck his head with both hands and gazed at him with revealed astonishment. 'Of course! That's it; they're *learning*.' He paused to let it sink in. 'Damn! I just never saw it, and it was staring me in the face. They're learning. The damnedest thing - they're learning!' His head fell back, awed at the discovery, and he shuddered with excitement. 'This is really hot stuff. Fantastic! But I get too involved in the damn details. - I'm always doing that. I keep falling over that same stupid conceit.' His fury consumed him briefly, before swiftly recovering. 'Typical male hormones driving headstrong into battle. I've got to knock that habit on the head. Just imagine what I'm missing out on here. Think I'm too smart, that's me. Well, I am, but I can be dumb as a melon too. I should have stepped back and seen the whole picture. Only you get so damn excited and wound up in what you're doing you can't stop yourself from falling in. That's the whole problem with obsessions – you can get too close for your own good.'

Silently, they finished their beer. Frank glanced at his wristwatch as if for something to do, and Freddy offered him another drink.

'Not for me. No. - I need to make a call.'

'Please, don't mind me, go right ahead.'

Frank called Nick, who verified that Ace was OK, the network was operating normally, and he would be heading for the club shortly. So far, everything checked out A.O.K, and Frank hung up and looked at Freddy toying with his pocket computer. - 'What happens now?'

'We're leaving,' he said, folding the computer and tucking it away. 'No, this way, we go by the side exit.'

It was a fire escape into an alleyway and Freddy pushed the handle-bar to release the door. Slouched by the exit was a dude fondling the strings of his old guitar with dazed precision.

'Who's he?' Frank asked.

'Just some bum who plays around here.'

The bum looked up at them listlessly, stoned out of his mind, and waved, saying he was serenading their spirits because their sprits were trapped and sad and wanted to be set free, like his.

'What he's doing?' asked Frank, holding the door ajar.

'Just jamming.'

'What's he on, dope?'

'It's not like that, Frank; not with him. It's more like a fetish than a fix.'

'He's choking.'

'Let him be.'

'But - '

'I said don't touch,' he said, insisting with a stern gaze, before easing into persuasion: 'Just trust me on this. OK?'

'But he could be dying.'

'He's in control. In a while he'll fall asleep. He'll dream some, twitch some, then later tonight he'll be on stage pumping it all out like time just hopped out of his dreaming bones, and he never noticed a thing. Time,' he said, smiling, 'it's all just music.'

Frank retracted his hand, mysteriously trusting to a strange, perhaps a lame, instinct. And he simply gazed, his emotions exposed and vulnerable.

'You get used to it,' said Freddy.

'Used to what?'

'This.'

'Frank shook his head, 'No. I don't think so.'

'It's just a mood thing, you see? Just a mood thing.'

'Look. His eyes are twitching.'

'He's happier than we are, Frank,' he said. 'What dreams mean to these guys, we'll never understand. – Easy now, don't let the door slide. Ease it back slowly till the lock catches. That's it.'

'Where are we going?'

'To find Roy.'

'At the club?'

'Yes.'

'Who goes there this time of the day?' he wondered. 'There can't be many?'

'You'd be surprised.'

Frank looked puzzled.

Freddy glanced at his wristwatch and reflected aloud. 'By the time we arrive, they should be just warming up. Did you drive?'

'I took a cab.'

'Here,' he gave him the keys to his car. 'Start her up. That one there. I'll be with you in a moment.'

Chapter 24

The kitten was having a manicure when her mobile phone - her mobie - started to ring. It was Roy, he was calling from the back of a cab en route to collect her. The cab driver's grizzled cadence had the immigrant slur of street slang: *Where ya wanna go, mester? Lef ere?...* that rattled Roy's eardrums. He anticipated arriving in around ten minutes time, as the rain was easing and the traffic flowing again.

'Are you almost finished, babe?'

'I need to do it perfectly, Roy, I want to be perfect.'

'Could you hurry it up, please? You're perfect enough already.'

'I know,' she said, laughing perfectly. 'I know.'

'Then could you hurry it up?'

'OK, Roy,' she agreed fussily. 'But don't rush me.'

And she hung up.

'Jen?' began the kitten, addressing her friend in the chair next to hers.

'Yeah?' Jen answered, her eyes covered with fresh strips of cucumber, her face masked with sandy-white cream, and her chin home to what looked like a slice of lemon.

'I've got to rush soon, Jen.'

'OK, honey.'

'I'll give you a call on your mobie.'

'Yeah, OK. I like this new model, it's so cute.'

'Yeah, I know, I'll call you on it.'

'And I'll answer it.'

'You're so sweet. Thanks, babe.'

'Ah, that's OK. Sure thing. What are friends for!'

'Yeah,' she mused, gesturing the manicurist to hurry. 'Yeah...'

The kitten was the quintessential cat that not only purrs to perfection, (has nine lives in hand and nine more in reserve) but can decorate a cake like no other, and that cake was her body. She paints her eyes, tints her eyelashes, colors her cheeks, shaves her legs, her armpits, her pussy – she likes him to do that, it takes a very delicate hand – adorns her toenails with tiny crystals, (she calls them dimples of luck), and smiles as the light sets them shimmering. And, to top it all off, she visits the beauty parlor for a make over and perm. Gosh! Ain't she the business? Ain't she lovely? Ain't she wonderful?

'Do you think I look beautiful, Roy?'

'You're something else, baby. Something else!'

'Do I make you feel horny?'

'All the time.' - His entire day was one long hard-on.

'Would you like to fool around a little... *Roy?*' She's a teasing little kitten, and winks at him.

'Maybe later,' he says, since he has a hard-on for a game of poker, but they still manage to fool around a little in the back of the cab. The taxi driver's an immigrant, Latino, the dream's still ticking in his dazzled stare, and he raised his envious eyebrows and gapes in the rear-view mirror. It's the American way: lucky guy, blonde bimbo, New York City taxicab, greasy driver – like a deck of cards, really. It's natural. Logical. It's American *cents* (phonetically speaking...) bankrolling life.

'Take the park route,' Roy told him as they cruised into Midtown.

'Sure,' grunts back the immigrant.

'And don't press so easy on the gas.'

'Ya da boss. Lef ere, hokay...?'

'Yes. And push the pedal a bit harder, would you, we're in a hurry.'

'Ya da boss. Hokay.'

'And keep your eyes fixed on the road ahead, *poncho.*'

He didn't take kindly to that remark, ethnicity being a touchy subject at the best of times, so he smarted and contented himself with peeping every now and again, voyeuristically, at that delicious bundle of blond luxury he could only drool and dream over.

'Careful, Roy,' cried the kitten. 'Watch my hair; you'll mess it all up.'

'Sorry, babe.'

'OK.'

And they smooched like teenagers on a first date. American-pie...
Squared.

Fifteen minutes later:

'Da ah be twenny bucks, mester,' said the immigrant tactlessly,
rubbing his money fingers together.

'Here you are,' said Roy abruptly, passing him fifty. 'Keep the
change, *poncho.*'

Roy was convinced he heard the universal trailer *Fuck You* rap out
in tune with the feisty engine as the cab yanked into gear and pulled
away. He stood under bunting with the kitten arm in arm and looked
up at the grey sky, cycling superstitiously: 'Rain, stop. Rain, stop.
Rain...' heaving bleakly: 'Stop! What the hell is happening to the
weather?'

'How's your English friend, Roy?' chirped the kitten innocently.

'Don't remind me, babe,' he lamented. 'Don't remind me.' And
gloomily shaking his head at the weather, led her into the club.

Inside, he spotted Freddy flirting with a waitress at the bar. They
shook hands and the waitress drifted off with a wink and Freddy's
telephone number. *See you later...*

'Where's Frank?'

'He went outside to do something.'

'What?'

'I have no idea; but said he'll be back shortly,' he explained, ogling
the kitten irresistibly.

'Who's this one, Roy?' she asked.

'Freddy.'

'Freddy. Hi!'

'Hi there.'

'Great name. Can I call you Freddy?'

'Sure,' he said. 'Be my guest.'

Roy asked him if Nick was around.

'The Brit? No, he hasn't arrived yet.'

'Come on,' he said, looking around, deep in thought. 'Let's take a
table further inside, closer to the stage. I prefer it there. I feel more
at home. I can think.'

'But it's noisy,' she complained. 'Roy!'

'It's not noise,' he turned to the kitten, smitten with her entirely, but frowning. 'It's jazz.'

Jazz. Lost in the music; lost in the sense of the sound. Hard to resist? Sure. Hard to forget? Yeah. Hard to let go of? Never. And..? And some.

Jazz. Jazzz. Jazzzzz...

As they were shown to their table the affected rituals kicked-in and the kitten purred and went meow and, excusing herself, said she had to visit the ladies' room to powder her nose and 'The bits and pieces we ladies do, you know.' Of course they know, what are they, mugs? Feminine beauty is a fiddly business, quintessentially urbane and one of those true wonders of the world perfectly depicting the superfluous, the unnecessary, the frivolous, the characteristically time-consuming ritual which without would make the world seem a pretty bland and miserable place indeed. Ladies are like jazz too, you know, full of a masterful piece, spontaneous, mesmerizing, the epitome of... *jazz*.

'She's a beauty, Roy. Where did you find her?'

'The kitten?' he smiled proudly.

'Yes.'

'I picked her up in Vegas,' he said, thumbing through the menu and the wine list and glancing at her empty chair realized he could never bear to be parted from her. 'She's like jazz to me now... What else can a man do..? but wonder and obsess.'

'But doesn't she make you feel horny all the time?'

Roy grinned: 'Life's a package. You take the good with the *best*.' They laughed heartily together – kind of a guy thing. Sure. The good with the best. 'What are you drinking?'

'Whiskey. - What will you do now, Roy?'

'Did you tell Frank everything; what you do; what's happening; what you did?'

'Everything.'

'How did he take it?'

He considered before he spoke, 'Philosophically, I'd say.' The waiters hovered around them and set the table. When they finished and left with the order Roy gave them, Freddy resumed, 'What happens now?'

'Confront them.'

'The guys in Paris?'

'I'm leaving tonight.'

'If I didn't know you, Roy, I'd think you were behaving strangely.'

'And since you do know me?'

'You're like someone acting out of character. Are you in the right part?'

'The part's right. It's the story that's all wrong.'

'This is beginning to sound too deep for me?'

'Imagine how I must feel.'

'Do you know who they *really* are? These guys; these hackers?'

Roy gazed intently at the stage: the musicians metamorphosed as the chorus of a drama, abstract things sounding the plot of life – not one narrative, but a thousand and more. And he, man in a daydream, communicated with the players in a spiritual unfolding of the story, as the soft processional sounds rose from them, he began to see a landscape emerge, to hear a story, and it felt... inevitable. 'Let me put it this way,' he said at length, 'I have a pretty good idea who they are.' Deep down, he felt, this was the only way the story could unfold.

'Can I offer you some advice, Roy?'

'Yes.'

'Make a deal. What these guys are doing with the technology is really innovative. They're pushing at the envelope. It makes you wonder.'

'What does?'

'Well...' Freddy gazed at him intriguingly 'where do you fit in to all this? You. And the others. What does it mean?'

Roy inhaled deeply. He felt the sheer weight of paradox upon him for the first time. It relieved him of his temper; shed him of rashness; exposing fears of what he may have gotten himself into. Rational hesitation, and a calm mind, would have made him more circumspect. Perhaps, in life, the best risks, the easiest dare, emerge from vagueness, from incomplete knowledge, of not really knowing the odds. Because some games are arranged with a deck full of blank cards; and you play, as it were, on blind will – with luck fashioned on the fly. These thoughts, surging up at once, made him feel numb with apprehension. But he shielded it well in the circumstances, so all that prying eyes could see was a resolute man - the occasional shudder notwithstanding. In any case, there was no going back. 'Thanks, Freddy,' he said quietly, ponderously. And they shook hands. 'Thanks for everything.'

The table next to theirs subsequently became occupied by an older, hefty looking gent and his younger, leaner, pretty looking bimbo; and as soon as they were settled in with the waiters fawning over them, their antics became flirtatious, bubbling over with exuberance: the old fella in the slick geezer's suit and bulging eyes propped up by meaty cheeks and a voice that reeks of money, lots of it, lots and lots of it, showers of golden dough and an endless laugh, *ha ha ha...* together with home-made self-confidence that smells of apple-pie, brimming over on the Yankee breeze of plenty. She's a honey beside him, and melts in his hands like he melts inside of her. The kitten looks on reproachfully and sneers – *What a sight, huh!* Roy amuses himself and looks, outwardly aloof but – *Oh, what a sight! Yes!* The riveting drama of money-coated Man was in full swing. *–Yes!*

The bimbo calls him Aaah-rie, her drawl is deep Dixie so Harry sounds like Aaah-rie, uttered with that carnival smile. He calls her chickie-bee, possibly because if he fondles her enough she might lay eggs – golden eggs, that is. Sure, he's a regular all-American Midas with the greenback touch, everything he touches turns to gold and a bimbo hanging on his arm and calling him Aaah-rie, you're soooo funnnnyyyy, Aaah-rie.

But she's a pro, a real turbocharged motor, knows the bends, the sharp turns, the long stretches and hairpins, vroooom, knows when to press the pedal hard, when to look coy, how to play the sophisti*cat*. Meow. She knows. *Meeeeeeooooooow.*

Her gestures formulate desire, even in a hand swept softly across her face teases riddles from bewitching gazes and she coos through the sound of lounge jazz and his wrinkled face charms her like oriental spice and aromas flood her mind and she feels near to it, to money, and is breathless at the fragile space separating wanton liberation from humdrum chores the masses have succumbed to.

'Waiter; your best champagne. You like that, chickie-bee?'

'And strawberries, too, Aaah-rie, we want strawberries too.'

'You heard the lady. A forest of strawberries. We want the best. – You like that, chickie-bee?'

Giggles pepper his wrinkled face as she creases-in her kisses, her pouting lips yearning with the frenzied things that words alone could never intimate. Ultimately, it is to discover this, that the intoxicating aspect of a woman to a man, lured by money and a breathless imagination, turns the world into a fever. And life is a dynamo for disease in endless suffering money can ever hope to cure. Pile it on. More and more and more...

'Here,' he hands the waiter five hundred bucks. 'Keep it rolling.'

'I want to drown in it, Aaah-rie. I want to drown in it.'

'Then drown in it we will. Gimme a kiss!'

Pop! The champagne foam overflows the bottle and the waiter sweeps it into glasses and the old-timer cries out: 'That's what I like to see. That's how it is. Pour it out, son. Pour the damn thing out. There's plenty more where that came from. Keep it rolling.'

'Let's use straws. Champagne and straws. Oh Aaah-rie...' Her exhilarating voice floods their world like champagne bursting from its bottle, as the spoils of riches draws out behaviors and the moods. Love is a promise. Money is a guarantee. And there is nothing as perfect as a sure thing. And as they drink champagne with curling straws sharing a glass, jazz sounds the features of impermanence, as the beat trickles down, and the bass sweeps on, the clarinet traces out an echo and the cymbals tantalize silence with a whispering *whoosh* as if to pluck it with a kiss, so emotions dance to the thrilling beat and lived today as though they lived forever. He fondles her breast and says something sweet. She replies with whispers, and chuckles, and disposes of the straws. Love is a riddle. Money a certainty. And there is nothing in the world more compelling than a sure thing.

'Are you having a good time, babe?' Roy lifted the kitten's hand, gently, and kissed it with playful tenderness.

'They're crude, Roy,' she protested. 'Crude.'

'I know. But it's a free country. What can we do?'

'Let's leave. - Freddy, don't you want to leave?'

'I'm all done anyway, sweetie,' he said, getting up to take his leave.

'If I can be of any more help, call me when you get to Paris, Roy, and I'll do whatever I can.'

'Paris!' shrieked the kitten.

Roy told her they were leaving tonight.

'Why didn't you tell me?' she rebuked him, frantically explaining she had to do a thousand things, oh, so many things he couldn't even possibly imagine, and arranging a trip to lovers' land so suddenly was so inept, just typical of men. 'It takes planning, you know? Lots of planning. Oh Fiddlesticks!'

'I know. I'm sorry, babe, but it all happened very suddenly and slipped my mind. Don't worry, I booked the late flight,' he looked at his wristwatch. 'We have plenty of time.'

Suddenly, he heard a warm voice cry out: 'Hey, Roy, is that you?' behind him as Freddy took his leave. Roy thought it was Frank, but King Stud approached with a beaming grin, gazing at the opposite table as they shook hands. 'All sorted out with the Englishman, Roy?' he said, waving to the kitten, and she excitedly waved back, suddenly very French with her gesture. She wanted to leave, and her expression made that clear.

'More or less,' he said.

'Good. - Hey, Harry,' King Stud strolled over to the neighboring table as Harry enmeshed his chubby hands with ckickie-bee's and excluded the world beyond them.

Harry lifted his fat head and frowned momentarily at being disturbed before revealing a grin. They shook hands like old pals and together erupted in a train of banter, yanking at the jokes of old, reviving and giving them a good spin, and chickie-bee laughed and coyly blushed at the flood of compliments lavished on her beauty, and she graces the performance with *Oh, you men, you're always teasing me...* brimming with neat gestures and the sultry look of desire, which whets the appetite of a man and sets his hormones on fire. What is a man, unless he burns?... But it's the woman who lights the match. Sizzle. *Men!*

'Hey, Roy,' King Stud turned and beckoned to Roy after indulging his fancies at Harry's table, and invited him to join them, 'I want you to meet someone.'

Roy grinned, shrugged helplessly at the kitten's silent appeals, and as she stared at him aggrieved he explained it would be impolite to refuse an introduction. So he went over.

'Harry, I want you to meet Hard Eight,' said King Stud.

'So you're the Eight?'

'So long as it's Hard,' said Roy, as they weighed each other up.

Yes, from Harry's happy face, the sleek contours of a thin man buried inside the profile of a fat one, the poise of self-disciple behind the scruffy facade of a sucker, you could tell he trained a poker hand and bested any number of guys sleeker and more handsome than he, but old Harry had the bimbo and, of course, the money, and, as he and Roy shook hands, Harry wet his lips and opened his eyes wide at the prospect of a game. He noticed Roy staring at his lady friend.

'Meet my friend.'

'Friend. Ah, the pleasure is all mine...' It was eyeball to eyeball and the prize was winning at poker, not the girl. But still, you can hardly help to gape and grovel over her: What are lustful eyes for? What is a drooling mouth for? Be honest, what is a woman like that for? Marriage, house in the suburbs, two-point two children, station wagon and SUV, a pet dog named Lassie, barbecue on Sundays, church choir on Mondays, the American *humble pie* dream?

A wet-dream, more like. Sweet apples and all. Yausa yausa yausa. And praise the Lord for women like that, and pass her along. Gimme gimme. Yes-sir-eeee. Yausa! Yausa!

It was as clear as gleaming daylight: shine and shine. She was the multi-purpose blonde bimbo with a heart of lay-in-the-hay gold and a screw-in-the-open mind to match with I've-been-there-before stretch marks but still has that impossible to resist horniness that comes of being a babe.

Yes-sir-eee, Harry's hit the jackpot this time, provided he's not a jackass.

Well, is he?

Harry is judge and jury and beckons the waiter with the broad-rimmed glasses and prompts him: 'Hey, four-eyes, bring us some beers.'

Four-eyes will bring them, rest assured, but he'll piss in them first. Beauty is ever the touchy subject, and Roy thanks him but no thanks, he's with someone.

'Oh,' sighs Harry, looking over at the kitten who fretted and frowned indignantly back at him, and she poked her tongue out, spearing him with a gesture. Harry ogles her moodily before shifting this attention to his pickle and reaches over and clasps chickie-bee's hand and smiles at her warmly. Is it love? Is it tenderness worth a life-time? - Wet around the ears, perhaps, drip, drip... But as long as it feels good, who cares? Drown in desire, baby. Drown. Drip, drip...

Roy watched the proceedings with a softly critical stare, conferring with King Stud before turning and gazing at the kitten. Strange, but it never makes him reflect on his own rendition of the incidental life. A bimbo he picked up at a game in Vegas – sure, she's been around, but so has he. Love, infatuation, must be viewed in this light as reshaping the landscape of relationships. The rule is: if love is blind, *to hell with it!* I want to be with her and that's all that matters.

'They call me Jack.'

'I thought your name was Harry,' said Roy.

'Around a poker table, I'm Romeo Jack. Well, how about it?'

Roy felt temptation stir. The Romeo part made him wonder, but the Jack part brought out a smile. Nevertheless, he saw it coming, and he knew that he couldn't resist. Anxiety and difficulties beyond his control afflicted him all day and he felt embattled, and this was one sure way he could unwind and relax. His life was a mess, sure, but he needed a break.

The kitten smarted angrily when Roy informed her, protesting that he never loved her, it was all a sham, a fake, a rotten shameless fake. – But at some point during her onslaught she seemed to relent and reconsider things in a broader context and graced him with a lovely kiss, and then went shopping and then home to pack their things for the journey to Paris, arranging to meet back at the club at six o'clock.

Roy glanced at the time: that left a good four hours.

'Are we ready then?' said Harry, pecking chickie-bee on the cheek and giving her several thousand dollars to amuse herself alone for a while. 'A couple of grand always buys you some time and a smile,' said Harry, as he watched her stroll out of the club. 'I bet your girl cost you more than did mine.'

'Never mind,' said Roy. 'I'll win it back at poker.'

When Frank returned from his excursion, Freddy had long since left and Roy was nowhere in sight. He asked at the bar and was informed Roy had gone upstairs to the poker room.

'He's playing now!' he shrieked with utter amazement. 'Are you certain?'

'Yes sir, I saw him go up there with King Stud and a fat gentleman I've never seen here before.'

'Is Nick around?'

'Who?'

'Never mind.' Embittered, Frank made his way upstairs. He rapped on the door and a hoary voice inside told him to get lost. He turned the handle and went in anyway. Roy leapt up and hurried over, excusing himself from the table – an emergency, he said, and drove Frank outside into the corridor and shut the door behind them.

Frank blasted out: 'What the fuck are you doing? Are you insane? What about Victor? What about Peeping Tom? Jesus Christ, Roy, are you out of your mind?'

'What am I supposed to do?'

'Asshole!'

'What do you want from me?' - No answer, only a seething contempt raging within him. - 'I'm all out of breath with this thing, Frank. I'm on the edge. I can only be myself. This is what I do. It's one way I can be honest with myself and cope. I'm not superman.'

'Christ!' He could have choked on that word, which he intended as an expletive but had the aura of forgiveness. Perhaps, in Roy's moment of confessed vulnerability, he saw his own limitations, and thus grew more forgiving.

'Frank, I'm going to Paris to confront them. I'm leaving tonight.'

'And Victor?'

'We have to tell him. I don't know what I was thinking this morning; I must have been insane to do what I did. Whatever possessed me?' He paused and reflected with a tide of regrets tugging at him. 'But it's done now; and we just have to run with it. What else can we do? Frank?'

'What?'

'Are you still with me on this? I need to know.'

Angst cut a grim expression on his face, full of doubt, full of consuming bitterness. Roy continued:

'Frank, we need some time. We need to keep Victor out of the picture for as long as possible. It's not perfect, but I have an idea. And I think he'll buy it. Don't worry; he won't wake for hours yet. He's out cold. Listen. Just listen to me for a minute.' And Roy explained his plan, which involved Frank persuading Victor that they uncovered a computer hacker who compromised their system, and that to counter him Frank and Victor would need to travel to San Francisco, where some documents would be sent to a post box, just some garbled codes, but should take several days to unravel.

'He won't buy it.'

'He will. He knows there is someone tampering with the system. He's aware of the same problems. I don't know how, but parts of it got duplicated, and he must have picked it up. He's more than likely to have guessed the rest; and chances are he suspects a hacker, probably an inside job.' Roy paused a moment to think, 'Victor doesn't believe in coincidence. That's what makes him so effective a trader, so he'll believe the hacker story, because he knows someone is poking their finger in his pie, but he doesn't know who or from where. That's why he's here. He thinks we've uncovered it.'

'Why San Francisco?'

'The main processors are made there. Let him believe you suspect it's an inside job, someone who worked on the hardware or has access to the designs, that the engineers had encrypted a hole in the processor, so someone with detailed knowledge of the design could break in at will. To find the hacker, you need to be near the source.'

'He won't buy it.'

'It's credible enough,' he insisted. 'It's enough. It's a chance; and we have to take it. Quit this bitterness, Frank; it's eating you up. He'll buy it. He doesn't have a choice. He's stuck with us, at least for a time. Listen to me! It doesn't have to be perfect. It doesn't have to be one hundred percent. It just needs to be enough. That's something you refuse to accept.'

Frank shook his head skeptically, 'What about Ace?'

'Don't mention Ace. Never! Just tell him the hacker went after the local system, the top layer. We throw some money to few student hackers to create a diversion, feed them some slick software that looks right but leads nowhere, and that's probably enough time to sort all this mess out.'

'And Nick?'

'One of us has to stay here in New York and coordinate.'

'And if Victor asks where you are?'

'Tell him...' he spun his thoughts frantically, 'tell him I'm getting married.'

'He won't believe it.'

'Yes he will,' he insisted stubbornly. 'He has no choice. None.' Then, pondering deeper on the repercussions, concluded: 'He will; in the beginning at least. We have the lead, Frank; small as it is; absurd as it is; so... we should use it. It's enough. Besides, it's all we have.'

'It won't work. It's crazy.'

'Do you have any other ideas?' He waited, staring hard at him. 'I thought not, and we're running out of time.'

'But you find time to play cards.'

'I'm all stressed out. It's therapy. Jesus Christ, give me a break!' he snapped, struggling to compose himself. 'And you had better do the same. You're not as strong or as smart as you think you are. Believe me, the best heroes know how to unwind, to step back; and we're nowhere near that.' He gazed at him earnestly. 'Look, Frank, we're fighting shadows. And now and again we may get in a punch; but it's useless anyway. Useless. We're playing against the clock; it's counting down. We're bluffing from moment to moment. What do you suggest we do?'

Frank, anxious and burdened with doubt, turned without saying a word and went back to the bar. And there he remained drinking beer after beer drowning his sorrows and quenching bitterness that sapped his strength, tumbler at a time. Sorrows were a dark weight he carried around carelessly with him, like sipping a beer, brooding over things and vague ideas: Peeping Tom, work, his life, a sports car; the spooky moon. What did they all mean? Nothing. Not a damn thing.

'Frank, what's going on? Where's Roy?'

'Hi, Nick,' he said despondently.

'Where's Roy? What's the matter with you?'

'I need another drink. Do you want one? Bartender... Bartender...'

'What did the cops say? Where's Roy? What the hell's going on?'

'Look. There's Vonnie over there.'

Nick turned swiftly and saw her sitting alone at a table, her hand demurely holding her chin, her elbow near a cocktail glass, tall and elegant. She spotted him and beckoned him over. He smiled back and before going turned to Frank.

'Where's Roy.'

'He's playing poker.'

'Poker!'

'He might as well,' he sighed. 'Besides, what else is there to do?'

'Are you OK?'

'Perhaps.'

'Frank - '

'He'll be down soon. He'll explain everything.' He tried to smile, but it felt lame. 'The clock is ticking away, buddy.'

The emptiness Nick felt revealed the vanity of things, the conceit of their endeavors, that painful recognition that events were not theirs to control. Their parody, for parody it was, expressed in gestures and words, a feeble game of pretend and dare, a boys-own boldness played with the miming of purpose, the pose of strength, and the reflex of contrived determination. What it all boils down to is who calls the shots. For them, someone in Paris was holding the gun, tweaking the trigger, controlling the game. Gazing blankly at one another, the bartender appeared and asked what they wanted. 'Same again for me,' said Frank, shrugging at Nick, who shook his head.

Nick was on the verge of descending into cliché and saying *Is there any point anymore?...* but wisely resisted and invited Frank to join him and Vonnie at her table.

'No,' he said, struggling to smile. 'Thanks. Maybe later. I want to just sit here a while and think. I....' His expression was a world holding all of six words, echoing and reverberating and filling it up: *Who do we think we are?*

Good question. But it's rarely that a man wants an honest answer. Unless it's silent, of course. Ssshhh.

Nick, with the tremble of foreboding stealing into his mind, gazed not at Frank but at his own reflection in the mirror behind the bar. It was the image of a man who in the past five days had changed so much, a man that wanted to feel happy. But he seemed worn, dimmed in the light by the bar; a closed book. Shaking his head, he dismissed this from his mind, turned, and walked away.

'You look tired,' said Vonnie, as she kissed him on the cheek. 'Are you OK?'

'Fine.'

'Shouldn't you be at work or something?'

'We broke early today.'

'Your friend Frank looks a little down.'

'It's his way,' he said, watching him drown his sorrows at the bar. 'Work; the pressure gets to us all at times, I guess.'

And he looked at his wristwatch, barely registering the time, looked at it again, and waited.

*　　　　　*　　　　　*

At the police station, Sandy noted the time and drew Forester's attention to it. He glanced at the clock and shrugged.

'So what,' he said, 'it's two o'clock.'

'I thought I'd bring your attention to it, that's all.'

'Thanks,' he said, almost on the point of yawning but it was boredom not sleep that plagued him, rubbing his eyes as they drifted absently over some files on his desk – all unsolved, and all pointing to Paris. Forester vented a groan of dismay in French and impulsively picked up the telephone. He dialed and waited. 'Hi, Captain, it's me.'

'Forester? I've been meaning to speak with you. Come to my office; I want to have a private word.'

Forester looked intriguingly at Sandy, and she raised her eyebrows at him – she's a peach, gorgeous, and looked so sexy. Telling her he would be right back, he promised to sing for her soul and enshrine it in poetry if she brought him a coffee with cream. She insisted on a complete elegy in French. He asked her:

'Street slang or opera?'

'Start with the slang, and close with opera.'

He winked at her and promised to do his best. One sugar. Thanks.

'Ah, Forester.'

'Captain.'

'You catch the fight on the telly last night?'

'What fight?'

'Shame on you!'

'Sorry. I had a lot on my mind.'

'Come in and take a seat.' He gestured to a chair. 'And close the door.'

'Captain, I wanted to mention that - '

'Just listen to what I have to say.' He gazed abruptly at him. 'The girl who vanished in Paris.'

'We're looking into it.'

'Just listen. Her sister has taken things into her own hands. Obviously, she felt we weren't doing enough. However, she left us a letter. Please,' he raised his hand, warding off further interruptions. 'Just listen. She's gone to Paris to look for her sister. – In situations like these people get emotional; they think the police aren't doing enough. That's understandable. But we end up with the headache. So...' he fell abruptly silent and fixed him with an intriguing stare. Forester waited, his lips twitching as the Captain picked up a file and leaned back heavily in his chair, marking time. 'You were going to say, Forester?'

'When do I leave?'

He tossed him the file. 'Tonight. There's a flight at ten. Be on it.'

'And Sandy?'

'My heart goes out to her, but I'm not running a travel shop here. Well...' he hinted, 'you know what to do. And I want daily reports.' Undecided whether to grin or frown, he chose to reflect instead. He thought of Forester's pop and their days together as rookie cops, and the bullet that took him down. That was a bleak, harrowing day. He offered him advice. 'Whatever you do over there, whatever happens, don't punch above your weight. Listen to the cops; it's their turf. Have the sense to keep your mouth shut and learn. The best cops listen and watch; they don't talk.' Forester smiled warmly. 'And remember, off the record, I want you to go out of your way and find this girl. I can't send you to Paris on a missing persons' brief, so you'll have to ride this one on the back of the official case. Just be careful you don't overload it. OK? Remember to close the door behind you.' The glint in his eye said good luck, and Godspeed, and Forester listened inwardly because it was sincerity with a masculine face, and comes from a cop's heart.

The first thing he examined in the file as he walked back to his office was the note left by the restless twin. The last person to see her sister, Zoë, in the United States was a man called Mr. Reinhardt, of New Jersey, a merchant in the import business: shoes, coats, brick-a-brac fashions and casual wear. The file contained his personal profile, home and business addresses, telephone numbers, and the most telling of all a clean sheet. He was some ordinary guy who happened to see her last. Forester decided to pay him a visit before he left for Paris.

'I was expecting you,' said Mr. Reinhardt, 'you're here to ask me about Zoë.' He was a broad sweep of a man who seemed a gentle giant, an avuncular face, brown eyes, and a quiet voice. He possessed the temperate sense of an honest man seldom beset by major troubles, and the archetypal anonymous hero who lives his life in quiet labor and retreat bothering no one. He was just another echo in the city unwilling to blare his presence to the crowd.

'We think you were the last one to see her before she went abroad,' said Forester, conversing rather than interrogating. He was polite.

'She said she was leaving for Paris the following day.'

'Did she seem serious about it at the time?'

'She had her passport. She showed me the ticket.'

'Why would she do that?'

'I never asked.'

'OK,' he said. 'That's OK.'

'She gave me a few tips on the card games. She liked poker; she talked about it a lot. She told me about the games, where she learned, where she played. That's unusual for a young woman.'

'Is it?'

'I think so.'

'Perhaps you're right.'

They paused and gazed at one another, something that just happened for a brief spell, until Forester picked up the conversion again.

'Will you be honest with me, Mr. Reinhardt?'

'Of course. I'll do everything I can to help.'

'Thanks. I appreciate it.'

'Would you like a drink, Detective? A beer?'

'Not while I'm working.'

'Coffee, tea?'

'Not for me. Thanks. – You mind if I take notes?'

'Go ahead.'

Forester cleared his throat and began. 'Could you tell me where you were that night?'

'At a house on a quiet street.'

'Who's the owner? Ah, it's OK; I've have it all written down here. Was there anything odd about this house?'

'No. The only odd thing, if you can call it that, were the presence of lots and lots of cat related ornaments everywhere: the lawn, the hallway, the bedrooms... and even a large black tom holding court in the sitting room.' He laughed softly. 'It looked funny.'

'And this was the *event* that you went to? Tell me about it.'

'It's a bit outside of the mainstream.' He blushed. 'Let me put it that way.'

Forester wondered for a moment what he meant. Then, the sigh of recognition, 'Oh, I see...' he got the picture and kept a straight face. 'Do you mind if I ask?'

'Go ahead.'

'Do you do this often?'

'No. And this walk on the wild side will be the first and last time. I guess, I'm not really cut out for this. It isn't me. It's not what I am. And you have to accept what you are.'

'What time did you arrive there?'

'In the evening; just after ten. Yes, perhaps a little later; I wasn't keeping time. I just drifted in; gazed at all the cat stuff, thought it amusing, then went into the lounge; and the first thing I saw was this gorgeous lady having a drink. She lit a cigarette, braced it with her lips; licked it with her wet tongue... It was magic. Her name was Alice. And believe me, she was the wonderland. That's what she called herself - Alice. It's hard to tell, really. We were all anonymous there. That's how we wanted it - all strangers on the wild side.

Alice was a world in herself, all things to all men. Some women are like that; it's a kind of art, with her soft skin, her hard-core eyes, a perfect ten! and her naive way of speaking... Well, when you mix lust with innocence like that, it makes hard men harder, and the gentle, gentler. Some women are a slow fire - to men, she was explosive. She confessed to me later that night she was realizing a fantasy. We all have one, I guess.'

'Oh?'

'It takes all kinds.'

'I guess so.'

'The drinks flowed freely and the ladies were lovely. I accidentally collided with a redhead who turned to me and smiled. I wanted Alice first, she became a kind of obsession, I guess, but there were others, and the redhead followed me around - flirted with me. So of course, when a pretty young thing with flame-red hair offers herself like that, it's hard to say no. So, like a cat to a bowl of cream, I said yes, and just lapped her all up.' He paused, took a tissue from the box and wiped his face. He wasn't anxious or sweating, it was just a gesture to make time, to pause the conversation, to reflect. Perhaps even to remember the redhead with affection, a fond tenderness. 'You know, Detective, being spoilt for choice can be a terrible burden at times.'

'What was on offer?'

'Fancy stuff, normal, threesomes, submissive, bondage... It provided me with the time of my life. They had it all there. And voyeurs lurking in the background.'

'Who?'

'All of us, I guess.'

'Spoilt for choice; was that it?'

'I was kind of... exploring, I guess. I suffered some personal setbacks. And to fill the void in my private life I wanted something different. Something mad. Something ancient, if you like. In the past, these things used to go on for days. It was part of culture. It was religion. And I was going through a very bad patch. I needed to reignite the spark. It happens to us all. The spirit goes dormant, and you need to set it alight again. And this event just happened to come along. It was a coincidence.'

'What about the girl Zoë?'

'The first time I saw her was at the bar by the pool. I never paid her much attention. I was in among a crowd of strangers experiencing a wet dream and ready to drown in it. I didn't care; I just wanted to plunge deep. I let go of myself the whole night long. - Then, as dawn broke, fatigue crept in and everyone retired to bed. I found myself snuggled up in an upstairs room with Zoë enjoying a cozy chat until she fell asleep on me.'

'How did you find her that night, during the party?'

'She seemed a normal, well-adjusted kind of girl. That impression stuck. - Slim, blonde hair, tanned and wearing just her underwear. I remember when she kicked off her sandals; she looked so... contented, so free. I envied her then... she made me seem so lost, so alone, so wasted. A spent force. - She has the most beguiling eyes. After a while, she stopped and gazed at me dreamily, and said that no one wanted to kiss her. I offered her my cheek, and she pecked me. She had an air of funny innocence about her, lost but not alone, dazed by her surroundings, yet comfortable inside. Most people get trapped by life, stranded, falter and remain stuck. Despite her fragility, as I got to know her she seemed to me unbreakable, quietly determined, in search of destinations, and that's what made her different. She was nervous, but not afraid, not jaded by the immensity of life. Confused, sure, we all are. But she wasn't afraid. That part of her was palpable.'

'Was she with anyone else?'

'Not that I noticed. No. I don't think so.'

'And what happened next?'

'It heated up. Full tongue kisses and her eyes go into slits like the girls at school used to.'

'Where was she?'

'On top.'

'I meant, where was she when the party got going?

'Oh, as I told you before, over by the pool. She was drifting among the revelers; we all were... She gazed at me and waded through them like in a dream, but she wasn't high. She didn't do drugs. Not even the soft stuff. – Detective?'

'Yes?'

'What is she after? Is it the experience, to test the limit, to try and push the envelope?'

'How do you mean?'

'She told me she had a lot of men that night, but only one orgasm. She never seemed to care that much. - Detective, do you think it mattered to her?'

Forester shrugged thoughtfully, and wished he had that beer now. 'Who knows...'

'It's not like a one-on-one affair, a relationship, something you can build on. Do we fuck like that because we're sad, because we fear, because it's a crazy world?'

He pondered thoughtfully and replied: 'Who can say...'

'Those days are over for me. Lust unchecked exhausts you. Sure, there's a lot of cynicism out there, but you have to look at yourself before judging others, and weigh up your own reality before you trouble with the crowd.'

'That makes sense.'

'Love is always there. You can screw yourself up, but not love, not respect. They remain. Even if you get washed up in the gutter, you know what you've lost, and it breaks you.' He paused, and reflected at length. 'Detective.'

'Yes?'

'When you find her, tell her she showed a man how to love; she taught him the value of self-respect; and to me she'll always be an angel.'

'I will.'

'And, Detective, one last thing.'

'Yes?'

'You can take a risk, and have a multitude of sins, so long as they don't break you.'

'Thanks for the advice. I'll remember that.'

And closing the door behind him, he left.

*　　　　　*　　　　　*

Frank brooded alone at the bar for almost an hour, declining to join Nick and Vonnie when they went into the restaurant for a meal.

'I'd rather wait for Roy,' he said.

'Forget him.'

'I'm not really hungry. You know me, Nick,' he said, 'I can't eat unless I have an appetite.' He managed a grudging smile, and tapped his glass signaling to the bartender he wanted another. 'Don't worry, Nick, I'll join you later.' He looked at his wristwatch. It was past three and he was working the time, although it was futile, but doing it quietly to himself.

Vonnie opened the menu and the waiter lit the candle. Nick watched the flame flicker in its glass ball as she ordered salad and sushi.

'Don't worry about him,' she said, unraveling the anxiety on his face. 'He'll win.'

He showed her a puzzled look. She laughed.

'Hard Eight. It's his game.'

'I had something else on my mind,' he said. She asked him to explain. He spun a tale of work-related woes, of the financial markets tumbling and leaving them short.

'It'll pass,' she said consolingly, touching his hand, embracing it with her own. She could see it was something else and felt the urge to probe, but resisted. 'I sometimes play poker,' she said. He smiled. He didn't know that. 'Not for money; just to understand the game; the attraction... To understand men.' And what did she discover? 'It depends on your hand,' she squeezed his hand. 'On the luck of the cards,' she kissed his cheek. 'On whom you are playing.' She lifted her glass, and drank. 'The answers come in droves, all vying to be believed,' she spoke deeply, her thoughts resonating in her words.

'Poker is just a game.'

'A *game*?'

'Yes,' he said, 'a game.'

'Understanding that is the most important thing of all.' She gazed as if searching for that sense of him which lay behind the cards. People are like a deck of cards - face down. But you must never play the cards: *always play the man.* That is the game. It is the player that invests it with meaning, who teases luck, who toys with the chips, who chances a hand, who antes and bets the whole pot, who *feels* what it really means to play.

Poker is the conduit. People are the journey. And the destination is to win. The friend. The lover. Life.

Ten minutes later events pulled a joker from the pack, and Roy came downstairs with a grin beaming from his face and the fat guy Harry trailing behind, a damp handkerchief in each hand wiping the sweat from his neck and face, and King Stud carrying a briefcase that he never carried upstairs with him. He tapped Harry on the shoulder and escorted him to a separate table while Roy strode in to the restaurant. This parting had the sense of an interlude, and every feature of "Game to be resumed."

'Nick,' said Roy, shaking hands. 'Vonnie.' He kissed her on the cheek. He took a seat. 'I'm going to Paris.'

'When?'

'Leaving tonight.' He glanced at his wristwatch. Still plenty of time. He grinned.

'Have you told Frank your plans?'

'Yes. Where is he?'

'Philosophizing at the bar.'

'We need you to remain here in New York. Vonnie will keep you company. Right, babe?'

'And Frank?' asked Nick.

'Can't keep Victor at bay forever, old chum. Frank will take him on a merry go round.'

'And?'

He shrugged his shoulders. 'We hope for the best.' He looked at Vonnie, who discerned the social code and excused herself, going to the ladies' room. 'What have you told Vonnie about this?'

'What have you told Barbie?'

'Nothing.'

'Likewise.'

'Good. Then let's keep it that way.'

'So what's the plan?'

'Frank learned about Freddy today.'

'He had to know sooner or later. We needed to test Ace. He understands. We needed an expert hacker, and if he knew that he would have behaved differently. You did the right thing, Roy. Don't worry about that. Frank will get over it. Let him sulk a bit. He's a pro.'

'Maybe he thinks we don't trust him.'

'No. He'd act no differently in the circumstances. Just give him a while to grind it though his system. Concentrate on Paris.'

'Freddy advises we confront them and make a deal.'

'What deal?'

'Share the code. Share the work load.' He lifted Vonnie's glass and drank, looking for any diversion to dilute the moment. 'I'll be perfectly honest with you, Nick; I have no idea what I'm doing. This is pure bluff, because we don't have anything to play with. Do we?' He sighed, 'I feel like an utter fool. What am I thinking? What am I doing...?'

'Then don't show your cards until you have to.'

'I have nothing, Nick. Nothing.'

'Even *nothing* is a card. Don't show them it. Keep it in reserve.'

'But this isn't a game,' said Roy intently. 'Nick?'

He pondered a moment, then replied. 'It *is* a game. Yes. That's exactly what it is - a game. And that's how you must deal with it.' He looked around, staring abstractly at things. 'Roy... it's just a game.'

They remained silent until they saw Vonnie approaching with Frank sullenly at her side, and Roy concluded: 'Then let's play.'

They never spoke much, and Frank carried his sense of disillusion to the breaking point and suggested they all go to Paris, ranting that they may as well break the bank there than elsewhere, but after some heated conversation to exhaust his fury and sweat out the resentments from his system, he breathed hard and said, 'OK, it was necessary. But that doesn't mean I like what you did.'

An altercation suddenly erupted at the club entrance; voices shrieked heatedly and tempers became frayed. The tone had a distinctly feminine purr. Just as the kitten alighted from her cab, a luxury limousine pulled up regally and out slides Harry's bimbo strutting her priority with all the pomp and ceremony of a queen, doling out liberal tips to the doormen and assistants that hovered around her like bees to a hive. The kitten caught her breath and shrieked:

'I was here first!'

Their demure postures strain to determine who is the most aloof, and their noses race each other higher to the summit of mutual disdain, and they sneer dismissively at the presumption of the other.

'Did you hear me, *miss!*' rasped the kitten. 'I was here first.'

'OK, *dear*,' chickie-bee retorts, chin to chin, eyeball to eyeball, bitch to bitch.

'Huh!' scoffed the kitten, and she saunters on inside.

Her rival retorts some spiteful but dainty aside and strides in at her ease, with a bevy of busy bees lapping at her every whim.

'What's the matter, babe?' asked Roy.

'That bitch!'

It was a short story, but with the uncanny capacity for prolonging itself at just the wrong time. Roy suffered the passionate distemper of a kitten in a filthy mood, and the frowns of disapproval she aroused from the other diners, so he took her to a separate table a manageable distance from Harry and his bimbo. Harry was in good humor and drinking champagne. His bimbo showered him with kisses and had her nose turned up whenever she saw the kitten.

'Just don't look at them, babe,' said Roy.

'I hate her! I hate her!' she fumed.

A few moments later King Stud appeared and sat down at their table. The kitten, understandably irate, asked him what he meant by inviting himself to a chair.

'Unfinished business,' he said, grinning.

'Go away; you're a bad influence.'

'Well, I try to be,' he said with false humility.

'What does he want, Roy?'

'I'm winning, babe.'

'You won?'

'No. I winning.'

'You see, sweetie,' King Stud cut in, 'the game's not over yet. You have to give the man a chance to win his money back. It isn't poker otherwise.'

'Roy!' she shrieked fitfully at him.

'That's the game,' he pleaded defensively.

'Awwwhhh, Roy,' she cried, 'you said you wouldn't.'

'No I never, babe. Besides, I'm just poking my toe in a bit, that's all.'

'Roy!'

'Five... ten minutes more, max. I promise.'

'Roy!'

'Here,' he reached in his pocket and offered her a couple of thousand and a kiss.

She sighed, smiled grudgingly, pouted fretfully at him, took the money and then looked at her wristwatch. She's timing him already - what a bitch! But he adores her so much he'll tolerate anything. Abuse is sweet when you're hooked on a blond kitten whose purr just takes your breath away.

'I love you,' he said.

'Ten minutes,' she replies.

And an hour later he's still there piling up the cash. But he easily forgives himself, because he's winning it all for her.

Meow!

Chapter 25

Jazz rattles, sound like a spirit's conceit felt but never seen, scratches like a bitch bites you raw like a whore flays you like a punk-slag lashing kicks at the mix of sound roaring like fire that you can't put out, not even with a deluge, hissssss... she blows you away, like a shot in the heart packing power into sound so defiant the meaning crushes like a hammer to the head, a whack instead of a stroke, a scratch instead of caresses... think she's your lover? Nah! Jazz is a hooker giving free lays and you're spent before you can cry *Hey! I didn't mean it* to this whore of a whore whose irre-fucking-sist-i-ble!

And you think you know what love is?

Come on!

That's jazz!

Cue to the club: Hard Eight weighs in at the table, deals, antes up the firepower and still it's a breeze; he's in good hands – his own – and on stage runs an improvised ride on a seamless journey from A to B to C to D... the destination remains unknown and the only certainty is the sound itself: Jazz. It started kicking-in as the lounge melodies were pushed aside and the stage became an animated bustle of lusting spirits in a soul machine whose vibe reverberated with the restless fact of life - enjoy, while you can; party, when you get the chance; let it roll let it roll let it roll, and the good times might just never end. Perhaps... You never know with jazz, you may just get away with the dream.

Ninety minutes later Harry folds and it's all over, bar the sound, which manifestly never ends. At the club entrance fresh customers were haggling for the best tables, while others of those inside were obliged by circumstances to take their leave. Bye bye.

'Frank, where are you going?' Nick detained him by touching his arm.

'To baby-sit Victor.'

Roy gave him the keys to his apartment, the kitten haggled with the cabbie and the doorman to take extra care with the luggage, that they were: 'Foolies, you people are such fiddlesticks and foolies...' and why couldn't they be more careful with the delicate things? It's the same every time, she complained, these people, they never learn.

'I'll be in touch,' said Roy, and the kitten waved them a cute little farewell with her cute little hand and blew them a kiss as the cab pulled away and glided into the traffic stream.

Frank, sulking, took his leave and walked along the sidewalk smoking a cigarette. He never wanted a ride, no thanks, he just wanted to think.

'Looks like trouble,' said Vonnie at length as she drove the car. Nick impassively sat beside her, just thinking, his absent stare floating over scenes beyond the window. To gaze into the world and not see a thing, to incorporate its essence, inside of you, yet not feel a thing. The world is too simple, too beautiful, too... mad to ever comprehend. One had to feel. Mind was the cage, feelings the key.

'Nick, are you OK? Would you like me to stop somewhere?'

'Shall I tell you about it?'

'No,' she said, 'I'd rather not know.'

'Why?'

'Does it affect our relationship in any way?'

'No.'

'You see,' she said, smiling. 'Used wisely, *No* can be such a constructive word, don't you think?'

'I suppose it can,' he wondered, gazing at the sunburst pouring through the breaking clouds, that sooner or later the rain was destined to abate, and the sun, waiting patiently, would dominate the sunset perfectly.

JFK. New York City Airport.

'Just here; pull up over here.' Roy directed the cabbie to a vacant slot at the Departures driveway. The cabbie was conscientious, all smiles and efficiency, alighting with a sprightly bounce and assisting them with their luggage. Roy pulled off a couple of hundred from the mighty roll of dollars he banked courtesy of Harry, and handed them smartly over. 'Harry and his chick-a-bee send you their warmest regards.'

'Excuse me, sir?'

'Keep the change.'

'You're a gent, sir. A real gent.'

'You know,' said Roy, basking in his own generosity, 'some guys seem to have lots of money, but it just happens to have my name written all over it. So what do you do?'

'Ask for it back.'

'You *win* it back.'

'How?'

He beamed proudly and said, 'With style!'

The cabbie laughed. 'You have yourselves a real good time, now,' his voice was full of warmth and friendliness. And the kitten, into the swing of things said, waving delightedly:

'Merci,' like it was the most natural thing in the world. 'Et vous aussi.'

'And some of that too!' he chuckled, climbed into his taxi and pulled away into the warm night of lush air and surround-sound blues with that dizzying smile bearing him into the mighty metropolis of NYC. N and Y and C... She's a homemade apple kind of pie. Take a bite of that, why don't you.

Mmmm....

Sandy moaned all the way to the airport: moan, moan, moan; with her bitching *par excellence* she excelled the car engine with her whining. Unlike a woman scorned, or one given to episodic fits, Sandy was tougher than that. She was a bruiser. She had a hard feminine edge, grinding facts down to their masculine essentials. She resented having to drive Forester to the airport. In her mind this added manly insult to feminine injury. It was a gender philosophy. Basically – sex.

'Am I your chauffer as well now?' she complained.

It was prudent to let her rant, besides, feminine steam must flow; sexually-dynamically it's a horny hurricane in the making, drama from a puff of femme-air. Just let the *old* air out of the *bag*, and soon this will all blow over. Besides, he grew tired of apologizing; it wore him down. How many times can he say *I'm sorry?* Sometimes, simply saying *fuck you* is a real blessing. Especially to a woman! *Particularly* to a W O M A N. Sexual bitterness bites - ouch! - and he wouldn't mind the flirting, only...

'We're running a bit late, Sandy. Can you hurry it along, please?' As soon as he opened his mouth he knew he'd put his foot in it – a massive boot to boot, size 50 at least, a real guy-size boot. Her reaction was swift and (being a woman) *exactly opposite* of what he intended. Pulling over to the hard shoulder she turned and confronted him. At this critical juncture, Pop kicked in with a rage: *Son, tell that bitch to shut her trap and move it. Grab her by the hair and throw her out of my car...* Forester stared passionately, but it was in vain. Sandy, fuming, couldn't get her words out; they must have been fifty feet thick and weighed fifty tons and expunging them from her throat an unbearable toil. She really needed about a thousand mouths with a million tongues to say what she wanted to say. And all superfluous. Every last syllable. But women... men still love them to death! And with jealous green rage exploding over her red inflamed face and sulfurous bile bubbling up within her. Tones do wonders for a woman, he thought, if only she would...

'Drive. Please, just drive.'

'Screw you, mister!'

'What the hell do you want from me? I'm just doing my job.'

'You cheat! You pervert! You freak in frogs' clothes!'

Son, Pop cut in incensed, *put a plug in that bitch's mouth. Ram it down her throat. I'm not standing for any more of this. Goddamn it!*

'Look, Sandy,' he tried reasoning with her, 'only one of us can go. You know that.'

'But why must it be you?'

'Must we go over this again? I speak French. I was assigned. I suggested it and, finally...' he almost put his foot in it again, but tied up his bootlaces instead and had the savvy to keep his mouth shut.

As a person Sandy can safely be characterized as resourceful (a tyrant?) persevering (thick?) a fighter (a man?) persistent (a bully?) and shyness she regarded as indignity: she's a cop, goddamn it, NYPD, a jealous bitch for sure, and not bad on the looks front - in fact, a great piece of ass for a cop - but she was a pro; all the way. With those fetching looks she can never be one of the men – but she's one of the guys. To subvert her femininity was a crime. And she knew, that the greatest power in the world as a cop, is flirting with a man's cock. And she's the one with the handcuffs! So, she glanced briefly at her wristwatch, and then at the clock on the car dashboard synchronizing the two. Suddenly, there was an all-points broadcast for a stolen car racing down the freeway towards JFK. Sandy, instinctively, was about to respond (A cop? Yeah, she's a cop; packing her gun, getting into her stride, the *Don't screw with me* frown, the *You're nicked, asshole!* growl. It kind of defines the essence of the masculine myth as all balls and fury signifying pussy).

'Leave it for the uniforms,' said Forester. 'Just get me to the airport. Please, Sandy,' he offered a peace-smile. 'Pretty please...'

A moment later she started the car, pushed it into gear, looked over her shoulder, pressed the accelerator and pulled away into the traffic stream, holding a speed of over a hundred with flashing lights and sirens heralding their swift advance. This *theatrical* gesture was perhaps testing him; but he kept quiet and just counted down the miles. Sometimes, you do the simplest things, even if you resent it, even if you hate it. Just bide your time certain in the knowledge that the tension cannot be sustained, and is a passing feature of the moment.

He alighted at the Departures Terminal and she stayed in the car, lowering the window. 'Is that all you're taking?'

'I travel light,' he said. 'Less to worry about.'

'Makes sense, I suppose.'

He smiled, 'OK.'

She smiled back, couldn't resist really, and held out her hand. He never shook it - that would be too formal - but held it intimately, warmly. 'You can be a real bitch sometimes,' he said.

'I know,' she grinned, with a measure of innate pride. 'I take after my mother.'

'OK.'

'Call me.'

'As soon as I get settled in.' He let go of her hand. And she waited until he passed through the entrance, mingled, and then vanished among the crowd.

*

'Roy, Roy, I want the window seat, Roy.' The kitten cried out excitedly, elbowing her way to the front of the queue. The kitten proved fastidious, insisting on a seat with the best view. When it was aired, politely, that during night flights there was little of interest to see, she responded as only a cat would:

'There's always the moon. Besides,' she concluded, 'I'd always rather have the best. Wouldn't you?'

Naturally, no one had a counter argument to that, and the several discerning grins endorsed her view. She was really rather witty as well as pretty and perky and full of ginger; and gals like her always bring a smile to your face. Well, it's the sex really:-).

Taking their boarding passes, they strolled, arm in arm, into the Departures Lounge, and the bar, where they ordered champagne cocktails.

'Roy.'

'What is it, babe?'

'That man over there keeps looking at you,' she said curiously. 'Do you know him?'

'Who?'

'Him.' She swung her glass round and pointed with her cheery at the man, and Forester, interpreting her action as a gesture, raised his own glass of beer in return, taking a sip as Roy turned to see and choked when he caught sight of him, almost toppling from his seat. Forester grinned coyly, mouthed something humorous, and at length alighted from his stool and strolled over to them.

'Mr. Riemann,'

'Detective.'

They shook hands. 'I wondered if it was you, but didn't want to intrude. May I?' He took a seat and smiled at the kitten, who asked him if he was there to arrest someone, and wouldn't it be exciting if he was.

'Sorry to disappoint,' he said. 'I'm off to Paris.'

'Gosh!' she exclaimed, biting deeply into her cherry. 'So are we.' She smiled, chewing excitedly. 'Are you going to arrest someone over there?'

'One never knows,' he grinned softly. 'Cheers.'

Roy could barely bring himself to drink, let alone utter anything.

He continued staring with suppressed astonishment, blinking hard several times to convince himself that this damn grinning cop who had been dogging him for days, presently sat at the same table contentedly drinking beer and waiting to board the same flight for Paris. And he was enjoying it! This pushed coincidence too far for Roy's gaming instinct to bear. He shuddered superstitiously, fearing what to expect next. Forester's presence jarred with everything positive he could imagine.

Forester began affably, 'So, what's the purpose of your trip, if you don't mind my asking?'

The kitten, her smooth, cute mouth just getting into its stride, and on the verge of offering a perfectly plausible, if more than a little self-flattering, explanation for their journey, suddenly found herself dwarfed into silence by Roy who panicked and burst out:

'We're getting married.'

The kitten was struck speechless and gazed with amazement. 'Roy!' she gasped. 'Roy!' She was in awe. 'Roy!' And for once, even she was speechless.

The timeless look of surprise, emerging on a man's face, is like art made perfect for a woman's heart: a masterpiece to get her paws on, to sharpen up her nails, and either to scorn or bask her triumphs in. And Roy, feeling gutted, gave substance to the unique male talent of putting his foot right down his own throat: a boot, size 50 plus, sole and all. And it went all the way down. He felt as if all the wind had been knocked out of him and gazed dizzily into the kitten's glowing eyes, wet with happiness, who naturally couldn't see even a smidgen of sorrow in him, but read his daze as the shudders of love and kissed and hugged him passionately, overjoyed and overwhelmed at this '... Most wonderful surprise, Oh Roy!'

Forester sighed approvingly, even looking on a little bashful, and lavished them with congratulations. 'I think this deserves another round of drinks. What shall we have?'

'Champagne!' cried out the kitten, blushing with pride. And so champagne, with a side dish of the reddest cherries, it was.

Chapter 26

Looking from the street up at the 22nd floor, NBS Tower, western face, Frank could see the lights of his office dimmed to a shade of privacy. It was dark in there, and it was just after 10 p.m. It couldn't be the cleaners unless, of course, they were screwing on the quiet (Frank laughed fatuously at his own joke. Sign of slob, that, but still, it seemed funny, so ha ha ha, he had himself a jolly old chuckle). Consequently, if it wasn't the cleaners cleaning up in the sexual positions (scissors, missionary, doggie, it's all work! hell of a slog...) it could only be Nick, he concluded quietly as he strode into the building.

The security guard was watching football on TV and passed him through with a shrug. Frank shrugged back and pressed the elevator button. Ping! The doors glide open, "*Hi there...*" chirps a simulated voice with a toneless pitch to match from surround sound speakers built into the elevator walls: "*What floor would you like? Please speak clearly.*"

'Take me to heaven,' Frank replied sarcastically, 'all the way up, mister.'

"*I'm sorry, I didn't quite hear that. Could you repeat that, please?*"

'Fuck you,' he retorted, being a man much too sensual to engage in repartee with a goddamn machine, and he pressed the 22 button instead, pouring scorn on the machine designers as clever little dicks, oh yes, clever little dickies eager to be witty, desperate to be cool, the *Hey, look what I can do: make a machine talk. Cool, hey?...* mindset. That's pure cliché with a dick, that is, and it makes men seem nonsensical. A hard-on endeavor, always trying to be sooooooo clever. However, on reflection, the designer may well have been a woman, in which case the f-word would need a good deal more meat on it. Something like *fffffffffffff* you, sweetie. *"I'm sorry, I didn't quite hear that,"* she'd say in her soft metallic way. *"Would you mind repeating that, please?"* *ffffffffff* you, sweetie. *"Mmmm, please..."*

Thirty seconds later the elevator coasted to a stop: *"Twenty-second floor. Doors opening. Have a nice day..."*

'Up yours!' Frank groaned as he turned into the corridor, walked routinely past several doors and a security guard on patrol. 'Hi there.' 'Hi.' 'You're working late.' 'Yeah.' 'They pay you overtime?' 'I hope so.' 'Is it worth it?' 'Sure.' 'Swap jobs?' 'No.' 'Thought not.' 'Well,' said Frank, 'it's become a habit.' 'I guess it has.' 'Goodnight.' 'Night, night...' and Frank entered his office.

'Hi, Nick.'

No answer. Not even a shrug of welcome.

'I got tired of babysitting Victor.'

Still no answer.

'He's out cold. Roy was right. But still, he flies off to Paris and leaves us with the headache. Nick..?'

No answer.

'I thought you might be here.'

Finally, a twitch of recognition.

'Nick, what are you doing?'

Nick, absorbed in something before Frank arrived, stirred gently, but only to massage his neck, his concentration fixed on something. Dim lighting about his desk fused into the nebulous glow from monitors casting shadows of grey metallic tints into the surrounding space. It seemed surreal, this gorgeous grey, almost tangible as Nick, moving his head a fraction when Frank complained about the dark and who, without consulting Nick, proceeded to switch on all of the lights. Frank's actions betrayed his vulnerability: he was a man beset by doubts and teased by intrigues he despised, and the bane of his nature is to express everything and hold nothing back. Some men carry their woes in public like a frown, others like a smile, yet others are ashamed of them and hide the fact, while Frank, well, he was given over to rash complaining for the sake of it.

'Nick, maybe I should go back and watch over Victor. What do you think?'

No answer.

464

'What are we doing here? It's pointless. – Nick...'

Lumbering with the weight of anxieties, he felt the same problems as Nick, but lacked the patience to unravel them. He had the yearning for instant answers, solutions at the press of a button, like a trade. His was a transaction mentality that presumed the possibility of things being always on tap, whenever you want, however you want - buy, sell, trade, an existence based on deals, cutting a deal, making the right deal. If only life's meaning could be bought... credits, debits, the heart and soul of the world. If only. Silly little if. Lame if. Frank was vulnerable because he was weak; and being clever, and lucky, did nothing to offset this. He couldn't trade his way out. He wanted to buy, but God wasn't a seller. *No deal!* And yet, he never felt *tested*, the way that tragedy tests men. He was more comfortable with farce. Cynical laughs. That figures. In his mind, it was just one of those things to bear and moan about, like a toothache.

Some men tackle a problem as though they were having a smoke, and so he tried lighting a cigarette to ease his problems away, puff at a time, but the spirit weighs heavy on a dispirited mind, and his woes seemed to weigh a ton. That's OK; men can bear it – what breaks them are not woes but self-pity and self-loathing. And Frank drew dangerously close to that threshold, giving himself a hefty push with his groaning: 'Nick, do you understand what Roy is up to? I mean, *really* up to? I think it's crazy. - Nick, are you listening to me? What is he trying to prove? It's crazy. Nick...? What are we going to do? Nick?' None of this seemed to register with Nick, there, stooped over his desk intently studying some papers, plunged in a strange, unshakable fixation. 'Did you hear what I said? Nick..?' Frank raised his voice. 'Nick?'

'It's uncanny.'

'What is?'

'They even seem to know what we were thinking.'

'Thinking?'

'Are they psychic?'

'Who?'

'Them.' Nick gazed at him oddly. 'The alias was coincidental, right? We just happened to mint it at the time. That's all we did. It has no *real* significance, has it?'

'What are you talking about?'

'The name.'

'What name?'

'The alias, the nick-name...'

'Nick!' he fumed, curiosity grating away at him. 'What is it?'

'We received an email.'

'From who?'

'From them. About an hour ago.'

'I'm going to explode in a minute. Just spit it out.'

'They sent us a message.'

'Who?'

'Tom.'

'Tom who?'

'Peeping Tom,' he said, and Frank shuddered. 'It's a message from Peeping Tom. That's what they call themselves. Can you believe it! How could they know? It's impossible.'

Stunned by the threat of surveillance, of being spied on, probed apart by someone out there, lurking invisibly amid shadows, encrypted in information streams pushing feelers into everything, in loops of cable networking the world - there, where is there, a foot away, a million miles away, Paris? Was that where *there* was?

'Peeping Tom...' Frank whispered anxiously. 'What did they say? Is it a *they*, Nick? Is it a him? A her? What the hell is it?'

'It's a riddle written as a poem. - Here, look.' Nick passed him the hardcopy and Frank studied it before reading it out:

'Ice blue; is warming to you.

Cool red; is derivatives led.

Cold green; on the turn of a queen.'

They waited quietly, nervously, fearing everything in the room, wondering if this very moment someone was watching them, listening, probing, downloading their private world and encoding everything into pixels and bits. The menace was intangible, invisible, impalpable – it was informational; pure data. Even their own fear was pure data, eye-to-eye, instinct-to-instinct, connecting them.

Confusion riddled them, each one suspecting the other and even their own selves, wondering: *Did they take the bait? Are they the bait? What is the bait? What the hell was going on? Boo!*

Despite the stillness of the room, where nothing stirred but the dim hum of machines, it seemed to grow quieter before Nick broke the silence and, taking back the hard copy, read out the riddle again, only more boldly.

'It's a deception,' Frank speculated defiantly, beating back his doubts. 'It's too absurd. What else can it be? It's absurd.'

Nick shook his head soberly. 'I thought that at first. It was just too ridiculous to be anything else. But now I think it's a signal.'

'That's crazy!' he cried, then whispered: 'Why would they do that?'

'Think about it,' he began, having considered the question in depth. 'We're not meant to know, are we? And yet Peeping Tom has let out his secret. Why would he do that?' He waited for Frank to answer, but only imponderable doubt colored his face with a frown. Nick continued, 'Someone is telling us that they poked their finger right into our eye, and we never noticed, even though we were looking, and they knew we were watching them.' He sighed incredulously: 'Why give that away? Why give anything away, especially that? Would you? No.' He shook his head warily. 'There's something very odd at work here, Frank. This means something.'

'We have to inform Roy.'

'I sent him a message,' he said, falling silent and fondling the hardcopy which, for some uncanny reason, handling it secured him some vague comfort, like holding the weight of an echo, or a whisper. 'In any case, it doesn't matter a jot where you are. You could be on the Moon, you could be sitting next to Peeping Tom himself having a drink at a bar. It's not *what* you know; it's what you *do* that matters. It's the verb, not the noun. They know everything we know, so all advantage lies with them.' He rose from his chair, fracturing the tension. 'I need to think.' Walking around the room, he felt less constricted as he sieved the pieces in his mind.

Frank asked him for the hardcopy, and reread the riddle. 'What does it mean?'

'*Ice blue.*'

'The guy in Paris?'

'Yes. I suppose so.'

'Why blue?'

'Maybe he's angry; maybe he's sad, and he's feeling blue.'

'OK... OK...'

'*Is warming to you...*' Nick continued.

'Perhaps he wants to cut a deal.'

'What deal? What do we have to bargain with? Nothing.'

'Then he's on to us.'

'Come on, Frank, he's always been ten steps ahead.'

'Bastard!'

'Perhaps he's changed plan, altered strategy, whatever that was.'

Frank shrugged gloomily. 'It could mean anything. Anything.'

'Perhaps he's improvising; making everything up as he goes along. Or maybe he's waiting for us to act; to make the first move.'

'Or a mistake. – Sometimes it's better to wait it out. Do nothing.'

'That's not typically you, is it, Frank?'

'I know,' he said anxiously, indicating the riddle, 'but neither is this. I can understand a game, Nick - but this? What does it mean? Where is this leading? It's not just unsettling, it's sinister. – It has me spooked and obsessed, and that's what's torturing me.'

Something spontaneous, some emotional swell of a strained mind, suddenly ruptured, and Nick began to laugh, a fitful chuckle more reminiscent of deep anxiety than pleasure. His feelings came tumbling out in a flood, and the giddy sensation yielded not relief but a dazed, floating mind, like a cocaine fix unhinged from present troubles and able to glean events from a clearer, deeper vantage, stripped of intrigue and the battles that macho egos are quick to instill in things. Reading the message of life had to be conducted simply, without the thousand skins of self-deception to riddle you with surprise or disillusion.

It was now perfectly clear to Nick there was no possible way forward without first taking a step back. He couldn't fail to glimpse, in his emotional amalgam of tension and suspense, the whole affair as a ludicrous but sinister game hinging on the conceit of someone with a talent for breaking another's will, for manipulating the human condition and destroying their resolve. The will's greatest enemy was not a monster, but a comedian - not the Ace or a King, but the Joker in the deck of cards. Nevertheless, he pressed on:

'*Cool red.*'

'My favorite color,' Frank looked more confused than ever.

'Red. That signifies... what?'

'A danger signal, perhaps.'

'Perhaps.'

'Or a warning.'

'And yet it seems like he's reeling us in.'

'I feel like a blind fish about to bite into the wrong bait.' Frank sweated it out. 'There are some incredibly smart guys out there. And you're never as clever as you think you are.'

'*Is derivatives led.*'

'He's locking us in to his trading program.'

'Or using us for bait. They're not fools. They know everything we know.' The ramifications continued to mount. It began to feel more like a task than a game, more a secret to uncover than a prize to be won. The foil was this – they were inevitably drawn to temptation. The desire to know. Everything seemed so easy to follow, yet indecipherable. And the sense of being so close to the source, yet so far from the light, made temptation grow in them. It is the light they never see that shines the brightest. And imagination is an eye the size of the world. Nick continued:

'*Cold green.*'

'*On the turn of a queen.*'

'Cold cards. Someone's been getting cold cards at a card game, perhaps. Ice may have lost some games. Think about it, Frank, he gambles, he plays cards, and he had a run of bad luck; a losing streak. It's not unreasonable for that to happen. He was dealt cold cards. Look how Roy behaves when that happens to him. It's possible. No one's luck can hold out forever.'

'And cold green?'

'Green... Greenbacks? It could be a reference to dollars, right? Maybe he lost a lot of money.'

'It's a pity Roy isn't here,' Frank groaned. 'It all feels very murky to me. I understand seedy. But this is intellectual seediness. I'm not used to that.'

'A queen symbolizes sovereignty, right? Power. A leader. Let's speculate a little here. Let's assume Ice played a game of cards for some really hefty stakes, and for some reason he overplays and loses

469

to someone in power, someone in authority. He could be seriously compromised by that.'

'And where does lead us?'

'I'm just thinking aloud, that's all. The queen signifies power over others. Even arbitrary power. That's scary.' Nick wrestled with the possibilities. 'It is feasible, I guess.' He gazed at Frank, who looked gloomy. But Nick wouldn't give up. 'What else could it mean? Green... Greenback... It *is* feasible.'

'You know what I think, Nick?'

'What?'

'Money is the poison everyone drinks, and wants to drown in.'

'You're a philosopher all of a sudden.'

'Well, if you knew someone blotted out of existence, murdered, it would make you think of the strangest things. And this message from Peeping Tom is strange. What's the connection?'

'Is there one? What are you getting at?'

'The queen of diamonds, and the joker.' Frank glanced at the time and wondered aloud, 'What's the worse that can happen?'

'We could be wrong.'

'That figures...' he sighed. 'It's getting late.'

Nick massaged his forehead. 'This riddle has many layers. Do you see what Peeping Tom might be up to, Frank? He's loaded the riddle with peculiar meanings; features we can identify with; clues that reveal as much about us as it hides about them. He knows what we would understand; our habits; our lives' vocabulary; what comes to us naturally. Gambling, especially card games like poker. Banking. Trading. Hierarchy. Everything is running in parallels.'

'But why write in riddles and rhymes?' argued Frank. 'What's the point? If he knows we know... what's the point? It's just stupid.'

'Plain language makes a perfect point, I agree. You can't beat simplicity.'

'And so?'

Nick answered with a feeble shrug, glancing briefly at the clock as he returned to the trading screens and followed the closing numbers in Europe and the Middle East. His thoughts, however, still obsessed with Peeping Tom. 'What's the point? I'd say he was covering his back in case he stumbles. Perhaps he's just hiding behind the rhymes, as kind of prop. Besides, maybe he's not really sure about us.' He turned abruptly and involved Frank: 'Who would you trust, if you started such a thing; you set it in motion and it began to unravel, and not because of technology, but human folly?'

'And that's what you think – it's unraveling?'

'No. I'm just guessing. It's just a possibility. I'm running with a hunch.' He chuckled whimsically, 'I picked that habit up from that cop Forester who kept snooping around.'

'Please. Don't remind me.'

'I give it fifty percent the message is a valid signal. A *strong* fifty.'

'Fifty percent?'

'A *strong* fifty. That seems reasonable in the circumstances.'

'But why use a riddle?'

'Perhaps he has a sense of humor.'

'Ha ha,' he groaned. 'Try laughing at that.'

'Peeping Tom wants to connect. That's a *strong* fifty.'

Frank took out a coin and spun it. He willed heads but it came up tails. He turned it over with his hand. 'Fifty percent is good enough for me. Should we send back a message?'

'I've been thinking that over.'

'And?'

'What should we say?'

'Let me try something,' said Frank, folding the hard copy away into his pocket. 'I have an idea. I have my own card game; and something else up my sleeve. And I'm going to pull Victor in.'

'As what?'

'As the joker in the pack. You said so yourself: it's what we *do*, not what we say?'

'Go ahead. I've hit a brick wall anyway. But we need to inform Roy in case it backfires; he has to know. We need a consensus on this. – Are you leaving already? You just got here.'

'I want to be back before Victor wakes up.' He started with haste, though that haste had precision and purpose. 'Besides, I have a few things I need to do. - I need a clean computer. Is there a spare notebook around here?'

'Here, take mine.'

'Keep your phone line open,' he said. 'I'll be in touch.'

She was reading a glossy magazine, glass of white wine at her side, the bottle kept chilled in a silver bucket of ice, and the breeze of a lush Manhattan evening tickling her arousal. Her fingers clipped the pages over, letting them sink into the polished folds to a soft landing on page ninety two, there, the advertisement for evening gowns, displaying chiffons and silks and oh so expensive, so pleasing accoutrements, a lavish accommodation to the rich that where mass brands are the lynchpin of the working masses, counterfeits the necessity of the poor, for the rich it was all of a singular piece. You buy, you consume not out of need, nor even of pleasure, but at your fancy, humoring a mood, feeding a whim, taking it all in your stride, like turning a page. She picks up the phone, makes a call, orders an outfit. 'Hi, Shirley, it's me, Vonnie, I want...' And what she wants she gets. She has the money. And when she hangs up, everything is done.

This woman is the embodiment of superior style, the physical delight in enjoying a cigarette, nipping it delicately with her lips, held between her fingers on the cusp of a V balanced delicately as if the world hung upon the lightest drag and softest exhalation. In her hands a cigarette is all part of a piece, a movement like a clock seductively in tow to the seconds of a timeless time, ticking away into the effortless sublime. For her, luxury flows as the indispensable part of the air she breathes, as the notes of a nightingale flirting with the sweetness of paradise. Perhaps, in a sense, she is the ultimate Buddha.

The tranquility is broken only when the rustle of keys, and the abrupt closing of a door, disturbs her inner peace.

'Nick, I'm out here.'

He crossed the hallway and through to the lounge, throwing his jacket on the sofa as he passed, loosening his tie, smiling when he finds her out on the balcony and embracing her hand before moving down to kiss her.

Her cigarette sat idyllically on the ashtray, burning down serenely to its stub. A cigarette is like a pet, in some enchanting peculiar way. It kind of kept her company.

'Is everything OK?' she said.

'Don't ask,' he slumped down in a chair opposite her.

Her eyebrows lifted like cats' ears, and he turned to her, then the wine, and then the view of the park in the distance, then her again.

'Roy's gone to Paris,' he said.

'I know.'

'He's getting married.'

'What!' she shrieked.

He looked at her with composed surprise, and reached smoothly for her wine and drank. It tasted wonderful. Chilled wine and the Manhattan skyline together tasted wonderful. Some things blend perfectly, and the cocktail is intoxicating.

'You're kidding me!' She pressed him: 'To the bimbo?'

'Her name's Barbie.'

The idea seemed so utterly preposterous to her she laughed out loud and said scornfully: 'Men have no idea at all, do they? No idea. You are so *totally* testosterone. Nothing but *thick*, overheated testosterone.'

'I think she's sweet. Give her a chance, Vonnie. Get to know her. You're not being fair. And she means everything to Roy. He's a different man since he's known her. Can't you try and be even a little bit happy for them?'

'Give me back my wine,' she snatched it from him hotly. 'Get your own, you testosterone junkie.'

'What's the matter with you now? They're getting married, so what?'

She looked at him hard and refilled her glass. 'If anything proves the point, this is certainly it. Men are not fit to make life decisions. They should seek the counsel of their mothers.'

He was on the verge of telling her she was crazy, but mindful of her temper wisely desisted. Besides, he was too hot and bothered with more pressing matters to take it any further.

'I'm going to take a shower,' he said, grumbling.

'There should be showers for the male brain, that semen-soaked organ of yours, and freezing bloody cold, to quench the testosterone from your system,' she thundered. 'And men should take one at least *ten* times a day. *Before* midday! *Every* day!'

473

Somehow, by relating this news he struck a raw nerve, teeming with jealous blisters, and once exposed she unleashed her venom. Although she continued to cut a picture of self-control, she felt vulnerable. But a woman in passion needs room to burn, he concluded quietly to himself, kicking off his shoes in the lounge, but she saw this and badgered him not to leave any clothes or footwear there.

'I'll throw them in the trash!'

She sounded like she meant it, actually, *as if she would enjoy doing it*, so he prudently picked them up together with his jacket and cried out defiantly: 'I'm not the only one around here who needs to cool down.'

She turned moodily to her cigarette, meaning to take it up and resume smoking, but noticed it had burned down to the stub, reduced to a frail pillar of ash. She considered a moment whether to light another, rousing briefly to do so but then suddenly stopped and took stock of the situation. Ever self-conscious of her appearance, she knew she must have looked frayed, and even a touch ridiculous, so she closed her eyes and, like the Buddha, counted to twenty in slow continuous steps. By the eighth turn, she was on her feet. By twelve, she was naked. By fifteen she joined him in the shower. And by twenty she blessed testosterone as the wonder drug as she came frantically and clutched him with such overpowering passion as though she would explode.

'Again,' she said, kissing him madly. 'Again.'

During nightfall, when they were in bed, he remained obsessed with the message that Peeping Tom had sent them. He wanted to tell her, but could only hint at his troubles in the abstract. Vonnie could sense something troubling him, but pressed him no further than to suggest he take a nap and worry about it tomorrow. She would rather wait for him to tell her in his own good time, and voluntarily confide in her – give him space, and let him bridge it - for that way, a man shows himself willing to share his power, and bestow his trust. Besides, it was not something in conflict with their relationship, and that mattered most. Prioritizing things, making a choice, it all seemed rational to her, and she preferred to keep things simple. In business, or on the trading floor of a bank, she'd probably be a killer, and end up owning the pot. *Then* the world would really see, who was screwing who.

'How do you play against a ghost, Vonnie? How do you compete against the invisible?'

'You mean, how do you play against yourself and not cheat?'

'Whatever. Yes.'

'Choose a game that won't let you cheat. Chess is no good. But a deck of cards folded face down... Then, even if you had ten identities, none of them would know what cards the other had. Until they all showed.'

That's the beauty of the cards. They won't let you cheat - even against yourself.

'What's the time?' he asked, kissing her.

'It's almost midnight.'

*   *   *

Downtown, in Roy's spacious, elegant apartment, with the lights dimmed to a bare visibility, Frank looked at his wristwatch just as the big hand of the pendulum clock slipped past midnight.

Cue to the mood: quiet, sober, slow motion just a touch above a yawn as Frank stretches out his arms, jerks his head, turns up the lights and pours himself another drink - whiskey with water, lots of water: he needed to think. Around fifteen minutes later the intermittent snoring from the bedroom stopped and the sleeper roused from his long slumber.

Time to face the music. Jazz, of course.

'Where is he?'

'Good evening, Victor,' said Frank. 'Or should I say morning? It's past midnight, you know. But hey, New York City never sleeps. – Would you care for some tea? I was just about to make some. A fresh pot. I'll even put a tea-cozy on. What color would you like: red, blue, yellow? I've even got a lime green... You'd like a lime green, would you, Vic?'

Victor's head ached; the five-point-five caliber burst of pure whiskey hitting the soft spot, as hangover short-circuits the brain and renders him wretched. Then, as the pain subsides, his throat stirs gruffly: 'Frank.'

'Yes, Victor?'

'Where is he?'

'Do you take sugar with your tea?'

'Where's Roy?'

'Paris.'

'Paris! Do you take me for Willy Wonka?' - He looked like the last man in the world about to start singing. Really. - 'Do I look like a dickhead?' Apparently not. God forbid. 'Frank!' That sounded hard, like a gunshot. 'Frank!'

'He's getting married.'

'Married! You expect me to believe any of that bullshit?'

'He's getting married.'

Victor glared at him, the raw rhythm of his breathing taut and agitated, but then suddenly the frantic force of it abated and he mouthed some curt remarks and grinned, his inflexible gaze examining a picture of Roy and the kitten partying at a casino in Las Vegas and holding the pot. That picture meant more to a man than a trophy or a victory. It was Cupid with a greenback smile, Venus dressed as Vegas with the dreamy seductive look that adores a winner; it was intimacy lavished with a buck, of boasted joys that he's a winner and he wants the world to know he won the pot, the girl, and the great big American Dream paraded with a smile flaunting the magnificence of it all. And don't you just love this guy? The picture said it all, and the kitten was as much part of it as he was. - Was this picture, then, incontrovertible proof that it is God who calls the shots, even in Vegas? Was that smile of a winner a stake not only on poker, but on a transcendental desire for greater meaning in a love affair, to share your life with someone? Was it, in a word, religion made manifest in the best flesh around, all blond and a perfect ten? - Nah, he's just one lucky son-of-a-gun, that's all. We'd all do the same given the chance, and Victor appreciated that. Why shouldn't he? He's made of testosterone like the rest of us. What a man! - Well, there is only one kind...

At length Victor spoke, his voice mellowed with irony:

'Shall I tell you something, Frank, old son?'

'I'm listening, Victor? I'm all ears.'

'It's against my better instincts to take the word of a dodgy geezer at face value, especially a bullshitting American one, but I think I probably believe you, old son.' He looked at him and laughed, lighting a cigarette, taking his time. 'Unlikely as it seems, and it stinks like something rotten I'm sure, but this marriage malarkey, well, she's a cute little chicken, and I think Roy's just stupid enough to go through with it. Yeah,' he gazed again at the picture, 'Roy was always a mug and a half. Especially that half...'

Frank grinned and cut in with some hopeful camaraderie. 'Well, you know Roy as well as I do, Vic.' He laughed, trying to humor him. 'Old son-of-a-gun, eh! What a geezer he is. Ha! ha! ha!'

'Indeed I do,' he said. 'And I'm pleased to see you making merry with the fact.' Victor seemed unusually composed, thought Frank, and this made him feel jittery. 'So,' said Victor coolly, stiffening, 'what's going on? Who's got their finger in my pie?'

'That's what we're going to find out, and put a stop to it.'

'I see...' he murmured impatiently, then raising his voice. 'Do I really look like bloody Willy Wonka?'

'Dread the thought.'

'Well!'

'All the client accounts are safe.'

'I should bloody well hope so. Or someone's balls will get added to the pot, mate, with a real dollop of seasoning. - Mark my words!'

'As for the system, we're taken care of that too. We backed up all the data and the code; filtered it for viruses; done all kinds of checks. It's clean. We're safe. There won't be any more poking about. All we need do now is find out who and why. We're on top of things, Vic. Trust me.'

'Ah, I see. And this being the case, with all this hectic activity going on, our *pal* Roy, not content with getting one in whenever he can on the old bag, decides to go the whole damn slog and get himself a ball and chain. And moreover, he heads for the frog capital, because no doubt he's becoming the true romantic sort, and nothing else will do but the land of champagne. I must have the face of a born-again mug! Do I look stupid to you? Am I bloody Willy Wonka? Have I got a lollipop in my hand!' he erupted, clutching his head as the pain surged agonizingly through him. 'I'm losing it, Frank. I'm bloody losing it with you, mate!'

'We shut the system down, Vic. Trust me, there's nothing to worry about. All we're doing is behaving normally. You know: going to work; doing the shopping; taking a vacation; getting married; visiting your mistress; drinking; gambling; whoring... all the normal things we guys do. Especially men in our position. Victor, please,' he tried reasoning with him, 'you have to look at it rationally. Despite what women imagine, we men are rational. We have logic all sized up. It's about six and a half cock lengths in total. I know. We're doing it the smart way. Don't you see? Routine is the answer. Come on... I thought about this a lot.'

'Routine? What are you yakking about now, you knuckle-head?'

'We don't want to attract attention to ourselves, do we? That's the last thing we need. Come on, Vic, look at it rationally. We've got to act normal. Don't you see? You, me, and the rest of the gang. Normal. That's the ticket.'

'But we're not normal, are we? Not normal at all. And you,' he pointed at him accusingly, 'and him,' he referred to Roy in the photograph, 'you two are about as normal as a donkey with a carrot stuck up its arse. - Wrong end, sunshine!'

Frank paused, considered a moment, and said: 'Well, Vic, that's not very flattering.'

'It wasn't meant to be, you dickhead!'

'Well... that's our plan. We've put enormous effort into this, you just can't imagine. And personally, I think it's a great plan. It's well-thought out. And I share some of the credit for that. Yes, that's right. Me.'

'Ahhh...so it's a *plan* now, is it? You clowns, you leave even God breathless with your dumb audacity. That's bold - oh yeah! Very *astute* that is. Oh yeah... God Almighty! If a dick had a name and a dickhead a face, you cretins would be it.' He could hardly believe his ears or restrain himself, but struggled against the urge to lash out, and Frank at length provided him with a summary of the plan. The marriage had a dual purpose: to uncover the French connection and the computer hacker in Paris and disable them at source, while he and Victor would go to San Francisco and do the same, leaving tomorrow. The flights were already booked, and... 'Nick will remain here and coordinate from New York. Trust me, Vic, everything is under control. This plan of ours, it couldn't be sweeter.'

'You know what I'd really love to do?' Victor began stretching out his arms as he moved toward the balcony, sliding open the wall-length windows and going outside into the warm evening air and immensity of Manhattan. 'I want to grab your rotten neck, my son; squeeze it ever so tightly; and toss your slobbering carcass over this balcony and into the gutter. Which, from up here, looks a pretty impressive sight indeed. It's amazing the effect that height has. It dwarfs a man; makes him feel miniscule and vulnerable, wouldn't you say? - Ah, what a beautiful view. What a glorious sight. Come out and have a look, Frank.'

'I'll give it a miss if you don't mind, Vic. I'm allergic to heights. Ahem! It runs in the family. I suffer from vertigo. Ahem! Even as a kid, I got sick on the slide. Funny, don't you think? Ahem!'

'Please, oblige me,' he said. 'I'm taking this all very calmly, wouldn't you say?'

Frank tentatively tip-toed forwards and out onto the balcony, keeping maximum distance from him. He feigned vertigo, but this failed to impress Victor.

'The way to conquer your fears is to confront them head on.'

'That's a real jewel of a proverb. I must think that one through,' Frank stumbled awkwardly with his words and actions, as though on the brink of doing something reckless.

'Proverbs aren't meant to be thought through. They're meant to be lived; experienced; and embraced.'

'You know what, Victor, I could *really* do with a nice cup of tea right now. It calms the nerves wonderfully. And you can't beat a cuppa in a crisis, can you?' He coughed with a nervous chuckle. 'Would you care for a cuppa, Vic? I was just about to boil some water. One sugar, was it?'

'A very sporting idea.'

'Well... you know me, Vic.'

'Yes, I do,' he said, marching firmly over to him. 'I most certainly bloody-well do.' He paused and stared sternly into his face, barely an inch away. 'I am, what you might call, compromised. I have to go along with your so-called *plan*, because I'm snookered and stuck with your little outfit. So, whatever your game, or *plan* as you insist

479

on describing it, is, it had better work. You had better pull the rabbit out of the hat; or I'll throttle the bloody lot of you. Understood?'

'Perfectly, Vic.'

'When someone grabs my plums and tries to make a fruit pie with them, I get a little peeved.'

'Who wouldn't? It's a bloody disgrace,' he said with questionable bluff, which grated Victor's temper. Realizing this, he swiftly grew serious: 'We know what our limits are. We're not trying to be clever. We're coping with a crisis. We push when we can; pause where we must; get help when it's necessary. This is serious, Vic. We know. This is no game. Sometimes, in the rough and tumble of events, that fact becomes obscured, and we're misunderstood. We don't mean to be. Getting it right. That's what counts.'

'And?'

'We're in this thing together. Joined at the hip. One falls, we all fall. No more games. No tricks. All straight down the line.'

'Good. And don't let me see a slip. Or I'll have you, mate! - Now, let me see...' he breathed easier and, although still wary, his temper abated because he knew only time would bring him the answers he wanted. Sometimes, risk is no more than a waiting game. And like all the best dreamers, he was a practical man and got things done. 'Since I've had my seven winks a lot earlier than I intended, and in circumstances I'd rather not recount: Ahem!' he threw him a hard stare, but it swiftly faded. 'I need to unwind. You cowboys have screwed up my mind. I need to think; and I can't do that unless I'm relaxed.' He stretched out his arms and yawned, flexing the muscles of his neck. 'Let's get out of here. This place reminds me of Roy, and I don't want him in my mind just now. That bloke is pollution. Everything I see, smell, touch. Yuk! Let's leave. Let's head into town. I need a breather from all this malarkey.' He turned casually and gazed at the skyline of Manhattan, and felt its million enchantments inspire his yearnings for excitement, for women, for life - the three that equals one. 'It's depressing in here. It's getting me down. I need the three that equals one.'

'I know exactly the place. Leave it to me, Vic. Leave everything to me.' And saying this Frank, heaving a sigh of relief, leapt back into the apartment before Victor changed his mind.

Chapter 27

'I want you to meet a friend of mine,' said Frank, introducing them.

'Hi. You must be Victor?'

'I see...' Victor eyed him warily. 'How did you guess that, I wonder?'

'Frank told me all about you.'

'Hmm...' turning to Frank. 'I see...'

'Victor, meet Frank.'

'What? Another one?'

'Better known as Double Kiss.'

'And why is that, I wonder?'

'Can't you guess?'

'He has double the lips of an ordinary bloke.'

'He plays pool.'

Double Kiss chuckled. 'Well, a bit of hustling here, some hustling there...' For a brief spell he was consumed with grinning. Then, more measuredly, asked him: 'Do you hustle for a living?'

'Only when I have to, sunshine,' said Victor. 'I bet I can guess what you're going to ask me next.'

'Well? Do you?'

'You drive the cue stick in pool; I control the cue stick in snooker. Your game is for hooligans, mate. Mine is a gentleman's game; a skill game. You wouldn't stand a chance.'

'A hundred says otherwise.'

'Make that five.'

'I've got ten money fingers. You care to double up?'

'I can beat you with one hand. Five'll do.'

They shook hands and withdrew into the poolroom where a pool table was already set up. Pairs of players competed at various stages of the game at ten tables neatly lined up in two rows, the rapping of cue balls colliding in the brinkmanship of numbers ranged across the colors of the table as the pockets swallowed them up, and the occasional cheer of triumph as the shot hit the slot setting the ambiance. Double Kiss prepared to spin a coin.

'Heads,' said Victor, just as he spun it, and took up his cue stick eagerly. 'I'll go first.'

A moment later the coin came down heads, but Victor already took the opening shot and the game was in full swing. He became more engrossed in the challenge than he normally would have, seduced by rivalry, tempted by victory. It was just a game, sure, nothing complicated in that. But winning is everything, especially to a man, and Victor was that man, fixated on the challenge: *They may be your balls, mate. But it's my game...* ran the mantra, which felt irresistible to him then. And so, thus absorbed, he never noticed Frank slip away to make a phone call.

'Hi Nick, it's me.'

'It's late. I'm sleeping. What do you want?'

He told him he composed a reply for Peeping Tom, which he read out:

> 'Ante the table,
>> A missing card,
> New deck is unstable,
>> Old habits die hard.
> Way out, way out,
>> Give us a shout.'

'What does it mean?' Nick sounded drowsy and bemused, Vonnie hugging him in her sleep.

'We're raising the stakes,' he explained excitedly. 'One of us is absent, Roy, the missing card; and there's a new man in town, Victor - that's the unstable part. He's rocking the boat. But we're still trying to continue as normal – that's the habit reference. And we want Peeping Tom to make contact. That's the request for him to shout.'

'To shout what, for heaven's sake? Never mind, Frank, I don't what to know.'

'We want to cut a deal, don't we?'

'What deal?'

'You know,' he fretted, 'a deal. Any damn deal.'

'Then why not just say so? Wouldn't it be easier?'

'Most probably, yes. But this whole thing has gotten completely out of hand, and I'm just going with the flow. What am I supposed to do? - Nick, this is where it seems to lead. Doesn't it?'

'What?' He sighed, and then fell silent.

'Nick...'

'Yes; I'm listening.'

'I'm suggesting we make a deal. I'm letting them know we're looking for a way out. That's the right thing to do, isn't it?'

The tempo of deep thought played with deep unease, before stirring with the murmur of breathing, and Nick said: 'I can't see anyone buying it.'

'Me neither. It's a bluff - pure and simple. But else can we do? We're smart guys too, aren't we, Nick? Nick..?'

Nick grumbled and hung up, a part of him simply ceased to care; after all, only time would tell, while Frank pressed on independently and sent the riddle from his phone to Peeping Tom. The network confirmed its reception, and suddenly everything felt irreversible. He shuddered briefly. It would have been more prudent to have agreed this with Roy first, but acting decisively felt more urgent to him then, so he composed a short message to Roy and sent it before returning to the poolroom where Double Kiss was counting out five one-hundred dollar bills to Victor who was grinning victoriously like a cat hugging a barrel of cream.

'You're a gent,' said Victor, full of triumphant smiles, 'and a pretty decent loser for a Yank, I must say.'

'Buy me a drink?'

'No, not really, mate.'

'Typical limey!'

These mutual insults were unmistakably blasé, and seemed natural *stuff* for this kind of masculine repartee. As a matter of fact, they jostled pretty evenly with compliments as a basis of lasting friendship (between men, that is), easily comprehended by a man as pretty normal in a pretty common setting in a pretty routine kind of way. Slurs often carry deeper meaning, and can be really rather redeeming - kind of a guy thing, that. And so they parted company, Double

Kiss flashing Frank a mischievous conspiratorial wink as Frank and Victor headed for the bar. Pretty common ruse - let the other guy win. Pretty irresistible really. Everyone loves a winner, especially the winner himself. Pretty OK, all agree - *for men.*

'Join us later,' said Frank, and Double Kiss saluted him with his cue stick, assuring them that of course he would, just as soon as he won *more* than his money back playing others at *his* own game.

'It's the American way,' said Double Kiss, doubling his smile to wider than wide.

'What is, mate?' said Victor.

'To win.'

See you later...

Inside the bar, the restless boozy atmosphere reverberated with the booms of ten TV screens featuring sports and news and finance: it was a man's world, a testosterone rich environment, the power of hormones everywhere muscling the mood into blunt compliance with manly things, manly time, manly space, the universal mantra of Made in the Image of Man stuff manufactured for the preference of men, yeah, guys, it's all Dionysian splash, and Hercules and Zeus' panache – and don't forget philosophy, man.

Men: the smell, the noise, the pit, a guys' world with girls on a leash, this masculine arrangement of furniture knocked up solidly, put here and there firmly, set in its place, like permanent obstacles to be tackled to visit the mens' room, or find a table, or a quiet corner to make that private call, or immerse himself in booze, alone. And men were everywhere, the few women either waiting tables or hustling for a John to earn some extra bread that night. - But it ain't all pretty, no sir, not here. Men in a bar, you can read the stories on their faces, the languishing lore of their lives, the privations, the agonies, the recurring themes repeating and repeating the same old hullabaloo narrative, the staring-you-in-the-face farce that account for their stay on Earth. Men, restless urbanites, hungry for a life-time yearning not for Nature but a clean break. An even break. But insofar as second chances go, give them a second chance and they'd invariably screw it up again - most of them, anyway.

Normal wear and tear, such as resignation with the run of things, passes as a fact of life, like genes programmed for eternity. Men.

'Frank.'

'Yes, Vic?'

'Get an eyeful of those drinking slobs. You can see their pitiful lives written on their faces; washed-out with beer, stained with tobacco...'

'Are we any better?'

'Excuse me?'

'Perhaps they're a grim reflection of our own deeper selves.'

'Well, who's doing the looking, us or them?'

'Judge not others until you judge yourself.'

He sighed glumly, 'That's a thought, old son. I never looked at it that way before.' He drank some beer, drowning the notion in a wave of alcohol, but like proverbial wind it floated up again in a virtual context. 'I mean, look over there at that mug-a-minute joe and that washed-out bimbo fishing for his jockstrap. Dumb bastard, it's probably where he keeps his money... And his brains too, the little that he has.'

'Yeah...' he concurred at length, 'it kind of makes you stop and think.'

And so they did, observing men in a bar, everywhere thick as a teeming slick of testosterone on a sea of swanky semen, they're mariners through life, these guys, men in a man's bar getting off on slopping around, playing the clown, *ha ha ha*, lifting themselves up by their boots off the ground, (especially when they're not wearing any). Frank and Victor watched them as they maneuvered and jostled and downed booze and yelled out "Hey, gimme another beer, Jack." "Put it on your tab?" "Yeah." "Gotcha!" reflecting on these guys, at the recurring tides of their lives, knowing their stories run and re-run of these boozing bums – it's simple math, do the sums, men in a bar make even Satan envy any one of these guys when he comes. For example, take that sucker over there, his burger-guts bulging over his pants as he orders two beers and is stuck like super-glue beside the cliché blonde with the junkie's eyes:

'Hey there, big guy...' she croaks, her gravelly voice creaking like it's been through the mill a thousand times and more. 'Do you wanna have some fun?'

'Yeeaah!' yaks the John, tied up with his own jock strap. He slams his mouth to the beer and swallows the lot. He doesn't drink it. He doesn't know how to. Just knocks it back straight from the bottle. Then he whistles and croaks, 'Bartender... Hey there, chief...' And orders another.

The readies fly after a fashion, numbers tally the mark as she offers him the menu: one-hundred for the basic; one-fifty teases you till you're nice and warm; two hundred gets you burning.

'What do I get for three hundred?' Jock-strap with a mouth, now he's talking.

'Three?' She's weighing him up, a sucker in her hands: weighs all of a gram; no problem.

'Yeah!'

'Dreams begin at five.'

Smiles galore hug the cry, 'Yeeaah!' He's not squeamish, this guy; just a mug, 'Yeeaah!' like words were lovers, like lovers were language and his tongue slips in and out with rapid ecstasy. 'Ahhh.'

'Time's up, lover boy.'

Suckers. Men, that is. He spaces out a moment then throws down the bills. Five hundred more. She smiles. He gasps. It's not a wet dream, it's a narcotic. Sex.

And it doesn't stop there. Oh no, the whole thing repeats. Everywhere there are men in abundance: Strip clubs; lap dancer bars, sex joints, brothels choc-a-block with willing flesh for the hungry boys to feed on, mistress to please, teeny to tease, yausa yausa yausa, she can shake 'em and break 'em and they'll always come back for more. Morning quickie, mid-day hump, afternoon shag, high-class courtesan in a chic apartment, dingy digs for the bargain hunter, seedy hives for the stalking mob and raincoat brigade, 'Hey, mister, are you looking for some action?' 'How much? 'What's your name?' 'Tom,' ...Dick or Harry it's all the bloody same. Dish out the readies and you get to taste the goodies. Brunettes, blondes, red-heads... 'Blonde. I'll take the blonde'. You want something different? 'Sure'. Nookie in the open. Haven't really lived till you've tried it. 'Yeah. Let's do it.' Sucker! Wife's a bore? He wants to fuck. He wants to talk. He needs someone to understand him. He wants to feel alive. 'Please, God, I want to feel alive, feel needed, wanted, alive!' Where to go? Sluthouse. Whorehouse. Fullhouse. Fairies flock and heathens rock. Punter's after pussy. She slides up and yanks at his sleeve. She wants him? She wants something.

'Do you want me?'

He ogles the meat, flesh is soft, silky, silvery, like a slick limousine cruising the top part of town, downtown, uptown, wham-bam thank you ma'am town. He thinks, but not too hard.

'Let's have a drink.'

'Drink?' She looks at the time, estimating her value in licker and cents.

'Yeah. I'm thirsty.'

'I'll order champagne.' She's pushing it. This girl's ambitious, or impossibly optimistic.

'Nah. Get me a beer.'

He's crude? Nah. He's just a Joe; Joe a minute Joe; geezer with a hard-on, licking his lips, looking at her tits. They're all the same, act the same, screw the same. It don't take a genius to figure out how the story goes. He tries to act cool, but it's a simple rule. Get in on and get it off and get it up and get out. Bang-a-boo. She can take twenty more like him, one, two... at a go! Easy peasy. But where to find the one that really pays?

'Was it good for you?' he asks. 'Did I do it for you?' he moans. 'Huh?' he yearns, in his own little way.

Gimme a break!

*   *   *

'Frank.'

'Yes, Vic?'

'Here comes Double Lips.'

'Double Kiss,' he whispered back quietly. 'He's very touchy about that. His name's Double Kiss.'

'Oh yeah,' he said, lighting a fresh cigarette. 'I forgot.'

Double Kiss pulled up a stool and ordered a beer. 'See anything you fancy?' he asked Victor.

'Quite a bit,' he said, and changed the subject. 'Only Frank and I were engaging in a bit of philosophy.'

'About what?'

'Whoring.'

'Sounds reasonable to me.'

'Men and whoring.'

'I agree, whatever the argument. I agree.'

Victor thought him pretty smug and guessed as soon as he joined them that he won his money back, and probably a great deal more besides, but he never asked, and Double Kiss never volunteered to say, but his demeanor hinted at the same. Frank cut in and fleshed out the conversation.

'We were considering men in general.'

'Yeah,' said Victor, 'pigs and blokes have a lot in common; and I'm not talking bacon, but the carnivorous tendency of your typical punter to eat any old bag, so long as he can get his end away.'

'I see.'

'For instance,' he said, turning to survey the bar, and picking out a punter, 'that one's a chain smoker. He probably fucks the same way, one hooker to the next to forget himself, to dilute his loneliness and pain in a shag.'

'It's a shame, eh?'

'Yeah. But who can resist a shag?'

'Point taken. Cheers.'

'Cheers. And so it all keeps going round and round. Beer, smoke, shag. Beer, smoke, shag... ad infinitum, until the money burns out, and the tap dries up, and his willy wanes – his waxing days are over. He can polish it with his hand, perhaps; but it's not the same, is it? And all that's left him is his rampant imagination and those tantalizing memories of beer, smoke, shag... to while away his remaining days to zero.'

'You know, Vic,' said Frank, sounding grave, 'I think I'll retire.'

'From what?'

He pondered this to himself, exchanging a solemn look with Double Kiss whose grin seemed permanently grafted onto his face, and conceded. 'Good point. I never thought about that. It just seemed like the natural thing to say.'

'Naturally. Smoke?'

'Thanks,' he took one and lit it himself.

'Another drink?'

'Sure, why not. Bartender, same again please; three beers.'

At length, Double Kiss suggested, 'So... how about a woman? Are you up for it?'

'Sure,' said Victor, 'we'll get to that. Let's observe these slobs a while longer. Their agony amuses me.'

'You're cruel, Vic,' said Frank, hiding a smile.

'It comes with being a philosopher. You can't avoid the hard edge. It's all part of the game. Cheers, lads,' he said, gazing into the faces of the crowd, their predictable dramas portrayed in endless flashes: the smiles, the gasps, the grunts, with the fold of every mannerism, how they lean over the table, how they drink their beer, how they laugh, how they banter together, how they piss, a long lazy release into the basin, hit the flush tap, drain it away, and then it's back to more beer, another glass, another pitcher, another barrel, another piss. And sex; sex is everywhere where the mind of man takes root. In a spaceship; in a pigsty; in a bar. Men.

Sex bustles in the cities, driving them around, driving us crazy: London, Rio, Berlin, Paris, Bangkok, New York, LA, Vegas, Riyadh. – *Riyadh?* Come on!

Johnny's about. Nab the sucker. They spill out of the bars and into the streets. Hookers breeze over to the edge of the sidewalk and throw their lines, fishing them in with pantyhose - or is it nets? Never mind. A web is a web, and they're out to get you, sucker!

'Hey, handsome, are you looking for a good time?'

He eyes her up like she's a piece of merchandise. She displays the goods. She's on show. Yeah.

'What do you want?'

'What have you got?'

'What do you see?'

'What do I get?'

'How much you got?'

'How much you charge?'

'What are you after?'

'What do you offer?'

'Depends what you fancy.'

'How long do I get?'

'How long do you want?'

'You got a friend? I fancy a double.'

'Sandwitch! Greedy boy. You got the bread?'

Shakes his head. 'Nah! I'll think about it.'

'Stupid bastard! You think this is the stock exchange? You think I'm cheap? Fuck you. Yeah, fuck you, asshole!' Currencies, metals, livestock, perishables. You trade your cock for what? Your dignity, your ego, your wristwatch? It's a thought. He looks at the time. Habit. Means nothing. Night's still young. Does the mind or the penis rule? Rod or nous? Roman or Greek?

'Hey, mister, you looking for some fun?'

'What do you offer?'

'What's your fancy?'

'How much does it cost?'

'How much have you got?'

…Ad infinitum. History is not cyclic, only feelings are. And feelings drive history in the random swirls and hurricanes of passion. So what is a love affair? What is a man? A hard dick? A soft dick? A small dick? A big dick?

'Hey, dick-head, you looking for some action?'

'What's on the menu?'

'Depends on the price.'

'I want someone to talk to.'

'Talk? About what?'

'About things. Life.'

'I know about things,' she slides up to him, pouting her lips. She hasn't listened to a word he's said. 'I've been around, baby. I can tell you about life. Come to mamma…'

It's an act. It's always an act. They can't act real because their real is an act, and they've lost the sense of reality to practice on, so only misery feels real. Put a price on anything, and it loses its intrinsic value. That's the dilemma of economics, and the agenda of power. It's the bane of a free mind. And the tragedy of the streetwalker and the sulking John who can't get enough because he can't figure out what he's looking for. He values the invisible, monetarizes the affections, when in reality value is not in the pricing mechanism of a buck, or a yen, or a euro. The currency of life, true life, is a wonderful round zero. Zilch! And that, as the wino knocking back the droplets from the empty bottle knows, is all there is. His problem is he copes badly with it. But he's closer to the truth than a whore, or a trader, or a carpenter, or a politician, or the pope, or the other hundred Johns preying the seedy streets for their kicks. I want pussy, he says, I want pussy. Pussy? What pussy? Come on!

'Hey, mister, you got a light?' She throws him the old routine, and winks lustily. Fake? Sure. But practice makes perfect.

'Sorry, I don't smoke.' And he looks away.

'Fuck you!'

It's street cred. It comes with the territory. Sure, it sucks, but what do you suggest he do – turn crazy and wipe them all out? Get real. Grow up. Knock some sense into your head. Go home and read a good book. Get some perspective. Christ! The world's bigger than your loneliness. It swallows you up.

The cab drops him at his apartment, turns around, and glides away. It's a quiet night. A silent night. Nothing seems to stir save his footsteps sweeping across the ground, a grizzly forlorn sound, then up the stairs, dragging it out, and into the apartment. Door shuts behind him. Thud!

'I'm home, honey. I'm home…'

Don't be a wiseguy. Think. Use your savvy. You've just got to make the best of it.

Capisca?

'Victor.'

'Yes, Frank?'

'Like another drink?'

'Sure.'

'Hey, fellas,' Double Kiss cried out excitedly, 'there's Boner over there.'

Frank laughed knowingly and Victor asked: 'Who's Boner?'

'Some guy from New Jersey,' he said, neatly stroking his pockets bulging with cash won at the pool tables. 'He tries... And it's hard... But you can never give a sucker an even break.'

And they all laughed mockingly as Boner left the bar, his head slouched lower than the glum-colored features on his careworn face, dreaming of aces, but hitting the grey deck of a loser.

Boner considered her place pretty decent for a walk-up. Said hello to the cat. Dodged the dog, and into the bedroom. Elena's waiting and hums him a song. Is she a mocking bird he wonders to himself? Nah! She passing the time. 'You got the cash?' chirps the lovely Elena, and the dog (the punter, that is) honks back to the bird. 'Yeah,' and hands over the readies. 'Get ready, then,' she says. So he drops his togs to the floor and positions himself on the bed. 'Ain't you gonna shower, then?' barks she. 'Oh yeah,' he grunts, and howls to high heaven as the freezing water petrifies him whole. 'Ain't you got no hot water then, love?' 'Nah,' says she, 'boiler's gone up the spout. Don't suppose you can fix it, can you?' 'Who me? Nah, love. Got a towel?' She throws him the nearest one she finds, there, lying on the bed. Guaranteed twenty punters have put their arses on that thing today and sweat and God knows what seeped into the soiled fabric. Smells of piss, actually (the things men do - shocking!) but he's too horny to complain and leaps back on the bed. 'You ready?' says she, lighting up a cigarette. 'Yeah,' he coughs, as the dangling poker between his legs stiffens for some action. 'We'd better hurry up, love,' says she. 'I'm going home in a minute.' Suits him up and lubes up herself, the action starts and the wrestling begins. Bong! It's all over before you know it. Merry wonder! 'Hurry up then, love,' croaks she, cigarette hanging from her mouth, it ain't been out since she shagged him. 'I ain't got all night.' Sees him to the door. The dog don't care. The cat don't care. 'Gotta rush. Bye then. See you next time. Take care.'

'Yeah.'

Love in a rush. Where'd it go? He's a mug in need of a beer. Passes a Diner; offers hot coffee and burgers.

'Yeah?' says the waitress by way of midnight greeting. 'What d'ya have?'

'Beer.'

'Ain't got no beer. This is a Diner, not a bar.'

'Burger and a cuppa, then.'

'Sugar?'

'Yeah.'

'Milk?'

'Yeah.'

'Onion with the burger, cheese, and sauce?'

'The lot. And mustard too. I wanna be sick.'

'Well, you've come to the right place.'

He's still horny and feeling dreadfully unfulfilled, imagination and reality clash, as they so often clash and knock back your hopes till feeling jaded becomes the hideous norm. And he'll go home with a bellyful of indigestions. The miss's will croak obligingly.

'What you been up to? Drinking?'

'Cuppa and a burger.'

'Liar.'

'I feel sick.'

'It's your own stupid fault. Get out! Get out!'

Wife. Hooker. What difference does it make?

Nothing, so he may as well hit the circuit and have another lay as he heads out to the city and besides, this time it'll be different. – Why is learning, even with the power of reason, so damn difficult? Because science has yet to master how to teach a man's dick the rudiments of logic. You have to try religion, because a dick is nothing but a double-headed animal. Our man Boner struts into bimboland seeking exotic experiences and believes what he hears, turned on instantly by her name.

Claudette: French (?) with a Tennessee accent (!!!!!!). It's all in the mind, anyway. Those horny bums'll believe anything. A bum believes what he wants to believe. 'Call me princess,' she says. 'Sure,' croaks the punter, and drops his pants faster than a speeding light beam hits the corner of his eye, and he's panting like an eager beaver, lighter by a hundred bucks (plus a twenty tip for princess and ten for the maid. Hey, what about five for the cat and two for the goldfish? Who needs a gold mine when you've got tits and an ass to die for?) Why do men do it? Because it excites them. Hold on a mo, she's run out of rubbers. Maid nips down to the local 7/11 and grabs a couple of fresh packs. 'Care for some flavors, ma'am? We've banana, raspberry, chocolate... but we're all out of vanilla.' 'How much?' 'Ten.' 'Ten?' 'Ten.' 'Nah, (punters aren't worth it) gimme the regulars.' She's got a bit of foresight too and buys some biscuits and soda while she's there, and milk, eggs and some smoked ham for breakfast. It's still early, and princess can take another five more punters before she yawns her little yawn and takes her seven winks.

Make that eight. At least eight. It's been a long night. OK. Next one. 'Are you really French?' the schmuck asks her with his wide gaping eyes. What a gorilla: but it pays. Yeah! 'Whatda ya want, mon-syer?' she asks. 'The grand tour?' answers he, gasping; and she replies. 'Three hundred. And twenty for the maid. And cat needs some grub. Ten; that'll do. And goldfish needs their toys. They get lonely in the tank. Wouldn't you? Five'll do. Get undressed. And oh, by the way, you can call me princess.' He begins sweating early, thinks he's in for a right royal rogering. She spots it immediately; he's going to be an easy one, this. Schmuck! He's priceless. It's princess and priceless. A match made in heaven? Nah... Still, let them have their kicks – as long as they pay...

Maid watches the TV, smokes, and the cat meows. *Shut-up, you fuck!* She tips some milk into his bowl, and sprinkles some fish grub for the fish. Not exactly a menagerie, but it's decent company when that's all you have. Sad? Maybe, but don't you get a feeling society wants it that way? Maid tries pouting her lips like she did in the old days, but it doesn't look good, it doesn't feel right. She coughs and spits up some phlegm. She was a beauty once, she persuades herself gazing in the mirror. She picks at a spot. Actually, she was a plain Jane, just an ordinary slut who had a dream for a month, before it burst and she woke up with some John inside her reeking of booze and having a hard time keeping it up. Why me?

At times, she envies the cat. She wishes she were a cat. Maybe even a Cheshire cat like the one in Alice in Wonderland whose grin is as wide as the world, or so it seems, but all she sees is the disabling, shriveled smirk of contempt on her own face, and reclines in a ragged armchair with her coffee and watches TV. Another game show. What the f----!

Bell rings; next punter hauls himself up the stairs. Gorilla's been drinking. 'Girl's busy,' said the maid. 'But you can wait if you want.'

'OK. Is she French?'

'Yeah.'

'Nice cat.'

'Yeah.'

'Can I smoke?'

'Yeah.'

'OK if I sit here?'

'Yeah. You wanna drink?'

'Yeah. Gotta beer?'

'Soda or coffee?'

'Coffee.'

'Sugar and milk?'

'Yeah.'

And they watch TV together. All three of them, that is, because the Cheshire's grown accustomed to the setting, and dozes in the all-American way by the box watching a game show - seldom answers questions, but meows sometimes when a dummy from Nowhereville on the panel gets a question wrong. Well, at least you can't call him a couch potato (a useless piece of dip-shit, perhaps. But it takes one to know one).

Enough said.

'Frank.'

'Yes, Vic?'

'I'm tired of this bar, looking at all these slobs trapped in their dramas with a hard on. Let's hit the road and find some decent sluts.'

'I know somewhere,' interposes Double Kiss, grinning. 'It's on my way home, I'll drop you.'

'Oh yeah...' Victor looks at him dubiously. 'What is it exactly?'

'A budget fuck.'

'A budget fuck!'

'I've seen it advertised.'

'Hmm... She's probably an old dog.'

'Let's go take a look anyway.'

'OK.'

He took the long route for no apparent reason, and when Victor enquired why he laughed and answered that he must have got lost, besides, it's killing time, and wouldn't he like to cruise around New York City in a swanky new car and see the town in style.

'Not really, mate,' he said. 'I'd rather have a shag.'

Double Kiss found that rather amusing, and turned the car around for the suburbs. He glanced at Frank conspiringly in the front seat beside him, before switching on the radio and listening to the news.

When Victor got out of the car, he gazed with awe. 'Is this it?'

'This is it,' Double Kiss grinned and winked at them, wheeling the car in a grand circle in preference to reversing. He honked his horn and flashed his lights at them before accelerating away down the long driveway of the mansion.

'It's a big one, eh, Frank?'

'And when a lady tells you that, you know you're in the right place. After you.'

They rang the bell and it was a B house, a bordello of substantial dimensions where 2 a.m. is considered early by both the girls and patrons alike. Buying sex is really but a mood, a state of mind, a distinct enterprise where the goodies are ferociously tempting and the appetite of men insatiable. Money is a measure of all things kinky, the refrain 'I want' common currency, the challenge 'Can you pay?' a test of authenticity, 'Give me everything' the road to pleasure, and 'Ahhhh...' means you've reached bliss.

'Welcome to the B house, gentlemen. Welcome to Bliss.' The Madame was a gamely looking wench, late fiftyish with a cute surplus of flab and enameled skin, not a bad package for her age, and for the Boners of this world she was an angel with a plump pair of tits.

Frank and Victor followed her into the selection parlor where a patron, recently arrived, was ahead of them. Commonly, men on the prowl grin at one another *You old whoremonger you...* as they wish themselves luck. However, this fellow was a lecherous specimen. He was an old codger with more money than potential in his pants. They were cannon balls once, big guns, weapons of mass fornication. He's a fella with an imaginary hard-on who still dreams of an all conquering dick, an empire of semen like a Roman army devouring the world, but his rooster went cold and now struggles to stay stiff, a willy-wonka in everlasting retreat, and now the only thing it sings is *cockadooladoo...* and licks on a strawberry lolly.

It is often claimed men can bear great hardship, their endurance a measure of their incredible stamina - but why bother when you can buy your way to heaven? Sex is mostly in the mind, anyway, so he convinces himself it's a cinch. He can take them ten at a time. Twenty. Thirty. Forty... How many do you want? (Caesar, seize her, Caesar... Gimme the lot...) His body trembled and his face beamed with fevered anticipation, his gloating eyes doing the real work these days since the rooster went *cockadooladoo* for the last time, proving, that for some, silence isn't golden but a f---ing endless headache. Well; it happens.

He was impressed when Madame reeled off the girls, thinking, lustily, that there must be something there to meet his eclectic tastes.

'Do you see someone that you like, sir?' she asked him with forced politeness. 'Is there a girl that's tickles your fancy?'

'I'm looking,' he said, staring on ravenously. 'I'm looking. Definitely...'

'What's the matter with you? Choose one, for goodness sake, and don't take all day. Can't you see..?' indicating Frank and Victor standing aloof behind him, looking perfectly blasé, coughing discreetly ahem! and feeling generally amused. 'There are other gentlemen waiting. It's also uncomfortable for the girls.'

'I'm getting choosy as I get older. Definitely...'

'More is less.'

'Ma'am?'

'Think with your dick, dear. It helps the girls enormously.'

'Excuse me?'

'Let the old-man choose, love,' she said, pointing to his private member. 'The sixth finger; get it to rise and pick one out.'

'He's growing fussy these days, ma'am. Definitely...'

'Fussy or not, please hurry up.'

'Definitely...'

'What is it you *really* want?'

'I want to *watch*.'

'Ah! A voyeur.'

'Do you have the facilities, ma'am?'

'Do you have the money?'

He pokes his bony hand into his pocket, and salivates. 'Yes.' He's a punter who pays, that's all. And, so long as he pays, it's all smiles and sunshine. Bliss is here to serve him.

'Couple; girl with girl; man with two girls; woman with two guys...?'

'Girl with girl,' says the lecher with easy money, fondling it with his bony hand. 'Definitely...'

'Slim, fat, plump, muscular, blonde, brunette...?'

'Plump. One blonde, one brunette. One must be clothed, the other naked and wear glasses. Here,' he handed her a script. 'Have them study it first. I want them to get it just right.' He grinned lustily. 'I'm a perfectionist, ma'am. Definitely.'

'Make your choice. The girls are waiting.' She hurried him up. 'Don't think, just use the sixth finger.'

Some call it the sixth sense, but it's the only *real* sense men have. And the connection between advanced mathematics and a horny guy? – Semen. It's a turn on. Turn it around, and you get algebra. Bend over and... Bliss will take care of the rest.

'Come on, dear, get a move on,' she pressed him again.

If his cock could salivate like his mouth, he'd be well in there – no doubt.

He chose the girls as only a voyeur would - from behind a screen with a peephole where his eye dangled like a frisky finger, spying on them as they sat, and chatted, and smoked. He chose Nicola, a tasty little number; classier than the house average - then perhaps not. Depends on the punter's state of infatuation. To the totally desperate or craven it all looks the same. The other girl was a china doll: the gorgeous Asian Amy with a totally infectious smile and small suckable tits. Amy is the proverbial pocket rocket! Curves in all the right places. Launches suckers into orbit - never fails, at least eight times a day. 'Mission control, I am ready for launch.' Knock knock. You pay your money and you take your shot. Moon shot? Mars shot? Any shot you like, as long as it's in cash. Yipeee aye yae! The Eagle has landed. And if that don't put a smile on your face, retire, become a monk.

'Miss,' said the lecher, groveling behind a screen as the girls performed for him.

'Yes?' said Amy, licking her fingers.

'There's something missing, miss. Definitely...' he breathed precariously, overexcited. 'Do you have another friend, miss, who

498

likes to be watched doing it? Mmm... Definitely....' He crawled out from behind the screen and winked at Amy lecherously. He wanted a third girl; voyeurism had become a numbers game. One. Two. Three. Wink wink wink...

'It'll cost you another two-fifty. Cash.'

'Ahhh...' Counting out the money with passionate hunger. 'Here... Definitely...' Adding fifty dollars more as a groveling tip, gratuity becomes gratuitous. But that's a wrap, if the geezer's a chap with a mac and an eye for the girls, who cares, so long as you pay, you get an eye-full of a lay, and a hey ho hum, diddley dum. And she smiles at him *OK*, but to her he's really no more than a loaded bum.

'Wait here,' she teased him. 'I'll be back before you can blink.' If eyes could grow, his would be as large as the world. An eyeful just isn't enough. He wanted to get up real, real close and suck her up with his eyes. Zoom into her moons and see the features in explicit detail. He might even venture a touch. - Forget deep space telescopes, nothing matches the eye of a lecher for resolution and accuracy :-)

She makes a quick call and it's all arranged. Meet Monique: tall, busty, sultry South American lady, a physical powerhouse nurtured in the arts of arousal. Coming out as a genuine 38 double D – a.k.a the contortionist. Makes an octopus seem legless. Her positions are legendary: she'd recite you Homer if you had a knack for the Greek, only you'd be none the wiser. But hey, it's the positions that count. Lovely girl. And those breasts! He's as happy as a fish dropped into her ocean – careful the sharks don't bite! Promises, promises... He knows it's been great and the thrill of a lifetime when he still has the shakes hours later and his willy wobbles with fond memories like in the grand old days of yore. Oh... way back when.

Victor and Frank took their turn and made certain to get a very close look at the rest of the scantily clad lovelies paraded before their lustful gaze. Drool and drool and drool. God, they would have loved to grope them. This, it was self-evident then, is what eyes were made for: ogle the flesh, smell the meat, taste it. Mmmm**men**!

'Now, gents,' said Madame enticingly, 'allow me to introduce our lovely girls.'

First to present are the professional troupe.
Let's meet them:

Cindy: Make-up overdone, pixilated looks. A real 'fuck me' face. Comes equipped with a hard-on body – testosterone driver. Made in heaven with a H for horny slut! Punters adore her. They'd leave their wives for her, sell their children, mortgage their own mothers, (father would do the same, so he's not worth a cent), whatever it takes.

Sally: Lovely eyes; great mouth, working words and willies to ecstasy. It's *hard* work, but hey, someone's got to do it. Right?

Jessie: So so looks, breasts decent, long brunette hair, tummy - stretch marks - appeals to the more fatherly kind of guy. Been there before. She's a slut, but he'll take care of her. Mug a minute, she weaves them like a spider, then kicks them out. It's a ritual become habit. Messy, but she can live with it.

Sandra: Kinky looks. Sex with her is hard. Rock hard. Metal hard. Flesh hard.

Lucy: Ouch!

Susie: The typical floozy; slut looks and shaved pussy screaming at you; oozes seediness from every pore. That's nice. Very nice...

Veronica: Slut-in-your-face Veronica. Everyone's fucked Veronica. Even if you haven't, well, you probably have because Veronica's been round and round so often she makes herself and those around her dizzy. Enough said.

Tara: Perfect bodywork. Perfect ten. The 'Hit me where it hurts' look. Painful! Leaves her men in agony. Not a mark on them. Their heart in tatters. She knows where to punch, and keep them coming back for more. With her looks it's money in the bag. She's a Vegas with tits. Born in the U S of A. (Nevada as it happens).

Jessica: Wears glasses; sports jet-black hair and all body-leather. In need of a slave. They're queuing up. Painful.

Maureen: a.k.a mummy to her girls, and Madame X to punters. Age counts, and fifty plus seems about right. Knows men inside out, and been both places. Seen it all, done it all. Jaded, but knows how to play a role – and swing it too. Limited skills now, but still durable.

Juliet: Not the one in Shakespeare. Older. Busty, a hand-me down chick (make that hen), could pass for a drag queen, perm-bleached blonde. Uses her hands a lot. Bit of a bush down there. Her regulars call it 'Forrest Gump!' and those of a seedier bent bend over for her pleasure. She's a swell broad, but would you marry her? - Nah!

Nancy: Takes all types, popular with the disabled, crippled, and those stricken with deformities. But who needs arms anyway? If it's embraces you're after visit grandma. Or buy a dog. Strong girl, does all the work. Good mind too. Loves her poetry and speaks five languages. Goes to night school. Never misses a class. Whore with a brain. Great.

Apple: a.k.a the chef: does great tricks with bananas, cucumbers, carrots, pickles and a range of exotic fruit. Mixed Salad is her specialty. Her caviar a treat. Dependable girl. She's strictly for the connoisseurs.

Mary: Catholic girl, wears a crucifix. Specialist school madame for the naughty boys, services the raincoat brigade. They love her, she despises them, which is the perfect match. They buy her presents, bring her flowers, wine, chocolates, clothes, jewellery, things, and she pisses on them. Strictly for the religious type.

Madchen: *Uber*-woman. *Uber*-face. A Saxon goddess in pink and white lace. Mythical bodywork. Legendary performer. *Uber*-honey dripping with *Uber*-sex. *Uber*-Nice. Guaranteed to give a man that *uber*-ouch!

Nicola: A tease. Tie and tease. Uniforms and toys galore – she has them all. Dresses up the punters too to make role-play feel authentic. Even has pre-drafted scripts for the loaded. Balls and money, that is. It's drama dressed up as sex. She's a real pro. Regulars love her.

Samantha: a.k.a the shrink. A 'tell me all your troubles' whore, pay, fuck me, and get lost.

Annabel: a.k.a The Doc (Mondays, Tuesdays, and Fridays); a.k.a The Therapy Queen (Wednesdays, Thursdays, and half-day Saturday). Sexual healing on-demand for the impotent and those who can't keep it up. She seems sympathetic. Even sincere. She has a website from which you can register to download carnal updates and upload your perversions for a fee. Not too pricey either. Overall, a better deal than the miss's at home any day of the week – including Sundays. Hey, you've got to believe in someone.

Martha: Past it. Long past it. Up, over and way down the hill and into the valley of time. Must have dragged her out of the knackers yard. But appeals to some, even some of the younger men. It takes all kinds...

Bunny and Mimi: a.k.a The Marathon Twins. Fantasy bimbos offering the two bird special – tweet tweet. Their motto: *Try us at least once in your life.* They perform a lesbian show too to fill the interlude, because no man can match them at their own game. But they won't stop trying. Men!

Charlene: Jesus Christ!

Jean: More like it. Ginger haired babe knows how to set a man on fire. And she knows just how to burn him. Combustible gal.

Sonia: A deviant's delight. Big, big woman. Melons overhanging the stupendous fat and drooping down like one-hundred weights of pure ecstasy. Most of her clients are thin. Makes sense? Ask any man.

Simone: Chick with a dick. Amazingly feminine. Men can't tell by looking. Women spot her at once, though. It's a behavioral thing. Women are women.

*Next to appear are the part-timers. Just as lovely as the rest, but with the tempting suggestion of nookie on the safe side as sweet relish for the man blessed with a full plate. Mmmm, ain't that a bite! It's not such a bad life after all, is it...***:-)**

Lilian: Blonde, slim, girlish, pretty face, lovely big smile, immensely sexy body. Probably faultless in a general kind of way. Deserves to be taken care of.

Lorie: a.k.a The Boxer. Knows how to deliver a knockout punch. Takes two at a time with ease. Three's no problem. A gang and a bang. Now you're talking. Her moves are classic and their numbers legion. She has great wit and intelligence that punters find very refreshing. They don't always go together. It must be the sex.

Jasmin: A sweet little package. If you're all on your own with an itch and a spare twenty minutes you can't beat this little number. She's a real pocket dynamo.

Irene: a.k.a The Split Personality. Slut or Virgin? Innocent features with the *come-in-my mouth* look. Cheeky. Sleazy. Nice. Also quite pretty and very natural looking, with fine features, full lips and the most amazing blue eyes.

Monica: a.k.a Pegasus. Always in a hurry. 'Let's just cut to the chase,' is her motto. A real shag-bag. Lovely! Saddle up and ride this cowgirl to the moon and back. Wow! A quickie with her leaves you with a smile on your face for a month. What a girl! Wonderful.

Angie: a.k.a the control freak. Don't touch. Stand there. Do this. Wash your willy again. Let me do it (!!!) Is she a paranoid director? And all the time she's nailed you with those 'fuck-me' eyes, never closing them until she comes. (Fake? Who cares.) 'Now clean up.' Romantic bitch! 'Round two.' That's more like it. What a great little buckaroo she is, has expert timing and turns the world on its head. Some punters even ask for her autograph. The perverts pay bucks for a sample of her pubic hair. She even has a sideline selling used panties, socks, bras, and other sweaty, filthy underwear to punters with a craving for the sordid and absurd. 'Well, as long as you pay, love.' And she wipes her ass with a hanky, and charges him a hundred. He can't wait to get home, and buries his face in it.

Kimberly: Bony, beveled looks, slim build, could do with an extra large dosage of protein. In her early/mid 20's, quite tall with shoulder length brown hair and legs that go on for ever which finish at a nice round, toned ass. Is she a gymnast practicing for the championships? Most guys would love for her to practice on their pole.

Kim: Fat old bag with sagging tits and yellow teeth, make-up fossilized on her face by now. Perfect piece for punters eking their pleasure from the seedier side of things. Capital S for seedy. Soiled as well. Some men love disgusting flesh. She provides it and with dollops to spare. Great one for investments, though. Spreads her bets and invests in a dozen different sectors from retail through beverages. Living proof that you can never judge a whore by its cover.

Angie: Brunette lady mid twenties with a great pair of melons. Rest of body shapely and nicely toned, ever so soft skin. Great mouth. A favorite with the lager crowd; they only wished her tits had the stuff on tap, paradise would be an endless intoxication. Well, even a slob has his dreams.

Allie: Attractive busty babe with brown eyes. Dress size 12, 34D bust, extra-large nipples, fairly tall. Friendly nature. Used to be a nurse. Got bored with giving enemas for free.

Charlie: Very sensual, very well presented and dressed, has the perfect wardrobe. Knows how to please. Top marks. Yes.

Last to appear are the punters: Groveling, sex-starved horny schmucks.

The punters: a.k.a men, a.k.a porno-sapiens, born and re-born again slut-worshippers (evolving *back* to homo-erectus? Dicey speculation that) a unique species of beings at their weakest, most fragile, most suicidal. A horde of cocks, hard-on schmucks every last one of them. Depressing sight. Makes you want to cry. But preferably in the lap of a cute blonde with lactating tits. Well, men, they're all just babies at heart.

And the world keeps revolving, round and round one thousand kilometers per hour. *Why?* some men ask. Good question! Let's leave it at that. They make their selection, lick their lips, and press on upstairs to the sin rooms instead.

Few women make full use of their greatest asset, their greatest power. To men, they're a drug; they're an addiction. Pump yourself into their psyche like pumping feelers into the veins.

Victor took one look at the ladies reeled out before him and remarked in aside: 'Well Frank, if you're looking for *demur* we've come to the wrong place.'

'Look *harder,*' said Madame emphatically, overhearing him.

'Ah! I see it now.'

Sex. It's all in the mind.

'Who's this one then?' asked Victor.

'The gorgeous Tara,' said Madame. 'A petite raven minx with a mega personality. Horny as hell; playful as sin; a lady of many talents.'

'Is that true, young lady?'

'Do you think I could ever kid you about that?' Tara pouted her lips at him winsomely. 'What you see is what you get. All one-hundred percent pure testosterone proof.' She smiled a sultry smile. 'And I ain't kidding.'

Victor's eyes bulged: *I must have me some of this Bliss, by God!* That's the one he wants. Dressed in tiny creamy togs that covered the bare minimum. With long raven hair and her gorgeous tan, which was really something yummy with that cream colored outfit covering her bits. Victor grew exceedingly impressed.

'I'll take this young lady for starters,' says he greedily, his brain running into overdrive at the thought of all those elastic positions that awaited him. Start with mish, spoons, then doggie, then sixty-nine add sixty-nine add sixty-nine and another sixty-nine for good measure, because sex is ultimately all about proportion – more is never enough, so you shovel it up in spades, moremoremore.

Frank waited to let Victor choose first before eyeing the babe with the short red dress on. Ouch! There was something about a single colored dress, a plain outfit on a pretty girl that really turned him on. Sometimes, a woman can look unimaginably lovely at her simplest: light make up, a simple dress, an easy smile... 'I'll take her,' he says adoringly. She cocks him a merry wink and flashes him a smile. And arm in arm they saunter to the bliss room with a matrimony pace, and soft lounge riffs working the senses with ticklish moods.

They did tie and tease for half an hour or so followed by body worship and then sex. Damn, she can grind away like she's trying to snap ya! Ouch! It left him feeling totally knackered and wanting moremoremore.

'Talk dirty to me,' she begs him breathlessly.

'Whore.'

'More.'

'Filthy whore.'

'Ah…'

Later she yanks at his plums – ouch! - And has him kneeling on the floor.

'Play with yourself,' he moans.

'I don't really want to touch it there but, ooooh, if I really, really have to...' she teases him to delirium. 'Ooooh, mustn't must I...?'

'You horny little thing,' cries he. 'Play with yourself.'

'With toys?' She had lots of toys with her - dildos, strap-ons, handcuffs, you name it. He went wild and she remained in control. It's all an act - but what an act! And then helped him to dress afterwards and pecked him on the cheek. Nice of her.

'See you later, love,' says he, tipping her a hundred. And she winks at him smartly and brushes her hand against his groin. Time is a bitch, if only it would hurry up and his balls fill up and the world spin faster and the ladies keep rolling and... and...

'You had your dirty little way I see, Frank?'

'I'm afraid I have, Vic.'

'Good. Let's shove off then.' And lighting a cigarette, he asked the receptionist to call them a cab.

The night was still young. Meaning, if you're a punter with a hard on, it's young, forever young as it happens. And time here lasts as long as you have money to burn.

They drove to Midtown, their bloated eyeballs feasting on the opera of lights, the dames, the sights, asking the driver to pull over by a bar. There; that one; easy does it. Stop here. Good man. And in they stride into the realm of pleasure, coasting with a Midtown ease, warm, soft, smiling as wide as the world – say cheese. Yeah!

'No touching the girls, fellas. OK?' croaks the avuncular host - he's uncle Bob to everybody this guy! And they laugh together lecherously, their gaping eyes drowning in hormones, the sizzling chemistry of horny guys and sexy girls reacting in their eye*balls* as they plunged deeper into the interior, pulled by its tidal power of sound and flesh and mesmerizing sex, expecting a whale of a time.

Further inside, even more lights assaulted them, not seducing, but raping the senses, vying in a dizzying dance across the auditorium and stage, brimming with a cast of delicious lap dancers, is a theatre of unrelenting gyrations and stimulations and intoxications and sensations and vibrations and fabulous, wonderful, gasp-for-your-breath-die-for-it flesh. Touch it, smell it, taste it, eat it, lap it all up, get up real, real close and just melt into it. Mmmm*men*.

Let's meet the performers.

Carol: late 20s, blonde(ish); beginning to droop a bit here and there; above average looks.

Roxie: Handsome lass, gorgeous hair and blue eyes; fantasy body.

Ellen: Leggy red-head, tall, smooth skin, knock-out looks, so so breasts.

Jodie: Slim but curvy, brown silky hair, velvet looks, fresh smile, smells sooooo good!

Emma: mid 20s, five-ten, attractive girl with sparkling mischievous brown eyes. Wow!

Jasmine: Slim, early 30's, short bobbed hair, lovely smile, great tan.

JoJo: Tall, slim, sexy, irresistibly tiny breasts. Most men find them (and her) irresistible. Naturally.

Misty: Knock-out looks, classier than most... Then, well, maybe not.

Nancy: Attractive, mid 20s, shoulder length hair, permed, perfect eyes, lovely boobs.

Erica: Waiflike, tattoos about the belly button, delicious legs, wanton looks, nice skin.

Roz: Lingerie blonde. Green eyes, knee-length boots, latex panties, leather straps. Whip.

Serena: Achingly sexy, ivory skin, perfect slut written all over her. Charmer. Lovely!

Vanessa: A drooler's dream. Megawatt porno brunette. Oozing with sex. Feel knackered just looking at her.

Jenny: Cheerful bunny. Sweet. Innocent looking babe in her late teens. Sports glasses and pony-tails. What's she doing here?

Rebecca: And God made women. He made Rebecca, and never looked back since.

Sarah: Smooth skin; smooth mouth; drool till you die, and still you can't get enough of her.

Mimi: Yausa! Yausa! Yausa!

'OK ladies, show time! Curtain call in one minute.' It's not high drama, OK, but a stage is a stage, and someone's got to tell them to get their butt out there and entertain the punters.

The security men (smartly dressed thugs, actually) hold back the hordes of ravenous men from surging forward. They're animals down there; it's like a hormone pit boiling with semen; hyper-excited male-types pressing against the stage, their money ready to push into the flimsy underwear of dancers teasing their senses off. No touching. Use your imagination. Sex in the head. It's all there among the fevered neurons, sloshing about. But she's in control. She blows him a kiss, shakes her tits in his sweating panting face, and like a blow to the head he goes to pieces and shudders explosively. But still, give the guy a break - he's in heaven.

'I love you. Marry me. What's your name? What's your name?'
'Rebecca.'

And God made woman.

Megawatts of simulated sex from start to finish, charging masculine drives up and up and up, combustible flesh pushed into his eager face, the ravenous eyes, the lapping tongue, he's all animal inside and out, he's a man with a cock more potent than a quasar, instinctively reacting to an overt tease setting him alight, detonating testosterone to helpless thrashing. The subtle vibes of romance are demolished by the visceral waves of yearning, as the tidal power of women draw and drench men with desire. It's a flood out there, wave after wave surging against the breakers of her oiled-up flesh. It's a fantastic deluge.

The ladies up the ante, becoming more daring, antics become foreplay. She'll fondle your thingy with her hand if that's your fancy, boys... The bouncer will turn a blind eye, cash on the side, she makes money, he makes money, the punter goes to heaven for a while, everyone's happy. Lots of stroking, (less petting), lots of nibbling, a bit of kissing, those provocative little moans of 'Mmmm, I want you inside of me, baby...' and not the wishful little echoes of soft seduction, but the thrill of pure orgasm. She knows how to work him up. Even pony-tails Jenny gets into the swing of things. Giddee-up! Knows how to act the whore, it seems. She's a wicked little tease, too. Hauled a punter on top for a game of *Let's-pretend-we're-doing-it...* routine, which set the house in uproar and started a riot. Mixing sin with innocence that way makes men go crazy! Like pouring testosterone onto the fire. She's playing the naughty schoolgirl role, see-through blouse, socks, achingly small skirt, fooling around to make some extra money but inadvertently worked them up to frenzy. Armed with long adorable pony-tails and pointed nipples spearing through her blouse – out they pop and blast the men to smithereens. She's killing them. Je–sus! She's turbo-charged the soldiers in their pants, and then up and ran away before they ravaged her. The cops were called, the bouncers pushed and shoved, and fights broke out and chairs thrown and mirrors smashed but the music played and played, on and on, because it simply couldn't stop itself. Yeeesssss!

'Frank, let's get the hell out of here!'

They guzzled down the beer because it was damn good stuff and raced for the exits avoiding punches, kicks, and a thinning grey-haired office type of animal with beady suburban eyes crazed by the overpowering atmosphere of his own burning lusts. What is a man? Answer: Put him in front of a woman and find out.

God made man first. Obviously the prototype. The real thing is the woman. Second. Or is that *first?*

'Frank. Watch out! '

'There. Grab that cab. You,' to the cabbie, 'get us the hell out of here. Step on it. Move. Move this damn thing. Move!'

The wheels of the taxi screech wildly and it races away, throwing up a plume of dust. It felt comical and classical at the same time, life scripted as farce. Frank begun laughing, a hearty laugh full of humor and insight. Sex is like that. Comedy made purposeful and compelling. So he continues to chuckle as déjà vu, or something to amuse, resonates in his head. He has a knack for that: squeeze him hard enough and his mind throws up sensational delights, and titillating sights, together with a plethora of weird and wonderful things.

'What's so funny?' Victor asked him irritably. 'I think we should call Roy.'

'In the morning,' he said, glancing at the time. 'When he gets to Paris and settles in.'

'What are you laughing at?'

'Things,' he tempered his laughter and, turning to the driver gave him directions for home.

'No,' said Victor. 'I've just got started.'

The cabbie agitated and told them to make up their minds.

'Just drive,' demanded Victor. 'We'll tell you where. Drive around the park for a while.'

He grumbled, but otherwise did as instructed.

'Why do these people always complain? Moan, moan, moan...' he breathed hard before coughing and composing himself. 'Frank, my old son.'

'Yes, Vic?'

'I understand you are the savvy one when it comes to fetishes?'

'Who told you that?'

'Roy.'

'The bastard!'

'Come now, Frank. Calm down.' He smiled knowingly. 'I think it's invaluable knowledge to have, After all, knowledge is power. And your knowledge is worth more than a plum.' Victor eased his privates by adjusting his seating position. 'It's the knowing that counts.'

'In that case, did you know Roy is a whoremonger?'

'We're all whoremongers, old son,' he said, grinning mischievously. 'We're all part of the same infamous guild - horny Romeos desperate for a shag; blokes going bonkers for a bunk-up. Everyone with a cock automatically qualifies as a member. And that includes you and me, old mate. It's a life-long membership that gets rolled-over into the hereafter. After all, it could be far, far worse. Just thank yourself fortunate you weren't born female. Or queer...'

Frank gazed warily at him. 'What are you after?'

'I have a fantasy that needs exploring.'

'Oh yes?'

'Yes,' he said. 'Frank, I'm not a particularly indulgent man, but on occasion our little indulgences need to be let out of their little boxes, now and again, for a little bit of airing, if you get my drift.'

'A little...' he replied. 'A little.' He leaned back in the seat and began to ponder. 'In my own *limited* way, I might be able to assist with some practical advice.'

'Limit or no limit, I'm after a bit of crumpet with a penchant for a whipping.'

'Receive or give?'

'She gives.'

'Naturally.' Frank briefly rubbed his eyes. He was growing tired and looked at his wristwatch: it was almost 3 am. 'I know a place.'

'You're a gent.'

'Don't mention it.'

'Is it far?'

'Is it worth it; that's the question.'

'Well, is it?'

'Sit back and relax. Let me give them a call first to make sure the house is open.' Frank made the call. There were several girls working the late shift: Erika, his favorite, was off, but business was relatively brisk, so yes, they could come over. He hung up and gave directions to the driver.

'Are you sure?' he complained.

510

'Just drive. Save your moaning for your wife.'

'I'm not married.'

'Then it's about time you were. Just drive; and we'll worry about the rest. OK?'

The cabbie continued to grumble, but eventually settled down, going fast, then slow, catching the lights as if to dare his passengers with the challenge: *Well, and what the hell are you going to do about it?* - Nothing, actually. They're just a fare kind of hitching a ride in the dead of night; geezers in Manhattan. So, he drove to their destination in relative quiet, pausing only to turn the radio on.

After a while, Victor turned to Frank and asked him.

'Are you up for a bit more hanky panky yourself, Frank?'

'No. I think I'll call it day.'

'Good man,' he said, grinning. 'I can see you're a bit worn out.'

Chapter 28

Frank checked the time and then looked for messages on his phone. Nothing, save a screen saver dotted with lovely droplets of golden rain showering a naked woman mouthing the words 'Cum inside me, baby...' It seemed a pretty cool download at the time, a diversion to amuse than an inspiration to act in kind. But coincidence is a strange thing, stirring testosterone in a man, blurring everything with carnal signals from a fevered brain fantasizing on lust and putting sexual feelers into everything he thinks and does and says, from sitting on the toilet to watching TV to digressing on a point of principle – what that principle was seldom counts, for when his dick grows hard it becomes the only fact of consequence that counts. Clearly, the ascent of Man parallels his descent to seedy orgasm of the third kind: one, you find a whore; two, you agree terms; three: Ahhh. The ultimate driver is the body, flesh the feeler of the world's delights, ousting the tendency to think rationally, even as Victor droned the while on the shenanigans of the markets and its shakers:

'Do you hear what I'm saying, Frank? Those bastards drove down the metals just as I got my finger out to do the business. They have no sense of timing. They're all just a herd of cocks stampeding into the sunset of profit after the market has past its peak. No wonder so many marriages fail and relationships fall apart. Most men just don't know how to trade. And women... well, I don't have to tell you, old son. Ahhh...' he shook his head with a faint gasp of disillusion. 'The real traders with a knack for the markets are few and far between. The rest, well... all a carnal pack of dodgy characters if you ask me.' He lamely dwelled on this a moment, and the 'plan' to recover from their losses that was... 'Confusing us all and costing me a great deal of money. Frank, are you listening to me?' The gripe was a real one but the expectation of fetish delights softened its cutting edge.

'Yes, I hear you. Loud and clear,' he replied, sounding distracted.

Victor, under the immersive spell of lust, asked for details on the bordello. Was it a house of plenty like a harem, an abode for deviants, a palace of pleasure? Had Frank ever indulged himself with any of the exotic fruits on offer at that tempting establishment? In brief, he wanted to know: 'Have you left your cock-prints at that place of infamy, old son?' Yes, he said, he sort of tried it out. 'Why?' Because someone had to. 'And?' Well, he went about this task very methodically, being a man especially keen on detail, so he dipped his toe in for a little bite of the goodies. 'Dipped your cock in, more like.' Well, it had to be done, Vic, it had to be done, he said. 'You're a decent kind of fella, Frank. I like you a lot.' Thanks, he said, as Victor patted him on the shoulder. 'And, in your expert opinion, was it any good, this place of infamy?' Oh yes, he had himself a jolly old time. 'And had he been through the extras on the menu with these delectable babes, and tasted all their sweetmeats? Was he grounded in their mill, done properly-like, manhandled by the big and the small, the brute wench and the tamed pussycat alike, big tits, small tits, shaven and hairy ones like a gorilla down below?' Well... Yes, every variation under the sun, he's tanned himself to a cinder you just wouldn't believe how hot it gets in there. Yes sir, every pickle in paradise the ravenous mind of man can dream of is within reach of those gamely mademoiselles - they bake sin like you wouldn't believe, cream cakes and pee, if that's your cup of tea, is all for the asking. French and wench, they don't only rhyme, declares Frank, these spices bite! 'I gotta get me some of that grub,' says Victor, licking his lips, thinking of the endless recipes. 'I'm a spice man,' says he, and he can have his cake and eat it too. So, he wants to know, 'What's the cream of the crop there like?' Inspiring, said Frank, as only a cat knows. 'Do I look like a horny connoisseur to you?' wonders Victor. You most certainly do, replies Frank, and he should know, old chum, he's a chef. 'Show me the menus,' says Victor, 'I'm feeling kind of peckish.' Well, Frank cuts in all knowingly-like, the girls work shifts because business is booming. They're enterprising vixens cooking up all kinds of dishes for the groveling men. 'And I'm one of them,' laughs Victor. Join the queue, says Frank, chuckling too, and remarks that the girls have various establishments at their disposal. They vary from day to day. He can't always count on his favorite piece of pickle being available when he's horny and wants to take a bite. Some savories play hard to get. 'Is that so?' Yep! bloody vixens! 'OK, I'm a businessman,' says Victor, and he respects entrepreneurs: enterprising characters are what make the world tick, whores among them included. 'What's the time?' Do you really want to know, asks Frank? 'No, not really,' he replies, he couldn't care less: *'Just give me a slut I can do business with - breakfast, lunch, and dinner; and snacks all day long.'* I can see you're a bit peckish, says Frank. 'You're spot on there, old son,' he confesses with a lusty grin. So, who would Frank recommend for a novice like him? Better wait till we get there and see who's on the menu, says Frank, rather enticingly-like. 'Lovely,' he said, wetting his lips, 'I can't wait....'

And Frank glanced at his wristwatch again then checked for messages. Time, signals: why can't they cohere when you want them to? He looked faintly anxious, but Victor paid him no heed. His taste-buds were drooling with anticipation for the luscious juice of fetish fruits going drip drip drip... and some wonder why men are crazy? Drip drip drip is carnal torture wrapped in flesh-dipped delights so thrilling for a man, that drip drip drip is everything to him. 'Did I ever mention, Frank old son, that rainy days make me feel horny. I wonder why...' Drip drip drip...

Meanwhile, at the establishment, which consisted of three double bedrooms with full en suite bathrooms, three singles with basic shower units, three dungeons amply configured and suitably decked out, and an attractive lounge set up as the waiting room with TVs, magazines and newspapers, including all the financials, internet terminals, telephones, self-service buffet and a sexual therapist on hand for those a touch too coy to dive straight in. Her name: Dr Softly with the soft voice and softer touch softly plying her trade. She looks sleazy like a slut, but tries her best all the same, and prides herself on her *handiwork*. After all, she's there to rouse the guy and spark a fancy in his wilted cock, not tidy up the rubbish in his head. The right worker for the right task: shrinks could learn a lot from her, and probably do; but being a businesswoman, absolute discretion is assured.

Typically, the clients are described succinctly as punters: *all men...* naturally. Here they come, one by one, dick, dick, dick... keeping perfect time. Something like the blind following the blind? Well, not quite. The cock following the cock more like in the blind craving for full-on sex. Ahhh, figures... Here, each guy gets to be baptized with a new name - *John*. Some guys see the joke and take it with a pinch of humor, but many don't and look upon it as a curiosity - duh! - and wonder what in heavens the hookers are about. Playing mamma, perhaps, to the rude little boys...

The ladies: the more interesting specimens by far, enterprising vixens each one of them, colorful as lustful rainbows spawning after clouds coming loudly in the upper reaches of the atmosphere. *Yes, Yes, O Yeeeeessss!* These babes get to tell their stories. Such as Rebecca in room 001, single room, en suite shower, and a fitted set of wardrobes for her accessories. Description – late 30s to early 40s, average looking, dumpy, quite short body; tits a bit baggy, dark hair; a bush that reeks of lube, lots to grab on to, though; biggish ass; acts friendly and seems quite willing. Punter strolls in tripping on the rug and gets right down to it. Didn't get the chance to get her fully out of her kit; some things are best left as imaginings. She gets his pulse racing and the soldiers warming up. Taps the dozy bastard on the head: 'Wake up, damn it; I ain't got all day,' and squeezes his balls: very sexy if that's your thing. (Rubs her tits all over him like she's sanding down a stone. He squeals as she pushes her nipple into his mouth, first the left, then the right. Randy as hell, he goes for her lips but she shakes her head.) Dummy's still got his socks on and she suits up his meat. 'You ready?' Ready or not, here we go; hump and pump and she looks at the clock. Jesus Christ, will he never come? Squeeze the soldiers out of him: *Quick march, you fuckers! Out! Out!* But she's been around a while, a well-used piece, and she ain't that tight anymore and it takes a lot more work than it used to. Eventually he reaches bliss and sneezes. She gives him a tissue. 'It's not for your nose, dummy.' He cleans up. She shows him the door. He grins, he grunts, and heads for the nearest bar.

'Gimme me a beer.'

'Bud?'

'Yeah.'

Next room. Next door, 002.

Mary, quite contrary - not your typical fairy. Calls herself the Chapel Maid on account of the service of thanksgiving she offers. Everything's included. In her mid 20s, pretty girl; trim body, nice proportions, medium waist, sexy legs, 34c tits, longish blonde hair, above average height, womanly in all the right ways, makes some men feel proud just knowing her. 'Come in, Sam.' One of her regular's strolls in and throws his coat over a chair. Misses and it falls on the floor. 'Leave it,' she pines, and he does, and dives into the goodies. 'You missed me?'

'Yeah, you bet.' He pauses and hands her the money. She takes it, swoons over to the next room, opens a drawer, packs the cash inside, and seals it with a key. By the time she's back he's piled his gear on the floor. His donk is up and ready, hard as a rock, nosing for action. She's cute and teases him with her smile. She always has a smile for him. He adores her. It's kind of sweet really because the old ball-and-chain at home has that forever-frown on her restive face, her hair in rollers all the time and mouth wide open bawling at the kids: *'Shut the fuck up!'*

It's not just the sex. It's therapy. 'You wanna roll in the sack?' Mary entices him.

'So long as it's not made of hair-rollers,' he grins, but the cynicism's glaring, at least for a while, until she comes over and kisses him, and life begins to roll. Yeah! She's loads of fun and very playful, fit as a pretty fiddle she's got talent galore, knows all the good moves on top and a sexy attitude to match. For a working girl she's a looker and in a good state of repair, beautiful soft skin, looks after the goods, her waist is just perfect for her height, and has a nice smile. Tonight she's kitted out prettily in sexy black knics, bra, stockings, smelling freshly spruced up and looking a sure thing, all woman, likes being with men, she makes them feel randy with the old come-on routine. When out of her kit he was raring to go, she performs some quick massaging on his back, ah, felt nice, and then rubbed her body and perky breasts over his front. She's good at kissing. Not the skimping type either, she does the deal and goes the whole way. Sprawling out on the bed she opened her legs for him. He maneuvers the module and docs into position. Ah, if it ain't love it's got to be science! The sex talk was never overdone and adds to the randyness. They both wanted the same thing. Went at it hard, gripping on each other with her hands pulling his ass and he hugging for dear life. He ended up underneath her being consumed by her kisses. What a princess. What a gem. She helps him to dress afterwards. 'How's your wife, Sam?'

'Nowhere near as lovely as you are.'

'Maybe you should speak with her.'

'Yeah,' he sounds resigned. 'Maybe; maybe…'

'See you next week, then.'

'You bet.' He perks up and plants her a kiss. And she waves him goodbye as he walks down the stairs.

It's delicately sweet in its way; a pathos that's charming; pain that is almost amusing; and when all is said and done, and the sum of his existence counted, it's his only real home, because it's his last pleasure in life. The ball-and-chain takes him for granted; the kids don't appreciate him; his mates suffer the same toils, so what's the use? - You know, maybe it's his own fault. But that's how it is.

On his exit through to the lounge he passes the new girl coming out of room 003. He's never been with this one before, a real candy girl from Dallas. Aye aye, she's a sexy piece, thinks he, she still isn't fully out of the door, but he winks at her anyway, says 'Hi,' and smiles lustily. She responds the same, and it's more than gesture as she offers him her business card. What a pro! Drumming up business for herself; proactive marketing, that's the ticket. If you have to sell yourself, and let's face it, we all do, thinks Sam, might as well sell yourself and keep the proceeds, then let someone else have the goodies. You know, if democracy made any democratic sense, she'd be elected President time after time: better a kitten in a Cathouse than a dog in a Whitehouse! Sure gets my vote, ol' Sam thinks knowingly to himself. Meow... He admires her card and reads (he'd never do that with a politician): *Cindy. The all-round pleasure doll. Graduated with a Masters in Sexology, Texas S & M University. All services catered for. Reasonable rates. Payment accepted in cash, credit card, or cheque with a banker's guarantee.* She has three phone numbers, a fax and an email address, even a private mailbox number in Sincinnati – Ooops! make that a C for Cin. Cindy has long straight hair that runs halfway down her back, she's petite, a size 8

518

with small but pert breasts. Curvaceous with picturesque looks, she has a real candy smile. In fact, if you pulled her on a night out you would have no problem taking her to meet your mother. 'Where did you meet her, son?' 'Don't ask, mum, don't ask.' 'Why does she call you John, son? Your name's not John.' 'Don't ask, mum, don't ask.' Cindy's a charmer when she invites you in that dreamy voice of hers, 'Will you take me from behind?' Pathway to heaven. Oh yes!

She's a variation of biologist by training, so he asks her a simple enough question. 'Have you heard of unnatural selection?'

'No. I can't say I have.'

'Unnatural propositions?'

'All the time. What are you after?'

'Piss on me.'

'A hundred bucks.'

'Done.'

Evolution often takes a sideways detour, proceeding horizontally along the line of a worm, spending several hundred million years there apparently before working up a nip to the humanoids, then around in quaint little spirals to nowhere in particular, then randomly meanders through various prototypes until you end up with a woman and a man who join not at the level of intelligence, or in the union of a kiss, but amid the gunk of their own feral desires and, fair enough, it suits them just fine. Life has become but a set of transactions. And it's business as usual. Down to the last cent.

'Can I have your dirty knickers?' he said.

'Sure. Fifty bucks.'

'Thanks.'

'You'd like a bag for that?'

'Nah. That's OK. I'll shove it in my pocket.' He smiles. Natural reaction. Doesn't hesitate and she cracked on.

'Did you enjoy it, John?' she asks.

'Yeah,' replies the mug, 'but my name's Sam.'

'OK, Sam.'

He sniffs it a little before storing it away, because he's always up against the clock, and for the price he can't be too unhappy with matters. He got a good deal.

Room 004.

If funky is your game, Vicky's your dame. She's around a size 12 with a reasonably sized natural bust. She comes equipped with red lips, stylish pantyhose, elegant shoes, more clocks in her place than a planetary month of Sundays (each one displaying a different time) an abundance of erotic gadgets and business cards for the gents.

'What are all the clocks for, luv?' croaks a punter.

'I like to pretend I'm at different times at different points in space, John.'

'Why?'

'Dunno,' muses she aloud. 'I just like it.'

'Like it? Well, aren't you a different pot of mustard.'

'Long as it ain't messin' with me pickles, luv. I'm partial to a pickle, I am.'

And he gets it on and she gets it off and off they go on a hell of a ride up down in out with around twenty different clocks going off during the encounter: cuckoos, bells, whistles, synthesized tones, you name it, it turned her on and got him moving as fast as the soldiers could burst from his plums and made his merry day.

'Call again, luv,' says she.

'I will,' says he. 'Any particular time?'

'Leave the time to me,' she laughs. 'You just bring the space.'

He makes his way to a bar and speculates on the physics of his encounter.

'Look at my wristwatch?' he looks at his wristwatch. 'Is this Einstein's time or Vicky's time? I ain't in no good mood for time travel, mate. Get it in and up and out I go. Phew! Seemed like days and days and now it's time for a beer, surely. What am I, a space-man?'

'You don't look like one to me,' utters back bartender Jack.

'Jack. Gimme a beer?'

Jack passes him a chilled one and he gulps it down like a beaver. 'I needed that,' says he, feeling quenched.

'Another?'

'Sure. Have one yourself.'

'Cheers.' - He whacks the bottle down and chases a punter that's dashed out without paying his bill. - 'Bastard!'

'Yeah...' says he, all knowledgeable-like. 'Fast raccoon, ain't he just...' And he looks around and sips his beer contentedly; rubbing his stubby chin and thinking to himself that tart had no knickers on - cheeky cow! Smooth as a baby's bot' her puss' was, and... 'Yep, I definitely need a shave.'

'Have time for another one?' says Jack.

'Yeah,' says he, looking at his wristwatch. 'Might as well.'

'Frank, is this it?'

Frank paid the taxi driver, whose grumbling stirred up again: 'Don't you guys have any smaller bills? I don't carry that much change with me.'

'Keep it. Keep the change,' retorted Frank, and the cabbie grinned and swiftly pulled away. Frank glanced around warily and led them inside. 'Let's take the side entrance,' he said.

'Why?'

'They don't have cameras around there.' His expression seemed to suggest: *And we don't want every Peeping Tom, Dick and Harry knowing you were here.*

'I see,' said Victor, following him diligently. 'I see... Good thinking, Frankie-boy...'

Inside the lounge there were about six men in attendance waiting for the 'hostesses' to finish with their current crop of male egos laid out in bedrooms, or otherwise strapped to the walls in replica dungeons kitted out for the modern man (modern!) with prehistoric trimmings – give the savage his space; a plain room ain't enough for some folk, especially city slickers.

A hostess, stylishly dressed and scented with tasteful perfume, greeted them courteously and asked them what their pleasure was. Victor spontaneously professed himself extremely keen to slake his carnal longings with a decent whipping from a sexy woman with an axe to grind. Frank cut in and tactfully restored their dignity by asking for whiskey and water. She smiled imperturbably and asked if they took ice with their drinks. Yes, said Frank, and she invited them to help themselves to the amenities in the lounge, the baser fancies of men never for a moment affecting her stride, proving that personal sophistication is just a form of superlative routine.

They took seats by a chap with white hair, about sixty years old, looking fit and perfectly dapper in his fine-cut blue suit. He recognized Frank. - 'Hi, do you remember me?' he said.

'Yes, you're mask and cream.'

'What's all that about?' asked Victor.

'It's how I like it,' he answered for himself and, offering his hand, asked if he were English.

'Indeed I am,' said Victor stoutly, shaking his hand. 'Indeed I am.'

'I spent a good many years over there,' he said, smiling. 'London, Manchester, Sheffield... I got about quite a bit, don't you know.'

'Well,' said Victor haughtily, 'you'd never know it.'

The man in white hair just laughed and said: 'Pleased to make your acquaintance, mate,' in a tone that was American but quaintly English in cadence, so its appeal lay in the native quality of its expression. It gave him an air of playful jocularity, all-American panache with English élan.

Just then, Victor saw half of an amazingly cute face peeking around a corner. 'Who's she?'

'The maid.'

'Wow!'

'She works on Sundays, but she won't go all the way.'

'What's she offer?'

'Soft massage and an easy stroke.'

'Is that all?' he sighed, staring at her lustily as she came into full view. Gosh, she's something he would die for to get his teeth into. Being smacked around by that beauty would really make his hair curl. And if baldness intervened? No worries, the toes will take to a good curly bending. In fact, his feet began to deliciously ache.

'I'm afraid so,' he said. 'But you learn to live with it.'

'Too bad. Just looking at her got me all excited. Can you take your shoes off in here?' said Victor, drooling over her, and the gentleman in white hair began to laugh. Victor asked him what he found so funny.

'Never mind her, mate,' he said ardently. 'It's Mistress Helga and her wicked nymph, Amy the Agony Maid in dungeon 101, that really boils your beans.'

'Go on. I'm all ears.'

'It's totally craven. Even just thinking of her knocks me out.'

'What does she cook up in there?'

'She crushes your balls; and that just the seasoning.'

'Amazing!'

'Vicious brute in it she is.' He stopped for breath. 'That woman is a thug with a whip. A bloody tormentor in high heels. Filthy bitch! But oh... what ecstasies she sweats out of you. They leave you breathless. She squeezes out that holy juice like only a true slut can.'

'Holy mother of...'

'She covers your face; wraps it in a mask.'

'Mask! What mask?'

'Must be at least...what? an inch think.'

'Good God!' Victor gasped. 'Are you exaggerating?'

'Not by half an inch, mate. Believe me, she'll give you a real roasting.'

'But it must feel like what... slaughter?'

'You can hardly breathe.'

Victor gasped for air, rolling back. You see, sex is all in the mind, chuck, although his dick begged to differ, and his was a real salivating bugger full of a shiverring desire for a ffff.

'Pardon me, but I really need to ask you about the mask. It sounds downright bloody evil. Do you mind?'

'Fire away.'

'Does she knuckle-down the straps?'

'Tight,' he said. 'And I mean bloody tight. Get her to use the steel buckle and strap. It's a brutal fit, hard as nails and you sweat like a pig. The bitch squeezes your bacon and juices you till you're as dry as a rock.'

'Inspiring!'

'Get her to pull it tight. Use the keyword – bravo, bravo. She'll have you choking in no time.'

They gulped breathlessly in silence for a time, awed by her résumé, overwhelmed with the promise of a good sweating. Drip, drip, drip... At length, Victor wondered aloud, 'If you don't mind my asking, how long have you been coming here?'

'After a single round with her in 101, it's a lifetime's worth of sweating, let me tell you that.'

'My God!'

'Make that ten lifetimes.'

'Ten!'

'That vicious bitch makes you drip, drip, drip... till you're dried out and raw.'

'Oh my God!'

'Fantastic whore... That's the ticket. Drip, drip, drip...'

'How can you stand it - all this exhaustion; this excitement? God! Doesn't it drive you mad?'

'Well, when your meat's raw and you're ready for a roasting, she's the one to stir the pot.' He reclined in his seat. 'If your gonna bake, you may as well burn to a cinder.' He grinned. He knew. He's been there. Tanned to a crust. A Sweating. Drip, drip, drip... and he still hasn't had enough. 'Ah,' he perked up, winking at Victor. 'Here she comes now.'

'Excuse me, gents,' said Victor, rising before everyone else in the lounge, 'I don't mind if I do.' And it took him all of ten seconds to tell her what he wanted, agree terms, and be led to the dungeon.

'Keen one, ain't he?' he said amusingly to Frank.

Frank glanced nervously at his wristwatch, and then his phone for messages. He heaved a sigh of relief. They were coming through steady now. Double Kiss reported all was quiet, and what should he do next? Frank replied with the message. "Go to plan B." He was wondering whether to call Nick when the man with white hair grinned at him and said.

'Aren't you going to taste the delicacies, then?' - Frank looked at the buffet, but the man laughed. - 'No,' he said, 'I meant the girls.'

'Oh. No, not tonight. I'll sit this out. I'm treating my friend.'

'Your mate?'

'Mate...' he echoed, thinking. 'Yes.'

'Have you ever heard of an establishment called The Whipped Cream? No. Ha! I thought a connoisseur of the S and M scene like yourself would certainly have paid it a visit.'

'Well I haven't. I've never heard of it.'

'There's a mistress there that would definitely take your fancy. She has no pity for the bad boys.' He emphasized stirringly: 'No pity. None. Not even a drop.'

Ouch! This spectacle aroused Frank's lust and imagination. The testosterone look worked its way over his face, and he asked:

'Who is she?'

'Her name's Joan.'

'Where's she from?'

'Well, she ain't French, and she ain't no saint, but by God she's got the devil on her side and does the business.'

Frank gasped with awe. 'Tell me more.'

'Pound for pound, it don't get any better that this. - Are you after a real roasting?'

'Yes.'

'Then she's your babe.'

'Go on.'

'Hard core, pound for pound the most perfect rump piece you're ever likely to taste. And I'm not talking fatty bits here, mate. No, strictly beef, prime stuff; lust flowing like gravy, delicious; spuds and peas, and I ain't talking Sunday roast, but a roasting you're sure to get. There's nothing quite like being on the receiving end of her. Heaven in a whipping is what I say. Heaven in a whipping; and hell can wait for afters. You know what I mean?'

Frank wet his lips hungrily with his tongue:

'The Cream, eh?'

'Whipped!'

Frank coughed. 'Does she work there alone?'

'The Whipped Cream? No, there's a stock of wenches to choose from.' He took a deep breath and looked over his shoulder. 'Creditable bunch of whores, you bet. Nothing beats them - not the miss's, not the kids, not the dog, not the football, not the beer, not your mates, nothing. For roasting your nuts, there's no one better. – What's your fancy?'

'Hard domination.'

'The real nasty stuff?'

'Yes.'

'Then go for Mistress Galore. With a capital G. Order her special. She gives you a real roasting. - You want the details?'

'Yes.'

'Hard, hard core. Mild pain ain't even in her vocabulary. I'm talking real mustard here, mate. She don't muck about. It's strictly connoisseur's stuff. The dungeon kit includes all the tools: rack, cross, irons, whips, canes, chains, a bevy of cruel teasers you can't even imagine what she does with - you name it. If it's torture you're after, she's your babe.'

'What's her lowest level?'

'Triple X; and I mean X X X, and some.'

'What about worship and submission? Does she know the routine?'

'She'll give you a real fry up, no worries.'

'And a whipping?'

'And rubs the salt in. Filthy cow rams her boot into your ass. High stilettos! You'll be begging for mercy. She bound me to the wall with chains and I kicked up a merry hell. So she thumped me one. I came out black and blue. Looked like a blueberry muffin.'

'Outstanding!'

'I deserved it. I was a real bad boy,' he said, sounding peculiarly remorseful. 'And watch her fingernails. The bitch gets carried away and scratches, like she's skinning a pig. That place is a proper little butcher's shop if you ask me.'

Unfettered desire soars, and lust comes along for the ride. Frank knows this brutal thirst of his can never be quenched, not even with the endless whippings that it feeds on, and it drives him crazy with the frantic urge to go go go and dive headlong into the ocean of XXX, his hot testosterone boiling and boiling... 'Holy cow!' It's irresistible as he scrambles in his pocket for his computer, lifts the stylus, and demands to know:

'What's her number? And give me the address.'

He recites it off by heart. Sweating, Frank calls her and makes an appointment. Yes, she's pricey, and won't compromise on the fee. (Good, it means she knows she's worth it and has more of them queuing if he doesn't agree. There are hoards of insatiable deviants in the world, don't you know. She does). 'Do you agree?' she asks tantalizingly.

Is sweat, wet? Of course he does. Frank confirms her address, hangs up, and orders some beer.

'Better get that inside of you, mate,' he warns him enticingly. 'You're gonna need every last drop. And don't bother about taking a piss. She'll sweat it all back out of you.'

Drip, drip, drip...

And before he's even finished his beer the cab is waiting outside, and in he slips en route for a quickie and planning to be back in time for Victor.

'Baby,' said Victor, gasping, his face covered with a leather mask. 'You are mistress, and I, your slave.'

He's just another John, slave to a fetish, that can't resist getting whacked by a brunette in shiny red leather togs and a white mask brandishing an oiled-up whip over his incarcerated willy.

'I want to see you, mistress. Please. Please.'

'Shut up, shit head!'

'I love you and promise to obey you.'

'Scum. Slave. You disgusting, filthy groveling piece of shit. What are you!?'

'A - '

'Shut up! Shut the fuck up!'

'Yes. Oh yes, I will. – Ouch!'

She grabbed his plums and squeezes them hard. He discharges a shriek of pain, of yearning, of contentment.

'Do it again.'

She spits on him.

'Yes!'

And to double up the punch she leaves the dungeon to find her clone; returning shortly after as the torturing duo, mistress and her merciless mistress twin, and they immediately set about him with a vengeance, professionally applied and scripted for the fresh ones.

'Look at the slave...' said the new girl Amy. 'He's getting all dirty now... Ain't you?' Uncovering his face, they smothered him with nasty kisses, dripping saliva everywhere, tightening the leather straps that impaled him to the wall. Was he a travesty of Christ, or just a freak? Both girls mangled their lips into him, disgorging words dripping with the gestures of assault, love as violence, and a delicious way of talking about him in the third person. They located the mirror where he could see himself humiliated and abased by these naughty nymphs. He was a voyeur turned-in on himself. He must see what other eyes see, feel what other bodies feel, as the center of arousal become consumed in his own frenzy. And they led him to his paradise… with exquisite pain.

He begged for more with lumbering screams, 'Bravo! Bravo!' and they dimmed the lights, teasing them down to just a tad above visibility so even they became shadows, with only their voices remaining distinct, mouthing obscenities in the darkness, lashing him with curses and whips.

Suddenly he felt cold, his flesh, in the unnerving coolness of imagined black, trembled in a cocktail of excitement and fear. Half the pleasure was to see himself abased, and now the mirrors, vanishing in the faded light, reflected nothing but the barest shapes meaningless in their blank form. They blurred his horizon and confused his vision, throttling his imagination.

Meanwhile, amid the shadows, he was unaware of strangers watching him. Then, a door yielded to, slowly, and a number of strangers entered the room, their steps engraving across the wooden floor clipping like a clock winding down to zero. Victor was startled, thrown into a surreal setting well outside his normal comfort zone.

'Who's there?' he cried out frantically.

The buckling crash of several tin cans, bottles, a tumbling stool, some implements thrown to the floor, brought a din of chaos to the moment, peaking at some breaking glass smashing like a cymbal thrashed in rapt finale. Then, just as abruptly, it went quiet again, save for his breathing, deep and agitated in a monotonous pleading gasp. Darkness lends a carrier frequency to fear, riding on a wave, amplifying it. Imagination is half the story - the important half, the part where fictions hold fantasy and, by an act of pure will, embrace the metaphor of the moment, and press out a thrill. Drip, drip, drip...

'We're been watching you,' said a man's voice as cool as the darkness was black.

'Who are you? What do you want? Amy, untie me. Amy. Amy. Where are you, damn it?'

'Here,' the stranger casually lit a match. 'In the beginning there was darkness, and God said, *Let there be light*. So… Let me light this for you.'

The light was meant to bring back a semblance of normality, but served only to confuse and plunge him in terror.

Then someone blew out the match, and jabbed him with a needle.

The following hours were a blur as he alternated between semi-consciousness and aching sleep.

The exhilarating aftertaste of erotic pleasure turned to panic when Frank returned and discovered Victor gone. He called Nick, he called Roy's apartment, he called Double Kiss, and then pressed the girls who robbed Victor of his dignity for five hundred bucks an hour.

'He left,' they said.

'Alone?'

'With some men. And a doctor.'

'What doctor?'

'We don't know him. We've never seen him before. They said it was Victor's birthday and they were surprising him. Playing a prank, they said. They intended to take him outside and embarrass him, and then bring him back. We get this *male thing* going on here all the time. You guys are just crazy. The things you think of.'

He could barely believe his own ears, that this pair of sluts think men are so utterly out of their minds that they would consent to something like this, to drug a man and carry him out on the pretext of a prank. It was absurd and terrifying at the same time. But they insisted more *bizarre* things had happened before, and it was all just a prank or other. Besides, Victor looked conscious when they carried him out, dazed a bit perhaps, sure, but everyone was laughing, even Victor, laughing like he was drunk and merry. It could have been his birthday party even! That wouldn't surprise them in the least. And hey, look, if he, Frank, was that concerned, he could always call the police and let them in on it. OK?

And steadfast in their reasoning, they returned to their clients.

Three hours later Frank was still trembling in his apartment when Roy called.

'Where's Victor?' he blared at him indignantly.

'I had this great idea, and I was using him for bait, and - '

'Where is he?'

'I... I don't know.'

'You idiot! Don't tell me you lost him?'

'No, Roy.'

'Then where is he?'

'He vanished. I was using him for bait. I had this great idea and then - '

'Screw your ideas. Just find him,' Roy seethed, and hung up with a deafening thud.

'I lost him...' he echoed into the phone, into a dead line, numbly whispering into empty space. 'I lost him...'

Chapter 29

Several hours of incessant rain set the mood, only lazily subsiding with the easing clouds to a drizzle, then lately tempered to the tail end of a thinning mist clearing gently as car horns and piercing shrieks in colorful French swelled in the abating rain. The sky seemed to take its time, to sweat it out, not a storm day today where dollops of rain pound the earth below. Oh no, today it was a slow affair, coughing up in dribs and drabs the brooding state of mind that is a grey day. It all seemed delightfully cast for poets and dreamers, but Forester, though a romantic, was not among them but had indulged the body and taken a late nap – very late. It was past 3 pm Paris time and the telephone rang, brrrr, brrrr... startling him awake. It was Sandy in New York who had just arrived at work, coffee in one hand, bagel in the other – breakfast on the move. She teased him a little with wily jibes making him feel self-conscious. 'I hope you got it right,' she said puzzlingly. *What the hell did that mean?* he wondered as she pressed on with business.

'We have an address in Paris,' she said swiftly, 'where the twin's sister, Zoë, was staying. You have something to write with? Good, take this down.'

Scribbling hard, the nib of the pencil snapped and he reached for another, which bore his irritation, and he asked her: 'Any more news yet on that guy we found in the dungeon?'

'The dungeon?' she sounded genuinely bemused. Then, 'Ahhhh...' the long knowing sigh catches her breath, 'the apartment of Mistress Correction where all the little *dicks*, sorry, I meant little *boys*, go to play. – What is it with men? What are you guys after?'

'Why don't you ask them?'

'I'm asking you.'

'Asking me what?'

'Why are men - *men*?'

'It's the sheer thrill and excitement.'

'Of what?'

'Of not being a woman.'

'Pig!'

He smiled to himself. Gotcha! - *Touché, son,* said Forester's Pop timing in on cue. *Don't let the bitch get one over on a man, especially a cop, especially if he's my boy and a cop. - What the hell does she think she's doing slopping around in a man's world for anyway?* She's doing her job, Pop, she's working? *Working! What the hell is she doing working? Shouldn't she be at home doing the goddamn cleaning and looking after the goddamn kids? That's the only kind of work a woman needs to know.* She's not married, Pop. *What is she, a lesbian?* No, she's straight. *But she's got tits, ain't she?* Yes, a real knock out pair. *Then why the hell ain't she married?* It's a mystery to us all, Pop; a mystery to us all... *Jesus Christ... I just don't get it anymore, son.*

'Hello, Sandy, are you still there? Did they finally identify him?'

'Yes. I'm just looking for the details. Wait a mo. Ah. Here we are. He's French; we were right there.' (We? What did doubting missy have to do with it? Better not start a commotion now, let her share the credit and finish). 'His real name is Charles Sennet, thirty nine, a lawyer, divorced with no kids - which is a blessing.' She paused a moment and seemed genuinely relieved at this, before restoring her gumption. 'The Paris cops have all the details. They're expecting you, like, five hours ago.'

'OK, OK,' he said grumpily, and hung up.

In a reflex action he turned to the window expecting to see the Eiffel Tower soaring into view – Oh shucks! There goes the dreamer, dreaming all day long; women try to understand him but hey, what do they know? Dreamers are a launch pad, not a landing slot. What comes down comes in its own time. He wanted to see it there, in the sunshine, towering into the sky. But he had to content himself with a field of view consisting of rain and a bleak confusion of buildings feeding his desire. Still, he's a dreamer, nothing will ever change that; a dreamer heralding the chant *Liberté,* because freedom is loving what you are, and knowing it, admitting it, saying yes to hope and no to despair, and he understood, like all dreamers, he was forever chasing the moment. Even while learning French he wanted to boast about it, but instead kept it secret from his colleagues But why? He was playing an act, he was meant to be all-male, all-American, all NYC, an ego in a jock strap. A cop with a punch line, smart-ass, big-shot, the *Get out of my way* hot-shot packing a piece and a badge, a pocketful of expletives, roaming the mean streets in his slick car, acting cool behind a wheel, scowling, honking his horn when a roving driver cuts his path - *Get out of my way!* But what the hell did he know? Courage, that's the thing. Honesty, there's the real power. It's looking in the mirror of the mind; it can blind you with lies, or opens your eyes. And the truth, though brighter than the brightest Sun, is a soothing thing at last.

Forester concluded it was a far bigger world out there, and Pop's death at the hands of a careless thug only drove the message home, and strengthened his resolve to master French. His only regret was that this ambition surfaced late in life. Making a choice, his own choice despite your peers and the begrudging little habits that populate their minds, the cynicism residing in their luckless hearts, despite the crowd, is, he determined, the only way he cared to hold dear. And he would have *his* way – *and eat it*.

Take a bite of that. *That's* what life should taste like. Apple and all.

He even brought along his favorite dictionary and a host of portable gadgets to practice his verbs. In French, you understand, perfection is never quite enough. You have to go beyond that – in fact, to leap beyond a frog (or *frogétte* for that matter!).

When he reached the police station and asked for his host and chaperone, Detective Claude Frasion: friend, comrade, chum, and best reference for French slang he'd ever come across, Forester was directed to the first floor and found Claude in full throttle packing the idioms of the Paris street and firing them at force, aimed with staged precision and the piercing way a circumcised-tipped verb can stab a hoodlum in the butt, and conjugate his nuts. That's talking! Claude was presently interrogating a shady looking character that he threatened with every conceivable sanction the law could inflict on a low-life hoodlum like him. Forester shook hands with Claude, who seemed perfectly adjusted to his task, smiled and shrugged knowingly before asking a uniformed officer to lock up the low-life in a holding-cell to ponder his options.

The low-life was a volcano of language in his own right and packed a flaming expletive or two back at the cops, protesting theatrically, *You corrupt wasters...* spiting out spittle and words like furied bullets, *Torturers! Tyrants! Frenchmen!...* and asserting his innocence before God, before witnesses, even before the American whom he assumed was an accomplice and let off a volley of abuse: *What the hell are you looking at, you tourist!...* and would instruct his lawyers to bring charges against the atrocious practices of the Paris Police Force. *Fascists! I am not saying another word...* That would be a blessing. Claude told him to shut up, which he refused to do until someone brought him a bottle of red wine and a vegetable curry. He was a vegetarian, he insisted, since he started flirting with Hinduism. He'd gotten a taste for it after seeing a show like the *Folie-Bergere* but consisting of penguins strutting around in blue tailored suits – it's was a rare sight, monsieur, these birds really had themselves a ball! - and he knew his fundamental rights as a Frenchman to flirt with anything he damn well pleased under the constitution of the *Republic Francais* which guaranteed him three square meals a day and a pack of cigarettes and chewing gum, a book, a TV, a video game, and something else he couldn't quite remember (a flashlight perhaps, he wondered, but couldn't quite comprehend why he should need one) and he settled down to a late lunch and a smoke.

'Remind you of home, Forester?'

Forester chuckled, and looked for a seat.

'Don't get comfortable,' Claude told him, picking up a file and his cigarettes and leading the way out. 'I was expecting you a lot earlier. Late flight, or late night? No, don't tell me, I have enough headaches of my own. We had better make a move; it's getting late.'

'Where are we going?'

'To the victim's apartment. And then his place of work. And...'

'Yes, Claude?'

'Welcome to Paris.'

'Merci.'

On their way out Forester, being in unfamiliar surroundings, was consciously noting every detail and observed a peculiarly long and grand sounding title on a door. It was a glass door yielding into a large room with about ten uniformed officers inside, stacks of technology, and several plain-clothes personnel. There was a *No Smoking* sign displayed prominently in red, but about half the group were smoking regardless. Forester detained Claude and read out the title: *'The Unit for Future Methods of Effective Urban Policing.'* He paused and considered it, noticing the cynical mocking expression on Claude's face and asked him to explain, which he proceeded to do with disdain.

'Look at these desk jockeys, prancing about like penguins in their air-conditioned offices and starch ironed uniforms. Get out on the streets and see what's really out there, why don't they? Look at them; they're just a mob of hormones with a stack of computers. Think they're video cowboys, do they? Ride on, you suckers!' he turned away in disgust and they continued down the corridor to the exit. 'They're relying on all this surveillance stuff, all this leading–edge technologies bullshit. But it doesn't work. I piss on the whole damn shebang! That's just how it is, Forester. You've got to be out there on the street, knocking up against it day in, day out. That mob of penguins is nothing but a bunch of voyeurs with a box of gadgets. Ahhhhh!' he sighed delightedly as they reached the street. 'Smell the air; smell the stench of criminality, the reek of low-life's making our lives hell. Isn't it great!'

'I suppose you have a point.' They walked to the car, which was parked further along past some quaint looking shops and charming boutiques and cafes oozing with delicious smells of gourmet pastries and hot piping coffee. Those tastes, those smells, were so thrilling they could lift you off the ground. And Forester's senses basked in their delights. It made him realize as they walked in silence, and he could see on Claude's face that the aromas, the sights, the sounds, the ambiance of the street afforded him not only pleasure, but fulfillment. And as a man that was, ultimately, the true test of living.

Claude was a supercharged Parisian cop with a natural talent for a pun – *As I always say, my American friend, a fart is more useful in this game than a computer. At least it leaves a signal you can follow; and I trust my nose more than anything. It has the mind of experience at its disposal. It has instinct at its service. It knows a cheddar from a brie. And no-one's fooling me, my friend. Never! Not with this nose. Can a computer do that? Ha!* - And a delight in two hour lunches – *Have you tried this season's wine yet? It's a pretty exceptional year.* - He also had a cop's eye for the street – *Look at her legs, mon dieu! That can only be Latin!* - The potbelly he boasted was deceptive: the correct interpretation for its bulk was a huge reservoir of energy for this effervescent cop-of-the-streets with a moral gripe against desk bound government - *Useless desk-jockeys; useless bureaucrats wasting time and resources on things they least understand. Relying on computers all the time – that's exactly how to lose your sense of smell. Ah! What's that? Onion soup!*

'The street,' he continued passionately, 'the street. That's where you've got to be, on the street. What is a cop otherwise?' As they casually turned a corner they passed two disputing pedestrians possibly on the verge of exchanging blows. Barely looking, or so it appeared, they strode by and he continued: 'Oh, by the way, have you been to the opera yet? No. Well, they've refurbished it from top to bottom. It looks wonderful. They've really restored its grandeur. I'll take you to have a look. I have a contact, a very decent fellow; we can get the best seats in the house. Opera! You can't match it for sheer spectacle.'

The verbal scuffle behind them was heating up, and Claude stopped, turned, and studied from a distance to see where it would lead. One of the two took offence at this and abruptly raised his voice at him, demanding to know what he was looking at. Claude modestly explained they were just tourists admiring the local architecture. The response was Gallic to a tee: *They should mind their own business and shove off back to their own country or they'll chop his nose off.* It sounded reasonable enough to Claude, who concluded the dispute would remain verbal and not descend to physical blows, so he and Forester continued on, Claude confiding his views on policing the street.

'I mean, you use your head; you can't be a cop and not slap them around a little from time to time when you have to. It's necessary.'

'The risk is you might get to like it.'

'You have a point there. But blame necessity, not lust.'

'If it bothers you that much, why are you a cop?'

'The same reason you are. Mind the traffic.' Claude grinned and they crossed the street.

So the raving, the complaining, the dilemmas, the quirky toils that beset a cop are like the props of his craft, his stage the ceaseless shuffle of the street, the cosmopolitan animated flux of human passions crammed together into a finite space. You jump into the frying pan, what do you expect? Not *The Unit for Future Methods of Effective Urban Policing.* You can shove that recipe you know where. A thriving society deserves better than that. Like onion soup for instance, with fresh crusty bread; and some cheese; and pepper; and.... *take it away. Yeah!*

As they walked towards his unmarked car he noticed a delivery van pull up alongside.

'Hey,' Claude remonstrated, 'you can't park there.'

'Fuck off,' came the retort in combative French. Claude smirked grumpily and let it alone. Not worth the hassle, this one. Live and let live.

At the apartment of the deceased, appointed with elaborate ornaments from Asia, together with exotic furnishings and decor, gave an impression of chic sophistication. A man with style.

'Did he live here alone?' Forester asked as he perused a shelf full of books, taking out several on literature and the psychology of the *I Ching* - in French, of course.

'Since his divorce; yes. She walked out on him.'

'Oh?'

'She works in travel. She's abroad, in Egypt.'

'Did she have anything to say?'

'No. She's no use. Which, to my mind, is a virtue of women in general these days.'

Forester smiled. 'You're growing ever more cynical, Claude. What's this?'

'It looks like a jewellery box.'

'It's locked.' He passed it to Claude who broke the lock open. It contained several strands of human hair, blonde, wispy, forlorn looking, mementos of a past tense, perhaps, past loves. 'He seems a quite refined man. Not the masochistic kind at all. – I wonder how he got there?'

Claude could sense the direction of his speculations, the misgivings, the stark incompatibility of the exterior man and his inner nature.

'He was disciplined, that's all,' said Claude. 'Some men are consumed by desire, are sex junkies, their lusts define not only their inner urges, but taint their lives and surroundings. This guy had a longing to keep them apart; a desire for calm beyond the routine of his work and the intrigues of his sex life. He was disciplined, that's all.'

This sounded reasonable, simple, effective, and Forester moved quietly to the window and opened it out.

'Why would anyone want to kill him?'

'Perhaps,' said Claude, at length strolling after him, 'it was a slip-up; a blunder; faux pas. I heard of a case once where a guy went to Berlin to buy some machinery, and he had some time to spare. He dials a number, and he makes it with a girl who owes a debt. By chance the debt collector is passing by that moment and knocks on the door. There's no answer but he hears muffled noises inside, the patter of feet and the sound of laughter. He's a proud, touchy character and hates to be ignored. It makes him angry, and he breaks in. The rest, as you can guess, is a tragedy.'

Forester paused and thought a moment, gauging the significance of his expression, and then asked him:

'Was that a true story, or did you invent it?'

'Sometimes,' he said, 'it's hard to know the difference. Very little that has people in the plot surprises me.'

Seen in this light the apartment was but one expression of a man than a manifestation of his total being; a replica of his tastes, his moods, his inner silences amidst the bedlam of the larger world; more the soft desires that go unseen outside the craved spaces of his sensual world. The human yearning for sanctity ceased being answered in the sanctum of a cathedral or a temple, and moved to home, the wired up, gadget crammed commoditized abode that is now home. One way or another, humans will always find a way to inner peace, a kind of modern prayer reinforced by need, and not pressed on a man by compulsion.

Claude noted the time and informed Forester they would have to get a move on, as the law firm where the deceased worked would soon be closing for the day.

On arrival, they met the deceased's secretary who erupted in a flood of tears. The other partners of the law firm portrayed sullen vexed faces and they had several questions they tended to ask all at once and that irritated Claude, who remarked bluntly that he was there to ask questions, not answer them. The lawyers received this rather in the nature of an insult and, feeling affronted in their own domain, their mood abruptly changed and they ordered him and his 'American cop friend' out. 'Au revoir, monsieurs.'

'Just answer me this one thing,' said Claude, addressing the senior partner. 'Who was he working for in New York? And why did he go there? Was it planned in advance, or arranged at short notice?'

'That's three questions there, not one.'

'So who the hell's counting!' he exclaimed irritably.

'Monsieur! How dare you come in here and... and... Out! Get out!'

'I'm sorry, monsieur. Please, try and help me out here.'

He stiffly took a handkerchief from his pocket and blew his nose, once, very loudly, which did the job intended, but he wheezed another two more times as if to say, "And what are you going to do about that, you damn cop?" Nothing apparently, for as he worked up a pose with his handkerchief and started folding it, he returned it to his pocket and looked at Claude with disdain. 'He was on vacation. But I believe he had some private business to attend to, of which he kept us in the dark.' He sounded much aggrieved at this. 'He told no one at all, it seems. Good day, monsieur.'

The secretary remained upset and in tears as she showed them out, and Forester offered his handkerchief, asking her at the same time:

'What did he like to do, madame?'

'To do?' she wept, stammering behind her tears.

'Did he have any hobbies, or obsessive interests?'

'Obsessive interests?'

'Anything he always returned to, I mean? Pardon me for pressing you, I know it's painful, but did he engage in anything regularly, whether or not he enjoyed it?'

'Well,' she thought, fighing back tears, 'he liked to play poker with those people.'

'Which people?'

'At the Blué Doux club.' She began whispering, even though no one could overhear. 'He often asked me to book him a table there, and preferred I did it discreetly.'

'Excuse me?'

'I used another phone line; a private one, not the firm's.'

'Why?'

'Oh, he was embarrassed, you see. Gambling for a lawyer is a very risky thing to do, especially when you handle clients' money. But Monsieur Sennet was a careful man. He never got into debt or anything of that sort. Oh no. And I truly believe he played poker only to meet with certain people and make connections. He was, ahem,' she looked around suspiciously, searching for spies as she entered naturally into the gossip routine, 'he was unhappy here at the firm, monsieur; and wanted to move on, as he said, and promised to take me with him.'

'I see. Did you ever personally speak with any of these people?'

'No. I just booked the table.'

'Thank you very much, madame,' and they turned to leave.

'Oh, monsieur, don't forget your handkerchief.'

'Please,' he said, 'keep it. I have a spare.'

Claude knew what he was going to ask and answered him even before he spoke:

'I'll run another check on the club and see if it's licensed. But there is no crime in playing poker, for whatever reason. And that secretary is a bundle of nerves; and I'd take whatever she said with a large pinch of salt.'

Forester was brooding as they reached the car and climbed inside. 'I need a pattern, and the club is a start. Where are we going now?'

'I'll take you to your hotel. By the way, some of the boys and I are going out on the town tonight; why not join us?'

Forester thanked him and they arranged to meet around nine in the evening at a bar. He also took the opportunity to mention the case of the missing twin.

'Is she underage?' said Claude.

'No.'

'Listen, Forester, in this world, there are adults, and then there are fucked-up adults. It's not our business to chase them around.'

'I understand that, but I have a hunch about this one.'

'Hunch? That's fair enough, but you may be taking on too much, have you considered that? Your captain sent you over here to do a job, and this other thing could distract you from the reason that brought you here.'

'I know, and so does he. But can you help?'

He sighed skeptically, 'I'll see what I can do.'

'Thanks, Claude. I owe you. Now, be a good friend and take me to this address.' He gave him the address Sandy provided earlier, and Claude shook his head hesitantly and turned the car around. Forester stared hard at the Paris rush hour, his thoughts fixed elsewhere as he said: 'I need to do this, Claude. Just take me there. And I'll meet up with you later. Thanks.'

The block of apartments had the elegant facade of classical Parisian chic, a feminine exterior on a masculine base, the romancing of stone made for those who believe if not in the values of a past age, then its sense of immutable style.

Forester skirted the elevator, climbing the two flights of stairs, not for exercise, not even to stretch the time, but to get a feel for the place, pacing an agile intuition. He pressed the doorbell and waited. She opened it at the same time as she asked 'Who's there?' as if she had been skipping and singing with subdued music playing in the background and half-expected someone to call. She seemed carelessly naive, her actions betraying her soft trusting eyes and athletic youthful physique. Somehow, one expected her to be graceful; she had the poise and look of elegance, but her animated spirit carried the careless airs of a young girl. Her contrary traits were fetching, enticing, and irritating at the same time.

Forester politely explained who he was, presented his ID, but she never seemed to grasp it all at once and pondered a while before deciding to invite him inside. Perhaps she liked the look of him more than what he said. She made decisions on a whim, careless perhaps, but she carried the sense that her luck would hold and fateful errors elude her. Some people are charmed that way. Like a cat with nine lives.

She offered him some herbal tea and, though he would have preferred a beer, it sounded fine. They sat and talked informally and she rambled on about America, how New York City was cool; how L. A. was more cool; how San Francisco was even more cool. He got the picture and guided the conversation around. He brought the subject back to the twin, Zoë.

'Yes,' she said, 'she was really... cool.'

Strands of festive red colored her mousy light hair. She had round naive eyes staring at the sense of things as simply there; incurious of the world around her.

'You know, I knew her, OK, but she left. You know... just like that.'

'Just left?'

She pondered with those wide telling eyes: 'I guess so.'

'Before she left, did you see her? Speak with her?'

'She left me Sara.'

'Who?'

'Her cat. Sara. She left me her cat. That was OK of her, no?'

'I guess so.'

'It's a nice cat. All white. A quiet thing it is; smooth as a kitten,' she smiled.

'Do you have any idea why she left?'

She shrugged, looking into her tea glass like a cat, teasing it, sniffing the strawberry flavor tea. 'She never let it be known. People are strange; not like cats.' She beamed. 'Cats are cool.'

'I'm a dog man myself.'

'You have a dog?' Her face lit up, intrigued by it all.

'No. Not at the moment.'

'Oh,' she sighed sympathetically. 'What a shame. Maybe, you know, you should get a dog. Dogs are cool.'

He returned the smile. 'Maybe...'

He thanked her for her time and the tea and rose to leave, when suddenly she cried out: 'Monsieur, I remember something.'

'Yes?'

'She used to say he was like a Tomcat. She said that often. Something about his moves; and how he played his moves.'

'Who? Your cat?'

'No. Some guy she was seeing. What do you think she meant? I don't know who he was, but...' she paused, wondering, 'his name was Tomka. It must have made it easy to call him Tomcat, I guess. - See ya!'

Outside, on the sidewalk, Forester looked at his wristwatch, fixing a stare on the dials. He had over three hours to kill till nine, and he was in Paris, with a load on his mind, and wondered what he should do. He turned left and, as he looked up at the sky, it started raining again.

Chapter 30

'Where are you going, Roy?' asked the kitten.

'I have to go somewhere.'

'Where?'

'I need to see someone.'

'Who?'

'Oh, just some guy.'

'Why?'

'About something.'

'Something?'

'This and that.'

'This and that?'

'I'll call you later.'

'When?'

'In a couple of hours.'

'Promise?'

He looked at her sincerely, with pride. 'Of course. Hey, come here you, and give me a kiss.'

'And a hug.'

'Sure.'

'Big hug.'

'Yeah.'

'Big, big hug...' she squeezed him tightly with the all the passion she possessed as though she never wanted to let him go, and he adored every part of her, her loveliness, her presence, her being. It made him wonder as a man: how does he hold on to all of that? *By being sincere,* his feelings softly confided back to him.

Outside, in the rain, he took cover beneath some retail bunting and made a call to New York City. Roy knew the answer even before Frank told him.

'I don't know where he's gone, Roy. One minute he was there, and the next...'

'Where did you go? Where did you take him?'

'I just put out some feelers and was using him for bait; soft bait.'

'You went whoring, didn't you?'

'It was his decision. I simply obliged. You know me, Roy, I was just playing my part. Being the good guy.'

He sighed with exasperation. 'And what's this stupid riddle you've sent me?'

'I sent it to Peeping Tom.'

'What for?'

'It's a coded message.'

'Why?'

'He sent us one.'

'And?'

'So...' he cross-referenced his intentions, 'I sent him one back.'

Roy waited, expecting something more. 'What else? Is that it?'

'Sort of,' he mumbled hesitantly, fidgeting. Then he snapped back. 'Why are you always so uptight over everything, anyway? I'm trying my best, aren't I?'

'Unbelievable!' He gasped. 'You're unbelievable. Have you ever considered castration? You ought to snap that prick of yours in half and throw the thing away. Get a bionic one, programmed to obey. - Where's your savvy, Frank? Frank...' he strained composure, 'where's Victor? Where is he?'

'I'm not sure,' he sounded confused, which infuriated Roy even more. 'Some people... they came and took him away.'

'He was abducted?'

Frank paused nervously, searching for the right words. 'Somehow, in the circumstances, that doesn't sound quite right.'

'What are you talking about? Where is he?'

'Someone took him?'

'Who?'

'I don't know.'

'This is crazy! - Who do you *think* took him?'

Recounting the details, he explained Victor's 'lady friends' were entertaining him at the time with their enviable titillations and amusements, and someone knocked on the door and whispered in their ear the most incredible nonsense. Well, you'd have to be a stupid whore to be taken in by any of that balderdash. However, they believed it, the stupid whores, presuming a gamely posse of Victor's chums were out to humor him with their jolly antics, and crept into the room while he was in a compromised position and, in a state of hushed hilarity, played a darling little prank on him, tickling Victor, so to speak, in a soft spot. These stupid nymphs had been in the game too long, swearing they'd seen it all before, and nothing that men did surprised them in the least: their antics were as ludicrous as they were legion, and it was all natural game as far as their dim minds could ascertain, so they simply stood by and giggled, thinking it was all a "boys own way of mucking about..." and he was sedated with a drug of some kind that left him feeling dazed and they bore him away: "In a right old state of affairs, I must say... You guys, ha, you're soooooooo funny!"

'And so, Roy, that's it. They ferried him away and never brought him back.'

'Where were you?'

'Me?'

'Yes, you?'

He coughed, and echoed timidly. 'Me?'

Roy had his answer and terminated the call in a blaze of bitterness before the slur 'pervert' flew from him. He was still possessed of his reason to appreciate Frank's indispensability, and antagonizing him would only make matters worse.

Thunder clapped ominously overhead, but despite the omens Roy pressed on through the rain and hailed down a cab, determined to find Victor himself and put an end to this *game* once and for all. No more Peeping Toms to vie with, no more intrigues and deception. Just the final stand-off of he and Ice; one last ante; and Roy was going to call. It was a testing moment internalized as drama as Roy rehearsed various scenarios in his mind – *Deal. Yes, a fresh hand. Five cards; three up; two down. Raise you. Are you in, Ice...? Well? - Don't blink, Roy, he'll notice. Be firm, but always smart. - It's your call, Ice, it's your call. I'm waiting...*

Roy struggled against rashness, controlling his temper as best he could. He realized the limits of his strengths and the perils of his weaknesses. Dueling with a rival often led to a deeper struggle with the self. Bitterness was a character flaw; he understood that but fought to tame it. Nick was spot-on with his characterization of Roy as temperamentally wanting. Bad luck is a bitch, hardship a whore. Sure. But, expletives aside, it befits a man in combat to step back and think, and not judge perils by his own lack of character and waywardness. However, the cards were drawn, and he had to play: the fantasy of personal power *had* to yield to the compromise of fact. There was no way back. It had to end here so he could get on with his life. And this proved the maxim: never mock normality. Understate it if you must, but never hesitate to hold the hand of routine, for it often saves you from your worst nightmares that are mostly of your own making. After all, when the curtain falls, we're still just guys; any drama of the world notwithstanding.

'The buck stops here,' he wrestled with himself, whispering, shifting in the back seat of a taxicab.

'Excusé moi, monsieur?'

'Do you speak English?'

'A little, monsieur.'

'Do you play poker?'

'*Pok-her?*'

'Cards, do you ever play cards?'

'Ah. Yes, monsieur. Cards. Yes, oui.'

'Do you like to win?'

'Yes, monsieur. I love to win.'

'Then stick around,' he said, 'because there are no more duds to deal. Only the money cards.'

'Monsieur?'

'Ante, my friend. Ante.' He breathed-in deeply. 'And this time, I'm going to call.'

The cabbie grinned in partial comprehension of this easy talk, the vernacular baiting of words one could fish up and digest with ease. He had nothing at hand to say so he hit upon the rain as a serene interlude for a tourist to remark on. But Roy said he liked the rain. It cleared the air; freshened it up. And it reminded him of home.

'It is good, monsieur, to have a home. Someone you can be with.

Somewhere you can always go to.'

'Yes,' he said. 'Yes it is...'

The kitten grew lonely and called him. He told her he missed her and he loved her and that he always would, and that he missed home, dreadfully, he missed it so very much.

'Are you OK, Roy?'

'Yes. I'm fine.'

'You sound kind of sad.'

'No,' he said, with a reminiscing turn. 'It's just the rain, babe. It's just the rain.'

'It reminds you of home?'

'Yes.'

'It's the ringing sound, I think. All those droplets coming down want to sing you something.'

'Yes.'

'Tapping on the windowpanes...'

'Yes...'

When the taxi arrived at the Bank's Head Office the cabbie spun a coin and asked Roy to choose: 'Heads or tails, monsieur?'

'Heads.'

'Bon!' He gave him the coin. 'For luck.' And grinning amiably, said *Salut!* and effortlessly pulled away in time to the gentle rustling of rain. A parting like a song; echoing in raindrops and the pleasing patter of home.

Self-consciously striding into the building, Roy was indifferent to the chic interior, the art nouveau design, the waterfalls shimmering with multicolored lights and the tropical fish weaving knowingly in a coral pond. He knew the routine: he told them his business, who he was, who he wanted to see. The reception staff made him a temporary visitor's badge and asked him to wear it at all times.

'OK,' he said, attaching it to his jacket lapel.

'Take the elevator, basement level three.'

'Thanks. I'll use the stairs.'

'As you wish, monsieur. To your left.'

'Yes, I know. Merci.'

Intuition, in the better guise of reason, should have guided him, but a hard determination engraved in rage drove him along a path

549

of makeshift fortitude instead. This was daring crafted in distemper. It was inevitable he would arouse curiosity, so he never pretended discretion or politeness. He wore a grave frown as a mask of his intentions. It amounted to effect - this challenge - to make an impact, to incite surprise, to set the opposition on tenterhooks. But amid the imminent struggle, he would need to counter the unexpected when it strikes with reason and resilience. Could he do that? Could he finish what he started? He had little time to ponder. Preparing for battle is much the same, you steel your nerves, you drum the moral into your mind again and again that fate favors the brave: those who dare, those who stand against the troubles that besiege them and hammer on the door of adversity, that you are the victor in this drama, the charmed protagonist, the one handed the lucky coin, now, pressing it between his fingers.

'Ice.'

'Hard Eight.' His expression was calm, untroubled.

Roy deliberately spun out time, waiting. Then: 'You don't seem very surprised to see me.'

'I'm astonished,' he said, coaxing soft wonder with his cool eyes. 'Are you paying us a surprise visit, or just passing through?'

'I'm getting married, actually.'

His face bloomed with genuine surprise, before cascading through doubt and derision. 'I see...' his psychic sense tracing the aura of suspicion. 'Have you met our wonder boy Michael Leoni?'

Roy turned to the wonder boy who gazed back with suppressed irritation and blushed. 'I'm always keen to meet wonder boys.'

'He's your fellow countryman,' said Ice.

'That doesn't surprise me,' remarked Roy as they shook hands. Though still wary, he began to relax. 'Tell me, *Mike* – can I call you Mike? Thanks a bunch. Have you been around here long, Mike?'

'About a year or so...Yes. No. Around that... We've met once before, haven't we?'

Unnerved by Roy's presence, Michael struggled with its absurd coincidence, unable to imagine it as anything but engineered, hatched quietly as a pretext for some ulterior motive, and he suspected Roy to be 'in on it' whatever *it* was that Ice was up to. Michael exchanged terse civilities with Roy, affable reminiscences on home, and New

York, and general trivia that lift away embarrassments and use up idle time. In this, Michael acted too formally, and Roy grinned, cutting himself a tease at his expense. 'You're way too glacial for an American, wouldn't you say? We're incendiary. We light fires; we don't put them out. What have they done to you?'

'He's found himself a nice French girl, Roy,' said Ice.

'Has he?'

'I believe he has. She's clearly tamed him, and eased the Yankee fire a touch.'

'Good for you, old sport,' Roy rapped him teasingly on the shoulder. 'Or maybe that's not so good. It depends on how horny you get. No? Testosterone. It sucks buckets, eh?'

How did Ice know about Sara? Did he see them together at the club, or dip into the pool of office gossip? Perplexed and irritated, he couldn't think straight. 'Excuse me,' said Michael hurriedly, 'I have some work to do.'

'Anything interesting?' Roy intrigued in a tone of insinuation.

'Just routine things,' he said, briefly looking away. 'Just nuts and bolts stuff... but it has to be done.'

'A bit tedious, is it, Mike?'

'No. Not quite. Besides, I try and put a bit splash on.'

'Good for you. Is there anything I might be able to help you with, perhaps? I'm good at making a splash.'

'That's unlikely, Mr. Riemann.'

'Please, call me Roy. It's as if we're buddies, after all. Just think how much we have in common. Are you sure I can't lend a hand?'

'That's kind of you, Roy. But no thanks.'

'Would you mind if I watch?'

'Watch?' He was taken aback. 'How do you mean?'

'With my eyes closed.'

He grinned nervously. 'You're playing with me.'

'He's being clever,' Ice cut in, 'aren't you, Roy?'

'I can't help it; it's my nature. – Can we smoke down here?'

'Michael, don't you think he's being clever?'

'I think I should go?'

'Do you know what I most admire about the eyes?' Roy detained him. 'Let me tell you. The eyes, they have infinite capacity. Even a

551

splash, when caught by the eyes, grows and grows. Eventually this gaping gaze multiplies in size, until all it seeks to do is suck up the whole world. And it all started with a tiny splash.'

'I don't quite follow.'

'Greed and gazing, Mike, they're birds of a feather. They have infinite capacity. They can swallow the world whole, and never have enough.'

A silence followed, framed more by hesitation than a thinking space. Eventually, Ice said:

'I don't suppose you can put that in French?'

'No... But I'm learning to master it in Greek.'

'Is there a riddle there?'

'Let's ask Peeping Tom.'

'Who?'

'Oh, just someone we all know.'

'Excuse me, Mr. Riemann, I have a meeting to go to.'

'Don't mind me, Mike. You go right ahead. I'm sure we'll meet up again real soon. In fact, I'm certain of it.'

'Good bye, Mr. Riemann.'

'Please, call me Roy,' he continued as Michael strode away. 'It's like we're chums already, wouldn't you say? *See* you later...' A sense of futility seized him then, for he suddenly felt his antics as absurd. What was he trying to do – be clever? Frustration with his actions left their mark, and he felt even more powerless than before. But he just wanted to hit back, and couldn't resist his own folly. Sometimes, even a punch thrown pointlessly at the unfeeling air lends weight to the moment, because human instinct abhors a cage, and will try anything to break free. In this sense, perhaps, his histrionics were a desperate prayer. And anything is worth a try; even the grim expression of fortitude when they were alone.

'What are you really doing here?' Ice asked him coldly while seeing him out.

'I told you, I'm getting married.'

'Really?'

'Really.'

'Married!' He broke out with genuine surprise. 'I never saw that one coming.'

Roy's fury convulsed and he turned on him powerfully: 'Perhaps you're playing the wrong game, *mister!*'

The mood abruptly changed. The deck was cleared. Call. All cards were shown. Face up.

'We need to talk.'

'Now!' demanded Roy. 'Right now!'

'No.'

'When?'

'Later.'

'When?'

'I'll call you.'

'When?'

'At eight.'

Roy looked at his wristwatch: it was six fifteen. He kept staring hard, playing for time, arranging his confused feelings as best he could. In a sense the pressure was off, yet it was on. He felt ambivalent, certain of his aim, yet doubting his motivation. He knew where he was going, but he was walking through the dark, and even the certainty of knowing where to go felt unsettling. 'You have my phone number?' he said bluntly. 'I assume you do.' It was a question posed resentfully as a failed threat. It annoyed him.

'Of course.' Ice was measured but circumspect, taking his time to answer, hoping to unnerve Roy in the exchange. It never worked.

While waiting by the elevator, Roy suddenly remembered Victor and asked Ice where he was? Ice never procrastinated or lied - this was a card he was willing to show, not giving it away, but sending a signal of his self-confidence, his own best hand. Perhaps as a foil.

'He's in London.'

'London?'

'Sleeping off a colossal hangover. Most likely, he'll be out of action for a few days.' He smiled as a challenge. 'You don't believe me. Call his wife. Or...' he paused deliberately, 'perhaps his mistress. He has a mistress, you know. She's quite a beauty. Would you like her phone number?'

Roy fixed him a stare and said with contempt. 'I'll call him myself.'

'And remember to send him my regards, won't you.'

When the elevator doors parted Sam, reading some papers, stepped out. Only slightly lifting his head he noticed Ice and began, 'Ice, I – ' but when he saw Roy beside him he stopped and stared intently. He seemed more than startled, his frantic gaze froze in horror as though he had seen a ghost.

'Sam, meet Roy Riemann from New York.'

They shook hands tentatively, each man shuddering in silence. Ice continued:

'He's getting married.'

'Why?' said Sam.

'Because we're in Paris,' said Roy, striding into the elevator before the doors closed. 'And that's what couples do here. Remember?'

Outside, under cover from the rain, he pulled the nametag off his lapel and was on the verge of throwing it away, but had second thoughts and slipped it back into his pocket. *Don't be rash, Roy,* he cautioned himself and, hailing down a cab, made his way back to the hotel, and the kitten.

*

'Damn it, Ice!'

'Look, Sam - '

'No! You look. Do you really expect me to believe this is all coincidence?'

'I told you; he just turned up. How was I to know?'

'Ice - '

'Sshhh,' he shushed him anxiously. 'Keep your voice down. You shouldn't even be down here. What if you're seen? – Quick, let's go in here.' Ice led him down the corridor to a vacant room. They went inside, he switched on the lights, locked the door, and then confronted him. 'Sam, just listen to me, will you?'

'It's bullshit.'

'It'll be fine; you'll see.'

'The cat's out of the bag, damn it!'

'So long as it's not a Tomcat, we're OK.'

'Don't get clever!' he snapped at him. 'What are you going to do?'

Ice sat down with deliberate calmness, self-conscious in his action. Sam remained standing, looming but looking volatile in his rages.

He repeated the question, and Ice coolly answered:

'It's very unwise to rush into things, especially now.'

'You'd better think fast, mister!'

'One step at a time.' Ice closed his eyes and pondered, the softness of his action giving weight to the sense that he had reached a decision, and was seeking a way to convey it. It seemed that the simplest things were the most troubling to overcome. 'Sam.'

'What?'

He opened his eyes. 'The game is over. We have to end it. We need to be discreet.'

'It's your head on the block, mister!'

Ice paused, his eyes hovering contemptuously over him. 'Don't threaten me.'

'Then do something.'

'About what, exactly? He's here to get married. If he causes any mischief we'll - '

'Mischief?'

'Call it whatever you like. If he causes any problems, we'll deal with it. As always, we'll deal with it.'

'You'll deal with it.'

Ice leaned his arms on the table, resting them deliberately, calmly, as if for a conference, but it was evident he intended to bring Sam in short. 'For a pretty respectable poker player, you're rather rash in a crisis, if crisis it be. It seems all your recent success really was no more than a rare spell of good luck. And I look forward to the certainty of winning all my money back.'

Sam glared with loathing, then marched to the door, seized the handle, turned it, stopped, swung bitterly around, and threatened. 'If I were you, I'd watch my back, mister.'

'I always do. Are you watching yours?' He wasn't going to be intimidated. 'If you push, I'll push back harder. And at the end of it all Roy will be left picking up the pieces and laughing all the way to the bank. – Sam.'

'What?'

'Wait. Where are you going?'

'I need to think,' he said, his whole being tormented, opening the door and driving himself out as if in a daze, unsure whether to turn left or right and starting left only stopped and went right then left again then right, languishing in a fevered choice that mattered not a jot, yet seemed to crush him.

To have everything one desires within reach, only for a rude intrusion from afar to clench away the dream: this proved a revelation in character, that men enchanted with easy wealth feel pain most not when a villain has a dagger at their throat, but when a straight guy in a business suit tries to slip a hand in their pocket, and steal the riches from them.

Ice remained alone feeling the emptiness of the room engulf him. He sensed only the stillness until his fingers started to gently stir and tap monotonously on the table, consciously following the period of a clock. Thoughts flooded into his mind. He knew time wasn't abstract anymore, it was counting down, and he would have to meet it. Thus, gently pacing himself, he lit a cigarette, inhaling deeply to stretch out time, holding it just so, before exhaling out completely until a faint smile emerged upon his contemplative face, and he felt... alone. Totally alone. Sam's disruptive passions he only briefly dwelled on. What preoccupied him was his own troubling tendency to act on the fly, like the turn of a card, and improvise himself out of crises, or even danger. A foundation of knowledge, like experience, is a great boon to a man, but he sometimes pushed his luck too far. The cards convey a riddle, and he answered with a bluff. And the rules, sure, there to be broken, we all do that, we're only human. But he failed to appreciate that they could break him too. *It cuts both ways.* He realized that now, and he shuddered, the tremble of understanding when you see before your eyes what your true limits are.

Ice suspected, reasonably, that Roy, for all his bluff, was clueless in the main. It was a fair bet that Roy was pushing in the dark, a blind man pretending to see, knocking around with his walking stick, irritating people. Ice could read the signs of desperate men, of human behavior under duress. The problem for Ice was, however, that irritation is often enough to undo an empire of ambition. Roy's threat rested not in knowing things in detail or even vaguely, but in provoking Ice to make a slip, to set the train of rumor in motion, knowing that an avalanche would result; in alerting people, the authorities; poking around, stirring the pot of mischief with that dumb blind stick of his. It was utterly ludicrous: how could he be beaten with this! He held all the cards, but alas! *the rules had changed*. Ice was devoid of plan B because he never really believed he would need to have, let alone execute, plan A. For him, only information counted, it alone had clout, it was worth any number of bets, and that would buy him out of any trouble, and erase his debts. It was his guardian angel, this information, his inexhaustible asset, the golden stock that in the market of ambition buys him anything he wanted, opens any door he needed, provides a shield against adversity. Always. You never imagine when you are up that you can go down. Yet now he cursed himself a fool because in poker he knew better: *It's not the cards you play. It's the player.* And whether you do so or not, the other guy's playing you.

At that moment, reminiscing, he remembered saying to his father as a precocious twelve year old boy: '*As I am so good at working things out, father, what should I be when I grow up? A mathematician? A scientist? A doctor?*' - '*Sherlock Holmes,*' said his father in amused, proud jest.

'Sherlock Holmes...' Ice echoed reminiscently, stubbing out his cigarette and, on his way out, paused instinctively to examine the room, saw everything was in its place, then switched off the lights, closed the door, and returned to his work.

Chapter 31

An itch... no matter how achingly benign, or irritatingly soft, an itch, even in a giant, demands to be scratched, or it will simply drive you crazy. Forester was no exception: his itch was a vexed mind sifting the puzzle of the case for clues, grasping in the dark for solutions. Examining his notepad, he mouthed the name *Bléu Doux*, stretching the vowels as if to snap them, despite that he knew the name by heart, habit, like an itch, he found difficult to overcome, and the notepad somehow seemed to define crime investigation as a set of clues drafted in your own hand. There's a reassuring sense of having been the author. He hailed down a cab and asked the taxi driver to take him to *Bléu Doux*.

'Would you like me to hurry?' asked the cabbie. 'Are you meeting someone there, monsieur?'

'No hurry,' he said, and looked at his wristwatch. He had time to spare, with nothing else to do, and had this itch that needed scratching. The cabbie droned about the weather; that the climate was changing for the worse; that the cost of living was spiraling; that women were losing their femininity and men were turning into Dorothy, and he was glad he wouldn't be around to see the decline of the world. It had a good old run over the years, he said, sounding full of pathos. 'I rather liked being a man. It felt good *not* to be a woman... Who the hell would want to be a woman after knowing what it was like to be a man?... You, monsieur?'

Forester shook his head, sympathizing with him in general, and asked him to drive around the city and include some of the notable sights of Paris: along the Champs-Elyseés; down to the Eiffel Tower, around the Arch de Triomphe, and then cruise along the bank of the River Seine - both sides.

The taxi driver chuckled. 'Who do you think you are? Napoleon!'

'Just a romantic,' he said, leaning back in the seat and gazing with awe at the spectacle. 'A true romantic. And a cop.'

'Le cop?'

'Yes.'

'American?'

'Yes.'

'Ah!'

'Romantic American,' he said. And time kind of plucked him a kiss and then stood still, romancing the moment and the imagination.

'Do you want to go around again, Mr. Romantic American?'

'Another time, merci. Now, take me to Bléu Doux.'

'*Bléu Doux*? OK, monsieur.'

And the closer he drew, the itch grew ever more tender and delicious, and he stroked it, just so, gently, and shut his eyes against the rain.

The exterior facade of *Bléu Doux* was a musical note in grey-blue: shades of grey with an aura of blue. A color that wanted you to guess: *What am I?* And you imagine to yourself: *Yes, I want to get to know you; to be close to you.* And you step inside and find yourself very much at home; the interior breathes and you marvel: *Go inside, there's more...* And it pulls you in, like a lover, like Billie Holiday singing a blues piece in that sensuous voice – Lady Day's a-humming. Trust the sound, the voice, as it take you to places, there – where? – this... other spaces, and creates new worlds, strangely reminiscent of remembered things, a déjà vu in blue. And all he has to do was let jazz set the tempo of desire, and the whole world falls into place.

Well, that's jazz!

Forester, breathing with satisfaction, strode deeper inside. And the interior, like a flower in bloom, opened out for him. This was a setting for those who knew what they wanted, aficionados of midnights and twilights, of surround sound jazz and blues, serene decor tailored for the senses, shades and shadows in suggestive poses not to linger under but to seduce you into a dreaminess of mind, not a home away from home, but a place to take you out of yourself, to throw off the skin, to unleash the unconscious drives and discover the deeper spectacle. You came here not to be yourself, but refashion yourself in mythology. If music was a metaphor for life, *Sweet Blue* was a metaphor for the senses: explosive, inquisitive, a million-million itches working all at once for your total attention. You came here to find an itch, and scratch yourself to delirium. *Ouch! times a million-million.*

He walked up to the bar. 'What a wonderful place you have here,' he said to the bartender, who answered him instantaneously with:

'Are you English, sir?'

'Are you American?'

'Let's just say we're both here in Paris. Agreed?'

'Sure.' said Forester, smiling. 'Sure.'

'Good. What would you like to drink?'

'Hmm... Do you have tea?'

'Tea! Not another one. Are you kidding me? For goodness sake, look where you are.' The bartender seemed distraught, and Forester absently replied.

'But I'm feeling a bit queasy.'

'That's the idea. Look where you are. Isn't it amazing? Go on, have a proper drink. What is it with Americans and tea lately? Have you lost your bearings? Do you need a compass? You're in magnetic heaven now, you know. Only jazz compasses work here. We're detuned out all the suffering stuff. And we have jazz to thank for that.'

'Give me a whiskey and soda.'

'That's more like it,' he heaved with relief. 'Pull up a stool, sir. Leave headaches and your skin outside on the sidewalk. Yesterday is a burned out cigarette. Ashtray? Please, have a seat and make yourself at home. Comfy? Good The show starts in an hour, and the restaurant is now open. Through there. Would you like me to reserve you a table?'

'Perhaps later. Have a drink yourself.'

He grinned: 'Don't worry, it's not tea. I'll have an orange juice, thanks very much.'

The bartender could see Forester wanted to chat, and since the bar wasn't very busy, he said cheers, your health, and waited for Forester to begin:

He took out his ID and showed it to him.

'I'm actually a cop from New York City.'

'That's interesting. Are you on vacation, sir?'

'No. I'm looking for someone. Perhaps you can help.'

'Of course, if I can. Fire away.'

'I'm looking for a young woman named Zoë Long. She's an American. I believe she once worked here?'

'Zoë? Yes, she did. She left a couple of weeks back.'

'I see. – May I ask what she did here?'

'Officially, she was a waitress.'

'And unofficially?'

'She used to get them things.'

'Who?'

'The patrons.'

'Oh, I see... What things?'

'Things. Dope. You know.'

'Oh... I see.'

'It's not what some of your more *genteel* patrons would want to be seen trading in.'

'I guess not.'

'*Patrons* is a fancy word, you know.'

'Fancy that.'

'They feel it lowers them to deal directly with the pushers. This sort of merchandise feels sweeter coming from a soft hand and a pretty face.'

'I guess so....' said Forester, not dismayed, or indifferent, nor even surprised, but in a world as corrupted as this one... well, same game, just a different street.

'Nasty business, isn't it, Detective?'

'Yes,' he said. 'Yes it is.'

'What can you do?'

'Nothing. Just don't let it get to you, that's all. You'd be amazed at the little things that can crush you.'

'How little?'

'Almost invisible.'

'That small?'

'Almost imperceptible.'

The bartender sighed and attended to another customer, returning shortly to resume the conversation. 'Did she do anything wrong in the States, Zoë that is?'

'No. She's missing. Her family is concerned, and I'm just trying to trace her.'

'Honest?'

'Honest. We just want to find her. Her sister's worried, as you'd appreciate, and is in town looking for her.'

'What does she look like, the sister?'

'They're twins.'

'No problem in spotting her then,' he chuckled.

'Can you tell me anything at all about Zoë? Did she take drugs herself?'

'No, not really. Well... only the very soft stuff. A few puffs at the end of the night; after work; to unwind; to relax. You know...?' he said, wondering if Forester believed him. 'Believe me; she *always* kept her wits about her. And I mean *always.*'

That sounded interesting, and Forester asked him to explain.

'Well, she had a passion for card games, especially poker. She tried her luck at a few of the top tables, but never really had the touch, and the serious players had no time for her. But she persisted; really worked hard at her game, and realized it's not just the game, but the players themselves. We have a *very private* room upstairs, wink wink; if you get my drift?' he winked at him. 'It's patronized by some of the heavyweights who dine here from time to time. You know, guys with money to burn. And I mean bonfires. Unless you're fire-proof, the heat is searing. These guys... they have the talent for the game; make no mistake. And it can get real hot up there, I hear.'

'Just rumors?'

'No, some guys are like that; attracted by the heat. It's a passion; an instinct; maybe even a fate. That's what they say, anyway. It makes you stop and wonder.'

'And Zoë, how did she react to getting the cold shoulder?'

'Hard at first; but she was ambitious and bit the nail. Nothing was going to stop her. She's not the kind to lie around and mope. She may be young, but she learns fast. And being Zoë, well, naturally, she wanted to play poker like the best of them. So she starts hob-knobbing with the top crowd whenever she could. You know, she started to attract them, the top knobs. And, once she got inside, she started to unravel them. To understand the men that play; how they weigh the odds; how they improvise; how they handle the cold cards and read the other players. She wanted to master those things that luck alone can't bring, and you're either born with or learn, if that's possible. So... she went with them. You know, she used her own trump card to get what she wanted.'

'Herself?'

'Yes.'

'Was she harmed in any way?'

'No. Not that I noticed. She was always focused on that one thing: the game. She said to me once, "When you know what you want, go straight for it." And she did just that. It must have been the essence of her learning these things.'

'The game?'

'Yes. The straight line is the simplest. You want it, she said, it's there. It's not going to come to you.'

'Why did she leave?'

He lowered his voice and drew closer to answer him: 'Rumor has it her learning paid off handsomely, and she really made a packet.'

'How much?'

'Enough to retire on.'

'When did you hear this?'

'The grapevine; about a week ago.'

'Do you know how I might be able to contact her, or know of someone who could help me find her?'

'Not off hand, no. But if what I hear is true, what would you do if you were in her place?' He hinted knowingly, 'Think about it.'

'I'm sorry, I don't follow.'

'Well, if it was me, the last thing I would want is to be found. I'd make myself scarce. Do you know what I mean?'

'From whom?'

'Everyone. The taxman, the lover, the loser, the scrounger, and people in general.'

'Why?'

'To keep it all. To make my money safe. After all, when it comes to money, who can you really trust?' He spoke persuasively, looking straight at him. 'Think about it.'

'But what if she lost it all?'

'Lost it? Where? How?'

'At a card game. Easy come, easy go. Besides, you said she was infatuated with the game.'

'True,' he said, wondering aloud. 'That never crossed my mind.'

'Winning is not the problem. It's knowing when to stop,' said Forester. 'Do you think she would know when to stop?'

'You mean *could* she stop?'

'Yes.'

He paused, trying to understand. Perhaps some enigmatic aspect of Zoë made him wonder longer than he would have imagined it possible – there are some things that hold your mind, that are trifling things, but in certain settings emerge as profound: 'No. I guess not. But that's only my opinion. I knew her; sure. But we weren't intimate. Just friends.'

The bartender withdrew to serve another customer, and on his return Forester asked him about the poker players she went with.

'Well,' he said, grinning, 'there's one of them sitting right over there, all on his own with a bottle of his favorite whiskey. Drown buddy, drown. - Looks like he lost a game or two, don't he just?'

Forester looked at him and asked who he was.

'That fella is Sam Tomka, alias Double Heads, his name at the poker table. And I bet he wished he had that other head with him now. - Are you leaving already?'

'I'm going to make myself acquainted with Double Heads.' He smiled at the bartender, who wished him luck and informed him:

'By the way, he's an American.'

Forester approached him, coughed to signal his presence, and said, 'Excuse me, my name is John Forester, do you mind if I ask you some questions?'

Sam threw him a cursory glance wondering who this man was. 'What?'

'Drowning your sorrows, I see. May I join you?'

'Who the hell are you?'

'John Forester.' He presented his ID but Sam took no notice and just guessed aloud:

'A cop?'

'Relax, sir, I'm just looking for a missing person.'

Sam scowled, which made him appear like a man rousing from a hangover.

'Are you a private *dick?*' he said sarcastically.

'I try *hard* not to be.'

Trying to laugh, Sam grunted instead and said, 'All right,' indicating with a careless shrug of his head, and Forester took a seat.

Meanwhile, as Sam poured himself another drink, Forester showed him a photograph. - 'Do you know her?'

'No.'

'Have you ever seen her around?'

'No.'

'Please, look carefully.'

He gulped down his whiskey, rudely seized the photograph, and scrutinized it hard. Hesitantly, he drew a faint smile of recognition, and flirted with a needless chuckle. Then he looked at Forester and handed him back the photograph.

'Well?' said Forester.

'Well what?'

'I'm looking for her.'

'Good luck.'

'May I ask you some questions? It won't take long.'

He stopped drinking and clutched his head intensely for a moment to get a grip on himself, then leaned back in his chair as if to say *OK, Mr. Forester, I'll tell you all I know. But don't push me, OK?*

'Sir, may I ask you some questions?' repeated Forester.

Sam shrugged his head in assent, languidly rubbing his eyes.

'Where did you first meet her?'

'Here; at the club. I met her here.'

'I see.'

'Well... She worked here. She gave me her card. Here,' he searched in his wallet, found it, and passed it over. 'It has her picture on it.'

'I see.'

'She looked sweeter in the flesh.'

Forester gave him back the card, and asked boldly. 'So you felt like having a fling with a pretty young thing?'

566

Sam smiled, the rhyme *fling-thing* caught his attention, and he was on the verge of enlarging it, but at the last moment stopped and just answered the question:

'There was nothing unusual about it; nothing at all. Sometimes we played cards here at the club, several of the guys and I, and she hung around until after the game. She pushed herself onto me. What would any man do?'

'Lucky you.'

'That's me,' he boasted with a flashy grin that somehow seemed to epitomize him completely. 'She came on strong. She was all over me.' He laughed needlessly. 'I don't mind flattery; it improves the art of fornication... more than you can imagine.' He paused (what was he waiting for, thought Forester, applause?) 'I'm only a man. It's gets to us all, I guess.'

'What does?'

'Flattery.'

'Oh...'

'Yes.'

'I suppose it does.'

'Do you think being a cop makes you any different? Or any less vulnerable?'

'I'm sorry, I don't follow.'

'Women are like a deck of cards; sometimes they show their hand; sometimes they don't.'

'What are you saying?'

'I'm not really sure. I'm only a man, remember? And we're mostly in the dark. - Is that all, Detective?'

'What attracted you to her? Why her?'

Sam reflected, his gaze following the smooth ripples of cigarette smoke rising serenely and vanishing into air – like the ghost of his presence, really. 'She had this very particular mannerism, like a little girl, that turned me on. Perhaps she could read me like an open book.' He smiled. 'I'm full of poems, you see, and all she had to do was dip inside, and pick at her fancy.'

'She must have found that interesting.'

'It's sweet in a way. I suppose, deep down, I'm a real big softie at heart.'

'And Zoë?

'Zoë's like fire. She's attracted to the heat. And yet... very gentle.'

'It made you stop and think?'

'Made me spin a bit. Sure. There's the hard side; and then there's the soft side. You need to see both; preferably at the same time.'

'Why? Most men wouldn't bother.'

'I'm not most men.'

'And what makes you different?'

'That's the only way to really see yourself.' Sam's smile waned to a mellow frown. 'Maybe I'm a voyeur. My eyes, you see, obsessed with gazing at the self.' His eyes conveyed the weight of confession, and he shrugged. 'At least I'm honest with myself. What about you, Mr. Forester?'

Together, they looked at her picture. She seemed innocent but had the teasing *You want to fuck me* look that makes men explosive and drives them crazy. Looking at that picture, at her sweetness, her vulnerability, one would imagine a girl out of her depth toying with emotional forces more muscular than she could handle, more formidable than she could ever comprehend. Some risks seem easy, because the outcome is certain, like a man holding all four aces who raises the stakes, round after round... It's a sure bet. Sure. Guaranteed. Just go with the flow. So you gamble and bet some more. Until it becomes a habit. And then you're more certain than certainty itself. That's when life steps in and checks your rise. Sometimes you're lucky. And sometimes, not.

'And what happened then?' continued Forester.

'We arranged to meet. I picked her up from her apartment.'

'And?'

'I took her to my place.'

'Directly?'

'We stopped at a bar.'

'Drink much?'

'Vodka martinis.'

'And?'

'She had a cherry.'

'That's sweet.'

'Well... we were just killing time.'

568

'How did you find her?'

'A sweet face; petite frame; very slightly older than her pictures, but not much. She has more maturity than the pictures suggest. But hey... still young.' He seemed to weigh his words, gesturing randomly to things around him. 'Considering the competition out there, she'd sit somewhere in the upper middle league. Pretty; yes. Beautiful; no. As I always say, it's character that's enduring.' He turned away and resumed smoking. 'She enjoyed the attention and loved a fuss made over her. You see, with women, they want to feel the world revolves around them, even if it's only someone taking them on a carousel ride at a fun park. But guys, well... A roll in the hay, that's all it takes to get them spinning.'

'And that's how it was?

'What?'

'You and Zoë?'

'Look, I have rules about this, and I usually stick to them. She was like a young puppy stranded in the world that I just happened to pick up, but which I seldom go for. I prefer women with a lot more meat on them, and more years too. But this one just happened to catch my eye. I get passes from women all the time. It's not a major event. This one was a little different, that's all.'

Forester had a hundred questions, but he shut up and let him talk.

'Some people you meet, and I don't know why, but their presence alone forces you to question your nature. And that makes life complicated. I'm too settled and savvy to carry the burden of self-loathing. I can't let a woman cloud my mind. I am, what you might call, a well-rounded guy that flirts with a square peg, but has no real intention of ever fitting into one. – At the end of the day, it's all just a game to me.'

'And so you play.'

'Why not – square peg and a round hole, it's just flirting...'

'Like birds and the bees?'

Sam sighed, an expression full of easy liquor. 'I know it's pushing the envelope, but I get a kick out of taking chances.' He looked at Forester bluntly. 'Don't we all from time to time?'

You can't knock a man for being horny, or single him out for lapping at the fresh young cream when there are oceans of it waiting to be drunk. His conscience holds him back, perhaps, but the yielding of the moral case is a perfect example of easy money finding easy sex a turn on. He continued:

'So, back at my place, she took off her clothes and, oh boy! it was now plain to see how young she was. I took a shower as she lay on the bed. I stayed in there a long time. So long that by the time I got out she was asleep. So I retired to an armchair, turned on the TV, lowered the volume, had a beer, and eventually crashed out. In the morning I awoke and she was gone. She took a cigarette from the fresh pack I left lying on the table, and left the rest.' (It was just a cigarette, but it made him think that, deep down, she took a hell of a lot more. She opened his eyes). 'Society can screw kids up. But some, they retain a moral sense; and guide their lives by it.' He paused, seeming more compassionate. 'She's a good kid, and she should go back home to college and settle down.'

'I don't suppose you mentioned that at the time?'

'No. It never entered my mind.'

'Then what did?'

'The conversation flowed easily, and I always find that a turn on. She was an interesting, articulate girl and, now I really think about it, wonderful in many ways. Given a fair chance, and some self-discipline, she could make a real go of it.'

'You struck up a rapport?'

Sam shrugged, reflecting aloud: 'It's just life. That's how it is. I never wrote the script; I just entered the scene. I played a part. We both did. I wanted a lay; she needed... whatever it was she needed. People bring things to a relationship; however brief. And they take them away, too. It might only be a cigarette. I never said I understood any of it, nor even tried to. So why make a song and dance over it? We were strangers passing in the night. We had a drink; some cigarettes; and took it from there. No plan; no end game. No real beginning; and no real end. Just a cigarette.'

'Did you finish the whole pack?'

'No... No I didn't. By the time she left it was almost empty, anyway.'

'Did you smoke slowly?'

'Sure.'

'And when it burned down to the stub, you stopped?'

Sam thought for a moment, and then said. 'All things considered, I felt it was the right thing to do. Some gulfs are not meant to be bridged.'

'Was she ever afraid?'

'No. Shy as first, sure, formal and polite at the beginning. But as time went on and we reached the apartment, just like a switch has been pressed she changed into a soft, sensuous pussycat. She did it right, all the way. But she wasn't a pro.'

'So you stayed in the shower?'

'Yes.'

'What did you talk about? What did she do?'

'She didn't say anything; just threw open the windows; put on the music; and turned down the lights. Then she undressed and lay on the bed. It was all like a motion one remove from reality. So I went into the bathroom and soaked it from my system.'

'And?'

'That's it. In a nutshell, that's all of it.'

'Tell me, what music did she play?'

'Why are you asking me that?'

'It was just a thought.'

'The stuff I had in the player. She just switched it on, danced a bit, smiled, and then removed her clothes. – The rest, you know.'

'OK. Thank you. – Oh, one last thing. Did she mention poker?'

'Strip poker?' asked Sam, glibly.

'No. The card game.'

'Not that I remember.'

'Did you know she played poker?'

'So what?'

'She's good at it, apparently. Very good.'

'So what?' Sam looked irritably at the bottle of whiskey on the table.

'That doesn't suggest anything to you?'

'No. Not a thing.' He broke out suddenly in a fatuous grin. 'Perhaps we'll meet up at a game some day. Do you think she'd win?'

'Let me put it this way,' said Forester, getting up to leave, 'she's most unlikely to lose.'

Outside, at the entrance to the club, there was a man in a casual blue suit meticulously wiping the tiniest blemish off the life-sized billboard of Cindy Gillespie. By his application to the task, the deft and nimble way he brushed with a pristine white handkerchief perched perfectly between thumb and forefinger, almost fondling the blemish to tease it off, one could tell at once this man was a perfectionist.

Forester casually walked up to the billboard, opening a pack of cigarettes, and remarked: 'Cindy Gillespie...' lighting up a cigarette as he looked at her picture.

'Have you heard her sing?' asked Anthony Leoni, folding away his handkerchief.

'No,' he began to smile with anticipation. 'No I haven't.'

'Then you're a schmuck!' he told him bluntly. 'Get with it; or get moving!' And coughing to clear his throat, strode on inside.

Americans! exclaimed Forester, frowning. *You ask them a simple question, and what do you get?*

A smart ass sonofabitch knowitall bum, that's what. - Son. Hi, Pop. Go ahead, I'm listening. *That bum ain't no New Yorker. He ain't from my town.* Oh? *You should have cuffed him one, son, right across the chops, just like I showed you. Whack! Whack! Do you remember? Whack!* This is France, Pop, I'd be arrested. *Nah! They arrest bums like him; not NYPD.* I'll bear that in mind, Pop, for next time. *Yeah! You do that... Whack, whack, and whack... right across the chops!*

'Taxi! Taxi!' Forester hailed at a passing cab, but the rain must have obscured the driver's view and he drove on, leaving Forester stranded there until the doorman reached for his phone and called him a cab.

'All you had to do was ask,' he said, smiling.

'Thanks.' He smiled back gratefully. 'I'll remember that.'

Chapter 32

'Hello, Charlie, how's it going?'

His name was *Charles*, the *ch* aspirated ideally as *zcher*, *a la Français*, concierge at *Bléu Doux*, who gazed peevishly at Anthony as he floated into the club on a cushion of crescendos. 'Ah... I'm siiiiinging in the rain... just siiiiiinging in the rain. Nice day, friend. How's it going?' winking as he coasted on stopping first at reception, 'Bonjour and merci, mon ami... How's it going today?' dropping off his briefcase, asking for any messages, 'Nothing today? Ah! Merci, mon ami... Merci. How's it going?' then striding up to the long bar, 'Been busy today, Will?' ordering whiskey and ice, and smiling at the bartender. 'How's it going today?'

'How many times must I remind you?' retorted the bartender. 'My name's Terry. Terry. Can you remember that, *please?*'

'OK, Will, have yourself a drink; and put it on my tab.' And thus enamoring himself to all and sundry, Anthony Leoni strode in to the restaurant and took his regular table where a waiter spotted him and gracefully glided into his presence:

'Bonjour, Monsieur Leoni. Have you had a pleasant day?'

'I most certainly have. It's been an all round great day. How's it going with you?'

He said not bad, and offered him a menu.

'Later,' he declined politely with a gesture and glanced at the stage. 'Have you seen Cindy around?'

'No, monsieur, I haven't. But I do recall seeing her sister? They look remarkably alike, no?'

'Where?'

'She went upstairs, I believe.'

'Upstairs?'

'To the private room.'

'The poker room? Do you mean *that* room?' he was astonished to learn this and jumped to conclusions. 'How long ago?'

'Just recently, monsieur.'

'Who else is up there?'

'No one, monsieur. Just her, I believe. She wanted somewhere quiet to work.'

'Ahhhh... I see,' he sighed with relief and lit a cigarette. 'Better let her be, then. She's a moody customer is our Amber, and I wouldn't want to get on her wrong side.' He paused and reflected obliquely to amuse himself: 'Come to think of it, her wrong side is probably more interesting. What do you think?'

'What is life but taking calculated risks, monsieur?'

'You've read my mind perfectly.'

'Hors d'oeuvres, monsieur?' he proposed temptingly, and it seemed to hit the spot.

'Hmm,' he leisurely considered, 'that'll be just perfect. Merci.'

The best waiters read the clientele, not simply their tastes, but their moods and moments too that define an evening of pleasure starting with the finest hors d'oeuvres, a bottle of wine - white, red, rosé, it depended on the moment, perhaps even the ambiance, what whets the appetite, what teases the palate. And it's smiles all round as surround-sound jazz permeates the space with lounge melodies honed for easy listening – this, the soft easy hour in prelude to the show proper, when restless percussion erupts with passion, and the hardcore beat sweats out from the essence of jazzmen, all fevered with lyrical fire and rapture and profound sound. Now was a soft phase, where even the waiters' footfalls seemed to harmonize with the patter pat patter of the drum beat, swaying to the mood, immersed in the vibes, as if gentle dance defined the meaning of the world.

The muffled chatter of a modest crowd seemed to woo jazz to a slumber, teasing it to softly play, sonata-like, not a single bar or note intruding on their pleasure, just harmony going with the flow, in sympathy with their needs, in step to the intoxicated spirit of a woman and a man capable of debauchery, but now abated to a calm and carried on the crest of style. Life - it's jazz. And jazz?... kinda like life, I guess. *Patter pat patter... Hmmm.*

Anthony watched the crowd simply, his gaze floating over the faces, discreetly dipping into a conversation or two at neighboring tables. Initially just humoring himself, he latched on to a party to his left, three men in their handsomely tailored suits. He had to admire the cut: they had style. They drank too much; sure, but that's normal for guys like these like heat from a fire – strike a match and heat up the hormones... *Sizzle!* It doesn't require a great deal of heat. No. Just a pinch. It's the fire that burns within that's crucial. Style is second nature for consumers with money to burn, and what does it cost? A couple of matchsticks. What does it give you? Style. Pretty priceless really, considering...

The party that Anthony watched was a trio of horny men clothing their sexual innuendos in waves of masculine banter. It's common knowledge with these guys, the cock carries the mind, the rear carried the sense, which leaves little of significance for the head, but the ears, when men go into listening mode. - "Hey, that sounds nice, doesn't it?" "It sure does." "Do you think so?" "I think so." "Me too." "Yeah..." was commentary that a gang of apes would make dressed in stylish suits and sitting at a table in a jazz bar.

Strike another match. *Sizzle*...

Anthony contrasted them with jazz. If they were akin to musicians, then they were suckers never knowing what it meant – a saxophone; a horn; piano. They improvise a solo like frothing wind up after a beer; they overplay like amateurs awed at the noise and the spectacle than delving deeper into the meaning of the sound or the rhythms of the piece. Don't they realize, music is sweet; the taste, exquisite? Dress sense aside, are they doomed forever to remain slaves to mere effect, never knowing depth in the music, chasing instant gratification? Is music to them no more than a fuck? Don't they realize, pure sound is love? Don't they? Can't they?

Anthony painfully listened as one ape remarked inanely to his chimpanzee chums.

'Circumstance and circumcision.'

'What's that all about?'

'It sucks!'

Grammar morons! To say something yet mean nothing of the slightest consequence is the bane of the world, and men in particular endowed with lame intelligence. It's really nothing but a self-gratifying chore in killing time. Perhaps, too, it was pain sweetened with luxuries and made to seem contemporary.

Anthony was not engrossed with what unfolded before him, but the vagaries of human nature fascinated him – even a fool could be spied upon with merit; but in measured doses, of course. Perhaps it was the slow unwinding way humans pass from one fuck-up to the next, the way their daft dramas unravel and it's something like a drunken spider caught in its own clumsily constructed web. "What are you trying to catch, your own fuck up?" Are some people predisposed to crassness, just basically inept, so blinkered that they can't even see the hole they're digging for themselves? It can't simply be explained away as stubbornness or habit, Anthony reasoned to himself. No. It was something more fundamental driving them - perhaps fear, fear of being alone, of failing, of... what? Boredom? Themselves? - The truth was, he didn't really care. He was just killing time, having a cigarette, amusing himself, eating hors d'oeuvres, drinking chilled wine...

Before long, Anthony was invited to the table of an acquaintance. He was reluctant to call him 'friend', an endearment reserved for the few, because he found it too embarrassing to ever contemplate. So, acquaintance it was.

'Anthony, it's good to see you, my old friend. How long has it been?' The acquaintance starts off very *friendly-like*. Evidently, the sentiment isn't mutual. 'Please, have a drink with us.'

'Thanks anyway. I'm full.'

The acquaintance coughed formally - here it comes: 'I'd like you to meet my fiancé.'

'Ah, I see.' Anthony behaved courteously, smiling warmly at the lovebirds, even as his mind waltzed with the jingle: S*ome men are born funny, like a donkey with a fanny. And some they just see love and bliss, in a bimbo as they're taking a piss – on them! A*gain!

The acquaintance: Meet Ray Monde, married five times, the first one a virgin, the last one a slut. And they all turned out the same way – they left him.

There's something of a well traveled chronicle in the story of a woman endowed with great breasts and a man with a wooly head. The shearing of sheep suggests a commonplace fact, as does rearing and the shepherding of lambs. Baaa baaa... The talk, like the story, is ever the same. Some men are never happy with their lot in life, crying foul at just about anything. In contrast, some women screw men up; plain and simple. Women. Men. Wool. Sheep. What's the parable here?

Power!

Women naturally take the art of deception in their stride – it's a culture step, the second being entrapment. Men just follow their dicks, and keel over with a hard on. Center of gravity? - *Ouch!*

But women are not to blame. No, give over - these mademoiselles, they're champions of the common will. Give a dog a bone, and she'll chew it. Ray Monde was that bone. And future wife number six was sitting right beside him heaving her bosom, sipping champagne and seeking sympathy for the flight of her finches.

'I left the cage door open to give them some fresh air, and they flew away. Oh Ray,' she cried, 'they flew away.'

'That's what birds do, baby. They fly. Don't you know that?'

'Fly?'

'High.'

'High?'

'Up to the sky.'

'But why? I loved them so much.'

He's a man, and so he *absolutely must* provide an answer. This is an imperative, like being able to keep it up, and words aren't mere seduction, but proof of his manliness. He takes a deep breath and here it comes, packed with fella-with-a-hard-on wisdom: 'Maybe... Maybe they'll come back.'

Anthony drank his whiskey and braced himself for the spectacle. It was so ridiculous it made him want to weep.

She started a lament that unraveled into nonsense about birds and finches and trees and the deep blue sea and the meaning of love and food left uneaten and tropical fish and the planets and the universe and the meaning of life in the suburbs. From a distance, say fifty kilometers away, it looked real enough: it's a strait-jacket case of the long suffering fake blond screwed around by men and regarded as a joke outside of the bedroom by most of them too starved of sex to ever care or give a damn.

'Do you love me, baby?' she coos with that wife number six whimper.

'Of course I do.'

'Really?'

Sure he does. Didn't he just say so? Schmuck a minute fondling his balls per hour and horny at least fifteen times a day he's too exhausted to be anything else. – A schmuck, that is. Love we leave for the saints. And the finches.

'Do you really, really, really love me, baby?' she whimpered.

He gazed into her adorable round eyes, the glazed blue of her irises quite picturesque – words can't convey what enterprise he carries in his balls, heavy with the load of life, and all he really wants to be is deep inside her.

The wise man passes her around. The soft one takes care of her. The philanderer never gives *it* a second thought. Guys – we all fit in somewhere. But him? Well... listen:

'Je t'aime,' he says.

And amen to that!

Just then, perhaps it was the lounge sound pushing up a gear, moving into phrasing mood of sweet bassoons and weeping sax, the swift cascade of a horn leaping in and alerting Anthony to the time, and excusing himself from the hopeless betrothed, he went upstairs.

Amber was sitting alone, with papers scattered over a table, and a computer running a screen saver – a scene of little male devils getting kicked around by girlie angels, and around them a weaving banner in dazzling red: *Men are demons. Men are demons...* And she was crying.

As he started to enter the room proper, she picked up a poker chip and threw it at him.

'What did you do that for?' he protested, keeping by the door. 'Amber? Where's Cindy? What's going on?'

'I hate it when *men* spy on me, follow me, press on me,' she seethed at him.

'They told me you were in here. Jesus Christ, Amber, what's the matter with you? Where's Cindy?'

'Leave me alone. Get out!' But he defied her temper and entered the room. 'Are you leaving?' He stood there solidly, waiting. 'Pig!

Get out of here.' And he swung the door shut with a crashing thud.

'Start talking,' he said. And at that point she threw another poker chip, deliberately wide of him and striking the far wall before cooling her temper and confiding in him. She related her encounter in Las Vegas, the ordeal of being stalked and the coincidence with Cindy's own experience in Paris. She expressed this obsessively and explained the role of the song and the lyrics, the changes she made and what they seemed to imply. Leaving no detail unturned, she speculated and drew a picture of menace, of stalkers, of imminent dangers suggested by the confluence of facts. What facts he asked? Facts, she said emphatically, pained by the refusal of men to hear her side, of men who wouldn't believe her, of the Las Vegas police – men! - attacking them as useless louts for their inaction.

He listened intently, and when she finished he mulled it over in his mind without making a sound, his expression only tenuously linked to her story and more intent on drawing his own conclusions. Finally, he began to frown at her.

'Are you even listening to me?' she cried fiercely at him. 'Pig!'

For an irresistibly sweet female, (especially with pony tails, she's a babe), her pretty eyes shining and lovely, her smooth skin, her delicious hair and sensual lips, she could turn into one hell of a bitch, and dealing with the devil would be easier, he reasoned, before addressing her fears with the retort:

'You're crazy.'

'Bastard!'

'Where's Cindy?'

'In her dressing room. Pig!'

'Coincidence doesn't work like that.'

'Get out.'

'It's fragile.'

'I said get out.'

'Coincidence is fragile.' He started to wander around the room - he just realized, he'd never been in here before, just heard the rumors of some splendid games running on for days. He picked up one of the poker chips she threw, and put it in his pocket. 'Amber, you aren't in a state to think clearly. You're too emotional.'

'Pig!'

'I, on the other hand, am perfectly able. Let me help you.'

'You?'

'Pause a moment and just think what you're saying. Amber, you're creating things out of thin air. I'm not saying that it's fantasy as such, no. But -' he noticed this thread of his reasoning increase her bitterness, so he put it more tactfully. 'What I am saying, Amber, is there's a catch. Something *uncanny* of that kind. Whatever truth there is, whatever the facts, is confused at best, misinterpreted more likely, and the pieces you're pulling together – OK, they sound spooky and I know you're frightened. But look at it objectively. It's absurd.'

'But the lyrics; the stalker...'

'If a stranger had grabbed onto a song, or even your ass, it would have reached a conclusion by now. You'd be in peril long before this.' He drew closer to her. 'For how long has this been going on? A while, I suspect. Ah!' She admitted it had; then he turned and walked over to the door. 'Come on, Amber, you're more gutsy than that. I know you. My guess is someone is playing a game, a prank perhaps, maybe even a jealous rival stirring the pot of mischief. It's not uncommon in this business.' Anthony avoided looking at her. He was thinking something over. 'Try and get some rest. I'm going to see Cindy.' And he left the room.

A torrent of expletives burst from her wonderful mouth, and he causally took them in his stride, never looking at her as he closed the door. Her luscious lungs were in full throttle and her spirit roused, and to his mind every woman needed that kind of catharsis now and again. And men? Well, a good shag should do the trick just nicely.

As he proceeded to Cindy's dressing room his thoughts were in some turmoil, but he never let on. After all, he could always be wrong, even if he was certain he was right. He used the interval in walking to her dressing room in planning what to do. Every able manger has a strategy for dealing with the unexpected, and he was no exception. But he was careful never to draw any conclusions until he saw Cindy and assessed her reactions. Putting on a reassuring smile he confidently knocked on her door and called out her name. Her voice was mellow, but otherwise normal as she invited him inside.

'Hi.'

'Hi, babe. How are you?' He briskly shut the door, and smiled.

'Are you hiding?'

'No.' She tried to smile too, but it was hard.

'Are you OK?'

'Yes. I'm fine.'

'Feeling good? Ready for the show?'

'A-ha.'

'Good. – I just saw Amber.'

'Oh...'

'She's a great song writer, and I love her to death. But she's always been a bit too inventive for her own good at times.'

'Oh...' she turned to the mirror and began to brush her perfectly combed hair, each stroke assured but pointless.

He advanced and kneeled beside her at the dressing table. They gazed at one another in the mirror, via reflection, an arrangement both intimate and safe at the same time, and most appropriate then. 'If you feel uncomfortable in any way, ill at ease, troubled, anything, and you want to go home... Listen, babe, it's OK. Really. We'll pack up and leave. It's as simple as that.'

'Oh...'

'Think about it. In the meantime, I'll look into these coincidences. I'm sure they're nothing; and will all just melt away.'

She remained quiet, thinking.

'Cindy, look at me. I need to make some phone calls. I'll be back in an hour or so.'

Looking directly at him seemed to give her strength. He took her hand and kissed it. And she managed a smile.

'Anthony.'

'Yes?'

She shook her head, 'Nothing. It's fine.'

'I'll be back soon.'

Returning back along the same corridor, Amber turned into his path, and her body visibly stiffened when she saw him. As they converged, she frowned bitterly and lifted her nose at him. It was such a pretty nose, he thought, but she was in no mood for a compliment, and he softly said: 'I know you really adore me... And you're such a sweetie,' even as she lifted her pretty nose higher, it only grew more inviting, and all he wanted to do was lean over and kiss it. But he had other more pressing matters on his mind. Calling his contacts in Las Vegas, among them some chums on the police force, took priority.

A kiss, notwithstanding a pretty nose, could wait.

Chapter 33

Ice lifted the telephone and dialed. It started ringing as he looked at his wristwatch, ahead by fifteen minutes and presently reading quarter to eight, so it was seven thirty. Someone picked up.

'Roy?'

'Ice. – I've been waiting.'

'That's not such a bad thing, is it, Roy?' the tone was leveraged for ruses and intrigue.

'It's getting late. I was beginning to worry.'

'Ah. Timing,' he said breathily. Ice was playing, perhaps not for time, but working the mind of an opponent. 'You know the rule of thumb about timing?'

'Refresh me.'

'The dealer always starts the clock; so we're just getting started.'

'Well,' said Roy, 'my dad always taught me never to double down on a ten when the dealer shows a face card.'

'Smart move.'

'I'm try to be a good boy. I listen to my father.'

'Touché.'

'Where are you?'

'Here, downstairs in the lobby of your hotel. And do you have any idea what I am doing right now?' he teased him. Roy remained quiet. 'I'm gazing at the perfect legs of a gorgeous brunette. Do you prefer blonds to brunettes, Roy?'

'I'll be right down.'

'Shall I hold the brunette?'

'No,' he said. 'Just the cards.' And hung up.

The kitten was soaking in the bathtub, miming a lullaby. He went in and she lifted her leg for him. He kissed her big toe and told her he'd be right back.

'Where are you going, Roy?'

'I have to sort out a few things... Just this and that.' He looked at himself in the mirror and combed back his hair with his hand. She watched him and he understood her suspicions. 'No women; just a colleague from the bank. I'll be right back.'

'OK.'

Ice was waiting for him at a table set between plain columns of white marble. He looked at Roy dispassionately and remained seated. They never shook hands. It was ordinary, yet strange; businesslike, but chilly.

'I ordered you a drink,' he said, sipping his drink. 'Is whiskey OK?'

Roy took his seat. 'What's going on?'

'How's everything?'

'Who's that jerk I saw in the elevator today?'

'Sam? Ah…'

'He seems to know me. Do I know him?'

He mused shrewdly, 'In a certain sense, I think you do.'

Roy sat impatiently, waiting. The competition with clever words had ceased, all pretensions at a game were past, and all that remained was the duel.

'OK,' said Ice, placing his drink on the table. 'All cards on the table. Face up. Are you ready for this?'

No answer; only the stern expression: just get on with it.

'There was a project to push computer trading to the limit. It was never meant to go live. We were doing simulations; that's all. It was never meant to go operational. But that plan got mixed up with my gambling habits. People got involved who never should have. I was in a bind. I let them in. And once in, they wouldn't leave. I could never pay them off. So I changed the plan; innovated; played the - '

'What the fuck are you talking about? Speak in plain English.'

'We started something. And it got out of hand. Is that plain English enough for you?' Ice raised his voice before regaining control. 'Look, these guys, they're not technical; they're not like you or I. They're jock straps in business suits who only know how to count money and believe what you tell them. Numbers to them mean money. Period. Do you get it?' He shook his head gloomily, at himself, at

584

Roy, at things... He seemed unwilling, or unable, to put up a struggle. Something deeper was driving him, perhaps fear, and he began to sweat. 'These guys will believe almost *anything* you tell them if phrased the right way, glossed in technical patois and the promise of money. Mammon sounded a dream. And I poured it on. I drowned them in buzz words. And that's the catch. That's how this whole thing became unstuck. Believing in what *you* want to believe. To shut your eyes and just listen to your own fancies, and lap them all up.'

'And what did you tell them?'

'That we pushed *through* the envelope. I persuaded them we could anticipate the outcome of any transaction, no matter how small or large, irrespective of margins or type of asset. That we could milk the markets – big-time. We could win big. Really big. I convinced them we had the technology, the skills, the means to manipulate anything with a monetary value attached. Spaceships. Buttons. Camels. The chair you're sitting on. You name it. Anything. This was a set of dice that always came up sixes. And they bought it. All of it. Every last word. Down to the full stop.'

'And?'

'And I needed the time. – Roy,' he said, beginning to falter, 'I owed them money. I was in debt up to my neck. And I needed the time to pay. Do you understand?'

Period. And all the pieces fell into place. The scams; the tricks; the bluffs; the buffoonery. Roy saw everything crystallized before him. It was true because it was simple. And it was ludicrous. Only a man in trouble could screw up like that. Only someone with a toy, that smashes it to pieces, and then cries foul when it's broken. Only Man.

'So you sold them this trading project, whatever it is?' said Roy.

'I used it to pay off my debts,' he confessed grimly. 'Very big debts. Colossal ones.'

'But it doesn't work. It's not operational. You just said so yourself.'

'Yes,' he said, leaning nearer to him and whispering intently. 'But they don't know that. - Roy, don't you see, I got in a jam, a truly massive jam. I had to improvise my way out. I panicked. I never thought it would go this far.'

'So you dragged me in?'

'No, it wasn't only you. Some of the things these guys bought, you wouldn't believe.' And Ice related the story of Cindy and Amber, the portfolio of songs and how the twin concept became a handle on the big greedy guys, how they were like ravenous giants that wanted to believe, that needed to consume, to gulp down everything, anything to get a bigger pot of honey and ram the riches down their throats. 'Roy, I tried to intervene. But they acted alone, independently of me. And to protect their investment they resorted to tactics that... OK, I closed my eyes to.'

'Why me? Why us? Why pick on us?'

'Because you were there.'

'But what did it mean?'

'Mean?' he looked at him uncomprehendingly. 'It meant nothing.'

'Nothing!' Roy gasped in disbelief, shaking his head numbly to and fro, a flood of thoughts, an avalanche of suspicious, rushing at him at once. 'Nothing?' Grasping his own insignificance was hard, it was incomprehensible, and he struggled with it. 'Nothing?'

'You were the first ones I thought of. - I'm sorry.'

Roy fell back in his chair bewildered and stunned. He continued shaking his head, looking for words that could express his fury, but the powerlessness of knowing disabled him. At length he said: 'Are they stupid?'

'They are just like the rest of us, Roy.'

'Stupid?'

'Ambitious, greedy, ignorant of the complications... Yes, all of those, perhaps. Temptation made them desperate. And it was just too great to resist.'

'Stupid! Stupid! Stupid!'

'I opened a Pandora's Box.'

'Stupid!'

'And it was too late to close it again. The demons crept out.'

'Stupid!'

'They saw something, and they went for it. – Wouldn't you?'

'No!'

'It's human nature, Roy. You would.'

'I'm not so stupid.'

586

'We are what we are. And you're no different.'

'You crazy bastards. Why suck me into this scam? Why?'

Ice gazed abstractly into space, uttering feebly: 'You just happened to be there at the time. I needed something. I looked; and there you were. It was just one of those things. A coincidence. And I seized it.'

For Roy, the compulsion to lash out was real, but the shocking emptiness of his cause exhausted him. Anger made him a mouthpiece of his rages. He knew everything now, everything, but the immensity of his insignificance crushed his spirit. 'You crazy, crazy, crazy, stupid bastard. You imbecile.'

Ice kept silent. He imagined he would feel relieved to tell someone, but only the dawning realization of tragedy befell his conscience then. He waited as Roy burnt out his rages. 'Roy - '

'What else?'

'Nothing.'

'Nothing! There must be something. There *has* to be.'

'No. That's it. That's everything. Just you and the others. You were props. All of you. Just pieces of a play. A game.'

'A game?'

'I don't know what else to say...'

'And the singer? What about Cindy Gillespie? Who is she? Why her? How is she connected with me?'

'She's not. - There's nothing.'

'*Nothing?*

'You were all just flotsam floating on the sea of life, that the tide of events had brought together for a time, and then dispersed.'

'What are you saying?'

'There's nothing, Roy. Nothing...'

'Nothing?'

Ice ran his mind into the ground chasing the recollection of events, dredging up dismembered parts and discontinued facts: 'By chance, I saw Cindy perform in Las Vegas. There was game.'

'And?'

'I was down four million to these guys that night. I needed an idea. I was desperate. I had to pull the rabbit out of the hat. These people,' he inhaled deeply, creating time for himself, 'they build the

587

story to suit themselves. I just gave them an idea and showed them the landscape. But they invented the plot. I ran with it, sure, I had to. I helped it along. How? It's simple. And that was the problem - *it was too damn simple*. We use big words, technology words, words that impress, that seem to tell a story to a man who wants to believe in that story more than anything else in the world. – It's that simple. They *wanted* to believe it. It was that powerful.'

'And all this stuff with the twins; what did it mean?'

'Nothing. I told you; it never meant a thing. It didn't matter what I said. When a man believes in something, he wants to believe in it despite everything else. That's the power of obsession, of dogma even. The chances of changing a fixed idea once it has taken root is almost nil. I could have sold them a goat, or even their own mothers, and they would have bought it all. I fed an addiction. I didn't start it.'

'You inflamed it.'

'I inflamed it. Yes. I saw a chance. I was in trouble, and I took it.'

'And?'

'And it just kept on growing; getting bigger... When it gets that far, everything but the end game is a threat to them. So they overreact and neutralize the threat. I tried to cool things down, to complicate the process when I realized how far they were prepared to go.'

'That's unbelievable.' Roy felt numb. 'Unbelievable...'

'Believe it. It's true.'

Roy shook his head in disgust: 'If ever there was a fuck-up idea, this is it. You crazy bastard, are you out of your mind?'

'That's the whole story, Roy. That's everything. And they believed it. All of it. They *wanted* to believe it. You, Cindy, everything. Her sister was a real bonus. They looked alike so much I played on the twin concept and the songs as carrying the launch codes for the market stampede. When they played them on the radio, in a particular sequence, the computer trading programs were supposed to kick-in and scoop the jackpot. – It sounds crazy to you, doesn't it? That it makes no sense.'

Roy was speechless. He looked dazed, and Ice continued:

'They believed it. *Everything*. People in power are not that smart. You overestimate them, Roy. We all do. I used a symmetry argument and it seemed to play in their hands. They were like children with a new toy. Try taking it from them and see what they do.' His thoughts drifted away, and then back. 'They bought it. And it bought me time, too. - I guess I'm just a puppet of conceit, like the rest... I thought I was so clever; that it would save me. And I just couldn't let go. - Money may be a false god; but we all worship at his shrine. Don't we?'

'The real twins, Ice? The waitress who plays poker?'

'That's pure fluke. It's things like that that make you want to believe in fate. And I loathe that. I really do. She turns up, a twin, right here in Paris, at a club where I happen to play poker. A twin that waits tables; and she plays poker as good as the best of us. I got hold of it, and just couldn't stop myself.'

'But it meant nothing?'

Ice gazed at him and echoed: 'Nothing... Nothing... Nothing...'

'Where is she now?'

'I don't know. She's around somewhere.'

'Is she in danger?'

'No. I wrote her out of the story.'

'And they believed it?'

'Yes. It even bought me some time.'

'Why didn't you write me out of the story?'

'How could I? You were the cards in their hands. I couldn't just take them away.' He looked forlornly at Roy, and said: 'It was the only way I knew to buy me some time.'

'Buying time.'

'Yes. Buying time. That's what this game is about, isn't it?'

'Game?' Roy seethed at him with disgust. 'What game?'

'Life.'

'But you forgot one thing, Ice.'

'What?'

'The rules are never the same. They change. Life isn't in the cards. Here,' he said, taking out a fresh pack from his pocket, removing them from the box, and holding out the deck for him. 'Cut.' He waited impatiently. 'Go on. Cut!'

'What for?'

'Why not? It's just a game.'

He laughed powerlessly. Roy packed the cards away and gazed at him with contempt. 'Asshole!'

'It was just a hoax. A bluff.'

'Stupid, stupid, stupid, stupid imbeciles.'

'And it got out of hand. Look,' he burst out, 'it happens.'

'Fuck you!'

'I predicted everything, except how people would react. That, it seems, you can never do with perfect accuracy. Humans are just too uncanny.' They gazed strangely at each other, a stare not to measure a man, but to measure oneself against him. The stare, in essence, was turned inwards. 'So I improvised. And it turned crazy. Really crazy.' He looked pleadingly at him. 'You know?'

'Why did they go on believing it? Why?'

'Because they *wanted* to. That's something you can't seem to understand, Roy.'

'People are dead, I understand that. Do you?'

'I know, I know, I know...'

'It must stop.'

'It will.'

'Sam and his gang have to be stopped.'

'It's not just Sam. There are others involved. Above him.'

'I don't care who it is. Turn it off. Now.'

'Turn it off?'

'Now.'

'You know of a way?'

'If I have to, I'll find a way.'

Gazing fiercely at him seemed to have no impact, for Ice uttered in a slow measured voice: 'There is only one way.'

'What is it?'

'We fold.'

'Fold?'

'Yes.' His lips parted faintly, not to speak, but to test the moment for spirits of silence, a prayer, perhaps, or a way to convey he was sorry, or that he wanted to rest, or pass the time watching butterflies fly in jagged ellipses. It was strangely serene when he spoke, searching for the words and uttered like echoes. 'With these guys... there is nothing else to do... but fold.'

'You're crazy.'

'Am I?'

'You're mad. You won't get away with it.'

'We were dealt a poor hand. The cards turned cold. It happens. We fold. We move on. '

'And who pays for the sins of this... this charade?'

'Sins...? What sins?' he said at length, lighting a cigarette. 'It went cold. We fold.'

'And what do you expect me to do?'

'Fold.'

'You're insane.'

'Yes,' he said coolly. 'Fold.'

'And just forget this ever happened?'

'Remember if you must. But fold. - Roy,'

'What?'

'Be smart. This is one you can't win.'

'Yes. But maybe one I can't lose, either.'

Roy got up to leave, and just as he was moving into his stride Ice cried out:

'What's her name?' Roy stopped and turned. 'The lucky girl.'

Roy hesitated, measuring the threat, weighing the bluff. 'You know, Ice,' he begun coolly, 'if people were a deck a cards, do you know what you and your careless friends would be?'

'Not kings, I suppose.'

'Jokers!' he said, turning away. 'The cards we smart guys throw away.'

'I'll be in touch,' he cried out after him, but Roy never looked back, pressing on despite him. But even if he did turn around, what would he see, what could he do?

Ice didn't wait to find out. He rushed to join him in the elevator, the walls panelled with mirrors. When the doors closed and they were alone, he began:

'There's a game.'

'What?'

'There's a game.'

Roy knew what he meant. 'I want to meet them.'

'It's high stakes.'

'Where?'

'At a private club.'

'When?'

'Tonight. After midnight. I'll pick you up.'

'I'll be waiting.'

'Good.'

It went intensely quiet for a while, then Roy uttered what they were both thinking, 'What do you expect I might do, Ice?'

Ice looked at him blankly, a feature he used too often. 'You have no idea, do you?'

'I'm like you, Ice, I improvise.'

'And look where it led me.'

The doors opened, Roy got out, and Ice pressed the button to hold the doors open. 'See you later, Roy.'

'Tell me, did your scam ever have a chance?'

'Scam?'

'Peeping Tom. The program?'

He smiled, faking power, and said. 'If we were machines, then yes, the world would be mine.'

'If we were machines,' continued Roy, without a doubt in his mind, 'we would be so consumed with trying to be human, that we would inevitably screw everything up. Especially ourselves.'

That's how it is, one way or another entropy is king, and chance rules. There was no way to play four aces other than on a fluke, and cheating doesn't count, because sooner or later you'll over-bet the pot and stretch yourself beyond your limit, and something is going to break, if not your wallet then your humanity or spirit.

'You should have trusted your instincts,' said Roy. 'The hardest thing to play is not the other guy.'

'No?'

'The hardest thing to play is *yourself*.'

As Roy continued down the corridor, Ice pressed the ground button and the doors closed, sealing him inside, alone, confronting his reflection in the mirrors. He seemed sad, tired, drained of the vibrancy he remembered as a boy. The invisible web of intrigues he spun about himself, believing it secured him and veiled his sins were seen, in that moment, to be the tenuous illusion he had always feared.

If he believed that the purchase of time on the run of a lie outlasts time itself, then gazing at himself he believed in it no more.

'Monsieur, this is the ground floor. Are you going up?' asked the waiter carrying a tray?

Silently, forlornly, Ice left the elevator, and the hotel, alone.

*   *   *

'Roy...'

As soon as he entered the suite the kitten started purring.

'Roy...'

'Get dressed, babe, we're going out.'

'Where to?'

'The last time I was in Paris I went to this great nightclub. Great singers; great sound; fabulous food. It's us, baby. You'll love it.'

'Is it for lovers?'

'Absolutely.'

She sauntered from the bathroom robed in towels. 'How should I dress? Sexy? Demure? Sultry. Sophisticated?'

He thought a moment and said: 'A bit of each, I think.'

'Red? Blue? White? Pink?'

'I leave it to your discretion.'

'And what about my charm?'

'Where would we be without that?'

'And my sense of style?'

'It's your call,' he said, smiling thoughtfully at her. 'Knock 'em out, baby.'

'OK. Be ready in a bit.' And she let the towels fall casually to the floor about her, and her nakedness was paradise.

The kitten: what can you say? That face: a million dollars; that body, a billion; brain: around the fifty dollar mark. But he adored her all the same. And he sat down in an armchair, lit a cigarette, and thumbed through a magazine.

Chapter 34

It was very bright in Cindy Gillespie's dressing room, the brilliance of polished mirrors and the soft luminescence of lights combining, until Amber dimmed them down to a shading hue. Cindy, if she noticed, never registered the change but sat quietly gazing in the mirror, absently brushing her hair. There are those silences that deepen just before an earthquake, and those other episodes of quiet that indicate a waiting state: something is expected to happen at any moment, but one seems careless of the details. Any tremor would be welcome, as long as it resounds of change.

Cindy looked thoughtfully at her sister, who gazed back with a rush of apprehension.

'He thinks I'm being paranoid. - Cindy, where did Anthony go?'

'In times of crises, he never lets you know what he's thinking,' she said, as a faint smile, a ripple of reminiscing, came over her. 'That's his way.'

'Does he think I'm crazy?'

'He's a good man.'

'I'm not crazy.'

'What would I do without him?'

'He said as much.'

'He's not afraid to show he cares, unlike some men.'

They were talking past each other, Amber consumed with doubt, while Cindy resigned herself to quiet self-possession, contemplating questions other than the anxious speculations of her sister who found it hard to becalm herself, and restlessly fidgeted around her. Cindy, mentally and spiritually, kept herself one remove from agitation and pondered in a mystic silence the thread of her life, her career, the constantly changing struggles to establish a foothold and keep a presence in a profession replete with pitfalls and false starts. Success as a performer was a maze of lucky breaks and hard work, of having dedicated people, the best people, on your side. It wasn't easy. It was damn hard work. She thought of all the effort and time expended by Anthony and his team to drive a path through the thick forest of toil and competition for her. Yes, for her. It makes you wonder what a friend is. What friendship was: a superlative form of mutual well-being, as the day befriends the night on equal terms with interests reinforcing one another rather than competing. To her, then, these were good thoughts. And if she could confide them to no one, then so be it, she would hold them ever closer to herself alone. Her reflection in the mirror echoed these sentiments in the silence and the stillness of the moment. A beautiful voice, a kind heart, a lovely face were insufficient pieces in themselves for sustained success. Someone had to be hardheaded, persistent; able to negotiate the rough with the smooth without relinquishing integrity in the art your spirit loves. You needed muscle and endurance and daring to stand strong against adversity, to put your neck out and clamor over the slippery rocks of misfortune. Many ask why it is so damn hard; but only the strong carry their bruises with fortitude.

Whatever the intrigues, whatever the fears, Anthony had protected her, cushioned her softness from the hard edges of a rough world. If this mysterious affair of stalkers harrying her and strangers meddling with her songs was more than fearful speculation, then it was time to break out of her shell and confront the demons.

Fear, in its thousand forms, had triumphed.

But no more.

'I'm not afraid,' she turned suddenly and gazed at Amber. Moving her eyes from the mirror to her sister brought out in relief their deeper resemblance. In Amber she saw her own fears shimmering like a billion stars. 'Not any more. If all this is merely illusion, then I'll burst it with a pin. If it's real - '

'Real! Oh, it's real all right.'

'If it's real,' she continued imperturbably, 'then confront it.'

'Confront what?'

'Whatever is there.'

'You're mad.'

In wars of the spirit one confronts not only an adversary of will, but one's own fears. These vie for contradiction: *one battles the self in order to master the self.* It's a paradox. And the only defense is freedom of action, to make a wise choice, not to be afraid.

'I'm going for a walk.'

'Are you crazy!' Amber shrieked at her, stunned for a moment before insensibly blurting out. 'My God! Can't you see it's raining?'

'Good,' she said. 'I like the rain. We used to play in the rain when we were young. Don't you remember?'

'Cindy.'

'Yes?'

She rushed over to her, stopped, gazed at her passionately, embraced her with all-consuming love, and then, too stunned to weep, gave her an umbrella:

'Here. You'll need this.'

She smiled warmly at her in turn. 'Thank you.'

Amber, in that tender, solemn moment, grasped the essence of her own vulnerabilities, and wondered what miraculous efforts would transpire to overcome them. Deep in thought, as Cindy left the room, she reasoned she should write a song, an exegesis of her sorrows and despairs, and so light away the long shadows that engulfed her. For echoing in her mind was the yearning, *I too want a way out.* And this emotion formed the basis of her song.

Thus, taking up pen and paper, she began composing a ballad of regrets and delights, of days and nights, of sunrise and the twilight, of herself and herself and herself... And she cried.

Chapter 35

'Roy.'

'Yes, babe?'

Emerging from the bedroom in rendition of a grand entrance, the kitten posed before him. 'Do you like what you see?'

She was dressed in exotic garb that made her look sexy and sophisticated, sassy and sleek, raunchy and regal, kitten and a lioness, with a meow and a roar, as magnificently adorned as any woman can be in the expression of her endless charms, and he was speechless gawping at her until he rose from his chair, swiftly advanced and kissed her, embracing and then swinging both her hands with his.

'What legendary marvel dazzles my eyes,' he said.

'Huh?'

'Aphrodite.'

'Is that legendary, Roy?'

'A woman of the highest caliber.'

'Woman!' she softly frowned, with a touch of jealously.

'A goddess born of the watery foam. You are a veritable Venus, my love.'

'I thought I was Aphrodite.'

He flinched there a moment, until a spot of quick thinking recovered the moment perfectly. 'They're twins.'

'Twins! Ah, OK.'

Outside she complained about the rain. 'My dress, my dress...' even though the hotel had ample bunting that sheltered guests from the weather, the slightest hint of ruin was anathema to her.

During the journey in a taxi she pressed the cabbie for a guided tour: Describe that astonishing building over there on the left; and those public ornaments on the right. Over there, do you see? And oh, he must drive to the river right away. Will he do that for her, please?

Yes, of course he would, he was at her service. She smiled and said she wanted to see the dainty boats decked out with multicolored lights and watch the patrons in their swanky garb sailing through an evening of pleasure. What a pretty sight they must be, even in the rain. Enchanted, she sighed and asked him:

'Is everything here French, monsieur?'

'The last time I looked, madam, yes, it was.'

'And Paris.'

'Madame?'

'From here it looks so enchanting; what do you think it means?'

'Most probably a great deal, madame.'

'Ah yes... And what about that huge building over there? Is that French too?'

'Only while we are in Paris, madame.'

'Is that true?'

'Down to the buttons on my shirt?'

'That shirt?'

'Yes, madame.'

'Ah,' she liked the look of his shirt, especially the color. 'OK.'

'Would you prefer I turn left, or right?'

'Ahhhhh... straight on, please.'

Oh yes, she purred, everything looked wonderful and inspiring and dazzling on a rainy night? Ever mindful of *overt* comparisons, she thought inventively: 'You know, it's not *quite* like Las Vegas,' and Roy sighed *Thank God for that*! the cabbie echoed his sentiments, and she concluded: 'But it's nice all the same. And I like it. Hmm. Yes, I like it a lot. – What's that building over there...?'

Ample umbrellas, enormous in size and superfluous in the soft cascading drizzle, were opened out for her benefit. She heaved with relief at not being stricken with a single drop of moisture on her outfit, she smiled a gamely smile and, taking Roy's arm, they strode into the club. The concierge, his perfect moustache a motif more than a humble sash of hair above his lip, remembered Roy and they shook hands warmly. They seemed to be on such good terms that the kitten irresistibly butted in and asked him how he shaved.

'With a mirror and brush, madame, held thus; do you see?'

'Like an artist.'

'Just so.'

'A-ha.'

'And a dash of eau d'cologne to complete the masterpiece.'

'That's great!'

'And you?'

She considered him a moment and then replied: 'I sometimes help Roy shave, you know.'

'And does monsieur help shave you?'

She laughed.

Suddenly, rising up from behind them, roaring peels of laugher leapt from a crowd of six boisterous men who jostled for space as they entered the club. One of them, presumably animated by an earlier bout of boozing, boomed in jest it was a police raid, and only a night of debauchery could save the club from being mothballed. Roy turned around and he flushed white as blood drained from his face - he saw that damn cop Forester in among this rowdy crowd and, spotting him, Forester raised his hands farcically in surprise, left the fraternity of inebriates, and joined him.

He was a hive of smiles and chuckles, and offered his hand in greeting. Roy obliged him, by way of dazed politeness, and the kitten too, though more in delighted humor. Forester observed:

'It's odd how we keep bumping into each other like this.'

'Yes...' muttered Roy, 'very intriguing.'

'Do you think it means anything?' asked the kitten breathlessly.

'It's a small world,' said Roy. 'Too small...' and taking the kitten's hand, they continued on alone into the restaurant.

The kitten excitedly suggested sharing a table with a fellow countryman in a foreign land. Roy said screw the fellow countryman in a foreign land, he looked happy enough with his hooligan chums, and they'd probably be imposing on their revels.

'Shall I ask?'

'No,' he said. 'It's just you and me tonight, babe.'

This cheered her up instantly, her blushing smile dazzled with a rainbow of delights, making her feel loved and special and, in a more practical setting, kept her tongue in check and provided him with precious moments to think. Roy knew this encounter was sheer coincidence, but was aware Forester would exploit every opportunity to further his investigation. He was a cop, nosing around was second nature to him, even amid the present extravaganza of fabulous food and festive entertainment, he was still a cop, and there would always be something tickling his mind to drive him to make contact.

They were shown to their table and presented with menus, which were all in French, beautifully typeset, and the kitten tried to read them. She struggled for a while, and Roy just watched her, until she signaled to a waiter, who diligently attended on her, and asked him if he were French (since everything else seemed to be, she concluded, so why not him too? - Contextually rational thinking, this).

'No, madame,' he answered courteously, 'I am Italian.'

'Really!' she gasped. 'You look Italian; doesn't he, Roy?'

Roy felt he had Slavic features, and remarked in passing to that effect, to which the Italian began speaking in Polish, before resuming in English and explaining at length that his mother was Polish, his father Hungarian, and he was born in Italy but now lived mostly in Germany because he built a house there, currently occupied with his two children and their again pregnant mother and *indomitable* grandmother who had mastered the art of complaining better than anyone he knew, and was particularly fond of reminding him he was a lazy goat in not working hard enough to earn more money, the purchase of things of no importance being a particularly obsessive hobby of hers; and he was obliged to be absent from home for considerable stretches at a time. He was a sentimental old soul, it seems. Ah... He added in passing that jazz added ginger to the mundane menu of his life, and spiced it up a treat.

'That makes sense,' said the kitten, requesting menus in English.

Roy glanced at his watch and decided to call New York. He excused himself and went outside.

Nick answered the phone. He was at the office, and everything was running smoothly. He asked news from Paris, and Roy informed him that events were progressing more slowly than anticipated, with few notable results. He was uncertain why he was sparing with the facts. Perhaps he found them to be so absurd he wouldn't be able to conjure up the right words. Expression seemed to fail him then, and he responded awkwardly:

'Well, I made contact. And that's got the ball rolling, I suppose.'

'That doesn't sound very promising,' Nick answered tactfully. 'Perhaps you're tired?'

Roy roused himself as if to laugh, but fell hesitant instead. 'How's Frank?'.

'He's here. Do you want to speak with him?'

'No. Just tell him that Victor is back in London recovering from his binge, no thanks to him. And Nick - '

'Yes, Roy?'

'Do you know what people are?'

'People?'

'Yes.'

'Just people, I suppose.'

'Sloppy. Stupid. Ridiculous.'

'That's a thought.'

'Damn stupid.' He sounded unnerved, it felt distinctly personal, and Nick sensed his unease stifle his emotions, so he took the initiative and spoke candidly.

'People, of whatever shade, crazy or sane, are just simply that - people. You have to accept them as they are. What else can you do?'

'Forget they even exist. You can't blame anyone for wanting that.'

There was the rustling sound of agitated breath, and then Nick said: 'It's never wrong to admit the truth; least of all for a man compelled by life to confront himself. At worst, it's a starting point. Looked at rationally, that's all anyone ever needs. To ask for more is to run the risk of disillusion. And you know where that leads.'

'I guess you're right, Nick. But some people... they sicken me. They disgust me. And I just want to lash out at them.'

'If you're wise, Roy, you'll realize nothing people do should ever surprise you. Confuse you, distress you, annoy you and get you mad, sure; that's part of life. Why is it necessary? I don't know why. It's just there. But nothing, when looked at honestly, should surprise you to the extent that it becomes disabling. It's the price of being honest with yourself.' He paused, then added as an afterthought: 'Truth is a test of what we are. Look candidly at others too. Don't put things into them that aren't there at the start, even if they're added later, or you're asking for trouble.'

'And never trouble trouble unless trouble troubles you.'

'Accept people as they are, Roy. Be a mirror; not a judge. Know what they are capable of – honesty shows you that. We all have our limits, but seldom want them tested. They throw up the most enormous surprises.'

'Know one's self - right?'

'Yes, and it often hurts.'

'Ouch!'

They chuckled together, humoring and remedial, and it felt therapeutic: a profound moment of man-to-man understanding, Women weren't excluded. No. They just weren't around. Nick asked him what he was thinking. It felt safe to answer, and Roy replied: 'It's the idiots that are the worse offenders.'

'Perhaps circumstances can cause a wise man to act like an idiot,' he said, thinking aloud. 'Perhaps even his own instincts undermine him. It's not unusual for a strong will to turn to willfulness. We've all seen it before; many times. Or even when a wise man loses the thread of his life, and he becomes the fool of circumstance. Life deals you the cards; and sometimes you would do anything to quit. But you can't leave the game. Deep down, you know that.'

'It's depressing.'

'It's life, Roy. It's just life. And people, being what they are, well, they try to be too clever at times, and their ambitions can implode in on them.' He was sounding genuinely philosophical, as if somehow he knew the facts. 'In a subtle way, it's good that life unravels our endeavors. The short-term keeps one in check. Long-term plans, unless they're flexible creatures, have no hope of success. To survive, every animal needs to adapt. And the best plans have the features of an animal.'

'Which animal did you have in mind?'

'The one we understand the least, but is closest to us.'

'And that is?'

'Try man.'

'And women.' He began to cheer up, climbing up out of his own sorrows. And comforting words, and memories, were the staircase to his salvation.

'How is she, your fiancé?'

'Don't remind me.'

'You'll regret it if you don't marry her.'

'And will I regret it if I do?'

'Are you asking me?'

'Myself actually.' Roy laughed nervously. 'Now and again, I find myself in perfect possession of my wits, and have to give myself a great big kick up the rear for being such an ass.'

'Try therapy.'

'Would you?'

'Perhaps.' Nick began a muffled laugh, and in the faint recesses of the telephone Roy overheard Frank's distinctive voice make teasing observations. Being the butt end of a joke is hard, but sometimes one is a joke, and Roy felt himself one then. He admitted it to himself. He only wished he could laugh too.

'Nick.'

'Yes, Roy?'

'I'm going to settle it all tonight.'

'How?'

'Over a game of cards.'

'Are you kidding me?'

'No,' he said, asserting himself, entrenching his sense of mission. 'Not one bit.' And he ended the conversation on a positive note and went back inside.

Pausing by the entrance to the restaurant, he stood and observed the kitten in delightful chatter with the Italian waiter. Roy folded his arms and watched them from a distance. He was concentrating hard despite the ease of his posture and never realized someone standing beside him. It took a while to dawn on him that he was there; and gently turning, saw him standing there. Somehow, Roy wasn't surprised, and merely took it in his stride.

'Well, Detective, we meet again.'

'Mr. Riemann.' He knew his first name was Roy, and that he preferred people who knew him to call him by that. And Roy, just staring blankly back at him, waited for Forester to begin: 'Roy.'

'Yes, Detective?'

'Would you like a cigarette?'

'No thanks. What can I do for you?'

'You never asked me.'

'Asked you what?'

'What I was doing here in Paris.'

'It's really none of my business.'

'But you must suspect it concerns the murder in New York; the one we thought involved your colleague Frank. As it turned out, the victim was French.'

'Should you be telling me any of this?'

'In principle - no. But I have a feeling you should know. Call it a hunch.'

'Some hunches can lead you astray,' he said. 'And I'm speaking from recent experience.'

'Not this time around.'

'No?'

'My Pop - '

'Who?'

'My dad,' he smiled warmly, 'he has a way of communicating with me.'

Roy gazed at him vaguely. 'I don't follow.'

'Like father; like son.'

Roy still didn't follow, but said, 'Oh,' just the same, and glanced at his watch.

'Roy, one last thing before you leave.'

'Yes?'

'An American went missing in Paris. A young woman; around twenty years of age. I'm sorry, I don't have a picture with me, I left it at the hotel.'

'What has any of this to do with me?'

'She plays poker.'

Roy's eyes lit up, and he smiled. Forester resumed.

'She's a twin. Her name is Zoë Long; and her sister is in town looking for her.'

Roy pondered this a while, thinking of Ice and his schemes, and then repeated: 'What has any of this to do with me?'

'Speaking as a cop – nothing. Not a single thing,' he answered him candidly. 'But I have a feeling I ought to tell you.'

'Tell me. Why?'

He shrugged warmly: 'Call it a hunch.'

Two pussycats were sitting at the bar. The only object to grace their hand a champagne glass delicately hung from the fingertips, unshakable, beautiful. Roy gazed at them and the kitten seemed upset. It was art, he said; women were art.

'Am I art too, Roy?'

'With mythology added.'

She never left it there, but shrewdly imitated the pussycats at the bar. The better lioness learns from the tigress the majesty of her culture, emulating to such perfection it becomes second nature. A kitten can't help but be jealous of the lioness – so she purrs and learns, because she knows, in time, she too will become a Sphinx.

'Look,' said Roy, turning eagerly to the stage and joining in the applause. 'The show is about to rev up.' Pleasure filled up his face. 'Fire her up, fellas.' He had an intuition of primordial sound about to explode, and he wasn't disappointed.

A soundscape of blues, of jazz, razzmatazz bursting into rhythm, booming out sound like kings of the samba tempo, rulers of delirious tango, knocking up riffs in phrasing aphrodisiac, the utterly amazing beat beat beating of a sexing drum that seeps into your fevered bones, and creates explosive time. Bones are the real soul – They shake ya! They move ya! They pick ya up and throw ya! *Ra-ta-ta-tat!* Convulsed by sound, the musicians became dynamic forms rattling space, spirits bursting out of rhythms, seismic states sublime in a blues piece set in sassy resonance and taken on a hurly-burly ride driven into the bones of men aching with rapture: Whack that soul! Whack it! Smack it! Whack whack wham! And weaved through with the seductive aura of a tenor sax.

'Roy, what's happening?'

'Jazz,' he said, feeling enraptured. 'Latin jazz.'

'Is that what's happening?'

'Yes.' He briefly glanced at her. 'Pass me the whiskey. Thanks.'

'Cheers.'

'Yeah...'

The musicians fractured harmonies and reassembled them again, working class style, rough cut, diamond hard, platinum coated man with a hammer of gold making silver rhythms encrusted with jewels, music to enrich, music to drench a man with ecstasy. The overkill overweight overbassed wantonness of obsession in the playing surround sound world made of nothing but sound as if sound were matter and supernovas nothing but percussion taken to excess. To overwhelm not with fire, but the essence itself is desire. Sound.

It was the sheer imperfections of the piece, its incompleteness, its obesity that teased the mind and made it seem sensational, provocative, like a half remembered dream.

'They're driving themselves crazy,' shrieked the kitten, struggling to make herself heard. 'Roy.'

He looked at her, exhilarated and dazed, visually asking what she wanted.

'They're driving themselves crazy.'

He laughed, shaking his head amid the surges of music storming the senses. The musicians, drenched with shimmering sweat, were the storm troopers lurching against sound and driving senses into submission, pushing the envelope of inner life, hammering the spectrum of sound into ferocious perfection, the echoes explosive, the burst of the beats going *boom boom boom* in a storm of restless energy, the percussional drive of *thud thud thud* lashing with the *swish swish swish* in a cymbals' fever of desire, animal intensive, relentless, the collective ricocheting of bullet-hardened whack bash thwack k-powww! Firepower unleashed, overkill in motion. Time, sound, space, and the human element. What does it all mean?

Sound.

Roy turned to the guy at the table next to his and said to him. 'They're really pushing the envelope.'

'They're fantastic.'

'Yeah.'

'It's push-pull. It's a driver. It's locked in. Look! See the sax-man pulling-in piano-man. The drummer can't wait to get a fix. He really knows how to shake it. Just knock up a few crescendos of the boomer and the rest just dovetails to the drum beat.'

'Magic!'

'Yeah! It's fire. Boom boom boom... flames made out of heat;

starlight that's pure beat.'

'Boom boom boom...'

'Yeah.'

What are they saying? Their feelings hug the rhythms of sound. Is this jazz as narcotic symbolism, or like a ra-ta-ta-tat bullet shot in the head junkie who just can't get enough of the musical fix? To live, he needs to burn. *Burn... in an inferno of sound.*

'I'm alive.'

'Yeah.'

Boom boom boom...

It was cryptic. What did it mean? Being alive amounted to more than breathing when music sends you breathless in euphoria.

Well... perhaps. Then again, it's all in the mind. Shot in the arm stuff. Shot in the head. Difference? *The music. The sound.*

Boom boom boom...

Fifteen minutes of relentless pounding, then applause, clashing hands like dynamos frantically clapping for moremoremore... And it's no wonder the universe drives itself into being, so it can listen to itself roar, and never dream to stop.

The band tops up with booze and nicotine: plenty of booze and a good smack of nicotine. It was time for a respite and the audience took a breather, the monotone of chatter picked up to a pattering session until the lights dimmed and she came on stage.

The applause mushroomed till it became deafening, then suffered for silence so she could sing.

The quirky dynamos of her voice booming arias to the money merchants plying currency swaps and derivatives as the bassoons erupt, and the gemstones adorning their mistresses, of pulp champagne and pussies wide open – she smiles:

'Oh Roy, you're got such great taste.'

'Gimme a kiss.'

Long and deep. 'Oh Roy... It's so wonderful.'

And he embraces her face tenderly with his hands. She is so beautiful.

'Ssshhh.' Their antics stir a couple who look annoyed and frown at them. 'Be quiet.'

'It's just a song,' said the kitten unselfconsciously. 'You know, it's just a song.'

'No. It's the voice,' said Roy.

'The voice?'

'Ssshhh...' they impatiently shushed them. 'Ssshhh...'

He nods: *Yes, it's the voice.* Dreaming of Callas at the Met and La Scala in Milan. The old days; the days of drama; of magnificence; of legend.

The stage-lights turned deep red for the fiery finale, and the artists pitched forwards as if to plunge into the audience like a spear. Swept up by a ballistic pace, packing the firepower of horns muscling the flutes into the synchronous throes of the punch of a drum – *ra-ta-ta-tat!* that voice summoned the greediness, the seediness, the lust and longing of a viper to pelt out its poisons and seize its prey: *Gotcha!*

It's that kind of song, made of diamond, sung like a shaker of spirits, tequila and bitters, written in stone, borne from the heart and delivered with voluptuous passion.

'You hear that, babe?'

'I sure do, Roy.'

'Don't it make you want to...'

'Sing.'

'Yeah... Sing...' he concurs at length, mesmerized by her presence; her voice; *her*.

On their exit from the club several hours later, Roy, while tipping the doorman, glanced back inside half-expecting to see Forester. But he wasn't there. The doorman, observant of these fleeting details, asked if he could be of some assistance.

'The cops,' said Roy. 'The drunken mob.'

The doorman grinned. 'They left about twenty minutes ago, monsieur.'

Without being asked, he presented Roy with a business card bearing the details of the French detective and Forester's chaperone, Claude. 'You never know,' said the doorman, 'it may be of some use to you.' And advancing to call them a cab, Roy stayed him and said they would stroll around for a while. 'As you prefer, monsieur, madame.' He wished them both good night, Roy shaking hands and the kitten waved ta ta, smiled warmly, and looped her arm through Roy's.

It stopped raining, the sky was a beautifully clear black and the stars were glittering with deep crispness. Booze and exotic pleasures erased their concern with the weather, and neither seemed to notice it had stopped raining as they sauntered into the starry night towards the River Seine.

'Do you know where we're going, Roy?'

He considered before he answered, looking at his wristwatch, the time, slowly pushing towards midnight, and with Ice resurrecting in his mind, contemplated the imminent ordeals ahead. 'Yes,' he said. 'I think so.'

'You think so?'

He smiled at her tenderly. 'Straight ahead.'

The profusion of predominantly French voices intermingling with copious other accents, principally European, gave an exotic feel to the night. The cafes were bustling at the seams, and to find a different more composed Parisian mood, they turned into an avenue running parallel with the river. The ambiance yielded smoothly from the pizzazz of the brilliant night to the fused twilight of serene street lamps, and the echoes of lovers' footsteps and muffled sounds. And there, just ahead, they spotted something out of context with a Parisian landscape. More in amused curiosity than exploring they strolled towards it arm in arm and paused outside the temple. The doors were open and His golden duplicates were everywhere in a variety of poses, from a solemn dance to a mesmerizing prayer, or in endless mediation.

'Is that the Buddha, Roy?'

'I believe so, babe.'

She stared quizzically: 'He's not French, is he?'

Roy grinned. 'Perhaps he tired of the East, and just packed up and left.'

That seemed disrespectful to her, after all, they were amid the splendors of Oriental spirituality, and she rebuked him softly, adding as an afterthought:

'I think he looks so sweet and kind and gentle and full of tenderness for living things.'

'Which are hardly the natural qualities of a Frenchman, babe!' He couldn't resist that jibe, but swiftly restored dignity to their surroundings and apologized for his irreverence. They went inside, barely into the entrance, to take a closer look. There were some monks kneeling, their hands clasped together in deepest meditation and prayer. Roy asked, spotting a Caucasian man in monks' habit:

'What's the white Buddha doing?'

'Meditating, I think.'

'What for?'

'To escape time,' said the kitten. 'They say it's to escape time.'

Roy seemed to grow particularly agitated at this. Trying not to be overheard by the monks and disturb their meditations, he nonetheless critiqued with passion the concept of leaving time. 'And that's what all this thing is about then, is it?'

'Something like that. - Roy, keep your voice down. Sssshhh...'

'So time is an illusion, is it? And meditation can sweep away the *fantasy* of time, and transport you to the reality of *true* timelessness? Oh yeah. Gimme a break!'

'What's got into you?'

'And what if he gets an itchy bum while he's mediating? Will that pull him back to Earth? What's more likely to grab your attention: timelessness, or relieving that itch? What's more real? – Gimme a break!'

'Oh Roy, but he looks so cute.'

'Well, give him a big hug from me, babe,' he said. 'On second thoughts, here – give him a thousand and tell him to put it all on Heaven Sent at the Kentucky stakes. I got a tip. He's a winner. Just like me.'

'Roy!' she blushed deliciously. 'You're so big hearted. I think it's wonderful.'

'I know. I can't help it.'

Back at the hotel, in their room, with the windows opened out onto the serene Paris night, the hand of the clock swept past midnight, and the mood changed. It grew quiet, tender, the will to forgiveness drew in. Paris spawned a sweeping panorama eclipsing all sense of isolation with a deeper communion, a harmony, the moon, the stars, the enveloping lights, the vastness of the city, its ancient echoes amid the bustle of modernity, and them – all part of a piece.

'Isn't it beautiful, Roy?'

'Yes... Yes it is.'

'Don't you just adore it?'

Life was short. Too short. Love too wonderful. Like the luscious fruit in its maturity that swells and bursts with exquisite richness, he gazed in awe at everything before him, and near to him, and then began to cry.

'What's the matter, Roy?'

'Why do we have to die and leave all this?' He held her closely, tightly, felt her softness melt into his own.

'Buddhists believe we never really die. That our essence passes on. On an endless journey.'

'What do they know?'

'They know something, Roy.'

'What?'

'Something...'

He just held her, until she began to cry too.

At length, as time pushed deeper past midnight and the weight of her tears and the long day ushered her into a deep sleep in his arms, he laid her on the bed, gently, covered her with the sheets, drew the windows to so they remained only just ajar, and, glancing again at his wristwatch, proceeded downstairs to the lobby to meet Ice.

Ice never looked the least bit troubled or tired. Perhaps it was adrenalin; perhaps a cocktail of pills provided him with a constant kick. In any case he sat, at ease, smoking a cigarette. They shook hands, a formality only, and Ice offered him a drink. He declined.

'Let's get this over with,' said Roy.

'I think, on reflection, you'll find it's already over. – Won't you have a seat?'

'No thanks.'

Ice stubbed out his cigarette in the ashtray. 'OK, let's play cards.'

'The only game I'm playing is an end game.'

Ice smiled: was this confidence or canniness? 'You play whatever you choose to play. And we'll do the same. – Remember, Roy, this is an invitation. You have nothing on these guys. Nothing at all. You couldn't find a spot with a microscope.'

'Yet it's strange, isn't it, how much they still stink.'

Ice had no clever response for that, and the smile melted from his face. He became more businesslike and led the way out.

For the entire duration of the journey, lasting over ten minutes, they never spoke a word. Presently, barely half way to their destination and waiting at red traffic lights for the green, Roy pondered on the game ahead, and what he would do; while Ice looked at his wristwatch, twenty to one, and thought of The Green Room which was where the men were gathering for a late game of poker.

At fifteen minutes to one, a burly American man in a Stetson hat strolled into the lobby of The Green Room. He was a regular, and the doorman clipped his cap in respect, pocketed his tip, and let him in. A young woman by the bar, long brunette hair but with blond roots, soft American accent, sipping bourbon over ice, beckoned the bartender and asked him:

'Who's the guy with the hat?'

'American. Texan. Rich.'

Confidently, she left her drink, went up to him, and smiled:

'Are you bald under there?' she touched his hat.

'As bald as an eagle.'

'I'm Zoë, from New Jersey.'

'Jersey..?' the name, like the State, has the flirty tenor of a Texan twang, but he felt she was a bit too young for him to woo. But hey, he's too polite to say Shoo!... so he flirts a little with her, to amuse himself, like. 'Here,' he offered her some money, 'buy yourself some candy. And try not to eat it all at once. Jersey girls fatten easily.'

She paused a moment. 'I've never been to Texas.'

'That's a damn shame.'

'Well, I'll get there eventually.'

'Why don't you just run along now, Jersey.'

She remained composed. 'I'm looking for a game.'

'A game?'

'Your game. My game. Our game. The best games are for sharing.'

'I don't follow.'

'Poker.'

'Ahhh...' he took off his hat – hell of a bald head, scratched it, and put it back on. 'You run along, now.'

'Do you know what I think, Texas?'

'I'm sure your about to tell me, Jersey.'

'Poker is a man's game.'

'You must mean me.'

'Sure, we both know that. And fundamentally what do men do? They fuck, don't they?' She was in bold mode. Texans, she felt, understood that. But he's a gentleman too, pitting politeness against her boldness. If only she were a guy, he thought, then...

'Do you know why women go astray, Jersey?'

'Fundamentally?'

'Sure.'

'Tell me, Texas.'

'They want to believe that Jersey is the size of Texas.'

'You're being polite.'

'Well, that's me, Jersey.'

'I can see that.'

'And we're the State with the *bulls*.'

'A pussy's as good as a cock.'

'Your words; not mine.'

'They're just different.'

'I see.'

'Like a hand to a glove.'

'Sure, Jersey, but I'm holding all the money cards.'

'I'll match your king to my queen.'

'That's better.'

'So, Texas, what happens now?'

'I'm here to play poker.'

'So am I.'

'You know what a cowgirl needs?'

'A cowboy.'

'And a roll in the hay.'

'Like a man.'

'Sure, Jersey, just like a man...'

'In need of a woman,' she said. 'You'll always be in need of a woman.'

'You're sweet, Zoë. Here, buy yourself some more candy.'

She took the money and looked into his eyes. It's not about winning, she saw, but compromise: 'Poker – it's like a relationship, really. Sex

615

aside, of course.'

'But still; it's a man's game.'

'In need of a woman. True, Texas?'

He smiled. 'Yes, true...'

'Then I want to play too.'

She offered him her candy hand, and he fondly shook it. After all, he was just too polite to say no. Texas, what a big ol'.....

Zoë, a.k.a The Butterfly, because she kicks so high and her kicks are coasting with the rich.

'Where did you learn to play?' he asked as they climbed the stairs to the poker room.

'New Jersey.'

'That home?'

'Home...' she wondered aloud. 'Yes.'

'Nice place?'

'Kind of.'

'Settle down there?'

'Sure. It's worth thinking about,' she smiled. 'I'll keep it in mind, along with the candies.'

'I'm from Texas,' he grinned, tapping his hat.

'A-ha. That figures.'

Without pausing he opened a door that led to a plush lounge, and variously greeted the others already gathered inside. Then, turning to Zoë, he introduced her: 'Gentlemen, meet The Butterfly.' They looked, they mused, they grinned with muffled laughter, asked if she was his niece, his daughter, his mistress, his mother – *mother!* Texas and the Butterfly sat on a couch next a man called Pierre. 'This guy's Russian, but has adopted a French name. And why not, it's just another fancy, and two are preferable to one.'

'What are you after?' he asked her.

'A game.'

'Just a game?'

'Yes. Just a game.'

'And after?'

'Coffee.'

'With cream?' He offered her a cigarette. She took one.

'Black,' said The Butterfly confidently. 'I take it black.'

'Fine with me.' He glanced briefly at the clock, and then addressed the others assembled in the room. 'They're on their way. Patience please, gentleman. Excuse me, and ladies too, of course,' he turned to the Butterfly. 'We're just waiting for a few more people to arrive. Our circle, you see, is not quite complete. Have a drink.'

'Thanks,' she said. And, reclining boldly on the couch, matched each man stare for stare until they accepted her presence as a fact.

There was a white door on the far side of the lounge, polished like ivory, and she noticed it when she first entered and never looked at it again until two men suddenly joined the group, and Pierre alighted from the couch and softly exclaimed: 'So you finally made it, Ice. We'd thought you'd melted.'

As Ice introduced his friend, Roy, a.k.a Hard Eight, The Butterfly gazed intensely at Ice as memories flooded back into her mind. She had seen him before, but never spoken with him. He threw her a curious look but seemed too preoccupied to pursue it any further and pressed on directly to the white door, the others following in his wake. Roy lingered behind, and Texas smiled at The Butterfly and wished her luck before joining the others. Roy never for a moment imagined she was one of the players, and was surprised when she asked him:

'What's the ante here?'

'Excuse me?' he said, looking startled. 'Are you American?'

'What's the minimum wager here? Five hundred? A thousand?'

He approached closer and spoke softly: it had still to dawn on him that she was part of their group, and quizzed her if she was with someone.

'Just my shadow,' she said, and strode into the gaming room alone. The others were already assembled round the table arranging their money, all cash, into heaps. The dealer went round exchanging them for gaming chips. Zoë took her time, getting a feel for the place, and sat beside Texas who smiled gamely and informed her that the minimum wager was a thousand. She wasn't in the least surprised as she unpacked a bundle of cash and arranged it on the table. When the dealer counted it, exchanging it for chips, she ended up with more stacks than anyone around that table would have imagined. Naturally, they gazed with varying degrees of surprise, respect, and amused awe, even a frown or two, but kept their thoughts private. Casting off assumptions and prejudices on the archetypal poker player is an extremely difficult thing to do for a man when it is *his* game. - Real butterflies aside, shouldn't *she* be fluttering amid the roses?

Roy, looking for a seat to be opposite Ice, was forced to settle for a place beside The Butterfly. During the brief prelude, as the players prepared themselves, Roy, having exchanged his money for gaming chips, couldn't stop himself from leaning over and whispering in The Butterfly's ear: 'You're a little young for this, aren't you?'

She leaned even closer to him and whispered back: 'Screw you.'

A stunned expression initially swept over his face. And then, as he caught his breath, uttered: 'OK... Let's play poker.'

When the dealer was ready he called time and play began, and all thoughts that prevailed before were expunged before luck, skill and the draw of the cards.

For Roy, the strangest episode of all was the sheer normality of the proceedings, baring the young Butterfly that held her game well, not advancing thus far, and any losses well within her means to bear. Ice seldom looked at him, and when he did, it was with a blank stare conveying the grim determination of a man intent on winning the game. This, even now, was his sole aim and obsession. The others, as players, were the anonymous rich that wheeled-and-dealed and are apt to believe the most extraordinary things when greed gets the better of their minds. There was Pierre, of course, suave and reserved; the arrogant pose more a part of his nature than an adaptation. There was Texas, grinning, who played poker with his hat on. There was Joshua who, unlike his biblical namesake, warmed to commerce over prayer and seemed happy to labor in his accounts all day – suspicion being his benchmark. There was Vaughn, like an aperitif, discerning in his tastes, refined in character, the face of a sophisticated man. And the others, sharing the common persona of generic gray man, rather pedestrian in appearance, respectable at the fringes, and even at this late hour looking immaculately normal. If Roy had met any of them at a poker game anywhere on Earth, he wouldn't blink an eye, not even for a moment. Yet here, something gave them a weight that was insidious, but in an odd way disarming. It was the interplay of events that brings you to a strange place, and you find that you are not really all that different from the rest.

After several hours into the game, with the fluctuations of poker taking its toll, especially on The Butterfly, who had mastered technique but lacked the refinements of experience that elevates intuition and risk into an art, was losing her assets by attrition, calling too often, over-betting the pot, failing to realize that these guys would not be intimidated at poker, not at any time. They had to be beaten, trounced by the best and not by intimidation. Novices, with an ocean of money, meant nothing to them. It was their game, first and foremost.

A game. For some, a last game, perhaps. But in each and every case: a game. Roy now realized what this ultimately meant, this game. Ice's *assertion* resounded with the fact: namely, there was *nothing* to bargain for, *nothing* to negotiate or deal with, *nothing* to do but play a last game and leave, win or lose, leave, because that was everything. *From nothing to nothing.* A credo in a deck of cards shuffled by the Joker.

When the cards are cold – fold.

As her assets dwindled, The Butterfly showed signs of quiet desperation. Self-doubt crept over her face, her fingers twitched and her voice softly trembled. They could all see she was thinking hard, as if thought alone would return her riches to her. She held the cards tightly; conscious she had to play against her rivals and not the deck. *What the cards hide, the human must find.* The thoughts running through her mind seemed confused but told her this: She must be steadfast, that her moments are untroubled, that she takes her place among those seeking mastery and ripens where the bulk of them pall. And if something in her stumbles or her life takes a blow, then it is no more than a bad day. Self-reliance, in the end, is the only way.

Pierre held the jacks, all four of them. Previously he hogged the queens - just three then - when he scooped the pot and, thus far, the highest The Butterfly reached was a triple ten, only the diamonds eluding her. And even as her favorite song played softly in the background, well, luck never played it for her.

'Raise you fifty thousand,' she said. 'And I'll see you.'

He smiled. 'Jacks!'

'Damn!' She cringes with dismay as the capricious cards beguile her expectations, and she takes another blow, loss upon loss wearing her down. Texas looked kindly on her and asked:

'How much are you down, Butterfly?'

Her fingers fondle the chips, superstitiously playing an invisible hand, moving them from pile to pile, and arranging them into roughly even columns that seem to be diminishing even before her eyes.

'We'll take a five minute break,' said the dealer, lighting up a cigarette. 'Anyone for a drink? Waiter, another round. Bring me an orange. And just coat the glass with vodka. Thanks.'

She salvaged what she could from what remained. She took off her wristwatch and traded it.

'How much does this buy me?'

'Only time,' he said, while dealing the cards, and pausing at her turn. 'Are you in?'

She tossed the diamond studded wristwatch into the circle, and picked up an ace. Her heart pounded with the cry: *Luck! What a bitch she is. I thought she closed the door. Now gimme more!*

'Raise.'

'Raise you.'

'Pass.'

'Call. And I'll raise.'

'I raise you too,' she said, taking her time, and held up two fingers to the dealer. She was dealt a king, and another ace. Luck was pouring in, but she held her nerve when her turn came around again. 'I'll raise.'

'Pass.'

'Raise.'

'I'm in. Raise.'

'I'll pass.'

She looked at them. They looked at her, at each other. The bald guy seemed to stroke the cards like he would a cat, the other guy was as stiff and impassive as a statue, until he twitched his fingers, weighed the chips in his hands, decided on more, sneaked a gaze at her, grinned, and threw them in the pot.

'Call. And I'll raise.'

'Pass,'

'I'll pass.'

Her ring was added to the pile. Her time was almost up. 'Raise.

And I'll see you.'

He eased back in his chair and revealed his cards, dishing them out on the table one at a time. 'Kings. Three of them. I never like to see them alone.' And he smiled at her.

'What happened to the other one?' she said.

'Who knows,' and he looked at the pot.

'Obviously, he prefers to keep better company,' she said, pulling out three aces and the missing King of Hearts. 'You never know what you're missing if the heart isn't in your hand.' And, as though reaching out to grasp her life, she swept out her arms, leaning forward, embraced the heap, and hauled the riches towards her. Yes!

'New deck,' cried out the dealer, breaking open a new pack as several players withdrew from the table and others joined, piling up their chips beside them loading their arsenals not for war, but something more formidable than that - poker.

Several hours later, and out of the initial number of players, only Roy, Ice, and The Butterfly remained, the others retiring with substantial losses, making way for fresh troops fully loaded with big guns. These guys, they always seem to be fully loaded.

When his eyes began to ache, Roy withdrew from the game, followed soon after by The Butterfly, who triumphed handsomely, and she took her winnings out into the lounge where Roy sat patiently on a couch smoking a cigarette. Ice persevered a little longer, holding about even and still hoping for a break. That was his flaw, to hope too far, and get in a rut. Knowing when to stop is as important as knowing when to start. Perhaps he knew this, rationally, but sometimes his obsessed heart wouldn't allow him to follow a sound head.

As The Butterfly arranged her winnings in stacks of fifty thousand, Roy became intrigued by her. He felt that uncanny turn of events inform him of her origins. He rose and walked over.

'You're a twin, aren't you?'

She stared at him, frightened, swallowing hard: 'How did you know that?'

'I'm Roy. Roy Riemann.'

'How did you know?' She felt threatened, shielding her money.

'A lucky guess, I guess.'

She glared at him, before daring to turn away.

'There's a cop looking for you,' he said. And she froze. 'No. It's OK. Really. Here, take this card. Call the number on the back. Ask for an American cop called John Forester. I believe your sister is in town. They're concerned. They just want to make sure you are safe and well.' She stared at him disbelievingly, struggling to hope, fearing to believe. 'They're worried, that's all. Really,' he said, trying to reassure her, holding out the card until she nervously took it. 'No one can force you. It's your call.'

Roy guessed immediately what her fears were: she had a lot of money, most likely a great deal more than what she won at the game, and probably all in cash. And she wanted to secure it without agents bleeding her with extortionate commissions, or the authorities asking awkward questions.

'I can help,' he said at length, after explaining what he did. 'I work in banking. I can help you move your money back to the States. Or wherever else you like for that matter.'

'You?'

'If you want me to. Yes.'

She stared at him intently. 'How much do you want?'

'Nothing.'

'Nothing!'

He smiled warmly. 'It would be a pleasure. I was beaten fair and square. You're not bad at the game. But you got lucky in there, more than you realize. Luck is only part of it. Remember that.' He gave her his card and his number in Paris. She asked him why he was being so helpful and so kind. He gazed at her with tired eyes and reflected on the absurdities he'd encountered, the ordeals, the struggles, the paranoia...and apart from the kitten, The Butterfly was the only unbroken, wholesome person he could think of. 'Everyone deserves at least one break.'

She offered him her hand to shake, but he kissed it instead.

'Thanks, mister. I mean Roy.' And she chuckled when he kissed her hand again. He said:

'I've realized, there's a lot more to being a man than just winning all the time. I want to help people, people who deserve it, to give them a chance. That's a fair bet, isn't it?' He smiled with sincerity, and a deep conviction. 'I want to feel I am a citizen of the world. I

622

want to do something. We can't always be alone, just chasing the buck; can we?'

She chuckled warmly. 'You're funny, Roy. And kind.' And she kissed him tenderly on the cheek.

The white door abruptly opened and Ice emerged. Someone shut the door behind him, and he stood there confronting Roy. Ice briefly glanced at The Butterfly, and then more enviously at her winnings, then he grinned and said.

'It's almost daylight, Roy. I think we'd better take our leave.'

Roy looked at The Butterfly and gave her the thumbs up. She smiled at him warmly and the two men left. As they descended the stairs, Ice began: 'Well, how did you fare; how did it go with you?'

'I lost more than I should have. But...' he smiled, thinking of The Butterfly, 'it went to a worthwhile cause, so it doesn't really bother me. Besides, I'll win it back, sooner or later. And next time, I'll spread it around.'

'I fared somewhat better tonight. I think my luck is picking up.'

'Evens, eh?'

'Evens.'

'And the others, what will they do, Ice?'

Pausing at the bottom of the stairs, the conceits of his arguments hammered the point.

'They'll find themselves another game to play.'

Roy exploded: 'Another game! They think this is a game? Are they stupid?'

'They're sort of unfulfilled.'

'Unfulfilled! Jesus Christ, we all are. But we keep a sense of proportion. For God's sake, when is enough, enough?'

'Mistakes and misunderstandings happen, Roy. That's life.'

'But we have to pay for them. It can't be like that, that you don't pay. Someone pays.'

'Where have you been hiding, in fairyland? Do you make a humble living like the vast majority of people out there? Give over, you're just like the rest us hacks. You look for cracks in the system. You exploit fools like anyone else – and why shouldn't we? You enjoy privileged income on the sweat and grind of millions saving and spending and working their whole lives day in, day out.' He was panicking, but it was controlled, because certain things of life he knew, even in a crisis, remain true and unbroken; the nature of human commerce being preeminent here. But despite this, perhaps for the first time, he was playing not for money but his deeper life, his integrity, and all he had to hand were a handful of arguments and words, words, words. 'The world was never a compassionate place for fools, Roy. And there's nothing you or I could ever do to change that. Life isn't a moral dilemma. It doesn't supply right and wrong answers like you think it does. It's all about survival. Not debt. There are those who seldom pay a thing for their mistakes. Well, not in the conventional sense, anyway.'

'And they just get away with it; just like that?'

'That's merely an interpretation.'

'What?'

'They pay a price of sorts.'

'Which is?'

'They suffer the personal indignity of getting it wrong,' Ice said. 'Of making a mistake.'

Roy gasped for breath at the sheer audacity of his argument. Absurdity seldom plunged such depths. 'Ah, I see,' he poured scorn, 'we offended their intelligence.'

'Their well-laid plans would be a better description of things.'

'And who gets the blame? Others, I suspect.'

'It doesn't really matter, does it, Roy?'

'Then what does matter?'

'Surely, you know the answer to that.'

'You're so full of crap.'

'Then I'll tell you: What matters is to be able to get up and play again.' The vigor of his expression paled beside his vanity. 'Look, Roy, I know - '

'Go to hell!'

'I know what you're thinking.' He was on the verge of panicking, but held his nerve. 'But stop and think.'

'No.'

'Stop and think.'

'And if I don't, what then?'

'Stop - And - Think.'

Something snapped, and it wasn't the fracturing of ice or stammer of heartbeats. It was impalpable thought driving insanely through Roy's inflamed mind. Holding the mirror of his judging eye upon himself, he stood amid the quandary that befalls men succumbing to a rash rage. Was he testing how brave he was, how outraged, how self-righteous he could seem to be? Or should wiser counsel reign, and he submit to an inevitability and act on that warning: Stop and think. – In a heated moment rashness provides the courage to dare against the odds; anger fashions the form of imprudent bravery; and the cry of passion the roar of intolerance to bullies. He reflected on his life, the kitten, Nick and Frank in New York, his family and friends, the unknown perils that could sweep out from nowhere and engulf them all, and fearing this more than he believed he could, he composed himself noticeably, and resorted to calm bluff.

'You know, Ice, there is more than one way to skin a cat.'

'And do you imagine for a second they don't know that too.' His answer was spontaneous, yet carried the measure of a sweeping conviction. 'Cats aside, it honors the man of common sense and firm will to think before he acts.'

'Oh?'

'Like you,' he said, a tone of confession seeping into his metaphor, 'I stick to a rule and I keep all of my cards close to my chest. That way I can play the man, and not feel seduced by the cards.'

The confrontation ended. The moment closed.

'Goodnight,' said Roy, turning and walking away.

Ice, at length, muttered goodnight; but Roy was out of earshot to hear it pass his lips and disperse into thin air.

As Roy crossed the exit and turned down the street, he felt a tepid chill seize his bones, and bracing himself against the strange burst of cold, he hailed down a taxi and drove to the hotel. The dawn had broken and it would be sunrise soon into a pure blue cloudless sky. And the rain - well - the rain was just a memory.

Battles are fought, and won and lost, every single day. Those who lose often live to fight another day - potentially; but many simply resign themselves and forget what they once struggled for, what they set out to prove, to be, what they may have become. Perhaps it was just time abating life's quest, perhaps a deeper motive, or a passion aborted and you simply ceased to care. Somewhere there amid these extremes Roy presently resided, and he knew it. Did that make him a coward? Did he yield his morality, and was that morality, on reflection, ever worth the suffering? The bottom line was this: what was being sacrificed, pride or innermost integrity? And does quiet compromise make him any less a man? It wasn't human spite or bitterness that could destroy the spirit of a man; it was his inner eye shining light beams on the shadows of the self and illuminating waif nothingness to substance. The revelation, for the most part, is surprising, perhaps even fated.

'Are you awake?' he whispered, closing the bedroom door behind him. 'Pussycat...'

'Roy... Where did you go?' the kitten, drowsy, looked up at him, her huge eyes sparkling awake. 'Roy...?'

'For a walk.'

'A walk. Why?'

'To thinks things over,' he said, sitting next to her. She continued to lie there gazing up at him.

'Things. What things?' Her soft wavering tone carried the faraway cry of weeping, as she imagined he had second thoughts of marriage, got cold feet and was going to end their relationship. Fortunately, he still had the presence of mind to sense these palpitations mar her lovely face, and quelled her fears by embracing her cheeks tenderly with his hands. 'I was thinking about where we should buy a house,' he said. 'Any ideas?' Her face lit up like a million candles. 'Perhaps we should buy an apartment over here, once we're married?'

'Perhaps,' she smiled warmly. And they kissed.

At length, after they made love, and lay there together, she sensed him brooding as they gazed at the sky, and said. 'Would you like to be left alone, Roy?'

'Huh?' he barely stirred.

'By yourself? Give you some time and space to think.'

'Think?'

'Shall I leave you alone?'

'No.' He was falling deeply in love. Intimacy and possession were growing indistinguishable, and he held her tightly until he began to cry inside himself. And then, as he burned, slept.

626

Chapter 36

As a truck hurtled past his apartment, Michael Leoni shuddered awake. His eyes, fighting the dimnesss of twilight, flinched, tilted left, and saw that Sara wasn't there, only the soft traces in her pillow where her head had rested, and loose strands of her hair entangled amid soft fabrics giving the flimsiest evidence she was once there. He lacked the emotional stamina to cry out her name, the reflexes of a scorned lover quitting him. Only the presiding sense of being used, of being a fool tormented his mind with painful riddles: Why? Why? Why? And shutting his eyes, bitterness consumed him.

Even the slightest provocation could make him react. And it was the soft tempo of a nightingale singing tweet tweet tweet that pushed him over the edge. He gazed frantically at the telephone, as if this alone would inspire it to ring. It didn't ring; and this crushed him. Cursing his impotence he seized the telephone and called his brother, but got an answer-phone. More crushing failure, so he tried the office. No answer. Someone should be there, he knew that, but too anxious to wait beyond the third ring he cut and dialed randomly. It started ringing. He waited anxiously, waiting, waiting... No answer. Damn! Throwing the receiver down, he flung himself back onto the bed; and the crushing sense of his powerlessness was complete.

His frantic gaze must have swept across it before, perhaps more than once, but he failed to notice and now, staring blankly at the window, the rain had stopped and a letter was attached to the windowpane. He leapt up and seized it. It was her handwriting; she said she was offered a plum new job in Geneva, a once in a lifetime chance, and she would be in touch. - Brief; a curt goodbye; an end written like a footnote. *Women!*

After rushing to get dressed, he drove to his brother's apartment and woke him and his lady friend. Anthony was fuming and wouldn't let him inside, detaining him in the corridor: 'What do you want?'

'Look at this.'

He read it. 'So what; she's gone. Women; they come, they go... Do you know how many fish there are in the sea? Shove off, sailor!'

'Baby, baby...' a delicious wooing from inside the apartment lifted an octave, from slumber to seduction, and stirred Anthony to divert his attention to its source and send back echoes of drooling delights that he would be right there. Furious with the intrusion, he confronted his brother: 'Here,' shoving the letter is his hands. 'Now get lost.'

'Anthony, wait.'

'What now?'

'Something very ominous is going on. I feel it, I know it. - Ice, you know, my boss, Ice, the one you saw at the club?'

'Ahhhhh... Here come the jokers.' He waited, like a tease, testing his reaction. 'You really have no idea, do you?'

'What do you mean? What are you saying?'

'I've been doing some digging of my own lately - oh, into this and that. And, well, being an old hand at the jolly old game of bluff, allow me the pleasure to spell it out for you, dear brother. - I smell me a fat rat the size of a cat crying *meow!* But don't think I'm going to take off my hat, no sir, and pull out a rabbit the size of a rhino going *roar, roar*... Have you got the picture yet, or not? Well, speak up. Don't stand there and gawp.'

'What in God's name are you talking about? Are you insane? Don't you understand how serious this is? Anthony, I told you, there is something ominous going on with the system at the bank, and I think we're irresistibly being drawn in.'

'Or having our leg pulled.' Anthony sensed how hopelessly incredulous he was, and tried to explain. 'Look, Mike, dear brother, I don't know the details, and quite frankly couldn't care less, but this *game*, this system you're talking about, it's just bluff and bullshit. I told you this before. Until machines can fuck, they'll never fuck anything up. Only people can do that - especially those with the nerve. Until a machine can pull a fast one, it's the guy pulling your leg you've got to watch. Do you understand? I couldn't give a toss about your super-duper computers. Behind it all are human beings playing a giant game of bluff of one kind or another.' He paused and yawned. 'You're wondering how I can say all this, aren't you?

Well, what are big brothers for if not to guide their siblings through the dodgy scripts of the weird and wonderful show called Life? Are you ready for this?' And he swept out his arms like an emcee, beaming with a razzle-dazzle grin of *The world is a stage.* 'It's all just showbiz, pal! Even real life; it's just showbiz. Yes sir! Next act. *Bong, bong, bong!* The show *must* go on. That's the only thing you *can't* bluff your way out of, because it's *real.* And it's coming your way. So roll on, sucker, or get rolled over. - Now, finally, go home and get some sleep.' And he withdrew inside with a huff.

With the *stage* door shut firmly on his face, Michael gazed into reality with somber bewilderment, wondering to himself: *Is everyone insane?* Anthony's depiction of events played like a heap of jumbled confusions in his mind. He felt as one stranded in a maze, wandering helpless, anchored to nothing but the vagaries of chance and, anxious what he should do, where he should go, Roy swept suddenly into his thoughts in a fitful surge of possibility. Why him? And how to find him? The last refuge of a stricken man is the familiar, even if he fears and abhors it. So, in that desperate interval of seconds that felt insurmountable, a shudder of hope burst forth in the guise of the project. Seizing on this he scrambled to the office, down into *The Vault* and logged on. A colleague was present reading a book and sipping wine, with only a restful toe dangling near a keyboard. Michael asked him what he was doing?

'Reading,' he said. 'Would you like some wine?'

Michael pressed on obsessively. Peeping Tom, as always, was actively simulating models of the markets. New York was a black spot on the screen, but then so was London, Sao Paulo, Athens, Shanghai and Madrid. Only Riyadh glowed in a lone desert of light. Like a riddle. Like a game. Like a bluff.

He left the console and turned to his colleague who, when he saw him moving, began to pour him some wine.

Michael asked him: 'Is there anything wrong here, Mark?"

'Your wine?'

'Thanks. Have you noticed anything odd?'

'Odd?' He mulled it over calmly. 'No, I can't recall anything odd. Should there be?'

'Has the system ever been used in real time; in any way? Has Ice done anything in real time?'

'Real time?' he wondered aloud, not curiously, but clarifying the question in his own mind. 'Do you mean *actually* hooking it up to the global financial system? To *actually* trade live? To go operational?'

'Yes. Has anyone?'

'That's crazy. We'd be swamped by too many variables. The unknowns would drown us. It would wash out the refinements. You'd end up with a mess.' He chuckled briefly. 'It would crash! It wouldn't last milliseconds, let alone a day; not with the weight of trades out there. We'd end up broke. Come on, you know, you can't let it run itself like that. We've finessed it too much. We stripped out the muscle. We wanted it to *look* good to be of any practical use. Well, not in the way you're suggesting.'

'But I've seen it myself,' he protested. 'It could handle it.'

'Perhaps, on a *very* small scale. But even that's pushing it. The only realistic way for the system to *play* in the bigger world is to duplicate it, many thousands of times. Ultimately, this system works only by interacting with its clones. It can't play the markets. It can't compete with a man, given all his instincts, his machinations, his schemes, his deceits. Humans are just too uncanny. That's asking too much. We can't duplicate that, Mike.'

'But the simulations. The tests. I've seen them.'

He began to laugh. 'Their fake. The data was massaged to impress the bosses upstairs to keep the project ticking over. This is an expensive game here, Mike. But,' he paused and looked mystified at him, 'I thought you knew that. Didn't Ice tell everyone?' He turned and looked at the monitor. 'It's just a game, really. At the end of the day, it's just a game.'

Michael's breath caught in choking stillness. The realization of events drained him of power, of his will, and he remained dazed for a time before he could stir a single syllable. 'No.... No...' he muttered, unable to comprehend what he was saying, and leaving the wine on the desk: 'No, he didn't.' And he proceeded to leave.

'Wait,' Mark cried after him, 'you haven't logged out.'

But he silently shut the door, and left.

'OK, I'll do it for you.'

Chapter 37

At around ten a.m. when Claude arrived at his office, he found Forester diligently going through the case files and drafting a report for his Captain in New York. Claude felt and looked weary, partly the result of last night's binge, and partly the crispness of the morning air – it was fresh and had no alcohol in it.

'Early bird,' he remarked, grinning at Forester as he poured himself some coffee.

'Bonjour, Claude.'

'The advantage of different time zones is you can nap and take your time, and not have to rush into work.'

'Habit,' he replied good-humouredly.

'You are in France now, my friend, and here one's indulgences are a fundamental right. Liberté, Egalité, Fraternité, and le Fun! - Fun, fun, fun.'

He laughed as Claude went to his desk and pored wearily over his messages. Then the telephone rang and he answered it. He frowned, and then grinned. It was a call for Forester.

'For me?' He looked surprised.

He passed him the telephone. 'It's a woman. American.'

Forester placed it cautiously to his ear and gave his name. The soft reply had a trembling sound that verged on trepidation.

It was Zoë Long, the twin, and she began speaking unstoppably, a torrent of words came gushing out as she explained that she was safe, she was fine, she was lying low, just keeping herself to herself, that she made some money, all honestly, but it was mostly in cash and she wanted to secure it before contacting her family in America, and she was sorry she put anyone to any trouble, but it was her money earned fair and square.

'What will you do, Detective?' she asked him anxiously.

'You're safe. That's what matters. That's my only concern.'

She gasped as if for air. 'Really?'

'Call your sister, and put her mind at rest.'

He heard her weep, the soft trembling of relief as it swept through her, and she cried out *'Thank you. I thank you so much. Thank you...'* earnestly several times. And then, wishing her well, he hung up.

Claude shrugged smugly as if to say, *There you are, that's another one sorted itself out,* and munched into a fresh croissant. Forester's old man had a word or two as well, and wasted no time in advancing them: *If you ask me, son, it's the selfless, simple, decent things like that that make a cop feel good about himself. Sure, you can nab a hooligan or two, bang him up and throw away the key. But the real lasting pleasure is a simple smile you bring out on the face of a decent person thankful that you're there for them when they need you.* Thanks, Pop. Thanks a lot. *Don't mention it, son. I'll always be here for you.*

Forester reflected, not only on Pop's elegy to life, but also on the nature of chance and circumstance that brought him here. Life is a stream of people, events and things in constant flux, and the sense of them drifting in and through each other's lives, seldom with any purpose or motive spanning years, but the fleeting circumstances of life, the nitty-gritty day-to-day transactions which for the most part pass for nothing but a trade, but sometimes pull you into a matrix that begins to resemble premeditation and a plot. Thinking along these lines, Forester said:

'People come and go, they meet, they exchange, and these incidental events make the world seem strange and puzzling.' He was beginning to lose the thread to mysticism, but worked his way back to reason. 'Just because events, things and people appear to coincide, it doesn't mean it was planned that way. It just happened.'

Claude concurred vaguely: 'In our business we get all sorts.' He downed a croissant and most of the coffee, and it brought a sense of freshness to his indolent face. 'I have files of missing persons never seen again. Stacks of them. I don't know why, but some of these people just like to disappear. Then there are the deceased, of both natural and dubious causes. You can spot the cases that will remain unsolved, so you quietly close them.' He alluded to the quiet actions conducted by everyone in a similar position. 'What else can we do? It's not in our hands. People aren't stupid; they know that. And... they accept it.'

Forester saw where this was leading, and came straight out with it. 'You think this investigation has been a waste of time.'

'It *has* to be investigated,' he said emphatically. 'I'm not disputing that. It's our job. That's what we're here for. But...' he shrugged, alluding to some *otherness*.

'And so some criminals go unpunished.'

'The legal system is not the only system of justice in the world. Things have a way, sometimes, of sorting themselves out. – Who knows, perhaps he deserved it.'

'And if he didn't?'

'Perhaps - even likely I'd say - we'll never know. But do we suffer because of it? Do we throw in the towel? No. You carry on. You do your best. Some crooks get away. Quite frankly, most crooks get away - those that use their heads, anyway.' He paused to give Forester an opportunity to respond, but he declined, so Claude continued. 'Just ask yourself honestly: who do we have locked up in jail? For the most part, stupid hooligans, right? People short of a few grams of gray matter. They've got the nerve, sure, but not the savvy. The majority of crimes are soft crimes. Wherever we compete for resources, there is crime of one form or another. '

Forester remained quiet, listening, thinking, a blank expression resembling understanding – or was it resignation? At length, Claude resumed:

'Ask yourself honestly: do we *really* want to catch them? For all the misdemeanors, big and small, smart and stupid, do we, as a society, *really* want to catch them?'

Forester remained still, and silent, just staring impassively at the sunbeams striking the surface of the desk.

'Sometimes you will; now and again you get a break, and you're a hero. Voila! But oftentimes, not. You plod along; and keep a lid on things.'

'We owe it to society, Claude. Compromised as we are, that's our job. Society wants them caught and punished.'

Claude pondered a moment, and lit a cigarette. 'As a society, I don't really believe we do. One way or another, the majority has its hands in the pot. – Think about it, as long as the system works, on any scale, large and small, we leave it ticking over, and ride out our lives in relative peace.' He paused, offering a moment's reflection, before concluding: 'This silent corruption, this quiet hypocrisy, like it or not, is a going concern.'

What is Man, but made in the image of the market? How many observers of the honest world would have countered otherwise, signaling belief in Man, in his innate goodness, in fairness, in the ripe old honesty of a buck, and the cash register of life? Stifling on their own dissent could cause a commotion, or a laugh. Yet the passing tide of realization dawns, that Man has settled for the compromise of civilization subject to the vagaries of his nature. Society embraces the lusts of Man, tamed at the fringes, harnessed for economy and commerce, at its disposal to use and apply. He is a fool who stymies his own strength. And the will to compete, by fair means or foul, reigns at the heart of his nature.

'If I weren't a cop, I'd say you looked surprised.'

'I am, Claude, I am.'

'A cop needs philosophy and good food. That makes for a good cop. In France, we have excellent cops.'

Forester braved a smile. It was reluctant, but genuinely set. For the world, amid its many tangible delights, was all about trade-offs, compromise, wheeling-and-dealing. Men are born to trade: their goods, their skills, their services, their morals, their values, even themselves. The commoditized nature of Man is the bane of his civilization, and its savior. It is like a coin: the head is inseparable from the tail. And all you can do with it is purchase and set it spinning. Life is a risk, of course; but a risk worth taking. Forester reached for the tail end of his feelings, and said:

'You're cynical, Claude.'

'Who, me?'

'You.'

He sighed philosophically. 'I'm a cop; like you, a lifer in this game. And I do my job as best I can. Why grumble? You know as well as I do the whole world runs on corruption of one form or another, or hypocrisy.'

'So what's the answer?'

He laughed delightedly. 'Here, have a croissant and a fresh cup of coffee. They're delicious. *Really!*'

End & Fin